PRAISE FOR ALICE BORCHARDT AND *BEGUILED*

"Alice Borchardt does the impossible; surpassing her brilliant debut novel, *Devoted,* with her even more dazzling second novel, *Beguiled.* I want more!"
—Bertrice Small

"A fine writer with a direction all her own."
—*San Jose Mercury News*

"Fans of Marion Zimmer Bradley and other purveyors of historic fantasy and adventure will enjoy the richly rendered historic detail with which Borchardt embellishes her baroque portrait of a turbulent, violent time."
—*Publishers Weekly*

"Like a medieval tapestry, the overall effect is bright and colorful. . . . Borchardt moves her tale along well, from intrigue to intrigue, striking a balance between big action scenes and small vignettes of life."
—*New Orleans Times-Picayune*

"I really found myself glued to the pages—and that's not common!"   —Marion Zimmer Bradley

"Relentless . . . an energetic scene-setter . . . a lively narrative with a great deal of action."   —*Kirkus Reviews*

"It should come as no surprise that Anne Rice's sister has more than her share of storytelling talent. But Alice Borchardt weaves her own special magic. . . . The sheer tenderness of the ending left me breathless."
—Susan Wiggs, author of *The Lightkeeper*

"Borchardt weaves an intriguing but traditionally historic and romantic tale about love and betrayal and the conquest of lands in 10th-century France. . . . *Beguiled* makes for interesting reading."   —*Baton Rouge Magazine*

PRAISE FOR ALICE BORCHARDT'S *DEVOTED*

"Love and treachery . ... marvelous. . . . Alice leads us into the irresistible atmosphere of the Dark Ages, into a vivid and deliciously violent realm of battle, love, and tragic entanglements." —Anne Rice

"A gem! This saga of witches, warriors, romance, and sex will hold you in thrall." —*Entertainment Weekly*

"Captivating . . . a feisty mix of Old World adventure and charm." —*Los Angeles Daily News*

"An absorbing, unforgettable novel . . . seethes with emotional intensity and sensuality, mysticism and grand heroics." —Penelope Williamson

"An ambitious and compelling first novel . . . presents a richly detailed world that will quickly engage its readers." —*Trenton Times*

"A joy to read . . . will move you to laughter . . . and break your heart . . . profoundly rewarding."
—Susan Wiggs

"A saga densely detailed, rich, and gripping."
—*Kirkus Reviews*

BEGUILED

Alice Borchardt

With an Introduction by
Anne Rice

A SIGNET BOOK

SIGNET
Published by the Penguin Group
Penguin Putnam Inc., 375 Hudson Street,
New York, New York 10014, U.S.A.
Penguin Books Ltd, 27 Wrights Lane,
London W8 5TZ, England
Penguin Books Australia Ltd, Ringwood,
Victoria, Australia
Penguin Books Canada Ltd, 10 Alcorn Avenue,
Toronto, Ontario, Canada M4V 3B2
Penguin Books (N.Z.) Ltd, 182–190 Wairau Road,
Auckland 10, New Zealand

Penguin Books Ltd, Registered Offices:
Harmondsworth, Middlesex, England

Published by Signet, an imprint of Dutton Signet,
a member of Penguin Putnam Inc.
Previously published in a Dutton edition.

First Signet Printing, January, 1998
10 9 8 7 6 5 4 3 2 1

To Katherine Rita Allen

I don't suppose there's much left now. I'm sure the coffin rotted and collapsed long ago. Some plastic lilies of the valley, a scrap of tulle, and, perhaps, a few very brown bone fragments, a bit of snaggle-toothed skull.

There are worse things. Being stuck into an airtight box of steel, bronze, and nylon until you mummify into something light as a dead leaf.

But perhaps it doesn't matter, and we three will join together and dance with the desert wind when the heat comes off the mountains and the cooling air roars across the barren waste being piped along to the wild cry of creosote and greasewood. Until we are flying free into the vast solar wind up among the stars.

To My Sister, Anne Rice,

a person of many possessions,
a thing that is no possession,
an offering of the spirit,
Hakon's tale

ACKNOWLEDGMENTS

My heartfelt thanks to Mary Jane Selle for her careful typing skills; Joyce Bell for friendship and encouragement whenever needed; Barbara Dawson Smith and Arnette Lamb for inspiration and belief; Susan Wiggs, a true friend, a friend in need and in deed; Michaela Hamilton for her vision; Lynn Nesbit for taking a chance in a risky business; Anne Rice for all her devoted encouragement and support; David Thomson II; Dean James for helping me shout for attention in a world where all artists have to shout to be heard, and for unfailing encouragement and good humor; and to Bruce and Gary of the B & G Plant Co. for flowers of the light. And may perpetual light shine upon them. To Karen O'Brien, all my love. But most of all, thank you to my beloved and patient husband, Clifford Borchardt. Truly all my life's joy is in you.

INTRODUCTION

by Anne Rice

Picture this . . . briefly, if you please. It's 1948. Two little
girls are sitting in a plain dining room in a smallish house
on St. Charles Avenue in New Orleans, talking to each
other in almost rhythmic whispers, as they page through
books or draw with crayons, or simply looking about the
room, reciting their words almost as if in verse. It's very
animated, this back and forth. Very important.

Now you can forget the picture.

The little girls aren't there at all. They are Alice and
Anne O'Brien, destined to be Alice O'Brien Borchardt,
author of *Devoted* and Anne Rice, known only too well
for a book called *Interview with the Vampire,* which is
one of about nineteen she has written. And I, Anne Rice,
am proud again to be introducing a book by my sister,
Alice O'Brien Borchardt.

Of course, these little girls of 1948 can't see into the
future any more than they can see the room around them,
with its routine oak furniture, sideboard, big, naked windows opened to the porch of the boardinghouse next door.

These girls are living in an imaginary world they have
created with each other, full of towers and turrets, and
peopled by the beautiful queens Mary and Madene and
those who endlessly court them, presiding over an empire
of splendid little offspring called the Slickery children,
who are so numerous and so cooperative and so clever

that they can build a new castle for Mary, Madene, and the Whole Court in one single day, each child taking one of thousands of bricks and putting it just in the right place at the right time.

It takes great energy and delight to create the world of Mary and Madene and Slickery children. Alice and Anne go about it with gusto, feeding in any new inspiration from a radio show or pictures discovered in a fairy-tale book. They draw their own pictures of princesses with coned hats, or lovely couches on which they might recline.

In the Court of the Slickery Children, there is suspense, conflict, victory, love. Above all, there is a sense of freedom and boundless possibility. The realm of Mary and Madene takes its delicate garments and battlements from the Middle Ages, the tenth century, the land of fairy tales, but Alice and Anne don't know it.

All they know is, they like this kingdom, and they can sustain its daily life for hours, weaving the story together, Alice providing three or four sentences, then Anne throwing in a couple to turn the plot another way, Alice perhaps inventing a terrible difficulty for the tribe in their wanderings, and on and on it goes.

Both Alice and Anne were born to tell stories, and it's so natural to them that it will be years before they realize that other people don't have "dream worlds," that everyone cannot at will slip into an active narrative fantasy, either with one's sister or alone.

Thank God there was no nanny about to say, "You ought to get your head out of the clouds, children." By the time school teachers try to clamp down on the wandering minds of Alice and Anne, the girls are too far gone.

As the years passed, they "lived" their after-school hours at the New Orleans public library, where Alice pored over books of history, science, philosophy, architecture, chivalry, and astronomy, raiding the vast upstairs adult section with her father's card. She had to do it. By the age of twelve, she'd read everything in the children's library on the first floor. Fiction she gobbled for breakfast, lunch, and dinner.

Let the rain fall; let the dishes sit in the sink. Devouring

Hamlet or *Macbeth* was much more fun for Alice, and just as easy for Alice as the Bobbsey Twins for other kids.

"What do you do with all you know? Why do you want to read all those books?" Those are common enough questions put to Alice and Anne. "What will become of you with all your reading and daydreaming?"

Alice didn't care. Her reading enriched her fantasies, as well as increasing her practical knowledge; all she learned inspired even more flamboyant characters and adventures, sometimes in fantasy lands, on rocket ships, on other planets, in other ages long before our own.

And two years ago, Alice's persistent, incurable dream world produced her first novel, *Devoted,* an instant success—chock full of joy of love and red clatter of battle, a tale as rich as it was readable, a feast for the lovers of such stories, and as fine as many a story Alice had read herself.

Now two years later, I'm proud to say we have Alice's second book to plunge into: *Beguiled.* Here again are the rugged and indefatigable characters of *Devoted*—Owen and Elin, and thanks to Alice's impeccable historical accuracy, we return effortlessly with them to tenth-century Chantalon.

Don't be fooled, however, by the gentle titles of these books, or their entrancing covers. In the tradition of *Braveheart* and *Rob Roy,* Alice's heroes and heroines spend as much time on the battlefield as in bed. Power and music are equal in Alice and in *Beguiled.* Once again I congratulate my sister on her accomplishment.

And again, Alice, let me ask you about your werewolf novel. People are pushing me for copies of this mysterious work—*The Silver Wolf.* When will we see you formally take the plunge into the paranormal so we can be the Weird Sisters in a new sense of the word?

THE CHARACTERS
OF *BEGUILED*

The Bishop's Household

Owen, bishop of Chantalon
Elin, his wife, a priestess of the forest people
Enar, Owen's best friend
Godwin, Owen's captain and cousin
Gowen, one of Godwin's knights
Edgar, one of Godwin's knights
Wolf the Short, one of Godwin's knights
Ranulf, a young knight
Denis, the bowman
Alfric, a monk
Ingund, Enar's wife
Elfwine, Ranulf's wife
Rosamund, a servant girl
Anna, an old, trusted servant
Ine, the half-wit

The Forest People

Alshan, the leader
Tigg
Sybilla
Ilo
Ceredea

The Vikings

Hakon, Owen's sworn enemy
Tosi, his second-in-command

Ulick, Hakon's spy
Ivor Halftroll
Osric, the Viking who imprisoned Owen
Holder, a low-life Viking
Llwyd, a giant

Elspeth's Household

Elspeth, the beauty who owns the neighboring stronghold
Reynald, her late husband who betrayed Owen
Bertrand, Elspeth's brother, an abbot who tormented Owen
Eric, Elspeth's son
Rauching, Elspeth's sly kinsman
Niethered, one of Elspeth's freeholders
Bettena, nurse to Elspeth's children
Corwin, a trusted servant, Bettena's husband
Clara, a servant

The Townspeople

Martin, a village priest
Arn, the tavern keeper
Routrude, his wife, the village gossip
Clea, the town's madam
Osbert, the stock dealer
Judith, a Jew and a moneylender
Lollas the Usurer, Judith's father
Count Anton, the former ruler of Chantalon,
killed by Godwin
Gerlos, Count Anton's good-for-nothing son
Gunter, the blacksmith, Ingund's father
Siefert, the tanner
Gynnor, Osbert's wife
Helvese, Siefert's wife
Rieulf, Judith's captain
Fortunatas, the drunkard

The Bretons

Elutides, a master manipulator
Gynneth, his niece
Cador and Casob, his sons
King Ilfor
Queen Aud

Chapter

1

*T*HE torches cast their bloody reflections into the black water.

"May the devil seize them alive," Martin said. "I believe you must see they are not gone, my lord bishop."

Lord Bishop Owen didn't censure the curse. Martin had endured enough from the men in the fortress to have a right to call any misfortune down on them he pleased. Owen even had a faint hope that such a curse, flung by a priest, might actually take. Martin would have to do penance, of course, but his bishop would see it was a light one.

The fortress was on an island in the river a few miles ahead. And it was obvious the Vikings were not gone. In fact, they were clearly involved in some sort of celebration.

"Beach the boat," Owen ordered. "We are nearly within sight and sound of them."

The boat slithered silently in the mud and came to a halt in a few feet of water.

Owen stood, turned to help his wife, Elin, and realized she was already on shore. Elin's friends, Sybilla, Tigg, and Alshan, had vanished into the forest. Owen leaped. His feet sank ankle deep into an unmentionable mixture of slime, detritus, and liquid mud. He pulled his feet free with two pops, jumped toward more solid ground on the riverbank, and joined the rest in invisibility among the black tree shadows.

Martin was the last to leave the boat. He landed on the soft riverbank with a mighty squelch.

Elin was the first to realize Martin was in difficulty. The big man's face was white with terror. His arms were swinging wildly, and, worst of all, she could hear the sound of oars slapping the water. Another boat was coming upriver. Indeed, in the distance, she could see torches lit along its sides.

"Oh no," Owen gasped. "He is mired like a bull in a wallow."

Elin ran back toward Martin, her feet splashing through the shallow water.

"No," Martin whispered hoarsely as she reached him. "I am trapped in mud up to my thighs. Run, my lady. Save yourself. They cannot track you into the forest."

"Get down!" Elin hissed at Martin

The light was growing brighter. The longship was closer.

Martin, his great strength turned against him, stared at her blankly.

"Down." Elin pleaded desperately with Martin, tugging, but without much effect, on his arm.

"Elin . . ." Owen cried softly.

"Punch him in the stomach," she whispered with bared teeth to Owen. "Punch him. Bring him down before he gets us all killed."

Owen punched. Martin folded forward, gasping and speechless. Elin began slapping mud on his back. "Roll," she whispered to Owen. "Roll in the mud." He saw what she was trying to do and obeyed. "Now, for the life of you, lie still."

From the corner of his eye, Owen saw Elin's people flip the boat on its side behind a screen of willows and throw some water weed on the hull. Resting keel down, it was not recognizable as a boat. It simply looked like another moss-covered hummock on the riverbank, while he, Elin, and Martin would appear to be part of the muddy expanse left by the dry winter's low water between deep channel and the shore.

The boat hove into sight at the river bend. She was small, no more than twenty or twenty-five feet, a fairly broad-beamed, shallow-draft scow intended for the coastal trade. But tonight, she was decked out within an inch of her life.

His cheek in the mud, his hand in Elin's, Owen watched her come and wondered what she could possibly mean. The dragon at the prow was newly repainted and glowed like some fine enameled jewel—scarlet, black, sapphire, and gold in the torches set along her sides. There was room at her gunwales for no more than a dozen rowers, six on each side. The men pulling the sweeps were freshly barbered and bathed, and wore clean clothing. They sang as the oars lifted and fell, carrying them upriver against the current.

The wood that framed the boat's body was freshly scraped, oiled, and gleaming. Garlands of glistening oak leaves, pale white-berried mistletoe, and lacy cedar hung draped along her sides glowing against the black wood. As Owen watched her draw closer and closer, he couldn't help but be awed by the ceremonial craft's beauty. The threatening but magnificent dragonhead loomed over him, blotting out the stars as it passed. In spite of the eerie terror of the prow, the chief danger they faced were the torches flaming along her length. They illuminated the river from bank to bank.

The three lying in the mud found their hands locked together. They forgot to breathe as she went by. Then she was gone, and the triumphant singing was succeeded by the sound of weeping, a ghostly sobbing that followed her into the night as the darkness closed in behind her.

Owen and Elin rose and helped Martin free himself from the mud. The three staggered ashore to join the rest of Elin's people.

They sat in the protected hollow created by the beached boat. One of Elin's people had thrown dry branches on the ground, and the water was able to drain slowly out of their clothing.

"Fire?" Owen asked Alshan. He was mindful of Martin's shivering.

"No," the old man said. "It is too dangerous. I have no high opinion of their powers, but should they see it, we might easily find ourselves in the same position as the men in the boat, blinded by our own light and easily taken."

They began passing food around—bread, cheese, and cold meat. Mouthfuls of eau-de-vie managed to combat the cold, and draughts of wine washed the food down.

The moon was in the last quarter, a faint crescent, a pale, eerie glow caught in the drifting fog that covered the whole countryside. Owen found he could see his companions well in its light. Personally, he was annoyed. *I am of noble birth,* he thought. *I am bishop of Chantalon. I should be sitting in my hall. My lady Elin, who is tearing cold meat and bread with her excellent teeth, should be sitting beside me dressed properly in a gown as a woman should, not wearing leather britches, cross-gartered leggings, a deerhide dalmatic, and a cap.*

Her friends, Sybilla, Tigg, and the old leader, Alshan, were beside her. Their attitude was the other splinter under his hide. When he'd rescued Elin from Viking slavery, he found they came with her. They were her dowry. And had proven a rich one. With their and her help he'd gone from being a minor, unregarded churchman, bullied by the count and the neighboring large landowner, Reynald, to becoming independent, rich, and the only remaining power in the city of Chantalon. His cellar bulged with stores intended to stand a siege if necessary, and his strongboxes were overflowing with loot taken in two battles against the Vikings. Now he was contemplating a third encounter and needed to know how many men were in the Viking fortress and whether the great raider chief, Hakon, remained with them.

Elin's people, her friends, had many names. However, it was common knowledge among the peasants who feared them, protected them, and sometimes worshiped them, that they had been part of this land forever. Before the Romans marched, their stolid tread tramping out stone roads; before the Gauls raided, fought, and threw up their green ring forts, Elin's people wandered under the trees. They gathered acorns, chestnuts, and honey to make bread. They netted fish in the streams and songbirds in weed-grown clearings in the dense forests, and took ducks and geese in the marshes along the coast.

When called upon by the wary peasants who lived at the edge of the waste, they could show even the unarmed and unarmored how to dig pits to defeat the tusked boar and the fearsome aurochs, wild bull of the woods. Restless as windblown thistledown, invisible as wind or trackless as the dawn mist, they came and went as they pleased, leaving no more trace of their passage than a fragrance broadcast into the summer wind by a mayhaw or a flowering quince. One thing, however, they not only didn't know how to do but wouldn't even try to do—they would not row. He'd found this out after a few moments' consultation with them when he'd proposed the expedition to the Viking camp.

He'd been married to Elin for some months and found it a very rewarding experience in most ways. But he'd quickly learned the punishing futility of trying to bring pressure to bear on either her or her people to obey any order they found unacceptable. Their approach to the fortress, as was explained to him by the old man, Alshan, was to travel upriver overland and then snag a large log. Mounted on this informal means of transportation, they would float downriver past the fortress in the night. They might ground it on the island occupied by the Vikings and make such observations as were to his liking and then push off before dawn. Home before dinner, Alshan explained. Why, after all, would one want to be so illogical as to paddle upriver? The river would not like it—the current was there for a purpose. Their hands would not like it—they would get blisters. And they might be caught by the Vikings, whose craft plied the river more and more frequently.

Elin committed the primal sin of a Christian wife. She first giggled, then laughed out loud at his entirely ineffective efforts to bring Alshan and her friends around to his point of view.

Hence, Martin. Martin was the really massive parish priest of the only fishing village near the city. The calluses on his hands had to be seen to be believed. He could begin rowing at dawn and still be found rowing at dusk.

Owen had given Martin two horses, a stallion and a mare. Martin was so poor that no one in his ancestral family for five generations had ever been known to possess such wealth. Every living relative out to the tenth degree of relationship came to examine this largesse and stand transfixed at the pasture fence. When the stallion was found to be willing, amorous, and fertile, and the mare pregnant, a solemn celebration was held.

All for miles around, whether related to Martin or not, felt Martin owed Owen anything he cared to ask. Hence, Martin, wet, unhappy, and probably much more afraid than he would admit, was here sitting in the cold, wet dark next to the bishop, wondering what was happening in the camp upriver.

The concentrated eau-de-vie warmed Owen and emboldened him. He passed the flask to Elin. "I wish you would stay here," he told her quietly, "you and your friends."

"No." She sounded adamant. "You and Martin aren't experienced night travelers. If you don't believe me, look at what just almost happened. Had I not known what to do, both of you might have been taken. And Owen, you know very well that if Hakon gets his hands on you, a moment later you'll be dead. When he captured you before, he yielded to Osric's greed and demanded ransom. This time he won't give money a single thought. He won't allow you a moment for prayer."

Alshan, the old shaman and leader among Elin's people, chuckled. "Indeed, this is true. He has promised your weight in gold to the man who brings him your head. In a recognizable condition, of course."

"I didn't know that!" Elin cried.

"I didn't, either," Owen said gloomily, "and I'm not sure I wanted to know it now, Alshan. Couldn't you have waited until I sat in my hall before a warm fire, friends and loyal companions at my side, before breaking the news?"

"You see?" Elin said as though it proved her point that he couldn't be safely left to his own devices.

Owen didn't, but he did realize that as long as Elin and her friends held to the same mind-set, he wasn't going to be able to shake them off. Though he hadn't communicated the fact to Elin, one reason he'd been willing to run this appalling risk was because no one could tell him if Hakon remained with the Vikings camped upriver. If he did, then Chantalon remained in deadly peril. "Is he there and still in command?" Owen asked Alshan.

"Who knows?" Alshan answered.

If Hakon remained, his strong leadership would hold the men of the camp together. If not, Owen and his captain, Godwin, could dangle bait before the mob of disorganized thieves, divide them into small groups, and cut them to pieces one by one. He had to know how things stood in the island fortress.

Hakon controlled the river. Owen knew that he who held the river in a very real sense ruled the valley along with the rolling limestone hills on either side of the fertile lowlands.

Timber grew well in the high fastness; deadfalls and winter kills contributed firewood. The broken stony slopes harbored elk, deer, coney, badger, and wild boar. Tame pigs could forage with the wild under the trees. But the true richness of the valley lay in the fertile soil, the bottom land along the river shore. There, the living torrent blessed them all. The rich, heavy, well-watered fields and forests along its length held water like a jug. In a bad year, they could harvest two crops; in a good, three. Only war brought starvation and suffering to the valley.

Compared to the more rapacious brigands who dominated the Seine valley to the south, Hakon was a very minor chieftain. He commanded the loyalty of only a few hundred men, as opposed to the many thousands controlled by those who had taken Rouen and raided up the Seine as far as Paris.

But Hakon's fortified island allowed him to send his brigands into the open country to the south, while he fed men and their camp followers on what could be stolen from those who remained in the river valley.

Even as Owen and his captain, Godwin, seized power in the city, Hakon raised the stakes in their struggle for dominance by seizing Reynald's widow, Elspeth, and gathering into his hands not only Reynald's stronghold but also what remained of those lands abandoned by both lord and serf scattered along the river between his island and Reynald's hall. He held, in fact, most of the valley length except Owen's town, Chantalon, and the farms and villages around it.

If Hakon could break Owen's power over his little city, the river would belong to the raider chief and with it, the whole valley.

But Owen's position wasn't as bad as it looked. Chantalon commanded the river mouth, controlling the rich marshes of the delta and the largest area of cleared fertile land in the entire valley. Compared with it, Reynald's hall was only a poor assart carved from virgin forest, and Hakon's island fortress a nest of thieves as like to be cleaned out by the next strong king who rose to rule in Francia, or even by Owen, should he gain the upper hand in his city by the sea.

"We're going together," Elin said flatly. "All of us. And another thing—the two of you have no sense of direction, and—"

Owen rose to his feet. Attempting to persuade them to accept any sort of discipline was a hopeless task, rather like trying to herd butterflies. He caught Elin's arms with both hands and pulled her toward him.

She gasped, admiring at the same time his quickness of movement. Her people called him a name that meant "cat." He was small, dark, lithe, flexible as a willow wand, and sexually driven. He did bring a tomcat to mind. He silenced her with a kiss.

"All right," he whispered into her ear. "Come with me. I suppose it's no worse than leaving you here. Promise me, though, if anything happens to me, you will flee with your people."

"Yes." She paused long enough for her lips to form the

words and continued kissing him. She had thought being dressed as one of her folk in the leather traveling gear would rouse disgust or perhaps indifference in him. She'd been wrong. Oh so wrong.

The night before they left, he'd come in and found her adjusting her leggings in front of the fire in their bedroom. He'd paused, hooked one finger in the front of the dalmatic, and looked down into the soft, linen camisole and what it contained.

"Quince," he said. "No, pear. No, they are too hard even when ripe. Plum. No, too rounded and the skin is tart. Peaches. Ah yes, that's it. Perfect, ripe, warm, velvety, and bursting with slippery hot juice." His hand fell to the crotch of the leather breeches. "Here," he said. "Let me rub my face in that warm, sweet juice."

She fled. He was faster. She wrestled. He was stronger. She pleaded, half in jest, half in earnest. He was merciless. She fought. He laughed at her and stripped her naked to the waist. The battle was lost. She was exhausted. He had the endurance of a timberwolf on the hunt. She made a last stand, clutching the breeches. He threatened to make her yowl and spit like the stable cat with a tom in her and scandalize the household. She yielded decorously and she found herself being pushed remorselessly toward surrender. The last sight she had of him before her final citadel fell was of him grinning down at her as her belly pressed against his, her eyelids fluttered shut. She entered the deep concentration of a long, pulsating orgasm and tried not to sound like the stable cat.

When he was finished kissing her, she found her knees loosened both by the kiss and the memories. She heard her people suggesting some things he ought to do to her right now before the end of their journey. They were an earthy folk and had fertile imaginations. She was glad he didn't speak their language.

Martin looked slightly shocked. Open demonstrations of affection between husbands and wives weren't considered dignified and lowered a man in the eyes of his peers. Not that Martin could ever think less of his bishop, but other men hearing of it might speak slightingly of Owen. "My lord," he said in a gentle, humble reproof.

Owen let go of Elin. He sighed and felt a surge of anger, both at Martin, for breaking up what had been a pleasant interlude, and at Elin, so precious to him and so stubborn and careless about risking her life. "I will take the lead," he said. "You, Elin, stay well back. Martin, I can do without your comments on my behavior. You will follow me."

Martin flushed, doubly shamefaced for being called down by someone he so deeply respected.

It was cold, wet work moving along the shoreline in darkness. The ground was soft and the going slow. At every step, Owen found himself mired to the knees in the sucking earth. Such grass as grew between the thick undergrowth of the forest edge and the water offered little better passage, being coated with slime that made the footing as treacherous as walking on a greased floor, forming a deceptive carpet over concealed mud holes.

After the sixth or seventh time Owen put his foot down on what seemed like solid ground and found himself crawling around in three or four feet of dirty water, he found his temper had cooled. He was simply too uncomfortable to stay angry. He also was unwilling to show either fear or discomfort to Martin, blundering along behind him.

They traveled at first by starlight and the faint glow of the sickle moon, but ahead of them, the light grew brighter and brighter.

Owen knew they were close to the camp when he was able to see a snag of stranded driftwood in time to keep from tripping over it. At the same moment, Martin put his foot into a stand of winter-killed alder. A dozen or so of the wandlike canes broke with a series of soft pops. "Take care," Owen said. "Don't be so clumsy."

This advice was somewhat marred by the fact that Owen tripped over a tree root he didn't see and plunged facedown into four feet of water. He paused to let the rest catch up with them and to clear the muck out of his eyes with his fingers. Elin and her kin moved like the very shadows themselves. He and Martin were the clumsy oafs in need of protection. He was likely spending his worry on the wrong people.

Owen didn't hear anything, didn't even feel a nudge as Alshan's voice spoke in his ear. Fright lifted him several inches out of the mud.

"We are very close to them," Alshan said. "The light is brighter. Can you not see it? And do not start so. They will hear you."

When Owen glanced back, the little man had faded into the concealment of the trees.

He found he was facing a small headland that projected out like a finger into the river. The nearly submerged bit of land was thickly overgrown by tall cattails and piled high with the broken remnant of a tall ash downed by the spring flood.

Owen stayed on his hands and knees, more to avoid falling and humiliating himself again than out of any idea of concealment. He climbed in and among the tree limbs, poked his head between the broken branches of the ash, and said, "Yeck!" He realized they'd reached their objective.

Martin, also on his hands and knees at his shoulder, asked, "What?"

"Be quiet," Owen whispered hoarsely, desperately. "For your life's sake be quiet."

Martin peered past Owen and hissed, "God protect us, it's them."

They both crouched, shoulder to shoulder, staring down at the scene. They were looking through the screen of driftwood and cattails at the camp and five mighty longships drawn up on the shore.

"Eighty feet if she's an inch, I swear it," Martin breathed in his ear. "Owen, these are oceangoing vessels, warships."

Owen didn't answer; he was too busy trying to master his fear. His mouth was filled with the sour taste of vomit, and his belly muscles fluttered against the mud under him. Yet, at the same time, his heart and mind were boiling with hatred. The bastards were so goddamned sure of themselves.

The nearest longship was beached just beyond the headland, only a few yards away. Owen's eye followed the curve of the prow up to where the cruel, fanged dragon head lifted almost to the lowest branches of the trees. In the fitful light of bonfires and torches, the gold-scaled neck, the scarlet head, and the slit pupil of the serpent eye seemed to stare down at him in proud malevolence.

Next to him, Owen heard Martin draw breath in awe. Despite being wet, cold, and afraid, Owen found he felt the same. It was a magnificent sight.

Torches blazed all along the stockade wall of the island fortress, their reflections dancing in the silent, black water.

Each of the five ships before him was illuminated by its own separate torch borne high in an iron basket, supported by a pole sunk in the sand. The ships' figureheads before him glistened with new paint. They dazzled the eye. Fangs jutted from their open mouths, tongues darted out, painted red and black. The mouths of the dragons seemed to drip clotted blood. The necks were scaled in gold, as the first, or metallic bronze or silver. Others were indigo blue. Each different, each beautiful in its way, burning against the night and the dark wood of the ships' bodies.

Their sides were lined with brilliantly colored shields bearing the devices of the chieftains who accompanied Hakon, golden dragons on fields of scarlet, knots of serpents coiled on azure circles. Others were emblazoned with the hammer of Thor or Odin's spear.

Rage stirred in Owen the way the beginnings of a volcano mutter in the bowels of the earth long before an eruption takes place. His mind began to cast about silently for something, anything that might turn the celebration into something a lot less pleasant for Hakon's men. Because celebration it was. Tonight they chose to flaunt their triumph over the helpless and wallow in the riches torn from his wounded and struggling people.

"They are at their revels," Martin whispered.

Yes, Owen thought. *They are.*

The ships were garlanded with branches of wild holly and mistletoe. From the far end of the line of vessels, he could hear the sound of singing, and the smell of roasting meat drifted to his nostrils. Men and women walked along the shore before the hulls of the giant war machines, laughing, talking, and drinking.

Bitterly, Owen added up what little they had to work with. He and Martin carried an axe and a knife. For whatever good it would do, he had his sword. The torches were set firmly on posts well away from the flammable rigging, and the sails were furled, wrapped tightly around the spars of each ship.

Martin was right. They'd best sneak back to the boat as quickly as possible and return to Chantalon with the news that an attack was almost certain before the end of winter.

Someone moaned.

Owen wiggled forward and heard another moan, then a sound of sobbing in the darkness near the forest just below the head of the closest dragon. Hidden nearby, someone, something was in pain. His hackles rose. He remembered that as the little coasting ship passed he'd heard the sound of weeping.

Owen pushed between the branches of the ash, through the brittle stalks of the cattails. They rustled softly above him.

Martin reached for him, but his fingers slipped on the slimy ooze covering Owen's back. Owen wiggled forward, trying to see into the shadows near the forest, and found himself sliding down the slight elevation of the headland to the beach below. He fetched up at the foot of the slope within hand's reach of the nearest longship, lying in the very shadow of the prow.

Beside him, the overlapping planks of the hull curved sinuously upward toward the dragon standard. He could see the outlines of the pegs that held them to one another and even the adze marks of the craftsman who fashioned the instruments of conquest.

Owen discovered that perfect terror casts out fear. From his position beside the prow, he was looking down the beach, past the ships' bows. Bearing down on him was Hakon, followed by a dozen chief men of the camp.

Owen froze. He couldn't move without giving himself, and perhaps Martin, away. He thought that when they plucked him from the mud, he would put up a fight, delay them long enough to give Martin a head start back to the rest, buy some time for them to escape. He had time to think perhaps this moment was meant to be. Hakon was there. If he came close enough to Owen, he could be killed. It might be worth it to end the raider chief's life even at the cost of his own. One hand was clenched so tightly in the sandy shore that when his fingers closed, it bit into the sand and his fingernails bled. With the other, he felt under his prone body for his sword. When he found it, he almost fell into the unforgivable sin. He almost cursed God. *How could you?* his mind raged. *How could you bring me so close and the blade be pinned under me?* He couldn't be sure he could free it in time to close fatally with Hakon before he himself was seen and killed.

Hakon was indeed in the forefront of the glittering company approaching him, the streak of silver in his dark hair gleaming in the torchlight. He wore the golden fish-scale cuirass, and his fingers were locked around a belt of amethyst and silver from which was suspended an inlaid sword sheath.

If he was the most resplendent of the men, the rest were similarly arrayed in mantles of brocade and heavily embroidered silk-covered armor aglow with precious stones. Everywhere on their bodies gold gleamed brightly; brooches, amulets, and the hilts of weapons dazzled Owen's eyes. Defiantly, they carried on their backs the successful plunder of a lifetime, loot torn from burning cities and shattered farmsteads, the price of slavery and murder, as if to say, "We go in glory because we have despoiled the world."

Hakon stopped within arm's length of Owen, and Owen thought clearly, *So, this is death.*

But the attention of Hakon and the others wasn't on a lump of mud on the shore. They hadn't looked closely enough to see the lump of mud had eyes. The pirate chief turned his back to Owen and pointed down at something in the thick growth of dried grass and weeds near the forest.

An old voice crackled, "Pleasing. They are very pleasing; all young and healthy. Very pleasing indeed."

Owen hadn't noticed her before. A crone, caped and hooded in black, she mingled with the splendidly dressed pirate lords like a crow in the midst of a flock of songbirds.

Hakon reached down into the path of weeds and pulled a woman to her feet. She was dark and her unbound hair fell down, half veiling her features, but Owen could see enough of her face to tell her skin was gray and her mouth slack with horror.

When she realized she'd been chosen, she began to scream, weak, rapid, high, thin, piercing shrieks, the screams of a person caught in a nightmare.

She screamed when the ropes were cut away from her wrists and ankles; continued screaming, each scream a nail driven into Owen's skull, as she was led below the prow of the ship that sheltered Owen; screamed when Hakon tore away her ragged shift in one brutal gesture, leaving her naked; and only stopped screaming when the rope closed her throat.

Her legs kicked violently as she was jerked into the air, and Owen saw the streams of yellow urine pour down her thighs.

When she dangled, twisting, face turning black before the red mouth of the dragon, the crone handed Hakon a spear. Hakon struck upward with the spear through the rib cage, still moving, still straining to draw breath.

Owen knew he must have closed his eyes but couldn't remember doing it. Because when he opened them, the form at the end of the rope was limp and the head of the dragon dripped crimson. Hakon, followed by the rest, was walking back to the patch of grass.

Still petrified with shock, Owen watched as Hakon dragged another victim to his feet. This one was male, not yet out of his teens, only a little younger than Owen himself. The boy howled and his body arched and twisted as he fought the ropes. Hakon's fist smashed into the side of the boy's head, and the slender body went limp. As he was dragged away, Owen could hear the screams and inarticulate pleas for mercy rising from the weeds where the rest of the victims were lying.

No! Owen thought. *No! Five ships, five human lives; no!* He understood the brief advantage his covering of filth brought him and chose to use it. He moved like a serpent up the beach, toward the forest and the voices crying out above him

The second victim was being hoisted into the air when he reached the pinioned bodies of the rest. Owen didn't look at or think about the two already dead. For them, it was simply too late. He crawled in among the others awaiting execution whispering, "Don't give me away," understanding even as he spoke the words that they were wholly superfluous.

As far as the crowd watching the second sacrifice was concerned, the prisoners were already dead, and no one paid the slightest attention to anything they did or said.

Two men and one woman remained. Owen crawled up next to one of the men. He stared at Owen in blank terror, the whites of his eyes gleaming in the shadows. For a heart-stopping second, he didn't seem to realize Owen's knife had freed him. Then he got his hands and feet under him and vanished, half walking, half crawling into the undergrowth at the edge of the forest.

The remaining two, a boy and girl, were quicker. Both rolled on their sides to let him get at the ropes on their hands and feet. When they were loose, Owen looked up from his crouch on the ground and realized Hakon and the chiefs, moving in a body, were almost upon him.

So, Owen thought, *the gray ladies had indeed intended the moment.* He was in a crouch; his sword was free. He drew.

He saw Hakon stiffen at the sound. Blinded by the torches, he still couldn't see Owen, but he knew the sword cry and was fully aware a warrior of practiced skill had drawn on him.

Owen should have killed him then, separating his head

from his body with one slice, but, hot as his rage might be, he had never contemplated such a killing in his life. He hesitated, a part of his mind stubbornly refusing to admit a life-taking of such stealth was honorable.

Hakon's eyes picked out his brown clothing even though it matched the forest. Against all odds, he recognized Owen. A band of firelight ran the length of Owen's blade.

Without thought, Hakon's sword cleared the sheath. His blade locked with Owen's, grip to grip, as he tried to use his superior weight and strength to throw the smaller man. But Owen slipped his sword into a smooth disengagement. Hakon heard Owen's steel whistle in the dark. He remembered one of Owen's favorite tricks with sick fear. He leaped, backflipping to the beach behind him. As he did, he saw Owen's blade slice through the air where his thighs had been. He knew, had his jump been a second slower, Owen would have taken both his legs off above the knees. *He will flee,* Hakon thought.

Owen didn't. He bounded into the open, following Hakon into the light, into the teeth of death, into the weapons of a thousand enemies who would compete with each other to slaughter him.

"I'm going to kill you!" he said to Hakon. And Hakon saw in his eyes the madness that made the slender young man almost universally feared, even among his Viking enemies.

Hakon gave him an honorable answer. "You will do what you can, and so will I."

They closed again, Owen coming in, seemingly heedless, trying to take Hakon's head off; Hakon going for the deadly stroke that clove a man's body from neck to waist.

They both missed. Hakon jerked back and Owen gave a lightning twist a snake might have envied, turning himself sideways. All Hakon's sword did was slice a strip from the leather dalmatic he was wearing.

Hakon realized the crowd on the beach was spreading out to give him room. Hakon was a deeply pragmatic man. He was profoundly annoyed that as he found himself confronted by a mad, dangerous enemy, all his friends seemed willing to do was be entertained by the engagement. He swore chain-lightning curses at his own stubbornness in being unwilling to sacrifice his honor and call for help. Even as these thoughts flashed across his consciousness, he realized Owen was moving to close with him again. Hakon was sure he could read the slender devil's intent. He was going for a disemboweling stroke, betting on sliding his sword under Hakon's cuirass to spill his guts on the ground before Hakon could cleave his skull to the teeth.

Hakon grinned. He was perfectly willing to bet Owen couldn't eviscerate him. There were things about his armor that didn't show on the surface.

A split second later, Hakon realized he'd been wrong. The groin had been Owen's target after all. The point of Owen's sword slid on one of Hakon's greaves. Owen had been hurried by Hakon's speed, but the blow Hakon aimed at Owen's skull also whined through empty air as Owen's body crashed into his knees. He was supposed to do a belly flop onto the sand, his neck bared to Owen's sword.

Hakon didn't. He somersaulted and came to his feet, driven upward by one blow of his left hand on the sand. His strength and agility sent him to his feet as though he were mounted on springs. But Owen had missed his footing. He was not booted but was wearing only the soft leather leggings of the forest people. Slick with mud, one of his feet skidded in water slime, and Owen's feet shot out from under him.

Hakon was above him, teeth bared, sword raised to strike.

Martin erupted from the cover of the cattails with a roar. He was a figure of terror, plastered with mud, dripping with slime and waterweed, red mouth agape.

Even Hakon quailed back, and the rest of the men scattered.

Martin was no soldier. He didn't try to seize a weapon but ran for the nearest of the tall torches that lighted the longships. He uprooted it from the soft earth and swung the red-hot iron basket in a giant circle, scattering coals everywhere. The men within the radius of that swing fled, even Hakon.

Owen could distinguish words in the roaring sound of Martin's voice, "Run, oh God, run!"

Owen didn't run. He darted for the torch near the second longship. He didn't have Martin's strength. The big pole wouldn't come up. But when he threw his whole weight against it, the thing tipped, emptying its basket of blazing charcoal into the longship. A few coals dropped into the furled sail and it caught fire.

From the corner of his eye, he saw Martin take his own advice. He dropped the torch pole and fled. He ran toward the two prisoners Owen had freed. They seemed rooted to the ground by terror, and seizing the boy by the wrist and the girl around the waist, he vanished into the darkness. Owen went down as the torch pole tilted away from him.

Freed from the necessity of single combat, Hakon roared, "Are you fools mad? Take him. Kill him. I myself will cover his dead body with gold. All for the men who finish him."

Owen was trapped between the advancing Vikings and the river, the burning longship behind him. His sword was gone. He had no other weapon, not even a knife.

The black-clad witch, the one who had pronounced the sacrifices pleasing to the gods, pushed her way through the knot of men advancing on Owen. She pulled at Hakon's mantle and pointed to Owen. "When he is dead," she screeched, "cut out his heart, roast, and eat it. His virtue and valor will enter you, and all the land between here and the sea will be yours."

Hakon stared down at the crone, and Owen saw the various expressions chase themselves across his face—horror, disgust, and fear, finally succeeded by cold-eyed resolution. And Owen knew before dawn his heart would be roasting on a spit and Hakon, however sickened by the necessity, would do the deed before the entire camp. He would, in fact, do far worse to achieve the prize he so desperately craved—possession of all land between the fortress and the sea.

Suddenly, fire seemed to rain down on the evil old crone. She screeched horribly as flames leaped from every fold of her dark wrapping.

Owen felt something fly past his shoulder.

Elin landed, leaping from the burning longship to the beach beside him. She pointed her finger at the Viking witch who was now rolling, clothes blazing on the sand. "I burn her. I burned Reynald. Alive, do you hear me? Alive. And everyone who touches my Lord Owen, I will burn alive—alive—in agony, alive."

The leather cap had fallen from her head. The spill of black hair framed a dead-white face with the dazzling blue eyes of a fiend.

They were grown men, strong men, armed men, but one and all, they quailed back before her. Not very far, but enough. She seized Owen's hand and they both pelted like lightning toward the huge ash deadfall and the dark forest beyond.

Hakon picked up the sorceress's flaming body and threw her into the river. "To the ship," he shouted. "Forget the bishop and his witch. Put the fire out. Get it out, damn you, before she burns."

In the darkness, Elin and Owen plunged through the forest, a few of the Vikings in howling pursuit behind them.

Without warning, the ground simply vanished from beneath Owen's feet. He let go of Elin's hand, fearing to pull her down with him. Down, down he went, crashing through what must be a deadfall of broken branches, in mortal terror that his descending body might be impaled on a thicker limb than the ones his body was breaking, until he came to rest in soft earth, the wind knocked out of him, in utter blackness.

2

*I*N the city of Chantalon, Godwin, Owen's cousin and captain, waited for news of his lord's success or failure in his foray to the Viking camp.

Godwin was sitting in the hall, eating sops of bread and wine. He wasn't worried about Owen. He wasn't worried about anything. As far as he was concerned, right now Owen and his rather peculiar wife might as well not exist. He sat there trying to look gloomy and bored, but he really wasn't either. He was watching Rosamund sweep the floor.

Rosamund was sixteen. She was one of the housemaids. When she wasn't being a housemaid, she was selling her favors to Godwin's knights for pecuniary and presentational considerations. Godwin had heard she had quite a bit of silver and jewelry in a lockbox under Anna's bed.

Anna was an ancient, rising seventy or so. She was doing mysterious things (at least as far as Godwin was concerned) to a large mound of flour on the sideboard behind him. She kept house for Owen.

Rosamund was a pocket porcelain Venus. She was less than five feet tall. She had wide hips, a tiny waist, small, well-formed breasts with big, pink nipples. Since she was working, her skirts and shift were rucked up to her knees with a leather belt. Her curly blond hair was pulled up to the top of her head, secured by a fillet, then allowed to cascade to the back and on either side of her face. She wielded a twig broom that tossed a lot of dust into the air and actually pushed other heavier detritus before it on the floor.

She radiated the energy, optimism, and happiness of sixteen. She seemed not just to push the broom but to dance with it—a little sunbeam trapped in the morning gloom of Owen's cavernous hall, not the least bit dismayed by her capture but still radiating color, light, and beauty into Godwin's morose middle-aged pessimism.

He could see, around her neck and under her dress, traces of the gold chain spaced with coral roses he'd given her. It was one of the few truly beautiful things she owned, and he'd been told by Anna that she treasured it. He hadn't given it to her for the usual services rendered. In fact, he and Owen were probably the only two men in the household who hadn't enjoyed her favors. He'd rewarded her for acting as lookout in the hall while he led his men to the church to kill the count.

As he watched, she began humming softly and a small smile played on her lips.

Godwin wondered how long it had been since he brought as much energy and joy to any project as this tiny one brought to the very mundane task of sweeping the floor.

Owen's hall was standard: front door opening into the square, public space, back door opening into a kitchen garden supporting a variety of winter crops in raised beds. Private space? Godwin would have snorted in derision. Half the town could easily find their way there if anything notable happened, even a knock-down, drag-out between a husband and wife counted as notable—any husband and wife, not just Owen and Elin. The yard ended in a little stone balcony with a splendid view overlooking the river.

The town was perched on a not very high rock cradled in the river end. Chantalon was a port, and shallow draft vessels sailing through the marshland at the coast could reach it without difficulty.

The little balcony over the river was chiefly useful for disposing of such garbage that could not be burned or composted away. Night soil went into the garden, thank you very much. They had not then given up that useful habit. And besides, no one ate raw vegetables. Most were too small, tough, nasty-tasting, fibrous, or tasteless to be eaten unaccompanied. They filled out the soup pot or the stew pot, where they were subjected to lots of boiling water and melted into the broth.

Enar, two peasants Godwin didn't know, and Ingund entered through the back door from the garden. Godwin made a soft sound of annoyance. Enar was one of his least favorite people. Enar was Owen's friend and he'd done Owen far too much faithful service not to be honored and trusted. But he went out of his way to annoy Godwin.

Owen hadn't taken him on his present journey because Godwin had asked him not to. "I will not deny he is a very brave and a most dangerous man," Godwin had told Owen. "But his greatest expertise is in starting quarrels. And it is my firm belief that one day he will initiate one he cannot finish. And I have found with such men that often everyone in the vicinity suffers grievously." Owen had slipped away, leaving Enar behind. And Godwin knew he'd earned Enar's bitter resentment.

Ingund, Enar's wife, Godwin liked better. The city had been attacked by the Vikings a few months ago, and she'd shown a real talent for warfare. She wore a mail shirt and a boar-tusk helmet. *Too bad,* Godwin thought. *She'd been an equally talented cook.* She was very given to the joys of the table, as was Godwin, and he'd been hoping she'd suspend her martial activities, at least until the Vikings attacked the city again. And return to cooking.

Godwin heard Anna, still working with the flour behind him, mutter something really nasty under her breath. Godwin turned and saw her shoot a very dark look at Ingund.

Enar, oblivious to these undercurrents, strolled over and sat down next to Godwin. He also took in Rosamund's graceful broom handling. He drove an elbow into Godwin's ribs. "Oh, she's a fine sight. Hey, my girl," he shouted at Rosamund, "pull that dress up a bit higher so my lord's captain here can get a better look at those soft, shapely thighs of yours. The old devil has been sleeping alone too long. He's as poisonous as a viper. I'll bet he thinks if—"

This was as far as Enar got. Godwin came to his feet with an inarticulate sound that was a perfect cross between a snarl of rage and a roar of fury.

Rosamund dropped the broom. Her face suffused with scarlet. Round her little heels might be, but she wasn't used to being treated so crassly. Owen and Elin always insisted an outward decorum be maintained.

Ingund whispered, "Oh no!"

Anna rounded on Enar. "Pig!" she snarled as she jerked his head back and placed a ten-inch butcher knife to one side of his neck. The knife nicked his skin, and a trickle of blood ran down, staining his shirt. Her fingers were locked in his nostrils. She wasn't bare-handed, but wearing heavy metal-tipped work gloves, and if he did move, she was capable of ripping his nose off.

He heard Godwin's blade clear the sheath. He gave an inarticulate cry that combined apology and fright.

"Not another word," Godwin whispered. "For Owen's sake I will not kill you, but I promise you will lose interest in sex—permanently."

Enar sat quietly.

"I am heartily sick of both of you," Anna told him. "All you do is eat, sleep, and drink. That was not so bad, but that is all your wife does, too. I have a household filled with lazy men to feed and keep clean, with but one woman to help me, and that one nearly a child—Rosamund. I will not have you louts annoying her. Get back to work, girl."

A goggling Rosamund immediately began sweeping energetically.

"Now, Ingund," Anna continued in a voice cold as winter-chilled stone.

"Yes, Anna?" Ingund replied meekly.

"You will . . . Come, I want to hear it."

"I will lay aside my arms and undertake to bake the bread and cook the meals again. Except for the helmet. I will not put aside my nice boar-tusk helmet. One of the knights or men-at-arms will steal it."

"Oh yes, you will," Anna replied grimly.

"I will not!" Ingund shouted, stamping her foot.

Enar made a gurgling noise.

"Shut up," Anna said.

"Yes," Godwin told him smoothly. "I wouldn't call attention to myself if I were you. Now, Anna," he said in a conciliatory tone, "the presence of the helmet wouldn't affect Ingund's ability to cook, and besides, I've noticed Gowen eyeing the thing affectionately." Gowen was the largest, most dangerous, and most ruthless of Godwin's knights.

"Hmmm," Anna commented, slackening her grip slightly on Enar's nose. "He's not usually interested in anything that won't feed him, fight him, or fuck him."

"True," Godwin replied, "but anyone who possesses anything, animate or inanimate, brute or human that Gowen casts a covetous eye on had best watch the object closely, or it will soon be gone."

"True," Anna said. "You may wear the boar tusks," she told Ingund. So saying, she let go of Enar's nose and took the knife away from his neck.

Enar leaped over the table and landed next to Rosamund and her broom. She ignored him and swept around him. She was sweeping toward the front door, the one to the square.

Enar stood, giving Anna a long thoughtful look. Anna tossed the pair of armored gloves to the table in front of Godwin. "Thank you," she said.

"You put her up to it," Enar said accusingly to Godwin.

Godwin smiled.

Nobody liked Godwin's smiles. Enar had been once heard to say Death himself would not care to be smiled at by Godwin.

"Discretion," Godwin said, still smiling, "is said to be the better part of valor. Or a word to the wise . . ."

"Do not drown me in proverbs," Enar said. He slunk out of the back door, giving Ingund an apologetic roll of his eyes.

Ingund was elbow deep in the flour, now dough. "What!"

she grumbled. "This is cold. How the devil do you expect it to rise? Where is the starter I left with you?"

"It died," Anna said with a really nasty snicker. "What am I? An expert in bread making? Before you and all of Godwin's killers arrived, I bought enough for a week from Arn, the tavern keeper. Now I have a household of hogs and," she added with a leer, "sows—who eat with both hands—and—"

"Well!" Ingund screeched at Anna. "Where am I supposed to get more starter—your old, smelly crotch?"

"Almighty Father in heaven above," Godwin roared. "Have mercy on my soul. What a vile idea. Rosamund, fetch Ingund some bread starter. Now!"

Rosamund's apron flew one way, the broom the other. She fled the hall at a dead run, slamming the door behind her.

"Does she know where to find some?" Ingund asked.

"If she values her life, she'll find out," Anna replied, and slammed the carving knife into the sideboard an inch deep. "I'm in a bad mood today."

"Dear lady," Godwin said, "I gathered that. And please wash the gloves. They were in Enar's nose."

Anna bore the gloves away.

Ingund indicated the peasant couple who were watching the high jinks with what Godwin considered commendable patience. "You'd best speak to them, Godwin," she said. "I know Enar can be the world's most ridiculous buffoon, but he's no fool, and they really have something to tell you."

Godwin invited them to the table. Ingund left the bread long enough to find them something to eat and drink. Rosamund returned with the bread starter.

The couple, it seemed, were the leaders of a delegation from one of the villages near the forest. They and others in the village, hardy souls that they were, had started out ready to get in a winter crop. And it seemed they were not going to be allowed to plant.

After the couple left, Godwin sat quietly for a few moments, frowning.

"What do you think?" Anna said.

"You know?" Godwin asked.

"Oh yes," Anna told him. She was lighting a fire in the bread oven near the hearth. "It's common knowledge. None have dared stay the night outside the walls. Already, valuable seed grain has been stolen. Any tool or implement left lying around vanishes."

"Hakon's men," Ingund contributed.

"Almost certainly." Godwin rose and went to the stair. It was pegged to the wall and went straight up to the second floor.

"What are you going to do?" Anna asked.

"I'm not sure. Talk to Ranulf, I think," Godwin replied.

Ranulf and Denis lived at the hall, as did the other three knights—Edgar, Gowen, and Wolf the Short. Thirty or forty additional young men served the household in arms. At any given time, five or ten would be resident here. The rest would be on duty at the walls, and the others at home with their families.

The principal weapons the lightly armed troops carried were the magnificent crossbows built by Denis. Denis had lost a leg in a skirmish with brigands the first year Owen was bishop of Chantalon. During his convalescence, he worked at his hobby of building crossbows.

The crossbow, known of old as far away as fabled China, was an imperfect weapon. The average crossbow was clumsy, slow loading, inaccurate, and almost useless in battle.

Not the crossbows Denis built. They were light; they loaded and fired quickly; and, so far as accuracy was concerned, they were stunningly lethal. The young men in Owen's guard treated them more tenderly than they did their wives. Every time Denis completed a new one, Godwin let it be known there was an opening among Owen's household guard. There was no dearth of applicants for the position. Denis had two young men apprenticed to him, both trying to learn his trade. So far, neither approached his skill in creating deadly battle weapons. Godwin had watched him in action and was convinced the boy had no secrets, only an intense drive for absolute perfection and an infinite capacity for taking pains. Denis

signed his bows with a little horse head. And Godwin
found it worrying that already some of Hakon's chiefs
were offering large sums to anyone able to obtain one.

When Godwin entered Denis's room, he found Denis
sitting on the bed, his artificial leg unstrapped, and Ranulf, the youngest of his knights and Denis's close friend,
beside him.

Elfwine, Ranulf's blond wife, was sitting in a chair chattering at both men. She was feeding her newborn child.
Godwin felt this hardly necessitated baring both breasts.

Ranulf was sitting forward on the bed, gazing at her
adoringly. Denis, however, had another sort of look on
his face.

"Madam," Godwin began forbiddingly, "if you will
excuse us for a few moments . . ."

"Oh," Elfwine said, pretending to be embarrassed about
her state of dishevelment. "I'm so, so sorry." Then, adjusting her dress, she simpered, fluttered her eyelashes at
Godwin, and returned across the hall to the bedroom she
and Ranulf shared.

Godwin watched her go, his expression deliberately
unreadable. He didn't like Elfwine. He found in her an
unpleasant mixture of cupidity and stupidity. Memories
rose from long ago. Memories of a woman he'd loved, a
woman who'd turned out to have the same traits in her
nature. *Nonsense,* he thought. *Richilda had been a noblewoman, cultivated to her fingertips.* Something dark and
ironic laughed in his brain. Oh, yes, to be sure, Richilda's
mother had taken care to stuff her head full of the more
repressive Scripture quotations about women and sex.
Large quantities of rags and tags of Latin and even a
little Greek poetry, yards and yards of homilies directed
at women about submission to husbands, churchmen,
their fathers, brothers, or any other male she happened to
encounter.

They rattled around in her skull like dried peas in a
pod. The small, ironic voice then tried to tell Godwin that
had he remained with what he still believed was his one
true and only love, a few years of what passed for her
conversation would have driven him stark raving, shriek-

ing, moon-howling mad. He refused to listen, pushing the idea firmly out of his mind, and addressed Ranulf. "Have you gentlemen heard tell of one Ulick?"

"Oh yes," Ranulf burbled cheerfully. "He has been hanging about the city for a week or so now."

Godwin smiled down on Ranulf. Ranulf paled and looked apprehensive.

Denis added helpfully, "Oh, everyone knows about Ulick. . . . We were talking about him the other day . . . with Routrude and . . ."

"Ranulf! Denis!" Godwin interrupted the flow. "Who am I?"

They glanced at each other, sure it was a trick question. "Our commander, sir," they chorused together.

Godwin nodded. "And don't you think you might have discussed this Ulick's depredations with me before taking your case to the biggest gossip in the entire city?" Godwin started the sentence in a moderate tone of voice but ended it in a roar.

"Oh, but we were only consoling them," Ranulf said. "They were both dressed in black . . . Clea and Routrude. And they were weeping mightily." Clea, the "widow," ran the local whorehouse. Routrude kept the tavern with her husband, Arn.

"Why were they weeping?" Godwin asked.

"Because they said you knew Ulick was there and hadn't done anything about him, and we were all doomed. We told her 'Oh, no, Godwin is just thinking of some way to settle him.' And that you would soon act."

"Nice," Godwin murmured. "Very nice if someone had thought to inform me." He closed his eyes and pressed the bridge of his nose with two fingers. "However," he continued, "no matter. I know now. And I do have an idea for settling Ulick. Now, how many of the men-at-arms can be trusted to keep a secret?"

Both young men looked guilty. No one ever seemed to mind selling information to the occasional representative of Hakon's army who managed to slip into the city from time to time.

Ranulf plunged forward earnestly. "It isn't as though

we haven't tried, sir. We sat the boys down and explained to them that bad things can happen if Hakon finds out about things we don't want him to know. But I don't think, I can't say if . . . they . . ." His voice trailed off.

No, Godwin thought. *The "boys" probably didn't understand. Many of them were poor enough so that a few silver coins could blot out both caution and common sense.* Still, he might be able to use even that. He gazed at the two eager and expectant young faces before him. They were happy now that his ill temper appeared to have faded. He took the chair Elfwine had quitted, pulled it toward the bed, and spoke softly. "Now, this is what we will do. . . ."

Chapter 3

*H*AKON greeted the dawn, leaning against the long-ship Owen had managed to set on fire. He'd already ascertained that this, one of the most precious of his possessions, was uninjured.

The air was cool and damp, the sun not yet up. A glowing white mist rested on the river. The forest shadows were fading from black to brown. As he stood watching, the big torches were guttering out. Just as well. They were unnecessary in the first gray light of dawn.

Tosi approached him. No one else had cared to since the fight. He glanced over to one of the fires where the cloaked and hooded priestess crouched over a few fragments of bone.

"She's still alive?" Hakon asked.

"A bit singed, no more than that," Tosi replied.

"Amazing," Hakon said. "Too bad."

Tosi laughed. "The bishop's witch saved you from a most unpleasant dinner."

"Yes," Hakon said, "and I would have eaten it. Not because it would have made any sense to engage in such folly, but because after she said it, the men would expect it. Take her to the camp. Let her mutter her spells and keep her out of my way."

"She casts the runes, Gyda does, looking for omens. I wonder what she'll say?"

"She'll say what I tell her to say," Hakon answered harshly. "I don't want to make this a religious quarrel. There are Christian men in the camp and pagans. The lady I married is Christian, as are her people. And I'll wager there are not a few in the city who are very slack about approaching the church altar. And ye Gods! Look at what our Christian bishop has taken to wife. Hell! She defeated our evil little Gyda on her own ground. I noticed a crowd of strong men who did not want to lay hold of her."

Tosi's eyes wandered. He behaved as though he didn't want to meet Hakon's stare. "She did burn Gyda and Reynald also," he muttered at length.

Hakon sighed. Tosi was his sister's son and closer to him than a full brother, but sometimes when Tosi talked this way, Hakon felt like smacking him. "The torch dropped pitch-covered coals onto the ship. The bishop's witch threw them on Gyda. They set that voluminous woolen cloak she wears alight. As for Reynald . . ." Even Hakon shivered a bit. "He went too far. He betrayed his friend, Owen, to me. I think his bad conscience brought him down. I saw him. His wife, and my lady now, Elspeth, hadn't been able to bury him."

Hakon stared out over the river. He remembered he'd gone from satisfaction to rage and frustration and then back to delight in a few days. Reynald had betrayed Owen to him for a high price, but Owen had escaped him. And then he heard Reynald, Elspeth's husband, was dead. She was at the home of one of her vassals and she'd sent for him. He'd left the camp riding like a madman. He'd not seen her before; Reynald kept her hidden. When he saw her, he'd understood why. What a beauty! Not that it mattered. Had she been a hunchbacked, half-witted one-eyed hag he wouldn't have let her out of his sight until he was lord of her lands. But this exquisite creature . . .

He struck with all possible speed. He made her his wife, without ceremony, within the hour in the room where they first met. Reynald's treasure, including what he'd paid for Owen, had, of course, been stolen. Hakon dispatched Tosi in pursuit of the thieves. He caught them and made sure they'd trouble honest men no more. He returned the treasure to Hakon and was suitably rewarded.

As for Hakon, he found Reynald in the ruins of his wing of the hall. Elspeth had not been able to persuade or even bribe anyone to bury him. Her brother, Bertrand, was hiding in the church. Bertrand began by cursing Hakon. That didn't last long. Bertrand had been a churchman, in fact, abbot of a monastery before the Vikings came. Hakon, by dint of a short conversation involving rocks and the bottom of the river, obtained his cooperation in quietly burying Reynald and being civil to Elspeth.

Then he moved into her side of the house. That night, he'd covered her naked body with Reynald's gold. Hakon had begun teaching her how to love him on a cushioned bench in the room where they first met, only a few moments after they concluded their bargain. He continued the lessons that night, giving her several more until she resembled nothing so much as a small, soft, fragrant sprite who lay weary, limp with absolute surrender in his arms. He considered by now she'd recovered from his last instructions and would probably be more than ready for a few more.

"Elspeth," Tosi said.

"Umm, yes," Hakon replied.

Then he looked up. Blood was caked on the dragon-headed ship's prow. The two corpses were still dangling in the trees. Hakon favored Gyda with another nasty look. "I didn't want to do what she suggested. Sending human beings to the one-eyed, red-haired lord of darkness is not my idea of . . ." His voice trailed off. "I think killing in the name of . . . of any god is . . . unlucky. An unlucky act."

Tosi glanced up at the two overhead. "I'll have them cut down, buried with rich gifts—oil, meat, wine, a dog with the boy, some jewelry with the girl. They won't walk. Their spirits will be content. If they'd toiled all their lives as slaves, they might not have gained so much."

"No, only a little time longer in the sun," Hakon replied sarcastically. He straightened and rubbed his back against the prow of the longship. "God, I'm dirty. My clothes are fouled with blood, soot from the fires, and sweat. I'll need to bathe before I go to Elspeth. I wonder if the dead feel anything or if they only remember?"

"Some say they don't even do that. But if I were you, Hakon, I wouldn't worry about it because we can't know until it's too late to do anything about it."

Hakon drew him into a quick embrace. "Ah, brother mine! Tell me, is Ulick still outside Chantalon and following orders?"

"Oh, yes." Tosi shifted his sword belt and looked down at his feet.

"Come on." Hakon made a beckoning motion with his fingers. "Out with it. What's wrong?"

"Ulick is beginning to think he can defeat and capture or kill Godwin."

Hakon looked off into the distance and his eyes changed. Tosi had seen them do that before. It reminded him of gazing into glacier ice. It seems transparent at first but then somehow the pale murk subtly increases until you are staring down into a sort of white darkness. He saw a similar obscurity creep into Hakon's eyes. He loved Hakon, but he didn't love that look. No one did. He wondered if Elspeth had seen it yet.

Hakon draped his arm over Tosi's shoulders. "Brother mine, let me tell you a story, and you may repeat this story to Ulick or not as you please. Once upon a time, there was a man in England, Wessex, to be precise.

"He was called Steiner Gold Gatherer, a mighty and successful chieftain of Gunthrum's. He'd grown rich plundering the realm of Saxon king Alfred of England. He besieged Godwin, then Alfred's commander of horse, in one of those mud-walled towns the English call burgs. The rain fell in torrents. The Saxon thanes with Godwin quarreled among themselves and fled. But still Godwin would not open the gates to him, would not yield the town.

"Steiner had spies within the town. They said Godwin was ill, rotten with dysentery; his men diseased, dying every day of starvation and the endless damp and cold. Their own lice devoured them.

"But still, every time Steiner tried to force the gates,

this Godwin cost him something. So Steiner, who was not called Gold Gatherer for nothing, decided to buy Godwin off. He offered a large sum, thinking Godwin, a landless man, held by but pledge of fealty to the English king Alfred, would be happy to take his gold and depart. The sum, or so it has been told, was more than enough to corrupt. Amounts as large had corrupted many greater and more loyal than Godwin.

"So he sent one of his spies to Godwin to make him an offer. Godwin returned the spy to Steiner less his nose, ears, and tongue with a placard around his neck reading 'This is how I deal with traitors.' "

Tosi whistled softly between his teeth. "A stubborn man," he whispered.

"More than stubborn," Hakon answered, "much more than stubborn. Had the story ended there, Steiner would still have considered himself fortunate."

"What happened?" Tosi asked.

"In disgust, Steiner raised the siege. He had a strong, well-fortified camp two days' march from the city, set in the middle of a river, as ours is. He meant to return there and sit out the cold, wet days of winter in comfort. Let Godwin rot, he thought, soon he will die and the city will fall into my hands like a ripe plum.

"When he arrived at the camp, he found shouts of welcome and warm fires burning beyond the walls. The gates opened and Steiner rode through followed by his men— into the teeth of a hail of arrows. Few escaped to tell the tale, and fewer still cared to tell it, being, as it was, a thing of shame."

"What happened?" Tosi asked. "What did Godwin do?"

"It seems," Hakon said, "the spy whose nose, ears, and tongue Godwin had cropped named the others Steiner depended on to Godwin. Godwin asked these spies—and I understand when Godwin finished asking, they vied with each other in answering—at any rate, he asked for the location of Steiner's camp. When he knew where it was, he mounted every man he had, even those who couldn't sit a saddle without fouling it, and proceeded by forced march to within bow shot of the camp.

"He and his men forded the river and waited in the shallows with reeds and branches tied to their bodies to conceal their presence, while he sent a few men up to the gates. Godwin's men cried out that they were wounded, that Steiner was following, that he'd suffered a mighty defeat, and that many among his soldiers needed shelter. The gates were opened, and Godwin and his men rushed in, overpowering the few defenders, and when Steiner returned, Godwin was waiting.

"Now," Hakon said when he was finished. "I cannot say if Ulick will profit by the warning or not. If he does, well and good. If not, his fate will serve as a warning to the next man to whom I assign his duties. He will treat Godwin with far greater caution."

4

O WEN woke somewhere near the top of a tree. He was lying athwart a big, pale, gray-brown, smooth-barked branch. The stub of one twig was digging into his ribs. Another was prodding him in the stomach. The sun was out and shining aggressively on his back. He had a crick in his neck, an itch in his crotch. His bladder was full.

He'd become separated from Elin in the dark when he tripped and slid down the bank of a ravine. In climbing the tree, he'd drawn on what he'd learned from the forest people. If you are pursued, go up if you can, especially in the night. Not one man in ten thinks to look up above his head, and in the dark, that tenth one can seldom see well enough into a tall tree to detect a man.

Well, he thought, *so far so good*. Then he smelled the smoke. He moved hastily, trying to get to his feet, and almost fell from the branch. He took hold of himself quickly. The branch he lay on was at least thirty feet in the air. If he fell, it wouldn't matter if the Vikings were nearby; he would be dead anyway.

He looked around cautiously. A water bird called softly. A flight of small ducks lifted and flew through the trees, rising toward the open sky. He gasped with surprise and delight as three elk, a stag and two does, passed below him, foraging for bark on the saplings. As he watched, one of the does lifted herself, placing her forehooves on one of the trees, dragged down a green strip, and ate it.

No, he thought. *They would never feed so casually with humans about.* Still again, he smelled the smoke. Cautiously, so as not to alarm the elk or fall, he rose to his feet. His was the tallest tree around. From his perch, he could see the entire neighborhood. The river glittered in the first light, sun-soft mist on the water clouding the thick vegetation at the banks. His perch was a mother tree. A crowd of her children, middling aspens, filled the space under her wide branches. The grove extended down the slope to the riverbank. The trees near the water, sheltered from the cold wind, still held their leaves, a mosaic of gold against the green water, brown forest, and blue sky.

More smoke. Wood smoke. Where was it coming from? The ground sloped upward toward a high hill. He made out a thread of white against the sky. He knew Elin's people well. They would not pick out the highest hill in the vicinity, light a fire, and inform everyone for miles around of their presence. No, only Hakon's men would be so bold.

He tried to remember what was up there. Yes, an old ruin, a Roman villa. He'd never been to the spot, but he'd been told of the place. He'd marveled a bit when he heard of it. Marveled at a world where a man could build an unfortified country house in such an exposed location and not be bothered by Vikings, brigands, or other lawless men. He wondered, looking at it, how long ago it had been abandoned. He decided the owners must have held out for a fairly long time. The cleared fields around it still showed only open ground, brush, and sparse, second-growth forest.

No, this was very bad. The moon was due to change tonight, and even if he made a wide circuit around the villa, he might be seen. Hakon would surely be looking for him.

He began descending the tree. A host of worries assailed him. Where was his sword? The scabbard rattled, empty at his side. Then he remembered. Oh yes. On the riverbank where he'd fought Hakon. It had been knocked from his hand. No doubt some Viking had it now. Owen only hoped whoever found it would treat the fine weapon as it deserved to be treated, and care for it tenderly. He resigned himself to its loss. Fear for his human companions troubled him more deeply. Where were they? Had they managed to make their way back to the boat? If so, had Martin sufficient strength to guide the vessel downriver? On balance, he hoped they hadn't returned to the small craft. He was sure Hakon's search parties would find it quickly and capture anyone nearby. Had Elin been captured? Oh God, no! Hakon hated her. He would kill her immediately, without mercy.

Resolutely, he pushed the idea from his mind. No, he would not torment himself with these horrible imaginings until he knew more about where she and her people might be.

He reached the bottom of the tree and found the spring. Yes! The tree was very old. The spring originated at its base, and once there must have been a low rock wall around it and a coping stone on top. But the spring had escaped them and formed its own winding track down to the river.

The place was very quiet. The strong, straight young trees and the carpet of brown leaves on the ground reminded Owen too much of a church for the worries that flocked in his mind like carrion crows not to be banished, at least temporarily.

The stones around the well had been worked. He could see faint markings under the gray-green lichen crusting them. But too many were covered by the tree or simply gone. He couldn't tell any longer what the figure had been. All that remained was a hand outstretched in a giving gesture. Elin's people weren't here, but he knew they would never drink without paying their respects to this ancient, sacred thing.

He remembered he had a bit of bread in his scrip. He crumbled it into the water and then drank. Ah, can there ever be enough thanksgiving for pure, clean water; clean, sweet air; and light? The sun sent its long, slanting rays through the last morning mist drifting among the saplings.

But when he finished drinking he found himself plagued with the sensation that something else was missing. What? Oh no! Elin's necklace. It must have fallen from around his neck as he lay crouched on the branch in the dark, trying to sleep. It was a lovely thing, butter yellow amber with chased gold beads so beautifully worked he was sure they must go back to Roman times. "They are love tokens," she'd told him when she gave him his, "and my people will recognize the tie between us." Owen began to search around the tree roots. Perhaps even though the sword was irretrievably lost, he could still find the necklace.

Then he saw the fungus. A really big one, it grew in the opening where the tree root forked. Owen had sometimes collected them in the wild when he was a boy. Lately, he'd only seen them in the square when the farm wives brought them to market. When or wherever found, they were a delicacy cooked and served in the same way as a tender piece of meat. This one was huge and, by the look of it, in its prime and bound to be delicious. He snatched off his dalmatic and wrapped it in his shirt. Then he laughed. In his excitement at finding such an exquisite treasure, he'd forgotten he had no fire to cook it with and no friends to share it. Then he gave a smile of deep pleasure when he saw the necklace lying in a heap very close to where the fungus had been. He felt uplifted with new hope.

How could he find Elin and his friends?

As the sun burned away the mist, birdsong began to fill the air. High overhead, he heard the calling of geese, their silvery cries wild music against the drifting clouds.

And yet, there was something very odd about one of those avian songs.

Then Owen realized. Lord above, he knew Alshan had very little respect for the intelligence of any so-called civilized man, but this was insolent to the point of recklessness.

"Good heavens . . . a nightingale."

A short time later, Owen found the nightingale. She saw him before he saw her. Her hand reached out of a thicket of bright holly and last summer's elderberry canes. It held his sword.

He took it and sheathed it with a cry and a sigh of thanksgiving. She pulled him in and he found himself walking along a ravine walled by thorny, red-berried holly bushes and floored by oak leaves.

Sybilla, who had been doing the nightingale, took one look at the big fungus and smacked her lips. "So large, and at this time of year," she said, "a true gift of the forest."

"Elin?" Owen asked anxiously.

"She's with us." Sybilla pursed her lips and blew another bird call. Sweet, soft liquid notes. Someone replied softly ahead of them.

"She knows you're alive now," Sybilla explained. "It was all we could do to keep her from running through the trees in search of you. We told her, 'Oh, yes. Play the fool. Hakon will lay hands on you, and this time, he will not think of what a high price he can get for such a young woman. He will have your head from your shoulders as quickly as ever may be. Owen will go mad with grief and be no use to anyone.' She was rebellious."

"She always is," Owen commented.

"But she listened!" Sybilla continued.

"Thank God," Owen said.

"Huh," Sybilla said derisively. "You better be glad she didn't listen last night when I tried to tell her not to go to your aid when the Northmen cornered you. She told me, 'In life and in death, it is my duty to join him.' Not a good way for a woman to think," she concluded disapprovingly.

Just at that moment, he saw Elin running toward him, and they were in each other's arms.

They entered a dell beside the river. It was surrounded by giant, tangled deadfalls washed up last spring and caught on the riverbank when the spring floods ended. They surrounded the shallow depression on three sides with high walls of uprooted trees and broken branches, all choked and thickly interwoven with leafless brush

dropped by the river or bushes grown up during the
summer among the heavier logs.

No one could possibly see them from the outside, and
the only way in was along the shallow ravine Sybilla had
led him through.

There was a low fire burning in the center of the depression. Martin and the two captives Owen had rescued from
sacrifice sat together on a log near the fire. Alshan and
Tigg had taken seats on the other side.

Martin greeted Owen with relief and joy. He rose to his
feet. "My lord, I'm so glad to see you safe and well."

Alshan and Tigg greeted the fungus with similar cries
of joy and delight. "Oh, look," Tigg said. "A meal in itself
and very delicious. We were sitting here wondering what
we would do since we were afraid to fish, net birds, set
snares, or even steal anything. Twice we have seen boats
along the river. They found the skiff, the one that brought
us here. We watched them towing it to the camp."

"And," Alshan added, "we have seen at least one large
party of armed men beating the bushes along the shore."

"All our food was in the skiff," Martin said, "and while that
is a very big ... ug ... thing"—he pointed to the fungus—
"what will we do tomorrow?"

Alshan chuckled and shrugged. He fingered the amber
jewel he wore around his neck. A big beetle was caught in
the gem, and the iridescent wing cases flashed even in the
dim light under the trees. "We will find something when
that day comes," he told Martin. "Let's enjoy what we
have now."

Elin bit Owen lightly on the earlobe. He yipped, then
turned and kissed her again. This time he tried to drag her
off back down the ravine.

Martin was scarlet with embarrassment. The two captives watched Owen and Elin with interest. Alshan,
Sybilla, and Tigg set about cooking the fungus.

Elin's lips were dry; her hair smelled of wood smoke.
A third kiss and he discovered he was wild for her. She
struggled, laughing and halfheartedly refusing to let him
get a good grip so he could throw her over his shoulder

and carry her off, when suddenly their feet were swept from under them by Sybilla's kick.

"Hush, you lecherous fools," she whispered fiercely. "You will get us all killed."

She and the rest crouched behind the screen of trees and brush looking out at the river.

The ship rowed close to the bank; the men on her deck were peering into the forest.

They all put their heads down and lay silent while she passed. When the splash of the oars faded away, Owen realized he could hear a very soft sobbing. He looked around and saw the girl they'd rescued from the Vikings clinging to Martin and weeping quietly. The boy clutched his arm tightly, hiding his face in the big man's shoulder.

"Who are they?" Owen asked.

"Who knows?" Elin told him. "They speak not one word of any language any of us can understand. And we have twelve among us. No telling from whence they came."

"They aren't very old," Martin said, "little more than children. We believe they are twins, or at least brother and sister. They favor each other in appearance."

They did indeed. Both were scrawny and nondescript, with dark fine hair, his cropped short, hers long. Both had large, silver-gray eyes.

"Well," Owen said, "we will need to teach them to talk. You'll be a rich man now."

"How so?" Martin asked.

"You have ten hectares of land, two horses, and two slaves."

"Two slaves!" Martin exclaimed. "I hadn't thought about them that way." He still comforted the girl, holding her in his arms.

Sybilla, Alshan, and Tigg all laughed and chattered among themselves for a moment.

Martin flushed and scowled. "They are talking about me, aren't they?" he asked Elin.

She smiled but wouldn't meet Martin's eyes.

He continued to glower at her.

"All they are saying," she explained gently, "is that the

fisherman priest needs a woman, and this one, if you feed her up—good bread and beer—will do nicely for you."

The girl was drying her tears and gazing adoringly at Martin.

"A month in my house and she'll be stout as a laying hen and the boy will strut like a rooster. We may not have much, but between the marsh and the sea, we have plenty of food."

"Yes, and we don't, at least right now," Sybilla snapped. "You two lovers come help me. We have a few minutes, when the Vikings aren't watching, to catch a fish or two."

Elin and Owen acted as lookouts while Sybilla fished in the shallows. She cornered three small trout and took them by hand. Twice during the fishing they all had to take cover—once, and most dangerously, from a party on foot, and another time when a ship passed by. Between the fish and the fungus, everyone had a decent meal.

"I'm worried," Owen told Alshan. "The Vikings are at the old villa and . . ."

"How is the mushroom?" Alshan asked.

"Delicious," Owen replied, mystified. "It is very like the leanest, tenderest of meat." Owen devoured another slice. "The thing is very big, and I would it had been twice as big. Why do you ask?"

"In the midst of such largesse, why are you turning your stomach sour with worry?" Alshan asked. "I believe I know a way around the Vikings, but we will consider what we will do this evening when we have all eaten and slept."

Owen looked around. They were all bone weary, drained by all they had experienced and endured. It seemed weeks, not two days, since they left the city. He bowed to Alshan's superior wisdom and concentrated on the meal.

When they were finished, he took Elin in his arms, but only to keep her warm. Martin and the captives curled up together. The small, quiet Tigg took the first watch while Sybilla and Alshan also slept.

* * *

When Godwin asked Enar which he would rather be, the woman or the man, he found out to his chagrin that Enar was delighted to dress as a woman. Godwin explained his plan to a suspiciously large number of people in the household.

He and Enar were to go to a ruined village near the forest. The Viking attack had devastated the outer, undefended villages surrounding the town. The Northmen swept through them with fire and sword, stripping them of anything of even marginal value. This included such mundane objects as bedding or chamber pots; then, whatever remained was remorselessly put to the torch.

So, unfortunately, there were many such tiny settlements suitable for Godwin's purposes. There they would pretend to be a family readying themselves to move back in and begin putting in the winter crop.

To sweeten the bait, they would bring along Godwin's hammer-headed, raw-boned roan warhorse and a large, gray mule donated by Osbert the stock dealer and tanner.

Enar thought it a fine joke to dress as the farmer's wife. He found a gown that would cover his rather massive bulk. Enar was a good two hundred and fifty pounds and six feet tall barefoot. None of it was fat. And he managed a really exaggerated pair of breasts, creating a sort of cleavage by the judicious use of white wool and linen poking a bit out of the top of the bodice.

Then he swaggered into the hall at dinnertime and began mincing around, telling jokes so vile they made even Godwin's hardened knights blush. Ranulf, Denis, and the women turned pale with embarrassment and horror. He then made himself obnoxious to Edgar, one of the bravest of Godwin's knights, but a man not known to be interested in women.

Edgar told Godwin he was considering giving Enar a possible fatal lesson in swordsmanship. Enar guffawed and invited Edgar to try in a shrill falsetto tone.

Godwin terminated the performance with a threat so horrible even Enar was taken aback. "I would not think a man would endure that and survive," he said.

"Would you care to find out?" Godwin invited him in a silken voice.

Enar decided he wouldn't. He sat down and ate supper with the rest. Quietly.

He and Godwin rode out near sunset. Not that either one of them could see the sunset. The air was blue. The weather had changed. The valley was clouded over. A misty rain mixed with sleet was falling.

Enar got the mule. It plodded along and showed not the slightest disposition to be energetic for either good or ill.

Godwin's warhorse was also an experienced and cynical animal. He resented being ridden out in this kind of weather. Godwin imagined horse logic suggested some form of insanity among the human species that made them prefer a ride on an evening like this to a nice warm stall.

"You did not tell me the trap part of things," Enar said.

"You didn't give me a chance," Godwin answered. "You were too delighted with your part in the masquerade." Godwin's only disguise had been to remove his helmet and wrap himself in a stained, ratty brown woolen mantle.

"And so?" Enar asked.

"We will ride in at sunset and take up residence in the house. Tonight Ranulf and the boys will sneak into the town and conceal themselves in the other ruined houses. When the raiders come to attack us and steal the horses, or rather horse and mule, the boys will fall upon Ulick and his men and destroy them."

The town came into view. Enar began to feel very uneasy. He felt his disguise would fool at least any distant observer, but Godwin's? No. His lean figure, long face, large eyes, and scrappy fine hair were too well-known, far too well-known. Godwin was a man with a reputation.

And he had helped the townsfolk defeat Hakon at the walls, then met him the next day in the field. True, he'd had Hakon at a disadvantage, but he'd administered a temporary trouncing to the Viking chief. A lot of men knew what he looked like, and his looks were distinctive.

Enar's uneasiness grew when they arrived at the chosen town. The wind had picked up. The rain had now changed almost completely to sleet. Godwin lit a horn-shielded lantern.

Oh wonderful, Enar thought. *Be sure to point out where we are. Just in case Ulick hasn't noticed.*

Through the fine, glittering mist of ice droplets, Enar could see what remained of the town. The dried and mummified carcass of a cow lay in the main street. Ice was beginning to coat the stiff skin and bones. Only one house could be seen to be left standing. The walls were five feet at their highest. Some clean straw was piled in one corner under the surviving rafters of a thatched roof that showed some recent work.

The remaining few houses were only piles of blackened timbers, some fallen into cellar holes, some not. A few dark shapes sprawled under the blackened timbers suggested that, like the cow, some of the villagers had not been able to flee in time and remained in the shattered remnants of their fallen homes. An empty eye socket seemed to peer at Enar as Godwin swung the lamp to look around. "I don't like this place," he said flatly.

"Don't be foolish," Godwin said jovially. "It's perfect for our purposes." So saying, he led Enar into the one house not completely ruined, where they took refuge in the corner.

Godwin lit a fire.

Just in case, Enar thought, *Ulick might lose track of where we are and need reminding.*

Godwin unsaddled his horse. The saddlebags held bread, wine, and meat from Anna. It transpired a lot of Enar's buxomness was beer. He unloaded himself and they had a pleasant time of it for a while.

Enar felt better when, under cover of darkness, he heard the soft clink of weapons, low voices, and the light crunch of footsteps in the freezing mud.

Ranulf's face appeared in the blackness over the wall. He whispered, "We are here."

Godwin whispered back, "Very well. Light no fires, but stay sheltered and warm. Await my signal."

Yes, Enar thought, taking another pull of beer, *and don't disturb the dead.* Then he retreated to the warm corner of the house by the fire. He left his mule saddled and kept his throwing axe where he could reach it easily, his sword hilt near his hand. At length, he slept.

When he woke, the fire had burned down. Godwin rested, one side of his face against the wall. He was sleeping deeply.

The fire was ash-covered coals. Enar didn't build it up. He was just as happy without the light. He crawled quietly to one of the walls and looked over. He could tell it was close to dawn. No stars were visible. The sleet had stopped, but the sky was thickly overcast. Occasionally, the fitful moonlight shone through a thinner layer of cloud like a lamp through gauze. In one of these brief illuminations, he saw Ranulf and the boys leaving the village. They were already far away on the road leading to the city.

"No," he gasped. "No." Then he turned and half scampered, half crawled to where Godwin lay. He shook Godwin violently. "Godwin, we are betrayed. We are . . . we are killed. Ranulf and the rest—they're leaving. We must ride out now—now, do you hear me?"

Godwin, rudely awakened, looked around bleary eyed. Then he crawled to the wall. "Why, so they are," he said. He seemed pleased. Then he turned to Enar and said, "Saddle my horse."

Enar ran to Godwin's horse and threw the saddle on its back. He was struggling with the cinch and the horse was filling his belly with air when, above his head, the thatch burst into flame.

Owen woke that evening. Tigg, Alshan, and Sybilla had divided the watches among themselves in order to let the rest sleep. Elin had her arms around him; his head was resting on her shoulder; his lips were against her neck. For a moment, he pulled her closer simply to have the comfort of embracing her. He knew there was no place they could really sneak off and be alone.

My, she was warm. Her body radiated heat. She felt and smelled like a round of hot bread, newly pulled from the oven.

Then he realized why she felt so warm. It was cold.

Even where he lay, he could feel the wind had changed. It was from the north.

· She felt Owen rise, even though he moved quietly. She knew he was trying to allow her a few more minutes of rest. She'd taken a horrible risk last night when she went to his aid. The risk affected more than one person. Elin carried a child in her womb. The child wasn't Owen's.

Before her rescue by Owen, she'd been captured and enslaved by the Vikings. In Owen's world, there were many who would condemn the tiny life before its eyes opened to the light.

In his world, the child was the offspring of rape and dishonor.

Elin and her wild kin did not share this belief.

In their language, the word for woman meant "soul catcher." Women kept the souls of individuals and the people as a whole. To give life was their sacred trust. Pregnancy simply meant a woman had been chosen to return the spirit of a deserving one of her people to the struggle of the world. ·

She'd first realized her condition in the stable enclosed by the Viking camp where she was imprisoned.

She had been from the beginning a most difficult captive, presenting herself to her masters as mad, filthy, stupid, sullen, and, in all ways, intractable.

They felt her hatred and returned it with interest. The night before she'd received a particularly vicious beating. She spat into the soup pot.

Elin herself considered this action a minor gesture of dislike, but unfortunately she was seen.

She awakened, looking up through the chinks in the stable rafters at the misty gray sky. One side of her face was sore and swollen, scattered purple bruises covered her skin, and her right arm and neck were a mass of scarlet flesh.

The contents of the soup pot had been emptied over her prone body after she'd been beaten unconscious.

It was barely first light; outside she heard the clatter of pots and women's voices calling to one another. Slave women were preparing the morning meal for their masters.

Elin smiled. The smile hurt her face because of the bruise on her cheek. But still the smile was one of satisfaction. Making breakfast was one task she would probably never be kicked awake to perform again.

She shared the stall with a gray mare, a stocky barrel-bodied little ruffian not much bigger than a pony. The mare, like Elin, was a most uncooperative slave. Elin was the only one who could get any work out of her. The owner of both beasts, horse and woman, was at a loss as to how Elin accomplished this feat.

In truth, the mare, who ignored punishment as beneath her notice, was a sucker for any sort of bribe. Apples worked really well.

The horse dropped her head and blew softly in Elin's face. Like many gray horses, the mare had a darker nose and mouth, almost black and soft as a whisper of velvet cloth. She brushed Elin's uninjured cheek with a gentle horse caress.

Elin rolled over. She moaned as her stiffened injuries protested. Then she began feeling around under the deep straw in the corner of the stall. She found three withered crab apples and a large heel of bread she'd stolen a few days ago.

She pulled out an apple for the horse, the bread for herself. The mean little animal was better protection than a vicious dog.

At night the unattached men of the camp came creeping around, trying to bribe or force such women as were left unprotected by a connection with the stronger warriors.

The mare bit and kicked without warning and without mercy. If surprised by an interloper in the dark, she engaged in both activities with enthusiasm.

Elin loved it. A few howls of masculine agony and rage cheered her immensely.

The mare accepted the crab apple with delicate gratitude; she savored it.

Elin tried the bread with her teeth and found her mouth too sore to chew it. So she tucked it down between her breasts and began the slow process of getting to her feet.

She would need to be out before the men to safely cadge a cup of porridge from one of the women.

She was sitting back against the rough-hewn wall planks when she looked down at her breasts, staring at the ragged shift that was all that remained of her clothing. Her body gave her the message as clearly, as baldly, as if its dumb flesh had the power of speech.

You're pregnant.

No! she thought. But her mind added up the evidence remorselessly. Her increased appetite, the enlargement of her breasts, thickening of the hips. Nothing noticeable to anyone else, but clear signals to her.

Her heart leaped with joy. It shouldn't have, but it did.

Her position was desperate. She had been forced into degrading slavery. Doomed, perhaps, to be sold far away from her homeland and kin to endure—not live—the rest of her life among these cruel predators who had stolen her freedom.

The life-receiving process in her body had been awakened by crude, violent, sexual assault. And . . . yet . . . she was filled with joy.

Since her capture, she'd fought despair with rage and hatred. But her greatest suffering and deepest fear had been that all those she loved—her family among the Franks, her kin among her mother's people, all—believed her dead. She was forgotten, abandoned, and alone.

At last . . . at long last, she was receiving a message of hope. Not from any human source. But from beyond the world, where the souls of her people wandered.

To Elin's people, a child did not belong to any man or woman, but was rather an offshoot of the divine force that created the universe.

If Elin survived for a few more months, the soul would enter the tiny body being created for it in her womb. She would know when it accepted its mortal resting place because it would begin to move, fluttering like a bird just leaving the nest learning how to use its wings.

Even now the soul hovered near. Waiting impatiently for the day. Waiting to begin its struggle toward the morning of life.

Triumph ran in Elin's own soul, in the throb of her heart under the swelling breasts, in the ebb and flow of blood in her veins.

She might be lost to the living, but the dead remembered. She was one of their people. And the spirit that called forth her womanhood to give it flesh was her companion. Succeed or fail, live or die, they would travel to freedom or beyond the gates of mystery into death together.

Sybilla's hand touched Elin's, rousing her from her reverie.

Elin's eyes opened and she found herself looking down into her own startled face: her own deep, blue eyes, her own thick veil of shimmering black hair.

Sybilla jumped away and Elin realized she'd shared the experience also.

It was as though, for a second, they'd exchanged souls.

Sybilla approached Elin again quickly. They joined hands and spoke in low voices.

"I'll be the one to do it," Elin said.

"No." Sybilla looked distraught. "No, Elin, the risk is too great."

"Don't argue," Elin commanded. "Feel the air. By midnight the dew will be freezing on the grass. You have three children all under ten. They'll die without your protection.

"If we don't act now, the rest of us will die on the return journey to the city. Without food to fill our bellies and wine to warm us when the weather changes, some of us will never reach the city alive.

"God! I wish Enar were here. I could trust him with this errand. But failing his presence, I am the only one with sufficient skill to accomplish the task.

"If I am killed, try to get Owen away. Help him defeat Hakon. And in spring, when the air is warm, and flowers shimmer like a fallen rainbow on the new grass, summon us both. Me and my companion. Bring us back to share the human struggle. To endure both suffering and joy again."

Owen stood with Alshan. Across the river, the sun was

crosshatched by bare forest branches. In long rays, it flooded the forest with red-orange light. The water was a sheet of beaten gold. Above, a thick flight of small, fluffy white clouds was obscuring even further the darkening sky.

"The weather's changed."

"Yes," Alshan said. He gave Owen a brief, worried look.

"Oh my," Owen said. "Now the future troubles you."

"No." Alshan smiled. "Not the future, the present."

Sybilla and Elin were extinguishing the fire and disposing of any leavings, fish heads and such, that might mark their stay.

Owen could see why his people so often thought they were supernatural beings. They left so few traces of their passage anywhere. When Elin and Sybilla were finished, the deadfall and the copse of holly trees would look as though no human foot had ever trod there.

As the two women worked, Owen noticed they had their heads together. They were obviously discussing some serious subject, one that didn't include him. When they were finished tidying the campsite, Elin and Sybilla embraced, further rousing his suspicions.

Then they gathered around Alshan. The sun was gone now. A salmon-rose glow remained on the eastern horizon, giving them only a faint light to see each other by. The cold wind was blowing hard now, not just nipping but biting at any exposed skin, at cheeks, nose, ears, and fingers. Overhead, the cloud cover was increasing steadily.

Sybilla sniffed. "The air smells of moisture. It will sleet or snow before morning."

Martin had, after the manner of his namesake, divided his mantle with the girl. Her brother also had felt the cold wind. He'd found a way to wrap his hands and face with some of the rags he was wearing. Wherever they came from, the twins looked like hardy souls, ready to do whatever needed to be done.

They gathered around Alshan. "We must go past the villa," he said. "And, as my lord bishop has observed, the Vikings are camped there. The best way past is actually the most dangerous. The thickest cover is closest to the villa itself. What was the old garden has been allowed to go wild, and after all these years, it's thick with runaway undergrowth and ornamental cypress that have turned into trees. I believe we can pass most swiftly and safely within a few hundred feet of the villa. Without the boat, we are afoot, and what supplies of food we brought, we abandoned when we left it. The weather is turning ugly, and we must return to the city as quickly as possible."

The light was almost gone when they fell into single file behind Sybilla. Tigg brought up the rear.

Twice they skirted the outlying fields of abandoned villages, the timbers of their ruined halls and shattered palisade fences standing, stark black shapes against the overcast sky. The moon was out, though. Its light reminded Owen of a ghostly lamp, its blue flame flickering among the swiftly moving clouds.

"Long after the villa lay in ruins," Alshan told Owen, "many people tried to work this land. Best we avoid those places. If any of the inhabitants survived the raids, they keep fierce dogs and sleep in fear behind barred doors, not even daring to show a light. The Northmen have tried to exterminate all human life near their camp that they may be more secure."

They left the farms behind them, plunging again into the embracing safety of the darkness under the trees.

What they traveled through now was more parkland. Though it was still almost always possible to stay among the trees, it was sometimes necessary to dash through a clearing. Owen noticed Alshan always put on a burst of speed when he did so.

They had just crossed a meadow near an abandoned farm—long ruined, probably many years before this set of raids began. No one within any of their living memories would dream of building in such an isolated spot now. Alshan stopped so suddenly that Owen nearly careened into him.

Owen asked, "What?"

Alshan whispered urgently. "Hush. We are . . . here!"

They were standing at the front of a hill whose top was ringed by a tonsure of trees and brushy undergrowth.

"Smell that?" Alshan whispered.

Owen sniffed; at first nothing, then wood smoke and horse dung drifted to his nostrils. His senses, cleansed by the air of the forest, were able to detect the man smell: sweat, leather, and even the sharp, somehow menacing, scent of iron.

"Follow me and be silent, for your life," Alshan whispered. He took the lead through the trees, Owen and Elin following. Owen was, by now, able to move almost as noiselessly as they, and he exerted all his skill to do so.

When they were through the trees, they confronted a ghost, or at least so it seemed to Owen, who made a short, sharp hissing sound between his teeth.

It stood on the hilltop, glowing pale in the dim moonlight. A Roman villa. Not the working farm of the Franks or even the Romans before them, but a summer retreat, the plaything of some rich, Gallic gentleman. Built for pleasure and relaxation in a secure world when the might of the imperium must have seemed invincible and eternal. As they drew closer, moving cautiously through the tall grass, Owen began to see how much of a ruin it truly was.

Only part of the atrium was intact. The pillared entryway had fallen, as had the walls of most of the rooms surrounding it. Now only green mounds, dotted with young trees, the growth of centuries, remained.

The spring that fed the reflecting pool still flowed, not surprisingly, for a spring is a thing of nature and indifferent to the rise and fall of empires. But the pipes that once drained the pool had clogged long ago, and the overflow undermined the left side of the villa and destroyed it. Yet, the pool itself was still intact, and Owen could see in it the white cups of water lilies lifted to the sky.

Beyond the pool, the marble entry into the once magnificent owner's quarters framed only sky. The walls and roof had vanished, fallen, scattering down the hillside, leaving not even rubble behind. All at once his awe turned into fear when he realized why he could see so well. The band of raiders was camped in the almost intact right side of the atrium.

The walls of a few of the rooms were still standing here, though the roofs were open to the sky. A fire burned in the corner of one, and the faces of Roman lords and ladies, gods and goddesses looked up from the tessellated mosaic floor, as if in surprise at the bodies of these strange barbarians sleeping on top of them. The Vikings lay scattered, their heads pillowed on their saddles, some in the room near the fire, others along the porch under the dozen or so fluted columns still left standing. Another fire burned on a still dimly visible mosaic of spring flowers near the pool.

The villa had been a big place. The room the Vikings were sleeping in must have been one of the smaller ones, yet a dozen men rested there without being crowded, with space for the fire besides. The ground around it was a veritable mare's nest of fallen masonry overgrown with young trees, briars, and brambles, all bearing thorns and concealing only God knew what holes and traps for an unwary foot. Even quick escape might be difficult.

Owen crouched amid the rubble on the opposite side, Alshan and Elin beside him.

"They have plenty of meat and wine," Elin whispered.

Owen understood what she planned to do and was horrified. "Was this what you had in mind all the time? Was this what you and Sybilla were whispering about? Are you mad?" He reached for her, but Alshan was between them.

He elbowed Owen away. "We must have food," the old man said, "and wine, if possible. We have no friends nearby. I cannot think of any other way to get it. She and Sybilla are the only ones among us any good at theft."

"Sybilla has three children," Elin contributed as though that explained everything.

High above, the cold wind tossed the trees. At least a dozen proven warriors slept at the villa, all armed to the teeth. Their bodies all bristled with swords, knives, and axes. Owen didn't have the foggiest notion of what he would be able to do if she were discovered.

Without any further discussion, Elin stood up and strolled out across the mosaic pavement and around the pool, then began picking her way among the warriors sleeping near the fire. She didn't find what she wanted, so she turned and coolly walked into the room where the rest were sleeping, stepping over one here, going around another there until she reached their provisions piled near the fire in the corner. She selected a full wineskin and a sack of food and turned to leave.

One of the warriors, lying near the door, sat up and threw his blanket aside. Elin froze, standing absolutely still.

Owen rose slowly to a half crouch, sword hilt in hand, thinking that if he could kill the man quickly, he and Elin might escape in the confusion that would follow.

But the man didn't turn or even so much as glance behind him in the direction of the fire, where Elin stood. He made a low sound of disgust, got to his feet, and shambled sleepily through the door to the edge of the pool, opened his trews, and began to piss, aiming the stream desultorily in the direction of a water lily.

Owen began to draw his sword slowly, very quietly. Surely the warrior would see Elin when he was finished and turned to go back to his blankets.

But Elin, as soon as she was sure the warrior was satisfactorily occupied, at once began to move as quickly and quietly out of the room as she had entered. She reached the door just as he heaved a sigh of relief and satisfaction.

Shake it, Owen thought.

The warrior shook it.

Elin slipped out of the door and began sliding, back to the wall, in the direction of the blackness inside the entrance of the next room.

Now, please, please put it away carefully before you turn, Owen prayed.

The warrior put it away carefully before he turned, just as Elin vanished safely into the darkness of the room beside the one she'd just exited.

Owen crouched down beside Alshan, shaking, and realized they were still in danger.

From the room where Elin had taken refuge, he heard the stamp of a hoof and the huffing sound of a horse blow. Of course, saddles; he should have known the horses would be nearby.

And the warrior who'd just relieved himself hadn't returned to his blankets but was fumbling among the provisions around the fire for what must be his wineskin, the one Elin had taken.

"You shouldn't drink so much, my friend," Owen snarled softly. "It might be the death of you."

The warrior didn't find the wineskin. One of the horses whickered softly. The warrior directed a look of outrage at his slumbering fellows, turned, and kicked one in the ribs.

The man awakened, and cursed the one who'd kicked him. But he jerked another wineskin from under his bedding and handed it up to the thirsty fellow, then turned over and, rolling himself in his blankets, went back to sleep.

The horses were silent.

Owen watched, fist clenched white-knuckled on his sword hilt as the man lifted his head and poured a stream of wine into his mouth, then crouched down and threw another log on the fire. He shivered a little; it was growing colder. But then he yawned, shook his head sleepily, and, with a glare at his fellows, threw the strap of the wineskin over his shoulder, carried it off to his bed, and settled down to sleep. Silence returned, broken only by the gentle hiss of the fires and the sound of insect voices in the long grass.

A cold breeze blew on Owen's face, drying the sweat that had broken out all over his skin when the warrior awakened.

"Give her the signal she may leave," Alshan whispered in Owen's ear.

Owen stood and stepped just out of the cover of overgrown rubble and beckoned.

Elin eased silently from the darkness of the stable room. A few moments later, they were moving downhill toward the river, the villa behind them.

*   *   *

Godwin ran up to his warhorse and unceremoniously kicked him in the belly. The roan aimed a bite at him. Godwin slapped him away and pulled the cinch tight. They exploded from the burning house together at a gallop.

The place was surrounded by a loose circle of men, all carrying torches.

The roof of the ruined house was burning brightly now. Godwin slammed his heels into the roan and rode like mad toward another small, ruined structure a hundred yards away. So little was left of it, Enar couldn't tell what it might have once been.

When they reached it, Enar realized it marked the confluence of two deep ditches. It wasn't possible to tell in darkness, but the village had been built on marshy ground. The whole area was deeply cut with ditches to drain it in wet weather.

Godwin looked up and down the ditch he'd just ridden through, an expression of shock evident on his face.

The knot of anxiety Enar had felt since he came to this accursed spot now expanded into his throat. He turned to Godwin. "What is it, old viper? Have you finally outsmarted yourself?"

"I believe that may be so," Godwin replied. He smiled at Enar. "How nice that you are here to share the moment with me."

"They were supposed to be in the ditch, weren't they?" Enar asked. "The others from the town were decoys, too, weren't they?"

"Just so," Godwin replied.

Enar glanced around at the warriors surrounding them. He noticed they were remaining well out of the range of his axe and Godwin's sword but were closing in slowly.

"Hoy, Godwin," one of the Vikings shouted. He was a thick-set dark man with long greasy black hair and beard. When he smiled, he showed a mouthful of rotten teeth.

"Ulick, honey eater," Enar said.

"My, a friend of yours?" Godwin inquired.

"Not if I can help it," Enar said. "Watch him, he's sneaky."

"Hoy, Godwin!" Ulick cried out. "Your luck's run out.

What happened? Is the devil asleep, or wouldn't your sister kiss his prick for you?"

"No," Godwin shouted back. "The evil one was too busy with your mother."

Everyone, including Ulick, seemed to find this sally marvelously funny. Everyone except the man sneaking up behind Enar and Godwin with a spear, because Enar caught him.

Godwin saw him from the corner of his eye. One moment the man had a head, the next he didn't. In a few seconds, Enar had scooped his axe from the ground.

The Vikings drew back. They all watched as the body slid slowly from the saddle and landed with a plop in the soft earth. The horse stood quietly with dragging reins, looking puzzled, shaking its head.

"What!" Enar shouted, brandishing the axe. "No one wants to kiss my pretty mistress? One touch of her lips and your troubles are ended forever. Each of you wants to spend Hakon's gold, but none of you want to earn it?"

"Gold indeed," Ulick yelled. "Do you know what a price Hakon has set on your heads?"

"Whatever it is," Godwin said, "those of you who try to take them will find it not nearly enough."

Just at that moment, the thatch roof burned through. The light became very bright as the broken rafters fell among the straw on the floor.

Slowly, like a noose around the two men, the circle was closing. Men on horseback and on foot moved up closer and closer. There were far too many for the two of them.

"I see they teach gentlemen how to die," Enar said to Godwin.

"I can't think that part of a gentleman's education is ever neglected," Godwin replied disdainfully. He drew his sword. "Shall we?"

"On your signal, my lord," Enar said. "I'll take Ulick. I guarantee his ghost will look like two men. He won't profit by this night's work. Here or in Odin's hall."

The bolt nearly killed Enar's mule. About fifteen feet away a man collapsed and died. Denis and the boys stood up in the ditch at right angles to the small building. After that, it was all carnage. The light from the burning house was too bright. Denis and the boys were able to reload too fast. All Enar and Godwin were able to do was get out of the line of fire.

"You looked in the wrong ditch," Enar accused Godwin, "and shaved ten years off my life."

"I did not!" Godwin shouted, shoving his face into Enar's. He didn't want to admit it, but he'd been so frightened his knees were weak, and, horror of horrors, he'd almost lost control of his bowels when the first crossbow bolt flew. The only consolation he had was that Enar looked nearly as shaken as he was.

"By the way," Enar asked more quietly, "why did you kick your horse in the belly?"

"He fills himself up with air. It makes it impossible to tighten the cinch properly. When you mount, the saddle slides to one side. You land in the dirt."

"Oh," Enar said thoughtfully.

The sky was showing long streaks of lighter blue along the eastern horizon. The wind was brisk, to say the least. It was freezing. Godwin rubbed his nose. It was beginning to show a dangerous rose color akin to frostbite. Enar's fingers were stiff and beginning to grow pale and blue.

"The boys" were plundering the Viking dead.

"Slim pickings," Enar commented.

"Hakon hardly would send the cream of his warriors to steal shovels and seed grain," Godwin replied.

Denis hurried up to Godwin. "I'm sorry, my lord, we weren't where you told us to wait. We did as you ordered, worked our way up the riverbank, then eased our way inland. But when we came to the place you told us to wait, we . . . me and the boys got worried. There was too much water in the ditch. We were afraid our bowstrings would get wet. So we moved to where it was drier."

Godwin gazed helplessly into the cheerful, valiant young face before him. There were armies that would punish Denis for moving on his own initiative. Caesar probably would have punished Denis, but Godwin didn't have seven or so Roman legions to play with. Besides, he was extremely grateful to Denis for telling him he had changed the archers' position. Godwin worried from time to time about his own mind. He was happy to know it was still in good working order.

Then Godwin shrieked as the roan horse finally found a soft spot on his buttocks and nipped him playfully.

Enar laughed. "Thank God I have a mule. They have more common sense."

The mule chose that moment to lean his neck against Enar's right shoulder and step on his foot.

Owen and the rest of his party reached the city the next day. He and Elin weren't speaking, even though he knew he'd lost the argument.

As the night wore on and the weather deteriorated further and further, they had found themselves traveling in the teeth of a shrieking ice storm. When they were finally forced to take shelter in a hollow log, they were unable to light a fire against the cold and rain. Some of the party might have become seriously ill or died of exposure had they not the benefit of the food and wine Elin had managed to steal. As it was, they were able to eat and drink their fill, not once, but several times. And their bodies had been better able to defend themselves against the bitter wind and pervasive damp chill that struck at their bones.

Even so, they were still grateful to meet Godwin, Enar, and a band of picked warriors on the road to the city. Godwin had horses for Elin and Owen and a dry cart piled with warm straw for the rest.

They stopped at the edge of the forest to let Sybilla go her way. "She must return to her children," Alshan explained to Owen.

Godwin had brought some provisions with him. Elin, in turn, gifted Sybilla with bread, oil, meat, and wine to help her on her way.

Owen watched. He looked sour and angry.

Elin kissed Sybilla and the small, brown woman vanished into the winter wood. Elin returned to her horse and swung into the saddle. She glared at Owen. He glared back.

The party started off toward the city.

Godwin sighed.

Chapter

5

WHEN Owen and Elin returned from the forest, no sooner had they shut the door of their room behind them than the quarrel had broken out between them. Full force.

"Damn it!" he roared. "Why in the hell did you take it upon yourself to rob those Vikings?"

"Who better," she shot back, eyes blazing. "The men, Tigg and Alshan, are, at best, clumsy thieves. And good God above, to send Martin or you would have been nothing short of murder. And, while we're on the subject of risk taking," she screeched, "why did you try to throw your life away and kill Hakon?"

She'd turned away then, half horrified. She'd sounded like the worst scold.

He had no answer for her, but instead he did something infinitely more hurtful.

He jerked his necklace off over his head and threw it at her. The beads smacked against her breast with stinging force, slid down her dress, and clattered to the floor at her feet.

Then he gathered up clean clothes and stormed out, going to the sweat bath in the courtyard to bathe and purify himself. Among her people, such an act was tantamount to divorcing her, in addition to being a terrible blow to her pride.

For a few moments, Elin sat on the bed and cried, giving way to self-pity and a sense of injury. After all, hadn't she practically saved their lives by supplying the whole band with food and drink?

When the tears passed, a storm of rage shook her. How dare he insult her this way after all she had done for him. Then the rage passed. She dashed further tears from her eyes, gathered clean clothes of her own, threw his necklace around her neck, then followed him to the sweat bath.

At first, he wouldn't open the door for her, but, at length, she prevailed. He was already naked. She'd never quite understood what drew her to him, what was so compelling about him that almost from the first moment she saw him she had felt in his nearness the pure quality of desire.

He was dark and slender. His body was well formed, with strong muscles, sinewy and agile rather than bulky and powerful like some of Godwin's knights. His eyes were a warm brown. His hair, cropped close, was curly and fine textured, rather like Godwin's. She knew, in a fight or in bed, he was much faster and stronger than he looked.

She undressed. She could feel his eyes on her.

The sweat bath was laid out simply—a pile of hot rocks in one corner and a tub of warm water near them.

She stood by the tub as steam rose from the rocks and, ever so slowly, bathed herself with a sponge while he watched. Underarms, breasts, belly. She took special care with her sex. The floor of the sweat bath was stone. The waste water trickled into a pipe that drained it into the river, so the floor remained dry at her feet.

He sat on the bench, staring at her, apparently unmoved. She watched openly and covertly and saw no movement between his legs.

She thought she'd lost until he rose, very deliberately took the sponge out of her hand, and embraced, then kissed her. He pressed the whole of her length against his body. Her breasts softly molded to his muscular webbing, her belly pressing his. Between her legs, she felt his full arousal. He was so hard. She felt, for a moment, she was riding him. His tongue explored her mouth.

Then, suddenly, before she could even dream of resistance, he had her hair in one hand and her wrists in the other. He backed up to the bench and sat down. As he did, he forced her to her knees. She found herself kneeling before him, both hands clasped in his, her shoulders caught between his legs. She also saw beside him something she hadn't noticed before—a big birch switch the tougher knights used to sting their skin when they bathed. It was a thick, flexible wand and could inflict a far more dangerous and damaging blow than a light sting. But then she realized that wasn't what was in his mind.

He tightened his grip on her hands. "You are my wife. Swear fealty to me."

She wouldn't meet his eyes. She turned her head toward the door, her long, black hair falling, tumbling over her breasts.

God, she is beautiful, he thought. Some shining creature from the very heart of the forest itself. She had dark skin, textured like the finest suede or velvet. She was pregnant how many months? No more than two now. It didn't show. She was flat stomached down to her sex. How could she take such a risk with herself and the child? And yet, she was right. Without the food, they might have died. And how could she send Sybilla? The woman also had responsibilities.

Elin twisted, trying to escape his grip on her hands and the pressure of his knees on her shoulders. She tossed her head and stared up at him defiantly, the blue eyes flashing.

He wanted her. He was taut as the prod of a crossbow with wanting her.

"Swear!" he said. "Why won't you swear fealty to me as your lord? Everyone in the household has, except you. There is no shame in it. Any free man or woman may, without shame, take an oath of vassalage to a protector."

She turned her head and wouldn't meet his eyes. "No. I won't and I can't."

He would love to have been able to beat her. Not to hurt

her for frightening him, but to compel obedience, to keep her from placing herself wantonly in danger. But he knew he couldn't. He'd never been able to strike anyone in cold blood. He and she were noted for keeping a normally quiet, well-ordered house in a violent world.

He released her hands.

She leaped to her feet and pointed at the stick. She was pale with fury. "What were you thinking about—that?"

He threw back his head and laughed. "No, I hadn't even noticed the thing." So saying, he picked it up and threw it onto the heated rocks resting on a grating over coals. The stick caught. "One of the knights must have left it here," he said as they watched it burn.

The anger faded from her face and was succeeded by relief. She hadn't wanted to believe him capable of such cruelty. She was glad he wasn't.

He stood and kissed her. A second later she was on her back on the bench. Her hands wandered over his body. Hers. He was hers. Like a well-used implement that, deftly placed, always brings pleasure. Oh, the fine hair, high brow, long eyelashes, chest, arms, body that reminded her of a panther. His sex, searing hot and hard in her hands.

"Oh, greenwood witch, greenwood wife, you won't promise me next week, next month, next year or even tomorrow. What have you to offer that I should love you?"

She looked up at him, the sharp planes of his face, the beautifully curved mouth. Her eyes glowed with the blue that is the hottest, brightest part of the flame. She gave a sharp intake of breath as he began to enter her. "I'm yours now," she breathed, "and for as long as you want me tonight, I'll be your abject, adoring slave. Is that enough?"

"For now," he replied.

He'd taken her at her word. The household was asleep, and they'd both been near falling down when they helped each other to their room.

They'd exhausted the fire and urgency of desire, and now their lovemaking was a gift of pleasure, one they bestowed on each other. Slow and deliberate, each rich moment to be savored and prolonged until they reached their goal—the flesh's ancient cry of delight in being flesh, the moment of withdrawal and union with the universe.

Once finished, they lay together in bed, spoon fashion, gazing into the fire flickering on the hearth. He cupped both breasts. They were firm and beginning to grow larger. "Sybilla may have three children, but you're pregnant."

She sighed. "Are you going to weary me with that again? If I live and prosper, the child will live and prosper. If I don't, it will die. In either case, we meet with the same fate. The fate of the mother is the fate of the child. Tell me, Owen, how often have you heard of a child surviving its mother's death in childbirth?"

He was struck dumb by the question. And as he searched his memory, he became aware he'd never heard of a single one. The hazards were simply too great. Perhaps some lived among the very wealthy where wet nurses could be produced more easily, but no family in or near Chantalon was even close to being rich enough to be numbered among the great magnates.

Among the poor, the only chance such a child had would be if a relative nursing her own baby would be willing to take the infant to her breast. But even then it often happened that the stepmother grew weary and the motherless little one would be weaned as quickly as possible. Bereft of the long nursing that gave infants their best chance of survival, such a child usually succumbed to disease and, often as not, neglect. And was carried to its mother's grave to join her in her eternal sleep.

He kissed Elin on the nape of the neck and drew her more tightly to him.

"For that matter," she continued, "how often have you been asked to officiate at the funeral of any child under three?"

"Not often," he answered quietly. "Those younger than three aren't so much buried as disposed of. Placed in a clay jar or wrapped in a blanket, they are laid to rest in the corner of a garden or near a cemetery wall, and very probably not a few go directly into the river." He knew the death rate among the very young was high, emotional investment low. They began their journey into eternity unloved, unmourned, and often even unnamed. She was right. Deprived of its most powerful protector—its mother—a newborn child would not live long. And in the wilderness, hunger and cold might kill her as quickly and cruelly as the Vikings would.

He hugged her tightly against him. She reached under her pillow, pulled out his necklace, and, half turning, flipped it around his neck.

"Very well." He reached under his pillow and drew something out. A string of dark beads was all she could see. Then he dropped them over her head.

She fingered the polished surfaces. "Amber?"

He indicated the fire, the only light in the room, with a nod of his head. She got up and walked naked to stand before the blaze and look into the transparent stone. He heard her soft whisper of awe and then rose and went to join her.

She was studying the clear, transparent brown beads. Each contained some once living thing. One bead held a tiny spider, another an ant, the next a piece of tree bark, still another a few fragments of dead leaves. The entire necklace was composed of reminders of how carelessly life's beauty and bounty is strewn about us.

"So beautiful, so powerful," she whispered. "No one has ever given me anything so wonderful in my life. We believe these stones have the power to protect their wearer in both time and eternity, in this world and the worlds above and below. It is an amulet of immense virtue, able to secure the safety of one of my order on any journey she may undertake."

"And of what order are you?" he asked softly.

She kissed him, and he felt his hunger for her begin to rise again.

"There are so many names." Her voice was hushed with desire. "And they all mean so little. Witch, sorceress, green wood queen are just a few. I am one of those who travel in other worlds, those worlds I spoke of just now. And so, my dear love, are you."

He clasped her hands as he had in the sweat bath. "I am your dear love, yet you won't promise me tomorrow."

"No one can promise anyone tomorrow, Owen. My people are the only ones smart enough to know that there are no guarantees. I cannot give you more. Neither of us knows what we may be called upon to do."

He released her hands and put his arms around her. "Elin, if you will not swear fealty to me, at least promise me this one thing: When your time is upon you, come to me, no matter how things stand between us. I will care for you and the child. If you should meet with some mischance, I will do the best I can for your little one."

"Oh, very well, I promise. Lord, you are a worrier."

He kissed her again and began stroking her in a number of places she seemed to like, but he was alarmed when she suddenly drew back.

"Hush." She pulled free and ran to the window. He followed quickly.

"What's wrong?"

"Nothing." She opened the shutter.

He heard the high piping cries. The moon was full and the earth and sky were drenched with its light.

"Wild geese," she whispered.

"Yes," he answered bitterly, "and one day I will find you gone and know you followed them across the sky into the north."

She turned toward him, seeming almost transparent in the silver light. Outside, a wedge of geese crossed the moon. "Love me," she whispered. "No night like this will ever come again. Wild geese and the moon. Love me. Love me now because . . . because whatever you believers in the mystery of time think, now is all we ever have. Now is all we ever get. So love me now."

He closed and bolted the window, shutting out the dangerous moonlight. His hands wandered over her body. She was a garden of many delights. God, he couldn't wait. Fealty be damned. He'd *take* her. He picked her up and carried her to the bed.

Chapter 6

*E*LSPETH sat in the great hall at Hakon's side. He had commanded that she sit beside him at the high table whenever he dined at her stronghold. She wore her jewels, at least as many as she could conveniently carry at one time, and had a long rope of pearls braided into her hair. Hakon had commanded this also, and she obeyed.

Her seven-year-old son, Eric, was at her side. Hakon hadn't commanded this, but he hadn't objected, and since she seldom let Eric wander far from her, she brought him here also. She understood perfectly how futile it would have been for her to try to protect the boy from any active malice on Hakon's part, but her fear for Eric was part of the vast, inchoate anxiety caused by this man, the Viking chieftain, who had so precipitously become his stepfather.

She carefully pulled strips from the breast of a roast fowl and set them on the child's plate, then added two spoonfuls of turnips cooked in their own greens. Eric began hesitantly to eat.

"Why can't he do that for himself?" Hakon asked.

Elspeth gave a slight start. Though no outside observer would have thought it, these were the first words Hakon had addressed to her since his failed attack on the city.

"I suppose he could," Elspeth said softly, "but his

father, Reynald, had little patience with children at the table. Eric has seldom eaten with adults, so he's timid."

Hakon's eyes flicked away from the child and stared into the big smoky room. His men and Elspeth's people were crowded together into the hall. Settled at the tables, they all ate as though tomorrow might bring famine. A babble of noise and conversation filled the room.

Elspeth sighed with relief that Hakon's attention was distracted from her son. She looked up guardedly at her new husband.

He filled the chair he sat in, six feet of massive muscle and bone. His silver gray eyes flickered around the hall with the alertness of a timberwolf. She could feel his tension. He seemed to quiver with it like a bowstring just before the arrow is loosed.

"I failed," he said.

Elspeth started again. She didn't know if the words were addressed to her. He wasn't looking at her, but out at the swarming hive of humanity stuffing themselves with dinner. And for a moment, she hated him for drawing her into his troubled mind, exposing himself so openly to her. She felt she had to answer.

"No," she said. "You suffered a setback. You are still stronger than that young firebrand—Owen of Chantalon."

Hakon laughed a humorless laugh. "You're like Reynald, your late lord. Go with the winner."

Elspeth felt the rebuff. Since his return from the city, he'd treated her more like a servant than a wife. He'd let her dress the wound he'd taken from Owen's crossbow.

It was a hideous scrape across the ribs, luckily with more bruising than blood. After she'd cleaned the wound, he'd shrugged into his clothes and stalked out, returning to his island fortress on the river. She knew he'd quarreled with at least one of the chieftains under his command. The man had loaded his ship and sailed away. But the rest of his followers remained. She could guess why. They were drawn by his promises of land. Land he'd gained by his marriage to her. Lands she held not only by her family's ancient right, but through her marriage to Reynald. By bedding her, he made good his claim to rule them.

The closeness of his people and hers was an uneasy one. Her people ate quietly, keeping their heads low, watching the Vikings fearfully. The Vikings ate and drank with the cheerful boisterousness of conquerors. As yet, they hadn't offended anyone. No man's daughter had been troubled. No one's land or property had been touched. So there were no fights. But they would come and soon. She wondered what Hakon would do. She didn't know if he recognized the strength of her people or not—a strength that lay in their power to give loyalty or withhold it. They had endured Reynald as she had, but she was sure they felt but little love for him. Now they looked narrowly at this new lord, this Hakon, and wondered what he would be like.

As for herself, Elspeth knew how they felt. She composed her features into the polite mask of a lady. Poised and courteous, much as she had been since her earliest youth, she waited.

Hakon spoke again, quietly, and it was as though he'd heard her thoughts. "I want to end our supper before my men get too far gone in drink."

"Certainly," she answered. "When you rise, I shall, of course, follow you out of the hall. The rest will take it as a signal to leave."

"Sooner or later," he mused, "there will be trouble."

Elspeth drew in her breath sharply and reached one trembling hand for her wine cup. She took two quick swallows. She knew she had to say something to him. Speak at least a few words and try to defend her people. But he terrified her. Terrified her as he had since their first meeting. She wanted to cringe and crawl away from him. Hide her feelings as she had from Reynald behind that ladylike mask of propriety. But Hakon wasn't Reynald. He hadn't dealt with her as Reynald had, treating her simply as a brood mare, keeping her locked away from all decisions about her estates. Besides, Reynald had come from among her people. He knew the rules, mostly unwritten, that governed their conduct. Hakon didn't.

The humble who ate so quietly with their heads bowed

had their own kind of power. If, by some action, he thoroughly alienated them, they would in small ways make life unbearable. She hoped against hope, in her own heart, that it wouldn't happen. So she must speak.

"Yes," she answered quietly, almost inaudibly, for his ears alone. "Yes, there will be trouble, and when there is, remember that a lord who does no justice is no lord."

There was a scream from the kitchen, followed by a howl of masculine rage.

A girl ran into the hall. Elspeth had time only to notice she was bare to the waist because she was at once followed by one of Hakon's warriors, a big, black-bearded man. His beard was more red than black, for blood was streaming from his nose.

The girl turned at bay in front of the high table. "Louse face!" she screeched at the warrior. She waved one of the big wooden cooking spoons.

"Not a very formidable weapon," Elspeth heard Hakon murmur. He was wrong.

She jabbed it at the bearded warrior's knee. He jerked his head back, but it had been only a feint. The girl was going for a much more tender portion of his anatomy. In a twinkling, she lowered the spoon and brought it up between his legs hard. He crashed to the floor with a yowl of purest anguish.

Two more Vikings dashed out of the kitchen. Both were bleeding, one from a torn ear, the other from the mouth. They advanced on the girl cautiously.

"Stop!" Hakon roared.

"Pig prick!" the girl spat at the fallen warrior. "Eat the maggots that ate your mother. Bat dung!" she yelled at the other two.

"Shut—your—mouth," Hakon said. He said it very quietly, but the menace in his voice silenced the whole hall.

The girl shut her mouth, though she still looked mutinous.

"Cover yourself," Hakon snapped.

The girl covered her breasts quickly with a torn gown.

"Slut!" one of the Vikings snarled.

"Brother to a rat, father of pigs, and son of dog . . . a mangy dog," the girl replied between her teeth.

"I said," Hakon snarled, "shut your mouth." He glared at the three men. "What happened? Did you try to force her?"

The room erupted into laughter, most of it coming from the benches where the Vikings sat.

"I can't think," Elspeth said, her face stiff with disgust, "that force was really necessary."

"Who is she?" Hakon asked Elspeth in a low voice.

"Your men used the word 'slut.' And that is what she is. Reynald purchased her a few months ago from one of the slavers. After a few weeks, he freed her. I can't but think he had some incentive to do so," Elspeth whispered, her hands tightening on the arms of her chair. "Her name is Clara."

Still clutching the dress to her breast, the girl pointed at the Viking she'd smacked in the groin. "He paid for a tumble; I don't deny that," she screeched. "But then his two friends joined him." She forgot her dress, put her hands on her hips, and glared at the offending Vikings. "I'll take on three, I'll take on a score, but I want my pay. A silver coin from each or you can go play with Mary five fingers and a hand gallop for you all."

The Viking she'd hit in the groin was on his feet now, his face scarlet with fury. "She owes me compensation for my knee and my . . ." He shot a look at Hakon's face, which was like a thundercloud. The Viking abruptly shut up.

"What are you worried about, Holder," the girl jeered, "your beauty?"

More raucous laughter came from the benches where the Vikings were sitting.

Elspeth noticed her people were strangely silent, and they all watched Hakon.

Holder turned to the Vikings sitting on the benches and shouted, "She's a boastful little slut, boys. Let's take her out behind the hay rick and see how many of us she can really take on before she begins squealing. I'll take out my compensation in trade."

As the men began rising enthusiastically from the benches,

he stretched out one big arm toward Clara, who, for the first time, looked really frightened. Covering herself with her torn dress, she began to back down the table where Elspeth sat with Hakon.

Elspeth glanced over at her own people. Their heads were bowed, but they seemed a forest of eyes, all staring at Hakon and the Vikings. She could see the anger move through them the way a sudden gust of wind troubles a flame.

Elspeth's nails dug into the back of Hakon's hand. "Stop this," she whispered urgently. "Please."

Holder reached out, grabbing Clara by the hair. She screeched like a rabbit in the jaws of a hound.

"Holder!" Hakon's voice roared. "Let her go. The women in this house are under my governance."

Holder directed a look of contempt toward his chief. "What are you?" he asked. "Pimp for the bitch?"

Before Elspeth could draw breath to gasp in horror, Hakon was up, his hands closed around Holder's throat. Holder was a big man, but Hakon dragged him up from the floor and across the table until their faces were inches apart. Then, almost negligently, he pressed down hard with his thumb on Holder's throat, right at the Adam's apple. Hakon threw him like a rag doll to the floor in front of the high table.

Holder's face turned blue and his eyes bulged in the sudden absolute silence. Elspeth could hear the dreadful wheezing shrieks as the injured man tried to draw breath past his bruised Adam's apple.

Hakon righted the wine cup he and Elspeth shared. Tapping the base of the cup lightly on the table, he said, "More wine, if you please, my lady."

Elspeth tore her eyes from the struggling man on the floor. She gripped the wine pitcher, white knuckled and two handed, trying to negate her own violent trembling and somehow manage to fill the cup. "He may die," she whispered.

"I think that might be no great loss," Hakon said. "He's worth more as an object lesson than he ever was as a man."

Hakon lifted the grail, drank, wiped his lip carefully with his napkin, and offered it to Elspeth. She accepted and took a quick gulp that burned on the way down to her stomach. When she lowered the cup, Holder was on his feet and the color was coming back into his cheeks.

"Have you anything to say to me, Holder?" Hakon asked, his voice cold.

Holder shook his head and staggered toward the table where the Vikings sat. His face was white now, not blue. He threw Hakon a murderous glance from bloodshot eyes and sat down. A neighbor at the bench pushed a tankard toward him and he began to drink, swallowing cautiously.

"I've dealt with the man," Hakon said quietly to Elspeth. "Now you take care of the woman."

Clara was crouched, whimpering, at the dais beneath Elspeth's feet.

"Stand up, Clara," Elspeth commanded.

She stood, pulling up her torn dress.

"Don't bother to cover yourself," Elspeth said. "Everyone knows what you are." Her voice was knife edged. "By your right, according to both law and custom, you are entitled to your pay. Now," Elspeth continued, "who wants her?"

Clara stood in front of the table, bare breasted, glaring at the men, both Elspeth's and Hakon's.

How many have had her? Elspeth wondered. *Or how many has she had?* With Clara it was difficult to tell the difference.

Most of the men wouldn't meet her eyes. Several of the women looked amused. No one said anything.

One of the Vikings, an older man, bald but with a long, silky black beard, finished eating and wiped his greasy hands on his beard. "Oh well," he said, and rose and walked toward the table.

When he rose and the torchlight fell on him, Elspeth could see he was hideously ugly. One eye was scarred and scabbed over. He was hunchbacked, with one shoulder higher than the other. His knees were crooked, his walk a shambling trot. He scurried over to the bench and pulled a silver dinar from the pouch at his belt. He held it up so that Hakon and Elspeth could see it plainly and then put it firmly in Clara's hand.

He turned and grinned a gap-toothed grin at the assembled company. "It doesn't bother me," he said. "I always have to pay." Then he led Clara off toward the kitchen.

She shot a truly poisonous look at Elspeth on her way out.

Hakon was grinning. Elspeth was pale and angry, but deeply relieved things had been settled quietly. She glanced toward the door and saw Tosi, Hakon's oldest friend among the Vikings, standing there with a visitor.

Holding him by the arm, Tosi marched him toward the high table. The stranger was a slender, blond young man, very richly dressed. He wore a gold-embroidered black dalmatic over a long-sleeved silk shirt. His trousers were dark linen, too. Instead of the cross-gartered leggings the rest wore, he sported soft leather boots topped by embroidered stockings.

"As I live and breathe," Hakon whispered in a low voice, "a courtier."

"Hardly," Elspeth answered. "My third cousin, Rauching."

"A kinsman," Hakon whispered.

"I have that misfortune, yes."

Hakon chuckled.

"He's a liar, a thief, and, quite possibly by now, a murderer," Elspeth whispered.

Tosi and Rauching reached the dais. Elspeth fell silent, but the look on her face was not a welcoming one. In spite of the roaring fireplaces on both sides, the big hall was cold, yet Hakon noticed Rauching was sweating.

"My dear Elspeth!" Rauching exclaimed with as much of a bow as he could manage. Tosi was holding him very firmly by the arm.

"I'm not your 'dear,' " Elspeth said. "What are you doing here?"

"Hoping for the hospitable warmth of a fire, a crust of bread, and, mayhap, the tiniest bit of beer," Rauching said, trying to sound winsome.

"Hakon," Tosi said, "this butterfly flitted in through the

gate with six other men. I wouldn't have let him in, but he says he's a kinsman."

"Where are the men?" Hakon asked.

"I put them in the stable," Tosi said.

Hakon nodded. "Good." He studied Rauching carefully. Rauching's eyes darted around, searching the table and the hall.

"Looking for Reynald?" Elspeth asked in an icy voice.

"I noticed," Rauching said, "he doesn't seem to be here."

"Reynald's dead," Bertrand, Elspeth's brother, said from where he was sitting among some of his priests at a side table. "Dead and most foully murdered."

Rauching looked both uncertain and crestfallen. "H-how," he stammered as he glanced from Hakon to Elspeth and then back again to Hakon. "How terrible," he said finally, getting the words out.

"Not for me," Hakon said with a broad grin.

"It certainly appears not," he said hurriedly.

"Reynald's ill fortune was my good luck," Hakon continued. "Elspeth is now my wife."

"My . . . how"—Rauching paused and glanced from one face to the other, taking in Hakon's grin as well as Elspeth's new jewels and blooming fairness—"very, very convenient for you both," he purred.

Hakon roared with laughter and staggered Rauching by reaching over the table and slapping him on the shoulder. "Never let it be said I turned away my wife's relatives from my door. Come up. Join us and sit down and have a bite to eat."

Hakon turned to the man seated on the bench next to his chair. "Move over," he said, "and make room for our guest of honor."

Rauching had to walk to the end of the high table and come around to reach the bench. While he was doing so, Hakon turned to Elspeth. "He isn't to be trusted, I take it."

"Hardly," she answered softly. "I suspect he's an unsuccessful criminal who thinks we are successful ones."

"Let's not disillusion him just yet," Hakon said as Rauching took a seat at his side.

Hakon filled Rauching's cup with his own hand. "Here,"

he said cheerfully. "Drink up. When you came in, you looked like a man who didn't know whether to offer congratulations or condolences."

"Whichever one, my Lord Hakon, is least likely to get me killed."

"Congratulate me," Hakon said, looking at Elspeth. "I couldn't be happier."

"I think," Elspeth said, staring out over the room and not looking at either, "Rauching, that you might congratulate me also. Save your condolences, if any, for Bertrand." She glanced over at her brother at the side table. His hate-filled eyes were fixed on both her and Hakon.

A lock of hair had slipped from Elspeth's jeweled coif. It lay like a curved, sooty shadow against her cheek.

Hakon reached up and brushed the soft wisp back, tucking it under with a touch almost unbelievably delicate from a hand as large and strong as his.

Elspeth turned toward him. Her lips quivered for a moment as though they begrudged the gesture, but then they curved into a smile. However, there was pain in both her eyes and her smile.

"Thank you," Hakon said, his voice so low it was inaudible to everyone but Elspeth and Rauching.

Elspeth looked quickly away as though ashamed to have betrayed herself so nakedly.

She trembles at his touch, Rauching thought, looking at them, *and he can barely keep his hands off her even here in the hall in front of the whole household.* Rauching cleared his throat quickly and reached for some slices of venison roast. "Alas," he said, "I witnessed that little contretemps when I came into the hall. You have a very hard hand, my dear cousin. I may call you cousin now, mayn't I? After all, we're all family here."

"I think not," Hakon said. "I much prefer 'my lord Hakon.' It has a certain ring to it. Don't you think? I rather like it."

"To be sure," Rauching murmured maliciously. "To be sure, my lord Hakon."

Elspeth leaned back in her chair, her fingers toying idly

with the wine cup. "Tell me, Rauching. What happened to your heiress?"

"My what?"

"Bertrada, the propertied woman you were about to marry when we first met."

"Oh, her," Rauching said. "We were married as we planned."

"And?" Elspeth questioned.

"My, what excellent venison," Rauching said, "and how delightfully prepared."

"The heiress?" Elspeth prompted.

"She died. It's something that seems to happen from time to time to some people."

"If she died," Elspeth continued, "how is it that you are not still in possession of her lands and property?"

"Oh, such a long tedious story," Rauching said with an airy wave of his hand. "I hate to bore my host and charming hostess. Besides, it's hardly cheerful dinner conversation, is it?"

"I'm not bored," Elspeth said. "Tell me."

"Yes," Hakon said, leaning back in his chair, thumb and forefinger curled at his chin. "I believe I'd like to hear it, too."

Rauching looked carefully at them from face to face. "Well," he said, "after all, why not? We're all family here . . . together."

"To be sure," Hakon said smoothly. "The heiress."

"Sweet Elspeth," Rauching said, "do you remember the lady at all? How well endowed she was, how fond of the pleasures of the table?"

Elspeth nodded. "Yes. She was both fat and greedy."

"Exactly," Rauching said. "As it happened, she seasoned her stew one night with a bad mushroom. A most fatal error. But since she gathered the mushrooms herself, and the stew was prepared by the cook under her direction, an error entirely on her part, I assure you."

"Certainly," Hakon said.

"Her brother, Ethewold. You do remember Ethewold, don't you?"

"He'd be difficult to forget," Elspeth said. "He's one of the largest men I've ever seen."

"Yes," Rauching said. "Lots of fat, but muscle under it. I believe he had his eye on his sister's property himself, but in any case, he adamantly refused to believe in my innocence. He had the temerity to haul me before the bishop."

"Heart rending," Hakon said. "And you in the midst of your grief."

"How inconvenient," Elspeth murmured. "But certainly you were able to withstand the ordeal?"

Rauching coughed delicately. "There was no ordeal. The bishop was kind enough to allow me to clear myself with an oath."

"How very understanding of him," Elspeth said.

"Yes, it was, wasn't it?" Rauching said, refilling his wine cup. "A man of true compassion. The serenity with which I took the oath, my obvious bitter sorrow, brought tears to the eyes of everyone in the church. Everyone, that is, except Ethewold. Can you credit it? He refused to believe an oath made at the peril of my soul on holy writ. The man began to dog my very footsteps. Every time I looked up, there he was, glaring at me from under those thick bushy brows of his. I began to doubt his sanity. Began to believe the poor brainsick unfortunate might do something rash. One night, he was set upon by three brigands."

"Tsk, tsk," Elspeth said, raising her eyes to heaven. "How very unfortunate for Ethewold."

Rauching managed to look rueful and sour at the same time. Having finished the venison stew, he loaded his plate with slices of stuffed pork roast. "As events transpired," he said, licking his fingers, "no."

"No?" Hakon repeated with an interrogative lift of his brows.

"No," Rauching replied. "Ethewold prevailed. Not a scratch on him."

"Ah, I see," Elspeth said. "One of the brigands lived long enough to talk."

Rauching shot her a very sharp look as Hakon chuckled. "Ethewold accounted for three strong men."

"And taken by surprise, too. You must have had a very fast horse, Cousin. Else you would not be here."

"I did leave the neighborhood rather quickly," Rauching said grudgingly.

"Where did you go?" Elspeth asked.

"Oh, here and there," Rauching said. "But, left destitute as I was, I found cold welcome. Even among," he sighed deeply, "my kin."

"Destitute, surely not," Elspeth said. "Bertrada was a wealthy woman, and some of her wealth was in gold and jewels."

Hakon chuckled. "Oh no, my dear, I can well believe destitute. Our kinsman's had quite a few out-of-pocket expenses haven't you, Rauching?" He glanced at Rauching, who avoided his eyes and concentrated on the pork roast.

"Let's see," Hakon continued, ticking them off on his fingers. "I imagine persuading the cook to season the stew so expertly cost something, but not nearly as much as bribing the bishop. Ecclesiastics charge an extraordinary amount for their services, don't they, cousin? And I imagine the three brigands wanted a bit in advance. They wouldn't attack a man like Ethewold for the fun of it. Yes, all in all, I would say our beloved kinsman has had a very bad year."

Elspeth caught her lower lip between her teeth. She stared out into the room with unseeing eyes.

Rauching's glare at her indifferent profile held pure murder.

Hakon caught the look. He slapped Rauching so hard on the back that he choked on the pork roast and almost fell off the bench.

"Never fear, dear cousin," Hakon laughed. "A man of your talents is able to make his way anywhere. I'm sure that in no time at all, your fortunes will be completely restored. I will personally see to it that the inconstant lady luck smiles on you again. However," he continued with a smile that showed every one of his teeth, "if you should ever favor my wife with that sort of look again, I'll gut you like a pig."

Rauching's reply was forestalled because at that moment Elspeth bade Hakon good night and left the table with her women trailing behind her.

Hakon remained. He pushed away the wine cup. He and Rauching spent a long time in very close, whispered conversation.

Once in her bedroom, Elspeth dismissed her maids and settled the children down in her big bed. A horn-shielded lamp burned on her dresser. She looked out through one of the narrow embrasures at the moon-drenched forest. As she watched, a ragged wedge of geese crossed the moon. She heard their lonely cry.

Would he leave, she wondered, and with never a word to her? Something in her whispered that she should turn away from the window, pretend indifference. Blow out the candle, lie down, and go to sleep. She had an early day tomorrow. It would be best if she got her rest.

Elspeth didn't listen to the mocking little voice. Instead, she began walking the floor quietly, pacing up and down as she often had when she was married to Reynald. Waiting. She wasn't sure what she was waiting for. Or even why she waited so patiently and so tenaciously. She only knew she did. She continued to walk, silent as a shadow, from the door to the window and back again.

Hours passed. The moon rode low over the treetops outside, and the room grew so cold her breath smoked a little in the still air. She heard a faint scratching at the door. She walked to the door and whispered, "Who is it?"

"Hakon," was the equally soft reply.

She slipped the iron bolt of the door that shielded her from the rest of the household. He slipped out of the darkened corridor and stepped into the room.

She was amazed as always by his sheer bulk and his presence. His shoulders filled the narrow doorway, and he had to duck his head to clear the lintel.

"What kept you?" she asked waspishly. "Did you stop to amuse yourself with Clara?"

She saw his frightening eyes glaze over with a film of ice. "I wouldn't lower myself to such as Clara," he almost snarled.

"Too bad," she said. "I was just going to ask you how she was." Her hand flew to her mouth, and the fingers covered her lips.

She turned away, so obviously shocked by her own words that Hakon's anger vanished. He knew he should be furious, but he couldn't sustain a decent rage around her. She had too much about her of the ferocious kitten. Something small and fuzzy, just learning it had claws and how to use them.

"I don't have to be curious about the Claras of this world," he said. "I know how she'd be. Do you?" He closed the door and leaned back against the panels.

"I can't imagine. I haven't the equipment," she said harshly.

Hakon chuckled. His admiring glance took in the way the soft linen bed gown she wore molded itself to her form and the dark hair coiled at her neck framed her small pale face like a storm cloud. "No, no need to worry about Clara," he continued. "I spent a lot of my time after you left with Rauching." A somber look shadowed his face. "Deceit and treachery are so easy to buy, aren't they?"

"From Rauching," Elspeth answered, "I imagine so. He has nothing else to sell."

Elspeth thought she was in command of herself until she realized that ever so imperceptibly she'd shrugged the gown from her shoulder to reveal one milky white breast to Hakon. She heard him catch his breath quickly, and realized his eyes were devouring her.

"Speaking of Rauching," he said. "My compliments, sweet lady, on the smooth way you pried the truth out of your slippery cousin."

"The truth isn't in Rauching," Elspeth said. "I got some kind of story, probably not the true one. But I wanted to give you an idea what sort of man he is."

His hand reached out slowly. He extricated the pins, one by one, from her hair until it fell into his hands. Elspeth swayed toward him, eyes closed, her lips parted.

Hakon released her hair. The back of his hand brushed her cheek, then fell and cupped her bare breast. His arms closed around her, and he lifted her from the floor. She seemed weightless.

Elspeth went limp with a surrender so absolute it terrified her. Hakon's eyes flickered over the children sleeping quietly in the bed; then with one hand, he jerked off his velvet mantle, flung it to the floor, and lowered Elspeth on top of it.

Her bed gown parted like a cobweb under his hands. Her fingers locked in his hair, sending a sharp burning pain through the scar on his forehead. To Elspeth's eyes, it seemed to grow white, then throbbed red with his urgency.

"You're mine," Hakon whispered into her ear. He parted her thighs with his knee.

"For the moment," she answered.

Hakon laughed again, but Elspeth could see that she'd hurt him. But then she felt his first intimate touch, and a devouring fire that had smoldered for days burst into flame, consuming her.

Like one shrinking from a precipice, Elspeth shifted and drew away slightly. "Shameless," she whispered, all the while knowing that would have been the word her mother might have used; Bertrand, her brother, would certainly have used; every disapproving adult in her life would have used, to accuse her.

"Shame," Hakon whispered, his lips close to her ear. "Show me any shame, woman, and I'll beat it out of you. Not with my hands, girl, but with my hammer." He chuckled. "How do you like my hammer?"

Elspeth liked it very much. The pressure between her legs brought wave after pounding wave of raw pleasure. She shuddered once violently, then yielded completely like a presenting mare beneath the weight of a stallion.

Hakon gasped, then laughed softly at the violence of her thigh grip and her inward pulsations.

She moaned.

"Sshh," he whispered, stifling her last involuntary gasp sweetly with his lips.

He was stiff, holding her head, resting on the crook

of her arm, when Elspeth realized the floor was cold and hard.

She could feel the stubble on his face cutting into her soft skin at her shoulder. She could see the deep-etched lines of fatigue and pain in his face. His eyes were puffy and bloodshot, shadowed by dark circles. The flesh on his jaw bone drew tight with strain. "Stay the night," she whispered, running her fingers across his cheek.

He shook his head. "No. I must return to the camp tonight. My men are an unruly lot, and right now they're frightened by my failure to take the city. If they ever begin to whisper I've deserted them, I will be lost."

Elspeth struggled to a sitting position.

Hakon leaned on his elbow, looking up at her. "I didn't expect this to happen," he said. "I only came to say good night."

"If you must go, you must," Elspeth said. "But leave a few of your men here."

"Why?" Hakon asked, looking troubled.

"Rauching," Elspeth said. "He's an evil man. I don't think you realize how evil. Be very careful of him."

"My sweet lady," Hakon said. "Little Elspeth. If Rauching ever lays one finger on you, I'll cut off his hands and give them to you for a present. I think I made that very clear to him tonight at the table. But in any case, you have no reason to be afraid now. I'm taking Rauching to the camp with me. Day after tomorrow I'm sending him to the city."

"You haven't given up on them, then?"

"Elspeth," Hakon whispered in a decidedly cold voice. "I don't give up. Either of the two men in the city could destroy me. The bishop Owen. I thought he was little better than a beardless boy, but then I saw him endure agonies that would kill some men and cripple others. He only emerged stronger and more willing to lead his men against me in a mortal combat. His captain, Godwin, is a proven soldier. The old wolf has never lost any fight he rode into willingly. How long do you think they would let me stand if I let them get their legs under them? How long?"

"They will destroy you if they can," Elspeth said.

"Yes," Hakon said, softly. "Do you know, you spoke rightly when I said you were mine and you answered 'for the moment.' "

Elspeth turned away from Hakon and peered over the footboard of the bed. The children still slept quietly.

"No," she said. "You don't understand; you're not one of my people. That question isn't asked or answered until . . . a certain time. It's a serious thing."

"I'll take your word for it," Hakon said. He looked up at her bemusedly, sitting there naked, with her long dark hair streaming over her shoulders, her face shadowed by the candlelight. She reminded him of someone or something long ago. And then he remembered. His sister.

She'd been his sister and his mother both. She'd shared her breast with him and her first child because his own mother was dead. He remembered that long after he was old enough to toddle around and take solid food, he would come to her knee, pleading to give suck, and she, laughing, would welcome him. So vivid were both the memory and the likeness that he almost seemed to see a drop of milk quivering at the tip of Elspeth's nipple. He reached up and pulled her down and took her nipple in his mouth, tugging at it gently with his lips, the way a child would.

"Ah God," Elspeth whispered, burying her hands in his coarse, dark hair and clutching him to her body. "Everything before you was a kind of sleepwalk; everything after you will be shadows. Ah God, why did you give me life only to have it end so soon?"

Hakon pulled away. Elspeth could feel his body shaking. She rose to her feet quickly and ran to get another gown to replace her torn one.

"Never, never, never," Hakon whispered over and over again as he got to his feet and began to straighten his clothing. He reached down, snatched up his ornate velvet mantle, and wrapped it around him.

Elspeth paused by the open clothes chest, clutching the torn gown to her breast, a nude woman of ivory and shadow. "Hakon," she said in a voice as soft as thistledown, but with a whisper of drawn steel in it. "Don't fail me."

Their eyes locked and held. His, glacial, filled with a memory of bitter pain. Hers, hard and flat, with terror.

"I'll take the city," he said, "and put my enemies to the sword or die in the attempt." Then, with a swirl of scarlet and gold velvet, he was gone.

7

GODWIN woke late. His room was near Elin and
Owen's. They had managed to rouse him several
times during the night. After each disturbance,
Godwin tossed and turned for quite a long time
before he was able to get back to sleep.

He knew himself to be envious. Enar, curse the loud-
mouthed bastard, had been right. It had been a long time
since he'd lain with a woman, and the lack of female
companionship was making him irritable. He thought about
the widow's ladies, then rejected the idea.

Though no one in the household knew it, and he would
never tell the story, he had spent some time as a slave.
He'd been able to escape and return to his own people and
regain his rank. But the widow's ladies were slaves, and
he knew by almost unbearably bitter experience how
helpless and cruelly treated most slaves were.

Rosamund had belonged to the widow. Elin had rescued her and the child was much happier now. But she'd
lived through years of sheer hell, and who knew what
scars were left on her spirit. He'd always been disgusted
by churchmen who condemned the sad wan young girls
forced into a life he was sure many had been taught to
regard as dishonorable. And he'd never condemned any
for doing what they had to do to survive.

He thought about Rosamund and found himself very

uncomfortable. He actually got out of bed, straightened his sheets and blankets, punched his pillow into submission before he crawled back in, and told himself firmly to go back to sleep.

At that precise moment, one of the married couples who shared the second-floor bedrooms with him began panting and moaning.

Godwin cursed audibly and fluently. He was sure the panters and moaners probably heard him, but it didn't slow them down one bit. There were quite a few pairs. Elin and Owen, Enar and Ingund, Ranulf and Elfwine. Not to mention Gowen and whoever he might have invited over from the tavern for the night. Godwin knew his chances of obtaining permanent peace were nil. So he clapped the pillow over his head and resigned himself to a sleepless night.

And, of course, woke up considerably after first light, his head at the foot of the bed, his feet on the pillow, and his rear end sticking out from under the blankets. That was what awakened him. He was literally freezing his ass off. The room was icy cold, the light bright, and he was sure the rest of the household was up and about their usual morning mischief.

He dressed and went downstairs. Ingund saw him coming and began to prepare his breakfast. A few moments after he sat down, she slammed a platter in front of him. The two poached eggs in a bowl and the buttered toast leaped several inches into the air. Godwin flinched.

She wore the boar-tusk helmet and one of Enar's throwing axes in her belt. Godwin had faced charges by berserks, assaults by any number of armed men, cold, hunger, disease, battle wounds, and death. He usually prevailed, sometimes bloody but always unbowed. Yet he could be cowed by the cook. He or she was, after all, in charge of his stomach, the only organ in his body he pampered. The only organ that sometimes gave him painful problems.

"Ingund," he pleaded, "please."

"Don't worry," she replied grimly, "it's to your liking. Eggs lightly poached in wine, seasoned with chervil.

Light toast, and just a bit of sausage seasoned with sage on the side."

He dipped his spoon into the eggs. "Aaaaah," he sighed. "Ingund, you are incomparable."

Alfric entered from the front door to the square. He was accompanied by a weary traveler. The man was well into middle age; his clothing and shoes were thickly coated with mud and dust. The stranger's hair was grizzled, his thin face lined by exhaustion.

Ingund was a good woman. She and Alfric hurried the stranger to the table and seated him opposite Godwin. Ingund quickly found the stranger something to eat. Bread, porridge, wine, a bit more of the sausage Godwin was eating.

"Thank you," the stranger mumbled through the food. He was gorging it. "I haven't eaten my fill in weeks."

"Go slow," Ingund warned. "Don't make yourself sick."

Godwin turned to Alfric, giving him a look of inquiry.

Alfric was the closest thing Owen had to a steward since Ranulf had abandoned the post to become a fighting man. He was a wandering monk, belonging to a community in Ireland, one long ago wiped out by the Viking raids.

Judith had found him sitting on the dock one day. A light rain was falling at the time. He had a small knapsack with some linen and a few coarse robes. He had a large box filled with books. Judith threw up her hands. She didn't know Alfric, but she knew the type. They showed up frequently at her father's table. Some called themselves rabbis, since she and her father were Jews. But sometimes the visitors were Christian. In any case, most had no interest in converting her father, any more than the rabbis did.

Instead, they sat up by candlelight until the small hours arguing about such important practical matters as how old is the world, did Noah have to load the ducks and geese onto the ark or were they allowed to ride out the storm on their own, how many languages were spoken at the Tower of Babel, how far away are the moon and stars, and is the earth flat or round?

Judith gave Alfric strong drink—he'd been chilled by the rain—and sat him down in front of the kitchen fire. The next day, Alfric found himself in Owen's hall listening to a violent quarrel between the civil authorities about whether to resist the Vikings or not. Owen's viewpoint ultimately prevailed, and Alfric took over his derelict chancery.

He was far better suited to the work than Ranulf was. Owen had been heard to say Ranulf never added a column of figures and got the same answer twice. Godwin was mildly surprised, since, frankly, he would have thought Ranulf could hardly add two figures, say one and three, and come up with the right answer. Ranulf had many virtues, but Godwin was fairly sure mathematics was a closed book to him.

As for Alfric, Godwin was well acquainted with his footloose countrymen. He knew most popes managed at one time or another to thunder anathemas at them and that the great monastic Benedict of Norcia held them in low esteem. But as far as he, Godwin, was concerned, he had never met one who wasn't intelligent, tolerant, and resourceful. Alfric had proven to have all of these characteristics in abundance.

Godwin finished his eggs. Ingund was fussing over the traveler, arranging a bath for him. Godwin followed Alfric into his tiny cubbyhole in the cathedral vestry.

Alfric, as usual, had a wax tablet in his hand and a pen behind his ear. The small man was tonsured after the Roman manner rather than the Irish, that is, a rim of hair encircled his bald head. He was small, dark-eyed, rather slight and in stature small, under five feet. He looked up from a large account book when Godwin entered.

"What are you doing?" Godwin asked.

Alfric said, "I'm trying to find a few pieces of silver. I have put aside an amount given over to the defense of the city, but I'm not sure this problem appears."

"Is this problem related to Enar?"

"Yes." Alfric looked surprised. "How did you know?"

Godwin pulled a folding camp stool from the corner,

opened it, and sat down. "Ingund nearly broke my breakfast plate this morning, and she is wandering around the house armed as though we're going to be attacked. Tell me what's wrong before she burns my supper and the griping in my stomach keeps me awake all night."

"It seems," Alfric said, "Osbert is unhappy about the mule. He wants to go to law about it and lay a complaint before the bishop."

Godwin made a snarling sound.

"I knew you would be annoyed," Alfric continued. "It seems Osbert claims the mule returned lame from your excursion to settle Ulick, and the animal is in a very depressed state. I have visited with Osbert. The mule is indeed lame. As to its depression, not being an expert on the mental processes of mules, I cannot say. However, the beast does appear unhappy. Osbert claims the mule stepped on Enar's foot. Enar retaliated and crippled the creature. Osbert wants ten silver pieces."

"No," Godwin said. "Mules never look happy, and the whole beast is not worth ten silver pieces. I saw what Enar did. It was self-defense. The mule may have a bruise, but it will heal. Give Osbert three silver pieces to compensate him for the beast's labor and tell him that's all he's going to get."

Alfric nodded and made a notation on his wax tablet. "Now, as to Enar. What do you want to do about him?"

Godwin showed all his teeth. "Several things, none of which I would even care to mention to a clergyman this close to the altar of the church. What in the name of the Prince of Darkness is wrong with Enar?"

"He also claims to be in a melancholic state. He has a swollen foot and has taken to his bed—"

"Indeed," Godwin interrupted. "He does his best work there. Between Elin and Owen, Enar and Ingund, Ranulf and Elfwine, and finally, Gowen and God knows who, I got almost no sleep at all last night. You tell Enar to shut up, since I paid Osbert; get out of bed; content his unhappy wife; and drown his melancholia at the tavern or I'll drag the bastard out of bed and swing him by his thumbs from the rafters in the hall! Do you hear me?"

"Godwin," Alfric temporized, "I imagine the whole town heard you."

Godwin calmed down. "Tell me about the traveler."

It was Alfric's turn to be surprised. "How did you know?"

"He came here escorted by you. I know you must have met him at Osbert's house. Normally, you'd have left him to Osbert's hospitality. The hall is packed full and I believe we have one family in the stable."

"Two, in point of fact," Alfric said, "but he told me he's carrying a letter to Owen from his father, Gestric. I asked him to say nothing about the matter until tonight after supper when most of the household has withdrawn."

Godwin stretched out his legs and studied the toes of his boots. "Christ," he muttered.

Alfric began searching for his pen and finally found it behind his ear. He lifted a parchment packet closed with rather muddy sealing wax from his desk. "I have it here if you want to read it."

"No." Godwin waved a hand negligently. "I know what's in it. You see, Alfric, no one ever expected much from the boy, especially after Bertrand imprisoned him in solitude for six months and his mind snapped. Do you know, it was the longest time before Owen could sleep without a light in the room? He would begin screaming in the most dreadful way if he woke to darkness.

"Clotild, Owen's mother, sent me here. She paid me to get Owen out of the city if I thought he was in too much danger. But Owen surprised all of us. He, Elin, and I were able to seize power. Elin and I helped, but he was the prime mover, pitting the majesty of the church against the corrupt civil authority of Count Anton and Hakon. He's shown an unexpected brilliance as both a soldier and a ruler. He's an asset to the family, and Gestric will want to use him. Who would have thought the quiet, retiring boy I knew would stand up to such a remorseless brute as Hakon. But he has and done right well."

"Elin had a lot to do with his success," Alfric said.

"Yes, but damnation on it, Gestric won't see it that way. He'll want to marry Owen into the family of one

of his strongest vassals. As far as Gestric is concerned,
Elin might do very well for a concubine, but not a wife.
He will argue she has no dowry and is without family
connections. He will tell Owen he must have been mad
to take up with such a girl. And that any bargain concluded between them is without standing in law or religion since no contract has been signed and she has no kin
to enforce it."

Alfric held the parchment packet between two fingers
and looked at it narrowly on both sides. "That's exactly
what it says," the little monk muttered, "except that in it
he mentions the names of two or three families who know
of the young bishop's growing reputation and would be
happy to place their daughters under his protection and
contribute both men and money to the defense of the
city."

"Amazing," Godwin commented, "and I can't see the
slightest evidence of tampering with the seals."

"Don't change the subject, Godwin. You know Elin has
a very large family and one I would be very careful *not* to
offend. And Elin may not come dowered with wealth, but
she has other darker abilities. She is of all of *them* I have
known, one of the most highly skilled and powerful. He is
far more apt to be in need of Elin's family and her talents
than in need of some simpering, overprotected child of a
wealthy lord, no matter how many men or how much
money she brings with her."

"That's your opinion," Godwin said. "I'm not sure I
share it."

"No?" Alfric's eyebrows lifted.

"No!" Godwin rose and walked toward the door. "I present my point of view tonight after he reads the letter.
But, by the way, thank you for preserving such an excit-
ing piece of news from general knowledge. It truly would
disturb my digestion to eat supper with half the town in
the hall, Clea and her ladies of joy hanging from the
rafters, and Routrude in my lap."

As it was, the hall was quiet that night. The traveler
emerged refreshed and much more presentable looking

from the sweat bath. His name was Wedo, though he had another Breton name unpronounceable to most of the Franks at the table.

Enar surprised Godwin by being fluent in the traveler's own tongue. Enar had been able to rise and take a little nourishment, two pounds of meat accompanied by bread, assorted greens, and about a gallon of beer. He translated when the traveler got lost in their foreign tongue. Godwin, for whom Enar could hardly do right, felt this might be a bit unfortunate since the message Wedo brought was hardly an encouraging one.

He was from Paris. Most were surprised by how far he'd come, and when they heard this, everyone was all ears. Ingund built up the fire and broached a cask of mead. Anna presented Godwin with a jar of wild strawberry preserves and a half loaf of fresh-baked bread.

Wedo, of course, had to explain he worked at a family business in Paris. He did well enough with the elderly owner, but when the man died, he and the son clashed. So he set off to return to Brittany and buy into his brothers' fishing business.

"I knew things stood ill in this direction, but I had no idea how ill. The whole coast is swarming with Vikings. Rouen is in the hands of Rollo. It is said he sets his table before the barren altar of the cathedral. His men drink and wench the night away in the desecrated house of God.

"He, Rollo, collects the same rents, dues, and tithes that once went to the church and the royal house. Men say there is a sort of count in the city, but he bows the knee to the Northman, and men swear the same fealty to him they once swore to their lords and the sons of Charlemagne.

"No one can blame them, since the great scoundrel at least leaves those living on the land a crust of bread, a few rags to cover their backs, and preserves the honor of their daughters." Wedo picked up his cup. It was empty. Five or six hands rushed to refill it.

Godwin, spooning preserves on the fresh bread, began to fear the fool might not shut up till dawn. "Tell us of the journey," he said.

Something quite different entered Wedo's face: a look

of bleak exhaustion. "Ho, well now, the journey . . ." His voice trailed off. He spoke a few sentences in his own tongue.

Enar translated. "He says he doesn't much like the idea of reliving the journey. It was very bad. He never thought he'd reach the city. He says men are camped about the city in the forest, and had he not been warned by a group of charcoal burners that Reynald's stronghold had fallen, he might have stumbled straight into Hakon's hands."

"The journey," Godwin insisted.

Wedo shrugged. "We started from Paris confidently enough. There were six of us, a fairly strong party, we thought: four fighting men, a small merchant who sold from a pack, and myself. We camped carelessly at first, lit a fire, relaxed by the roadside. We should have been warned when we found the first place we were to lodge, a Benedictine house, only a pile of charred ruins. It was some months abandoned, I would say midsummer at least.

"That night we were not so bold. We lit a fire only long enough to cook a hot supper. The next day we saw smoke in the sky. It took us the rest of that day and most of the next to reach the spot from whence we saw the smoke rising." At this point Wedo lost his command of their language and wandered away into a Breton dialect even Enar had trouble unraveling.

Enar told the story. "There must have been about fifty in this party. Possibly some women, but by the time they got there, no one could tell much about the dead. The corpses were working with maggots and black with crows. They'd had two traveling carriages for the women and four wagonloads of provisions. The carriages and the wagons had been burned. That caused the smoke."

Godwin sighed and pushed away the bread and preserves. Not that what he was listening to bothered his digestion—he'd heard and seen worse—but the sheer horrific predictability of the tale discouraged him.

The travelers learned quickly enough any sort of order had broken down in the Seine valley. It had become a true no-man's-land. Each day they saw smoke rising, burning farms, villas, monasteries, or perhaps only outlaw camps.

They never knew the difference since they avoided all such sites. Each night they lay in the dark, not daring to light a fire no matter how cold or wet it got, subsisting on dried meat, cheese, and bread.

The one bright spot on their journey was a visit with Gestric and Clotild. They and a few others, the archbishop of Reims for instance, were bulwarks against the general disorder. Many other lords and churchmen fled, abandoning their tenants, free and serf, to the marauders, who were already claiming the helpless peasantry as their own, either subjecting them to ruthless extortion or simply treating them as a superior sort of cattle, to be rounded up, shipped out, and sold as slaves.

The rest of the travelers remained with Gestric. Wedo alone pressed on, hoping to find things better in Brittany, now ruled by Alan the Great, who had lately cleansed, at best, part of Brittany from the Viking hordes. Warned by the charcoal burners, Wedo had approached the city with great stealth.

"You say they are all around us, camping in the woods?" Ranulf asked.

Wedo nodded. "I was hard put not to be seen and heard by them, but I had the good luck to encounter the one-legged knight, Denis, and a patrol of archers on the road, and they brought me safely to the city."

Then Ranulf turned to Godwin. "What good did it do to slay Ulick? No one will be able to get in a crop, in any case."

Godwin had found some nuts. He cracked one walnut with another. "Go to bed, Ranulf." He was sitting at one end of the table, Owen at the other. Their eyes met. The hall was silent. No one seemed to want to look at anyone else.

Ranulf glanced around, bewildered. "But . . ."

"Ranulf," Denis said, "help me up. My leg is off. Let's do as Godwin suggests. Go to bed."

Wedo was swaying where he sat. Mead or simple weariness, Godwin didn't know, but Ingund boxed Enar's ears playfully, then helped Wedo off to his bed. The rest, except for Owen, Godwin, Enar, and Alfric, drifted off to their slumbers.

When they were gone, Alfric rose and handed Owen the letter.

He stood up and looked at it, surprised.

"Wedo was a good man and did as I asked," Alfric said. "I believed you needed to see this only among your most trusted counselors." He turned to Godwin. "You know what I think, but I can see your side also. Perhaps you're right. We may have gone as far as we can alone." Then he left to seek his bed.

Owen opened the letter. He spread out the paper on his knee and began to read by the firelight. He smiled at the first page. "Well," he said, "two elderly relatives died. Several children have been born to some people I'm not sure I remember. Clotild's right knee is still bothering her. Tell me," he asked Godwin, "is she older than my father?"

Godwin nodded. "By a few years."

"How odd," Owen said. "I've never thought of her as getting old. She was always just . . . my mother. The letter says she can walk well enough but can't kneel in church any longer."

"I don't think kneeling to anyone, even God, was one of Clotild's favorite activities," Godwin said.

Then Owen began to read the second page of the letter. Suddenly, he crumpled it in his fist, almost as though he were going to throw it into the fire. But then he rose to his feet, smoothed out the parchment, and read it again, very slowly and carefully, holding the missive down where the light was bright, close to the flames. Finally, he folded both sheets carefully and placed them in his shirt.

He turned to Godwin. Their eyes met. They both knew that if they discussed this in the hall, by tomorrow there would be open speculation in the tavern about whether Owen would divorce Elin, who he would marry if he did, and what Elin would do to the new bride if she were feeling vengeful.

"All rather boring," Owen said. He sat down heavily on a bench beside the table and stared into the flames. "I had hoped that after we defeated Hakon he'd lose control of his men and most would wander away in search of easier pickings."

Godwin nodded. "I hoped, rabble that they are, some might turn on him and put an end to our troubles. But, it's not to be."

Enar laughed and wiped a mustache of beer from his upper lip. "I never thought so. I do hear tell"—he gave Owen a sly glance—"that he quarreled with one of his minor chiefs and the man took his people and sailed away, but the rest are sticking like burrs to boar's bristles. And besides, he has sent a little smarter man than Ulick, to hang about in the woods and keep us penned inside the city."

"Who is it this time?" Godwin asked.

"Tosi, his nephew," Enar said.

"Damn!" Godwin snarled. "Who says?"

Enar grinned and lifted the tankard as if in salute. "Ah, the incomparable Routrude. My Lord Godwin, had you wanted to know about Ulick, you should have asked Routrude. But that is one of the disadvantages of high nobility. A great man like yourself wouldn't be caught dead in a tavern bending the elbow with vulgar men like me. So alas, you are the last to know."

Godwin turned and looked at Owen. "How in the hell do you stand him? I'd have fed him to the crows within a week of making his acquaintance."

"Enar," Owen said. "Since you seem to know so well how things are with Hakon, tell me why you think his men won't go."

Enar grinned. "Go ask Routrude."

"Enar, would you like to move your bed to the stable again?" Owen asked.

Godwin laughed.

Enar sighed. "No, my lord."

"Indeed," Owen said. "Then answer the question."

Enar emptied the tankard, Adam's apple working overtime, then put it down. "In my youth, when the priest told us how the world was made—"

"These were not Christian priests, I take it," Godwin interrupted.

"I have never understood," Enar said pleasantly, "why Christians take such an unchristian pride in being Christian."

"It is the religion of all civilized men," Godwin answered.

"Indeed," Enar said. "He is a very convenient God. You need only do Him honor for a short time on a Sunday; the rest of the week you are able to be out and about getting into even more mischief than the poor pagans."

"Enar," Owen said sharply. "Bed. Stable. Get to the point."

"As I was saying," Enar continued with a lofty look at Owen. "In my youth, when the priests explained to us how the world was made, they said it was composed of earth, air, fire, and water. And they said we would always remember these four if we would but think of woman. The spirit of air and desire. Red gold, born in the blossom of fire; silver, cold companion to water; and, last of all, black soil, the sweet earth itself. Of the four, I think black soil is the strongest. And that is what men want the most."

Godwin nodded. "Elspeth's lands," he said.

"Yes," Enar answered, and looked at Owen. "I wager, Lord Christ Priest, there are not a dozen who follow their war chief who weren't brought up behind a plow. I dream of the land, myself, of tall wheat, rippling in the wind, the fairest gold in the world. In sleep, I touch my lips to clean water, sweeter than all the silver ever coined, nourishing my land, my soil. And last and best of all, the woman seated at my hearth. He who takes this earth, gains all."

Godwin reached up and caught the bridge of his nose between the tips of his fingers for a second, then lowered his hand to his lap. "Much as I hate agreeing with you, Saxon, I think you are probably right. No, Hakon will not go away. Not without a much harder fight than we have given him."

"Soon, very soon," Enar said. "The people hiding here in this town will need to go out and plant the winter crop. Do you think Hakon will let them?"

"No," Godwin answered. "He won't. I think by then he'll be ready to attack the city again. He will bring destruction. He will draw his men up in the fields, build a catapult, and begin to rain fire down upon us. And we won't be able to do a damned thing about it."

Owen looked away, into the darkness.

"I think Hakon will do what I have said because, were I in his shoes, I would do the same. This whore's son Hakon is a great many things, but"—he glanced at Owen and met his eyes—"neither of us has any reason to believe he is stupid. Would that he were. And as long as he can hold his force together with the promise of Elspeth's lands, one way or another, he'll be a threat to us."

Owen frowned and steepled his fingers. "You are a pre-eminent battle lord—"

"Skip the flattery," Godwin said. "I know I understand the art of slaughter better than most. Get to the point."

"How many men would we need to meet Hakon in the field?" Owen asked.

"About two hundred," Godwin answered.

"How many have we?" Enar asked.

"About seventy-five," Godwin answered.

"There are many strong men in the town," Enar objected. "They defended the walls."

"To defend a fortress is one thing," Godwin said. "To hazard one's life in the field against battle-hardened soldiers, quite another. For that you need troops with similar experience and training. I wouldn't lead the citizens out against Hakon's Vikings. It would be a slaughter."

"With another hundred we would win, then?" Owen asked.

"No," Godwin answered. "I never said we would win. But we wouldn't lose. When those sons of Odin retire bloody from the field and can't count high enough to number their dead, they don't return. It's notable that though the people of Paris saw it as defeat when their king betrayed them and allowed the Viking fleet to sail past and plunder Burgundy, they did win absolute freedom from Viking depredation. No chieftain, however mighty, has turned his eyes in their direction since. They know it would be too costly to face the rage of the Parisians again."

Godwin turned and stretched out his hand toward Owen slowly, the fingers closed and clenched into a fist. "Give me another hundred men, Owen, and I'll put the fear of God and the devil both into Hakon. But without them, well . . ."

He left the sentence unfinished and turned back to stare into the flames, flashing and dancing among the logs, jumbled on the hearth.

Owen also continued to stare in brooding silence into the yellow-and-gold flames. Enar, who had retired to crouch near the hearth, looked up inquiringly at Owen. "What will you do, Lord Christ Priest?" he asked.

Owen touched the letter where it lay above his belt next to his skin. The parchment crackled. "I think I won't say. The estimable Routrude knows too much already. There are too many ears nearby."

"Yes," Godwin commented. "And all attached to winged tongues which will spread any tale to the four winds. I am looking at one of the worst now," he said with a glance at Enar. "Those conversations with Routrude don't go all one way, and I imagine Hakon knows every time a townsman braves the cold by night to go to the privy. Whether that one squirts or pisses and whether upwind or down. Now go upstairs and comfort your patient wife, lest she be tempted to use her spiked mace on your head."

Enar looked stung. "I know Ingund is a dangerous woman, and some say she is unnatural. But her strength seems good to me, a complement to my own.

"I took the sword," Enar continued, "not at seven years, but at birth when I slipped from the womb. My mother carried me from the birthing stool to the wall, and before my lips touched her breast, my hand touched steel. When I was old enough to stand and walk, she sent me to a lady of the wood; my task, to learn all the arts by which cold steel drinks warm blood. And when I had satisfied my teacher by my first killing, she lay with me and taught me the art of manhood. At the dawn after a night of carnal combat, the witch set her seal on me. A geas, her promise was that when I wielded the axe I would never miss if the target be human. And as you know, Godwin, I don't. She, like Ingund, had red hair. I have always loved women with such hair, and I will always remember her. So you see, I yield nothing to you in training or in valor. I was not brought up to avoid a fight."

"Saxon," Godwin purred. "I find you amusing, annoying, and dangerous, and I don't care to find out how dangerous tonight. Does that content you?"

Enar finished the beer. Even with his nose in the tankard, he and Godwin watched each other like a pair of rival wolves.

"Enar," Owen said, "go to bed. I won't decide anything here and now." Something warm—trust and friendship perhaps—leaped between Enar and Owen for a second.

Enar flashed a wicked grin at Godwin, then said, "I believe it does." Then he set the tankard on the sideboard and deliberately sauntered upstairs.

"He's one of them," Godwin said. "Hakon's cursed breed. Certainly you know that."

Owen chuckled. "Of course, he's the worst liar in Christendom."

"By that do you mean the most transparent or the most constant?" Godwin asked.

"The most transparent," Owen said. "He pledged faith to me by the lady Freya herself."

Godwin moaned and shaded his eyes with his hand. "How in the hell did you manage to accept his oath with a straight face?"

"My back was hurting," Owen said. "And he'd just saved my life. That carried some weight in the matter. Now I believe I'd best go to Elin. I left her with Anna, fitting a new dress, but she will be tired of waiting by now."

After he left, Godwin settled himself back in the chair. He might have his worries about Elin and the city, but he was still full of wine and a very good dinner. He was soon in the midst of a truly excellent dream involving a ripe young woman. She cooperated enthusiastically as he removed her ample garments one by one.

Godwin was down to her shift and he had every expectation of getting that off soon when something in his mind that never really slept warned him there had been a change in the room. Under the table, Ine or possibly one of the dogs, whined and scratched at a flea. The torches were out. The room was lighted only by the hearth fire. But he knew he wasn't alone. He could feel a presence in the darkness. Eyes were fixed on him from somewhere.

"Who's watching me?" he snapped loudly. "Come out and show yourself, now."

Rosamund scurried out of the shadows and presented herself for inspection about six feet from Godwin's chair. She wore only a shift that barely reached the tops of her firm graceful thighs. She pushed her hair, a mop of gold fleece, out of her eyes and stared at Godwin.

"What are you doing here?" he growled.

"I'm waiting for them," she glanced at the ceiling, "to go to sleep. You see, I can always tell," she continued rapidly. "Wolf the Short lies flat on his back and blows up through his mustache, and Gowen curls up tight with his hands around his nuts."

The two men in question were Godwin's toughest knights. Rosamund shared their beds, though Godwin privately thought Gowen was the senior partner in the arrangement. Gowen was something between six and seven feet tall and 270 pounds stark naked. If he shared Rosamund with Wolf the Short, it was not out of the kindness of his heart. He had no heart, only a vast indifference to anything that did not serve his immediate ends. To him, Rosamund was simply a convenience. And, Godwin reflected, if Rosamund died tomorrow, Gowen would replace her with the same indifference he showed toward sharing her with Wolf the Short.

"Why do you care if they're asleep?" Godwin asked testily.

"Because if they're asleep," Rosamund said breathlessly, "they don't bother me. And I can always tell because of the way they look, with Wolf blowing and Gowen clutching."

"I know, I know. I've spent many a cozy hour around the campfire with both of them."

Rosamund glanced at the ceiling again. "The way Gowen acts about his balls, you'd think someone was trying to steal the big smelly bags," she said resentfully.

"You never know," Godwin said with a perfectly straight face.

Rosamund lifted one foot and scratched the calf of her other leg with it. The bells on her anklets tinkled.

Godwin buried his nose in the wine cup to keep from seeing that Rosamund's toes were blue, and thinking about how cold she must be.

She began to shift from one foot to another rapidly in a way that set her ankle bracelets to tinkling.

"Stop jingling and jangling. Who gave you those cursed things, anyway?"

Rosamund planted both feet firmly and looked down, frowning. "I can't remember."

"Ah," Godwin commented, and took another sip of wine.

Rosamund looked up at Godwin, a slow flush burning her cheeks. "You're trying to shame me," she accused. "You're trying to shame me because ... because ... of what I do. Why do you care what I do? I have no kin to look out for me, so I must take care of myself. But I'm not ashamed," she finished defiantly.

"Rosamund," Godwin said in tones of deepest menace, "you are annoying me."

She took another step backward. The bench and table were right behind her.

"Rosamund," Godwin said in a voice of iron. "Stay where you are and stand perfectly still."

She froze like a frightened bird.

"Rosamund," Godwin continued in the same tone. "Do not fall over the bench and table behind you and bring the household up in arms."

She turned and looked. "Oh, I was about to, wasn't I?"

"Yes," Godwin said.

"I'm sorry," Rosamund said, easing toward him again, sliding her feet along the floor.

"What are you doing?" Godwin asked. "Are you suddenly crippled?"

"I'm trying not to jingle," she said indignantly.

Godwin set the wine cup on the floor and drew his fingers down his cheeks wearily. "Rosamund, go to bed."

"But," she said, looking up anxiously at the ceiling, "I don't have—"

"Take my bed. Presently, I'm not using it. Only let me snatch two more hours of sleep before dawn."

Rosamund looked overwhelmed. "Oh, I couldn't. If Anna ever caught me . . ."

"If Anna catches you, tell her I gave you my permission."

"Why should you let me have your bed?" she asked. "Edgar says you are a very cold man, that you could drink water and piss snow. I know, I'll leave the door unbarred so you can come up later and . . ."

Godwin ground his teeth. "No, don't leave the door unbarred. Go upstairs and go to bed."

"But . . ." she protested.

"Rosamund, what do you say when I give you an order?" Godwin asked.

"Yes, my lord." Rosamund retired.

"Fine," he said. "Practice saying that as you go up the stairs. Walk, don't run. And do not, I repeat, do not fall over anything."

Rosamund did as she was told. With some restraint, she walked quietly to the stair, but she turned at the foot and looked back at him.

The basilisk stare she got hurried her on her way.

Godwin snuggled himself down into his mantle and drifted off to sleep. To his unabashed delight, the lady he had been dreaming about returned to finish the dream. He was only mildly annoyed that she wore a pair of jingling ankle bracelets.

Chapter

8

A FOGGY dawn was whitening the world when Owen and Elin slipped past the sleeping Godwin and out into the square. The town had long ago grown up around the bishop's palace, the cathedral, and the Roman fortress high on its rock above. Elin looked up at the fortress, at the smoke stains on its walls, and shivered.

"It's empty and a ruin," Owen said, turning her face from it with his fingers. "Gerlos burned it the night he left, and I don't think anyone's been up there since."

"Judith has," Elin said.

"Judith," Owen said. "The redoubtable Judith."

Judith was, in the absence of her father, a Jew named Lollos the Usurer, a veritable merchant princess with a finger in every commercial pie in the town.

"What was she doing up there?" he asked.

"She made me an offer for such unburned timber as she could salvage," Elin said.

"You didn't accept, did you?" Owen asked, alarmed. He didn't distrust Judith exactly, but he didn't quite trust her, either. Theoretically, Elin couldn't handle any matter of business without his permission. But Elin knew, and no doubt Judith did as well, that he wouldn't dare repudiate any agreement Elin made. To do so would be to humble her publicly. But their hold on the town was tenuous in the extreme. Any public rift between them might be dangerous.

"No," Elin said. "I found the offer too low and told her so. She grouched and griped, then said she would have to pay for the labor of tearing down the hall and the walk-ways along the battlements. And then, of course, she went higher."

Owen threw back his head and laughed, a strange sound in the empty street.

"But I told her I'd have to speak to you," Elin continued.

"What did she say?"

She sniffed and said, "Husbands are so convenient sometimes."

Owen laughed again, more softly, and looked around. "Strange," he said. "No one is out this morning."

Elin stretched out her hands, palms up, and stared into the billowing whiteness around her. A few drops of mois-ture fell on her hands. "It's the fog," she said.

"Indeed," Owen said, looking around. The fog shrouded everything. The colorful shop fronts facing the square shone through it dimly like jewels seen through muddy water. Behind them the cathedral and the bishop's house they'd just quitted were almost lost in the blowing white mist.

"How did it come to be there?" Elin asked, pointing back at the cathedral and the hall. "Who built them?"

"I don't know," Owen said. "Godwin tells me this was once the site of a Roman camp and a magistrate's seat. The cathedral was a basilica where the Romans sat in judgment. What's now the bishop's house was the magistrate's resi-dence. The house was destroyed after the Romans left. The basilica still stood, but without a roof. When the Franks had conquered and brought peace to the valley, Christians in the city repaired the building and turned it into a church. The house is newer, built for the bishop in Charlemagne's time."

"Charlemagne?" Elin asked. "How long since he died, Owen?"

"Not even a hundred years," he said. "I cannot say if Godwin is right, but the cellars of both house and church show the kind of stonework the Romans made. So does the fortress."

They walked on together toward the Roman wall. They paused by the granite pillars and looked down at the spill of burned-out houses that stretched down to the wooden palisade, now the town wall.

Even through the obscuring mist, Elin could see that many of the ruined houses had tents stretched out over their foundations. Some were clearly being rebuilt. She leaned her veiled head on Owen's shoulder, and they stood together in the strange morning silence.

"You know what I have to do, don't you?" Owen asked.

"Yes," she said quietly.

"I'll leave the city tonight or tomorrow. Godwin says with a hundred more men, he can knock Hakon back on his heels. I'm going to get more warriors. You and Godwin will have to hold the city until Enar and I return. So sell the timber in the fortress, if you must."

Elin laughed a little shrilly. "By all means, the timber in the fortress."

"Elin," Owen whispered. "My mind's made up. There is no more to be said, except one thing." His body stiffened, and he turned to rest his back against the gate post. Elin drifted a few steps away from him and looked down the cobbled street that led to the palisade gates.

"What is the other thing?" she asked. "I thought it was fairly simple. You will ask your father and brothers for the men, and he will send them."

"No. It's not that simple, and you know it," Owen said. "I'm almost certain my father will have to call on his vassals to raise such a force. He can't do that without something to bargain with." He handed her the letter. She was amused by the first page as he had been, but when she reached the second page, she froze in her tracks.

She is beautiful, Owen thought. Her black hair, where it emerged from the cowling veil, was bejeweled by moisture. It set off her skin with its faint rose flush. Her lips were slightly parted.

"You don't belong to yourself, do you Owen?" she asked.

"No," he said. "I belong first to the city, then the church, and when I come supplicant to my father Gestric's hall, I will then belong to him and Clotild, my mother."

"And last of all to your green wood wife. Yes, I can hear them asking, who is her father, her mother? When did they give their permission for you to wed? And what sum of gold and jewels did she bring as dowry to your hall?"

"Elin," Owen said. "I have nothing to offer except myself. And I'll offer that self if I have to."

"Do that, Owen," she said. "Please—if taking a rich wife will win you the men you wish. I will leave on silent feet as soon as I learn her name. I will wander far with my people, but in the forest, when the fires are lit on the feast when the dead are unbound, I'll make a doll out of the last sheaf cut and call it by her name."

Elin made an abrupt throwing motion with her hand. "I will cast it into the fire. And she will wither in your bed like a flower cut in its prime or a green sheaf in a drought, one that never sees the harvest. You will be alone."

"You could," Owen said, "but you won't. I know your nature. You are too just. You wouldn't curse an innocent unknown over so small a thing as a man."

"I think you know me too well," Elin said. "No, I wouldn't. And you'll do what you have to do to get those men."

"Besides," Owen said. "There's many a slip twixt the cup and the lip. Many an affianced wife has never seen the door of her husband's house, much less his bed."

"You'd make a bargain, Owen, and not mean to keep it? You really don't belong to yourself, then."

Owen turned his face away as though he couldn't bear to look at her any longer. "I'm trying to warn you."

"Yes," she said. "But I could destroy her in the hall were it not beneath me to try. I'd need no magic. Many a concubine has stolen a wife's place in her husband's bed. And I know I light a fire in your flesh that sets you whimpering like a dog. If I crooked my smallest finger, you

would come, and a drop of poison in her cup, some night,
would do the rest."

"Yes," Owen said, his fists clenching. "Yes, you could.
All true."

"I'll tell you another thing that is true, Owen. It would
choke me if even for one day I had to live a lie. So that if
you return to me and even a promise has passed your lips,
I will go—never to return."

"Even so," Owen said.

"Yes," she answered. "Even so."

"Then it must be," Owen said. "But I'll tell you something, Elin. Even should I promise and wed, I'll draw you
back to me, green wood wife. And the lady will be bereft,
because I'll have no other."

Elin drew in a sharp ragged breath. She stretched out
her hand and placed it on his chest. He could feel her nails
through his shirt, cutting into his breast. "That sounds like
a curse," she said.

"Curse or blessing, be it what you will. We are what we
are to each other, green wood wife. I'm not sure that even
death will release us from our vows. And were you a
lesser woman than you are, I wouldn't have told you what
I planned to do. I wanted you to know, so that you could
act accordingly when the time comes."

Elin drew back a little from him. He was handsome.
She could feel it even in her almost blind rage. Small,
only by a few inches taller than she, fine featured and
dark, he reminded her of the forest she loved. The dark
shadows under the trees. The clear pools tasting slightly
of the oak tannin released by the brown leaves that
floored them. Then her rage faded and was succeeded by
sorrow. "The church curses passion and says it leads only
to grief," she said. "Now I know why."

"Better grief than nothing," Owen said. "Better grief
than never to have known you. Not to have known you
would be not to have lived. But!" He seized her wrist.
"Godwin says with another hundred men we can offer
battle to Hakon. Break his power and lift the siege. Elin, I
won't lie to you." He pulled her wrist. She stiffened her
arm, crooking her elbow. He used her own resistance to

pull her closer to him. "We can last a few more months on what's stored in my cellar, but no longer than that." He shook her arm. She was so rigid her whole body quivered. "Tell me, Elin, when you asked to be part of my fight, was it to teach me how to surrender?"

She jerked her arm free. "No! But this is going to hurt. And don't tell me any children's tales about how you will get around this marriage."

"They aren't children's tales." He took her in his arms. "Among the great lords, marriage is a pretext for many things. It doesn't hurt the girl, my very love, not to be bedded. She's divorced, well paid, and soon finds another who suits her better." His kiss was a devouring one. It seemed to carry the whole burden of his lonely need, and she knew he was telling his soul what it needed to hear so that he could gather the courage to go and do what he must to save the city.

No, she thought. *No, I will never teach you how to surrender. How could I? I never did. Not even in the bath when I wanted him so. Nor before in the Viking camp. Or even to the marriage my parents wanted me to make. I will lie down in my grave and let them throw dirt on my living face before I will permit myself or you, my long, long love, to yield ourselves beaten. To hell with Hakon. To hell itself with him. If it costs me my love, my peace, my hope and plunges me into everlasting sorrow, I—will—win!*

Her kiss was as fierce as his own. He pulled free. Then they both became conscious that they were not alone.

"Well," Elin said softly. "I can't say I didn't know when we met what owned you. The city."

She looked down toward the gate and realized the mist was clearing. She could see the shops and houses now, and even a few people stirring about, near the tavern and the widow's house. And beyond the gates reared a solid wall of mist.

"Come," Owen said, "the fog will burn off in a few minutes."

"Hush," Elin said. She looked down the sloping street toward the palisade gate.

"What?" Owen asked.

"Can't you hear it?" she whispered.

"Hear what?" Owen asked, bewildered.

But Elin had already begun running down the street toward the few sleepy archers on duty near the gates.

"Get your shields up!" she cried. "You're under attack."

Alan, one of Godwin's younger knights, hurried out of a cellar hole. He stood for a second gaping at her.

"You fools," she screamed more loudly. "You're under attack."

The flight of arrows flashed out of the fog like a rain of death. One man fell with an arrow through his throat while another gasped in astonishment at one sticking out of his arm.

"Fire!" Owen screamed at the young crossbowmen.

"My lord," one of them shouted. "We can't see anything."

A dozen crossbow bolts were loosed into the mist. Alan seized the young man who was still staring stupidly at the arrow in his arm. "Go rouse Godwin," he shouted. The man bolted up the street.

Owen could hear now what he was sure Elin had heard, the thunder of hooves on the earth. He could guess what the enemy was doing. They were riding in to fire their arrows and then riding out before the crossbowmen could loose their bolts.

The man struck in the throat was down, blood pouring from his mouth and nose. His heels drummed on the packed earth behind the palisade.

"To the wall!" Owen shouted at the top of his lungs. "Everyone to the wall." Then he snatched up the fallen man's shield and turned to Elin. She'd tossed aside her mantle. She had a crossbow in her hands.

Unceremoniously, he snatched it away from her, threw her down, and covered her with his shield just as the next flight of arrows crossed the wall. He felt the thunk as two of the arrows hit hard on the shield. Then Godwin was beside him, closely followed by his four knights.

Owen looked the length of the palisade. As far as he could see in the mist, men were at the walls, most carrying shields and spears. The crossbowmen were reloading their spent bows as quickly as possible.

Godwin turned to Ranulf, the youngest and least experienced of his knights. "Go back to the hall. Secure all the approaches to the city. Rouse Judith and her men at the river. Move!" he barked.

Elin ignored Owen, who was crouching nearly on top of her. "It can't be many," she whispered to Godwin. "If he'd planned a sneak attack, I would have known. My people would have told me."

Godwin nodded. "Stay down," he said. "Under your husband's shield."

Elin gave a short, sharp snort of laughter. "I'm most useful here," she said, pressing her ear to the ground. "They are coming again."

"Crossbowmen to the walls," Godwin said. "Press your bellies up against the wood. They can't hit you there. They'll have to shoot over you. Wait until they loose their next flight of arrows, then fire at will."

"Here they come!" Elin screamed.

The crossbow bolts whined through the air. Elin heard a loud animal scream. The flight of arrows rattled among the defenders at the gate again. Then they were gone.

Elin lay listening. "I think," she whispered, "they're withdrawing, riding away. The hoofbeats are muffled by the plowed land."

For a moment, Owen stood, peering into the murk beyond the palisade. He realized why the attackers were leaving. The fog was burning away, and even as he watched, he realized he could see further and further into it.

Owen looked around. The entire town seemed to be at the walls. Two women were shrieking over the corpse of the young man who had taken the arrow in his throat.

"I hope he never knew what hit him," Owen said.

"I think it quite likely that he did," Godwin murmured. "But there was little he could do about it as he strangled on his own blood."

Elfwine arrived and joined the two women, kneeling over the corpse, keening.

Godwin shuddered violently. Routrude pressed a cup of wine into his hand. Godwin tasted it quickly and found it a better vintage than he had heretofore believed the tavern boasted. He remembered threatening to hang Routrude the night before. *I must,* he thought to himself, *threaten to hang her several times a year if it produces this kind of result.*

"Alas," Routrude said, gazing at the corpse. "Poor young Ricard. He was a fine man. He and his sisters were orphaned early. It's heaven's mercy his parents did not live to see him perish. He was in every way a pattern of a man. He helped his sisters to prosperous marriages."

The body was being placed on a litter. Elfwine shrieked again. Wolf the Short was standing next to Godwin, leaning on a spear. He nodded approvingly.

"The two ladies weeping over him are his sisters, I suppose?" Godwin asked.

"Yes," Routrude said. "Elfwine is a close friend of theirs."

Elfwine's next yell froze Godwin's blood.

"She does him much honor," Wolf the Short said.

"He might be pleased," Godwin said, "but I could do without it."

Everyone within earshot looked profoundly shocked. Wolf the Short's eyes rolled, and he gestured against the evil eye. "Don't say such things. His spirit may hover near. He must know we mourn."

The body was carried up the street toward the church. Elfwine's cries faded into the distance. Godwin sighed with relief and sucked down some more wine.

"I must say, though," Routrude continued. "He picked a most inopportune time to die. Bretwala is late."

Both Godwin and Owen found this statement incomprehensible. Ingund and Enar, who were standing behind them, apparently didn't. Ingund wore her boar-tusk helmet, and the spiked mace was over her shoulder. Enar was attired in linen drawers and carried an axe.

"How late?" Ingund asked.

"Two weeks," Routrude replied.

Elin was standing now, properly wrapped in her mantle and wearing her veil. "Is she usually regular?"

"As sunrise," Routrude answered.

"Send her to see me," Elin said. "If matters go further, I

will intercede with the sisters to grant her some share of Ricard's property."

"That would be fair," Routrude said as she started back up the street.

"What was that about?" Godwin asked Enar.

Enar grinned. "It seems Ricard left some small token of his existence with us before he shuffled off this mortal coil."

Godwin noticed Routrude had left the wine jug behind. Enar was holding it.

"Things just stick to your fingers, don't they?" Godwin said as he gently but firmly removed it from his grasp. He refilled his cup. "Explain it to me," he said, "without the poetry."

"Bretwala is pregnant," Elin said. "Routrude knows."

Godwin moaned.

Edgar, another of Godwin's knights, stood nearby. He wore a purple silk dalmatic embroidered with white flowers. His lips and cheeks were rouged, his eyes shrouded by a heavy mixture of lamp black and fat. The look clashed incongruously with his short, curly black beard. He reeked of sandalwood and carried a drawn sword. "What I would like to know," he said, "is what Hakon wished to accomplish by this attack."

"Did you have a late night, Edgar?" Enar asked. "I didn't see you at the hall this morning."

"I passed a pleasant evening with friends," he replied with unruffled calm.

"As just another link of the daisy chain, no doubt," Enar suggested snidely but in a low voice.

Owen put an elbow into Enar's gut, hard.

"Saxon," Godwin murmured. "I'm pleased to note you're suicidal. Edgar is a premier swordsman. I would not like to fight him myself."

Enar had regained his breath. "That's because you're getting old."

Godwin, always in a black humor in the morning, rounded on him. Just at that moment, Enar let out a howl and spun around. Ingund had him by the ear and started leading him up to the city back to the hall.

"Come," she said. "I must get breakfast. I cannot understand how you have lived so long. You are so contentious a man." She drew Enar along with a firm grip on his tender ear.

Enar howled. "Let go. I'm bigger than you are."

"Return to the hall with your wife," Owen said in tones of ringing command. "And don't give her any more trouble."

"He's been looking for a chink in your armor for weeks," Edgar said with aplomb. "I see he finally found one."

Godwin glared at Edgar, red-eyed with fury.

"I am what I am," Edgar said calmly. "I make no excuses or apologies. Certainly none to such as Enar."

The rage faded from Godwin's eyes, and he adjusted his gold inlaid helmet.

"I would still like to know," Edgar continued, "what Hakon hoped to accomplish by that attack."

He'd no sooner finished speaking when there was a loud banging at the gate near the ground and a voice called, "Sirs, gentle sirs, please let us in."

Godwin's sword was out of the sheath in a moment. "Who are you?"

"Fugitives from the Northmen," said the voice from beyond the gate.

Standing in the hall a few minutes later, Godwin cursed inwardly and realized that he'd, as usual, lost control of the situation. No sooner had the six men standing before him come through the gate than the entire town was at his back. And there was plainly nothing else to do but shepherd them through the crowd up to the hall, and there they stood. Godwin would have liked to have a little private talk with them. Not with their leader, a beautifully dressed nobleman, but with the five down-at-the-heels wretches who followed him.

Godwin never had any trouble persuading people to tell him the truth. He wasn't particularly proud of the fact that he was a terrifying individual. He felt it cast an unhappy reflection on his character, but all the same, it was useful at times.

He was certain he could have had the five who followed the young nobleman singing like a tree full of birds in five minutes. But no hope of that. Not in front of the entire town.

Lord, but they were a ragged-looking lot. All except for one were old and appeared beaten by life. The fifth was a young man, but his eyes were those of one who has seen too many horrors. Flat and a little mad.

Not so the nobleman who was even now bowing over Elin's hand. "A sweet lady," he was saying to her. "The warmth of your hospitality is only exceeded by the beauty of your person."

He was exquisitely dressed, looking well fed and bejeweled. He clasped Elin's hand while he kissed her palm, her wrist. He was about to extend the same courtesy to her elbow when Owen cleared his throat, loudly.

"Sir," he said. "May I ask your name?"

"Why, Count Rauching," he replied, letting go of Elin's hand.

"Count Rauching?" Godwin asked. "Count of what?"

"Why," Rauching said, smiling, "this district hereabouts."

Up to this second, there had been a loud babble of voices in the hall. Suddenly there was complete silence.

"Just what we need," Enar growled from his position next to Godwin. "Just what we need, another one of those courtly thieves."

"I suppose you have some proof that you are who you say you are?" Godwin asked.

"Alas no, good sir," Rauching said.

Enar smiled and fingered the axe in his belt.

As usual, the household was gathered near the stair, except for Ingund, who was still bending over the fire, doggedly cooking her breakfast. The townspeople were at the doors to the hall.

Godwin saw Gunter the smith accompanied by Osbert the stock dealer. He wondered where Siefert the tanner was and then remembered the leg wound he'd taken a few weeks ago in the Viking attack on the town. It was said his wife, Gynnor, had refused to let him out of the house until the leg was completely healed. She must still be keeping him at home or he would be here by now. The three men were an unofficial trinity of power among the merchants in the town, and Godwin was glad they were here to judge Rauching for themselves.

Godwin's brows lifted, and he continued to stare inquiringly at Rauching. "No proof?" he asked again.

"Alas, no." Rauching took another long pull at the wine. He glanced over the cup at the faces of the household and the massed ranks of the townspeople at the doors.

"Elspeth," he explained, "is my cousin. Last night I rode up to her gate. At that time, you understand, I had a suitable escort; twenty men and more, all hardy souls."

"To be sure," Godwin murmured.

Rauching stepped into the center of the hall, away from Godwin and Elin, away from his men. There was a quick stir at the door, and Godwin saw Judith arrive. Rieulf, her captain, cleared the way for her.

"Alas," Rauching groaned, raising his arms and eyes to heaven. "Alas!" he cried loudly. "Alas!" he cried even more loudly. "Alas!" he screamed, and fell dramatically to his knees.

"Fond of the word, isn't he?" Alfric said from beside Godwin.

Enar chuckled. Elfwine moaned. Routrude fell to her knees, weeping.

"So much sorrow," Enar said. "And they have not even heard the story."

Tears flowed down Rauching's cheeks.

"What happened?" Owen asked.

"Alas!" Rauching cried. "I did not know how things stood with Elspeth."

Routrude beat her breast and moaned.

Godwin contented himself with grinding his teeth. He was in no position to yell silence.

"To tell it simply," Rauching said.

"*Deo gratias,*" Godwin whispered.

"Once inside the gates, we were attacked. My men

fought valiantly. Many a mighty blow was struck. Many a brave warrior will no longer look upon the sun. Too many a strong heart did the Viking devil's men bring cold death. But alas, alack. We were, in short, ambushed, and stood no chance against the numbers arrayed against us. At last we stood," he pointed to his breast, "and these few pensioners back to back against the triumphant force that encircled us. And I was forced to surrender to save not myself, but these time-weary servants of mine. I felt," he said sanctimoniously, "that they ill deserved to have the many years they have spent in my service rewarded by death.

"I was imprisoned, no doubt destined for some grim fate. But our guards drank heavily and sank into deep slumber. I and my friends forced our way out through the roof and escaped. We were, as you saw, pursued. Thank God we reached the cover of the city walls in time.

"Dear lady," Rauching turned to Elin, "far be it from me to impose on your hospitality. The count's proper residence is the fortress, is it not?"

The question was posed with such sweet innocence that Godwin's suspicions immediately reached their highest pitch. Owen and Godwin exchanged glances. *Maybe,* Godwin thought, *sending Rauching to the fortress wouldn't be such a bad idea.* When Gerlos, Count Anton's son, abandoned it after Godwin killed the count, he burned it. True, the walls were stone, but the walkways and the building that had served as Count Anton's residence were wooden. The reception rooms were a gutted shell. The exterior walls were standing, and the count's bedroom.

Rauching might be able to make himself comfortable there, but his men would end up camping out among the fallen roof timbers in what had once passed for the count's hall.

As to the fortifications, the place couldn't be defended against a cold wind. The count had never maintained the walkways and lookout points. Now they lay a jumble of burned and rotten wood at the foot of the walls. One big gate was missing, so the giant doors at the entrance couldn't be barred. It would take more than Rauching had with him to render the place habitable, much less defensible.

"Yes," Godwin said slowly. "I see no harm in your taking over the fortress. Do what you can to repair its ruined condition and help with the city's defense."

The next day when Godwin heard Rauching had purchased bedding and wall hangings, he grunted, saying, "Well, apparently all the son of a bitch wants to do is make himself comfortable. I don't think we need worry about the fortress being turned against us."

Rauching wasn't planning to make himself comfortable. He was planning seduction. Elfwine, Ranulf's wife, was already in the bed. He was making love to her.

She isn't bad, he thought as her body moved voluptuously under his. She was already wiggling and moaning on her way to a second orgasm. *God,* he thought. *She's a bawdy little bitch.*

Rauching was having trouble restoring his love lance to complete the act in order to let her enjoy herself. He did hold back, however, since he was proud of his abilities as a lover. During the brief times he was invaded by self-knowledge, he often felt it was the one thing he did well. His prowess in the sport of the bedroom had allowed him to marry not one but three women. Yet despite his best intent, all three marriages had been disastrous for him.

The first was to a wealthy Lombard woman. To his chagrin, Rauching found even after the marriage she kept the reins of power firmly in her hands. She managed her own estates, and the fighting men who surrounded her were loyal to their pay mistress. Rauching had no more authority than her spoiled, overfed lap dogs. So the Lombard lady began to suffer a mysterious and debilitating illness. Rauching began to extend his authority, gaining control of her estates. Unfortunately, nemesis arrived in the form of a young, lean gimlet-eyed Greek physician. He understood perfectly well the origin of such an illness as troubled the lady.

One day Rauching was summoned to her bedroom. He found the lady sitting up. She was regaining her health rather rapidly since the physician had begun to oversee the preparation of her food.

The lady was surrounded by her maids and a large part of her personal guard. All the men were armed to the teeth.

"My dear Rauching," the Lady Wilgefort said. "My physician here feels that I will enjoy far better health if you depart from my estates and never return."

Rauching hemmed and hawed, made excuses, and finally ended by pleading and begging. The lady was unmoved and continued to wear the same expression of benign contempt.

Stavros, the physician, and a large part of her personal guard accompanied him to the edge of her lands. The last thing Stavros said rankled Rauching the most. "I will remain and take care of her health and other things. I know a soft berth when I see one."

At the beginning, his second marriage looked to be rather more successful than the first. This wife was somewhat older. She doted on him and allowed him to do anything he wished. Unfortunately, she had an extremely young, attractive daughter. Rauching unceremoniously forced his attentions on the girl. She confided in her mother. Her mother didn't believe her. She confided in her fiancé. He did.

Rauching reluctantly decided the girl had to be gotten out of the way. So one day, he went out hunting with the rest of the family. Rauching slipped away and retired to the house. He found the girl there alone. He had knocked her in the head with the hilt of his dagger and was lifting her neck into a noose suspended from the ceiling beam when the fiancé burst into the room. Rauching managed to get his dagger into the boy before the young man got his sword into him. But at that moment, the hunting party returned to the house. Rauching was caught, as it were, red-handed.

This time Rauching was barely able to escape with the shirt on his back. Both the girl and her fiancé recovered. They talked about things like hanging, weighted sacks, rivers, and even crucifixion. Rauching never ever intended to visit the area again. *The world*, he thought philosophically, *is a very big place*. But he found after this adventure that, big or not, word gets around.

Getting yet another woman to marry him was a lot more difficult. And when his third marital adventure ended in the unhappy way he had confessed to Hakon, he knew there were not many places where he was welcome. In fact, his visit to Elspeth had been something of a last desperate expedient. When he arrived at her gate, he had only a few rather disreputable followers, some handsome clothing, and a few jewels. But Hakon promised to repair his fortunes if he completed his assignment successfully, and Rauching wanted that very, very much. The encouraging thought restored his hardness.

Elfwine's body bucked and she seemed almost to convulse with desire as she lunged against him. Then, drenched with perspiration, she relaxed, and so did Rauching, with a mighty heave of his chest. He spent his passion and rested on her body quietly.

Elfwine wiggled free of Rauching and sat up, curling her legs under her. "Oh, that was wonderful. That fool, Ranulf, hasn't touched me since the child was born."

That fool, eh, Rauching thought, realizing his task might not be as difficult as he had feared. And Elfwine really was an enjoyable toy. She was beautiful in the light of the one candle that illuminated the room. Slender, well-shaped, she was a true honey-blond. Her hair held dark strands to give it the color of polished wood. It had the texture of raw silk in his hands. But her breasts were truly the most erotic thing about her. Breasts big on her small form, heavy with milk, the nipples dark with large brown aureoles.

"My God, but you're lovely," Rauching said.

"Flatterer," Elfwine simpered. "You're a great man. Surely you've had all sorts of beautiful women. Noble ladies come to you dressed in silks, wearing jewels."

Rauching drew one velvet arm toward him.

Elfwine curled her fingers quickly. "I have calluses," she explained.

"Ye Gods," Rauching whispered. "What blasphemy. What an obscenity. I would no more expect hard work from a fragile creature like you than I would expect it of a goddess. You were born to be worshiped."

Elfwine smiled at him a little uncertainly. No one had ever spoken to her in this way before. Mostly, men had seemed to her like dogs or bulls. All they wanted to do was catch you behind a haystack or a hedgerow, throw you down, lift your skirt, and have their way with you. And once they got it, they became even more like dogs, following you around, ready to give you presents, mostly cheap things, a hare snared at the edge of the forest, a few eggs still warm from the nest, a lead brooch. And each time wanting you to spread your legs for them again. Always whispering "I love you" as though it were the most important thing in the world. She eyed Rauching suspiciously. "What do you want me to do?"

"Nothing," Rauching said expansively. "Only stay as beautiful as you are. And come to my arms as frequently as you can."

"Liar," Elfwine said, easing out of the bed and hurrying toward where her clothing lay piled on a chair in the corner.

Rauching saw all of his carefully laid plans leaving with her. "Wait."

Elfwine paused. She stood, naked, looking at him, a smug expression on her face.

Rauching longed to slap her silly, but he forced his face into a smile. He patted the bed beside him. "Sit down. Have some of the roast, a little wine, and we'll talk."

Elfwine sauntered over to the bed. On a silver tray beside it stood a platter piled with cold, larded roast beef. She poured some wine into a cup and helped herself to a little of the meat.

"I do have something for you." He reached under one of the pillows and produced a gold fillet set with cabochon rubies.

Elfwine had only to glance at it to realize that it was the sort of thing high-born ladies wore to hold their veils in place. She threw down the meat and snatched it eagerly. Rauching noted with new disgust that the thing almost slipped from her greasy fingers. She tied it around her forehead. Rauching concealed his revulsion and handed her a silver mirror.

Her hands smeared the back as she peered eagerly at herself on the polished silver surface. The eyes that stared into the mirror were as cold and impervious as blue glass. "I know about money," she said of the fillet. "It's pretty, but not worth much. Besides, I'll have to hide it. Ranulf knows I have no fine jewelry."

Rauching stretched like a cat on the silken coverlet. He tried to look confident. He tried to feel confident, but he was beginning to believe that in choosing Elfwine as the object of his arts of seduction, he might have chosen a little too well. She was not a practiced criminal, but she had all the right instincts. He decided to take a chance.

He reached under the bed. The thing clinked in his hand. As soon as Elfwine saw it, she forgot the mirror and made a dive across the bed for the massive chain of red gold. Rauching spread one hand flat on her belly and pushed her away, laughing.

"Not yet, my pretty," he said.

Elfwine gazed avidly at the thing dangling from his fingers.

It represented wealth incalculable to her. Enough to allow her to buy horses and land, and to eat and drink sumptuously for the rest of her life. All these thoughts flashed through her mind as she took in the splendor of the thing swinging slowly back and forth in the candle-light. A necklace weighted down with gold, big-petaled flowers of the precious metal, each set with a huge ruby. She gazed, and then she pounced. Not on the necklace, but on Rauching, straddling him with her hips.

She tore her eyes away from the necklace and looked down into Rauching's face. "What do you want?" she asked, naked greed in her eyes.

"Hakon wants to take the town."

Elfwine rolled off his body, sat up, and turned away. "Keep it," she said. "Money is no good to the dead."

Rauching sat up and placed the necklace in her hands so she could feel its weight, then chucked her under the chin. He looked ingenuously full into her blue eyes with a smile on his face. "My pretty. My sweet," he said. "Those silly people at the hall have been filling your head with all manner of nonsense about the Viking chief."

"Nonsense is it?" Elfwine asked. "Is it nonsense that he sent a horde of howling killers to our walls and was only beaten off with great difficulty? Is it nonsense what happened to the women in the village attacked by the Vikings? I don't think so. You'll give me this, but I won't get to keep it long."

"Yes, it is nonsense. It's the bishop and his witch who will get you all killed." He cupped and kissed one of Elfwine's breasts. She purred and stretched like a cat.

"He only wants the town to submit to him as Elspeth's people have. None of them have been raped or murdered, have they?" he cooed persuasively. He transferred his attention to her other breast. She really was, if one ignored her low birth and sloppy manners, a tasty little morsel.

Elfwine's clutch on the gold tightened. Rauching's mouth dropped to the place between her legs as Elfwine tried a petal of one of the golden flowers with her teeth. She yelped with pleasure. She fell back on the bed, shuddering with enjoyment. "Stop," she moaned. "I can't think with your tongue up me."

Rauching stopped and wiped his mouth. She drew her legs together, feeling the heat and swelling between them.

"He only wants to become your overlord," Rauching said.

This made sense to Elfwine. If the city were looted and destroyed, it would be a one-time profit, but the rents and dues paid by the citizens represented an income. Hakon would be continuously enriched.

Rauching could tell by her expression that he had won his first point.

"So where do I come in?"

"Sometime in the next week," Rauching said. "You will season the supper well with a white powder I will give you."

Elfwine's skin grew cold and desire drained out of her body like water from a broken jug. "Poison them all?" she squeaked.

But Rauching noticed she still kept a tight grip on the gold. "No, no," he said. "Everyone knows the Viking chief is a highly moral man. He wants this done with as little bloodshed as possible. It will only make them sleep, deeply. While they sleep, I will throw a rope ladder down over the walls and let the Vikings into the city."

Rauching knew this was a tissue of lies, but he gambled that Elfwine, not a soldier, wouldn't know this. When he reached the city, the first thing Rauching had done was to scout its defenses. He'd come to the conclusion that Godwin, whom he'd found a depressingly good commander, had all possible approaches tightly covered. They were in the hands of Ranulf, Elfwine's husband, and Alan. Two of the most reliable men Godwin had.

Torches were set near the fortress wall at night, and anyone climbing rope ladders into the city would be shot down by the crossbowmen. Rauching's position in the ruined fortress would be of no advantage to Hakon at all. It was then that he conceived the idea of recruiting Elfwine. So Rauching was prepared to counter any of her objections with benign promises. Certainly, he would say, though Elin would be whipped and driven out of the city, she would survive. Godwin had noble kin who would, no doubt, ransom him. Owen could continue on as bishop if he would obey Hakon and recognize him as count. All of these words were on the tip of his tongue and more, but Elfwine didn't ask.

She was thinking about the gold. Considering what it would mean to be a rich woman. She had been wild with delight when Ranulf was made a knight, but she soon realized his change in status meant little to her. She was still expected to do her part of the heavy work involved in running the household. Besides, Godwin still seemed to look down on Ranulf and used him only for such tasks as guarding the walls and helping Denis and Enar to train the other young men who flocked to Godwin.

This thing in her hands represented more money than she'd ever seen in her life. She could use it to buy at least two houses in the city, and maybe it would even stretch to a manor in the country and a slave woman to wait on her.

She thought contemptuously of Ranulf. He was loyal to the bone to Godwin, to Owen. He would no doubt defy Hakon and thereby bring about his own death. Well and good: when he was gone, there would be many, many new and wealthier suitors. She could pick and choose among them.

Rauching, studying her face, grinned and decided not to push his luck. He'd won and knew it. *She doesn't want to know,* he thought. *She doesn't care. After all, when we throw a sack of newborn kittens in the river or leave an infant in the baptistery of a church or by a hedgerow, do we really care to find out what happens to them? She was thinking only of what the precious object in her hands could do for her.* And that was the way he wanted it.

"Yes," she said.

Rauching gave a crow of delight and flipped Elfwine over on her stomach with her legs spread. A second later she felt Rauching's weight on top of her. She wiggled with delight. She liked vigor in her men. But then she realized the thing forcing itself between her legs wasn't Rauching. It was large, cold, and hard, and it tickled her in some deliciously frightening unfamiliar places. She tried to push free, but Rauching was holding her down by her engorged, tender breasts.

"Spread those pretty legs of yours as wide as you can, you little bitch, and do as I say or I'll slap you silly."

Elfwine did. She hovered perfectly balanced between pain and pleasure for a moment; then, as her body lubricated the thing between her legs, she slipped over into pleasure and began thrashing and moaning her way into another orgasm.

Elfwine slipped down the street from the fortress. She was wrapped tightly against the cold and any prying eyes that might see her. Her heavy old woolen mantle covered her head and upper body to her knees. She felt bruised and slightly humiliated by Rauching, but she had liked it. Gentleness was pretty much lost on her. She preferred dominance in men.

Her heavy breasts were leaking milk into her gown, and she knew she must hurry back to her child. The baby was in Bretwala's care. It was she who had brought Rauching's message to Elfwine. Only fair since Elfwine had been Bretwala's go-between during her romance with young Ricard, who had been killed that day at the wall.

Elfwine was nearly as contemptuous of her as she was of Ranulf. If there was any justice in nature, Ranulf and Bretwala would have gotten together. Both of their heads were stuffed with moonbeams. As it was, there wasn't. She had snared Ranulf. And handily, too.

He wasn't her first, or even her fifth or sixth. In fact, she had been limping from a savage beating administered by her father when she first saw Ranulf. The boy was pointed out as being a trusted servant of the bishop.

Elfwine had earned the beating. She'd fallen in with a wine merchant from Paris and agreed to run away with him. Her father and brothers had borrowed horses and ridden after them. Elfwine's father and brothers were formidable men. They were armed only with staves, but the wine merchant gave Elfwine up quickly enough when he saw them. Elfwine's father whacked her with a hoe handle until she screamed for mercy and promised not to run away again.

She hadn't meant to keep her promise, but she did. Not out of fear of her father but out of fear that what he said about the wine merchant was true. That the man only intended to take her as far as the nearest large town and there sell her to a brothel keeper. Elfwine believed her father was probably right, and had been on her best behavior when she saw Ranulf.

She decided it was time for her foot to slip again. Ranulf was a novice at the monastery where Owen was studying for his ordination. The fact that he belonged to a community of men consecrated to God meant nothing to Elfwine. Ranulf was philosophical about it, too. She persuaded him to give her a ride on his mule one day in the fields near the monastery. The mule had not traveled five hundred yards when Elfwine had Ranulf down and in a haystack. Fast work even for her.

Ranulf was a virgin. He was innocent, gentle, and filled with the rapture first love brings—and the sexual urgency of the very young. Within a week he was vowing he would love her forever. Within a month she was pregnant, and he was damn well going to, whether he liked it or not. Elfwine felt sure her father and brothers would see to that.

When her father learned of her connection with Ranulf, he didn't whack her with the hoe. Instead he dipped into the family's small hoard of silver and bought her the first real dress she'd ever owned, along with a string of blue beads. Elfwine understood she'd done well.

As indeed she had. She and the most witless of her brothers, Ine, were firmly ensconced in the bishop's household. She was married to an up-and-coming young knight.

But Rauching had shown her it was possible to do better. Without the sum promised in hand, she had told him she would not act. So he had given it to her, along with a number of veiled threats about what would happen to her if she failed him. The threats hadn't mattered, not really. Elfwine had sold herself to him when she lay with him. In a town as small as Chantalon, no one could carry on an intrigue for long without half the town finding out. Ranulf might be the last to know, but eventually he would know, and her little game would be over. So she had to be rid of him soon. Him and the rest.

She dithered for a moment about where to stow the treasure she carried in a cloth wrapped around her waist. Then she decided on the only place possible—Judith's. A good three-quarters of the town had valuables on deposit with Judith. She kept them in packets in the iron-bound chests in her strong room. She sealed the packets and did not look inside. She charged a flat yearly fee for keeping them safe.

Wind from the river funneled down the narrow street where Elfwine walked. The cold blast pierced the mantle she wore, chilling the wet spots on her breasts where her milk leaked out. The two cold wet spots reminded her of the baby, Ranulf's child. And for a second she saw her husband's face clearly in her mind. Elfwine shuddered and a sick sensation of dread stole over her. For a moment she was sorry she'd ever taken Rauching's gold. She wished she were strong enough to return to the fortress and throw the necklace in his face. But she knew she couldn't.

The gold represented too many things she wanted, needed. Besides, if she didn't help Hakon get into the city, someone else likely would, and they would reap the terrible Viking chief's reward, not her. And she wanted that reward: warm clothes, food on the table every day, safety and freedom from the want that had dogged her footsteps since as long as she could remember. An assurance that she would be safe, secure, cared for. An assurance that for all Ranulf's protestations of love, he could never give her.

Naked greed and fear won. Elfwine, a small figure in a dark cloak in a narrow, dirty street, hurried on alone toward Judith's counting house. So wrapped up in her own thoughts, she didn't notice the growing commotion behind her.

9

*E*LIN was having problems of her own. They started with Elfwine's brother, Ine. Ingund had sent him to chop wood for the fire. Strong and ever enthusiastic, he chopped it into kindling. This occasioned some mighty oaths from Ingund, but Ine was impervious to curses.

Enar, sitting on the back steps of the hall near the pile of firewood now kindling, began laughing. Incensed, Ingund slapped Ine. Ine thought about the slap for a moment, then slapped Ingund back.

Ingund turned to Enar and screamed, "What kind of a husband are you to sit by and watch another man hit your wife?"

Enar was eating a cold meat pie and didn't want to be interrupted. "A pleased one," he said. "A little slap will do you good, woman. Teach you not to be so free with your hands."

Ingund slapped the meat pie out of his grip and snatched up a log of firewood, one Ine hadn't gotten to. It was solid oak and three feet long. Enar took off running. Ingund was fast, but Enar had the stamina and speed to run most horses into the ground. He considered the chase a mild form of exercise.

Ine scooped up the remains of the meat pie from the courtyard flags and ate it, dirt and all.

"Do you eat anything?" Elin asked.

"Anything," Ine replied happily.

"Stop!" Elin screamed at Enar and Ingund. They ignored her or possibly did not hear. Edgar, standing near Elin, doubled over with laughter. Elin buried her hands in her hair and pulled. Edgar, seeing Elin was really at her wit's end, straightened up.

Enar flew past him with Ingund a pace or two behind. Edgar tripped Enar, who gracefully somersaulted to a stop and simultaneously snatched the firewood from Ingund. They both stood, panting and laughing, in front of Elin. Ingund's short burst of temper had been worn out by the chase. She fisted Enar in the ribs. "You cannot live one hour without making trouble."

Elin took her hands out of her hair and wiped her damp palms on her skirt. "Enar," she said sternly, "Judith has purchased a load of grain from a merchantman at the docks. She will be here with it soon. Go to the cellar and start making room for the sacks. And you, Ingund, go help Anna with the noon meal. Godwin is feeling queasy today, and she must cook twice, once for him and once for the rest of the household."

"Queasy," Ingund said disapprovingly. "I hear tell he made a pig of himself this morning while he was at Gynnor's talking to the men. Honey cakes, about a dozen of them, and some of Gynnor's homemade wine."

"He met Iltrude," Edgar said. "I met her once, too. Only a very old woman could get away with some of the remarks she made."

"No wonder he has dyspepsia," Elin said.

Judith clattered into the courtyard driving a wagon pulled by a team of mules. As she jerked them to a halt, she let fly with a string of blistering curses that singed the air around Elin's ears.

"Pardon me," she said as she climbed down from the wagon. "It's the only thing they understand." Her captain, Rieulf, arrived just behind her, driving another wagon. He, too, addressed the mules in an objurgatory fashion but didn't ask anyone's pardon.

"Elin, I hope you appreciate all the trouble I went to to

get this," Judith said. "The ship's captain was an absolute tartar. The bastard refused to come down to a fair price until I invited Rieulf and his men aboard ship. And even then I had to tell a lot of lies about how hardhanded and ruthless Lord Godwin is."

"Don't be so sure they are lies," Edgar muttered.

Elin went down to the cellar to supervise Enar. She found him already distracted by a jug of beer. Sternly, she ordered him back to his task and stood over him while he completed it. When he was finished, she sat down wearily on the cellar steps to await Ine's arrival with the grain sacks.

His big bare feet slapped loudly on the stone floor. A grain sack was tossed over his shoulder. There was a medium-size hole in the sack. Rosamund trotted along behind him, holding a bowl under it to catch the spill. "Judith says we can feed it to the chickens," she remarked brightly to Elin as she bustled by.

Elin buried her face in her hands. When she raised her head, she realized Edgar was sitting beside her. "Didn't anyone think to tie a knot in the sack and close the hole?"

"Probably not," Edgar said.

Elin gave a discouraged sigh, rose slowly, and went out to inspect the grain sacks for leaks. The sacks were porous and a few were rotten. Rosamund and her bowl were pressed into service frequently.

Both of Judith's carts were almost empty when Elin heard the scream from the house. A terrible, muffled, masculine shriek. *My God,* she thought, standing up in the wagon. *We're under attack.* She lifted her skirts, jumped from the wagon, and ran for the house at top speed, followed by the rest. The shriek had come from Godwin. Routrude was climbing him like a tree. She had him by the hair. Everyone stood at the back door, gaping in astonishment.

As they stared, Arn, Routrude's fat husband, darted into the hall waving a two-foot-long carving knife, screaming "Bitch, whore, adulteress, hag!" Arn ran out of words at this point, took a slice aimed at Routrude, and very nearly succeeded in cutting Godwin's head off. He missed by inches. Gowen, Wolf the Short, and Ranulf came charging downstairs.

By now, Routrude was nearly sitting on Godwin's shoulders. She slowed because she couldn't get much higher. Arn caught his breath and took aim again.

Godwin roared, "Ranulf!" The boy skidded to a stop next to Arn and snatched Arn's arm straight up. Godwin reached over and rather casually plucked the knife from Arn's fingers.

Godwin got Routrude firmly by the back of her dress and removed her, holding her, dangling at arm's length, the tips of her toes on the floor.

She hung there, wiggling and screaming. "I am not. I protest. There was no harm in it. You have gone mad. I am married to a madman."

"I caught you," Arn howled. "I caught you in the act with Fredgar."

"In the name of Jesus Christ," Godwin roared. "Man, I adjure you, in the act of what?"

"Adultery," Arn gasped out.

Dead silence fell.

"By all that's holy," Judith whispered to Elin, "who in the world would want to commit adultery with Routrude?" Elin slammed her elbow into Judith's ribs.

Routrude took a deep breath and screamed, "Bring on the red-hot irons. I will prove my innocence. Heat the ploughshares. I will walk over a dozen and more to prove I am a virtuous wife."

At this juncture, Fredgar arrived, dragged along by his wife. He staggered to his knees before Godwin. His face was covered with blood from a deep cut on his forehead.

Arn yelled, "Heat the ploughshares," and tried to attack Fredgar. He nearly dislocated his shoulder. Ranulf still held him.

"Don't let him go," Godwin ordered Ranulf between his teeth.

"No," Ranulf said, getting a firm grip on Arn.

"She lies," Arn yelled. "I found them together. I caught them in the act. She was half naked."

The crowd that had gathered at the door gave a gasp of

barely concealed delight. Godwin looked at Routrude, then glanced at Fredgar's wife. She reminded him of a horse. In fact, her face made most horses look pretty. He could see how Fredgar might think Routrude attractive.

Godwin had vivid memories of Fredgar and his wife. The cursed man always seemed to be in the wrong place at the wrong time. A few weeks ago, he'd almost started a riot by announcing publicly that Hakon was building a catapult to burn the whole city. For one happy moment, Godwin entertained himself with thoughts of hanging Routrude, Arn, and her purported lover together in the town square but then dismissed the idea as impractical. Attractive, but impractical.

To Judith, Godwin's expression suggested that he might be finding the idea of running Routrude up and down over red-hot ploughshares pleasant, even entertaining. So she decided to come to the rescue. "Routrude," Judith said, "are you guilty?"

"No." Routrude seemed almost surprised at Judith's calm tone. The hubbub around the door near Godwin died down.

"Then," Judith continued in an exasperated tone, "will you stop caterwauling about red-hot ploughshares and explain to your husband what you and Fredgar were doing?"

"I have some burns," Routrude said. "I got them when Hakon attacked the city."

"We know," Judith said. "What about them?"

"One of them is on my back in a hard-to-reach place."

"My mother," Fredgar chimed in, from his place near Godwin's knees, "had a sovereign remedy for burns. It is made of lard and garlic."

"I undid my dress at the neck," Routrude said. "So that Fredgar could smear some between my shoulder blades. I was not immodest. I was covered, but for a small place on my back."

Godwin released Routrude and looked down at his hand. It was greasy and, indeed, the entire hall reeked of raw garlic.

"Arn saw us," Routrude continued, "and attacked Fredgar with a three-legged stool. I ran in one direction, Fredgar in another. The stool is broken," she wailed. "Who will repair it?"

"Sir," Godwin said to Arn. "Are you satisfied with your wife's explanation?"

Arn pulled himself out of Ranulf's grip and strutted toward Routrude. He inspected the spot on her back, then turned to Fredgar, still cowering at Godwin's feet.

"Yes," he said in a dignified manner. "I am. But in the future, if my wife needs ointment on her back, I will put it there."

Routrude gazed at Arn, hands clasped, stars in her eyes.

"Now," Arn said, clearing his throat. "There is this little matter of the stool."

Godwin's teeth ground together audibly.

"Fredgar is a carpenter," Judith said hurriedly. "He will repair the stool."

Fredgar again nodded vigorously.

Arn took Routrude's arm and prepared to lead her back to the tavern when someone in the square shouted, "Vikings!"

The crowd at the steps melted away. The entire household, with the exception of Elin and Godwin, charged the door, tripping each other in their haste to get out and see. Godwin strolled toward the table.

"Don't you want to know what's going on?" Elin asked.

Godwin seated himself at the table. "Elin," he said. "I have here a lovely fat capon stewed with parsley and leeks." He removed the cover from an earthenware pot on the table and inhaled the aroma rising from within. A look of ecstasy came over his face.

Owen entered from the church, armed and wearing his helmet. "Godwin," he said. "Come on."

"And do what?" Godwin asked testily.

"The Vikings are on the river," Owen said.

"Yes," Godwin said. "Hakon heard about the merchantman selling us grain. He is going to seal the river mouth so that no further assistance can come to us by sea."

"You're sure?" Owen asked.

"That is what I would do if I were Hakon. Now, children, go up to the parapet in front of the fortress and watch the pretty ship pass. They are," he mused, picking up his spoon, "very beautiful, those ships with their painted prows and black hulls. But I have seen them often before." He raised his heavy-lidded eyes. "I do not want to see another until I can burn it."

10

*E*LIN and Owen strolled together up the ramp next to the fortress walls until they reached the parapet in front of the fortress gates. The crowd made room for them at the low wall at the edge. Despite a fairly long residence in the town, Elin had never had occasion to go up to the fortress, and she was surprised at the fine view it gave of the town and the surrounding countryside. The brown-stubbled fields stretched out all around the city. She could look directly down on its thatched and tiled roofs.

From here, Chantalon seemed to be very small, lonely, and lost. The forest began quickly beyond the plowed fields around it. Across the river, the woodlands came right down to the shore.

She and Owen stood together, watching the Viking ship make its stately way past the city. The ship was, as God-win had said, beautiful. The blue sky was flocked with hundreds of small, puffy white clouds, and the fitful sunlight made the ship's prow gleam like some fine cloisonné sword hilt. The roaring dragon's tongue seemed to be a spurt of flame. The hull itself appeared to be of oiled black oak, and it set off its bejeweled bow the way a dark velvet gown displays a magnificent jewel. She tussled with the current, her crew pulling at the oars. The sail was furled.

Denis the archer watched its progress with his cross-bowmen. "Should we fire, my lord?" he asked.

"No," Owen said. The graceful ship was keeping to the shallows well across the river from the fortress walls. She would be within bow shot for only a few moments. The men at the oars had taken cover behind their shields, and Owen didn't think in those few moments they could do much harm.

Denis nodded and steadied himself with his crutch. The quiet man was the linchpin of Owen's small but deadly force of archers. "Then, with your permission, I will return to my post at the walls." He withdrew along with his men.

The Viking ship vanished into the thick trees and brush that cloaked the shoreline. The rest of the crowd, seeing no further excitement was in the offing, began to drift away, leaving Elin and Owen alone.

"They aren't worried yet," Owen said.

"They don't understand yet," she replied.

"Yes," Owen said. "We talked to Godwin."

"I can't think Hakon's blockading the river matters much," Elin said. "Godwin told me the Vikings hold Bayou Reims and most of the other towns along the coast. Block-ade or not, we will get little help by the sea."

"Yes," Owen said. "Once a great many ships called at this port. But I've noticed in the last few years the arrival of even one is an event. We are all but forgotten."

"Hakon bestirs himself to little purpose," she said. "The grain Judith bought was only a few hundredweight, two cartloads and very poor quality. Not much better than animal feed." She looked down at the roofs surrounding the fortress toward the square. "The city of God."

Owen began laughing. "Augustine. Where in the world did you ever hear of Augustine?"

"My mother. She used to read to me from it. She had a copy or some abstracts. I don't know which. She said it was a sacred book. I . . . I didn't like his mind."

"His mind?" Owen asked.

"A man's mind is in his work," Elin said.

Owen shrugged. "Whatever your thoughts, I can't think this is the city of God. Right now, the widow is probably selling one of her girls to a man, likely as not one of my priests. Arn is no doubt hard at work watering the wine he sells. Osbert is probably cheating some peasant out of a hide, which he will sell to Siefert at a fat profit."

"Everyone is up to their usual tricks."

"I hope so," he chuckled. "When they're up to any unusual ones, Godwin hears about it in short order."

"You saw Routrude," Elin said accusingly.

"I saw her and fled," Owen answered. "I feel," he said, with a perfectly straight face, "that I should let Godwin handle all civil matters. He is an excellent judge."

"Coward."

"Where Routrude is concerned, I own it." Owen laughed, then sobered abruptly. "Elin, I'm leaving now."

Her face paled. She turned away quickly. The distant trees across the river blurred as tears filled her eyes.

"I've been with your people all morning, Elin. They feel they can get Enar and me to my father's stronghold by secret ways known only to themselves. Perhaps if we travel quickly, we'll be there within a few days."

"I detest good-byes," Elin said.

"Hold the city, Elin."

"Yes," she answered, her voice thick with tears. "The city of man."

"Augustine," Owen said. "He was so certain about the city of God. But Elin, I'm not certain of anything. This may be all we have. Don't let it be destroyed." His voice pleaded. For a few seconds, she heard the sound of Owen's footsteps on the stone ramp; then there was silence. Elin stood facing into the wind, letting her tears dry. She must show nothing of her feelings when she returned to the hall. The rest of the household would guess where Owen and Enar went and why. She would swear them to silence but knew that, sooner or later, word would reach the town gossips. She hoped Owen and Enar would be well away by then, safe and traveling with her friends through the deep woods.

Likely he would return a man pledged to another. Her chin lifted and the world blurred again. She felt the pain like a knife turning in her heart. Owen had said, "You know the rules, and there are always rules."

She did. Owen would never get the men he wanted without a pledge. And the only thing he had to offer was himself. The town was a rich prize, and many might be willing to throw for it. But they would want his oath strengthened by a blood tie. A tie that would cost her dearly. *Well,* she thought, blinking back tears. *Cheap at the price.* She would not fail him or the city. And the victory would be hers, untarnished if forever unsung. *We give, not take, from those we love.*

Elin bowed her head, fists clenched, and in her mind she made the sacrifice and felt her heart at peace. Then she unclenched her fists and set them on the parapet's stone rail. For now she was a leader, and a ruler must act like one. When she lifted her head, she realized she was completely alone.

The sun was moving westward toward the horizon. The rays were long and golden; the supper hour was near. Her responsibilities drew her back to the hall. She envied Owen. She was sure he was running now in the freedom of the forest with her people by his side.

She turned back and looked up at the fortress's tall gates. One of them hung by only a hinge. It was blackened by fire. The other was missing. Through the gates, she could see the dim pile of what had been the count's residence. It was both more squalid and in better condition than she'd thought, a dim square-built hall of heavy timber, smoke drifting up from a hole in the roof.

Elin shivered. Lost in her own thoughts, she'd forgotten there were men inside now. Rauching and his people.

The heavy gate moved as if stirred by some vagrant breeze, and a man stepped out from behind it. She recognized one of Rauching's followers. In the dim light of the hall, she had thought him old, but now seeing him by daylight, she realized he wasn't really old but only so scarred and battered that he seemed of greater age than he really was.

He was filthy, his matted yellow hair hanging in tangles around his soot-smeared, greasy face. She recoiled instinctively. She could smell the green hide armor he wore from where she stood. She was repelled but not really afraid.

A supper-hour quiet had settled over the whole town, but she was sure they would react, and violently, to a woman's scream. The vacant blue eyes that peered through the tinged hair held no malice, only a rather vacuous amusement.

She wrapped her mantle tightly around her, covering the lower half of her face. And then, unwilling to give in to her growing sense of unease by a show of fear, she strolled toward the ramp leading toward the hall.

She was halfway down when a sound behind her made her turn quickly. The man stood at the top of the ramp. It looked like he held a large black spider in his hand.

"Elin!" Edgar screamed as he lunged from the deep shadows near the fortress wall.

Something dark and swift flew toward her. She flung up her mantle-wrapped arm. She felt a cut like a whip across her forearm as she deflected something into the stones of the path. Edgar drove his sword hilt into the side of the man's head.

The black spider thing fell from his hand, clattered down the ramp, and came to rest at her feet. She had never seen anything like it before, but she knew instantly what it was. A tiny folding crossbow. She looked at her left arm and realized blood was running down it and dripping between her fingers.

"God bless Iltrude," Godwin said.

Elin sat on a bench in the hall, Anna tending the cut on her arm. She clucked and fussed over it. Denis examined the crossbow, folding and unfolding the tiny iron wings that formed the prod. Finally, he shot the bolt into the table with a whack.

"A very deadly thing," he said.

The man who had shot the bolt at Elin lay near the hearth. He was still unconscious. Edgar had hit him hard. His feet were toward the fire.

"I'll keep this," Denis said to Godwin. "I'd like to duplicate it, if I can."

"As you like," Godwin said.

Denis turned the small weapon several times in his hands. "If the bolt had struck home, Lady Elin, we would likely never have known how you died. You notice the bolt has no fletchings. And the head is thin and razor sharp. When it enters a human body, if the wound closes quickly, the person struck would simply have been seen to collapse and die. Cause unknown. Unless someone had the courage to take a knife to your corpse. And I doubt if any here would. It might seem like some sort of natural death."

Elin turned pale and placed one hand on her breast.

"Oh, be quiet, for heaven's sake, Denis," Anna said.

"No, Anna," Elin said as she put one hand on the other woman's shoulder. "He's right. It was very clever, and but for Edgar being close by, it almost worked."

"My being near you was not an accident," Edgar said. "That's why Godwin said 'thank God for Iltrude.' She felt Rauching might be here to kill you."

Elin noticed he didn't mention Owen. She realized he knew Owen had gone and must have guessed why.

Godwin's eyes swept the hall. Besides Anna and Elin, none of the other women were present. Of the knights, only Ranulf and Edgar remained. The leaping flames in the fireplace were the only light.

"Some things," Godwin said quietly, "are best done in the dark."

Anna sat down and scratched her hip. "Shall I send for Alfric?" she asked.

The man on the floor opened his eyes. Edgar caught him by the armpits and pushed his feet toward the fire.

Elin whispered "God" and turned her face away. The man's mouth opened wide in what seemed a soundless scream until Elin, looking through her fingers, saw that past the stubs of his rotten teeth, he had no tongue.

"Stop," Elin whispered. "In the name of heaven, don't. He can't speak. Look, he has no tongue."

Edgar ignored her until Godwin raised his hand. At the

gesture, he stopped. Godwin stared down at the man at his feet, studying the pure animal terror in his eyes. "Cut our friend loose," he said almost benignly. "Anna, give him some wine."

Edgar cut the man loose. Anna returned with an earthenware cup. She put it into his hand. He drained it in one gulp. She filled it again, then stepped away, silently. The man giggled.

Elin gave a slight start and realized that but for the eerie little sound, the hall was silent. The man giggled and drank again. Elin saw the cup was empty.

"Refill the cup, Anna," Godwin said.

Silently, Anna refilled the cup. This time the faint giggling went on even as he gulped the wine. Edgar looked at Godwin. Elin saw their eyes meet over their prisoner's head. Godwin nodded.

Edgar drew his sword and used it so quickly that Elin saw it as a flash of light before her eyes. A second later, the tousle-haired head rolled at her feet, wine still dribbling from its open mouth.

Elin gasped. She felt the air rush into her lungs, then force its way out with a moan as the pumping trunk spread a fan-shaped splash of blood over the floor. She turned away from the sight. The fire behind her flared as Edgar tossed on another log. She found herself looking straight into Rosamund's eyes. The sixteen-year-old sat cross-legged on the table.

Fist in her mouth, Elin whimpered. "You shouldn't have seen that."

"I have seen worse," Rosamund said. "Didn't you know what Lord Godwin was going to do?"

Elin didn't answer. She had guessed but hadn't thought he would do it with such dispassionate dispatch.

"Where are Wolf the Short and Gowen?" Godwin asked.

"Drinking at the widow's," Edgar said as he wiped his sword clean. "Clea and Wolf the Short are keeping company."

"Go fetch them," Godwin said. "Tonight we're going up to the fortress to kill Rauching."

"You can't," Rosamund said quietly.

"Why not?" Godwin asked.

"Because he's not at the fortress," Rosamund said. "He's at Osbert's hall. He gave Osbert a magnificent present, a beautiful brooch. Rauching has money." Her voice was flat, unemotional, cold, not the voice of a young girl at all.

"How do you know these things?" Godwin asked.

"One of the widow's ladies is a friend of mine," Rosamund replied. "I saw her today. Some of the girls were hired to entertain the men."

"So, Rauching has set about corrupting the townsfolk," Godwin said.

"He is talking to the farmers," Rosamund answered. "If that's what you mean. They are all murmuring, saying if they can't get past the walls to plant a winter crop, we will all starve. The girl told me Rauching is saying nice things about Hakon now. Saying Hakon only wants to be our overlord, and the defiance he meets with from the bishop and his wife will get everyone in the town killed."

"Poor, misunderstood Hakon," Godwin said. "The man of reason. The paragon of accommodation, compromise, and peace. Do you believe him?"

"While the Vikings had me," Rosamund said in a soft but tight little voice, "I saw one landowner try to surrender to them. The ship's captain offered him terms. The men on the ship cut his throat."

"The captain's?" Godwin asked.

"Yes," Rosamund continued. "Then they burned and slaughtered at will. Hakon's men would not let him spare us even if he were so inclined. The city is too rich a prize." Rosamund jumped from the table and fled, her anklets jingling.

"What are we going to do?" Edgar asked Godwin.

Godwin sat down in his chair by the fire, his shoulders slumped. "The little girl knows a lot about those devils, doesn't she?" Godwin said to Elin.

"They brought her to the city and sold her to the widow," Elin said.

"Godwin," Edgar repeated. "What are we going to do?"

Godwin gestured toward the headless corpse on the

floor. "The first order of business is to throw this dung in the river. Call Ine."

Ine arrived a minute later and stood looking attentively at Godwin. Godwin pointed to the corpse. "Take the body and place it in a sack, then throw it in the river."

"Head?" Ine asked.

"Yes. The head, too," Godwin replied.

"Sack, stones, river." Then Ine paused, studied the floor, and said, "Mop?"

Godwin put a silver coin in his hand. "I like you," he said to Ine. "You always grasp the essentials immediately."

Upstairs, Elfwine retched into a chamber pot. Her skin felt icy cold, and she was weak with terror. She'd heard everything that had happened below and noticed Godwin had no answer for Edgar. If the townspeople decided among themselves to open the gates to Hakon, Godwin would have no way to stop them.

She retched again, dryly, and realized her stomach must be empty. The pain in her lower belly went on and on. Elfwine remembered in panic her abandoned lovemaking with Rauching. Had she yielded her body too soon after having the baby? Was something wrong? She wiped her mouth, then washed it out with wine and spat into the pot.

No, she decided and sipped some more wine. The pain was receding now and almost gone. She had an assignation tonight with Rauching in the church. She had two things to tell him. First, that Godwin had killed one of his men. Secondly, that Owen was gone.

RAUCHING was half drunk as he crept through the street toward the church. Most of the town was safely in bed by now. The only lights were in the tavern, the widow's hall, and Osbert's house.

The light from Osbert's house flowed out into the street accompanied by shouts and loud laughter. The feast had degenerated into a drinking bout after the women withdrew. The presence of the widow's ladies lent it the trappings of a mild orgy.

Most of the farmers were Osbert's customers, and he was a man to cultivate his customers assiduously. Rauching had a number of very satisfactory talks with them. These talks usually began, "Well, I'm no friend of the man, but ... I think the bishop and Godwin misunderstand him."

Soon he found he was preaching to the converted. He was telling these men only what they badly wanted to hear, convincing them that if they made peace with Hakon, they would be allowed to plant their crops and generally get on with their lives.

These landsmen not only wanted peace, they needed it. Everywhere among them hovered the unspoken fear that if both sides remained at odds, starvation and disease would be the next visitors to the city. Rauching was happy to agree with them until wine and beer drowned all possibility of coherent conversation.

Humming cheerfully, he moved from shadow to shadow across the square toward the church and Elfwine. When he found her, she seemed almost one of the paintings on the church wall. Except that her face was too pale and stood out against the reddened pigments of the others. He caught her in his arms, feeling the strain of his erection in his thighs. He could hardly wait to get his horn into her. The fact that the church was a sacred place only added fire to his need.

She pulled her mouth away from his and turned aside. "Godwin has killed one of your men."

Rauching laughed. "So soon? What did he do?"

"He tried to kill Lady Elin with a small crossbow."

"So he failed," Rauching said. "I promised him ten pieces of gold if he succeeded. How did Godwin kill the fool? Slowly, I hope."

"Quickly," Elfwine said, smiling a little. "Edgar cut off his head."

Rauching laughed. "Better than he deserved."

"There's more. Owen is gone."

Rauching's fists tightened on her arms, painfully. "Gone? Gone where?"

Elfwine gave a little moan of terror. "I don't know. Stop. Stop, you're hurting me."

"Bitch," Rauching whispered. "If you don't tell me all you know, I won't just hurt you. I'll strangle you."

She tore free. "You stop," she babbled, "or I'll scream and bring the whole household down on us. I mean it, I really will."

Rauching stood where he was, listening to the thud of his own heart in his ears as he realized he was sober and shaking all over. Mastering himself with an effort, he managed to speak calmly to Elfwine. "Now, now," he said softly. "My pretty, my sweet. I'm sorry if I hurt you. You only startled me, and I don't know my own strength."

Elfwine, reassured, crept closer. Rauching put his arm around her, and a second later, she realized his hand was up under her shift caressing her between her legs. She stiffened, then relaxed. His touch was the most expert she'd ever known. Unlike other men she'd lain with, he seemed to know the exact spots on a woman's body that would drive her absolutely wild. A moment later she was whimpering, thrusting her sex against his hand, and she was holding him, nails digging into his back.

Rauching pulled his hand away. "Tell me," he breathed.

"I want you," Elfwine whispered.

"Tell me first," Rauching panted. "Then you'll have all you want, more than you want."

"I really don't know," Elfwine gasped. "But Anna says he's gone to get more men. Gone likely to his father."

Rauching gave a soft crow of triumph and forced her to the floor.

Hakon and his men set up camp on a large sandbar near the river mouth. The coast was utterly wild, and the area where the river entered the sea was a dense maze of swamp, salt marsh, and thick, thorny tangled undergrowth. The space where the Vikings had chosen to camp was the only clear area for miles.

"It doesn't seem to be under water at low tide," Tosi said, looking around the sandbar. A few stunted trees and bushes grew in the center.

Hakon grunted.

"Hakon," Tosi said, slowly and deliberately. "If we're going to put a fortress here to stop the traffic upriver, we're going to have to think about things like that."

"We aren't," Hakon said. "That's what I want Godwin to believe."

Tosi scuffed the sand with his foot. "What are we doing here, then?"

"We're waiting for Rauching to send us a message," Hakon said. "I sent him to make mischief in the town. I only hope he succeeds."

Just at that moment, two of Hakon's men entered the camp, dragging a sack. "This came from the city," one of them said. "It was bigger than the other trash they threw out, so we brought it to you." They emptied the sack at Hakon's feet.

"It seems," Tosi said, "the Lord Godwin is not so easily put upon."

The body had a well-washed, livid look. The severed head seemed strangely peaceful. The stiffening ligaments had closed the mouth and eyes.

"He was Rauching's?" Hakon said.

"Yes," Tosi replied. "And a lot cleaner now than he was in life."

No one even suggested a grave. They gave him to the ebbing tide and rowed back upriver to take their position under the fortress.

"It would be just as well if the next were Rauching and in the same condition," Tosi said as he and Hakon sat by the fire, sharing a jug of wine. But the next wasn't Rauching and this one was alive, if only just partly. He clutched an empty barrel. The letter to Hakon was wrapped in leather and chained around his neck.

Hakon, who could read well enough, didn't share the contents of the message with anyone, not even Tosi, except to say, "The man has, I think, been worth his pay."

Tosi knew he wasn't referring to the wretched creature vomiting water on the sand spit.

"Man the boats!" Hakon shouted. "The bishop is escaping."

Owen never saw Alshan and Sybilla. In the time he traveled with them, he had almost come to believe he was as clever at woodcraft as they. But he never found them when they didn't want to be found and never saw them when they didn't want to be seen. So he spent an hour or so blundering around in the marsh until they found him.

"My feet are already wet, Lord Christ Priest," Enar complained.

Alshan stepped out from behind a tree and said, "Yes, the ground is very damp. Why do you not ride like your lord?"

Owen was mounted on the red stallion he'd taken from

the Vikings. He rode him with only a small hackamore
and a saddle cloth. No one in the city considered the stallion a natural beast. He wouldn't, for instance, abide a bit
in his mouth. But around humans, he behaved as tamely
as a dog. Owen had brought him at Elin's insistence. "He
is no warhorse," she had said. "But he can go like the
wind if you can get to the open plain. Nothing can run
him down, not even Enar. He will have you at your
father's stronghold in a day. And he's obedient, if handled
gently."

"I don't like horses," Enar said. "Not even that one."

Alshan walked toward Owen.

"Where are the rest?" Owen asked. "We're ready to
travel."

"Nearby," he said.

Something flashed at the corner of Owen's eye, and he
saw Sybilla. She had been standing near a bush covered
with brown, dead leaves. He hadn't realized she was there
until she moved. "We sent the children away," she said.
"We are also ready."

Tigg appeared. He was sitting on a huge deadfall of
mixed broken limbs and tree trunks cast up by the river. He
slid to the ground and walked soundlessly toward Owen.

Owen dismounted and the five of them came together,
sitting quietly on their heels: Owen, the mail-clad warrior; Enar, his companion, wearing only a heavy woolen
tunic, trousers with cross-gartered leggings; and the three
forest people clad in deerskin dalmatics and leather
trousers. Their skins were almost as dark as their clothing
in the shadowed swamp.

"You know where I wish to travel?" Owen asked
Alshan. "You know my father's stronghold." Was Alshan
their leader, their chief? Owen never had been sure. The
rest obeyed him and seemed to follow him willingly.
The little man never gave anything that sounded like an
order nor used force on any of his companions. Owen had
never seen as much as a blow exchanged between any
of them.

The three of them chuckled and spoke musically among

themselves. "Yes," Alshan said. Owen wore the amber-and-gold necklace given him by Elin. Alshan was adorned by a polished amber teardrop strung by a thong around his neck. Alshan fingered the jewel like a charm. "Yes, we know him. Gestric, your father, is a proper man. When we travel near his stronghold, we let ourselves be seen. And then summer or winter we find a feast spread for us near a sacred spring on his lands. He never lets us leave hungry. I think we will be welcomed if his son brings us to his hall. Though it is said he has let the priests pour water over his head."

"My father's been baptized. Yes," Owen said.

"To capture the Frankish girl, Clotild," Alshan said. "He let himself be washed by the priests."

Owen was a little annoyed by Alshan's comment but thought it very likely a true assessment of the situation. When Clotild was approached about the match, one of her conditions had been that her prospective husband be a Christian. Openly, he kept his word and the old ways were never spoken of among his men. But Owen knew that in Gestric's hall, as almost everywhere else, things went on in secret. He hadn't believed Gestric had any part in them, but if Alshan was correct . . . well, Owen knew his father kept his own counsel about a lot of things. Perhaps Clotild did, too.

"How will we travel?" Owen asked. He was anxious to be off.

Enar looked around cautiously. The whites of his eyes flashed in the green gloom. "Hakon is on the river," he said. "We saw his ship pass."

The woman, Sybilla, laughed softly. Her green eyes were as dark as a thicket of scrub oak. But they seemed light against her brown skin. "If his patrols are as noisy as you, Saxon, we will have no difficulty in dodging them."

"We will travel by day following the river," Tigg said. "Until we reach open country. This is the dark of the moon. We'll make a dash through open country to your father's stronghold. Hakon could not stop us when we brought you back to the city. He cannot stop . . ."

Owen watched Sybilla's eyes. They gazed speculatively at a spot near Enar's feet. Owen saw the snake the same way he had seen the woman herself—when it moved. He grabbed Enar and jerked him away.

The thing was patterned like the carpet of leaf litter around them. It seemed almost part of the forest floor. Enar stared at it for a moment, then reached for the axe in his belt.

Sybilla shouted, "No!" A second later she straddled the thing and reached down.

"Stop!" Owen shouted. "It may be deadly."

"It isn't," she said. "I know the kind. He comes to bring us a message." The snake came to her hands like a tame pet, the enameled coils reaching her elbows. She held it in her hand just below the head.

Enar, standing next to Owen, stared into the thing's eyes in dumb fascination. It looked fixedly at Owen, then turned its head toward Enar. The brown, narrow head with its fix-lipped reptilian smile turned in Sybilla's hand and looked upriver. The black forked tongue flickered in and out. Then the head turned and looked down toward the coast. The brown coils tightened. The serpent flowed over Sybilla's hand down toward the muddy riverbank. It slithered through the tall grass and into a pool filled with brittle reeds and away toward the ocean.

"I don't know where we're going," Sybilla said, watching it vanish. "We'll travel along the river as we planned, but not to your father's stronghold."

That night at supper, Godwin made Elin take Owen's seat at the head of the table. He seated himself on the long bench beside her. The men and women all ate together. The household was embattled and everyone of them knew it.

Anna served Elin the way she would have served Owen had he been there. From time to time, Elin stared at the bandage on her arm and then at the dark stains near the hearth.

"Try to forget it," Godwin said.

"Why?" she asked, softly.

"What was I to do with him, Elin? Turn him loose so he could try again?"

Elin worried her lip with her front teeth for a moment, then applied herself to Anna's soup, a rich beef broth laced with onions, and last week's bread and cheese.

Even across the square, she could hear the celebratory shouts coming from Osbert's house near the Roman gate. "Osbert and Rauching are feasting the farmers again tonight," Ranulf said. He was seated at Elin's left hand opposite Godwin. "So much for loyalty." He spit out the last word like a curse.

"Don't blame them too much," Godwin said. "Rauching is telling them what they want to hear."

The knights were seated in a row next to Godwin, Edgar with his short black beard and pale face, then Gowen. Gowen, with his massive chest and shoulders, towered over the smaller men. *There is,* Elin thought, *enough of him for two men—and he eats like three.*

"I still think," Gowen said as he downed the soup in one gulp, "that we should go to Osbert's house, drag Rauching into the street, and kill him."

"No," Godwin said. "We will not make a mockery of Osbert's hospitality. Make a mortal enemy of one person in this town and you create a blood feud with them all."

"It's true," Ranulf said miserably. "Osbert wouldn't forgive you, and he's close kin to Gunter, Siefert, and the rest. They may quarrel among themselves, but offend one and they would crowd together to shut us out."

"My brothers would help them," Elfwine said. "They are deeply in debt to Osbert. They see themselves as his men. They often do the slaughtering for him, and when they do, we eat well from the bones and tripes no one else wants."

Ingund, her face dark and brooding under her crown of red braids, brought a platter of ducklings cooked with quince and citron to the table and set it down with a bump.

Gowen speared two of the ducklings with his knife and was reaching for a third when he felt the prick of Edgar's knife against the back of his hand.

"Leave some for the rest of us," Edgar said quietly.

Gowen looked down at him, his large blue eyes expressionless as glass. "Take the knife away, or I'll break you like a sack of dry sticks."

"No, you won't," Wolf the Short said. "Leave the ducklings alone, or I'll ram my knife at the nape of your neck, up through your brain."

Elin froze where she sat.

Gowen was facing Edgar at his right, and Wolf the Short seated at his left did indeed have the point of his knife at Gowen's neck.

"Gowen," Ingund said. "Were I you, I would forget the other duckling. I have a whole ham stewed with cabbage in the pot. You wouldn't want to miss that."

Gowen turned back to his food, tore a duckling in half with his bare hands, then began to eat it. He rolled an eye at Wolf the Short, who also went back to his food. "You're getting cranky. What is it? Clea won't speak to you or let you have free use of the girls?"

"She has forgotten me since Rauching came. She prefers that painted snake. So do the girls. He's very liberal with his gold."

Elin relaxed and asked in a whisper, "Godwin, do they always combine against him?"

"Yes," Godwin said. "They have some rudimentary intelligence. No one can possibly stand against him alone. He's tired of Rosamund or she's tired of him. He needs another woman. Killings at suppertime spoil my appetite."

"What about Rauching?" Elin asked in a whisper.

Ingund, who'd seated herself next to Wolf the Short near the end of the table, was drinking beer from an earthenware cup. She slammed it down so hard it shattered. "Don't speak in whispers. Say what you have to say out where the rest of us can hear it."

"Shut up, Ingund," Anna said. "You're drunk."

"S-s-s possible," Ingund said, and hiccuped.

Elin looked angry, but Godwin continued to be calm.

"She's lost her heart to the Saxon brute, Enar, and now he's gone," Anna said philosophically. "Who knows if he will return?"

"He's not a brute," Ingund snarled. "He never laid an unkind hand on me." She burst into tears.

"A perfect man," Anna said, tears starting in her eyes.

Elin noticed the old woman looked a bit under the weather herself. The two cooks had been tippling among the cooking wine.

"No." Ingund sobbed, her head on the table. "I'll not hear Enar abused. He's just as hasty as the next man, but he's afraid of my father."

"I think that quite likely," Godwin murmured.

Suddenly Ingund leaped to her feet. "Let's kill Rauching!" she shouted.

"Sit down," Godwin roared. Ingund sat. "Now," Godwin said. "We will discuss Rauching." His eyes swept their table briefly. The glance was a quelling one. "I know what Rauching is saying to the farmers. And I know they're listening."

Ranulf started forward as if to speak. So did Edgar. Godwin held up his hand. "But," he continued, "I don't think anyone is so rash as to want to run down and throw open the gates to the Vikings. At least not without some firmer guarantees than Rauching is offering at present."

"No," Rosamund said quietly from her seat near Elfwine. "Now he only hints and suggests."

"Yes," Godwin said. "And I don't think anyone in the city will do anything simply on the basis of hints and suggestions." Godwin turned to Ranulf. "Are the archers at their posts?"

"Yes, my lord," Ranulf said. "Denis is with them. I'll go down in a little time and release him for the night watch."

Elin noticed Ranulf's arm was around Elfwine, supporting her. The girl looked pale. She was very fair and the skin around her mouth was blue.

"Very well," Godwin said. "I think the presence of armed men will discourage any ill-considered action on the part of the townsfolk. In the meantime, no one is to do anything to Rauching until I give the word. Sooner or later, he'll have to declare himself openly, and then I'll deal with him."

It was plain from the mutinous expressions on many faces that agreement was far from unanimous, but no one was so forward as to contradict Godwin openly, and the rest of the meal passed in sullen silence. When Elin started to rise from the table, Ranulf caught her sleeve.

"My lady," he said. "I'm worried about Elfwine. She's bleeding again."

Elin called Anna, and they helped the girl up the stairs. When Elin finished examining her, she left with a face like a thundercloud, followed by Anna, to confront Ranulf in the hall.

The boy was arming himself for his stint at the gate. He pulled his hauberk on over his quilted tunic and was buckling on his sword when he turned to confront their accusing eyes. "I didn't, I swear," he said. "Do you think I'd do anything to harm Elfwine?"

There was so much sincerity and love in the boy's voice that Elin's conviction of his guilt was shaken. Anna's hard old face remained stubbornly skeptical. "Are you sure," she asked, "that both of you didn't get carried away one night and . . ."

"No." Ranulf's body stiffened. His mouth tightened. The blond, boyish good looks vanished, and Elin found herself staring into the face of a man. His blue eyes met hers, steady and without flinching. "No," he repeated. "I'm aware of the danger. She means more to me than life itself—she and the child. I wouldn't allow it even if she asked it of me. Never. No. Never. I'll swear no oaths, Lady Elin, but as I am a man, I would fall on my own sword before I would lay one hand on Elfwine until the proper time had passed and we could be as husband and wife again." He bowed his head. His features softened and became those of a boy again. "Elin, I'm so afraid. I was sick when she told me. In God's name, will she be all right?"

Elin looked into his tortured, frightened eyes and took both his hands. "The bleeding is minor. Perhaps she exerted herself too much the past few days. We'll put her to bed. Anna and I will watch over her. Now go to the gate. Godwin expects you."

Ranulf nodded, turned, and strode out through the big doors into the square. Elin and Anna moved toward the hearth where they could speak privately. The knights were gathered at the table. Alfric was telling them a story in a low voice. Snickers and soft chuckles were rising from the group, and Elin surmised the story was probably one Alfric considered unfit for a lady's ears. "A saintly man," Elin said.

"A saint who knows a lot of bawdy stories," Anna commented darkly. "Elin, I'd swear a man had been at Elfwine. And maybe a man a lot rougher than Ranulf."

"Oh God," Elin said, and laid a finger on Anna's lips. "Hush, Anna. Don't say it. You don't suppose . . ."

"I don't suppose anything. I know what I saw when I looked between her legs. And as for her overexerting herself, that girl never overexerted herself doing anything. Rosamund is half her size, and she can do twice the work in half the time."

"In heaven's name, Anna, hold your tongue. It would break Ranulf's heart. He loves her to distraction."

"He should love her less and beat her more often," Anna growled. "Let me at her, Elin. I'll get the truth out of her with a horsewhip. Find out who the man is and put a stop to it before Ranulf finds out what's going on. He's not a man to wear a cuckold's horns with a smile. He'll kill her and maybe the child, too."

Elin realized she was so close to the fire, the heat was scorching her legs. "A horsewhip," she whispered. "Anna, I couldn't countenance . . ."

"Bah, Elin. You are like Godwin. I believe it's the gentry in you. Far too tenderhearted and soft." The old woman hooked her thumbs in her belt and eyed her with grim amusement. "Elin, I was gotten in some bushes along a stream bank. My mother wore a serf's collar around her neck. Starke the Strong, Owen's grandfather, claimed every child borne alive by any woman he bedded— If such a polite word can be used for my begetting. My mother's swollen belly made her fortune. Like as not, he made some mistakes from time to time, but no matter. My point is I know how cunts like Elfwine think. If someone dangled a

pretty present or enough money in front of Elfwine, she'd
be off like a bitch in heat, ready to show her backside to
anyone.

"Like as not, Ranulf wasn't forward enough for her. If
the boy hadn't been so careful of her health, so solicitous
about her welfare—in other words, if he'd fucked her
blind—she'd likely have stayed home and not gotten into
mischief. So leave this to me. I'll beat the truth out of her
and put a stop to it. Surely you'd rather that than have the
matter come to a killing."

Elin nodded. "Yes, but not tonight. The girl is too sick.
I wouldn't want you to be the death of her."

"Ha," Anna said. "I wouldn't mind being the death of
her. I'd like to be the death of her. The little bitch should
know better than to bring scandal into the household at
such a time. I'll sleep beside her tonight. She'll have no
man in her bed while I'm there. In the morning, I'll take
her to the stable and find out what she's been up to."

"How will we explain the marks to Ranulf?" Elin
asked.

"We won't," Anna said. "There won't be any marks.
The little twat is as guilty as Judas Iscariot. She'll begin
sniveling and confessing as soon as she sees the whip in
my hand."

Staring at Anna's grim, hook-nosed old face, Elin found
she could well believe it. As she watched, the lines and
wrinkles in Anna's face softened into a smile. She put
her arm around Elin's shoulders, and together the two
women walked toward the door. "You're Owen's aunt,
then," Elin said.

"I doubt it," Anna chuckled. "I said I felt Starke made a
few mistakes, and I've always believed I was one of them.
My mother was a woman with plenty of company. She
had five legal husbands and was working on a sixth when
an untimely fever carried her off. That's why I said I
understood Elfwine. Mother lifted her skirt for any man
who offered her enough. And I can't say I was all that
choosy either in my youth. I wouldn't give a good loud
fart for all Elfwine's lechery if she hadn't picked the
wrong man to play games with. She's a married woman.

And Ranulf won't pass off the horns with a shrug. When I was married, I behaved myself. So should she."

"The devil with Elfwine," Elin whispered. "The devil with all these contretemps. I wish I were with Owen. It's at times like this that I'm sorry I was born a woman. He will be in the forest now. I wish I could go and run beside him. There is no moon, and the stars will seem so close you'd think you could touch them if you climbed into the topmost branches of a tree."

Anna laughed. "Did you ever do that? I mean climb into a tree to see if the moon and stars came closer."

"As a child I did," Elin said.

"So did I," Anna said. "My God, how the hall stinks, cooking smells, unwashed bodies." She shot a glance at the men gathered at the table. "And the damned chimney smokes."

Elin shrugged and pushed open one of the big doors to the hall. "All chimneys smoke," Elin said with resignation.

The night air came wafting in, cold, clear, and fresh. "I'll stand on the steps," she told Anna, "look at the stars for a moment, and then come in and go up to bed." She slipped out and stood on the broad top step overlooking the square. Anna joined her.

The tavern was still brightly lit, and there were lights in the windows of the widow's house beside it. Farther down the street, the doors to Osbert's hall were open. The shouts of merrymakers within the hall were carried by the wind to Elin's ears.

"He's feasting the farmers again," Anna said. "And pouring his poison into their ears."

Elin looked out at Osbert's hall at the light shining into the street, her face enigmatic. Then the glow on the horizon caught her eyes. "It can't be dawn," she whispered. "Oh my God, my God!" was her anguished cry.

Then, leaping away from Anna, she ran across in front of the church and up the ramp to the parapet in front of the fortress gates. The rail stopped her headlong plunge, catching her at the waist. From there she could see far out over the darkened countryside. The stars above were obscured by the glow rising from the forest upriver. A second later, she was joined by Edgar, Anna, and the rest of the household.

"Look," Elin screamed. "My God! Owen! My God!" she shrieked. "The forest is burning."

*E*NAR smelled the smoke first. He had been uneasy for at least a half an hour before, sensing something wrong. They traveled quickly along the river with the forest people leading the way. The route they took seemed unnecessarily circuitous to Enar, but he was wise enough to know they must be careful, dodging all human habitation. So he went along with them quietly.

But he remembered the snake. He hated snakes, but he respected them, too. They were sons of the dragon who lived in the sea. The dragon whose head adorned the prows of Viking ships. They carried tales to their father and whispered in his ear. With cold lips and forked tongues, they told about the doings of men. They were his messengers. The three veiled ones, whose names he would not speak, used them, too. The veiled ladies spun the thread of a man's life from birth to death and cut the thread when they chose.

"What's wrong?" Owen asked. He ran beside Enar. The horse followed at an easy trot, rather like a dog on the hunt.

"The snake knew something, Lord Christ Priest. I'm glad I did not kill it. I'm afraid."

"You? Afraid?" Sybilla laughed.

"I'm always afraid," Enar said testily. "Afraid when I don't know what there is to be afraid of. When danger presents itself, and I find I can deal with it, I have the courage of a wounded boar."

Sybilla said something to Tigg and Alshan in a low voice and they stopped. The five were near a spot where a tributary flowed into the bigger stream. A jumble of fallen trees, branches, and other trash washed down by the small stream had nearly blocked its mouth, creating a logjam that towered over them. The waters of the tributary exited through the screen of branches and logs in a series of tiny waterfalls, pushing their way through, out to the sea.

"What do you feel, Saxon?" Alshan asked.

"I don't know," Enar said. "I wish we had some light. The hair is standing up all over my body."

It was growing dark. There was light still along the hills surrounding the river. The treetops blazed with it. But the river valley was in shadow. The greenish brown gloaming of a winter forest.

"It is very quiet," Sybilla said with a shiver. "I can't hear a sound. All the birds are silent. I'm sure the Saxon is right."

"I smell smoke," Enar said.

"Someone's cooking fire," Owen said.

"No." Alshan shook his head. "No people live hereabouts."

The stag shot from the forest on the other side of the deadfall like a stone loosed from a sling. His leap took him across over the big knot of trees and fallen wood from the forest. The antlered head lifted above the timbers. He scrambled for a foothold for a second; then his leg went down among the broken branches. Owen heard the bone snap.

The stag bellowed, his voice a roar above the forest stillness. And then the antlered head went down. The water turned scarlet as the shattered leg emptied itself of blood. The stag bellowed again once more as the final silence drew him in. And then Owen heard him no more.

A doe and her spotted fawn, more cautious than the stag, spilled across the deadfall, picking their way over the shattered wood. When they gained their footing on the other side, they fled past Owen and the forest people, ignoring them, as though they had been so many tree stumps.

Owen charged forward. One leap brought him to the top of the deadfall.

"Be careful," Enar shouted. "Remember the stag."

In a second, he was back down on the ground. He realized now that he had seen the fire, that the air was hazy with smoke. "We're trapped," he gasped. "The fire is all around us. Our only hope is the river."

Enar pointed to the deadfall. "If we can pull one of the tree trunks free, we can ride it to safety."

As he spoke, a tall pine near them burst into flame, exploding into a fireball before their eyes. The needles burned away in a flash, leaving the tree a blackened flaming skeleton outlined against a dark sky. Owen and the rest dodged back toward the river to escape the cascade of resinous embers.

Enar clutched the stallion's bridle as the horse reared and seemed to trumpet a challenge at the flames. Knee-deep in the river, Owen could feel the current tug at his legs. Peering into the forest, Owen could see flames beginning to appear among the winter-felled weeds and undergrowth. He felt the first stirring of blind panic. They could never swim the river here. The water was too deep, the current too swift.

"It is as always," he heard Alshan say. "First the pines burn, then they set alight the hardwoods, oak and ash."

"And we'll be roasted alive when they do," Tigg said. "Or forced into deep water where we will drown."

There was a shout from behind him, and Owen turned to see two men in a small rowboat. They held torches in their hands. As he watched, almost stupefied by surprise, one of them raised a bow. The arrow was pointed at him. From the corner of his eye, Owen saw Enar move, the axe a flash of steel in his hand.

The top of the bowman's head vanished. Still upright, he toppled like a falling tree into the water. In one motion, Owen stripped off his hauberk and hurled it toward Sybilla, the nearest one of the forest people.

He went into the water as cleanly and smoothly as an

otter. He felt the battle rage fill him the way clouds suddenly fill up the sky before a storm. Owen knew he would make no mistakes. He surfaced beside the boat. The remaining man inside bashed at him with the torch. Fire seared the side of his face, but his hands were already clamped at the gunwales. The small craft tipped and the warrior went into the water with a splash that drowned the torch. The man was armored. He sank like a stone.

Swimming with one hand, Owen towed the capsized boat toward the shore. A few seconds later, Enar, waist deep in water, was beside him, helping him right the boat.

"I lost the oars," Owen panted. "But the boat may take us to the other shore or to a ford where we can get clear of the fire."

Enar saw one oar floating in a shallow whirlpool near the deadfall. He lunged toward it, a dangerous move since the deadfall was catching fire. Wet, it smoldered rather than burned, sending out clouds of thick, black smoke.

"What can we do with one oar?" Owen shouted.

"Leave that to me," Enar said.

"The horse," Owen gasped.

"He can swim almost as well as you can, Lord Christ Priest," Enar shouted above the roar of the flames.

They all stood waist deep in water now. The whole riverbank was a sea of fire trees and underbrush burning fiercely. The forest people clambered into the boat, using the rings to tie the horse's head to the stern.

Enar darted forward and knelt at the bow. With a push of the oar, he shot the boat into the current. But even as he did so, Owen saw flames flickering between the tree trunks on the opposite side of the river.

Elin lay on her bed, surrounded by her women. Rosamund washed her face with a damp cloth. Gynnor, Siefert's wife, steeped herbs in wine at one of the tables. Anna stood in front of the fire, warming her backside. Ingund held Elin's head.

"Bring me my clothes, the ones I wore into the forest," Elin cried.

"No," Anna replied. "Hakon somehow found out about

Owen leaving the city. His men will be out all up and down the river."

Rosamund slid from her seat at Elin's side and went to her knees on the floor. She put her head in Elin's lap and embraced her around the waist.

Elin understood the truth. They were right. She had no choice but to remain here. He said hold the city, and whatever happened, she must. A pang of unspeakable sorrow coursed through her, sharp as a spear driving through to her heart. With the pain came knowledge, a knowledge sure as is the certainty of death. *I cursed him for belonging to them,* she thought, and saw the irony of her life. *I belong to them, too. As much as he does or more. They command my allegiance.* Elin swayed where she stood and sat back down on the bed.

Judith appeared at the door, carrying a covered cup. "I have a posset, Elin. You will drink it."

Elin surrendered, and as always when she did, her surrender was absolute. She let them undress her and comb her hair. She drank Judith's posset and the herbs Gynnor steeped in wine. As she drifted into sleep with Ingund and Rosamund still watching her, she thought of Owen again. She remembered she'd once asked to be part of his fight. Now she knew she might lead the only fight left—the last one.

"This is no natural fire," Enar shouted at Owen. "Hakon's war snakes will be on the river."

At that moment, the dragon ship hove into sight. The forest on both sides of the river was ablaze, and the big ship seemed adrift on a river of golden light. The gold-embossed sea-serpent head glittered in the bloody light as though it were made of real precious metal, not paint. The wide-open fanged mouth seemed to drip blood.

Owen saw Hakon run to the prow. He heard his shout above the crackle of fire. "Surrender, Owen. Surrender or die."

Enar looked back at Owen's face. He knelt in the stern, the horse's reins in his hands. His face was dead white, the eyes glittered with madness. Enar knew they were not going to surrender.

At that moment, an eddy current in the river brought the small boat into the shallows. Enar could feel the fire's heat sear his flesh. The boat grounded and the stallion stood up. He half reared in the shallow water, jerking the reins out of Owen's hands. He floundered for a moment and then, getting his legs under him, he plunged into the fire.

Enar watched, horrified, as Owen and the forest people followed him. Enar jerked his mantle from around his shoulders and threw it into the river. He picked it up and flopped it around his face and neck. It was a man's duty to follow his lord, even into the mouth of hell.

He leaped from the boat and found it not as bad as he expected. The brush he ran through was dry and blazing, but the ground under his feet was cool. The grass, damp and still green in places, hadn't caught fire yet. The pines all around him were blazing, and he knew it wouldn't be long before the hardwoods followed. Even though his eyes were tearing from the thick blanket of smoke that flowed among the trees, he saw Owen and the forest people ahead of him, following the horse. Abruptly the horse vanished.

Enar picked up his pace and caught them just in time to see the horse take the sloping sides of a ravine on his haunches. Owen and the forest people tumbled down after him. Enar skidded on his backside, and they found themselves standing at the bottom of a small watercourse that led into the river.

Enar splashed toward Owen. He flipped the mantle from his head and shoulders and was horrified to find it nearly dry. He threw it down into the trickle of water in the bottom, then back up over. "This is no sanctuary," he shouted.

At that moment, the horse began to run again, upstream toward the very heart of the fire. Owen, Enar, and the forest people followed blindly. It seemed every step they took carried them deeper and deeper into the flames. The fire seemed to grow brighter and brighter as they went.

Upstream, the hardwoods joined the blaze. They passed

a grove of beeches, white-hot, spitting sparks surrounded by a cloud of fire. A dead pine ablaze from root to crown crashed down into the ravine behind them, the broken trunk splitting into a piled bonfire of fragments, cutting off any chance of retreat. The light around them was brighter than full sunlight. On the high banks of the stream, the forest became a wall of flame, a furnace blast of heat. Ahead of them, the horse charged forward at a gallop.

Suddenly the sides of the ravine sloped down, and it ended in a shallow pool at the base of a falls. A small lake fed by the spring. The pool was surrounded by an oak grove. The trees had trunks thicker than the length of a man's body. The sturdy-branched roots gripped the ground like fingers, and the massive trunks were a dam holding back the fire in the forest beyond.

The horse stopped, knee-deep in water, and stood still. Enar stepped down in the cold water and splashed it over his hands and face. His cheeks and hands were blistered. Owen stood quietly, his arm over the horse's back, Tigg beside him. A kind of bleak resignation was in Owen's face.

"This place was holy once," Tigg said. "Sacred time out of mind."

Owen knew he must be right. The oaks were so old some of them must have sent forth their first shoots from the acorn before Caesar marched into Gaul.

"He is heedless and rash, this Hakon," Tigg said. "His fire profanes all things. He will have no luck from it."

"Neither will we," Owen said. "When those oaks go, and they will, this pond will be the center of an inferno. We won't survive." Even as he watched, the trunks of the other trees began steaming. The leaves covering their crowns blackened, curled, and crumbled, filling the air with fine ash. Tall pines around the oak grove began to let go. They snapped explosively, sending a fiery rain of blazing fragments, small branches, and pine cones among the oaks. One split in half with a sound like a clap of thunder, and its blazing top shattered, falling among the oaks.

Then one of the oaks nearest the fire succumbed. Enar watched in horror as the enormous trunk smoldered for a moment. He could see light flickering through the coarse bark as it exploded into flames, sending a column of fire thirty feet into the air.

Enar seized the horse's bridle and led him toward the waterfall. Owen was right: the oaks would catch slowly, but they would burn with a white-hot ferocity the pines could never match.

Alshan and Sybilla stood in a shallow grotto carved out by the aeons-long flow of water from above. "Saxon!" Alshan shouted urgently. "Put your back against this stone." He pointed to what appeared to be the solid wall at the back of the grotto. "Put your back against this wall and push."

Standing huddled in the flow of water with Owen and the rest, Enar looked back at the pond. The water was a bright evil mirror filled with flames and only partially obscured by a thick pall of smoke drifting in through the trees. As he watched, bubbles began to appear at the edges of the water. The hair on the back of his neck stood up as he realized the pond was beginning to boil.

With a strength born of terror, he heaved his shoulders against the rock in the grotto. His feet slipped on the wet surface under him, but the rock gave a slight lurch and moved. Enar braced himself and put his whole being into the next push.

Almost the entire wall of the grotto slid away, and with a screech of absolute terror, he plummeted backward into darkness.

13

*E*LIN slept late the next day. When she did awaken, she became aware that her head buzzed, her ears rang. When she moved, she found the buzzing passed into actual pain and she was dizzy. She was up and bathing her face in cool water before she realized her mouth tasted like the bottom of a sewer.

When she came downstairs, she found Judith and Gynnor sitting at the table in the hall. Both looked guilty. Anna tended the fire.

Elin staggered from the stair to the table, flopping down into Owen's carved chair. She clutched her head and moaned. "Oh, my God. Gynnor, what did you give me?"

Gynnor avoided her bloodshot eyes. "A little something people hereabouts call eau de vie and some valerian."

"Christ," Elin whimpered. "Anna, is there some cure for this?"

Anna chuckled. "There is for the eau de vie and the valerian, but I'm not sure about the opium Judith put in the posset."

"We only wanted to guarantee you a pleasant night's sleep," Judith said defensively.

"I'm sorry, Elin. I didn't know about Judith's medicine. And she didn't know mine would be so strong," Gynnor said. "We are very sorry."

Anna banged the outside of one of her heavy kettles

with a wooden spoon. Both Gynnor and Judith gave a start. "Had she not come down with at least a semblance of life in her, I would have made you even sorrier. Very well, you may go home now. And I charge you," she continued with a nasty laugh, "to take care of Hakon's health in the future."

Judith rose to her feet in high dudgeon. "I will not stay here and be insulted." She wrapped a magnificent blue mantle around a yellow linen dress and stalked toward the door.

Elin looked at Judith and thought of several incantations that were said to bring at least mild trouble to their targets. Then she glanced at Gynnor's pleasant, penitent face and her malice ebbed away. "Please, Judith, don't go away angry," Elin said finally.

Judith turned and walked back to the table with an air of injured dignity. Rosamund came downstairs with a bowl of water and a clean cloth. She put the cool cloth on Elin's head.

Judith kissed Elin on the cheek; Gynnor kissed her on the forehead. "We were worried about you," Judith said.

"I think I'll be all right," Elin said. "Thank you for your concern. I believe I would accept either of you as physicians, but not both at once—please." The two women departed arm in arm into the square.

"Probably for some of Gynnor's honey cakes," Anna said.

"Oh God in heaven above," Elin said. "Don't be obscene, Anna."

Anna set a cup and a bowl in front of Elin. Her stomach heaved, and she gagged. "First," Anna said. "Drink what is in the cup, then try the soup."

Holding the cloth on her forehead, Elin took a sip from the cup. Her stomach accepted it without shooting it back into her throat. She drank the rest slowly. She felt better. She then applied herself to the soup in front of her. It was a light, clear chicken broth with pieces of white meat seasoned with parsley. When she was finished, she set the spoon in the bowl. "What was in the cup, Anna?"

"A hair of the dog that bit you," Anna replied. "Ingund made the chicken soup. She said you'd need it."

"Where is everyone?" Elin asked, looking around the big room. She and Anna were the only ones present. It wasn't often the hall was this empty by day.

"Godwin and the knights are conferring with Routrude."

"Drinking in the tavern, you mean," Elin said.

"Godwin doesn't need to go to the tavern to drink," Anna said. "Routrude sees all, hears all, knows all, and tells all. I noticed he dispatched Ingund to her father's house also. Half this town gabbles and drinks at the tavern; the other half gabbles and drinks at Gunter's forge. When Ingund returns and he's finished with Routrude, he will know what Rauching is saying and who is listening. He will also know who is not listening and thinks Rauching should have his throat slit right now."

"Who's on our side and who isn't," Elin said.

"Right. Alfric is in the scriptorium, trying to put Owen's accounts in order. Not an easy task. A rather monumental task, in fact. That man of yours isn't one to keep careful track of anything. Denis is in his room, building another crossbow."

Elin got up from the table and strolled toward the door. She moved carefully. Her head still felt rather delicate, and the room tended to spin if she moved too quickly.

She opened the door to the square. A cold, gray rain fell. It was slow, steady, and dismal. The sky was deep gray, the cobbles in the square were gray, even the brightly colored walls of the shops and houses seemed pale and washed out. "Ugh," she said.

"A good day to stay indoors," Anna commented. "Alan and Ranulf are on duty at the walls, and Ine is heating the sweat bath for you."

"For me?"

"Yes. An hour or so sitting in the steam will do you no end of good."

Elin rested her hand on the door frame and peered into the misty horizon beyond the town. She could see only the dark outline of the forest in the distance. She was still afraid for Owen, but not as fearful as she'd been last night. By day, and in Anna's calming presence, her common sense reasserted itself. She trusted her people. She had seldom seen them trapped by anything. They were as at home in the forest as a man is in his own house or a woman in her own kitchen. She didn't think they could be cornered by Hakon's crude tricks. She was sure they'd found a way to lead Owen to safety.

It took her a long silent moment to question her own confidence. The certainty was like a quiet place at the center of her being. A place she could retreat to and find peace. But why was she so sure? The question returned, and with it, the answer. There was a connection between her and Owen, a connection that defied time and space. She had felt his anguish the night he had been trapped in the cage by Osric. Felt his agony and joined with him in defeating it. Now she was equally certain he was safe among friends.

Wind took the rain and set it to undulating. It reminded her of a gray silk curtain, drifting between heaven and earth. The connection between herself and Owen was as tenuous as the rain but as eternal as the cloud's love for the green earth. They were part of its being as she was part of Owen's. He was the wind and the rain, she the flowering tree.

Anna threw a heavy mantle over her shoulders. "It isn't good to brood," the old woman said.

"He's safe, Anna. I know it. I would feel it if he weren't."

Anna put one arm around her. "I'm sure you would. They say it's often so with lovers." Then she turned her around, shut the door, and began conducting a still bemused Elin toward the sweat bath.

As they passed the fireplace, Elin paused, mindful of her duties as a housewife. "The noon meal," she said. "They will arrive hungry as bears or wolves."

Anna pointed to the fireplace. "I have a kettle of soup on the hearth, and for supper we have a magnificent dish." She indicated a gigantic earthenware pot, resting on the coals. "Ingund's famous loin of pork cooked with honey, wine, and wild mushrooms. Osbert killed a pig today, and Ingund took both loins.

"It's nearly done now. In a short time, I'll take it from the fire and let Ingund reduce the sauce and put the finishing touches on herself when she returns from her father's house."

Reassured that provision had been made for the household, Elin let Anna lead her away.

The back door closed with a slam, and the hall stood empty for a second. Until Elfwine came creeping down the stair. She held Rauching's packet in her hand, and her eyes were fixed on the two pots hanging over the fire.

Elin and Anna were crossing the yard toward the sweat bath when Elin thought of Elfwine. "What about the matter we were discussing last night?" she asked.

"I haven't had a chance to get her alone yet," Anna said in a low voice. "I was too worried about you. She rose this morning fresh as a daisy, acting as though butter wouldn't melt in her mouth. She told me the bleeding had stopped in the night. And hurried away to help Rosamund with the cleaning. It's the first time I've ever seen her do any work without specific orders from me. She's up to something all right. Up to no good. But she won't stir a hand or foot out of this house while I'm watching her. Don't fret yourself about that. So steam yourself to your heart's content.

"When you're finished, join me in the cellar. The load of grain Judith brought will rot unless we get it into clean, dry sacks. I've had Rosamund cutting and basting some together all morning. They should be ready when you've finished your bath."

When Elin stepped out of the shed that comprised the body of the sweat bath, she found the rain had stopped and a stiff breeze was blowing. The sky was still slate gray and an even darker misty overcast was drifting in from the sea.

She wrapped her blue woolen mantle tightly around her body and walked toward the cellar. Just at that moment,

Anna came out of the stable with a pile of sacking folded over one arm and a wooden shovel in her hand.

She joined Elin and followed her down the short flight of steps into the big room. It was almost impossible to move around in the cellar now. It was stacked full of the provisions Owen had collected against the Viking siege.

Grain sacks were piled up to the ceiling, four deep against the walls. Hundreds of sausages hung from the beams. In bins against the far walls, there were piles of turnips, dried apples, onions, and other root crops. Big clay jars of oil occupied the front of the cellar toward the square, stacked six deep. In the middle of the floor, piled almost to the level of the sausages, were cheeses and barrels of beer, mead, and wine. The only clear space was near the cellar door. The grain sacks were heaped there.

Elin looked at them in dismay. It was clear the ship's captain who'd sold them to Judith hadn't taken any care of his cargo. The sacks were rotten. Elin could see that since she'd had Ine pile them there, several more had burst their seams and spilled their precious golden contents.

"I wonder if it's worth the trouble," Elin said, hands on her hips, as she contemplated hours of backbreaking work.

"Elin, we are feeding over thirty families now," Anna said. "I think before this is over, we will need every ounce of wheat we can get our hands on."

"I'll hold the sacks open. You pour."

They set to work. When the first new sack was filled, Anna ran her hands through the wheat. She cupped some and brought it to the single barred window that let in light from the yard above ground.

"What do you think?" Elin asked.

"Not bad," Anna said. "Very little chaff and dust. It has taken no hurt as yet from being in the damp sacks. We have—"

Elin heard a low, moaning sound. She turned, alarmed. "Something is in here with us."

Anna tossed the wheat back in the sack. The cellar had a dozen ventilation ports that let in air and a small amount of light from above ground. The main part of the room was dark.

The moaning sound came again.

Anna looked around for a weapon and decided the shovel would be ideal.

Another moan.

Elin seized a long-neck jar used to draw wine for the table. She brandished it like a club. The next sound was a sobbing cry of pain.

"Near the beans, I think," Anna said. She marched toward the beans stored in sacks beside the root crops.

They found Ine. He was curled in a ball on the brown lumpy sacking. Between moans, he whimpered like an animal. To Elin he sounded depressingly like a dog. A dog that'd been kicked very hard.

Anna threw the shovel down in disgust. "Half-wit!" she shouted at Ine.

"Anna," Elin said in mild reproof. The insult was only too true.

Anna ignored Elin. She seized Ine by one ear and hauled him to his feet by force. He offered no resistance but followed with a screech of pain. He shuffled along, propelled by Anna's grip on his ear, howling, still half doubled over. Anna dragged him to the corner of the cellar where she stored her herbs.

"As though we didn't have enough trouble," Anna complained loudly as she flung him down near the window to the yard.

"He has eaten something noxious, Elin," Anna spit. "He eats things that would gag a foraging boar. I'll wager anything you like that he's gotten into the dried beans and stuffed himself."

"God," Elin whispered. She was staring down at Ine's face in horror. His skin was an ugly gray, his eyes were half rolled back in their sockets, and long slobbers of drool poured down his chin from slack lips.

"When the beans swell," she gasped in horror, "that could kill him."

"Right," Anna said. She rolled up her sleeves quickly. "I'll mix the emetics; you hold his nose. And keep a firm grip on his hair."

Neither woman was gentle. A few moments later, Ine's

bucking body pulled away from them and he began to vomit. Heaving spasms shook his whole body as he emptied his guts on the floor.

Elin pulled up her skirts and stepped quickly back as the yellow brown liquid splashed in copious amounts at her feet. She had a moment to realize she was not seeing beans, and then she was distracted because something really horrible was happening to Ine.

When he finished vomiting, he fell to the floor on his side, then rolled over on his back. His eyes went white as they fell back in the sockets. He let out a loud sound like a scream as the air left his lungs. Then his body arched as he tried to stand on his neck and heels.

Elin clutched at Anna in terror. Anna pushed her away. She straddled the puddle of vomit, reached down, and caught Ine by the belt. "Help me get him on his side, Elin, so he won't swallow his tongue."

Elin's grip on Ine's ankles and Anna's on his belt was enough to turn him on his side. It seemed an eternity to Elin before the spasm stopped. But at length it did, and his body relaxed, cheek against stone floor. "Anna," Elin said, clutching a fold of her mantle. "Anna, he isn't breathing."

"I cannot see what we can do about that, Elin," Anna said. "We will wait and see if he starts again."

Ine did begin breathing a second later, deeply, like one in a heavy sleep. "Oh, thank God," Elin whispered.

"Your thanks are premature," Anna said, and Elin realized Ine's body was beginning to arch again. This time he vomited a spewing stream that burst from his mouth and splattered against a hogshead of beer five feet away. His whole body jerked again and again, violently, so violently that Elin could hear his joints crack. Then he went limp.

Again Elin waited, fists clenched, nails digging into her palms, trying to will the breath into his lungs. Slowly, he took one deep breath, then another, and settled into something that seemed a kind of sleep. Elin realized her hands were shaking and her body was drenched with sweat.

Anna left and went to the stable, then came back with a horse blanket. They pulled Ine away from the mess on the floor, wrapped him in the blanket, and pillowed his head on one of the clean grain sacks.

"Should we leave him here?" Elin asked.

"I can't see how we can get him anywhere else until the men come back," Anna said. "Then they will no doubt complain loudly about the task. I'm sure you noticed he's filthy. He pissed on himself and emptied his bowels, too."

Elin had noticed. The cellar reeked of discharged human waste and vomit. She went to one knee and rested her left palm down on the cellar floor. She raised her right. "Mother," she said. "This is only a poor innocent. Very unimportant in everyone's eyes, but give him life. Please, I beg you." Then she rose. She found herself shivering. The sweat was drying on her skin and she was cold. She pulled the mantle tightly around her shoulders.

"Elin, don't make prayers like that around the household," Anna said. "They may have doubts about who you're praying to."

"You don't have any doubts, though, do you, Anna?"

"No. Not a single one."

Anna stood over the puddle on the floor, studying it narrowly. "These aren't beans. It's difficult to tell about such vile stuff, but I'd almost say Ine got into Ingund's pork."

Elin looked down at the mess and agreed. There were definite fragments of pale meat floating in the liquid on the floor. "Could the pork have been tainted?"

"Impossible," Anna said. "The pig was fresh, killed this morning. We had to let the meat cool before we could cook it."

"What about the mushrooms?"

"Nonsense. Ingund learned the kinds to gather at her mother's knee. She was a farm wife for seven years. She could pick them blindfolded. Besides, mushrooms don't take a man so quickly as this took Ine. The only time he could have gotten into the stew was while you were having your bath. I returned from taking you to the yard and found him in the hall. I ordered him back to the stable. It seems he came here instead. When one eats a poisoned mushroom, it is many hours before the first pains begin."

Elin glanced at the still sleeping Ine. She felt her skin crawl. "There is darker work here than spoiled pork or a bad mushroom," she said softly. "Let's go upstairs and get the stew."

It took all the strength the two women had to wrestle the big pot out of the fire, across the yard, and into the cellar. The pot had a curved bottom, an excellent shape for cooking on the coals, but it didn't balance upright.

Elin and Anna braced the big pot against the side of the stair. When Elin pulled the lid off, a few drops of liquid spilled over the rim and splattered on the floor.

"What now?" Elin asked.

"We cannot use the cat," Anna said. "Godwin calls her the Countess. Her highness sleeps in his room. He says she's his liege woman, and he feeds her from the table. He would not forgive us. Never mind, I'll find something."

Anna left, and Elin went over and studied the still unconscious Ine. Color was beginning to come back into his cheeks. He was breathing more easily.

When Anna returned, she carried a ladle and bowl in one hand and led a dog with the other. Elin recognized the dog. It was one she had seen often, scavenging for scraps of garbage in the square. The beast was very old. Its muzzle was gray and it had an opaque film over its eyes.

Anna put the bowl on the floor and poured a ladleful of stew into it. The stew was still hot. The dog sniffed at it once. Its nose jerked back, and it whined softly.

"I suppose we could be imagining things," Elin said.

"If we are," Anna said, "then no harm is done. We put the stew back on the fire. Nothing more need be said."

The dog buried his nose in the cooling stew and gulped it down. It licked the bowl and even lapped up the one or two splashes of liquid that had fallen from the tilted pot.

Nothing happened. The dog sat down on his haunches and grinned up at Elin, his tongue lolling. It looked expectant.

"Oh, all right," Anna said. She poured another ladleful of stew into the bowl.

Elin went limp with relief. The dog gulped the second bowl of stew. Elin took a cloth, straightened the pot against the side of the stair, and put the lid back on. "No more, Anna. Ingund would kill us if she saw us feeding her precious dish to a dog. Maybe Ine ate something else. It's impossible to tell from that mess on the floor."

Full fed, the dog lay down on the floor, rested his head on his front paws, and prepared to go to sleep. Its tail thumped twice on the stones.

Anna still watched him.

"God, what a mess," Elin said. "I hope Ingund doesn't come back before we can get the stew upstairs. We need to tend to Ine, get him washed and into bed."

Anna turned away from the dog. "Don't bother about Ine. I'll have the men dunk him in the horse trough. As for the floor, Rosamund is upstairs cleaning with bucket and brush. If she can scrub the floors upstairs, she can scrub this one. Here, you," she shouted at the dog. "Out. I want no fleas in my cellar."

She slapped her dress at him. With a resigned look, the dog dragged itself to its feet and started up the short flight of steps into the yard. To Elin's eyes, its legs appeared to fold up under it. The dog slid down the three steps it had climbed and lay motionless on the cellar floor. Its breathing stopped as Ine's had. Its body bowed itself back, nose to tail. Froth appeared on its jaws. Then its body relaxed as the seizure passed. It jerked once, twice, and lay still.

Elin staggered toward the cellar steps. She sat down. To her, the whole universe seemed to lurch. She'd broken her arm once as a child. She remembered falling from the tree and seeing the odd crooked angle of her wrist and wondering at it for a moment. Until the pain came. She felt that way now, and sat, waiting for the pain to come. She lifted a length of her mantle and threw it over her head in absolute grief. She sat very still.

Anna raised her hands and covered her face for a second. Then she staggered back and sat down hard on the humped side of a wine barrel. "I've led a long life," she said. "With many troubles. I'd believed I'd seen everything, but this . . ."

Instead of grief, a blind hatred and rage filled Elin. Not for whoever had done the poisoning, but for Hakon. *Why can't he go away and leave us alone?* "What is it?" she snarled at Anna. "Some disease in these Norse people that they can never be content with what they have and always must go stealing, fighting, and killing. I have already lost Owen's love to him. Now he seeks my life. Why? He has Elspeth's broad lands. Why does he need more? Aren't they enough for him?"

"Elin," Anna said sharply.

Her rage passed. She remembered who she was—mistress of the household. "Anna," she said. "Go fetch Godwin and Alfric."

Anna gathered her skirts and darted past her up the stairs and out into the yard. Elin had a few minutes to wait. She heard a buzzing sound and looked up. Flies were beginning to gather around the pile of vomit on the floor. Ine still slept. Elin tried not to think. Tried not to think about who would have so lightly taken the lives of the entire household.

Godwin stepped past her. He looked at the dog and then at the big stew pot and lastly at Ine. His face remained expressionless.

"Had we eaten the pork, we would all have died," Elin said.

"I know. Anna explained." Godwin turned to Alfric. "Go fetch Rosamund. Do it quietly. Don't alarm her."

Rosamund came bouncing down the cellar steps a few moments later, mop in one hand, bucket in the other. Elin stood next to Godwin, Anna beside the stew pot. Rosamund found herself surrounded by a ring of grim faces. She looked at the stew pot, the dead dog, and the unconscious Ine. She set the mop and bucket on the floor and turned to face Godwin.

He shifted his body until he was between her and the stair. His mouth was set into a tight line, his heavy-lidded, dark eyes fixed on her.

Elin saw the girl's face flush scarlet and her breast begin to rise and fall. "I didn't!" Rosamund screamed.

"We know," Godwin said. "Who did?"

She tried to dart past Godwin. He took her by the shoulder and pushed her back easily. Rosamund's face went perfectly white. She hissed like a snake, and a second later her knife was in her hand. Both of Godwin's hands moved. The right slapped away the knife, the left landed hard on her cheek.

She flew backward, landing upright against the pile of grain sacks against the wall. She stood frozen, staring at him, her hands knotted together against her skirt.

"Never pull a knife on me again, girl, or I'll show you how a knife is used. And no whining and whimpering. I didn't hit you that hard. Had I wished, I could have killed you. I want the truth, girl. Who is Elfwine's lover?"

"My lady!" Rosamund cried.

"Don't look to me for help, Rosamund," Elin said. "You knew about this, knew and didn't tell me." Elin was shocked by the raw fury she heard in her own voice.

"Ranulf would have killed her," Rosamund sobbed out. "No one cares what I do, but she's a man's wife."

"Yes," Godwin said. "Law and custom both allow a man to kill an adulterous wife. But it seems," he continued, nudging the dead dog with his toe, "adultery is the least of Elfwine's crimes. Rosamund, she meant to kill us all."

"No," Rosamund wailed. "No."

"Stop that, now." Godwin's voice cracked like a whip.

Rosamund gulped down her sobs, gasped, and said, "Rauching."

"Yes," Godwin said. "Pray continue."

"One of the widow's ladies saw her at the fortress. Then she brought something to Judith."

"What?" Godwin asked.

Rosamund shrugged. "Who knows? Judith isn't Routrude. She doesn't tell about her business. She's very close-mouthed when she's dealing with other people's secrets. My lady," Rosamund said, turning to Elin, hands out-stretched, pleading, "I don't like Elfwine, but I didn't want to see Ranulf kill her."

"No," Elin said wearily. "No, Anna and I didn't, either."

"A conspiracy of women," Godwin said coldly.

"Be fair, Godwin," Alfric said. "Who would have guessed Elfwine would do something like this?"

"She wouldn't have," Anna said quietly, "if it hadn't been for Rauching. He must have given her the poison. . . . I don't keep anything this powerful among my stores, and Lady Elin doesn't, either. He's the instigator, the real culprit."

Rosamund sidled along the wall toward Elin and cautiously took her hand. Elin realized she was standing rigid. Slowly, she forced herself to relax and took Rosamund in her arms. Rosamund closed her eyes and rested her head silently against Elin's breast.

"Will Ine recover?" Godwin asked.

"I think so," Elin answered coolly. "I believe Anna and I got to him in time."

"Thanks be to God," Alfric said. "Elfwine is not a murderer."

"Yes," Godwin said, looking at the ceiling, "but not for want of trying. Elfwine. Elin, I believe you and I should go up and get her. We'll have to decide what to do with her. Ranulf must be told."

"I'll tell him," Alfric volunteered.

"No, I will," Godwin said. "Rosamund, where is Elfwine?"

Rosamund pulled away from Elin. She sniffed once and wiped her nose with the back of her hand. Elin saw blood on her hand and realized Rosamund was bleeding a little from Godwin's blow. Elin remembered the girl's nose had been broken a few weeks ago during the attack on the city. Perhaps it wasn't completely healed yet.

"Godwin," Alfric said reproachfully. "You shouldn't have hit the child so hard."

Godwin looked at Rosamund for a moment, his eyes opaque, face expressionless. "Get her knife," he said to Anna.

Anna searched a moment, found the knife, and handed it to Godwin. He lifted Rosamund's hand and slapped the hilt of the knife into her palm.

"This," he said, holding the knife in the classic over-hand position pointed at his chest, "is tactically unsound."

Rosamund stared at him, cornflower blue eyes wide with shock.

"I'm giving you a lesson," he said. "Please pay attention."

She nodded quickly.

"Good. It's especially tactically unsound when the man is wearing a mail shirt like I am."

He bowed her hand and placed the knife in an under-hand position, pointed at his belly. "This is better, but still a dicey proposition if the man is armored. Better yet if you go lower and sink it into his groin. A knife blade there will give most men pause—possibly forever." He checked the sharpness of the blade gently with his thumb. "Very good," he said. "Did you put this edge on it?"

"Yes," she said proudly. "With a whetstone."

He placed the knife gently back in its sheath at her belt. "Don't," he roared, "draw the damned thing unless you are in mortal peril and plan to use it."

Rosamund scuttled hurriedly back toward Elin.

"And never, never try anything like that with me again. Understood?"

"Oh, yes. Yes. Yes," Rosamund said, hiding behind Elin.

"Good. Where is Elfwine?"

"In her room," Rosamund whispered. "Lying down. She said she felt weak."

"Anna, find some chains," Godwin ordered. "We'll have to confine her until we can decide what to do with her. Elin, come with me. We have a very unpleasant task ahead of us."

The next half hour was never very clear in Elin's memory. Elfwine must have known the moment they con-fronted her. She must have read the knowledge of her own guilt in their faces. The baby was in its cradle. Elfwine ran toward him, but Elin blocked her way. Elfwine flew at Elin, hands upraised like claws to tear at her face. Godwin caught her from behind and twisted her right arm up between her shoulder blades.

Elfwine began to scream. Not in pain, because Godwin wasn't hurting her any more than he had to in order to control her. She screamed in rage and hatred. She ignored Godwin's grip on her arm and poured out her venom on

Elin. The vengeful, concealed bile of a lifetime. The concentrated hatred and envy of the poor and powerless for those who, as they see it, have won the game of life and have all they desire.

Listening numbly, Elin knew she would remember Elfwine's screams, her rage, her despair for the rest of her life. She would remember and hear them echoing in the darkest of her nightmares. She had believed she hated, that she was vengeful. Now, as was, she thought, only fair, she had malice and hatred thrown back in her face. She saw the sheer ugliness and cruelty of them. And worst of all, the utter pointlessness and futility of repaying hatred for hatred and wrong for wrong.

Godwin ignored Elfwine's rage, and when her rage turned into hysterics and the hysterics into tears, he ignored those, too. He marched Elfwine down the stairs, still screaming, and into the cellar.

Anna had the chains fastened to one of the stone pillars that upheld the house. Anna and Elin searched Elfwine, removing anything she could use to harm herself or anyone else. Then they chained her hand and foot.

She was sobbing now, the deep gulping sobs of a child crying itself into exhaustion. She sat back against the stone post, hair over her face, and refused to answer any of Godwin's questions.

Alfric pulled a few of the grain sacks away from the wall and made himself a seat beside Elfwine. Then he took her in his arms.

"Alfric, I believe you would try to save the soul of the devil himself if it were in your power," said Godwin.

Alfric smiled up at Godwin, then looked sadly down at Elfwine. To Godwin's surprise, Elfwine rested her head in Alfric's lap and became quiet at last. He stroked her hair as her sobs eased away into silence.

Elin and the rest turned away and went upstairs into the hall. Elin sank down in Owen's carved chair and buried her head in her arms.

The knights, Gowen, Edgar, and Wolf the Short, came in, followed closely by Ingund. Godwin took them aside and acquainted them with the facts. He spoke in a low voice.

"My pork!" Ingund shouted. "She ruined my pork."

"Oh, for heaven's sake, Ingund!" Anna exclaimed. "Ine nearly died, Ranulf—I don't even want to think what this will do to Ranulf. And Rauching is still out there spinning his webs." She pulled the soup kettle away from the fire. "Here, you men, one of you take this and dump it in the river. And I wouldn't sample any of it if I were you. If Elfwine got to the stew, there's no telling what else she might have tampered with. I'll have to throw away every scrap of food in the house. So stop going on about your pork."

"Gowen, go dump the soup," Godwin said. "Edgar, go fetch Judith. Tell her the whole story and ask her to bring whatever Elfwine left with her to the hall. Ranulf is not going to believe any ill of his wife without proof—incontrovertible proof. I believe that proof may be in Judith's keeping."

Elin heard something. She raised her head, ignoring the voices around her in the hall. She glanced up at the ceiling toward Elfwine's room.

The rest looked at her face, and hearing the sound, they fell silent.

The sound she heard was a high thin wail. The baby. Crying for the comfort of his mother's arms and breast.

Weeping, Elin tried to stop her tears and found she couldn't. Then she tried to put her hands over her ears and blot out the infant's cries. She found she couldn't do that, either. They went on and on and on.

OWEN slapped the horse on the rump. It leaped forward into the crack Enar had opened into the rock. Owen and the forest people followed.

Enar landed on his hands and knees. The drop really wasn't that far, only a foot or so, but he had to scramble out of the way to avoid being trampled by the others. He could see very faintly by the light of the fire outside that he was crawling on a stone floor.

When they were all inside, Alshan caught him by the shoulders before he was fully on his feet and shook him. "Close the door, Saxon."

Enar rose and put his back against the rock. He could see smoke streaming in like a thick black veil. He hazarded a glance at the pool. The outer ring of oaks had caught and were blazing furiously. The tree trunks of the inner ring were spewing out clouds of scalding steam as the wood heated. A blast of air that felt like it came from the mouth of a furnace seared his face.

The little pond was a place of death. Smoke stung his eyes and half blinded him. He threw his shoulders against the rock and heaved. The rock shuddered and fell back into place.

Enar sank down on his heels, exhausted. Owen struck a light with flint and steel, and a torch flared in the darkness.

Enar looked up. "Gamaaa!" he exclaimed.

"What's wrong?" Owen asked.

Enar was halfway to his feet, hands covering his eyes, looking through his fingers. He realized Sybilla was studying him with a grin on her face. "Turn around slowly, Lord Christ Priest, and look behind you," Enar said.

Owen turned and gave a violent start and backed toward Enar. "We have come through hell to visit the dead."

Across from the door stood a low altar, only a thick, crudely squared block of stone. Above the stone, a dome had been chiseled out of the rock. They were ranged rank on rank around the dome. Not skulls, but the heads of men.

Owen drew closer. He felt something vibrate within him, a vibration like the lowest string on a harp set too loose when the pitch leaks sound and becomes something you cannot hear but only feel in your belly.

"Don't light them any better," Enar begged. "I don't want to see them so well."

The heads had evidently been exposed to some kind of preservative. Tight flesh still covered the blackened bone, but the lips were withered, drawn back, teeth set in the final smile. Here and there on those who'd weathered the ages best, eyes still gleamed in the eye sockets, flat and shimmering like stones. All were clouded with the mist of death, but it could still be seen that some were blue and others dark. Some heads still wore helmets with the deep cheek pieces Romans used. One near the center had a crested helm, the horsehair brush still in place, still scarlet.

Owen drew his sword and saluted them.

Enar clenched his teeth to keep them from chattering.

Sybilla doubled over laughing. "Saxon," she chortled, "you are the color of fresh milk."

Enar was annoyed. Sybilla had found him hysterically funny since a particular incident a few weeks ago when the women of her tribe had captured him and teased him. "I simply believe that the dead should keep to their own world and leave the living alone."

"They do," Sybilla said. "It is we who have invaded

their domain and ask their hospitality. Would you rather go back outside and fry?"

Enar half turned. He didn't feel right about turning his back on that dreadful altar, not completely. He placed his hand on the rock. It was warm. He didn't care to think about temperatures that could strike through two feet of solid stone. "We are best off. Where are we?" he asked.

"They will not disturb us," Alshan said, indicating the heads ringed around the altar. "The battles they fought took place long ago. The men who killed them are dust and one with their enemies. It no longer matters who won and who lost."

Owen sheathed his sword, turned away, and stood near Alshan. "I think it mattered at the time," he said. "Who were they?"

"Swordsmen. Romans, you call them," Alshan said. "The people you call Gauls did not yield their hearths easily to outsiders. The battle went on longer than men know. They fought from the forests and the mountains. Long their priests, the druids, walked among the trees and called the young men out to war. They hid here between battles and took the lives of those prisoners on that stone. They struck them down and read the future in their death struggles."

Enar shuddered. To be killed was one thing. To have one's death used in such a way, another. "This is a place of terror," he said. "I can feel it creeping into my bones."

"The heads of those who gave them favorable omens they placed above the altar," Alshan continued. "They feasted then and poured out oil and wine to their spirits. All men respect a brave enemy."

"They lost in the end," Enar said. "Let us be glad."

"I don't know," Alshan said. "They understood many things. The Romans understood nothing. Only conquest and loot. When their conquests ended, the Gauls died of sorrow."

"What did they understand?" Owen asked.

Alshan played with the jewel on his neck and looked up at the heads. "The distance between friend and enemy is not so great, and the dead walk always among the living, even as the living stretch out their hands to the yet unborn."

"The distance between Hakon and ourselves isn't nearly great enough," Enar said. "You have that right. We can wait till the fire outside burns itself out, then leave."

"No," Alshan said. "We can't."

Owen nodded. "Hakon will comb the burned-out forest, wanting, if nothing else, our charred bodies to assure him we're dead."

"We must go deeper into the earth," Sybilla said. "Try to find another entrance and slip away."

Alshan pointed to his left. "The cave widens out here. Follow me."

In the wider part of the cave, they found torches piled against the wall. Owen loaded them on the horse. He stood docilely enough and allowed himself to be made a packhorse.

At the end of the cave, a flight of shallow stone steps had been cut into the rock. The horse went up them like a mountain goat. The steps ended at a broad cut-rock path next to an underground river. It flowed slowly past, ink black, gleaming like obsidian in the torchlight.

"You knew this cave was here, didn't you?" Owen asked Sybilla and Alshan.

"We didn't," Sybilla said, pointing to Tigg and herself.

"Yes," Alshan said. "That's why I followed the horse. He was running in the right direction. I didn't want to come here. It is as the Saxon says, a place of terror and some—no, little evil. But"—he shrugged—"we had no choice."

"Why didn't you explain?" Enar asked.

"Oh yes, explain," Sybilla said. "Stop and argue with your fears while the fire reduced us to charcoal. It's as well he didn't explain. You might have turned and run right back into the flames."

"I might at that," Enar snarled. He could feel the darkness pressing in on him. The torches sputtered, sometimes burning high, at other times spitting, crackling, and almost going out. He was sure he saw things at the edges of his vision. Dark, hooded shapes that faded away when he swung the torch toward them. He felt the weight of the earth above his head, pressing down, ready to entomb them.

They followed the underground stream by torchlight for what seemed like a long time. Owen could tell that the path had been built and worked by men. He could see chisel marks on the limestone under his feet and places where obstructing rock ledges had been battered down.

Here and there heads had been placed in niches in the walls, perhaps as guardians. Owen saw the first not three feet away, a brown-haired man with a short beard. He jerked to one side so hard, he nearly went into the river. When he mastered himself, he stopped. He refused to let the fear that chilled his bones control him.

The other's beard and mustache covered the lipless mouth, giving the head an almost living appearance. The dark eyes were still intact. They had the dead crystalline appearance of a statue's eyes in the torchlight. Over the hair was the helmet of a Roman foot soldier.

"They liked to keep a lot of them around, didn't they?" Enar said nastily.

"That one marks a boundary, Saxon," Alshan said.

"Does he?" Owen asked. "What?"

"We are close to the end of the path."

"What then?" Enar asked.

Alshan shrugged. "No one knows."

"I don't find that reply comforting," Enar complained. He felt even less comfortable when the path they were following came to an abrupt end.

"This is as far as they penetrated into the cave," Alshan said.

The stream they were walking along went around another bend in the tunnel.

"Must we continue on?" Owen asked.

"Yes," Alshan replied. "Hakon's men will be swarming like angry bees around the river, and we no longer have the forest to protect us."

Enar decided to quarrel vigorously with this assessment. "We can outwait him."

"Not if it rains," Alshan answered. "When it does, this cave fills up with water. Not the top, but that won't matter to us. The current is fierce and the water icy cold. Why do you think they placed the heads so high?"

Enar made a strangled sound, and Owen's face looked grim in the ruddy torchlight. "I see," Owen said. "We're in a race against time. How deep is the water?"

"Now it will only just come to our knees. But, as I said, if it rains . . ."

Enar waded cautiously, leading the horse. The rest followed. Travel wasn't difficult for the first few miles, though the tunnel narrowed and the light from the torches no longer reached the ceiling. The streambed carved out over the centuries by the spring was smooth and offered good footing. They were all heartened by the fact that they seemed to be going slowly uphill. Closer to the surface, they hoped to find air and light.

But then abruptly the roof sloped down. Enar gritted his teeth and kept on going. Owen was so frightened he was nauseated. The forest people were very quiet.

Enar eased the horse past the narrowest place in the tunnel. The stallion went through, his flanks and withers rubbing the walls. The passage widened again and Owen realized they were standing in a big room—a gallery so large the torchlight couldn't find the roof or walls. The underground stream they'd been wading along ran through the center.

Owen strode forward, following the stream until he realized it simply vanished right into a stone wall. They had followed a blind tunnel and this was the end.

15

A FEW moments after the baby began to cry, Elin heard the sound of Denis's wooden leg moving around above her. He came downstairs, carrying the baby in one arm and a crossbow in the other. "Where's Elfwine?" he asked.

A knock came at the door and Godwin enlightened him while Elin went to the door.

Ranulf came into the hall. He stared around at the ring of shocked faces. "Elfwine," he cried, and ran for the stairs.

Godwin intercepted him. He stood in front of Ranulf, blocking his way, and took him by the arms. Ranulf stared up at Godwin. "I want your sword," Godwin said.

The boy began shaking. "She's dead," he said helplessly.

"I want your sword," Godwin repeated.

"If only she were," Ingund said bitterly.

Ranulf turned his stricken gaze toward her.

"Silence," Godwin roared. "I'll handle this. Your sword," he repeated.

Ranulf reached down and unbuckled the sword belt with quivering fingers.

"The knife, too," Godwin said, and took it. He put Ranulf's weapons on the table in front of Elin. He led Ranulf away, through the back door into the yard.

Outside, Elin heard Ranulf shout, "No!" She heard
Godwin's voice, murmuring. Ranulf shouted again. There
were no words in the cry, but Elin felt she heard it with
her whole body. It pierced her like a sword, and then there
was silence.

Rosamund began to cry. Ingund took the baby from
Denis. They all looked at Elin. She rose to her feet. Her
knees felt like liquid, as though they didn't want to hold
her up. She rested her hand on the back of the chair. "Is
the baby hungry?"

"No," Ingund said. "He just needs changing."

"Change him, then," Elin said. She turned to Anna.
"How is the bread?"

"We baked four days ago. I wouldn't think she was
able to get to it."

"The cheese?" Elin asked.

"You can tell when a cheese has been interfered with,"
Anna replied.

"So we have food for tonight?"

"Yes," Anna replied.

"Good. We can't send out for more. Not without bringing the whole town down on us." Rosamund still sat,
weeping quietly. Elin embraced her. "Hush," she said
softly. "Be still. It's going to be all right. I don't know
how, but I'm going to make it all right."

Rosamund quieted. They all went about their tasks
silently. The baby was changed, the suspect food disposed
of. Fresh cheese was cut and a new sausage was brought
out. Rosamund, her eyes red, her face still tear streaked,
set the table.

Elin looked at them going about their appointed tasks
and remembered her mother, Wilsa. Elin had heard her
story at her mother's knee. Wilsa had been rescued by
Elin's father, Roscius, when the forest people left the
crippled child to die. She had been only a serving girl in
his household when her father's first wife, Sophia, fell ill
with a wasting disease. All of Wilsa's skills learned from
the forest people were useless against the disease. But in
the end, as a reward for her efforts, Sophia sent Wilsa to

Roscius's bed. She told Wilsa that the life of the household must continue, and she knew Wilsa would never dishonor her.

Elin had not understood how Sophia could so easily turn her world over to another. Now she did. Men might have time to wallow in grief or allow themselves to be paralyzed by it, but women never. Too many needs had to be met on a daily basis. A child cried; it had to be fed. Meals must be scraped up. The washing done. Life went on, and women who were the guardians of life had to see its continuance. It was their burden and their honor, an endless responsibility.

They were almost ready to sit down and eat when Edgar entered with Judith. She carried a cloth-wrapped bundle in her hands.

"Go fetch Godwin," Elin said.

Wolf the Short left quickly. Godwin returned with Ranulf. The household silently gathered around the table. For a second, Elin met Ranulf's eyes. In them she saw blind, devastating grief. For a moment, Elin almost regretted that Elfwine's plan had not succeeded. Death would have been less cruel than this. Elin remembered Ranulf as he had been—a boy happy in his marriage, pleased at his progress in learning the military arts from Godwin, and overjoyed to have a newborn son. She looked into his eyes and knew she would never see that boy again.

Judith set the bundle on the table. It was sealed with the emblem of her father's house. "You understand, I yield this only under protest and at the urgent command of our warlord?"

"I do," Godwin said.

"Have done," Ranulf whispered in a barely controlled rage. "Open it."

Godwin fixed Ranulf with a hard eye. "Play the man," he said. "This is a matter of business to Judith."

"The business of our lives!" Ranulf cried out in agony.

"Even so," Godwin said. "We will observe the proper formalities. Open it, please, Judith."

Judith glanced at the somber faces around the table,

broke the seal, and opened the package. The gold necklace winked and glittered in the dim light of the hall.

"He did not buy her cheaply," Godwin said.

"No," Judith said. She lifted the necklace, weighed it with one hand, then valued the cabochon rubies with her eyes. "I should say at least the price of a manor or two, not to mention a fine house and perhaps a few slaves. She meant to do well out of this."

"I suppose," Judith continued, "it belongs to Ranulf now."

"I don't want to touch the dirty thing," Ranulf said between his teeth.

"I wouldn't say so," Judith murmured ironically. "Gold is the cleanest metal I know. It never rusts. Blood rolls off it."

The necklace passed from hand to hand, down the table until it fell with a heavy sound in front of Ranulf. He sat down on the bench and buried his face in his hands.

Alfric let himself into the hall through the back door. He approached Godwin and stood at his shoulder. "I have been talking to Elfwine," Alfric said. "She tells me she never intended to poison us."

"No?" Godwin said. "What, then, did she intend to do?"

"It seems Rauching spun her some wild tale about putting us all to sleep while he let Hakon's men into the city."

"She can't possibly have believed that," Ranulf said bitterly. "What did she think the crossbowmen at the walls and near the fortress would do if Hakon's men tried to sneak into the city?"

Godwin sighed. "You wouldn't have believed it. I wouldn't have believed it, either. But she's a woman, and not a very smart one."

"I suppose," Judith said, "that the question is what do we do with Elfwine now?"

"We?" Elin asked softly.

Judith glanced defiantly at her from the corner of her eye. "Yes, we."

Godwin, however, chose to let Judith's implicit inclusion pass. "Ranulf is her husband. It's his right to speak first."

Ranulf lifted his head. Ingund was still holding the child. "Give me the baby," he said.

Ingund placed the infant in his hands. He cradled it between his palms and looked down at the sleeping face, the closed eyes with the tiny blond eyelashes resting on its cheeks. The small, clenched fists. He glanced up at Anna.

"Is it mine?" he asked.

"Mercy of God!" Anna exclaimed. She raised her eyes to heaven and pressed her palms together as if praying. "What a question. Yes, if the gossips are right, and usually they are, it's yours. She conceived only a few weeks after meeting you, and everyone was sniggering about how well behaved she became after snaring the bishop Owen's servant."

"We can find a wet nurse for him," Ingund said stonily.

"I suppose so," Anna said. "But even the best wet nurse won't care the way its mother would."

"Find a wet nurse for the babe," Gowen said, "and kill the wench."

"No," Wolf the Short said.

Elin was surprised to hear the blond Saxon knight speak up. "If you must have done with the mother, have done with the child, too. My mother was similarly cast away by my father. I grew up to hate him. This child will live to hate you, too."

Ranulf handed the child back to Ingund. "Don't bring him near me again for a time. I am too filled with grief and rage. I might dash out his brains. It was well that Godwin took away my weapons. I might have taken all three of our lives. Hers, the child's, and mine. Perhaps I still should." He began to weep again, softly, hopelessly.

Alfric sat down beside him and let Ranulf's head rest on his shoulder.

"I don't see," Judith said, "how you can do anything to Elfwine. At least not without creating such a broil that it will rend this city asunder." There was a murmur of protest from the table. Judith continued inexorably. "Elfwine's brothers will not believe this tale of poisoning. They will say Ranulf, having been honored by the dignity of knighthood by Lord Godwin, became displeased with

Elfwine because she was of humble stock, and wanted to put her away and find himself a wife with more property.

"My lord Godwin, Rauching has been whispering his lies into their ears for days now. Your influence is hanging by a thread. Some will side with you, but many will side with Elfwine's brothers. If the townspeople begin fighting among themselves now, the thread will snap. Punish Elfwine, privately or publicly, and you will play right into Rauching's hands. You might as well turn the town over to Hakon."

When Judith finished speaking, dead silence fell in the hall.

"It seems," Elin said, "we have a decision to make."

"I'll be her advocate if you like," Alfric said.

"Speak then," Elin said.

Alfric still embraced Ranulf. He lifted his ravaged face from the small man's shoulder. "I don't want her to suffer," Ranulf said softly. "Please, Elin, don't make her suffer, whatever you do."

"No, Ranulf," Elin said, taking his hand. "No, I promise she won't suffer."

Ranulf rested the back of Elin's hand against his cheek. She could feel the dampness of his tears.

"Don't be a fool," Ingund said to Elin. "Leave her to me—and Anna. Some of the stew is still left in the pot. She seasoned it. It's only fair she eats it."

Godwin was silent. He stood a little apart, hand on his sword hilt, watching Elin narrowly.

Alfric disengaged himself from Ranulf. "My lady," he said. "The girl believed Rauching's lies. She's young, inexperienced—little more than a child. She must have been putty in the hands of a man like Rauching. He supplied the poison. He—" Godwin began to laugh. "Please," Alfric said. "Not right in my face."

"You will drag the Vices in chains at the car of mercy, won't you, Alfric," Godwin said.

"I suppose you could put it that way," Alfric said. "The girl is sorry."

"Elfwine," Ingund said, biting each word off as she spoke, "is sorry she was caught. She is sorry we are not all dead. She is sorry we will punish her one way or another."

"Yes," Alfric said, smiling sweetly. "She has a number of reasons for penitence. Those are a few."

"Alfric," Anna said. "I'm glad to see that though you're a good man, you're not a complete fool."

Someone banged on the door. "Oh no," Elin said. "Can Routrude have got wind of this already?"

"You can be sure she has got wind of something. Half the town heard Elfwine screaming. The news of a commotion in your house preceded Edgar's arrival at my counting house," Judith said.

Godwin pointed to the gold necklace still resting on the table. "Get that thing out of sight at once."

Anna scooped up the necklace, put it on the sideboard, and covered it with a cloth.

Godwin walked to the door and threw it wide. Elfwine's father and three brothers stood there. Behind them, as supporters, curiosity seekers, and spectators, stood half the town. Principally the male half, though Routrude and her usual beer-soaked entourage of tavern sots were in conspicuous attendance. Elfwine's father shifted his feet and would not meet Godwin's eyes.

"Yes?" Godwin asked.

Elfwine's father was a tall man, muscular and work hardened and weatherbeaten. Every muscle, vein, and sinew seemed to stand out on his body in the torchlight. His skin had the slightly oily tinge of one who doesn't bathe much. His blond hair had long ago gone silver gray.

Elin was horrified to realize she didn't even know his name.

Godwin wasn't about to make it any easier for them. "What is your business with this household?" he asked.

"My lord." Elfwine's father shifted his feet and backed into his oldest son. The young man stood his ground, glaring at Godwin. "My lord." Elfwine's father cleared his throat and continued, "We have heard evil reports of my daughter's husband, Ranulf."

"What reports?" Godwin asked forbiddingly. "And from whom?"

Elfwine's father glanced down and across the square at Rauching. He stood a little apart from the rest, surrounded by a dozen of the farmers the siege had forced into the city. Rauching was smiling. But the men surrounding him looked truculent and defiant. Two of Rauching's servants stood near him. One of them was the young man Elin remembered. The other was older. He swayed where he stood and looked drunk.

"We have heard," Elfwine's father continued, "that her husband has rejected her and plans to put her away, believing she is no longer good enough for him. We have heard today he beat her and even now she is imprisoned."

Elin walked toward the door. She heard a rustling behind her and realized the entire household was stepping up with her like a wall.

"Well he should," Rauching shouted from where he was standing. "This bishop keeps a most irregular house, and its women would make the widow's ladies blush."

There was a shout of laughter from the men around Rauching. Godwin noticed it wasn't echoed by the rest of the people in the square.

Elin felt the blood drain from her face.

"These are very serious charges," Godwin said quietly, his eyes on Rauching and the men around him.

Rauching strode out of the group of men he was standing with and stood in front of them. "For a godly house, the bishop harbors a most ungodly bunch of sluts."

"Sluts," Elin heard Ingund whisper between her teeth.

"Liar!" Ranulf screamed. "Take a step forward and I will prove it on your body."

"Be silent!" Godwin roared.

"No!" Ranulf shouted back at him.

It was plain to Elin that the boy's grief had turned to rage. She turned toward Ranulf, who was behind her, but Godwin, as usual, was faster. He spun and stretched Ranulf out on the floor with one blow. Dazed, the boy blinked up at him.

"Are you my man?" Godwin asked.

"Yes, yes," Ranulf stammered.

"Then show it by obeying me. Be silent."

Ranulf got slowly to his feet. Edgar put one hand under his arm and helped him.

Elin faced Rauching again. All over the square, people were lighting torches. In the increasing glow, Elin watched Rauching. She saw him turn to the men behind him and murmur a few soft words. Elin sensed something hung in the balance. The wrong move by either party could tip the scales.

She turned to Ingund and spoke in an undertone. "Go get Elfwine and tell her if she wants to live, to hold her peace, to be silent." Elin could feel and see the entire town watching her.

Rauching, emboldened by what he saw as the support of his own party, spoke up again. "Sluts," he shouted. "Sluts, every one."

Elin heard Anna's breath exhale in a hiss behind her.

"Look at them," Rauching continued. "The smith's daughter, Ingund, consorting with an adventurer, a man from God knows where. She calls herself his wife? I'm told she showed scant courtesy to her father before the wedding. The housemaid, Rosamund, tumbles the knights for pay. The Lady Elin has a bun in the oven and no one can really say if the good bishop is the baker. Anna . . ."

Now Rauching turned to his followers. He winked and nudged the nearest in the ribs. "She's too old to offer much sport, but no doubt she's able to instruct the younger ones in vice."

At this moment, Ingund arrived holding Elfwine by the arm. The girl looked blank and detached as though she were in shock. Ingund pushed through the household crowded around the door and came up to stand beside Elin.

"At last!" Rauching shouted. "The beautiful Elfwine. The lady I saw disporting herself with two of my servants—not one, my friends," he shouted at the people in the square, "but two. Two," he repeated, holding up two fingers, "at the same time."

A brief volley of uneasy laughter swept the men surrounding Rauching, then died away. The square was silent except for the hissing cressets in the hands of the people. Elfwine fainted. For once, Elin didn't think she was dramatizing herself. The girl's fair skin was ashen, her lips blue. Elin could feel that her own face was bloodless, not with shock, but with rage.

"The accusation is public," Elin said. "So, we will refute it publicly. Tomorrow, Elfwine, who is a true wife, will carry the hot iron three times around the bishop's chair. Here, before everyone in the entire city."

"And it will burn her to the bone!" Rauching screamed. "Painted little harlot that she is."

Elin began backing into the hall. Godwin and the knights followed. Godwin was the last in, and he slammed the double doors behind them and dropped the bar. Ingund half dragged and half carried Elfwine to the bishop's chair at the head of the table. She sat, blond head lolling like a broken flower.

"Sluts. He called me a slut," Ingund said.

"Don't feel singled out," Anna said. She walked to the fire, added another log, and poked at the flames with a piece of kindling. "I fared no better. Neither did Lady Elin."

"Anna," Ingund said, slumping on one of the benches beside the table, "was I a bad wife? Was it my fault they died?"

Anna sighed heavily. "No."

"Who died?" Elin asked.

"Her whole family," Anna answered. "Nearly the entire town knows the story, but it was before your time."

Elin walked toward Ingund and rested her hands on her shoulders.

"Rauching may have done himself some harm by including Ingund in his accusations," Anna continued.

Ingund raised her head in the firelight. Elin could see the tears sprinkle her cheeks. "When I was sixteen I wed a farmer," Ingund said. "We were very happy. We had three children." Her teeth ground together and she was silent.

Anna's voice took up the tale. "They lived together with his parents and two of his sisters. Ingund and her husband had one of the best farms in the valley. Until the plague came.

"Gunter became alarmed when a few weeks had passed

and none of the family had been seen in the city. He visited the farm. Gunter found . . . they were all dead. It was clear she'd tended every one of them to the very last. Some she'd been able to bury, some she . . . hadn't.

"He found her on the kitchen floor in labor with her fourth child. Gunter carried her back to the city. She was not well in her mind. The child was a stillborn, a girl."

"Don't be so nice, Anna," Ingund said. "I was mad. And was wandering in my wits for a long time thereafter. In the end I came back to myself. My father let me do what I liked. Maybe a little too much. He spoils me. He felt if Enar was what I wanted, I should have him. I believe my father is now Rauching's bitter enemy."

Elin couldn't think of anything to say. She lowered her head and pressed her cheek against Ingund's. Her hands tightened their grip on Ingund's shoulders.

"Sluts," Ingund whispered. "Tomorrow I will kill him."

"No," Godwin said. "You won't. I will. Elin, I believe you have put Rauching right where I want him. Can Elfwine carry that iron?"

Elfwine was waking up; color was coming back into her cheeks. "I can't . . ." she whimpered. "I can't. . . . Please, don't make me."

Elin turned away from Ingund and walked toward Elfwine. Her face was like the fall of night. She caught Elfwine by the chin and jerked her head up. The girl's eyes were wide and unfocused. "You can and you will. I'll show you how."

Elfwine screamed and slapped Elin's hands away. She struggled to her feet, oversetting the chair behind her. "I can't!" she screamed. "I can't! I'm guilty!" she shrieked.

Ranulf strode out of the shadows past Elin. Whatever remained of youthful sweetness was gone from his face. Elin knew it would never return. He was a disillusioned man. He seized Elfwine, his hands closing into fists on her upper arms. He shook her violently. "You are my wife." He spat out the words between his teeth. "My wife," he repeated, and shook her again.

Elfwine's eyes were glazed, her jaw slack with terror.

"Yes," he continued in the same terrible voice. "You

are guilty. Guilty as Lucifer, guilty as Judas. But you are my wife, and I will not let Rauching take anything of mine. You will do as Lady Elin tells you and as I tell you—forever more." Ranulf's hands tightened. "Do you hear me?" he roared.

"Yes!" Elfwine screamed.

"You will obey."

"Yes. Yes. Yes," Elfwine howled. "I will. Before God, I will."

Ranulf opened his fingers deliberately and let her go. She collapsed, sobbing, in a heap on the floor. Ranulf drew back one fist as if to backhand her across the face.

"No," Godwin said. "Enough. She will probably never disobey you again."

Ranulf's hand dropped. "Yes," he said quietly. "I believe you're right. I had hoped things would be otherwise between us, but I see it was never meant to be."

"Do you know why I silenced you in the square?" Godwin asked.

"Yes. If I had tried to do anything to Rauching, his followers would have clubbed me down."

"Just so," Godwin said. "We weren't ready for him. But we will be tomorrow. When Rauching arrives to view the little spectacle Lady Elin has arranged, he will find he has walked into a trap."

Alfric tried to comfort a sobbing Elfwine. "Alfric, you will say mass in the cathedral and bless the bishop's ancient throne. Then we will carry it in procession to the square," Godwin said. "While the procession is coming out of the church, Denis, I want you to choose the most reliable of the archers and lead them to the upper windows of the bishop's house. When Elfwine is finished carrying the iron . . . ." Godwin turned to Elin. "I trust she will be able to carry the iron successfully?"

"She will," Elin answered.

"Very well. When Elfwine is finished carrying the iron, you, Alan, and Denis will open fire on Rauching and his men. Kill as many of them as possible."

"My God," Elin said. "The men with Rauching are farmers. They come from the villages around the city.

They have friends and have been among the townsfolk. You will create bitter division among us."

"What would you have me do, Elin?" Godwin asked.

"Let me deal with Rauching."

Godwin sat down in his chair before the fire. "Can you?" he asked.

"I think so," Elin said.

Rosamund stood at the sideboard, cutting bread. "Rosamund, what do you think of Rauching?" Elin asked.

Knife in hand, Rosamund turned and faced her. "His words were a scourge. I felt them on my body. I had no choice about my life. I was but thirteen when I was sold into dishonorable slavery."

"Stop weeping on the board, girl," Anna said. "None of us loves Rauching. Elin, what do you have in mind?"

"You'll see in the morning," Elin said. "Godwin, I beg you, have Denis stay his hand unless all else fails."

"Ranulf?" Godwin asked. "You are the offended party. The choice is yours."

Ranulf took Elin's hand and gazed into her eyes. His heartbroken face was almost more than she could bear. She reached up and touched his cheek. "I'm so sorry, Ranulf," she whispered.

"Lady Elin, I could have forgiven her for Rauching. It would have been difficult, but I could have done it. What I can't forgive is her trying to kill us. I can't believe she didn't know what Rauching really intended. I want to believe it, but I can't. Oh, God, I can't. What shall I do?"

Godwin answered. "Live with her and try to turn her into some semblance of a human being. When you claimed her as a wife before the entire town, you broke her will to resist you. I've seen it done before. Never with such speed and brutality. It is as I said: she will not disobey you again. That may be all you can ever hope for from her. Maybe with time and mercy you will get more. But for the child's sake at least, bear the pain. Play the man."

Ranulf let Elin's hand drop. He stepped back. "I will do as you ask, Lady Elin," he said. "I'm loath to kill any, except Rauching. I hate him and with good cause." As he turned and walked away, Elfwine threw herself at his feet sobbing. Ranulf stepped back as if contaminated by her touch. She collapsed, moaning facedown on the floor.

Ranulf looked at her for a few heartbeats. There was nothing left in his face besides despair. Alfric gathered up Elfwine and hurried her away.

Chapter

16

OWEN approached the far wall of the cave, torch held high. The stream seemed to trickle between a crack in the rocks into a pool on the floor. Enar followed him across the cave. The rest came with him.

Alshan dropped down on his heels beside the pool and stared into the black water. Sybilla seized a torch and began circling the room, looking for a side entrance. Tigg dropped down beside Alshan.

"There is still time for us to retrace our steps and return the way we came," Enar said hopefully.

"No, there isn't," Alshan said quietly. "Can't you see?" He pointed down to his feet. "We were dry shod only a moment ago."

Owen stared down in horror at the floor. It was true; the pool was widening. Owen glanced around for the second time tonight, prey to blind panic. His mind added up the facts bleakly. This room would become a whirlpool exiting into the tunnel they'd just passed. The five of them couldn't possibly survive until the water level fell again. The current would be too rapid, the water too cold. Even if they could keep afloat for a time, in the end, exhaustion and the frigid water would finish them.

Enar clutched at the neck of his shirt, his eyes tightly closed. Owen realized he was trying to master his terror.

Sybilla returned carrying the torch. "Nothing."

The horse, perhaps sensing their fear, whinnied loudly. The sound echoed like a thunderclap against the stone. Enar's eyes opened, and the four of them looked at him.

"There is," Owen said, "one last chance. I don't plan to die without trying it."

He dived into the pool. The weight of his mail shirt and sword took him to the bottom immediately, but the weight gave him some purchase against the current trying to beat him back. He swam strongly forward. When he opened his eyes, he realized the water was shallow. He could just barely see by the light of the torches in the hands of his friends above. Before him, a black hole gaped.

He plunged forward and went in. The current buffeted him, taking him to the ceiling of the tunnel. He realized he was going down into a siphon. He could feel the pressure against his ears. His lungs hurt, burned. But he hauled himself down into the siphon doggedly. Dragged down by the weight of his sword and armor, his hands pressed against the slimy ceiling, he made his way slowly.

It was a shock when the current let go. He had passed the bottom of the siphon and was on the other side. The chain mail held him down. Terror gripped him like a vise. He felt his bladder empty itself.

Even without his volition, his hands tore at the hauberk. He needed air. God, he needed air. His feet scrabbled for purchase on the bottom, and he stood upright, trying to tear his hauberk off over his head.

Owen sucked in a breath of sweet air through his mouth and nose so violently that he almost strangled on the water dripping down over his face from his hair. He was standing in no more than two feet of water in another cave. His head spun and there was a roaring in his ears. It took him a second to comprehend what it was. Rain. He was standing only thirty feet from the mouth of a cave. Outside, the rain poured down.

Light, there was too much light. He cleared his eyes with his fingers and saw a lone figure beside the pool, holding a torch. Owen saw by his clothing that he must be one of the forest people he'd never seen before. A boy.

"A rope!" he roared. "Have you a rope? The cave on the other side is filling fast!"

The other didn't hesitate. He ran toward the entrance to the cave and returned with a length of plaited rawhide rope. A few dark stalagmites ringed the pool. Owen tied the rope to one of them. Then he unbuckled his sword and laid it on the ground.

He shook all over with terror and cold. The temptation to stay where he was was overwhelming. He knew if he let himself think too long, he would never master his fear. If he went back, he might not be able to return. The current might already be too strong.

He picked up one end of the rope and plunged into the water. The journey back was quick. The weight of his hauberk sent him down like a rock, and the current shot him into the other cave like a cork.

He hit the bottom of the pool running. He bolted out of the pool on his feet. The water at the bottom of the cave was ankle deep. Enar and the forest people surrounded him with joyous cries.

"What's on the other side?" Alshan shouted.

"A way out," Owen gasped. "Grab the rope. You have to pull yourself down for a few feet, but then the passage widens and the current is not so swift. Hurry. More and more water is pouring into the cave by the minute. The current is growing stronger and stronger. In a few minutes, there will be no escape."

Alshan ran and wedged his torch into a crack in the rock. The three forest people plunged into the pool and were gone. Owen snatched at the horse's bridle and led him into the pool. He tied the end of the rope to the hackamore.

They stood knee-deep in the water now. The whole bottom of the cave was filled, and it was beginning to swirl round and round, ominously. Within no more than a few minutes, the cave would be a whirlpool of death.

"You go first," Owen said to Enar. "All you need do is follow the rope down. When the current lets go, swim for it."

Enar stood where he was, frozen eyes empty. "Lord

Christ Priest," he said softly, almost apologetically. "I cannot swim."

There wasn't time to argue. Owen flexed his fingers and knotted them together. He brought the doubled fist hard up under Enar's chin.

The Saxon's head jerked, his eyes glazed, and his knees buckled. Before he could fall, Owen had his neck in the crook of his elbow and both hands on the rope. He pulled himself down, hand over hand. His lungs were burning again. Light flashed before his eyes. Enar's body was a dead weight. The current now seemed almost a malevolent living thing, trying to tear Enar away from him. Then he felt the current quiet for a second as the turbulence decreased.

Owen knew something upstream must have dammed the flow. He seized Enar by the scruff of the neck and pushed him forward. He could see the torches through the water and Enar's body drifting upward when a rush of mud and rock carried by the water took him full in the face and blinded him, sweeping him back the way he had come, into the siphon and the water-filled cave beyond.

Darkness. Owen stood gasping for breath on the other side. The light was gone. The torch Alshan had slipped into the rocks had been drowned by the rising stream.

The cave was waist deep in water now. The rope was gone. It had been torn from his grip when he was plunged back into the cave.

Darkness. The horse reared and screamed. The echoes confused him. One end of the rope was tied to the bridle. The rope would be tight, he knew. The forest people would be on the other side. He knew they wouldn't abandon the horse or him without a fight. But how to find the horse and the rope in this absolute blackness?

He could still hear the muffled thud of hooves on stone. Owen reckoned there was one chance. If he stood frozen like Enar, he would surely drown. He plunged into the water, his hauberk weighing him down as he swam along the bottom into the current. The horse screamed again. Hooves seemed to pound the stone floor all around him.

Owen surfaced to get a breath of air. The horse snorted

and struggled again as it was dragged into the deeper water.

Owen's whole body shook with cold, the absolute terror of death and sheer fatigue. He knew he could dive again, but one more time was all he had in him. If he didn't find the rope and the horse, he would die there.

Darkness, he thought, but he would dive one more time for Elin.

Owen took a deep breath. In the darkness, the only thing he could be sure about was the direction of the current. It pounded against his chest. He swam directly into it.

Sounds were louder underwater. Abruptly the crash of the horse's hooves against the stone floor stopped, and he realized the forest people must at last have pulled the animal into deeper water.

Owen lunged forward and something brushed his face. For a second, he fought the entangling strands until he understood it was the horse's tail. Then he grabbed on. A hoof lashed out, gouging Owen's hip, but he clung like grim death. His head banged lightly against stone, sending a scattering of sparks before his eyes. And Owen knew they must be in the tunnel between the two caves. He was lost in silence and darkness. All he could feel was the pounding in his temples, the burning in his lungs, and the turbulence created by the violently struggling animal in front of him.

Owen locked his fingers in the coarse tangle of the stallion's tail and prayed. As if in mocking answer to his prayer, one of the stallion's hooves caught him hard in the belly. The little air remaining in his lungs poured out in a rush. *So this is death,* he thought as his numbed fingers slipped free of the precarious handhold. A second later he saw light. An eddy brought him to the surface.

The whirlpool at the entrance to the other cave spun Owen wildly. His body was numb. His arms and legs didn't seem to belong to him. He could see Enar and the forest people standing on the shore, torches in their hands. One of them shouted and pointed. They formed a human chain.

Owen felt the suction pulling him down. But a second

later, an iron grip closed on his wrist. The sucking whirl-pool let go with a snap. He was almost flung away by the force of the pouring water, and he was towed ashore. Gasping, retching, and vomiting, he staggered toward the gray light at the entrance to the cavern. The rest followed.

In the other room, the stallion waded out of the swiftly filling pool. He stamped once and snorted in fury. Then he lunged forward at a gallop past Owen and the forest people and out into the rain.

Owen vomited again, emptying more water out of his belly.

"I can't say I blame him," he gasped. "If I could, I'd run, too."

A half hour later, they were sitting around a fire just inside the mouth of the cave with warm blankets wrapped around them, sipping some sort of soup Sybilla managed to put together.

"What's in it?" Enar asked, eyeing the bowl in his hand suspiciously.

Owen fished a mussel out of the bowl with his fingers and ate it.

"You don't want to know," Sybilla said.

"No, I don't," Enar said.

"No," Owen said. "The less I think about certain things, the better it is. Shut up and eat."

Enar fished something out of his bowl and squinted at it appraisingly. "Looks like a small octopus," he said.

"It is a small octopus," Sybilla said as she removed the dangling object from Enar's fingers and swallowed it.

Enar shuddered.

"Where are we?" Owen asked.

"In Amajorkia. Brittany, you call it," Sybilla said. "Near the green mound. The tomb where the king gifted you with your sword belt."

Owen remembered. He had fled Hakon's captivity here and sheltered in a chamber tomb. Owen looked down at the golden belt at his waist.

"I think he calls you back, that king," Alshan said.

Owen stood up and walked to the door. It was dusk, made all the deeper by the rain still pouring down.

Behind him, most of the inner cave was submerged. Their fire burned in the other one near the entrance. Owen's whole body ached. He relaxed and rested his shoulder against the rock as he peered through the thick tangle of creepers obscuring the cave mouth.

"Any chance of Hakon finding us here?" he asked.

"No," Alshan said.

"Your people found us," Owen said.

Sybilla chuckled. "Oh, that one," she said. "If you think I'm secretive and elusive, I meet my match here. She knows the caves and has explored all of them. She believed that since we were frightened by the fires she saw in the distance, we might flee underground away from them."

"She," Owen said, puzzled. "I thought her a he, a boy."

"More boy than girl," Tigg said.

"Something other than either one," Alshan said.

Enar fished some meat out of his stew and eyed it suspiciously.

"Chicken," Sybilla said. "Someone left two of them near one of our offering stones. They were scrawny and tough. I put them in with the rest."

Enar drank off the remainder of the liquid in his stew and began carefully inspecting the morsels in the bottom. "How can someone not be a man or woman?" he complained. "Every person I ever met was either man or woman."

"You never met any people like us before, have you?" Sybilla asked.

"No," Enar replied. "And I can't say I've always enjoyed the experience."

"Boy or girl," Owen asked, "can she catch the horse? Tomorrow I plan to turn and try to reach my father's stronghold again."

Alshan rose. "Yes, she will catch the horse. And she will return in the morning to tell us when she's hidden him. But you won't go to your father's house."

Owen was silent. He studied Alshan thoughtfully. "Remember the sword belt," Alshan said.

Owen looked down. He was used to wearing it by now. It was a mass of fine chain in graduated colors of gold, white, yellow, and red secured by inlaid latch knots along its length. Owen remembered the dead king in the tomb. He had made an offering to the king, and the sword belt slid from the bier a moment later.

"Gift or theft?" he asked Alshan.

"Gift," Alshan said. "We touched none other of his treasure. He wanted you to have it and be his man. Now he has summoned you. He has something for you to do."

Chapter

17

*E*LSPETH woke early. She'd watched the fire last night in terror lest the wind change and destroy the villages surrounding her stronghold.

She'd stood with the rest of her people on the earthen rampart behind the palisade surrounding her fortress. Stood clutching one of the sharpened stakes and watching the flames leaping above the trees in the distance. Along with the smell of wood smoke, she had smelled the stench of fear. Theirs and her own.

Hakon's men massed in the center of the bailey. They were roasting the carcasses of three deer and two pigs taken in flight from the flames. They ignored her fear and that of her people, saying they were ready to start backfires should the wind change and bring the fire near her villages.

When some of her people lamented the destruction, the Vikings laughed and said that there would be all the more freshly cleared land along the riverbanks for the spring planting.

The faces of Elspeth's people grew grimmer and grimmer as the fire raged on. She knew why. In the hall they ate beef, venison, duck, and chicken, not to mention other wild game taken in the hunt. But in the villages, her minions, the peasants, depended on the pigs that foraged in the woods for the winter supply of meat.

At length the rain began. It was only a fine mist at first, but then it became stronger and stronger. Hakon's men took their cooked meat and retreated into the stable. Some made signs against the evil eye. Others, the Christians among them, began to cross themselves and say the witch at Chantalon was interfering to protect her lord, the bishop.

But Elspeth stood for a long time, letting the rain run down her face and soak into her mantle and linen dress, feeling the icy touch of winter against her skin. It was the cool, clean feel of heaven's beneficence. Elspeth hated fire, but wasn't that what Hakon was? A fire lit in her body. A fire that wouldn't be quenched by any earthly rain. Fire.

Now, as she stood looking over the wall of her stronghold, she remembered the fire she'd seen from the road.

She spurred her horse to full speed at the sight of the glow through the trees against the sky. The men accompanying her held back, afraid their horses might slip on the icy road, afraid they might ride into an ambush if the stronghold were under attack.

But she galloped forward, heedless of the danger, thinking only of the children. She hadn't thought of Reynald at all.

She dismounted, running. The big double doors of the hall stood open. The overturned benches and tables showed the signs of precipitous flight. The air was gray with smoke, smoke that stank horribly.

Reynald had always been so strong. Perhaps that was why she found her way to his room first, calling his name wildly. She stumbled over the heavy oak bed frame. Hot as the fire was, the wood hadn't burned through, and as the heat from the smoldering oak seared her ankle, she looked down.

He was recognizable, just recognizable. She realized that afterward, but she hadn't known what she was looking at until she saw the teeth and eyes. Teeth gleamed where the flesh of the lips had burned away. The eyes were baked to a muddy orange by the heat of the fire and stared up at her from the charred timbers of the bed.

Elspeth's throat closed. She couldn't even scream. The next thing she remembered was standing in the hall, screaming for her children. The rasp of the smoke in her throat and lungs turned her screams into harsh, croaking sounds. She fell to her knees, gasping for clean air near the floor.

"Mama?"

Eric crouched in the shelter of one of the heavy trestles, his arms protectively around his sisters.

"Mama?" he whispered as she clutched them all against her body in desperate relief.

"Mama, don't be angry."

This brought her back to her senses. Sobbing, she wrapped them in her heavy mantle and hustled them outdoors.

The dozen or so men she'd left to care for Reynald were gone, the lure of his treasure box having proven too much for them.

Bertrand raved so violently at those who remained that the women fled, and the men began to mutter angrily among themselves, threatening to desert her also.

In terror now for the safety of Eric and the two girls, Elspeth used her jewelry to bribe the soldiers. She knew what a pathetic figure she cut, standing in the bitter cold, the icy rain dampening her hair and soaking her tattered, golden dress, the children clinging round-eyed to her skirts.

Bertrand completed her humiliation by turning on her, calling her a weak, shallow fool for spending what little of her substance remained on these lazy cowards.

But her gold, distributed so lavishly, brought at least a small measure of temporary loyalty. The men formed a united front against Bertrand, who retired to the relative comfort of the church outside the walls.

A freeholder called Niethered took command. He conducted Elspeth and the children to the stable, making beds for them in the straw of the loft. He undertook the dismal task of entering the hall to cover Reynald's body and get enough food and drink for a modest supper.

Elspeth ate nothing. She fed the children and bedded

them down for the night. She did her best to control herself before the children, but once they slept she gave herself up to the tidal wave of despair that welled up from the
bottom of her heart. She crouched, shivering and weeping, in the straw until near midnight.

The storm outside blew itself out as did her grief, and
she lay there, staring up at a few scattered stars that shone
through the broken chinks in the roof. She was too numb
to plan, to think.

Eric struggled in his sleep, cried out, and kicked off the
covers. Elspeth abandoned her own despair to go to him,
lying down beside him in the straw and taking the small
body in her arms. He didn't awaken. Whatever nightmare
troubled his slumber passed. He breathed evenly again as
he slipped into deeper sleep.

But she lay quietly for a long time holding him, brushing the downy dark hair with her fingers, inhaling the
sweet, innocent scent of his child's body.

The girls were too young to understand what had happened, and Elspeth was thankful for that. But Eric was
seven; she couldn't be sure how much he'd seen of
Reynald's death, how much he knew.

Her arms tightened around him. He squirmed, independent even in his sleep, and moved away. Of all the children, he was so much like her there seemed nothing of
Reynald about him. He was dark-haired as she was, but
with the same creamy, fair skin and brown eyes. She
believed he shared much of her own gentle nature and had
feared for him, knowing that he must leave her soon, to be
given into the care of strangers and begin his training for
manhood.

She worried less about the girls. Even at three years
they were growing into stocky, mischievous editions of
Reynald, blessed with the same interior toughness that
he'd had.

She looked over at them, heaped together, sleeping
comfortably as puppies wrapped in a downy comforter.
Eric, curled in a ball at her side, was rolled up in the fur-
lined mantle she'd worn to the city.

From below she could hear the hushed voices of the

men who tended the fire. Its light made a gentle shadow play on the slanted roof beams above. She stared up at it and the distant stars beyond.

A new terror entered her dull mind. Soon Niethered and the rest would realize her lands and person could easily go to the strongest among them. She wondered if they weren't already eyeing each other, estimating strengths and weaknesses, ready to begin jockeying for power.

Fear, grief, and even despair were luxuries she couldn't afford now. At whatever cost, she must find another husband, the strongest one possible, a man able to defend her lands and her children. Whatever she had to endure at his hands she could bear, if only she knew Eric and the girls were safe.

One hand lay on the straw beside her, the other on her breast. Slowly they clenched tightly into fists. If he promised that, she would do and be anything he asked of her. God knows, after nine years of Reynald she knew how to be an obedient wife.

In the morning she rode out, accepting Niethered's offer of hospitality until the hall could be aired out and Reynald's body buried.

At the freeman's manor, she bathed. Once clean and dressed in the best that remained to her, she sent a message to Hakon.

From her window on the top floor of the house, she soon saw only a party of men ride in from the icy forest beyond the farm.

Hakon was downstairs now, speaking with Niethered. When she told him where to send the messenger, the shrewd old eyes had studied her gravely.

"He may be the best choice possible," Niethered said at last.

"I've never met the man," she'd answered calmly, "but he's said to be strong and keeps his word."

"True," he said, "but how a man behaves toward other men and how he deals with women are often two very different things."

She'd nodded. "I know," she said, and climbed the stairs to await Hakon's arrival.

She stood quietly by the window, nervously clasping and unclasping her hands.

It seemed like Reynald had been dead for years. How long had it been since he'd last come to her bed? Sometime before the two girls were born, and they were three years old. She was a small woman. Her pregnancy had been a difficult one.

On the pretext of consideration, Reynald had moved his rooms to the other side of the hall, aping the great lords by turning her side into a makeshift women's quarter. He didn't sleep alone. She'd never known or wanted to know how many women shared his bed, when he bothered with a bed, tumbling his paramours as readily in the stable or in a field behind a hayrick. He never made even a token attempt to treat her as a wife again.

She hadn't had the courage to confront him with his infidelities, feeling that her only salvation lay in silence and a pretense of indifference. When she wept, she did so alone at night, when the children were in bed, walking the floor by candlelight, into the small hours of the morning, sleepless till the sun rose, hiding her pain and putting on a brave face for the world, hoping that someday the pretense would become fact and she would no longer care what Reynald did, or with whom.

Bitterest of all days were those when certain rites were celebrated among the green sheaves of the new wheat and the rising dust of the harvest. Those days didn't exist as part of the calendar span of the year but were set. Time was suspended. In the spring, bonfires burned, the tall points of flame dancing high under the stars. The night winds were soft and fragrant, scented by wildflowers and orchards bursting into bloom. Groves near the edge of the forest sounded with the laughter of lovers—she sat alone.

Elspeth hated Reynald then, and again in the autumn when the big yellow moon shone through the skeleton branches of the trees. He shut her up in the women's quarters, saying she was too delicate a lady for such festivities as these. If he'd only known how gaily, how gladly she'd have gone with him. She could have forgiven him for the rest—anything—nothing else he did would have mattered had he given her her rightful place in his arms, let her be the first to know his embraces, carried her away from the fires, off into the darkness, before all the rest.

But he'd denied her even that ancient right, a right belonging to the woman of the hall. Denied her, making her nothing in the eyes of her people when they saw how he slighted her and she suffered his insults without protest.

But Hakon might be worse, probably would be worse. At least she would know what to expect of him.

She turned and faced the door at the sound of his heavy footstep on the stairs.

Hakon opened the door cautiously, hand on his sword hilt. His gray eyes scanned the room suspiciously. What he saw reassured him. It was sparsely furnished, with no hiding place for an enemy.

Certain that he hadn't been enticed into an ambush, he walked to the table and turned his full attention to Reynald's lady.

Impossible, he thought. *Fate is too grim a hag. She hates me too much to toss this much good fortune into my lap. But here she stands, Reynald's lady, mine for the taking. By all the gods, a flower, blessed by Freya in her mother's womb.*

The woman before him was slender, yet so beautifully proportioned that she gave the impression of being taller than she actually was. Her legs were long. Small hips rose to a tiny waist, breasts two perfect rounded cups, her face exquisite, large brown eyes, long lashed and melting. Chestnut hair, highlighted by a faint shimmer of dull gold, so heavy it curled, hanging in ringlets around her cheeks, escaping the binding fillet of silver. The soft feathers of white fur that trimmed her long blue mantle brushed the skin that reminded Hakon of an apple blossom, a clear translucent white with just the faintest blush of rose.

The chill of the night's ice storm still hovered in the air of the room, but she clutched the mantle more tightly around her than was warranted by the cold.

Hakon sensed she was afraid of him. *All to the good,* he thought savagely. She might be as treacherous as her husband, and being so beautiful might make her only that much more dangerous, since there were times when he'd have to trust her. She was a Frank, and Hakon was astute enough about his own reactions to know that she intimidated him.

These Franks intimidated him. The houses with their closed rooms, glass in the window, carved furniture, books, wall paintings, even the food of their feasts, rich in taste and smells never dreamed of in his own land. And now this perfumed, delicate woman, her face lovely as a flower above the blue mantle, confronted him with her strangeness, her fear. He could see it in her eyes. She looked at him as she might a wild beast threatening her with its claws.

She spoke first, breathlessly. "You are . . . Hakon?"

He bowed slightly. "I am Hakon. You sent for me."

"Reynald is dead," she said.

"I know," he answered, "and Count Anton. Reynald at the hands of that witch woman of the bishop's, and Anton slaughtered by Owen's kinsman, Godwin."

Elspeth nodded. "Do you have him?"

"Who, the bishop?"

"Yes," she answered. "They said Reynald sold him . . . for a sum of money."

"Yes," Hakon laughed unpleasantly. "The story is true enough. We had him and, yes, Reynald sold him."

Elspeth seemed to shrink into herself as if she'd received a blow. "I had hoped . . ." she said, turning toward the window, "I had hoped the witch lied. He's dead then?"

"If only he were, you and I would both be better off. But, no, he's not, though I have hopes he soon will be. My nets are spread wide, wider than he knows. The sad fact is he escaped and is even now in flight. I have spies in the city. They say he hasn't returned. If I catch him first, he won't."

She seemed not to hear him as she stared out at the cruel glitter of the frozen forest. "I suppose I knew the truth from the first. I didn't want to believe it, not even of

Reynald. I wanted to believe the witch cursed him out of spite. Oh, he was false. False to me, to his friends, true only to his greedy heart."

Hakon's cheeks flushed. "What is this whining! Reynald had no friends. He was a treacherous, covetous, cold-hearted bastard, callused as a ploughman's foot. To him everyone, man or woman, was an object to be used for pleasure or profit. And God help the tool that turned in his hand as the bishop did. Reynald sold him to Osric's tender mercies. He looked at him, then at me—and chose the one he thought would be the winner. Just, my fine lady, as you do now!"

Hakon walked to the table and rested his hand on the back of the chair.

Elspeth felt the strength, the power of the man in the very yield of the floor itself. She didn't need to look at him.

She hadn't expected to be quite so afraid of him. The hand holding the mantle under her chin tightened. She felt the pulse, pounding in her throat, flitting against the tips of her fingers.

She'd looked for a little politeness between them, a pretense of regret for Reynald's ugly fate. He refused to allow that. Instead he'd laid her motives bare with an acuity of perception that terrified her.

"My brother, Bertrand . . ." she whispered haltingly, "he"—she grasped at straws—"so did he."

Hakon laughed, a laugh that grated as cruelly as the scrape of a knife against bone. "Worthless! Men fly rather than serve him. He has cost you several that would otherwise be loyal. I wouldn't be here if you weren't utterly bereft."

Elspeth thought of her children and tried to find some courage. But, oh God, what hope had her children when a man like this ruled the household?

She turned slowly to face him, the very picture of fear, her lips white and shadowed by a faint blueness around the mouth. Her cheeks appeared sunken, bringing out the ashy circles under her dark eyes. The fabric of the blue mantle stirred with the rapid, shallow movement of her breasts.

Her beauty's faded, Hakon thought. *I've gone too far.* Suddenly he wanted that beauty back. He hadn't realized how fragile it was, how quickly he could snuff it out with a few words. Elspeth saw an expression of disbelief flicker across his face, followed by a slight frown. Suddenly his expression softened and he became almost handsome. The scar that traced a silver line through his hair, then sliced down across his cheek and nose didn't detract from his even features but rather seemed to lend them definition and distinction. The body, under the gold fish-scale cuirass and the heavy fur mantle, was muscled like that of a dangerous predator, a wolf or a bear. And he had an animal gift of swift, sure movement, effortless and powerful.

He shook his head as though puzzled. "You're terrified of me?"

"Yes. Isn't that what you wanted?"

"No, not yet."

Some of the color returned to her cheeks and lips. "I haven't denied the truth of anything you've said."

"Why should you?" he asked. "Why should we two bandy words? You sent for me and saw how quickly and eagerly I came. Don't trouble me about Reynald. I watched him sell his best friend. You were married to him for years. I've never known a woman who didn't understand her husband's mind."

"I understood Reynald better than I wanted to," Elspeth said, looking at the floor. Hakon's odd eyes frightened her. That clear, transparent stare seemed to look through her with a cold, self-confident intelligence.

"Then enough said."

Hakon raised a hand as though to beckon her closer. "Come here! Cast aside that mantle; let me see if the stem is as lovely as the flower it bears."

Elspeth's first reaction was astonishment. She didn't think well of her own charms. No one had ever given her reason to. To her father she had been only another girl to be married off as advantageously as possible. Her features had been completely lost on Reynald. Then she realized the meaning of the sudden softening toward her, the intensity of Hakon's stare.

She walked toward him very slowly. As she did, she released her grip on the folds of cloth in her hand until the cloak fell open.

Under it she wore only a simple brown dress ornamented with a running pattern of gold embroidery at the hem and neck.

Elspeth moved with an unconscious elegance and grace. In a kinder world she might have been a dancer. As it was, each gesture she made flowed into the next with the seamless smoothness of rippling water.

Hakon was suddenly hard put to control his breathing.

The clinging softness of the gown highlighted the curves of a body that made the bodies of every other woman he'd seen seem misshapen and thickset. The hand that had rested on his sword hilt instinctively slipped off and hung at his side.

She paused a few feet from where he stood, looking up into his face.

He lifted his hands, placing one on each side of her waist, fingers spread as if to measure it, pulling her closer. He moved her whole body as easily as he might have a feather, and looked down at her with a buyer's greedy appraisal. His eyes traveled slowly down to her feet, then slowly upward, until they met hers again. And he received the shock he'd once received as a boy when ice he thought of as solid broke and dunked him into the freezing water below.

Her expression was one of bleak resignation and acceptance.

"At least," he said, "we know where we stand."

She nodded.

"You dream of lands, forested and tilled, of a stronghold, of being a lord among my people, lording it over my people. But"—she licked suddenly dry lips quickly with her tongue—"there are conditions."

His hands dropped quickly from around her waist, and he stared down at her with detached amusement.

"Conditions," he snorted. "The victor dictates the terms of surrender, not the vanquished."

Elspeth jerked back, eyes blazing with the first fire he'd seen in her since he'd entered the room.

"I have children," she said. "*My* children. You need me," she continued, "and you'll need my help to rule here. These are my people and some, a few of them at least, are still loyal to me. It's said you want to take the city. By now everyone knows of your designs, and I don't think you'll find its walls so easy to breach, whatever army you have at your back.

"That cousin of the bishop's is the devil's own blood kin. Oh God, he killed Anton as though he were a dog or a rat. Lured him within reach of his hand, then struck—"

She stopped, breathless, conscious of the pounding of her heart, then turned half away from him, one hand pressed tightly to her breast.

Hakon's hand rested again on his sword hilt. He gave Elspeth a concentrated stare. His eyes chilled her.

"I'm wondering," he said slowly, his left hand fingering the sword hilt, "if you're worth bargaining with."

The hand at Elspeth's breast rose suddenly to her throat and she laughed wildly, then spun toward him, eyes aflame.

"I don't know that I am. I can only offer you what a woman offers a man. For my children, I'll yield you my lands, my loyalty, my body, my life."

Hakon continued to stare at her with those strange wintry eyes of his. "Never," he said quietly, almost contemptuously.

"Yes!" She shouted the word at him fiercely.

"What do you want for these children of yours?" he asked.

Elspeth relaxed and brushed at her forehead with one hand. "That the girls be well dowered and properly married when the time comes."

Hakon nodded. "That presents no difficulty. Men will cut each other's throats for the privilege of wedding even my foster daughters. I would not do less for any woman under my protection. And the boy?"

"I don't know . . ." Elspeth said hesitantly. "I've thought of sending him to my kin near Paris to be fostered . . . but now—"

"No," Hakon shook his head, "such a journey is out of the question, at least for the present."

He looked puzzled; he frowned, running his fingers through his hair with a quick nervous gesture.

Elspeth was surprised. The fearsome raider chief seemed to be trying genuinely to do justice. He looked past her, deep in thought, at the crystalline beauty of the sky beyond the window.

Then he snapped his fingers. "I have it. I'll give him his choice. Lands and a stronghold, or a longship and crew. A gift of immense value, that, my lady. I don't know if you realize how much it costs to outfit a ship and hire a skilled crew to sail her. Should neither one strike his fancy, he may take gold up to the value of one or the other.

"I can't expect the boy to love me, but I won't give him any reason to hate me, either. How's that?" he asked.

"Have I your word?" she asked. He was being generous, too generous. It roused her suspicions.

"Yes," he said strongly, "you have my word. But," he laughed suddenly, looking down at her with a cold smile, "you don't believe me."

"No," she said bitterly. "Men's promises to women are easily made and even more easily broken."

One of his hands shot out and caught her chin, forcing her to stare into his face. "I had wondered if you were worth bargaining with, poor little bird."

His voice was tinged with an angry mockery that belied the sympathy of his words. "Poor dove, struggling in the talons of a hawk. What sureties could I give you? Upon what gods could I swear? I, a pagan. We share no common gods, you and I.

"I've sworn no oath of fidelity to your king. In truth, I never swore such an oath to my own king. I left my land a despised outlaw, an outcast. Hunted by my brothers. Reviled by my kin. Men of the same womb that bore me, of the seed that gave me life, sought to destroy me.

"I cannot offer you even the protection of my own customs, my own laws. Think how little yours mean to me, my fluttering dove." Hakon's voice was soft, but as he spoke, an infinite menace crept into it.

Elspeth tried to pull away, but the grip of his fingers on her chin held her. His eyes narrowed, holding a cold that burned and flayed.

"But," he whispered between his teeth, "I have no reason to parley with you. Reynald's body had not yet stiffened in death. His flesh smoldered still when word was brought to me by spies among those people whose loyalty you boast of that he lay dead. I could have ridden then, burned the house down over your head, taken your life and the lives of your children, seizing your lands and people for my own to rule as I pleased.

"Were I the deceiver you think me, it would be done now even as I speak."

His fingers dropped from her chin. He gave her a light, almost contemptuous shove.

Elspeth stared up at him, still gripped by the commanding gaze fixed on her.

I've hurt him, she thought. *I've hurt his feelings.*

In all the years she'd lived with Reynald, she'd never felt for one moment that anything she could say or do would hurt him.

"I see," she said in a low voice, "that I can trust your pride if nothing else."

"Pride!" he exclaimed. "Pride, is that what you call it, shadow woman? Reynald's shadow, now offering so humbly to crawl into mine? Is there anything so strong about you, in you, as what you call my pride? Have you any such virtue wherein I can place my trust?"

Elspeth's eyes fell from his. She was shaken, but not as afraid as she had been. She'd seen the man, his vulnerability.

"I don't know," she said, looking at Hakon again.

Her eyes were shadowed by a pain so naked, so deep, and so long continued as to be a thing of use, an endless, weary loneliness.

"For nine years," she continued uncertainly, "I was Reynald's wife. You know what his promises were worth. . . ."

"I said I saw him sell a friend," Hakon answered. "Even as I watched and smiled—I had to smile, Elspeth, his treachery was to my advantage—I wondered how he could bring himself to do it. No one, and nothing, governs me."

Hakon threw back his head, and Elspeth saw in his face the pride of the damned. It glowed with a luminous intensity in the gray, bitter eyes, the weather-beaten skin stretched over his cheekbones. Blood pulsed in the scar that traced a line across his forehead and nose; then it faded to a tight white slice across his flesh.

"Long ago, when I was flung out as a bird into a storm wind, alone, trusting to my own strength and courage to survive, I vowed there was one thing to which I would always be true, and that one thing is myself. Never have I requited good faith and loyalty with deceit and treachery. What I promise, I will perform. Otherwise I wouldn't let the words pass my lips. I extend my protection of you to your children and offer your son his fair share of whatever is to be won here when he is of an age to be called a man. You may depend on it. I'm not given to subtle shifts—"

Elspeth laughed, then choked, her voice full of tears. "My lord Hakon, you have the subtlety of a thunderbolt." She shook her head. "Even I can see that."

A sudden warmth flooded his eyes, a hint of laughter that astonished her as much by its presence as by its rapid departure.

"You may rest easy, my lady. I'll keep my word. Now it's time you kept yours."

Elspeth blinked at him in surprise, not understanding what he wanted. Then she did. "What! Here! Now!" She stepped back with each word. "He's not buried yet, not dead even one day. I won't, I can't."

Hakon studied her, a perplexed expression on his face. "Can't?" Hakon asked. "Are you with child? Is it your time of the month? Do you bleed?"

Elspeth stared back at him, the hard, scarred face, the powerful shoulders, conscious that he carried the breath of the frozen woods with him. The scent of fresh cold air hung around his body, clinging to the folds of his heavy furred mantle.

She could find an excuse to put him off. She wanted to find any excuse to stop him. But the fear of what he might do when he realized she was lying made her flesh crawl.

"It's indecent," she protested.

"Indecent?" Hakon repeated. "How indecent?"

She gestured at the window behind her.

"It's broad daylight, the sun is shining . . . and I . . . I've never been with a man in daylight. Even Reynald came to me in the night, in darkness."

Hakon's eyes rolled upward in impatience. "What folly is this? Is there some deformity about you, something hidden and secret that you don't want me to see?"

"Oh no!" Elspeth gasped out in horror. "I am formed as"—she groped for words—"as are all other women."

"No!" Hakon said appreciatively. "Much better."

"It's too soon," she pleaded.

"Too soon? What?" he asked. "Are you afraid the house churls will laugh at you? If they do, if they dare show so much as a smile, bring them to me; see how long they laugh at my fist."

He raised his right hand, big as a mace, and closed the fingers.

Staring at him, Elspeth was suddenly obscurely tempted to smile.

"I'll agree," she said. "Your fist is no laughing matter. But must you be so headlong? Wouldn't tonight be soon enough?"

"No! If tonight, why not now?"

"The room is cold."

"Anger me by any more resistance," Hakon said quietly, "and presently it will grow much warmer for you."

He regretted his words instantly. Her eyes seemed to grow larger and darker as her face paled around them. She was too easy to frighten.

He turned away with a sharp sound of disgust. "Waste of a good bath."

"What?" Elspeth said, startled.

"Here I am," Hakon said. "No sooner did I receive your message than I must jump in an icy river—too impatient to wait for my men to heat bathwater—thinking that if I can't please this Frankish lady I can at least keep from offending her, while all the rest stood on the riverbank laughing at me. I know I'm no beauty, but this much coyness . . ."

Elspeth did smile then, and dimpled beautifully.

"Is it funny then, my jumping into a river before I'd even seen you?" Hakon asked. "Lovely lady, I'd jump into ten rivers gladly, the better to please you."

He was wooing her. Elspeth couldn't help but feel flattered.

Ah, now. That's the way, Hakon thought.

The morning sun streamed into the room. Elspeth, caught in its light, was radiant.

The clinging folds of the brown dress suited her much better than the stiff cloth of gold she'd worn yesterday. Its very somberness highlighted the purity of her skin, and the soft dark mass of her hair misted with a coppery shimmer made a more glorious ornament than any diadem.

He could see she was weary, but even the lines of fatigue around her mouth and the faint shadows under her eyes only seemed to accentuate the sweet, gentle curve of her lips and turn her eyes into pools of velvet shadow.

Before all the gods! Nine years of Reynald. How did she stand it? She was born to be loved. "Come," he said, stretching out his hand as he had before.

And she came, not called by his voice but fascinated by what she saw in his eyes. Even when she stood before him, he didn't embrace her at once. He only loosened the fillet that held her hair and let the soft dark mass of it fall around her shoulders. Then he turned her around and began to undo the dress at the back. When he started to slip it down over her shoulders, she gave a short, sharp outcry.

"Couldn't we find a bedroom?"

His lips brushed the back of her neck. "Such a craving for darkness."

She shook her head. "I've never been alone with a man by day."

"Ah, indecency again," Hakon said. "The indecency

to my mind would be to hide such beauty as yours in darkness."

She held the dress against her breasts while he unarmed himself, shrugging off the fish-scale cuirass and laying it and his sword belt on the table. Under it he wore a tunic of ivory silk, embroidered at the neck and sleeves with blue flowers.

She made a small sound of surprise.

He smiled. "It's as I said. I bathed at once and donned my best clothes when the rider delivered your invitation."

Then he began to slide the dress down over her shoulders again.

"Couldn't I wear it?" she asked plaintively.

"No!" his voice held the sharp sound of command.

She lowered her arms and the dress fell to the floor at her feet.

Then all in one movement he sat down in the chair and set her on his knee.

She wore a wrapping of silk at her breasts and between her legs.

He peeled away the cloth on her breasts.

Elspeth closed her eyes and buried her face in his shoulder. She was more disturbed by her own nakedness than she thought she'd be.

But he stroked her neck and back gently. "What's wrong?" he asked patiently.

"I'm ashamed," she muttered. "Ashamed that you should see me like this."

"Oh," he answered. His voice was distant and dreaming. "I have seen you before and often since my earliest youth."

Elspeth raised her head to stare at him in surprise. "Where?"

Hakon caressed her neck with one hand while the other stroked her breasts and stomach. "This neck of yours." His hand moved, sending a delicious thrill of relaxation across her shoulders and down her spine. "This neck, proud as the arching rise of my ship's prow, smooth as a dolphin's leap, I have seen and touched it often.

"And your body." His voice quivered with desire. "Ah,

that I knew from the first time in early spring. I went on snowshoes to the high pastures of my father's lands and saw mountain flowers blooming through the snow. The delicate petals dusted by its powder, glittering with frost crystals, yet each a form of exquisite beauty, the blush of springtime over a frozen earth."

His hand found its way between her legs. He stroked her gently through the silk.

Elspeth leaned back over his arm. His voice was hypnotic, soothing away her fears, lulling her into a trance of desire.

Then she looked up at his face and her desire faded. His eyes, cold as the hoar frost that clung to the eaves outside, devoured her with a predatory intensity.

He wants me to love him, she thought. She was suddenly afraid. Her breath caught in her throat. She hadn't loved Reynald, and he'd stripped her of pride and self-esteem, reducing her to a nonentity within her own household. What would this man do to her? she wondered.

With one quick movement he pulled away the last scrap of silk covering her body and put her on the bench.

His clothing dropped to the floor beside hers.

She felt a surge of warm pleasure when he entered her. That was all she'd ever felt with Reynald and all she expected to feel.

Her legs curled over his hips in a practiced way and she relaxed.

This seals the bargain, she thought. *He is, after all, no different than other men. Is this all my life? First, Reynald's embraces. Then I pass from his arms to the next man's and from him, perhaps, to the next.*

She stared up at Hakon's face, wondering if there was anything more lonely than this thing called love. He, too, looked detached and remote, though his face showed the struggle of pleasure. His eyes seemed to watch her from a great distance, as if evaluating her performance. She closed her eyes and sought his lips with her own, hoping to find some tenderness—if not love, at least a momentary kindness—for the pleasure her flesh gave him, hoping she would at least have that memory when he, like Reynald, was gone.

But his face evaded hers. His breathing quickened. The speed of his thrusts increased as he completed the act.

She felt the spasm of pleasure surge through his powerful frame. His muscles knotted, then relaxed, then tightened again until he lay quiet, body resting between her thighs, head on her breasts.

After a few moments he got to his feet and released her. Elspeth sat up, head bowed. She didn't want to look into those strange frozen eyes. She reached for her dress.

His hand closed on her wrist, stopping her. His grip was powerful and, though not painful, impossible to resist.

"It's cold," she said.

"Yes," Hakon answered. "I felt it."

"Let me go," she pleaded.

"No, not until you keep your part of the bargain."

She stole a glance at him through her lashes, then looked away.

"I have," she said desperately.

"No," he said. "You promised me your lands, your loyalty, your body, your life. I want all of them. I want a wife," he shouted. "Not a bitch who makes love like a whore."

"Whore!" she screamed. With one quick movement she tore free of his grip. She stood facing him defiantly, as fear, rage, and despair all came together in one blinding, red flash in her mind.

"Whore, you bastard? I'll give you whores. It's you who came whoring to me. I'm not a woman to you any more than I was to Reynald. Look at me," she screeched. "I'm lands, a stronghold. I bought you. I'm buying you. Not the other way around."

He leaped toward her, teeth bared, eyes blazing with fury. Both of his hands snapped around her wrists in a tight grip.

She lunged away from him, then toward him, her nails raking at his face. But he held her easily while she kicked, scratched, and twisted at arm's length until at last her rage was spent and she stood heaving and gasping with exhausted, impotent fury, spitting out curses.

"God damn you. God damn you to hell. Damn you. . . ."

"I do the buying," Hakon said. His voice shook with rage. "I do the buying, Elspeth. Not you."

Her shoulders slumped. She stopped struggling to break his hold on her wrists. She laughed through her tears. "Hakon, you wouldn't buy me if I were offered to you for sale."

He felt a thrill of pure triumph. *I have her,* he thought in wild elation. *Before all the gods, my beauty, I'll make you love me now.*

"You don't know?" he said. His voice was soft and filled with amazement. "You don't know how beautiful you are? Woman, you are Freya herself, come from Asgard, walking among the flowers, to purchase the necklace of the dwarves. If she looked as you, they must have thought that magical ornament a cheap price to pay for one immortal night of love."

Elspeth's head turned toward him slowly. Her eyes were swollen with weeping, her cheeks wet with tears. Yet there was something in her face, something just beginning, that to Hakon's eyes seemed as glorious a thing as sunrise.

"Woman, you are a field of wheat, heads bending heavy with the glume, awaiting the gathering arms of the reapers."

He drew her toward him slowly. "An orchard of ripe fruit, sweet and succulent, that falls at the touch of a hand."

He released her wrists but caught her upper arms, pulling her closer. "I wish you had come to me, bought and paid for. Then you'd have no reason to doubt the passion you rouse in me. I've had you once, but that was nothing."

He shook her lightly. "Nothing, I tell you. Insults from your lips are sweeter than words of love from most women's."

She looked into his eyes. The ice was gone. Instead they raged like storm clouds. She could feel the heat of his flesh against her breasts. His skin seared hot with desire.

"I wish some merchant had sold you to me. I can see the man, see his strut, the sure knowledge in his face that he would soon be much wealthier.

"Taking me by the arm, he'd have spoken quietly into my ear, for beauties such as you aren't sold before a camp of leering fools. 'Come,' he would say to me." Hakon's voice was low, almost more intimate than the touch of his hands.

" 'Come, but bring all of your gold for this sublime beauty. This prize of war will command the first asking price.' I would come and not be disappointed. You'd be waiting in his tent, stripped, bathed, and perfumed as you are now. Those smooth eyelids lowered, long lashes against your cheeks, afraid to see what sort of buyer might enter."

Elspeth's eyes were closed. Her body pressed against the full length of his as he stroked her face with one hand. His fingertips brushed her eyelids gently.

She felt helpless. The animal heat of his body seemed to enter hers. The sound of his voice in her ears swelled like the roar of a cresting river, drowning out the world, the past, the future. Dear God, where was he taking her?

"The merchant would begin with the loveliness of your hair, inviting me to feel its silken perfection."

Both of his hands were in her hair, drawing her head back slowly, irresistibly.

"Ah, the color and texture of the finest sable. Men die among the blue ice floes, trapped by winter storms, striving to win the priceless treasure of just a few of those pelts.

"And your lips . . ."

Elspeth's eyes opened. She stared up at him, half in fascination, half in delight at the ardor that quivered in his voice, his face, and in those storm-tossed eyes.

"Lips, pink with the spring flush of the wild rose, sweet to my own lips as its scarlet autumn fruit."

And Elspeth didn't doubt then that he would have

bought her and reveled in his use of her, even as he was doing now.

Hakon eased her to the bench, then down on her back. His hands explored her body shamelessly, indifferent to her faint protests. Her hands kept meeting his, but they didn't seem to stop him from doing the things he was doing.

"Of course," Hakon said, "the man would make a point of your birth."

"My birth?" Elspeth half whimpered.

"Yes, your birth," Hakon said savagely. He was savage now. Elspeth felt something like rage building in him. Whatever world of desire he had taken her to, he was there with her.

" 'Look at her,' he would say. 'Take note of the slenderness of wrist and ankle, the whiteness of her skin, pale as the blossom of the blackthorn. Touch it,' he would invite me, but I would already be availing myself of that pleasure, cursing in my mind the man's chatter, wishing him gone and willing to open my purse wide and pay any price he asked.

"For touching you would be as it is now, like running my fingers over the finest silk. No, not silk. Softer, smoother still. It's as if I stroked the new catkins of a willow."

His fingers were doing things to her breasts that were . . . Oh God, there were no words. She felt as she had when bearing her children—as though her body were under control of some dark power, driving it toward an unguessable completion.

"Oh, but the man would babble on. 'Ah, pity the poor lady, bred to be the consort of princes and kings, now sold to be the plaything of a pirate chief. Your plaything, Hakon.' "

His knee was between her legs, parting them.

"And you would be my plaything, for I would pour my gold out at the man's feet and give him extra to leave us alone immediately."

His hand moved slowly, gently down her stomach, falling lower and lower.

"And you would know, in shame, then in delight, that this Freya's temple, this fountain of love, this most intimate part of you, belonged to me."

She shuddered with pleasure at the caress of his hands and voice.

"And I would enter as often as I pleased and remain as long as I liked. Not at your will, but at mine."

He filled her. The sensation was electric, just this side of pain.

Her body arched against his in a first spasm of pleasure.

"Ahhaaa," Hakon sighed. "You are a honeycomb heavy with the distilled essence of a thousand summer flowers."

Elspeth tossed her head from side to side and gave a sobbing moan as his movements built a magnificent heat in her loins.

Her body was his. She no longer controlled it. Her hips lifted to impale her body to the hilt on his stallion's manhood. It twisted to enjoy the hot delight of him moving within her. Her breasts tingled with pleasure each time they brushed the hard muscles of his chest. Her hands roved his body, caressing, stroking, urging, goading him on.

"You are the earth," Hakon whispered, "the earth after a soft spring rain, warm, soft, ready to yield its bounty to the hard horn of the plow.

"Ah, Freya, oh my goddess, oh my lovely, lovely goddess woman, Elspeth. This body of yours, this magnificent instrument, it sings to me. I will adore you, teaching you all the glorious arts of desire. My hands, my lips will caress every inch of you until your flesh melts with pleasure at my touch, until you are lost in ecstasy at my approach."

"Oh God," Elspeth screamed, and threw her arms around his neck. "Am I dying? What is happening to me?"

Their bodies seemed to melt together.

Hakon felt the beginnings of her hot, womanly caress, the love touch that flows from the womb, drawing him after her to the heights, the white fire of joy.

"No, not death," she cried out, a cry of surrender and triumph at once. "Life!"

* * *

When memory released her, she had begun to weep. Her women pulled her away from the wooden wall and led her, sobbing, to bed. They made soft, comforting noises. "Come, the rain will drown the fire, sweet one," Bettena said. "It's freezing. You will catch your death." None of them really understood the reason for her tears.

Dry and warm, drifting off to sleep, she could still feel the apprehension that shadowed her consciousness. *They will destroy him,* she thought. He saw her people only as tame creatures, born to be used and ruled by such as he. He didn't realize they had their own kind of power. Had he remained within certain boundaries, he could have been a tyrant. *God knows,* she thought, *they and I have had much experience of tyranny living under Reynald.* But when he savaged the forest from which they drew so much of their sustenance, Hakon had trespassed beyond the boundaries of their broad forbearance. He threatened their very survival. They must needs flee or . . . tame him.

Elspeth rolled on her back. The room was in darkness. The moon sent a ghost light past the edges of the shuttered window. "Tame him," she whispered.

She saw the outlines of an idea in her mind. Only the outline. She saw it in much the same way she saw the shapes of furniture in the soft moonglow.

I am a woman, she thought. *I have power.* Reynald had tried to deny her that power. He had shut her in his so-called "women's quarters" away from her people. They knew what Reynald had done and how she suffered him for their sakes and her children's.

They waited as only they could wait. She had seen cold watchfulness often enough in their eyes.

Now Reynald was gone. And Hakon. This magnificent man-beast was as innocent as a babe about the ancient ruling powers that held the land he wished to own. How long? She guessed. Before the Romans, perhaps even before the Gauls, the land was consecrated to its people. She was their descendant, keeper of the flame.

Is woman power? she wondered. She had always seen man as power. The warrior, the slayer, the taker. He of the iron fist.

But her people had yielded the land first to the woman. Of the hearth, tender, peacemaker, child bearer, lover, begetter of life.

They left her to choose the man who would be in her arms. Her womb sanctified him with immortality. *She* could choose. She could be assured this Hakon would be only an interloper in her bed, remembered as Reynald was, but not regretted. Or she could choose him and save him.

Outside a small cloud covered the moon. The room became utterly dark.

Elspeth's eyelids slipped down. The lashes brushed her cheeks. She sighed once, deeply. Consciousness with all its questions flickered out—she slept.

Chapter

18

*I*T took her some time to become aware of the silence in the house. Then the uneasiness changed to alarm. She had not expected the trouble to begin so quickly. The three children who shared the big bed with her were still asleep. She rose, naked, shivering at the morning chill in the air, and hurried toward the window slot.

The sun was rising. Its red orb seemed caught in the branches of the trees. Elspeth knew the sounds of the waking household should surround her, the clatter of pots in the kitchen, the snorting of horses in the bailey being led out to do the daily work, the chattering of the scullions and kitchen maids. But she heard nothing.

She dressed and hurried out of her room. In the hall she found the trestles lying against the wall, the table boards beside them. The dirty rushes of the night before crackled under her feet. She knew they should have been swept into the yard and fresh ones laid. At least a few torches should have burned on the walls. None did. The hall was dark and filled with echoing silence.

She ran to the kitchen. A few slaves, including the girl, Clara, crouched near a small fire on the cooking hearth. Elspeth stopped and stood, panting. They cringed away from her, all except the girl, Clara, who gazed up at her with cold-eyed insolence. Elspeth refused to demean herself by asking where the rest were. Besides, she was sure she knew. And because she knew, her heart was hammering with terror.

"Get up, you lazy clods," she snapped. "You, Clara, see to my children. Don't wake them, just be sure that if they do waken, they don't wander off."

Clara began to get to her feet slowly, still staring at Elspeth with the same contempt. Red rage burst in Elspeth's brain. She snatched up one of the fire pokers and smacked Clara across the back with it. Clara squealed much more loudly than the blow warranted, Elspeth thought. Then the girl ran off toward the bedroom where the children were sleeping.

"Glad to see there's some life in you," Elspeth muttered.

Then she turned to the rest, still brandishing the poker, and gave orders to have some food prepared and water heated for Hakon's bath when he returned. Wrapping herself in a heavy mantle, she left the hall.

Elspeth's stronghold was built on an island in the midst of a shallow lake that had once been part of the river. A narrow earthen causeway connected it to the tilled fields and pastures surrounding it. She crossed the causeway, turned, and started toward the river.

A small but sturdy house stood on the high part of the riverbank before it fell away into the water. The ground was wet and her footsteps squelched in the damp soil, sounding very loud in the morning silence. When she reached the house, she wiped her damp palms on her dress and knocked on the plank door.

As she knocked, the door opened. It wasn't latched. She peered into the darkened interior. The house was lit by one parchment-covered window and the louvered smoke hole in the roof. The hearth under the smoke hole was blackened but bare, swept clean. No fire burned there. The curtains that separated the sleeping quarters from the rest of the house were gone, and she could see the big bed with its leather strapping was stripped, blankets and bedding missing. Straw was piled in the corner. Otherwise the house was abandoned.

"No," Elspeth whispered. "No! Christ, this can't happen. God, don't let this happen. Please."

She stepped back from the door and called, "Corwin. Bettena. Where are you?"

She turned, walked around the side of the house, and looked toward the edge of the forest.

"Corwin. Bettena. Please!" she cried. "Come out. Answer me."

Her voice echoed in the morning stillness. A slender man stepped out of the woods. His skin was dark, varnished by the sun of thousands of days in the outdoors. But his hair and beard were gray. Deep curved wrinkles scored his cheeks. Elspeth knew he'd lost most of his back teeth, but the front ones were as white and even as a young man's.

"Corwin," she breathed softly. "So, you haven't left. I was so afraid. . . ."

Bettena rose to her feet and followed her husband toward Elspeth. She was a matronly, gray-haired woman wearing a soft white veil. She approached Elspeth and embraced her.

Corwin settled down on his heels, staring at Elspeth.

"Bettena," Elspeth whispered. "The children will miss you."

Bettena backed away, sobbing, wiping her eyes with her veil.

"What's wrong?" Elspeth asked.

"My lady," Corwin said softly, "you know very well what's wrong."

"Hakon," she said quietly.

Corwin nodded. "He has no respect for us, this man of yours. When we first saw you come home with him, we decided to wait. We thought, even though he is a foreigner, he might be a good lord to us. And at first it seemed so. He did not let any of his men insult our women. He kept them well in hand. Moreover he appeared to be even more serious than Reynald. He was very quick to reward the industrious among us. But now he has burned the forest, the very woodlands from which we derive part of our livelihood."

Corwin stretched out his hands toward Elspeth. "Time out of mind," he said, "we have held this land sacred. It gives us life; we give our lives back to it. It soaks up the blood from our cracked and bleeding feet when we plow. The sweat of our brows soak into it at planting and harvest. When we die, it dissolves our flesh and cradles our bones. We anoint its sacred stones with honey and oil. We leave bread and wine beside the sacred springs. But he, an outsider, comes here and in his anger at the bishop, he scorches the forest with his wrath."

"The forest will grow again," Elspeth pleaded. "Richer than before.

"The new growth will be fine fodder for the wild creatures, for your own horses, cattle, and pigs. Saplings will spring up in the burn, and in a few years everything will be as it was."

"We know that when the earth is wounded, she will heal herself. No, my lady, it is not the consequences of his act we dread, but what it shows us about his heedless and cruel heart."

"But he isn't," Elspeth insisted desperately, "he isn't heedless or cruel. He has been a better husband to me than Reynald ever was and a better lord to you. He was angry." She was about to say frightened by the bishop and his dangerous captain, Godwin, but she couldn't bring herself to confess Hakon's fear to these people. At any and all costs, they must believe him strong.

Elspeth looked at the forest edge and saw that she, Bettena, and Corwin were no longer alone. At least twenty others and perhaps more were standing silently among the trees. She bent down, took Corwin by the hand, and led him a little apart. "Yes, you can go," she said to him. "You can run away and abandon this place. I know."

"It's not supposed to be possible," he said with a quiet smile. "Serfs belong to their lord and are at his mercy."

"Not here and we both know it," Elspeth said. "Some of you will come to grief, but most will find other places where they are welcomed. Although it is hard to begin again at your time of life."

Corwin nodded, his face grave.

"I ask you, please," Elspeth said, "let Bettena return to the house with me to care for the children as she always

has. I will speak to my husband and see if I can bring him
to a better understanding. I know you for a man of influence among our people. Try to persuade them to wait a
little before they run away."

Corwin gazed out over the fields shining in the new
sun. The furrows of the last plowing were hazed with the
clear bright green of new growing things and covered by
long, low draperies of mist.

"We know," he said quietly, "that you have much influence with this man, Hakon. Reynald slighted you, but
Hakon does not. Several of the serving girls tried to make
themselves more agreeable to him. His eyes slid away
from them. When he comes here, he always seeks your
room first, and Bettena takes away the children quickly.
His last stop before he leaves is always your apartments."

"Yes," Elspeth said. She was looking at the fields.

Corwin gave her a speculative glance. "It's almost time
to prepare the earth for a winter crop."

Elspeth looked back at him. Their eyes met.

"Bertrand will hide in the church, make loud moans,
and pray for our souls as he always does at such times,"
Corwin said.

Elspeth squared her shoulders and gave Corwin her
hand. He took it gently between his palms. Elspeth's fingers tightened.

"Why didn't you ever demand this of Reynald?" she
asked.

"He ignored you," Corwin said. "We couldn't trust
him. We hid most of our doings from him."

"Try not to hurt him too much," Elspeth pleaded.

Corwin bowed over her hand and kissed it. "The new
wheat will sprout in your footsteps," he said.

Chapter

19

*E*LIN was grinding herbs in the cellar by the light of a smoky oil lamp, finding it a grim task. Christ's message of forgiveness and love had never taken root in her heart. She was by nature and temperament inclined to revenge. She wanted to kill Elfwine.

Near her, a child's voice spoke. "None of those are poisonous."

Elin gave a slight start and realized one of her people sat on a pile of sacking she and Anna had intended to hold Judith's wheat. She recognized the child, Ilo.

"What are you doing here?" she asked, thinking of Owen.

"Waiting to see you," the child answered. "I've been here a long time, but someone was always with you. I saw what happened. She tried to kill you." The child came into Elin's arms. "I'm afraid. I wasn't afraid before, but I am now."

Elin tightened her arms around the little girl and kissed her on the forehead. "What are you doing here?" she repeated.

The child looked up at her. Dark curls peeped out of the leather cap she wore. Her eyes were two midnight lakes in the lamplight. "Alshan left me here to keep watch on Reynald's lady, though she's not Reynald's lady anymore, and her lover is Hakon."

Elin's lips pursed. Although she knew among her own

people children were often trusted with much greater responsibility than among Owen's, she disapproved. "That's no errand for a child," she said.

"Alshan said I was the only one he could spare. Besides, I was safe enough until Hakon burned the forest."

Elin's embrace tightened on the little girl. "Were you out there?"

"Yes," the child murmured. "Until I took shelter with an old woman who lives on the edge of the waste. This morning, I slipped away from her farm and came here. But after I saw what Elfwine did, I'm not sure I should stay. Are you going to poison her?"

"No," Elin said. "Tell me, what is Hakon doing?"

"He's in a lot of trouble," the child said. "Elspeth's people are talking of leaving him. Elspeth may persuade them to stay. I don't know if she can."

Elin took the child by the hand and led her to the foot of the stair. "Anna!" she shouted.

A minute or two later, Anna came down out of the yard. "Good heavens," Anna said. "Where did she come from?"

"Never mind," Elin said. "Take her to the hall and give her something to eat."

"Will she be staying the night?"

Elin knew her own people. Imprisoning them was impossible. They either escaped, or if they could not escape, they died. The child would only stay as long as she wanted to. "I don't know," Elin said, looking down at the child. "Will you?"

"Yes, if I can sleep with you."

"You can," Elin said.

The child nodded, took Anna's hand trustingly, and followed her. Elin turned back to the herbs. A few moments later she was steeping the herbs in a bowl.

A long, narrow cleared aisle led through the stored provisions. Elfwine sat with her back to one of the pillars holding up the house. She was nursing the baby, flanked on one side by Alfric and on the other by Ingund. Elfwine's face was puffy, and her eyes were red with weeping.

As Elin approached, holding the bowl in her hand, Elfwine finished with the baby and reluctantly handed him to Ingund. She seemed to have gotten some of her courage back, and she faced Elin defiantly. Her chin lifted.

"Is that my death you carry?" she asked.

"No," Elin said. "I'd have no trouble accomplishing your death without any fuss at all if I wanted to."

"Then how does it stand with me?" Elfwine asked, her voice trembling.

"I think you're a vicious little bitch," Elin said. "But I won't see the town torn apart by a blood feud because of you. Your father and brothers would never admit your guilt. They would gather as many of their relatives as they could and maintain your innocence until the end. As quickly as he repudiated you, Ranulf would find his party also. The two groups would fight to the death and probably drag the rest of us down with them. Elfwine, I won't let that happen. Tomorrow, you will carry the iron around the bishop's chair three times in token of your virtue. I've come to show you how."

Elfwine tore her gaze from Elin's face and glanced uncertainly at Alfric. "He says if I am truly sorry for my sins, he says it is the same as if they were never committed. My heart will be pure."

Alfric went to his knees. "Yes, my sister," he said softly. "God is all forgiving and merciful. He will purify your heart for the ordeal you must face tomorrow. Have faith in his mercy; offer up true contrition. Now, my sister, let us pray."

Elin and even Ingund bowed their heads in silent prayer as Elfwine began to whisper her confession to Alfric. After a time, he raised his hand in silent absolution.

Elin knelt down beside Elfwine and told her to take a few sips from the bowl. Then she began. Elfwine was a difficult student. It was late before Elin finished. The whole town was silent, and she and Elfwine sat alone in the deep late-night stillness. Elfwine's head was in Elin's lap. "I don't believe Alfric is right about my sins, Elin."

Elin stroked her flaxen hair gently. "Why not?" she asked.

"I don't feel any real contrition. I'm not sure I wouldn't

do the same things again if I were put to it. You see, Elin, I'm afraid of being on the losing side."

Elin felt Elfwine's nails dig deeply into her leg as the girl spoke. "Alfric says it's wrong to lie," Elfwine continued. "Well, I don't feel like lying now. Hakon's much stronger than you are. He will win, and then what will happen to me?"

"If the Northmen take the town, they will probably kill Ranulf, dash the baby's brains out, and sell you as a slave."

"I can see you don't believe much in lying, either," Elfwine replied.

"No," Elin said.

"I didn't think Ranulf loved me so much," Elfwine sighed. "I thought I only trapped him with the baby. I don't think anyone could love someone else the way he loves me. Oh, Lady Elin, have I lost him?"

Elin leaned back against the pillar and closed her eyes. She was sunk deep in weariness and grief. Grief for herself, for Owen, and for the girl whose head rested in her lap. A girl who knew so little about love that she had not even been aware of the gift she'd been given. She had not known how to value what she possessed.

"I'm not a good person," Elfwine said. "I'm only doing what you tell me because I don't want to die. I don't want to die the way they kill an adulteress—led naked through town—then strangled and thrown into a swamp."

"And Ranulf doesn't want you to die, either," Elin said. "I don't think you've lost him. The first step toward winning his love back will be to carry yourself well tomorrow. He wants to believe in you. He wants you to let him love you. He wants to be proud of you, of your honor as a woman. If you can't be courageous for God, do it for Ranulf."

Elfwine raised her head from Elin's lap and looked at her. "I don't know about God, Elin, but I do understand about Ranulf. I hurt him more than all the rest."

Elin levered herself to her feet. "Don't leave me, Elin," Elfwine pleaded. "I don't know what I'll do if I'm alone here."

Elin lifted the bowl from the floor and offered it to the girl. "Drink the rest of this," she said. "It guarantees a good night's sleep. Follow me. You can share my bed tonight."

She found Ilo in the hall. The little girl was safely ensconced in Godwin's lap. She was asleep, her leather cap askew on her dark curls. "I'm beginning to understand how you know so much, Elin," Godwin said as he handed the child up to her. "She's been telling me all sorts of interesting things about Hakon."

Then he glanced up at Elin and Elfwine. They reminded him of two fighters who have fought to a finish and haven't been able to kill each other. Their hatred exhausted, they were almost friends now.

Elin nodded and cuddled the little girl close. She stirred sleepily but did not awaken. "She's one of my people," Elin said. "She needs protection and shelter now."

"There was a time when I wondered if your people were human," Godwin said. "Now I see they are only too human. She is very much afraid of Hakon."

"So is everyone else," Elin said bleakly. Then, carrying the child, she led Elfwine up the stair.

20

OWEN woke worried about the horse. The animal was both a prize and a talisman to him. Enar and the forest people still slept when he slipped out of his furs and eased toward the cave entrance.

The young man who had helped him last night appeared out of the mist. Owen felt an instant of mild disorientation, not quite believing what his eyes told him. The boy was no boy, but a woman, and one he knew well.

Suddenly, she dropped forward and stood on her hands. "Ceredea, the tumbler," Owen said. "We've met before. You entertained my father's guests many times."

He remembered the high-pitched cry of the flute, the rhythmic, throbbing tabor. Owen had clapped with the rest, in time to the drum, watching Ceredea as she leaped and cartwheeled in seemingly impossible feats of acrobatic grace, her smooth limbs glowing in the yellow light of the fire.

She laughed, then did a backflip and landed on her feet. "Yes," she said, "these are my people."

"How strange," Owen said, "that no matter how disturbed the times were, you and your friends always came and went at will."

She smiled. "Now you know."

Owen looked around. "I can barely see the ground at my feet. How will we find the horse in this murk?"

The forest growth was as dense as any Owen had ever encountered, dominated by oaks, untouched by the hand of man. The branches spread wide and lifted high above them. Their tops were lost in the low white clouds of moisture that billowed all around, obscuring the sky above, blurring to shadow anything more than a few feet ahead of them.

Owen knew the sun was well up in the sky because the fog was pale. Against the whiteness, the stark black trunks of the trees stood out, enormous and brooding, deeply stained by patterned growths of lichen, scarlet, brown, and dark green.

Overhead, the trees forked into branches nearly as thick as the trunks themselves, festooned with dense tufts of foliage. Among them, the long pale wands of mistletoe stood out, chartreuse against the crisp, jade surfaces of the oak leaves, each long switch of the parasite encrusted with berries white as the fog itself.

The few clearings they came to had to be avoided. They were densely overgrown with brambles and the long trailing canes of wild roses.

Owen paused at the edge of one open glade and lifted the stem of a rose carefully to avoid the sharp black thorns. "They're still in bloom," he said, "though it's winter."

"A few flowers linger here," Ceredea said. "It doesn't grow very cold."

The soft blossoms, saffron at the center, were a pale rose edged in white. The fragile petals clasped pearls of dew at their hearts. Owen dropped the branch and stood quietly for a moment. The forest was hushed. No bird or insect called. The fog muffled everything. "So silent here among the trees," he whispered.

"This is our forest," Ceredea said softly. "Alshan knows many songs about how things began. But there are no songs about this forest, except that it is said that here the first tree grew. When it was of an age to bear fruit, blessed by sunlight and watered by rain, all living things came to birth among its branches."

"A pagan story," Owen said, "and blasphemous." The

words had an odd sound in his ears, and he realized to his horror that he was quoting Bertrand.

Ceredea turned toward him. He met her eyes. In this light they seemed green, a dull green, dark as the lichens that clustered on the boles of the trees. "Isn't there something about a tree in your Christian story of the world's beginning?" she asked.

"Yes," Owen answered softly, speaking as much to himself as to her. "Eve, the mother of all living, plucked the fruit of the tree of knowledge. First, she ate of it, then gave it to Adam so that he shared her fall. God drove them from paradise because of their sin."

"She stole knowledge from the gods and gave it to mankind?" Ceredea asked, frowning.

"Knowledge of good and evil," Owen answered. "The tree was a forbidden one."

"How can such knowledge be forbidden?" Ceredea asked. "If men knew nothing of good and evil, how could they live? They would fall into fire thinking it safe, know nothing of what's nourishing to eat, what's a poison. How would they understand whom to love or hate? Who did well by them or harmed them? It sounds to me as though the woman was too clever for this God and he hated her."

"Before that," Owen answered, "men were the sons of God and He protected them."

Ceredea shrugged. "Your god must have wanted a dead son, then. It seems to me, this first man did well to listen to the woman. She gave him the means to protect himself." Then she turned away and walked on, her footfalls soundless on the thick black carpet of dead leaves that covered the forest floor.

Owen followed, remembering his own reaction to the story of creation when he'd first read it in the Bible at the monastery. He was glad Ceredea hadn't said any more because he had his own doubts.

The God who drove Adam and Eve from paradise hadn't seemed the loving and all-wise father that Bertrand claimed he was, but arbitrary and vindictive. Owen tried to turn away from the idea and its implications but couldn't. That God had seemed afraid—afraid of mankind. Mere creatures whose aspirations reached so high that they would fly in the face of divinity itself in order to achieve them.

Ahead of Ceredea something huge loomed up among the wraithlike curtains of mist. The hulking black shape was the largest oak Owen had ever seen. Three men couldn't have spanned the trunk with their arms. All around it the low limbs stretched, brushing the ground like the legs of a giant spider.

A spider caught in its own web, Owen thought. The boughs were thickly overgrown by a tangle of blackberry and wild rose. Other vines and creepers settled into a skein of almost impenetrable growth surrounding the giant trunk.

Ceredea led him under the tree limbs, down a winding path beneath the living burden of the splayed boughs toward the trunk.

When they reached it, Owen realized the monstrous oak was nearly dead. At some time in the past, it had been torn by a bolt of lightning, nearly splitting the trunk in half.

The tree, as if in defiance of the command of heaven, still lived, too strong to die, even when blasted by such a mighty force. But the lightning-scarred portion rotted, leaving a big hollow in the trunk. The stallion was stabled in the hollow.

Ceredea had knotted a rope hackamore and placed a deerhide over his back to protect him from the cold and rain. When the stallion saw Owen and Ceredea, he raised his head and trotted toward them.

The stallion gazed at Owen out of long-lashed brown eyes, blew softly from his nostrils, then gave him a horse kiss on the cheek, the velvet nose brushing his skin gently.

Suddenly the stallion lifted his head, both ears perked, listening. He jerked at the reins, trying to rear. "Whoa!" Owen shouted, pulling down on the bridle.

The stallion reared straight up. "Christ!" Owen shouted, "he's determined to break free."

The horse lunged forward, dragging Owen along by the rein. From far off, Owen heard a high whistling neigh.

Owen stripped the deerskin blanket from the stallion and vaulted onto his back.

"No!" Ceredea shouted, "without a bit you'll have no control over him."

Again came the equine cry from the drifting mist. The stallion bolted, running out through the vine-covered green tunnel Ceredea used to enter the clearing near the tree.

Owen bent low over the stallion's withers, head alongside the neck, hoping he wouldn't be swept off by low-hanging branches or a trailing loop of vine. The horse took the narrow passage at a gallop, then broke into a flat run when they reached the open forest.

The sun was beginning to strike through the fog now, filling the forest with a glorious golden light. The stallion ran with a relaxed, unconscious power that filled Owen's heart with delight—a gait so effortless that the horse seemed to float rather than run, and only brief glimpses of the shadowed tree trunks as they sped past allowed Owen to gauge their speed.

When Owen judged the stallion had worked off his excess energy, he began to pull in on the rein. This time the stallion answered the command of the bridle. He dropped to a trot, then a walk.

They were out of the forest into more open country, moving among copses of beech and poplar. Their leaves burned scarlet and gold against the patchy gray fog. Owen tried to stop the stallion or turn him back into the forest, but the horse resisted, pulling against the rein. Owen found that what Ceredea said was true. Without a bit, his control was limited.

Then, without warning, the stallion stopped. He whickered softly and a black mare appeared out of the haze, trotting up to him. Owen looked down at the stallion and said sternly, "So!" The stallion ducked his head and tossed his long red mane in what almost might have been a gentle gesture of apology.

The mare was saddled and bridled in red leather, trimmed with gold. She was nearly as beautiful as the stallion and obviously someone's beloved prize. Her coat was curried and combed to lustrous black silk perfection, mane and tail braided with scarlet ribbons to match her trappings.

In the distance Owen heard a voice calling. "Jewel? Oh, my Jewel, where are you? Come back! Please come back!" The voice was a woman's, and even in the distance, Owen could hear her distress. He reached down, caught the mare's reins, and rode toward the woman.

The girl was stumbling along, weeping so bitterly that she didn't see him until he pulled the stallion to a stop beside her. Even then, she had eyes only for the black mare.

She wiped away her tears and ran to the horse, throwing her arms around the sleek neck, burying her face in the mane. "Oh, Jewel, you wicked, wicked girl. Why did you play such a terrible trick on me?" She finally turned her attention to Owen, who was still holding the mare's reins. Her eyes widened in fright. Her grip tightened on the mare's bridle as she stared up at him.

At first Owen had thought she was a child. Upon closer examination he realized she was a little beyond childhood, but not by very much. She was, he decided, about fourteen, and very beautiful. She reminded him of a flower, its exquisitely delicate petals unfurling in the first sunlight of life's morning.

Her skin had that velvety freshness that nature bestows only on the very young. Dark hair flowed down over her back and shoulders; dampness curled the ends into a mass of chestnut ringlets. Her long-lashed brown eyes were clear and bright, filled with a limpid innocence.

"Oh!" she exclaimed. "But you aren't one of the huntsmen. Are you a brigand?" she asked breathlessly. "If you are, sir, please take my brooch. It's gold and very valuable, much more valuable than my horse." She reached up quickly and began unpinning it. Her fingers trembled with anxiety and haste.

The brooch held a dark woolen mantle that covered a long green velvet riding dress trimmed with sable. The brooch itself was a golden crescent set with cabochon emeralds and did look to be more valuable than the horse.

Owen realized that the horse wasn't the only treasured beauty lost in the woods. His eyes scanned the fog-shrouded countryside. Where were her menfolk? If he was any judge, the girl was not just well born but noble and shouldn't be riding unattended in such an isolated spot.

She extended the brooch toward Owen cautiously with one hand, still keeping her body between him and the horse, seemingly oblivious to the fact that he held the mare's reins.

"I'm no thief, my lady," Owen answered gently, trying to put her fears to rest. "I want neither your brooch nor your horse. Here." He placed the reins firmly in the hand that held the brooch. "Have a care she doesn't get away from you again."

The child stared up at him, still puzzled. "If you aren't one of the huntsmen and you aren't a brigand, then who? Oh!" she gasped, and backed precipitously away, pulling the mare after her. "You must be one of the good people." Her voice and expression were balanced perfectly between alarm and delight. "Of course you are," she continued. "What mortal rides a steed as fine as that, bareback, with only a light rein? And your dress is like theirs also."

"No." Owen smiled as he shook his head. "I'm no spirit. With your permission, lovely lady, I'll be on my way." His fingers tightened on the stallion's reins as a voice spoke behind him.

"You may have her permission, but you don't have mine. Stay where you are. I have a crossbow bolt aimed at your heart."

Though the voice came from behind Owen, he sensed movement on both his left and right. He remained absolutely still, keeping his hands well away from his sword.

"If you're not a thief or a spirit," the voice continued, "then you have no business in my lady's forest. Give me your name and how you come to be here. Do it quickly. And don't lie to me. I have a short way with liars, short as the road to hell. If I catch you out, I'll put your feet on that road with one pull on the trigger of this bow. Your name, sir!"

The voice rang with authority and assurance. For a second, Owen tried to think of a convincing lie, wasted another second regretting he wasn't a good liar, then answered, "Owen, son of Gestric. Lord bishop of Chantalon."

The man behind him didn't answer. The skin on Owen's back twitched as he expected to feel the bolt tear into his spine. But the man behind him rode his beast around the stallion, placing himself between Owen and the girl, holding the crossbow pointed at Owen's heart.

Had he been on foot and unarmed, Owen might have judged him a peasant or even a slave. He was as tall as Godwin but even leaner, hook-nosed, and lantern-jawed. His clean-shaven face was very dark, the eyes black. His head looked as though it might be shaven also, but it was difficult for Owen to tell because it was covered by a leather cap that came down over his ears, hugging his skull tightly.

He wore a coarse black woolen tunic split at the back and front; the sides covered his legs and hung to his ankles. A single, vivid scarlet stripe edged at the sleeves and hem. He rode not a horse but the biggest mule Owen had ever seen. "Very well," he told Owen, "half my question's answered. Now, how do you come to be here?"

"I was trying to reach my father's stronghold. I need men to help me in a fight."

The lean man lowered the crossbow and said thoughtfully, "Owen, son of Gestric. I've heard of you."

Owen relaxed, but not enough to allow his hands near the hilt of his sword. He glanced right and left and was immediately glad he hadn't decided to either run or fight. He was flanked by two of the largest men he'd ever seen. They looked like trouble, bad and worse. *Christ,* Owen thought. *Their necks are bigger than their heads.*

Both were equipped with spears, swords, axes, knives, and crossbows. "It doesn't do," Owen said mildly, "to ride about unarmed."

"Oh no!" Bad boomed from his right.

Worse on his left added, "This forest can be very dangerous." The two looked identical to Owen.

"I'm finding it so," Owen said. "The mare strayed. I returned her to the lady. I did no harm and intended none."

Bad and Worse looked at each other. It was as though one stared into a mirror. They both had full black beards and long black hair flowing down their backs. Appropriately, both wore bearskin shirts. "Do you think he's telling the truth, Elutides?" they asked, addressing the clean-shaven one with the crossbow.

Elutides rubbed his lips back and forth with one finger. His intent eyes analyzed Owen's dress and attitude. "Yes," he said.

Suddenly there was the sound of hoofbeats and someone yelling, "Whoa! Whoa! Whoa! God damn you. Stop!" The rider burst out of the mist. The horse came to an obedient halt beside Elutides' mule. The rider continued yelling, "Stop! Stop! Stop!"

"He's not moving," Elutides said.

The horse aimed a disgusted bite at the rider's foot, missed, and rolled his eyes. "This horse hates me," the rider complained. He was a corpulent, gray-haired man with a beefy red face and a wide, bulbous, scarlet nose. He wore a green velvet riding habit stained with the remains of at least the last fifteen or so meals he'd eaten.

Elutides grinned. "May I present King Ilfor."

King Ilfor peered at Owen. "Who is this? What's he doing in my woods? Are you going to shoot him, Elutides? If you are, do it now, so we can get on with the hunt. Though I don't see why you should bother to shoot him. After all, you can't eat him. Or can you? Do your rules allow that?" King Ilfor apparently found the idea amusing, because he burst into raucous laughter at his own joke, then asked again, "Who is he, Elutides?"

Before anyone could speak, Elutides' hand reached out and seized the headstall of Owen's horse. "He's our guest," Elutides said quickly.

"I am?" Owen asked, then saw the warning in Elutides' eyes. "I mean, I am!"

"He is?" Bad and Worse chorused.

Elutides continued smoothly, "My lady Gynneth, being grateful for the return of her horse, invited the stranger to our feast." He turned to the girl who stood behind him, still holding the black mare's reins.

"Oh yes!" she said sweetly. "I did. For better than my hawks and hounds, I love my Jewel." She stroked the mare's neck and bestowed a smile, dazzling as a ray of sunlight, on Owen.

"My lady Gynneth," he said, inclining his head.

"These are my sons," Elutides said, indicating the two giant warriors, "Cador and Casgob. Casgob's the handsome one."

Owen looked left and right again. The one on his left had a nose bent in the middle from being broken, and two cauliflower ears. The one on the right didn't. They both smiled at Owen, displaying a dazzling array of big, blunt white teeth. The smiles didn't reassure him. They looked perfectly capable of dining on him before or after Elutides shot him.

More and more people arrived, either mounted or on foot. Most carried game.

A red-haired woman galloped out of the fog and brought her horse to a rearing halt beside Owen. "A stranger!" she whooped with delight, and kissed Owen on the mouth, shouting, "welcome to our kingdom!"

Owen noticed the woman was well padded. A second later, enveloped in her embrace, he realized the padding was well distributed. He returned the kiss with a right goodwill.

She released Owen and shouted, "Let's drink to our new friendship!" She unslung a wineskin from her shoulder and squirted wine all over his face. Most of the wine went into Owen's eyes, nose, and lungs. He gave a wheezing gasp, coughed and sputtered.

"Don't drown the man, Aud," Cador rumbled.

"What, Aud!" King Ilfor screeched indignantly. "Will you seduce the man while he's yet in the saddle?" The king's horse reared, nearly unseating his rider. "Elutides!" the king screamed. "Help!"

Elutides reached out one long arm, caught the bridle of the horse, and brought him down gently. "I know, I know," Elutides said placatingly, "but be patient. It's only for a little while. He hates to ride!"

Owen, wiping the wine out of his eyes, realized that

Elutides wasn't speaking to the king but to the horse. The horse appeared to be listening, because the animal lowered his head and stood quietly.

"My aunt," Gynneth told Owen in a subdued voice, "Queen Aud."

"Yes," Owen said hoarsely. He was just getting his breath back after being half strangled by the wine. "I gathered that she was some sort of relative."

Aud leaned back, all the way back. Her body arched over the cantle of the saddle, her head touching the horse's rump. "Could it be done in the saddle? By God, yes it could! What a merry sport!"

"Not for the horse," Elutides said darkly.

Aud squirted a good quantity of wine into her mouth. "S'truth," she said as she sat upright, then stared at the stallion. "By God, what a beauty. Elutides, I must have a foal of him. I hope at least one of my mares is in season." She sounded as though if she found the mares unwilling, she might take the stallion on herself. "By Christ and all the saints, what an opportunity. But like as not, all my ladies will be cold and distant," she moaned. "Elutides, I cannot understand the ways of horses."

She threw up her arms. "I am always in season. Why has not God given my mares the same gift? Elutides, we must keep him here until I can be sure of at least a few foals." She looked in Owen's general direction, but he wasn't sure if she meant him or the horse.

Owen burst out, "But my lady, I must—"

"Be quiet," Elutides hissed at Owen under his breath. "Come, ride with us to the feast," he said loudly. Then more softly to Owen, "Come, you are under my protection. There is no stronger thing in this land, though I think you might have to lend out the stallion."

"We will have a great feast," Ilfor crowed happily. "All the game we have killed will be eaten tonight."

"I'll drink to that," Aud yelled joyously, and had another go at the wineskin.

"You'll drink to anything," Ilfor said.

"I'll drink to nothing," Aud answered with a wink at Owen. "I don't need an excuse."

The crowd around them continued to grow as more and more hunters straggled in from the forest. Owen counted at least a dozen deer, besides the one Aud had slung over her saddle. The footmen carried a magnificent variety of game—woodcocks, pheasants, ducks of all kinds, wild geese, and swans and uncountable hares and rabbits.

Aud turned her horse, dropped the strap of the wineskin over her shoulder, and blew a loud blast on the horn. Six men trooped into the clearing, the carcasses of three wild boars slung from their carrying poles. With Aud riding beside them, they led the procession.

Owen toyed with the idea of running away, but Cador and Casgob rode immediately behind him. The stallion was fast, but he'd need a good head start, and Owen didn't think he'd get it.

"Better a guest than a prisoner," Elutides said.

"Yes," Owen agreed, "but where are we going?"

"To our city, Idris," Elutides said. "You will attend the feast. It's an important one."

Gynneth bowed her head sadly. "I'm to be betrothed."

"No, not necessarily," Elutides said. Cador and Casgob laughed.

"But uncle," Gynneth looked at Elutides in distress, "if the king has agreed, what can we . . ."

Elutides chuckled knowingly. "Ilfor agrees with everyone," he said. "Have faith. Didn't you hear me tell the stranger that my protection was the strongest thing in this land? Did I lie?"

"No," Gynneth said softly.

"Fine, then. Now, smile and make your old uncle happy." Gynneth smiled beautifully up at him.

Someone thrust a wineskin into Owen's hand. There were at least twenty or so being shared out among the crowd. He took a pull and gave it to Elutides. Owen began to relax. The wine glowed in his veins and warmed him. Elutides was right. Better guest than prisoner. He was riding to a feast. Perhaps after the feast he could extricate himself from Queen Aud and King Ilfor and be on his way. *Besides,* Owen thought, *who could remain downcast on a day such as this?*

Though the fog still hung thick in places, the sun was beginning to shine and the party rode through patches of warm light. The meadow grass was long and green and so tall it brushed the horses' bellies and Owen's stirrups.

The trees and bushes were spangled with diamond droplets of dew. The moist air around him was heavy with the myriad scents of the wildwood, verdure, and autumn flowers.

A hunter walking beside Owen said, "The wine is nothing. Try this." He handed up a rude bottle made of bark, enclosed by leather. Owen drank cautiously at first but then with enthusiasm and delight. Mead! Mead of the finest kind, perfumed with the dark, sweet scent of wild honey, the essence of the forest with its impenetrable thickets and untrodden meadows alight with flowers.

He drank deeply, seeming to feel the liquor fill every vein in his body. His blood foamed with pleasure. His fingers and toes tingled with the heat of its passage into his flesh.

"Hey, be careful now; that's heady stuff," the man who'd handed him the mead shouted good-naturedly.

Owen capped the bottle with a sigh of regret and handed it back to its owner. He was a thin, dark man dressed in leather, like the rest of the huntsmen. He carried a double stringer of wood doves over his shoulder. As he held the birds up for inspection, Owen counted at least fifty, if not more, of the small, tasty gray-feathered creatures dangling from the leather. The huntsman smacked his lips. "For the feast."

"You will be there?" Owen asked.

"Everyone will be there!" Cador shouted.

"Dying men rise from their beds and send away the priest to come to the feasts we give!" the huntsman yelled.

"Pregnant women taken in travail jump up!" Queen Aud cried out. "They pat their bellies, say 'wait a bit,' and come running."

"Husbands abandon their wives, wives abandon their lovers to make merry with us!" King Ilfor shouted.

"Mourners leave the wake," the huntsman crowed, "and a time or two the corpse has been known to follow!"

Everyone shrieked with laughter at this, and Owen, well warmed by the mead, thought them a convivial and merry company. They passed from sunlight into a patch of pale, ghostly fog, still laughing.

The stallion shied as a post loomed before him. The thing at the top still had most of its long, black hair, but the face was of bone. The lower jaw had fallen away. Only the top teeth remained.

Owen reined the stallion in, but the rest of the company continued on unconcerned. "What did he do?" Owen asked.

King Ilfor stopped and scratched his head. "That one I can't remember. No matter. Whatever it was, he won't do it again," the king chuckled. "Who was he, Aud?"

She, too, paused. "I can't tell," she said with an indifferent shrug. "There's not enough of him left." Then she brought the wineskin to her mouth, took a swig, wiped the bloody liquid from her lips, and rode on.

The next head they came to had most of his hair and beard, but no nose and no eyes. His skin was a leprous green. "He stole one of my mares," Aud said.

"We look with great disfavor on horse stealing," King Ilfor said primly.

"I can see that," Owen said.

They passed more posts, but Owen averted his eyes and stopped asking.

They were riding in the open now, through pasture, and the sun was high and the mist gone. The city stood before them, perched on the rocks beside the sea.

King Ilfor gestured expansively toward it. "Idris, the greatest city in all Brittany, and the fairest."

Owen was about to point out that some other places in Brittany had claim to fame. Then he remembered the heads on the posts and decided he'd better sing its praises. God alone knew what they considered a mortal insult. "How beautiful a city," he said truthfully.

Idris drifted like a chimera in the light from the sea. The walls and rooftops were a warm rose in the rising sun. It seemed a place of light, cradled amid the jaws of black rocks, the brown of the wide fields stretching out around it, the emerald sea beyond. A big square Roman fortress crowned the rock, and the houses spilled down the boulder-strewn slope all around, ending at a wooden palisade like the one at Chantalon. At a distance the fortress did look majestic, commanding the valley by the ocean. As they approached, the squalor became apparent.

The fortress was a ruin, at least half of it fallen down a steep cliff into the sea. Few of the houses retained the original tile roofs; most were now covered with thatch. The orderly Romans had attempted a grid plan even on the steep slope, but the later settlers blithely ignored it, adding houses and rooms to already existing dwellings of timber, wattle, and daub, turning the once broad thoroughfares into narrow twisting alleyways mired in mud.

Yet the city had grown since the Romans left, and even if poor looking and dirty, it was filled with the bustle of life. People ran from the gates to greet the returning hunt party and escort them home. Nearly all of them carried more wine, and here and there was a container like the huntsman's, filled with mead.

As they passed the gates, a girl stood on Owen's stirrup. She offered him a kiss and another drink of mead. Owen took both, telling Elutides, "It's a pleasure to know I won't die of thirst."

"No," Elutides answered, "something else possibly, but thirst, no."

Pigs and children wallowed in the muddy street. It wasn't always possible to tell the difference between them. Chickens squawked and flapped as they dodged the horses' hooves. Once the whole party halted while a cow ambled out of one house in front of them, blocking their way. She stopped, turned her head, and considered them thoughtfully with large, liquid, bovine eyes.

Queen Aud addressed the cow in a wheedling tone. "Come, Ester, you're blocking the street. Move along now. There's a good girl."

The cow stayed put. There were shouts and curses, and the stallion was jostled from behind as those members of the hunt party farther back tried to find out what was blocking their progress.

"Damnation, Aud," Ilfor shouted, "give her a cut with your riding whip."

"What!" Aud screeched. "Take a whip to the finest milk cow in Christendom? Not I." The cow was a beauty, a deep cream color with the rather bony build but full bag and teats of a fine dairy cow.

Ilfor shouted, "Elutides!"

"Restrain yourself, Ilfor," Elutides said. "She will move in a few moments."

"Talk to her, Elutides," Ilfor pleaded.

"I have no influence with this particular beast," Elutides said. "She's very self-confident and fully cognizant of her own worth."

"Are we discussing the mind of the cow?" Owen asked.

"Why not?" Elutides said. "They have minds and wills of their own. Some listen to me, some don't."

The hunt party stared at the cow. The cow switched at a fly with her tail. Suddenly, the tail lifted and the cow made a deposit that plopped twice in the mud of the street. Then she strolled unhurriedly through the door of a dwelling opposite.

Around the next bend a plow horse joined them, walking along amiably with the rest of the horses. Queen Aud slapped him on the flank and greeted him affectionately by name.

Owen was grateful for the stallion's good manners. He picked his way delicately past children and pigs and didn't kick at or step on either one, didn't shy when chickens flapped at his face.

Owen twice had to stop him from entering houses. He seemed to believe that a horse could come and go as humans did and appeared surprised and pained to be restrained, looking with gentle hurt back at Owen as if asking why he shouldn't be allowed to seek further companionship among the humans he obviously accepted as being only another if lesser kind of horse.

Aud treated both Owen and the stallion with a proprietary air, never letting him get very far away from her. This wasn't lost on the crowd.

A woman leaning out of an upstairs window pointed at

the stallion and shouted something at Aud, something Owen
didn't comprehend immediately. When he did understand
the woman's remark, he felt his face burn until the heat
reached the tips of his ears.

Aud doubled over in the saddle, screaming with laughter,
then shouted something even worse back at the speaker.

Owen averted his eyes from both women and stared
down into the mud in an agony of embarrassment.

King Ilfor slammed Owen in the ribs with his elbow,
tears of mirth streaming from his eyes. "Did you catch
that? It was very funny."

Since the joke concerned sodomy and bestiality, and
cast grave doubt on the queen's chastity and marital
fidelity, Owen didn't quite know what to reply. "I suppose that . . ." he said uncertainly. His reserve seemed to
amuse the king even more.

"By God, another wooden-faced Northman. It must be
the climate of that hellish land of theirs," the king bellowed. "Nine months of the year they sit staring at the
snow and ice, freezing their fingers and toes, pricks and
balls, belching and farting from the beer they swill to
keep warm. It's said that the women's cunts are as cold as
their hearts and almost as cold as their hands. And I've
been told that they make love but two months of the
year—that being in June or July, when a man may safely
embrace his woman without fear of being taken with a
mortal chill.

"They have naught to eat but fish: fish salted, fish
dried, fish frozen in the ice that must be thawed over a
fire for two hours before it can be cooked, smoked fish,
and moldy cheese. A terrible life," the king sighed. "They
must be accursed for living so close to hell and being
pagans."

Owen cringed. At its very lowest register, King Ilfor's
voice was a shout. Owen estimated his remarks carried for
at least a half a mile. He devoutly hoped that none of the
aforementioned Northmen were within earshot.

The king's elbow slammed into Owen's rib cage again,
nearly knocking the wind out of him as he shouted, "Have

no fear, boy. Remain long enough among us and you'll soon be like your other friends, laughing at everything!"

A bare-breasted woman leaned out of a window above the king and threw a garland of flowers around his neck. Then she complimented Ilfor on his attributes as a man and, lest anyone fail to understand which attribute she referred to, she added measurements—length and breadth.

Ilfor blew her a kiss, returned the compliment by calling her his inspiration, and concluded with a brief but colorful description of the type of activity she best inspired.

Owen had gone cold when Ilfor mentioned his "friends" the Northmen. While Ilfor was occupied with the lady, Owen eased the stallion up beside Elutides. "What 'friends' have I here?" he asked him. "What did the king mean?"

"Ah," Elutides whispered, "we have as our guests one who calls himself Ivor Halftroll and twelve companions of his who call themselves berserks."

"Berserks?" Owen hissed between his teeth.

"True," Elutides said. "These guests have somewhat overstayed their welcome, but no one wants to brave the consequences of asking them to leave."

A sudden hollow feeling appeared just below Owen's ribs in the region of his midsection.

"I take it," Elutides said, "that the king was mistaken. Ivor and his friends are not acquaintances of yours?"

"No," Owen said.

"Strange," Elutides continued. "They know you. Ivor described you to me only yesterday at dinner and promised a very large reward, a reward to be paid in gold I might add, in return for your head."

Ceredea followed the hunting party until she was sure Owen wasn't going to break away, then returned to the others.

Enar sat beside the fire staring across the flames at Sybilla. Ceredea hunkered down between them. "He's been taken," she said.

Enar reached for the beer. "This is a jest. You're making game of me?" he said. "Tell me this is a jest."

"No," Ceredea said. "I'm not."

Enar stared into the flames, then took a long drink of beer.

Ceredea continued, "Queen Aud and her priest have taken him to the city. He went with them peaceably enough but not willingly. He needs your help."

"Not mine," Enar said, taking another swallow of beer.

"He's your lord," Ceredea said.

"No," Enar said, his expression stony. "Now, as of this moment, I'm quitting his service. I want nothing more to do with him."

"You swore an oath," Sybilla said.

"A pagan oath," Enar said. "Now that I plan to turn Christian, that oath is no longer binding. Even he would agree with me and never ask me to follow him. And that's probably why I will," he sighed. He looked out the cave entrance. "Is it cold outside?"

"No, damp," Ceredea answered.

"Raining?" Enar asked.

"No, mist," Ceredea answered.

"You know where this city is?" Enar asked.

"Yes."

"How do they behave toward strangers?" Enar asked.

"You will be in more danger from the women than the men."

Enar brightened at once. "I think I'll be able to defend myself."

Every muscle in Owen's body tightened as the full impact of Elutides' words sank in. The blood left his skin, and the battle rage washed over him. Everything but Elutides' face blurred away before his eyes. His reply was very soft but with the menacing rasp of a serpent's scales across stone. "I will not go, living, into their hands again."

"Please, Father, don't frighten him," Cador rumbled softly from behind him. His words surprised Owen by being a plea.

Then Casgob surprised him even more by adding, "If even half the stories about him are true, he's a very dangerous man."

Owen relaxed a little, remembering that if Elutides

wanted his head, he could easily have taken it when they first met.

"We mean you no harm," Elutides said as he studied Owen with a stare of such intensity that Owen felt the lean man looked not only at what he was but tried somehow to see what he had been and what he might become.

Owen spoke to the look. "I'm trying to save my city. No more, no less. I can't imagine what stories you might have heard but . . ." He broke off as they entered the town square.

The cobbled street was cleaner here. At the center of the square, a fountain played, pouring clear water into a basin. Beyond the fountain stood the tall white colonnade of a Roman portico. Once, the oval row of columns had embraced a wide open plaza that framed the entrance to the magnificent sprawl of an ancient villa. It was a building that, along with the crumbling fortress above, must have dominated the town and countryside beyond it—a building calculated to impress the conquered savages of this poor benighted province with the sanctity of Roman order and the might of Roman arms. It was a building now rendered much less impressive since the poor benighted savages had got hold of it.

The Britons had bricked up the spaces between the columns, forming a solid wall, and roofed the open plaza with an enormous cone-shaped structure of wattle and daub.

Ilfor and Aud rode toward the door. The rest followed. At the entrance, Owen paused to dismount.

"No," Aud said. "Bring him right in, and let's see how she likes him."

So, with a shrug, Owen guided the stallion up the three shallow marble steps and entered.

The Romans were a sublime legend to Owen. It was generally conceded that the world had gone steadily downhill since their day, tottering slowly toward a final fall at the day of judgment.

Owen wondered what the orderly, sometime conquerors of the world would have thought of it, then decided he'd prefer not to know.

"We have beautiful mosaics," Queen Aud said proudly, "all over the floor."

Owen looked down. Any mosaics present were covered by a deep and suspiciously lumpy layer of rushes. In addition, the huge room was dim. The smoke hole in the roof let in only a little light.

Even in the gloom, Owen could see the pale glimmer of the white columns that formed part of the wall. Following the curve of the colonnade were stretched benches and tables. In the center of the room, under the smoke hole, a square white marble fish pond served as a fire pit.

"Wait until you see it at night," Aud said, walking toward the fire pit, "with the logs blazing and torches burning on the walls. Our hall is the fairest and coziest in Brittany."

Her whip cracked, and a pig leaped out of the fire pit with a honking screech of distress and scuttled away under the table toward the darkness near the colonnade. "Are you stupid?" Aud shouted after the pig. "Do you want to be roasted before your time? Wine!" she shouted. "Build up the fire! Give our guest a fair welcome!"

No one hurried to obey. Instead everyone crowded around the stallion. If Owen had any lingering doubts about the identity of the honored guest, they were dispelled at this moment. He was virtually ignored while the experts on horseflesh discussed the stallion's conformation in highly technical terms. Others, feeling that aesthetics outweighed mere mundane matters of bone structure and carriage, rhapsodized about the color and texture of his coat, the delicacy of his manner, his fluid grace.

The stallion arched his neck, lifted his tail, and pawed the rushes under his feet lightly, managing to look almost like a girl primping herself in front of a mirror.

"You are vain," Owen whispered.

"He has reason to be vain," Aud said in stern rebuke to Owen. "How did a scruffy fellow such as yourself become the owner of so noble a beast?"

"Aud!" Elutides said. "Fetch the mare."

"The mare!" Aud screeched. "I almost forgot the mare."

She turned and ran toward the shadows at the colonnade where the pig had taken refuge.

Owen dismounted cautiously. The rushes under his feet were springy, very deep. Something small darted away from the weight of his feet through the loose top layer, thus confirming his suspicion that not everything residing among them was quietly dead.

"How long since we lifted the rushes, my sweet?" Ilfor shouted at Aud.

"I don't know," Aud called back over her shoulder. She had reached the colonnade. The soft whicker of a horse greeted her.

"Should we not do it again sometime soon?" Ilfor asked plaintively.

"No," Aud shouted. "Not till spring. It is a most filthy job. Once lifted, there always remains the problem of disposing of them. We threw them into the sea, and the fishermen complained so I ordered them burned in the square. You and everyone else walked around holding your noses, yammering in my ears about the stench." She led the mare out around the long table toward Owen. "Besides, lifting them disturbs the mice. A horde of them descended on the household, always underfoot and gnawing everything. I killed five in my own chamber one night. I don't sleep well when they begin running about on my coverlet."

"Mice!" Ilfor grumbled. "If this keeps up, we will soon have rats."

"No," Aud said. "You need not trouble yourself about rats. The dogs kill them."

At the word "dogs" a lot of something stirred near the fire pit. Owen looked closely and found himself staring into enough pairs of yellow eyes to form a medium-size wolf pack.

Owen stripped away the stallion's bridle. The two horses stared at each other. For a few seconds it seemed as if nothing would happen.

Owen's eyes had adjusted to the dim, watery light of the hall. The long rays of blue daylight streamed down through the faint haze of smoke from the fire pit.

In the gloom, the stallion was a horse of bronze, the mare a darker shadow beside Queen Aud. Then the stallion snorted and stamped his feet silently on the thick rushes. His neck arched beautifully and his tail bannered a swirl of silk threads at his haunches. His nostrils distened as he caught the scent of the mare's heat. The veins that traced the contours of his face stood out as they filled with blood. The crowd drew back to give him room.

He began to prance slowly toward the mare. So smooth was the movement of his hocks and cannons that he seemed to have springs in his legs.

An awed sound arose from the crowd.

Elutides, at Owen's side, said softly, "He is fine, possibly the finest I've ever seen. Where did you get him?"

"In the camp of the Northmen," Owen said. "He saved my life."

"So that story is true, then," Elutides whispered. "It is said by some that the gods dispatched him to serve. . . ."

"No," Owen said. "I believe he was brought up a pet in his master's household. He's used to human beings, entering and leaving their dwellings at will. He—"

The stallion reared with a ringing scream. The mare followed, plunging, tearing her lead rope from Aud's hand, then joined him in a mad rush through the door out into the square.

"Male and female He created them," Elutides whispered.

Aud leaped into the air with a yell of delight. "She is ready."

Owen and the crowd ran to the door, following the horses. They galloped together side by side beyond the arc formed by the hall's intrusion into the square. The mare was nearly as beautiful as the stallion—a blood bay the color of polished wood with darker legs and face. They jostled each other with their shoulders as if in a test of strength, and bit playfully at each other's necks.

Then suddenly the gallop became a race in earnest. The mare stretched herself out, mane and tail flying, but the stallion passed her, matching her stride for stride; then he took the lead.

At the end of the square they turned and thundered back

past the crowd at the door, around the fountain, and came to a stop. Without further ado, the mare presented her backside to the stallion, and he mounted her.

"Now, there's a beautiful sight," Aud breathed.

Elutides sighed.

"She should get a foal of this," Owen said.

They were standing back—away from the stallion's cheering section at the door.

Elutides gave him an unhappy look. "First the horse, and then the rider."

"What do you mean?" Owen asked.

"You know perfectly well what I mean," Elutides said. "It won't take Aud long to notice your wiry good looks. Or the ardent promise of those hungry, dark eyes."

"I believe," Owen said, "that she just called me a scruffy fellow and all but named me a horse thief."

"Pha." Elutides waved a hand negligently. "How long do you think it will take for her to look beneath the worn clothing and see the man, a hero come riding out of the sunrise to—"

"Hero!" Owen hissed, "are you out of your mind? I'm no—"

"He's modest, Uncle," Gynneth spoke up. He hadn't realized she stood right behind him.

"Modest? No," Owen said. "Believe me, my lady, I have every reason not simply for modesty, but for humility. I failed my people badly, and—"

"Not a hero?" Casgob said. "Man, the whole coast rings with your exploits. Tales of how you captured a wild woods witch, bedded her, and brought her people to your side, then slaughtered Osric in his own hall. The Viking camp itself wasn't strong enough to hold you."

"I didn't capture Elin," Owen protested. "I rescued her. She accompanied me to the city of her own free will."

"That resounds even more to your credit," Elutides said. "A rescue no less, in the teeth of the Northmen's fury, of a high-hearted and beautiful woman."

Owen remembered Elin as he'd first seen her and almost laughed. The situation was perfectly ridiculous.

He felt as if he'd blundered into a bog, was already mired to the knees, and sinking deeper every second.

"As for Osric," Owen said stubbornly, "when I escaped from his prison, I didn't know my friends were on my track. I believed that I was alone, and resolved to die bravely rather than be hunted down like a wild beast. So I fired the hall and—" Owen broke off in confusion as he realized they were hanging on his every word.

"Aud will want him," Gynneth said, shaking her head in the affirmative.

"Is the king jealous?" Owen asked.

Gynneth cocked her head to one side and asked, "Why should he be jealous?"

"It's dangerous to frustrate Aud," Elutides said. "She rules here as much or more than the king does." Elutides laughed as Owen fingered his neck. "Yes, either one of them can separate your head from the rest of you and place it on a post."

Owen's eyes swept over them: Gynneth, the petite girl standing beside the two warriors; Elutides, lean as a sword blade and, Owen suspected, nearly as dangerous. "You brought me here. Why?" Owen asked in a low voice. "Or was there a reason, besides sport, like coursing a hare with hounds?"

"We brought you here because we need you," Elutides said. "But right now what I need, damnation upon it, is a distraction for the queen."

Owen looked out across the square. He saw Enar and Ceredea approaching together.

Queen Aud's gaze lighted on Enar a few seconds after Owen's did. She watched him coming over the backs of the mating horses, a gleam of interest in her eyes.

Elutides smiled very slowly. "Is this your companion, the axeman?"

"My friend," Owen said. "Enar. A good friend. I would take it amiss if anything happened to him."

Ceredea pushed through the crowd, watching the horses, and kissed Elutides on the cheek.

Enar followed, looking uncomfortable. Aud followed Enar. She looked him up and down, then back at the straining horses. "Ah," she whispered, "if only human life could be so simple." Then she threw her arms around his neck and kissed him. "What a pleasure to welcome two such handsome strangers to our city." Then she backed away very quickly. "He looks like a god but smells like a goat. By Saint Erbo, I itch just looking at him. Elutides!" she shouted.

"Yes, my lady, have no fear. I'll see to it right away."

The horses were finished now and standing side by side, nuzzling each other's faces. Aud caught the mare's lead rope and led her back into the hall to her place near the colonnade. The stallion followed with docile affection.

Elutides motioned to Cador and Casgob. "Bathe him," he said, pointing to Enar. Enar's shoulders hunched. He looked as if he might be getting ready to make a fight of it.

Owen caught his eye and shook his head. Enar sighed and relaxed.

"All over," Elutides said, "hair, everything, and burn his clothes. Fumigate him."

"Now wait . . ." Enar began indignantly.

Owen brushed past Casgob, put one arm around Enar's shoulders, and spoke into his ear. "Did you see the occupants of those posts near the city?"

"I didn't examine them closely," Enar said. "Their appearance didn't invite it."

"They incurred the queen's displeasure," Owen said.

"Ohoooo," Enar said, his eyes widening, "did they? How unwise of them."

"Yes," Owen said. "You don't wish to displease the queen, do you?"

"Oh no!" Enar said earnestly. "No, no, no, not at all, not for all the world would I want to fail in courtesy toward the good lady."

"Then bathe," Owen said, "and let them burn your clothes."

"But, Lord Christ Priest," Enar said, in some distress, "I've often been told that it's unhealthy to get wet all over. I much prefer to sweat."

"We will introduce you to the tepidarium," Casgob said from Enar's left.

"May I present Cador and Casgob," Owen said. "Casgob's the handsome one."

Enar looked left and right. "Handsome," he said, "in comparison to what?"

Casgob took hold of Enar's arm and relieved him of his knife, saying, "A clever fellow, Brother."

"Yes," Cador said, taking hold of the other arm, "but it's as the queen said. He's dirty." He removed the axe from Enar's belt.

"Oh, very rank," Cador said. "I'll strip him, Brother. You catch his clothes and burn them quickly before they can crawl away and hide."

Enar looked left and right again. His reaction to Cador and Casgob was the same as Owen's. "Oh, well," he said, scratching his ribs, "I've been looking forward to a good scrubbing."

*I*T was near dusk when Hakon's horse thundered into the yard. Hakon was soot-blackened and soaked to the skin by last night's rain.

He knew there was trouble. The villages he and his men had ridden through on their way to the stronghold were empty. From the gateway to the bailey he could see all the settlements. No lights shone in any of them.

Hakon stood for a moment, shivering in the night wind. He was both enraged and frightened. All the more enraged because he was frightened. Then, his strange eyes frozen, he strode into the hall. His men were seated at the almost empty tables. Only a few torches burned on the walls. The men ate silently, almost furtively.

As he passed through the hall, Tosi, his closest friend, rose and plucked at his sleeve. "Hakon, don't go to see her the way you are now," Tosi begged. "Wait till your anger has had a chance to cool."

Hakon turned and glared at Tosi. Tosi's hand fell away from his shoulder, and Hakon continued his progress toward Elspeth's room. He didn't kick the door open. He pushed it back quietly.

Elspeth was standing by a steaming tub. A light supper for two was laid on the table. At least a dozen torches flamed on the walls.

After he'd won Reynald's lady, Hakon had lavished his

wealth on the household, especially on Elspeth's bedroom. Between the torch brackets on the wall hung bright colored tapestries, the plunder of a nameless Iberian town. The bed coverings were ermine and sable. The furniture was cedar, hand polished and inlaid with ivory. He had intended the whole place to be the setting for a precious gem. The gem it held was Elspeth.

But now he stared at her through a murky red haze of absolute fury. He entered quietly enough, and very deliberately barred the door behind him. "What's going on here?"

Elspeth approached him cautiously. "My lord," she said softly. "Let me unarm you."

He pushed her aside. Elspeth staggered back against the bed and stared up at him. Hakon eyed the steaming bathtub and the supper laid for two on the table. "I see," he said. "My lady." He spat out the words in a rage. "A nice bath, a little supper and then what will you do? Offer me your body? Perhaps I won't notice that two-thirds of your people are gone."

Elspeth slipped to her knees. She trembled violently. Hakon stood watching her with his frozen eyes. Elspeth was too frightened to speak and almost too frightened to think. "Let me unarm you," she repeated. She reached up and her hand fell on the hilt of Hakon's sword. The sword was a beautiful thing, the silver hilt encrusted with jewels.

Hakon's fist closed very deliberately around hers. He crushed her fingers around the metal and stones. Elspeth didn't scream. She couldn't. Hakon's grip was too terrible. She sank to the floor, one arm outstretched, her fingers squeezed by Hakon's around the sword hilt. After what seemed an eternity, he let her go.

"Never," he said between his teeth, "never touch one of my weapons again. "Now," he said, beginning to strip off his hauberk, "do what seems good to you. Weep, run away, slit your wrists, or hang yourself, but whatever you do, be silent."

Elspeth scrambled to her feet, her face ashen. She stood clutching the wrist of her injured hand and staring at him. He pulled the hauberk off over his head and tossed it to

Elspeth. She caught the heavy thing and staggered under the weight of leather and metal.

"I see," he said. "You won't pretend to be too injured. Spread it out on the bed. I don't want the metal to rust."

The leather backing of the overlapping metal plates was damp. She felt it as she carefully spread the shirt on the bed.

"There," he said, throwing his filthy linen shirt at her. "I like that better. Sweet submissiveness becomes you, Elspeth."

His trousers and linen stockings were damp and muddy also. His face was sweat streaked and blackened by soot. The look in his pale eyes was terrible. When he was finished, he stood naked before her.

She avoided his eyes as though they were hot irons that might sear her skin. A fine silk Persian carpet covered the floor near the bed. Elspeth carried the filthy clothes away and piled them in a corner so they wouldn't dirty the silk rug. When she was finished, she turned and walked back toward him with downcast eyes.

Something like a red poppy seemed to bloom in the complex knotwork of the carpet. Elspeth focused her eyes on that and tried to calm herself. She was sick with fear, not just of Hakon but of what his words and his rage meant.

When she reached him, he caught her by the bodice of her gown. He shook her once, lightly, as a lethally playful cat shakes a dying mouse. He exerted little of his strength, but enough to snap her head back.

When she saw his face, she knew that for many men this had been their last sight. His lips were drawn back from his teeth, the skin stretched tight over his bones. His icy hoarfrost eyes were like still frozen wells. They glittered with implacable rage. He looked a man who, sword in hand, reaches out to strike an enemy down.

"Tonight," he whispered, "when I've finished my bath, you will dress for riding. I will want you to see what fruit the trees will bear. The oak will not carry acorns; the ash will not set its winged seeds adrift. Instead, they will be ornamented by hanged men. And you," he shook her lightly

again, "you, my sweet, will watch—each—one—gasp—
his—life—away. Treacherous bitch, treacherous and untrue
like all your people. My men will hunt them along the river
through the forest and on the shore. Every other one I catch
I'll hang. The rest will be flogged! They, like you, will
know who is master here." He flung her away.

Elspeth fell and lay on her side, her cheek against the
silken nap of the carpet. She heard the water splash and
Hakon's sigh of pleasure when he slipped into the tub.
She stroked the carpet with her fingers, thinking of her
children. She'd given them to Bettena. If she died tonight,
Bettena would get them safely away.

She grieved for her only son, Eric, more than for the
two girls. Women always seemed to find men to care for
them and somehow make do. Besides, the girls were too
young to remember her. But Eric would remember and
suffer. He would know he had once had an inheritance
and a loving mother. She thought of him and felt a pang
of sorrow so strong it was almost physical in its intensity.
Then she pushed the memory of her children out of her
mind lest it drive out the rage she needed to feel—the
blind fury that would propel her into action.

Hakon washed his face. His sheathed sword leaned
against the side of the tub. He was blinded by water when
he heard the sigh of his sword being drawn. He dashed the
water out of his eyes, looked up, and saw Elspeth.

She stood before him, clutching his own sword in her
two hands. The tip was only inches from his breast. Her
face was as terrible as his had been only a few moments
earlier. Her skin was gray and her two dark eyes were tun-
nels leading into endless night.

I'm a dead man, he thought. His back was against the
curved end of the bathtub. If he tried to move forward, he
would spit himself on the blade. If he tried to jump back,
he might easily disembowel himself getting out of the tub.
He felt like a man who pushes into a thicket thinking to
startle a hare and instead finds himself face-to-face with a
she-wolf.

Deliberately Elspeth pushed the sword forward until
the tip rested against his breastbone. A small ruby droplet

appeared. "Now." She gasped out the words. "Now! You
will listen. I was brought up to be the proper wife of a
nobleman. Trained in my youth never to cry out in pain. I
bore my children in silence. When Reynald beat me, I
never screamed, though I wept in anguish at his cruelty.
I'm not afraid of you, nor of any death you can mete out
to me."

He could feel the sword quivering with her fury. "When
Reynald was too drunk or too besotted with his women, I
rode out to put meat on the serfs' tables. And when I did, I
didn't back away from the stag's antlers, the wild boar's
tusks, or even the fangs of a cornered wolf. I'll accept your
blows, stand silent while you curse me, look away from
your rutting, and if I live, I'll give you children, biting on a
rag in labor so as not to disturb your drunken sleep. But I
will not take the blame for your stupidity.

"I tell you, if you begin these hangings, the horror will
never end for me or my children. Oh, I know my people
won't all get away. You'll catch some. But the rest will go.
And they will find themselves welcome elsewhere. Some
are skilled craftsmen. Chantalon will embrace those. Other
lords will stretch out their hands to men and women who
will till the soil and increase their wealth."

Elspeth took a deep breath, and Hakon marveled at her
ability to hold his heavy sword steady. He began to have
some hope of life. He could see color beginning to come
into her cheeks, and her eyes had stopped staring like a
madwoman's. He stirred slightly, moving away from the
sword tip.

"Be still," she whispered, jabbing the point at him. "I'm
not finished." Her voice quivered with the soft warning of
a serpent's hiss.

"If you begin these hangings, within a year your fields
will yield only crops of thistles and weeds. Yellow broom
will blow where the houses once stood. Those vaunted
men of yours are better at drinking than plowing, better at
stealing than working, and better at killing than bringing
life from the soil. They will desert your starving stronghold in search of more prosperous chieftains. And you
will be left alone here among moldering ruins." Elspeth

lowered the sword, letting the flat side of the blade rest on the edge of the tub.

Hakon again felt an uprush of terror. The foot of the tub was higher than the back. If she let go of the hilt, the falling sword would shear through his body. But now he could see the white-hot fury that drove her was draining away into exhaustion.

There were tears in her eyes. "I didn't ask for your love," she said sadly. "I didn't expect to have even half a life with you. Now I can't imagine life without you. But if you destroy my people you will breed white-hot a hate in my heart. You will have to kill me before I can find a way to kill you. And I would rather feel your steel in my body now, tonight, than see you destroy all I love in your folly."

With those words, she drew the sword back and cast it aside. It fell on the carpet beside the bed with a ringing sound that was almost a cry of regret. Then she turned her back and walked away from him.

Hakon climbed out of the tub. He was shaking with equal parts relief, terror, and, he realized to his own horror, pride. He could feel his belly muscles fluttering, feel the mixture of warm water and blood running down his stomach.

He caught up to Elspeth in two strides and grasped her hair with his left hand. He didn't pull the hair or jerk her head back. He only let her feel the power of his grip. She turned her head toward him. He saw only mute resignation in her expression.

He lifted his right hand, fist clenched, and shook it in her face. "I can kill a man with one blow," he said. "I didn't know that when I was young. I found out on my first voyage. One moment he was a man standing before me, challenging me, the next he was a rag rolling in the bilges, face a mass of blood, oozing into the filthy water. You're a rag, too. Like he was. A silk-and-velvet rag. Silken hair, velvet skin, with a basket of fiery coals at the fork of your thighs."

Elspeth's eyes slowly closed. An expression of triumph transfigured her face. She was naked. Hakon wasn't sure how she had so quickly disrobed, but naked she was, and he was throwing her onto the bed.

He hesitated for a second, thinking he didn't want to rape her, and then realized her legs and thighs were clasping his buttocks, forcing him forward and in. She was as ready for him as he was for her. The pleasure carried him higher and higher, almost to the very threshold of pain. Then desire was what a breaking sea is to a drowning man. The pulsations of her raw fulfillment drew him down and down and down.

He came to himself, gasping on the pillow. She was stretched out under his body. He could feel the quiet ebb and flow of her breathing against his chest. His lips and face were pressed against the long silken tangle of her hair. "I blundered," he said. "I never should have set that fire."

"You're so warm," she said. "Hot in fact." Her arms were around him, one hand resting on his neck. The other stroked his back gently.

"I'm a heavy blanket," he said.

"You certainly keep out the cold," she said.

"I blundered," he said again.

"Not seriously," she said. "All they're worried about is the pigs."

"What?" Hakon shouted, levering himself off her and rolling aside. "Is it just the pigs, the damned pigs?" he roared.

Someone rapped on the door. Elspeth recognized Bettena's voice. "I'm fine," she answered. She was off the bed, scooping up her gown and slipping into it.

"My lady." Bettena rapped again anxiously.

"Don't worry," Hakon snarled. "Your little falcon is holding her own. I can see now why the male is only a tiercel. Go away."

Elspeth sat down on the bed, giggling as Bettena's footsteps scurried off.

"The pigs," Hakon muttered as he dug through a clothes chest and pulled out clean trews, stockings, and a shirt.

"The pigs may be a small matter to you," Elspeth said

as she began combing her hair. "But they are the winter meat supply for the villagers."

"I see," Hakon said.

"Do you?" Elspeth asked.

He was pulling the shirt on over his head. "Yes," he answered. "I really do. I may have killed a few with the fire, but there must be at least a hundred or so more rooting around in the lowlands near the river. I can set my men to hunting them, and in a few days I can promise the head of every household a fat porker for his table. Do you think that will bring them back?"

Elspeth nodded as she pinned her hair up. "Yes," she said emphatically. She paused for a second and looked into the silver mirror in front of her. "God," she whispered. "That was worse than childbirth. Is it always necessary to hold a knife to your throat to make you see reason?"

Hakon picked up his sword. He flourished it in his hand, examining the blade for water marks and the tip for traces of his own blood. It was clean. He sheathed it. "You took a terrible risk with me," he said. "I almost killed you when I came out of the bath."

"The way you killed the man in the longboat?" she asked. "With your fist?"

"Yes."

"How did it happen?" she asked as she was giving the finishing touches to her hair.

Hakon shrugged and walked toward her. He looked over her shoulder into the mirror. "We were many days at sea," he said. "There are better accommodations for chieftains aboard a dragon ship, but I wasn't one of those who enjoyed them. I was an outlaw, a landless man hunted even by my own kin, only another hand to pull an oar, a body to be thrown first into the breach in a fight. I didn't even own a sword.

"By day I rowed with the rest. By night I slept on the decks. After a good many days at sea, we were often hungry and always cold, wet, and afraid. Tempers flared easily.

"Nearing the English coast, we had only some oat porridge and a little bread left. I put my bit of bread down to swallow the porridge, and when I looked up, I saw him gulping it down. The rest began laughing at me. I smashed my fist into his face. He died at once. I think I broke his neck. I cannot even remember his name, if I ever knew it. The sea was his grave. A cold gray grave, the sea, and none to mourn the fallen who lie there."

Elspeth's eyes locked with his in the mirror. "You learned not to hit out without thinking."

Hakon smiled. She was always surprised by his rare smiles. They seemed to lighten his features and give them a good-humored, boyish cast.

He squeezed her shoulder lightly. "Yes," he said. "Everyone else was impressed. I was sorry. It seemed a poor exchange—a man's life for a piece of bread. Until then I'd been ignored by the rest. After that, the starving rabble aboard the longship went out of their way to avoid provoking me. The whoresons were impressed. Tosi told me that on that day I took my first step on the road to command, to good fortune. That is, if command of scoundrels awed by a quick killing could be considered an accomplishment. I don't even know if I lead my men. They may simply use me, someone strong enough, wise enough to steer them past the rocks in a torrent. If my luck or wisdom fails, they will probably cut my throat, cast me into the river, and choose another."

He turned abruptly and said, "No one loves a tyrant. My men would never follow one, and I can see your people won't, either." Hakon eyed the table and the covered dishes on it.

"You understood my plan perfectly," Elspeth said. "A bath, a little supper, and then offer you my body."

"We skipped supper," Hakon said. "I suppose the food is cold."

"No, that's why it's covered," Elspeth said as she drifted toward the table.

Hakon sat down opposite her. The table rested on another of Hakon's fine silken carpets. He dug his bare feet into the nap and wiggled his toes. He sighed with pleasure when she uncovered a larded capon stuffed with a forcemeat of breadcrumbs, butter, and black mushrooms. Elspeth lifted a gleaming table knife and carved the capon.

Elspeth finished carving and placed meat and stuffing on his plate. He had good table manners. He sat upright at the table, ate the stuffing with a spoon, and when he drank, he used the napkin to wipe the cup he and Elspeth shared. "You made much of being a noblewoman in the little speech you made while you had me trapped in the tub. Does it matter to you that I am nothing?"

Elspeth's lowered lids lifted, and she stared him full in the face. "Whatever your birth, you are not nothing. And no, it doesn't bother me. I only meant to show you I could be brave, too. That I have my dignity also."

Hakon nodded. "Why didn't you kill me? My men wouldn't notice my absence till morning. Maybe not even then. I imagine most of them are well on their way to a drunken stupor even now. You could have been far away by dawn. A lot of my wealth is in this room. You could have taken it with you."

"Didn't you understand a word I said?" she asked bitterly. "Without you, I don't care to live. I'd as willingly kill you as myself. I might as well. I'd die, too."

Hakon stopped eating, rested his elbows on the table, and clasped his hands. "Before I met you, I dreamed of you," he said. "Sometimes when the camp wearied me, I would go ashore and walk in the forest along the riverbank. The forest is never really silent. Birds sing. The trees speak to each other as the wind takes them; sometimes they only whisper. At other times they sigh with contentment, feeling, perhaps, the warm sun, the clear cool air. I have heard even in my sleep the roar of welcome they give a summer storm as it rolls its black clouds over them.

"I would walk among them, listening to their ever changing voices, and dream. Sometimes I would take the thick, black soil in my fist and feel the crackle of last winter's oak leavees against my palm. And I would think, I want this to be mine. Mine and my son's sons, forever. But how can I make this dream a reality? Then one day, I heard Reynald was dead. Even before I got your message, I was already preparing myself to act.

"When I saw you, I couldn't believe my good fortune. Perhaps that's why I was so angry with you tonight. I'm always looking for the worm in the apple, weevil in the bread, or maggots in the meat. Perhaps this cup, wherein I drink all my desires, may yet be snatched from my lips."

"You didn't catch Owen," she said.

"No," Hakon answered. "Elspeth, do you know they say among my people 'better a fool and coward with luck than a wise man without'? Of a certainty I have no luck with the bishop."

"He hasn't had any with you, either," Elspeth said. "It may well be you're simply not destined to face each other. Some whim of the fates keeps you apart. It doesn't mean you won't take the city in the end."

Hakon nodded and continued eating. "I can't do that with treachery at my back." He felt again the black rage rising in him as he remembered the empty villages.

"What you see isn't treachery," Elspeth said earnestly, pleadingly. "It's only a protest against your disregard for their concerns. They will be back tomorrow. I promise. If only you will promise me no one will be harmed and the fat porkers will be on their tables."

Hakon was finished eating. He banged the spoon down on the plate, rose, and began to pace. "I promise. I won't hang anyone," he said.

Elspeth rose also. "That's a cheap evasion," she snapped. "Worthy of Bertrand. You said nothing of flogging, branding, or . . ."

Hakon froze where he stood, and she could see she'd angered him again. The scar that coursed down from his hair, crossing his forehead to the bridge of his nose, flamed dangerously. "I don't deal in cheap evasions, but if you prefer, my lady, I'll give you a more general promise. No one will be harmed."

Elspeth's eyes closed. She sighed deeply with relief. "Thank God," she whispered. "Now," she said, "there's one more thing." Her eyes opened and she saw Hakon's bad temper had vanished. He was advancing on her with a grin on his face.

"One more favor . . . ?" he asked, taking her in his arms.

"Give them a little feast," she squeaked. He lifted her dress.

"Oh, a little feast, is it?" He nuzzled her neck.

"Yes, it's almost time to put the winter crop in."

"I'll give them all the feasts they want," Hakon said. "Now shut up about it." His nostrils were distended. He was breathing heavily.

She could feel the rise and fall of a chest sheathed in iron muscle pressed against her breasts. She was naked. "Put out the torches," she whispered.

"Why do you always want to darken the room?" he complained. His fingers were doing exquisite things to her breasts.

"It's wicked to do it in the light." Suddenly she felt herself thrust back, away from him. "What . . ." she whispered. "Did I do something wrong?"

"No," Hakon said. His eyes were dark as storm clouds. A flush of desire burned his cheeks. "Get your jewels."

"You want me to get dressed?" she asked in sweet confusion.

"No," Hakon said. "Forget the dress. Only your jewels. I've been toying with you up to now. Before I leave here in the morning, you're going to find out what wicked really means."

Chapter

22

*A*FTER Cador and Casgob led Enar away, Gynneth took Owen's arm. "Come," she said, "let me show you the villa. It's very old and very beautiful."

"I will accompany you," Elutides said.

Halfway through the tour Owen concluded that the villa had never been intended by its builders as a dwelling. It must once have been the opulent administrative center of a Roman province.

The few remaining habitable rooms were big and elaborate, with floors of marble bound in bronze intended for heavier use than they would have been subjected to in a private house.

The queen's chamber was circular. Plugs of glass in the domed roof let in the light. The walls were decorated by a painting of the god Pan pursuing maidens through a garden. Owen studied the painting thoughtfully. "Very . . . attractive," he said.

"Oh, but how inappropriate, don't you think?" Gynneth said softly. "Properly speaking, to make Aud completely happy, the maidens should be pursuing him."

Owen looked at her quickly, but her face was the picture of sweet innocence and purity.

"Intelligent girl," Elutides laughed.

They strolled from the queen's room out into the atrium. The garden had been kept up, though the flower-loving

Romans might have found some parts of it strange. Onions, leeks, and turnips clustered around the marble pedestals of gods and goddesses. Peas were trained against the Doric columns supporting the porch roof. In beds surrounding the formal square's central pool, cabbages were swelling happily in the sunshine.

The only flowers that remained were herbs, the high yellow heads of yarrow, spikes of blooming gray sage, white-and-gold chamomile, and the blue brushes of tall mints. Even in the pool, sweet flag stood above clusters of butter-flowered watercress. Low mats of thyme clumped between the flagstones of the path, its scent drawing bees and perfuming the warm air.

Owen found it relaxing and beautiful. The statues, though, were faintly disturbing. He found their graceful nudity shockingly pagan.

Elutides paused before one. The sculptor had represented the goddess of love as a young girl, her rounded breasts just budding. She cupped a plump beauty lightly with the fingers of one hand, offering the nipple to a dove perched on the other.

"Are you a Christian?" Owen asked Elutides abruptly.

"Yes," he answered, raising one eyebrow inquisitively. "Why?"

"I'd think Christians would want to be rid of such things."

"Oh," Elutides said, "really, I can't think so. Look at her face. Wouldn't it be a shame to destroy such beauty?"

Owen raised his eyes to the statue's face. She was lovely. The pale, marble oval was surrounded by ringlets. The hair and features were so exquisitely molded they almost seemed real. She smiled down at him with pagan gentleness. Owen tore his eyes away and quickly walked on.

Elutides and Gynneth followed.

"Yes," he said to Elutides, "she is beautiful, too beautiful. A painting is flat. It lies against a wall. But she looks as though she might come to life and speak at any moment."

Elutides chuckled. "I think that may be the problem. She does speak to you and of things you'd rather forget."

"My people were never conquered by the Romans. I find them less easy to admire than you do," Owen said stiffly.

"Perhaps," Elutides said smoothly, "that was your loss."

Gynneth laughed. "Never debate my uncle; he always has an answer."

"Shush, girl," Elutides said, grinning. "Don't offend our prudish hero. We need him."

Owen paused. They were nearing the end of the long garden. Beyond the marble portico he could see the open sky and hear the rush and crash of waves. He felt humiliated and very angry. He realized his cheeks were scarlet. Elutides had rebuked him as a wise elder might a forward child, and he felt the sting of the reproof. "A prude, am I?" he asked bitingly. "Yes, I suppose I am. I find it offensive that such loveliness could be so crassly set forth for any passerby to gape at. When I looked at her I felt . . ." Owen faltered.

"Desire stiffened your flesh," Elutides finished the sentence for him. "That's natural in a young man. I would that I were so young again myself. She is very beautiful."

"She's more than that," Owen said. "She's a reminder of all they were and all we are not. They built palaces to live in—"

"Not for everyone," Elutides said.

But Owen rushed on. "They conquered an empire. I cannot win the security of one city and the few farms that surround it. They—"

"Sowed the wind," Elutides said, "and we have reaped the whirlwind."

Owen was brought up short. He was used to the theories he'd been taught by Bertrand being accepted as givens in any conversation. "How so?" he asked.

"By destroying every powerful state around them," Elutides said, "and opening the floodgates of barbarism."

Owen was completely bewildered. "Then you don't think our present troubles are part of God's plan?"

Elutides shook his head. "On the contrary, I think everything is part of God's plan. But . . ." He raised his hand. "I'm not sure that I or any other man understands the mind of the Almighty or what He intends for us. And further, he who tells you he does is a liar."

Owen's mouth opened, then closed. He was completely confounded.

Gynneth, however, took his arm affectionately. "Come, Uncle," she said demurely. "He's a hero. Heroes aren't supposed to think. They're supposed to fight, and by all accounts, he does that very well, don't you?" she asked, giving Owen such a long-lashed look of admiration that his knees nearly melted.

"You just insulted me," he said, "and I didn't feel it."

"Did I?" Gynneth answered guilelessly. "I can't think so. All I see in your reaction to the Roman beauty is respect for womanhood. Is that a bad quality in a man? But come, you haven't seen the best part of the villa, our walk by the sea." She led him from the garden, through the portico, into the sun.

The high porch he stood on now followed the edge of the cliff overlooking the ocean. The floor here was mosaic, a beautiful pattern of fruiting grape vines. The glass tesserae of the twining growth gleamed in the warm light, the deep amethyst and scarlet fruits glowing against the green leaves.

The porch was railed by a waist-high wall of masonry that supported tiny Corinthian columns of marble topped by a light roof of trellis laths. The roof allowed light to enter freely but broke the worst of the midday sun.

Through the laths Owen could see the crumbling fortress that towered high above them. Below, the waves boiled the water a shifting emerald and aquamarine amid the jaws of rocks black as ebony.

The wind blew hard, yet it carried with it the cool fresh caress that blesses only air that has flown long over open water. It was scented with the sweet breath of endless freedom.

Gynneth walked to the rail and, winding one arm around a pillar, looked down into the sea below. "Sometimes," she said, "when I stand here at the moon tide, the waves leap so high I can taste the spray on my lips and feel it dampen my hair. Truly, is this not the most beautiful part of the villa?"

"Yes," Owen said, but he was looking at her, not the sea.

The breeze molded the dress against her young body and brought a flush, fair as the first light of dawn, to her cheeks. He realized why the young goddess standing among the flowers had roused not only his lust but his protective instincts. Seeing her, he'd looked not upon cold marble but at a living, young girl naked and waiting, asking to be loved. A girl like Gynneth.

Elutides broke in on his reverie. "Have you a wife?" he asked.

"Yes," Owen replied.

"That's a problem," Elutides said.

"Why?" Owen said. "I'm not looking for another one."

A high wind-driven wave broke hard against the rocks below. Some mortar at the base of the column Gynneth's arm rested on crumbled and fell into the sea. The thin shaft of the marble shifted with a loud grating sound.

Owen gave a cry of alarm and reached out to draw her back from the edge. "This place is dangerous."

A hard gust whipped Elutides' mantle, snapping the fabric with a sound like tearing cloth. "Yes," he said with a smile, "in that and other ways. This porch will soon fall into the sea, as much else has here. Come, I'll show you."

He led Owen along the walk until they reached a flight of marble steps that led curving against the side of the cliff into the water below. The emerald sea was so transparent in the sunlight that Owen could pick out the place where the mosaic began again at the foot of the steps. Vine leaves and fruit, purple and green even with the shallow water covering them, continued down and down into the depths.

The moving waves stilled between one crest and another, and through the glassy surface Owen saw the outline of buildings and courtyards, only shadows now, lost forever in the changing movement of the ocean.

"Yes," Elutides said, "in time all this will be gone. Tell me, do you like Gynneth?"

"I like her very well," Owen said, "but . . ."

"Good," Elutides said. "I need a husband for her, and the man must be a hero. You're the closest thing to a hero I've come across in some time."

Owen felt a cold sweat break out all over his body. He'd suspected that Elutides might be dangerous. He was certain now. The tall old man in his black robe with the bloody stripe was like a figure of death in the sun, his lean lantern-jawed face saturnine and raw-angled as a skull in the bright light from the sea.

Owen didn't know if he could fight his way out of here, but he stood the best chance now if he took the old devil by surprise. The thought of Enar gave him a pang of regret, but the queen liked him, and the big Saxon was well able to fend for himself.

His left hand dropped to the scabbard of his sword as his right crept toward the hilt. "No," he said. "I have a wife, and she pleases me well."

Elutides drew back up one of the two steps.

Owen was taut as a bowstring, the skin drawn tight over the bones of his face.

"Think for a moment, my hero, before you cut me down," Elutides said quietly. "I'm not so inhospitable as you suppose. If you truly mean no, I'll let it go at that. In a day or so you may be on your way. And Gynneth will fall to a berserk."

"A berserk?" Owen whispered.

Elutides nodded. "A great lover of the battle gods, her suitor is. They have marked him as their own."

Owen sagged against the rock beside the stairs.

"He is a horror," Elutides said quickly. "I will see her dead before I let her enter his embrace."

"Old man," Owen whispered back, "who do you take me for? Alexander? Charlemagne? Even were I as fearsome a warrior as they are, how could I ever prevail against these killers? I have only my sword and no other arms or armor."

"A mere detail," Elutides said. "One that can be dealt with easily. You have only to trust me and—"

"Trust you?" Owen hissed. "An hour ago I had not met you. Leave the girl alone. Many as innocent and beautiful as she have gone to worse fates and with less ceremony. We live in troubled times. They may even make a match of it somehow," he finished lamely.

"Impossible," Elutides said. His mouth hardened. He stared out over the ocean. "This man is in love with death. She is the only mistress he has. When you see him you will understand. Gynneth is a great match. The city and the rich lands around it go with her hand. That's why he wants her. The moment they are wed, Hakon will send his Vikings to take over the city. It will be the end of all of us, and you, too. There is a harbor nearby where he can base his longships. How long will your people be able to stand against him then?"

"They hold other harbors along the coast," Owen said. "Yet they trouble us little or not at all. No, my city needs me. Now, stand aside and let me pass."

Three steps up, Elutides' lean figure towered over him, stark against the white marble. "Coward! I offer you a kingdom and more than a kingdom, a chance to prove your manhood in deeds of unsurpassed might and valor, and you stand before me cringing, knees knocking together, and cry for homesickness. You look on the last vestiges of Roman glory and would in barbarian prudery destroy that glory because it reminds you of how small you would have been in their eyes.

"How little you understand of how those Roman glories were bought and paid for—the risks taken, the blood shed for prizes won and lost."

Owen was stung almost to rage. "Quickly enough, old man, you'd use that barbarian prudery of mine to persuade me to fight your battles, to fight for a woman who—"

Gynneth appeared at the top of the steps. "Are you quarreling?" she asked. "You are quarreling, over me?"

"No," Elutides said, staring down at Owen with contempt,

"I'm being instructed. The lord Owen is instructing me in sniveling weakness and worldly expedience."

Gynneth didn't speak. Instead, her fingers played with a strand of her long hair as she looked sadly from one man to the other. "He's refusing to help us, isn't he, Uncle?" she asked quietly, with a look of sorrowful resignation on her face.

Owen thought again of her as he'd seen her standing under the oak in the first light of morning, the mist bejeweling her hair, and of the pale pagan maiden in the garden—youth at the threshold of life caught by the skill of the ancient sculptor frozen in marble forever.

He thought of what he knew of the berserks, those blood-spilling lovers of darkness. They would crush the beauty that stood in the clear, bright light from the sea as easily as a man's hand crushes the life from a butterfly.

Owen lowered his head and rested his hand against the black rocks of the cliff face by his side. "There are," he said slowly, "some kinds of cowardice that take more courage than I have. I'll do what I can to help you, old man, but I think you overestimate me. I can't fight twelve men alone. I'll be slaughtered like a suckling calf. She will fall to this Ivor . . . in spite of all I can do."

Gynneth looked at her uncle. "Is that true?"

"No," Elutides answered. He stared at Owen, but Owen avoided meeting his eyes. "We have Cador, Casgob, myself, and your large friend, the axeman, Enar," Elutides said.

Owen raised his head quickly. "Berserks!" he said, "twelve of them, old man. The odds are still better than two to one. What of your people? Are there no men among who will fight?"

"We have suffered the same Viking raids your people have," Elutides said. "Most of our warriors are away. They ride with our king. He fights on the borders of our land. Even had I the power to call them home, I have no assurance they would return in time."

"These . . . these," Gynneth's voice quavered, "creatures of hell descended on us but three days ago. So far Aud has hedged. She flatters their leader and feasts him.

Ilfor makes promises and looks at their gold with covetous eyes. When I first saw you in the wood I thought, I hoped, you were one of the good people come to carry me off . . . to save me, to . . ." Her face twisted and her breath came faster and faster. "Oh, Uncle," she gasped, "I know you told me to be brave but . . ." She sobbed now. The tears streamed down her cheeks. "Oh God, I'm disgracing myself in front of our guest. I will lie with him, Uncle. I will wed him rather than see brave men die." She turned and fled.

Owen's head bowed wearily. He stared down at the steps at his feet realizing the blocks that formed them were cracked and lay askew, the crevices between slimed with waterweed as the sea had slowly begun to reclaim them, too.

"I can't think," Elutides said quietly, "that the creature wants to lie with her. I doubt she'll survive her wedding night, nor will any of the rest of us if he has his way."

Owen raised his head and stared out at the blue haze of the horizon, at the ocean basking in that magnificent clear light that seems to defy time and distance, making every image of possibility a near reality. Then he turned and struck the harsh rock of the cliff face with his fist and bowed his head against his arm. "What of my city if I help you? What of my city if I die?"

"What of your city if Hakon takes mine?" Elutides asked. "What of your city if the berserks hunt you through the countryside here?"

Owen turned slowly to face the black-robed man standing above him on the steps. He saw power and an ageless certainty glowing in the dark eyes.

Elutides smiled. "How long would you live?"

"Long enough for Elin and Godwin to accomplish their purposes," Owen said.

"I promise that even if you fall, you will live as long as it takes for Elin and Godwin to defend the city and the citizens who daily await your return."

"How?" Owen asked.

Elutides reached down and seized Owen's arm in a powerful clawlike grip. Owen was suddenly glad he hadn't tried to fight his way past him. Elutides virtually compelled Owen up the steps and down the walkway at high speed, saying as they went, "We have no time to lose. Come. You will die unless I can teach you what you are."

"Not a berserk!" Owen said, trying angrily to break free of the iron grip.

Elutides threw him a look of icy contempt. "No! The berserks learned the uses of the battle frenzy from us! Now, don't argue any more. You've chosen to help Gynneth. I saw it clearly written on your face when you looked at her, when you saw her grief, her despair. You are utterly without guile, one of those for whom deception is almost impossible. It's a trait that will make your life miserable at times, I'm afraid, but one that will . . ." He broke off as they entered a room that faced out into the atrium garden.

Elutides' lair was the strangest room Owen had ever entered. The ceiling was hung with dried herbs as his own cellar was, but along the walls were stacked more books than Owen had ever seen in one place in his life. Accompanying them were glass beakers and bottles of liquid, all dark and vile looking. More jars rested on the table. Most were earthenware and opaque to his eye. Dried bats, mice, and even the ophidian eye of a serpent or two stared out at him from the gloom.

On a bench running beside the long table, Ceredea was comforting Gynneth. She rose when they entered, a look of anxiety on her face, her eyes wide, lips parted. "You have persuaded him?" she asked.

"Not I, you!" Elutides said. Gynneth sank back onto the bench into Ceredea's arms. Elutides spun Owen around and dropped him into a chair placed against the wall.

"Yes, and the more fool I for it," Owen answered.

"Then whatever happens," Gynneth breathed, "Ivor will not prevail."

"Not if I live long enough, beautiful lady," Owen said. He glanced around the room. "Where is Enar?"

"Bathing," Ceredea said, looking at her knuckles.

"Still?" Owen said.

Ceredea giggled. "The queen is helping him."

"Oh!" Owen exclaimed.

"It was very funny," Ceredea said. "Casgob said, 'Strip.' Your friend growled and grumbled but did. Cador carried his clothes to the furnace that heats the baths saying, 'I feel these should be disposed of at once, lest the inhabitants become alarmed and seek safety in flight.'

" 'Murder,' your friend said, trying the water with his toe, 'are you not ashamed taking so many innocent lives?' 'No,' Casgob said, and shoved your friend into the water. He stood up and said, 'Well, at least it's warm.' Then the queen stood up and shouted, 'Surprise!' Your friend let out a yell and crouched down in the water up to his chin.

"So Aud jumped on his back and ducked him. Up he came, sputtering and screeching that she would drown him. But she sat on his shoulders, saying nice things about his size and strength, and unbraided his hair, washing it as she did, while Cador and Casgob poured fragrant oils into the pool.

"She was scrubbing his body when I left. He was still making noises, but more pleasant ones, and didn't seem to mind that he was wet all over."

"The king?" Owen asked.

Ceredea seemed puzzled. "He's visiting the lady who gives him fragrant garlands," she said.

Elutides pushed aside some of the junk on the table, clearing a space around a big iron mortar and pestle.

"Tell me," he asked Owen, "are you always so easily persuaded to commit suicide?"

"Oh, Uncle," Gynneth gasped.

Owen jumped to his feet. "Old man, you're a wonder. You contradict yourself every other breath. One moment you're praising the Romans to the skies. A few moments later you're telling me they're to blame for all our troubles. A short time ago you were begging me to help you. Now I'm a fool. . . ."

"Sit down!" Elutides roared. Owen found himself sitting down. "I didn't say you were a fool," Elutides muttered as he began measuring ingredients from several bags and bottles on the table into the mortar. "I merely wondered at your willingness to put your body between us and our troubles." The tall man's brows drew together in a frown.

"I heard you praise the old imperium," Owen said. "Had those Romans not their share of barbarian auxiliaries willing to fight for them, lured by gold and the shining splendor of a civilization they barely understood? I believe that was how the Franks first came here."

Elutides laughed. "Cynic."

"Yes," Owen said. "Consider me your barbarian auxiliary."

Elutides gave him a quick grin of approval. "You have some education," he said.

"I learned of the Romans at my mother's knee," Owen answered. "Of Caesar's conquest of Gaul, and the Book of Gregory, bishop of Tours, who did write of the Frankish kings and their doings."

"Not always in praise," Elutides said.

"No," Owen said, "but then they were rude, unlettered men who couldn't speak in their own defense. While Caesar wrote his own book, he would hardly include anything discreditable to himself."

Elutides threw back his head and howled with laughter. "Oh, how I would love to have you as a student of mine," he said, wiping his eyes.

"Are you a teacher?" Owen asked.

"Yes, among other things," Elutides said, beginning to pound the mixture in the mortar with the heavy iron pestle. "Your mother must have been a Frankish lady of quality."

"Yes," Owen said, "Clotild was of good family. She told us that while we must be skilled in arms, she would not have us hang our heads in shame among the Frankish lords or before any man of wider understanding."

"Indeed, a great lady," Elutides said, "and married to a man who might be kin to this Ivor who troubles us."

Owen was on his feet in an instant. "Old man, don't think to carry your insults too far. And don't mention my lord and father, Gestric, in the same breath with the off-scourings of a chamber pot like Ivor. My father is a proper Christian, temperate, just, and generous. He is a scourge to his enemies, with a strong arm to defend his people, and a comfort and a prop to his friends in adversity. Whatever his lineage be—"

Elutides smacked the pestle against the side of the mortar. The metal rang like a bell, bringing Owen's tirade temporarily to an end. "Oh, sit down. Save your energy for Ivor. Don't take offense where none is intended. I agree, whatever your father's lineage, his son is a credit to him, brave and loyal." Owen, mollified, began to sit down again until Elutides added, "But proud, stiff-necked, hot-blooded, and obstinate."

"If you want me to fight for you, old man, stop baiting me," Owen snapped back.

Ceredea, sitting beside Gynneth on the bench, broke into a silvery peal of laughter. "Impossible." She leaped to a handstand on top of the table where she began to walk its length, still on her hands, picking her way expertly among the clutter toward where Elutides stood pounding the contents of the mortar. "When?" she asked Elutides.

"Tonight," he answered, "at the feast. I like to settle my accounts quickly."

There had been kindness, affection, and compassion in his face when he spoke to Owen. All of these drained out of his features. The black eyes held the inexorable chill of a winter night which spares nothing its cruelty. His lips had the grim set of the executioner who listens to pleas for mercy and watches the sufferings of the condemned, his decision unaltered, then ruthlessly lets fall the axe.

And Owen knew, whatever his personal fate might be, Ivor would die tonight. "You're not a man of passion," Owen said.

"No," Elutides answered, "the passions, after all, are but the servants of the will. My will is too strong to allow them free rein."

"Besides," Ceredea said, "Owen will want to hurry home to his witch queen." She leaped to the floor and undulated suggestively. "You know how her kind can beguile."

"Indeed," Elutides said. "The wonder is she took an honest Frank and didn't choose to instruct Hakon, the Viking chief."

Anger burned in Owen's breast. "Old man, you are my host and I am your guest, but don't try my good nature by insulting first my father, then my wife." So saying, he turned and stalked out of the room, through the courtyard to the porch over the ocean. He gripped the balustrade and looked out over the sea, oblivious to all else until he heard the sound of a sigh.

Gynneth stood beside him. She was silent, her eyes downcast. The wind ruffled her long hair.

"What is it?" Owen asked angrily. "Is your uncle afraid I'll run away? Did he send you to bring me back?"

"No," she said, raising her eyes, "but he did say stand near you that you might look upon me."

Owen understood perfectly what was in Elutides' mind. He invited Owen to make a comparison between her innocent beauty and Elin.

No, Owen thought. *Elin was not innocent. There was no innocence about her. Whatever age she might be in years, Elin had never been as young as this girl.*

He remembered her as he'd first seen her—naked, kneeling on the wolf skins by the fire. The gold of the firelight enhanced the ripe wheat color of her skin, a darkness bequeathed to her by her mother's people. Her blue eyes seemed to concentrate the light of the sky in their depths.

He'd asked her why she didn't bar the door. He was shy. Proud, as Elutides said. Stiff-necked, especially where women were concerned. Had she barred the door he'd have turned away. Frustrated, bitter, and angry he might have been, but he would never have forced the issue. Not in his wildest dreams could he imagine himself doing that. But she hadn't barred the door. Instead, she'd stretched out her arms to him and spoken of life.

Her words went straight to his heart. She had trusted her bruised body, marked, scarred by cruelty, to his hands, and he hadn't failed her, meeting that trust with tenderness and love because he had scars of his own. He, too, had tasted the ultimate pain and defeat one human can inflict on another, short of death. In the midst of that darkness, he had chosen, as she had chosen, life.

And Christ, there had been darkness. Oh God, what darkness. He'd lain in the cell where Bertrand penned him, staring into the blackness that sealed his open eyes like a coffin lid. His whole soul yearned, prayed for one pinprick of light, if only to remind him that somewhere it was morning, somewhere the sun still shone and men went about their work and days in happiness.

He'd lain in the darkness shivering with the cold, damp chill of the stone cell, smelling the musty scent of the clothes rotting on his body, the stench of his own foulness. In the end, he'd soiled himself again and again, having neither the strength nor will to rise and clean the filth from his withering flesh.

Yet he, too, had clung to life, even in his final descent into utter madness when he'd almost forgotten who he was, what he was, or that he had ever been a man. Even in that extremity, he'd held fast to living. Even a desert of endless pain was preferable to nothingness.

Beside Elin, Gynneth, for all her beauty, was a pallid shadow.

In his youth, he had loved the storms that rose on the horizon during the harvest. Working in the fields with his father's men, he would lay down his scythe to watch them come, black against the gold of the ripening wheat, the high clouds' crests almost crystalline in their purity against the blue of the sky while below they boiled with the dark fury of the rain, the splendor of bursts of lightning.

He loved Elin the way he loved the storm. She was a fierce woman. Her spirit followed him into the cage. That had been no dream. He was sure of it now. She had stretched out her hands into the darkness and refused to let him die, infusing him with her strength and not caring if the spirits she summoned were from heaven or hell. She'd called the battle god to aid her and brought him to Owen's side. She attacked his enemies with whatever powers were at her command and destroyed them. She had given Owen her promise and would hold the city until death.

Elutides' voice broke in on his reverie. "Surely you know you cannot wive such a woman as Elin? If indeed

Elin really is her name. She may have lied in that. A wild wood witch probably would lie in that as in much else. You were not her first man, nor will you be her last."

Owen spun around, a scream of rage on his lips. His hand closed on the sword hilt as automatically as he drew breath. A foot of steel cleared the sheath. Then, Elutides, with a faint smile, stepped in. His hands clamped suddenly around Owen's wrists. Owen found he couldn't move.

Elutides held him as easily as a strong man holds a child, frozen, sword half out of the sheath. Owen heard the ragged scrape of breath from his mouth and nose as they struggled silently. Elutides' eyes, inches away, locked with his. His dark gaze was strangely mild as were his words, "Don't do that. You'll regret it."

Owen already regretted it. His hands were numb. The crushing force of Elutides' grip increased every second. He shifted his weight, trying to throw him off. A mistake. An instant later he found himself pressed against the masonry of the parapet, one arm pinned between his shoulder blades, looking down at the sea foaming against the jagged rocks below.

"Now," Elutides said in the same conversational tone. "Do you believe I have anything to teach you?"

"I hope," Owen said, eyeing the jumble of boulders at the foot of the cliff, "that yes is the right answer."

Elutides chuckled. "I see your sense of humor doesn't desert you even under very peculiar circumstances." Elutides released him.

Owen turned back to face him, studying the tall man very thoughtfully. "So far Elin has kept every promise she made to me. I cannot say the same of you."

"In other words, talk is cheap." Elutides chuckled. "I see already you've developed a certain discernment and judge others by what they do rather than what they say."

"Compliments again," Owen said. "One minute you're about to throw me into the sea, the next . . ."

"Oh no," Ceredea said. "He wouldn't have tossed you down on the rocks. Possibly he might have broken your arm or dislocated your shoulder, but kill you, no. Elutides is a just judge and never exceeds the measure of an offense."

"I didn't want to do any of those things," Elutides said, "only demonstrate to you that I'm a man to be reckoned with. And when the time comes to face Ivor, I can do more than talk."

"That's a pity," Owen said. "I was planning to fetch Enar. I had hoped that between the two of you the unfortunate Ivor might easily be worried into his grave without ever the sad necessity of a drawn sword."

Elutides threw back his head and howled with enjoyment.

Ceredea smiled. "I agree. Elutides could easily talk anyone to death."

Gynneth cried, "Please, Uncle! I'm afraid." She shuddered. "Those men with Ivor. Every time I look at them, I'm seized with such terror that I can barely breathe." She covered her face quickly with her hands for a moment, then spun around and stared at Elutides, clutching his mantle in her two small fists. "Uncle, please! Ceredea says I can go into the forest, hide among her people."

The laughter vanished from Elutides' face, replaced by a look of tender concern. He placed his two big hands over hers. "My little one," he said softly, "have I ever failed to protect you?"

Gynneth, her face pale, stared up at him in silence for a moment, then slowly shook her head. "No," she said, "but Ceredea . . ."

"Impossible," Elutides said. He directed a sharp look at Ceredea. "Don't put such ideas into her head. She couldn't live your life. It's too hard."

"Perhaps," Ceredea said. "We know many hiding places. She would be safe among us."

"Impossible," Elutides repeated. He paused. "Only as a last resort. If I die, flee with Ceredea then. Now turn and speak to your champion." Placing a hand on Gynneth's back, he pushed her gently to face Owen.

The old devil, Owen thought. He gazed at the mute appeal in the girl's eyes as she approached him slowly.

All Owen saw in the lovely young face before him was death. There were so many obstacles. How could he ever surmount them? The shadowy figure of Ivor loomed before him. Beyond the berserks lay the city, his embattled city. Hakon would be ready to begin the assault. And if they survived Hakon, there was still the long winter, with its icy rains and cold winds.

For a moment, all the forces ranged against him by man and nature stared at him, reflected in the two clear, beautiful, desperate eyes that looked so searchingly into his.

Then the chimera dissolved, and Owen understood the wonder and terror of all beauty and all human accomplishment. It was created from the clay of suffering, bound with the blood of men who would not let it perish no matter what they had to endure, no matter what they had to do.

"I have dreamed of love," Gynneth said softly, "love tender and kind, the love of one who would feel for me what those warriors of old felt for their ladies, an Arthur of Britain or Tristan of Lyonnais."

Owen reached up and cradled her face between the palms of his hands. "Gracious lady." He faltered. "Life is not a poem or an old tale told by bardic singers in a hall. I have seen suffering that I would give my life—almost my very soul—to end. Much of that pain I cannot help," he whispered. "Much I cannot even touch. But what little I am able to ease, I must, because . . ." He hesitated for the space of a long breath, then continued, "because that is what I believe God asks of me. So if I can stand between you and Ivor, I will. Whatever happens, he shall not escape my hand."

He saw she believed him. The life and color flowed back into her face. He looked at Elutides over her shoulder. "I think," Owen said, "we have some important things to discuss."

23

*E*LIN woke before dawn. The house was very quiet. The fire on the hearth had burned to coals, blinking through a coating of gray ash. Trying not to disturb Ilo and Elfwine, she rose quietly, pulled on a dark blue dress, and coiled her long hair at the nape of her neck. She found Godwin standing quietly before the fire with Edgar, Wolf the Short, and Gowen.

Ranulf stood to one side, warming his hands at the blaze. The boy's eyes were puffy and swollen. His nose was red, but his face was serene. He wore a dark mantle.

"I called on my in-laws, Elfwine's family," he said as Elin arrived at the hearth. "I gave them my promise that I did not plan to abandon Elfwine. My son is still my son. And she is my wife. They believed me."

"Do they have any inkling of the truth?" she asked.

Godwin laughed. "What is truth?"

"Pilate's question," Elin said. "Will you want some water to wash your hands?"

"No," Godwin said. "Rauching isn't Christ. He dies today."

"Don't dignify him with death," Elin said, walking toward the door to the square. "Let me deal with him."

She unbarred the door, opened it, and stood looking at the silent city. She thought of Owen, and a wave of violent desire coursed through her entire being. She could see his face: the intense dark eyes, the firm yet generous mouth, the cap of fine, dark hair.

Her eyes closed and it was as if she could feel his hands on her body, pulling her toward him, compelling her. She shuddered. Her knees loosened. Her lips parted. The thing was soft, yet hard at the same time. She had never outgrown her wonder of the thing men had. None of the words in any language were adequate to describe it. "Manhood," "stiff rod," all seemed to carry the implications of something man-made, hard, cold. But it wasn't hard or cold, more like muscle sheathed in silk. It fitted into her body the way a key fits into a well-oiled lock, turning, twisting, thrusting.

Elin was suddenly glad her back was turned to the room. None of the men could see her face. She moved slightly. Her gown brushed her breast tips. Somewhere, somehow, Owen was making love to her. The ancient triangle of desire flared in her body, reaching up from her groin to her nipples.

Elin leaned her shoulder against the door frame to keep from falling. She felt helpless. The first explosion coursed upward through her body. Then almost unbearably intense, a second and a third. Elin shuddered and bit down hard on her lip to keep from moaning. Then the fire died slowly, leaving her resting, limp and exhausted, against the door frame.

She remembered Owen's words on the morning in the square before he left on his journey. His promise that he would never let her leave him. Now she understood the full implications of that promise.

She would never really leave him. He would always be with her, and she knew that even when she grew old, her body dry and useless with age, he would be able to call up the spirit of youth and the many moments of love they shared together. He reached out to her across the miles that separated them, and so he would reach out across the years, turning her blood to flame in her veins. She might flee as far as she could into the great northern forests that beckoned to her heart, but he would always follow her.

His eyes would meet hers across the campfire, his arms and kisses lead her into the darkness.

She heard a faint sound behind her, and Godwin spoke. "Elin?" he asked. "Are you all right?"

"Yes," she said, and then realized the tears were coursing down her cheeks. She dried her eyes with her mantle. "No, I don't suppose I am."

"It's too sad," he said. "I can't even put my arm around you. There's too much chance someone might see and think I'm helping myself to the bishop's lady."

"I know," Elin said, wiping her face with her mantle. "Perhaps it's just as well. If you did, I might sit weeping all day. Owen is safe."

Godwin didn't question her certainty. He acknowledged her statement with a nod, then turned. "Ine!" he barked.

Ine appeared. He climbed out from under the table, gnawing on a large bone.

"I see he's well," Elin said.

"Better than well," Godwin said. "In a fine fettle. I consoled him for his brief illness with a visit to the widow." Godwin turned to Ine. "Begin heating water. Your mistress will want a bath and so will the other ladies."

As Ine bustled toward the fireplace, Godwin spoke to Elin in a low voice. "I've already met with Judith. She and the other women are busy organizing a magnificent ceremony for later in the day. She has your dress picked out. Elfwine will wear white. Rauching and his followers won't enter the church."

Godwin showed his teeth briefly. "He's heard tales of what I did to Count Anton in the church. So he's hiding behind the townspeople. Clever man. He won't let me near him. Me or any of my men."

"He thinks he's being clever," Elin whispered back. "If what you say is true, he's doomed."

Then she spoke up. "Ine, heat the sweat bath for me. I'm going to bathe separately. I need to be alone."

"What are you going to do?" Godwin asked.

Her tears were gone. Her eyes were set, and they had a strange remote look in them. "Godwin, what fate does the false accuser face?" she asked.

Godwin drew back a little, giving her a half smile. "Custom allows him to be punished. The punishment varies. Sometimes he must pay compensation; sometimes he loses a hand. Sometimes—"

"I don't need a book of law, Godwin. Punishment is in order, is it not?"

"Yes."

"Very well, then," Elin said. "As you are our lord, it will be as you say. He will be punished."

Elspeth woke early. The room was cold and Hakon was gone. He'd returned to the camp upriver where most of his men were based. He had awakened her briefly to kiss her good-bye. Then she remembered what had happened after he promised to teach her about wickedness. She could feel the blush covering her whole body. *God, where did he get such ideas?* she thought. Some of the things they'd done still made her quiver and shrink, but not with horror. She licked her lips. Simply thinking of them heated her flesh.

She slipped out of the bed and pulled on an old dress. She covered herself with a dark mantle, then hurried out. She stopped at the door to the room where her children slept. One lone torch was burning in the hall. By its light, she could see the huddled shapes of Bettena and the three little ones in the bed.

She went in and touched Bettena lightly on the shoulder. Bettena awoke, eased herself away from the bodies of the children, and followed Elspeth from the room. The two women faced each other in the hall under the guttering torch, Bettena blinking sleep from her eyes, Elspeth standing proudly.

"I take it you succeeded with him," Bettena said.

"I am not dead," Elspeth said. "But it was a very near thing."

Bettena shivered fearfully. "If he were to guess how we plan to deceive him . . . to humble him, he would likely kill us all."

Elspeth took Bettena's hand and squeezed it. The torch above burned low, the flame blue. Neither woman could see the other's face in the sudden darkness. "He will either pass the test or fail it," Elspeth said. "If he passes, well and good. If not, he must die and we must all flee. I don't know if I'll be able to get away. If I can't, take care of the children. Please."

The torch flickered once, lighting the alcove brightly enough for Elspeth to see Bettena's face briefly. "Yes," Bettena said. "The children. They are innocent. The wrath of the Northmen must not fall on them. I will go now and carry the word. They await me at the edge of the forest."

Elfwine and Elin were alone in Elin's bedroom. As Elin put herbs on a brazier, Elfwine breathed the smoke. Elfwine felt light-headed, dizzy, as though her body did not belong to her. Her hands and feet were numb. She looked at Elin across the brazier in the heat rising from the coals. Elin's face seemed to shimmer as though it were trying to dissolve.

"Are you afraid?" Elin asked.

"No," Elfwine answered. "I can't seem to feel anything."

Elin smiled, a grim, tight smile.

"Am I going to die, Elin?" Elfwine asked.

"Not if I can help it," Elin said.

"I know I'll drop the hot iron," Elfwine said. "I know it. I'm guilty."

"No, you won't," Elin said. "When you receive the sacrament, you will no longer be guilty of anything. Those whom God has forgiven are free of sin."

"They say," Elfwine continued, "to receive the holy bread into a guilty body is the greatest of transgressions. I have been told a scoffing, adulterous woman once wanted to convince her husband she was innocent, so she took the sacrament with evil in her heart. When the flesh of God touched her lips and tongue, they scorched her as though she had been burned with fire. She died at the altar of the church, and the devils dragged her soul away to hell."

"Maybe that will happen," Elin said. "Maybe it will not. If it doesn't, you may take it as a sign from God that your heart has been purified by penance."

Elin's face seemed to recede into the distance, but her voice was only too close. And Elfwine, turning, realized

Elin was at her side, leading her out of the room toward the church. Toward the terrifying ceremonies beginning there.

Alfric joined Elin at the top of the stair and took Elfwine's other arm.

"I've used every trick I know," Elfwine heard Elin say to him. "And I'm still not sure of her."

"I am not a woman of resolution," Elfwine said sadly. "And my heart is not pure."

"God can purify it," Alfric said.

"Why should he bother?" Elfwine asked.

"I don't know," Alfric answered. "But usually, if asked, he does. Do you ask, Elfwine?"

She couldn't seem to find the stair treads under her feet. She floated down more like a wraith than a woman. Alfric's question echoed in her mind. She wondered if she really wanted the purity of soul promised by Alfric. All her life she had been happy to leave sainthood or even heroism to others. She wasn't brave or noble and didn't want to be. Yet Alfric's words seemed to suggest she might have to embrace both if she wanted to survive.

She liked her vices. Lust. She had enjoyed it since she first knew what it was. Enjoyed. She had reveled in it. Rauching had been a treat. Though given what he'd done in the square, the insults he'd hurled at her, she now loathed herself for having desired him.

Sloth. Elfwine was utterly lazy. Brought up with the brutal necessity of working the land, the unremitting labor that stretched from first plowing to harvest time, she hated the very idea of work. She was more than happy to bully, manipulate, or whine until others, in exasperation, threw up their hands and did the household chores in her stead.

Greed. Oh God, she was more than greedy. She remembered long stretches of hunger so intense it was painful. Since she had lived in the bishop's house, the luxury of having sufficient food set before her each day had represented a victory beyond her wildest dreams.

She was painfully aware this was the sort of heart she had to set before God. She was clothed today in white, but her soul was black with sin.

She found herself trembling in terror that God would strike her down at the altar rail in the same way he had destroyed the woman in the story she had told Elin. She was almost hoping he would. At least it would be quick. Being flogged through the city, strangled, and thrown into a ditch would be humiliating and agonizingly painful. Her flesh shrank from the whip, and her mind completely dodged the thought of the cord tightening around her neck.

Her stomach was empty, but if she thought too much about that, she might disgrace herself by vomiting on the floor in front of the whole household. To fail today meant death. Her father and brothers might strangle her with their own hands. If she failed, they would be ruined. Their profitable connection with the bishop's household would be cut off.

Twice Elfwine had been afraid her father would kill her. The first time was when he caught her lying with one of the count's huntsmen who had offered her a few hares. She had been savagely hungry. Their meager supplies of food from the last harvest had been used up, the new year's crops not yet in.

When her father bent over her in the barn after chasing her lover away, she'd seen death in his eyes. He beat her with his belt and then with his fists until she was unconscious.

The same had happened when she ran away with the wine merchant from Paris. A daughter was a man's property and not supposed to give herself without her father's permission. So she got scant sympathy and no one tended her bruises—even though both eyes were swollen shut and her mouth battered almost beyond recognition.

If she were returned to her father now, such abuse was the best she could hope for. No, her only hope now was God. And Elin's tricks.

She was aware she was still walking. Alfric and Elin were leading her through the vestry and into the church. Elfwine tried to pull back, but Elin forced her to a space cleared for them in front of the altar.

Elfwine looked around. She seemed to see everything with a bright unnatural clarity. Nearly the whole town had assembled in the church. After the open challenge Rauching had thrown at the bishop's household, no one was going to miss this.

The bishop's chair stood on carrying poles before the altar. In front of it, between the altar and the chair, lay a cushion. Elfwine understood. It was there she was to kneel.

She felt Elin's hand in the small of her back, ready to push her forward if she resisted. But she didn't. Instead, with the same floating sensation she'd felt on the stair, she drifted forward and knelt.

A few moments later, Alfric appeared on the altar. The soft buzz of conversation in the church died out and the mass began.

Elfwine seemed to feel every eye in church on her. She alone was dressed in white. The pure white dress draped her from neck to her ankles. Elin made sure the sleeves covered her from shoulder to wrists so as to hide the bruises left on her arms by Ranulf's grip.

Alfric's mass seemed to pass in a dream until at last the moment came when she was to receive the sacrament. Elfwine raised her head. Here was the chance for God to strike her down.

She remembered her father's face, distorted with anger, the hard leather belt in his hand. Then she thought of Ranulf, his gentleness and the pain and despair in his eyes when he'd looked at her last night.

Alfric stood in front of her, the host in his hand, ready to place it on her tongue. For a moment she hesitated, her lips sealed. Behind her the vast throng in the church seemed to hold its breath.

Her father hadn't loved her. She was only his property. Lady Elin didn't love her. She was desperately trying to hold the town together against the Vikings. Of all the people she had ever known, only Ranulf had ever loved her.

Did God wear Ranulf's face?

I'm sorry, she thought. *But you must take me as I am.* She looked deep into her own heart and remembered Rauching's lies about the poison being only a sleeping potion. *Yes,* she thought as her final offering of truth. *I knew he lied, but I didn't want to know, so I didn't.*

Then her lips parted, and she took the sacrament into her mouth. She swallowed the dry bit of bread, then sipped the wine Alfric offered. There was a soft, collective sigh from behind her.

Alfric stepped back to the altar and began the prayers, indicating the mass was ended. Elfwine slipped forward from the cushion and prostrated herself on the floor, her arms outstretched in the form of a cross.

Elin stood nearby. She bit her lip, anxious and afraid. Was the gesture too dramatic? Would it lose Elfwine the sympathy of the watching crowd? Then she saw the tears running down Elfwine's cheeks and realized her actions came from the heart.

Elin breathed a sigh of relief and began to pray. To her, a hierarchy of powers ruled the world. Some could be bought, others commanded, but the final power was beyond all human reason and couldn't possibly be controlled. To Elin it was certainly feminine. The world, the woman, keeper and sustainer of all life, fecund as the burgeoning springtime. Terrible as a winter storm sweeping in from the sea, blasting all before it with rain, ice, and snow. Uniting in itself, herself the final truths of birth and death, carrying all races of living things into an unknowable future. To it, Elin prayed. *You owe me vengeance. I am your instrument. Deliver Rauching into my hands.*

Elfwine felt rather than saw Alfric standing over her. She raised her head and saw his hand end the blessing. He had chosen a purple dalmatic to say the mass. In that purple, there was more than a hint of blood.

Elfwine got to her feet slowly and faced the congregation.

"Do I need to take your arm, Elfwine?" Alfric whispered.

"No," she breathed. "I will go alone. The sin was mine; so shall be the atonement."

Elfwine's brothers slipped out of the crowd. They had bathed and were dressed in their rather ragged best. The four men picked up the carrying poles under the big chair. Their progress cleared a path for her through the crowd and out into the square.

Elfwine passed Judith, who gazed at her as if to say "You are in the greatest danger a woman can face, but stand fast and all will be well." Near Judith, Bretwala, who had passed the first messages from Rauching to Elfwine, stood weeping. Feather-brained little bitch. Her tongue was hinged in the middle. She knew the truth, and she certainly hadn't neglected to tell the whole town.

Elfwine lifted her chin. She must behave in such a way as to make the truth seem a lie. If she didn't, it might destroy them all. Her father and brothers, her husband and her child.

Courage, she thought in wonder. *This is courage. I have it. Certainly courage is a terrible thing born of intolerable pain and desperation, but I have it now and I will win.*

Elfwine's brothers carried the chair down the church steps and placed it in the center of the square. Elfwine stood beside it while the crowd flowed out of the church and surrounded her.

Rauching stood on the opposite side of the square surrounded by his friends among the farmers. They were laughing and joking among themselves, and Elfwine knew Rauching must have paid for a few rounds from the tavern keeper's stock. She could see Rauching's insolent eyes fixed on her.

Gunter stood beside a fire burning near the tavern. Resting among the coals was a big iron bar. Elin told her there was a trick to it. Gunter, the smith, specialist in metals, knew how to forge a bar of such low conductivity that the ends would stay cool even if the center were heated white-hot. "You cover the cool ends with your hands," Elin said. "The center of the bar glows, people see it and think the metal is hot to both ends. Yes, you get some burns, but nothing a person of resolution can't stand. Yes, there is some pain, and you must bear it. I'll help you."

Elfwine could feel the heat of the sun on her back. It shone down from a cloudless blue sky.

Elin approached her. "I will get the bar from Gunter and place it in your hands."

"He's staring at me," Elfwine whispered back.

"Forget Rauching and look at your husband," Elin hissed softly.

Elfwine glanced at the steps of the hall and felt her knees loosen with terror. They were all there. Anna held the baby. Ingund was beside her. Rosamund was clinging to Ingund's arm. Godwin and his knights were behind them. Still farther back, above them on the top step of the hall, stood a dozen of the archers, crossbows pointed down but drawn and ready. Rauching must be mad, she thought. Even as she held the thought, she realized he wasn't. He and his men mingled with the townsfolk. If Godwin ordered his archers to fire on the crowd, he would destroy not only enemies but friends as well. In a town as small as Chantalon, where everyone was tied to everyone else by blood or marriage, they would never forgive him. Some of the archers' own families were among the people in the square. She wasn't sure they would fire even if ordered to do so.

Ranulf stood beside the archers. The marks of grief were gone from his face. It was pale, set, and still. His eyes met hers. She saw in them neither grief nor reproach but only a steely expectation. An expectation that she would do her best.

Elfwine rested her hand on the back of the bishop's chair. It was an ancient holy thing. Carved from a sacred oak, it had been felled by the first Christian missionaries when they came to the valley. The story went that the first bishop of Chantalon sat in it and redeemed it from its pagan origins.

Strength seemed to flow into Elfwine's hand from the old blackened wood.

Gunter lifted the iron bar from the fire and placed it in Elin's hands. She held it by both ends and turned to face the crowd. Even to Elfwine, who knew the trick, the effect was impressive. Elin seemed to hold a red-hot iron bar in her hands and feel no pain. She carried it toward Elfwine and placed both ends in her hands. Elfwine's eyes met Elin's for a shocking second. She seemed to drown in their blueness.

"You will feel no pain," Elin said.

And she didn't.

Elfwine started around the chair. The journey was an

eternity and a second. The first time was easy. She'd forgotten the crowd; she'd forgotten the world. The only reality was the object in her hand. The second circuit of the chair was worse. Elfwine could smell her own flesh burning, and she was aware of the absolute silence, so intense she could hear the flames fluttering over Gunter's fire.

Elfwine staggered as she passed Elin for the second time. Pain was beginning to creep through Elin's drugs, and in agony, Elfwine could hardly hold her pace to a stately progress. She was finding it almost unbearable when she reached Elin for the third time. But from a place she had not known existed within her, she found the strength to pause before Elin and place the bar in her hands.

Elin took the bar and whispered, "It is finished." She carried the bar toward the center of the square before the watching crowd. Elfwine staggered toward the steps of the hall. She felt an arm around her, holding her upright, and realized it was Ranulf's.

"Elfwine has shown the strength of a virtuous woman," Elin shouted as she held the bar aloft. She was about to shout "Let the accuser stand forth," but Rauching darted out of the mass of his supporters and faced her.

"It's a trick," he shouted. He pointed at Gunter. "The iron's not hot. It's a trick, I tell you." He was still pointing at Gunter. "The smith is in the pay of the bishop's witch!"

He had a moment to realize he'd blundered when he saw the look of savage triumph transfigure Elin's face. "You are delivered into my hands," she whispered as she laid the red-hot center section of the iron against Rauching's cheek. There was a loud hiss and a sharp stink as the red-hot metal seared through his skin to the bone. Rauching began to scream and sank to his knees. The women of the household charged him. Rauching managed to get to his feet and tried to run into the shelter of the watching crowd, but Gunter stood between him and safety. Gunter's blow caught Rauching on the uninjured side of the face, sending him into the arms of the women.

"Call my daughter a slut, will you?" Gunter shouted.

"No man ever had a truer or more faithful wife than Ingund."

Elin stepped aside and watched Rauching writhe, screaming under the nails, fists, and feet of the women. Some of Rauching's supporters surged forward. Ranulf raised his arm. The archers' bows came up.

"Stay where you are!" Ranulf shouted. "Every man has his target picked. Rauching is a false accuser and is justly punished."

When Rauching was naked, sobbing and bleeding from dozens of gashes inflicted by the women, Godwin called a halt. Rauching lay on his belly, pissing and puking in the street, unable to speak.

Ranulf stood with Elfwine. She swayed slightly and looked down at the burns on both palms near the thumbs.

He supported her with one arm. "Does it hurt?" he asked.

She looked up at him and nodded. She seemed numb. Numb and broken like an animal that has endured so much suffering at the hands of cruel humans that it will never have the courage to offer any resistance to whatever burden it may be forced to bear. *Elfwine,* he thought, *may walk for the rest of her days, head bowed, an outcast, forever despised.*

"You knew?" he asked.

"Yes," she nodded. "I never wanted to look into your eyes again . . . and know how I'd hurt you." She looked up. Their gazes locked and held. . . . She was broken and he understood what had broken her.

Pain, he thought. This is why pain entered the universe at the hand of God—because of its sheer, raw, efficient, savage teaching power. It reached us not through our rather weak intellects but struck at the pit of the stomach and chilled the blood in our veins, the marrow in our bones.

And the lesson it brought to Ranulf was that however carelessly love is given, it may never be taken back. He had thrown his love away in a hayfield tumble that roused him to a pitch of sheer fleshly lust so unbelievably powerful that it obscured even the sun for him, driving him into the arms of a woman he had never really known .. forever. The gift had leaped from his hands into her seared ones. She had fully admitted her guilt to him. She planned his death. She was at his mercy.

Ranulf pushed her away from him. She rested her back against the wall near the bishop's house door. Her face emptied of everything, even despair.

"Wait here," he told her.

The women were finished with Rauching.

Ranulf plucked a crossbow from one of Denis's men. He strode down the steps and stood in front of Rauching.

He was getting his voice back, whimpering and pleading for mercy.

"Rauching!" Ranulf spoke loudly enough to cut through the other man's terror and pain. Rauching looked up at him, almost more in annoyance than with any other emotion. It was clear to the watching crowd that Rauching was more afraid of Godwin and the women behind Ranulf than his paramour's boy husband.

"Rauching," Ranulf continued, "those stories you told about Elfwine and the other women of my lord's household—they were lies, weren't they?" Ranulf's voice was flat, unemotional. He almost might have been discussing a particularly heavy rainstorm with Rauching.

Rauching's eyes wandered away from Ranulf's face. And Ranulf understood the evil little reptile was trying to figure out some way of retrieving the situation.

"Rauching!" Ranulf prompted.

"Yes, yes," Rauching whined. "Yes, I suppose they were lies."

"Thank you," Ranulf replied quietly . . . and fired.

Godwin, who'd been standing close by watching the drama, found his whole body jerked with surprise.

The crowd gasped.

The crossbow bolt lifted Rauching from his knees several feet into the air, spun him around, and deposited him facedown on the cobbles. The bolt, having gone through his body, protruded from his back, covered with still quivering shreds of what had once been his heart.

Godwin was amazed and a bit pleased to note that no

one, not even himself, had observed that the crossbow was pointed at Rauching's chest, that Ranulf's face had not changed expression, and not one flicker of any emotion had shone in Ranulf's mild, hazel eyes. "Very good," he commented.

Ranulf handed the spent bow back to the archer. He returned to Elfwine's side.

"Elfwine." Ranulf spoke to the people, and especially to the men who had supported Rauching. "Elfwine is my wife!" he said loudly. "Mine!" His glance swept the square, and he experienced an odd phenomenon. No one would meet his eyes. Each man or woman found someplace else to look as his gaze touched them. "I will," he continued, "send any man who thinks he can make free with my wife's person or reputation on the same journey I sent that offal." He pointed to Rauching. "And to the same destination. And I will do so at whatever cost to myself. Even if the cost be my life."

Then he turned, lifted Elfwine into his arms, and carried her into the hall.

Chapter

24

*H*AKON'S men cursed him for making them pig drivers. He cursed them back with equal fluency and then asked them if they wanted land and women. They assented with silence and a great deal of industry, so much industry that they gathered enough pigs to last for months.

The bailey of Elspeth's hall resounded with porcine squealing and the clamor of men and women engaged in butchering the animals and salting the meat.

Farther downriver near the threshing floor, preparations for the feast were underway. Several of the biggest boars were roasting on spits. Barrels of mead and cider appeared to quench the thirst of Vikings and villagers alike. The general atmosphere was a rather deceptive one of brotherhood and joy, spiced with a touch of expectation on the part of Hakon's men. Several rather lascivious rumors floated around about the kinds of things Elspeth's people did to ensure the fertility of their fields. The Vikings looked forward to the celebration.

Elspeth was startled to find Hakon sitting in the great hall alone, a wine cup in front of him. The almost window-less hall was dark by day. Hakon slouched, brooding in the big chair that had been Reynald's, staring at the bright square of light in the doorway. His face was deep in shadow.

Elspeth gave a little start as her eyes picked him out in the darkness. "My lord," she said, surprised, "shouldn't you be out supervising the slaughter?"

"Killing a pig isn't difficult," he replied. "Your people are experts. They need no help from me. I loathe the beasts. Oh, I'll eat pork quickly enough if that's all that's to be had, but in general I prefer the meat of any other creature, even fish or fowl, to pork."

"So I've noticed," Elspeth said, drawing a little closer to the table.

Hakon nodded. "Yes," he said. "You seem to notice a great many things you don't speak of. What are they?"

Elspeth studied him with grave dark eyes. "I've noticed you seem almost afraid of my son, Eric."

Hakon laughed softly, unpleasantly. "Elspeth, I was fathered by a man who hated me. My mother died bearing me. My father told me the size of my shoulders tore her womb and she bled to death."

"My God," Elspeth whispered in horror. "What kind of man would tell his son such a tale? You didn't ask to be given life."

Hakon stirred uncomfortably in the chair. "If my sister, Asa, hadn't plucked me from between my mother's legs, cut the cord, and taken me to her breast, my father would have had the life out of me soon enough. Do you know what Outburied is?"

Elspeth shook her head slightly. "I've never heard the word, but I think I understand the deed."

"Yes," Hakon said. "The unwanted babe is placed in a cradle of ice, its first cries stilled by a mouthful of snow. In the cold of our northern land, life ends just minutes after birth. Perhaps it should have been so with me. Do you know what my father said when he saw me at my sister's breast?"

"How could I?" she whispered.

"Guess, Elspeth," he said tauntingly. "Guess."

She fixed her eyes on his face. "I think he said something like 'Thank you for giving me time to work my revenge.' "

The scar on Hakon's face pulsed, reddened, and then

turned white. "You understand the old brute's mind. Those were not his very words, but close enough. He said, 'You have given him time. Time to suffer. Time to pay all the forfeits I will demand.' And, before all the gods, I did. I was no older than sixteen when I could outwork the strongest of my brothers and all the slaves. I'll wager I could outwork any man who tills your lands. My hands are no stranger to the plow. I can fell trees with the best, cut brush, dig until my back breaks, and clear the newest field of rocks and stumps. I didn't yield to your expert persuasions last night only out of love. You showed me your people's minds, and I saw in them a mirror of my own.

"I, too, have known hunger when it is not only appetite but pain. I, too, have felt the lash across my back and the curse of the driver. But I tell you, Elspeth, if it hadn't been for, as I said, your expert persuasion, there would be more screaming in the bailey than pigs, and not all the bloodshed would be animal."

Hakon rose. He pushed the chair back, strode around the table, and stepped down from the dais to face Elspeth.

She drew away from him and bowed her head.

"What is it, Elspeth. Have I frightened you?" He stretched out one hand and turned her easily to face him. "What is this mummery? You looked dressed for a funeral. Is it mine?"

Elspeth looked down at her dark gown and mantle, then reached up and adjusted something on her hair.

Hakon realized she was wearing a finely woven crown. He reached out, touched it, then drew his hand back with an exclamation of pain.

"The darkness is playing tricks with your eyes, Hakon," she said. "My gown is not black but brown. The mantle is gray."

"The crown?" Hakon asked, sucking one of his fingers.

Elspeth laughed. "Thistles and holly. I'm dressed as the winter queen, though I am no hag as she is reputed to be."

Hakon backed away from her. "You didn't tell me it was that kind of a feast."

"There are no other kinds."

Hakon caught the slight hint of strain in her voice. The

shouts from outside came to his ears. "The winter queen?" he asked. "And do all men desire the winter queen?" His voice was thick with rage.

Elspeth grew weak with relief. *He's only jealous,* she thought. For a few moments, she'd believed he suspected something.

"No. Nothing like that happens. I don't know what stories have come to you and your men's ears, but this is all in fun. Besides, no one loves the winter queen. She is honored. Nothing more. My people would be afraid not to honor her. I'm dressed to call them to the feast; then the winter queen's part ends. I blow a horn at sunset."

Hakon moved forward and embraced her. "I don't know why you rouse such darkness in my soul, but you do," he whispered. "I think it must be because you remind me of Asa. I haven't loved many people in my life, but Asa was one of them. She gave me her breast. She gave me life. She was my sister and my mother. The wise woman who sent me from my home said the double tie was too strong and would always rule me unless I escaped it. The cold irony is I have escaped it in your arms."

Elspeth rested her head against his breast. Hakon felt the crown prick him through his shirt. "Doesn't that hurt?" he asked, concerned for her.

"Only a little," she confessed. "Most of it's on my hair. What else did the wise woman tell you, Hakon?"

He tilted her chin up so he could see her eyes and face in the half-light. It seemed a double face—one side cloaked in shadow, the other in light. "She told me I would love immoderately if I loved. She told me to beware. I might pass on the curse my father laid on me to my sons. I have dared to love you, Elspeth. Now I tremble with fear that somehow the cup of all I wished for in life will be dashed from my lips. You said I was afraid of Eric. I am. I'm afraid I might be as much of a wolf to him as my father was to me. And when I touch you, I fear the wrath of the gods who hate me. I can't make myself believe you won't betray me in the end. I can't believe you aren't as treacherous as Reynald. You were only too willing to come to my arms after he died."

She pulled away from him and walked toward the door. The late afternoon sun shone in, creating a lake of golden light on the floor.

She stood in its glow, and he could see the brown dress and the gray mantle. The only touch of color was the holly berries glowing in her crown of carline thistles.

"The gods don't hate you, Hakon," she said. "Your father did."

The words hung between them. Hakon became suddenly aware that it was silent. The noises from the bailey had ceased.

Drenched in the late afternoon sunlight, Elspeth was a commanding presence. Her features glowed against the brown gown and the soft gray mantle. She seemed larger than life, a fairy woman stepping out to block a wayfarer's path in a dark wood.

"The gods don't make our destinies," she said. "We do, and Hakon . . ." She seemed to barely breathe the words, yet he heard them clearly. "Hakon, the gods await you tonight."

Hakon sat quietly in the shadowed hall, sick with fear and a dark guilt that knotted his stomach. He knew what Elspeth's words meant. He knew he should call his men and ride away, back to the safety of his island fortress in the river.

Her words were as clear a warning as a man had ever been given. But he didn't rise from the table. He only emptied the wine cup once or twice.

The barrels of cider and mead had been stacked in the yard in front of the fortress. He heard his men's shouts of joy as they began guzzling the precious contents of the mead casks.

Hakon understood that he should either run or fight. But if he ran, he knew sooner or later he would lose Elspeth as surely as the sun rose. In the end she would turn from him, either to her people or to some other man. As for fighting, how could a man fight the dark powers he was certain she had invoked?

So he sat quietly and watched the evening shadows

gather in the garden until at last he stood up and walked into the bailey. Across the river the edge of the dying sun entered the treetops.

A lot of his men were unconscious, the rest staggering drunk.

Tosi stood beside the fire in the center of the yard. When Hakon reached his side, he said, "This is treachery. Look at them, Hakon. These are hard-headed men. I've seen some of them drink all night, but a few cups of this stuff and they're blind drunk, falling down drunk."

Hakon nodded.

"Are you mad?" Tosi shouted. "We must leave this place now." He caught Hakon by the arm and shook him. "In a few minutes, those remaining on their feet will be unconscious. Get your horse. We must ride now!"

"No," Hakon said.

"She! That woman! Her people! They're planning something, even now. Forget these fools here. I tried to warn them. The mead was a new drink to them. I told them to go easy. If they're doomed, it's their own folly that destroys them."

Hakon dragged his hand down his face. "No," he repeated. "Her husband's body was yet warm when I took her in my arms. I burned the woods to try to catch the bishop. I took her lands and her people. She said the gods waited for me tonight. Her gods, her land."

He caught Tosi by the shirt and almost lifted him from his feet. "I want her. I want her lands. Is my heart so faint, so white that I won't face them to win her?"

Tosi pulled away, staggering. "Well and good," he said. "I have ever been your friend. I'll stand with you till the end. Don't send me away."

"No, I won't, but you can't come with me, either." Hakon suddenly felt an icy calm as though all of his doubts had been resolved. He was going forward to place himself in the hands of fate, without fear and without regret. "Stay here. Build up the fire. Keep watch and wait for me to return."

"And what if you don't return?" Tosi asked.

Hakon shifted the sword on his hip. "Then do what seems best to you." With that, he strode out through the gate.

He crossed the causeway leading toward the villages and set out into the fields. Then he paused as he saw Elspeth.

She was walking across the plowland some distance away, still clad as the winter queen. Her step was regal and she carried a curled ram's horn in her hand. Hakon understood. She was going to summon him along with the rest.

In the west the sun touched the hills. The red orb seemed caught in a tracery of branches. A light breeze fanned Hakon's face. It was cold, presaging the chill of a clear winter night.

Above his head a few early stars began to light the dark blue of heaven. He eased back on his heels and felt the thick clods of a first plowing press against the soles of his feet.

It will need another plowing before the sowing can begin, he thought. In the distance, he heard the soft, endless rush of the river between the high banks. *But then,* Hakon thought, *winter is a time of silence. Silence and clear light. A light that picks out the contours of every object, strips the trees naked, and even seems to peer into the darkest corners of our own souls. Winter is the silence that enters our spent bodies after love. The silence of a despair so profound it cannot drown its pain even in a sea of tears or blood. The silence stares at me,* he thought. *The silence and the light. They show me what I hunger for, what I long for. So simple, really. The river singing its eternal song, the forest I touched with profane hands, the woman I perhaps can never possess, and the earth. The earth I know so well I can measure its needs through the soles of my boots. I want these things. If I hazard my life tonight, what of it? The cost is not so much. If I fail, only a little pain and I am one with the silence and the winter light forever. If I succeed, I have won a world.*

In the distance, Elspeth reached a high bluff overlooking the river. Beyond, on the hills, the sun was only a last ember flaring against the twilight.

She is waiting, Hakon thought, *for the powers. They reside in the moment of passage between night and day, sunlight and shadow, sea and land, life and death.*

The sun vanished, though its rays still glowed against the sky.

Elspeth blew the horn.

When Hakon reached the woman standing beside the river, he was not sure it was Elspeth. She still wore the crown and robes Elspeth had worn, but her face was covered by a wood-and-leather mask. It was the face of a hag—twisted with anger and lined with age, all protruding teeth and wrinkled skin.

Its voice, however, was Elspeth's. "You cannot say you were betrayed."

The winter twilight was blue around them. The river breeze tossed the long, gray locks attached to the mask and veiled the cruel face for a dark moment. So gowned and masked, Elspeth was a hideous caricature of a woman. But there was power in the leather-and-wood face she wore— winter's power to bind the hills in icy chains, seal the sap in trees, and chill seed into dormancy in the earth. Something ancient and instinctive in Hakon bowed to the power.

"Are you yourself, Elspeth?" he asked.

"Tonight," she whispered with a touch of the hag's evil cackle in her voice, "I am more than myself. But even the winter queen could not let you come here without a warning. You know what you undertake?"

"I do," Hakon said. "The girl receives the seed, the woman bears the child, the hag is midwife."

Elspeth brought her hands together in a clap, loud in the silence as the crack of doom. In the distance, Hakon heard the pipes and the throb of the tabor.

"Put aside your sword and knife," Elspeth said. "They have no place here."

"Only for Elspeth do I unarm myself," Hakon said. "She once held the sword at my breast and did me no harm. Not for the hag. For Elspeth."

"The hag binds, the maiden loosens, the mother completes the cycle. We are three, we are one. We are Elspeth. Hand us your sword."

Hakon placed the heavy scabbard and the hilt of his scramasax in her hand.

She walked toward the threshing floor as the dancers emerged from the wood.

They were led by the lord of the dance himself. He wore the horned head of the bull of the woods. Between his legs dangled the gigantic balls and phallus. He came leaping and capering with the authority of one who is the fructifier of all things.

The pipe's tune was a joyous cry. It seemed to carry the dancers along with it, their feet leaping to its tune.

The men were not masked as Elspeth was in a representational mask but rather in ordinary leather masks that covered enough of their upper faces to make them unrecognizable. The women danced forth boldly, faces bare, eyes sparking, carrying torches in their hands.

The hag set Hakon's weapons to one side on the threshing floor and awaited the rest as they danced, wending their way through the plowland.

Hakon looked down and realized the threshing floor was made of gigantic stone slabs, unmortared but fitting so tightly together that none of the precious wheat could escape when the newly cut sheaves were slapped against it.

In the four corners of the floor and in the center, fires were laid, each awaiting the torch.

The music the piper played in the distance sang to Hakon's heart. He felt he had heard it before, skirling and wailing in his dreams. Perhaps while he slept in a ship on a pitching sea, one hand gripping a spar against the roll of the boat, those pipes had cried in his dreams.

The sound of the accompanying drum was his heartbeat in a moment before battle—the thud and throb an endless challenge to death. *No matter,* he thought, *but I have heard it before, and all my life I have awaited the horned dancer, the horned masked priest who carries with him the power of life.*

Then, the horned dancer was at the threshing floor, touching his torch to the fires.

The people crowded onto the floor, standing apart from Hakon and Elspeth at one end. The music ceased and the only sound was the bubble and rush of the river below and the faint night breeze stirring the brush along the riverbank.

To Hakon's surprise, the people ignored him. It was as though the spot where he stood was empty. And then he understood he was the neophyte, the outsider come to witness a sacred rite, asking to become part of their world.

Elspeth's people gathered in a circle around the fire in the center of the threshing floor.

Silence! They were silent. They also partook of the winter silence. An eternal silence, not of doom, but the silence in the forest and the sky before an awakening. The silence of the moment before dawn.

Then the hag, Elspeth, and the horned priest pushed their way into the center of the circle. They began to dance. Elspeth danced against the sun to the left, the priest to the right as though summoning the summer. The pipes began again. This time it was a high thin wail—a cry of bottomless grief.

Elspeth and the horned priest passed each other slowly—the hag on the inside near the fire, the horned man on the outside, his back to her, the thick grotesque prick and balls an assertion of manhood.

Then, slowly, one by one to the tune of the piper, the younger women in the crowd began to join Elspeth. Holding hands, they began to circle the fire round and round.

Then the young men came forward and clasped hands with the bull-horned dancer, and they also danced, facing the women, with the women circling to the left, men to the right.

The music changed. The cry of the pipe was now a joyous jig. Laughter and delight bubbled in the music.

Suddenly, Hakon realized one of the dancers was one of his own followers—a young man, landless and poor, named Kalt. He had attached himself to Hakon some months ago. Apparently not all of his followers had joined the drunken spree. If things went badly for him, he might have at least one supporter here.

A second later, his hopes were dashed.

The music stopped. A young girl broke ranks with the other women. She embraced Hakon's young friend shamelessly. Kalt looked shocked and dazed for a second, but the girl was very pretty, small and dark with long, silken hair and doelike brown eyes fringed by soft, curling lashes.

Kalt recovered in a second, and realizing his good fortune, he seized the girl. They fled away together into the darkness surrounding the fires.

The dance began again. This time Hakon saw the signal. A girl raised her arm. This young man wasn't as slow as Kalt had been. In a twinkling, he seized the girl, threw her over his shoulder, and was gone into the night accompanied by a great many snickers and guffaws from the watching crowd.

When the dance began again, the dancers revolved faster and faster. Twice more they stopped and women chose partners.

The pipe shrilled to a high note. The dancers stopped, standing rigid with joined hands raised for the length of the pipe's cry. Then their hands dropped.

The men stepped away from the fire and began to mingle with the rest of the women.

Suddenly, Hakon realized the women were gone. It seemed to him that they had simply vanished. Later he understood that some of them must have slipped away during the dance and the rest, putting the fire between themselves and their menfolk, left when the dance ended.

Hakon felt a stab of rage. Jealous rage. Where was Elspeth?

He didn't mind her playing these games, but if she'd gone off into the night with the bull-masked dancer, he'd—

But no, the bull-masked one was standing in front of the fire—a terrifying silhouette.

The mask had been made from the horns and skull of an aurochs, the wild bull of the woods. The horns spread out fully three feet on either side. The face of the skull had been covered with the stiffened hide, the nostrils painted scarlet. It seemed an almost living thing. The rest of the hide had been stiffened around the limbs of the dancer. He wore it like armor. Between the dancer's legs dangled the bull's pizzle and balls, tanned and stuffed to full erection.

No, Hakon thought, *the bull dancer is still here, but the women are gone. Why?*

He tore his eyes away from the dancer and looked at the men around him. They were all masked. Hakon folded his arms. He understood how alone he was. His men were drowned in drunken slumber. Tosi might try to help him, but even with the best of intentions, he could do little against such numbers. There were a full forty large, strong men gathered on the threshing floor. They could smother any attack by a lone man by sheer weight of numbers.

In fact, Hakon found himself hoping Tosi would stay away. Any interference by him might be seen as some form of treachery and could mean the end of both their lives.

Hakon was determined to show no fear. If he died tonight, he would die with honor.

"Greetings, man who would rule us," the bull dancer said.

"Greetings," Hakon answered, inclining his head as to an equal, though he knew the man he was facing was by day a serf or even less, perhaps a slave. He understood instinctively that here between the fires they were all equals.

"Who are you?" the bull dancer asked. "And I warn you, answer only from the heart."

Hakon did. "I am no one. The name I bear is not the one my father gave me. I repudiated that long ago. I come as a wanderer longing for the thing all wanderers long for . . . a home."

"The earth rejects you wanderer . . . wargus," the bull dancer said, "because you haven't given her your heart. Do you still dream of the sea? Of rowing? Of gold and silver won by your sword?" The bull shook his giant horns in the firelight. "You cannot win dominion over the earth with a sword."

Hakon understood the answer weighted his life in the balance. He clenched his fists, closed his eyes, and searched his heart for truth. No man would ever say Lord Hakon died with a lie on his lips.

He opened his eyes. His hands dropped almost helplessly to his sides as he answered. "The sea never troubles my dreams. The whale road is a dangerous one. She takes and keeps her tribute from the wild rovers. Yes!" he shouted ringingly, "I do dream of gold. Fields shimmering with fair wheat, white gold in the sunlight. And of silver—forest, river, and meadow dreaming, at peace beneath the moon. My fields, my wheat, my woman in my bed beside me. This is my victory and all my lust, my desire, my pleasure, my life."

The bull dancer roared and capered. The horns and the savage mark of life swinging between his legs glowed in the firelight. "Are you then willing to pay the price?" he shouted.

"Yes!" Hakon roared back. "Once now and forever more. Yes!" Hakon felt the hands of the men around him, bearing him down.

25

*E*LUTIDES sent Ceredea and Gynneth to warn Cador and Casgob to be ready. "And tell them not to let Aud get that big Northman too drunk to fight."

Owen bristled when he heard Enar called a Northman. "Enar is a Saxon!"

"Indeed," Elutides said with an expression of mock astonishment. "How do you know?"

"He says he's a Saxon."

"Amazing," Elutides said. He returned to the mortar and pestle on the bench. "Do you believe everything people tell you?"

Owen felt the first flush of anger stain his cheeks but realized how pointless it was to defend Enar's honor to Elutides. He shook his head and laughed. "I don't believe anything Enar tells me. I don't know where he comes from or care." He continued more soberly, "But so long as he serves me as faithfully, he may call himself whatever pleases him best."

Elutides, working up a sweat pounding at the mortar, nodded. "Very wise," he said.

Owen walked to the door and stood in a square of light the sun cast into the dim room. He stared out at Elutides' garden.

"She brought him to me," Owen said. "He has proven himself more than a servant, a good friend."

"She?" Elutides asked.

"Elin," Owen answered. "How strange are the chances of life. When I first saw him, I said to her, 'You might have brought me better gifts.' Now . . ." He broke off, deep in thought.

Elutides stopped pounding and touched the mixture in the bowl delicately with one finger.

Hearing the steady thudding stop, Owen turned his head. "What are you doing?" he asked. "Is it a secret?"

"No," Elutides said. He walked away from the mortar, around the table, and sat down near Owen. "You wouldn't understand what I'm doing, not without long study of arts which I'm sure are as yet unknown to you. But I'm preparing a little surprise for our friend, Ivor. I hope it's a very nasty, final, and fatal surprise. You are part of it, and so is the mixture in the bowl.

"I plan to present it to him at the feast tonight. The mixture heats while it's being ground, so I must let it rest for a time for fear it might catch fire."

Elutides leaned forward and frowned at Owen. "You keep calling Elin your wife. Surely you know you cannot marry such a woman."

Owen rested his back against the door frame and stared out at a statue of Mysaris almost lost in a thicket of long rose canes. Among the shiny heart-shaped leaves the male organ of the satyr was erect amidst the curling marble hair of the groin. The lips of the statue's face was curved in a smile of ancient lust.

Owen's nostrils distended at the heady scent of flowers entering the room on the warm breeze. "My wife is my wife," he said.

Elutides sighed. "A man must rule his wife, and you cannot rule her. She brought Enar to you, pagan that he is, and what else? Answer me man, tell me what else she has given you!"

Owen straightened up. His hands clenched on the sword belt, the links of the mingled chains biting into his palms. "When I lay captive in the Viking camp, Osric, the man I killed, tortured me. He didn't try to break my body, for that is quickly and easily done, but my mind."

Owen looked down at the floor. "I was going mad, as he wished, with pain and sorrow." He threw his head back, wanting to hide the tears in his eyes, the words coming hard to him, almost torn from his throat. "For know, old man, all this has been done to me before by . . ." He couldn't speak the name. "By someone else.

"I wanted to die, to die and escape the shame of it. For that's the worst. The shame. The shame that your pride, your heart can so easily be broken." Owen took several deep breaths, then continued. "But she came. At the time I believed I dreamed. She brought the . . . battle god with her. I saw and spoke with him, the one-eyed carrying his cloak and staff. We stood together in the springtime. Elin carried flowers in her hands and pointed to him standing at the edge of the wood. He taught me how to escape, first my suffering and then the cage."

"As I thought," Elutides mused, his voice low, "you have mastered the battle frenzy."

"No!" Owen said, making a gesture as though flinging something away from him. "I sinned in my despair. In my rage against Osric I sinned. I offered my life to Christ in atonement. He didn't choose to take it, but I hope He has forgiven me, for He is my true king and Him only would I serve."

"I know," Elutides said. "I heard your words to Gynneth. You spoke as a lover speaks of his beloved, but not to the girl. I believe you would defend her if she were an ancient hunchbacked crone."

"I hope that I would," Owen replied.

Elutides stood up. Rubbing his big jaw thoughtfully, he walked to the door. "Once I'm finished with the mixture on the table, there are things I could teach you about yourself, if you wish to learn them."

"I don't," Owen said. "I am a man and will face Ivor as a man."

Elutides, standing at Owen's shoulder, turned his head and looked into his eyes for a long moment.

Owen met his look with one equally level and determined.

"Meet Ivor and die?" Elutides asked.

"If I must," Owen answered. "I will not become a creature of the one-eyed, yielding my soul to an enemy of Christ so that I may be strong in battle."

"Why is it that all that is noblest in men also is the most dangerous? I find that very perplexing. But no matter." Elutides began to pace. His long legs took him the length of the room and back toward Owen. He still fingered his jaw, a frown on his face. "Odin and Christ, eh?" Elutides muttered. "You make it a choice between them."

"Isn't it?" Owen asked.

Elutides stopped pacing. "No! For I do not believe in many gods. There is only one God. The universe couldn't have room for more than one such omnipotent intelligence. That which is imminent and transcendent, omnipresent, omniscient, and eternal is by default, also"—Elutides grinned and raised a finger triumphantly—"alone."

"Christ—" Owen began.

"No!" Elutides exclaimed. "We are mortal and understand only what our senses tell us, so he must present us with a face we can understand. When we are brushed by that fount of light that is the Holy Spirit, we experience the glory but don't comprehend it."

Owen looked away from Elutides into the sunlit garden. He was filled with revulsion. "Are you saying the one-eyed is of the same divine spirit as Christ? This I cannot believe!" he said indignantly.

His brooding eyes fell on the statue of a nude Gaelic warrior dying on his shield, head bowed, the sword fallen from his hand. Clustered around the statue's base were the thick, woody stems of rosemary. A yellow-and-black butterfly visited the small blue flowers nestled among the dark green leaves of the shrub.

Elutides strode to his side and pointed at the statue. "What do you see?"

"A defeated warrior," Owen said bitterly.

"No!" Elutides said. "That's but a thing of stone. I mean the living creature."

"A butterfly," Owen said with a shrug.

"How do butterflies come to be?" Elutides asked.

"Is this some trick?" Owen said. He turned to Elutides.

"Every farmer knows they come from the pestilent caterpillars that eat the leaves of plants."

"Ah," Elutides said, "and how does it happen that one creature turns into quite another? Can you also cover yourself with silk and fly with the birds?"

"No, of course not. It's not the nature of man."

"Aha, then," Elutides said, resting his hand on Owen's shoulder. His strong black gaze fixed intently on Owen's face. "You do understand how the leaf-eating caterpillar becomes the butterfly cavorting among the flowers. If so, I beg of you, please explain this phenomenon to me because I don't understand it myself."

"I don't . . ." Owen said.

The butterfly left the rosemary bush and drifted down to the clump of thyme growing between the stones of the garden path.

Owen gazed at it, perplexed, and floundered on. "The butterfly is a different kind of creature than . . ."

Finding a damp spot between the cobbles of the path, the butterfly uncurled his long proboscis and set it down into the earth. Opening and closing its wings rhythmically, it drank.

Owen stopped speaking, sighed deeply, then whispered, "So complex a creature, yet also so insignificant. But you're right. I don't understand him."

Elutides threw up his arms and raised his eyes to heaven. "God and the shade of Socrates be praised. He has reached the beginning of wisdom. He realizes that there are things he doesn't understand."

Owen felt dizzy. The sunlight in the garden seemed suddenly too bright.

He staggered back. Elutides caught him, then eased him to the bench beside the table. Sitting in the cool, dim room, Owen regained his composure.

Elutides poured something into an earthenware cup and offered it to him. "Mead," he explained, "of my own making. It calms the mind an brings ease to the troubled heart."

Owen drank. The fragrant beverage seemed weaker than that he'd so enjoyed on the way to the city, but after a few moments he felt a deep relaxation flow quietly through his whole body. He stared down suspiciously at the mead.

"What's in this?"

"Verbena and elder flowers," Elutides said.

In spite of Owen's limited knowledge of herbs, this seemed a harmless enough mixture. He sipped slowly, savoring the fragrance of the flowers steeped in the honeyed wine.

"I admit," he said to Elutides, "you have shaken my faith in Bertrand's teachings about the old gods, but . . ."

"Bertrand!" Elutides exclaimed. "Was he the one who made you suffer so grievously?"

Owen didn't answer. He stared stonily past Elutides into the sunshine of the garden. Pride sealed his lips.

"You needn't reply," Elutides said. "I can read the truth in your eyes."

He reached out and touched Owen's forehead gently, brushing his skin lightly with his fingers. "How dare he lodge such darkness in a young man's mind? Has he not read the parable of the millstone?"

There was so much indignation and compassion in Elutides' voice that Owen was almost unmanned. He covered his eyes with one hand for a moment before looking up at Elutides again.

"The one-eyed," he reminded him.

"To be sure," Elutides said. "Do you want my own thoughts on the matter?"

"Yes," Owen said. "I can see those opinions have value. I wish you had been my teacher, not Bertrand."

Elutides looked both troubled and taken aback. "I greatly fear you won't find me a gentle mentor, either," he said, "but I have offered you your choice: go or stay."

"I stay," Owen said. "The one-eyed."

"Very well."

Elutides stepped back and pointed to a leather case on the wall at the end of the room. "See my harp? Go fetch it and play me a song of your own people. Sing to me of the glorious Charlemagne or of Roland of Roncesvalles."

Owen gave him a quick look of surprise. "A song! I, sing

to you and play a harp? I can barely pick out a tune on a wooden flute. The skills of the bard are quite beyond me."

Elutides nodded. "Men are not all the same, but variously talented. Tell me, does your friend Enar share your ferocity in battle?"

"No," Owen said. "Though he is brave, I believe his nature is cooler than my own."

Elutides nodded. "Then isn't it possible," he said, "that these things that you have done are rooted in the passion of your own heart? Part of God's wide creation placed in your hands to do with as you will?"

"No," Owen protested stubbornly. "Elin brought the one-eyed to me in the cage. I saw him. I saw her. I cannot doubt her powers. She has killed Reynald, ill-wished him into his grave by hatred and malice alone. She set her face against a man, a strong man, and destroyed him." He drained the cup and set it with a bang on the table. "Explain that, if you will?"

Elutides took two quick strides toward the door, then turned back again toward Owen, standing in the light from the garden. The scarlet stripe glowed against the somber darkness of his long tunic. "Very well," he said mildly. "That a man may be killed or made to suffer terribly from such a curse, I have no doubt, for I have seen it happen and even broken a few curses myself. But . . ." He raised his hand. "That it is entirely the witch's doing, I do not believe."

"She killed him," Owen said. "He died. She—"

"She, she!" Elutides shouted. "All I hear is 'she.' What of him?"

He threw up his hands in disgust and exasperation. "Owen, all our lives we struggle against our own baseness. Admit it." Elutides pointed a finger at Owen. "Admit it. Would you not like to flee now, return to Elin's arms, to the comfort of your kinsmen of Chantalon?"

Owen gazed down at the floor. "I suppose . . ." he began.

"No suppose about it," Elutides snapped. "Wouldn't you?"

"Yes," Owen admitted, "but to do so would be to break my word, my promise to both you and Gynneth."

Elutides smiled slowly. "So," he said, "why don't you break that promise? I won't stop you. Run! The stallion is in the hall. Drag Enar from Aud's bed. Run!"

Elutides waved one arm at the open air and sunlight behind him. "Run! To safety! To freedom! Run away!"

Owen leaped to his feet. His heart hammered with fury. His hands clutched at the sword in his belt.

Then he remembered Elutides' skill and speed.

The tall man was poised, legs slightly parted, balanced on the balls of his feet.

"Old man," Owen said savagely, "I believe you to be a mighty opponent in war or in debate. But you try my patience sorely. To flee now would be to forfeit my honor. I would carry the stain of wrongdoing forever in my heart. I couldn't forsake Gynneth. Her eyes would follow me wherever I went. I couldn't escape them."

"Is it possible," Elutides asked softly, "that you would judge yourself and find that self wanting, as did Reynald?"

Owen's rage drained away, leaving him limp and feeling a little sick at the thought of Reynald's suffering.

"He sat in judgment on his own deeds," Elutides continued, his voice very gentle. "Who knows what he found? But we do know the result."

"Then Elin's curse wasn't important?" Owen asked.

"Oh, but it was!" Elutides answered. "His crime was secret, hidden in darkness. When Elin cursed him, he stood guilty before all men. I wonder. Did he see his treachery and bad faith mirrored in their eyes? Hear the subtle change in their voices as doubt crept into their hearts? Imagine others thinking the lord bishop was his friend, yet he was sold, his living body delivered to torture and death. What might he do to me, if I, like Owen, earn his displeasure?

"My lord Owen, remember the butterfly and consider, if you will, how infinitely more complex are the workings of the human heart."

Elutides walked over to the bookshelves on the wall and selected a volume. He placed the book in Owen's hands. "Here," he said. "Examine this while I finish my little surprise for Ivor."

Owen carried the book to the door, opened it, and began studying the pages in the light.

Elutides returned to the mortar, considered the ingredients thoughtfully for a few moments, then selected a few more bottles from the shelves behind him. He added a little of each and resumed grinding.

"You do nothing without a purpose, old man," Owen said as he looked up from the pages of the book and stared at Elutides. He gestured with the book. "What is the purpose of this?"

"Who is the maker of that book?" Elutides asked.

"Questions," Owen said, "always questions."

"I beg your pardon." Elutides grinned. His teeth were a flash of brightness in the gloom. "I find men learn best when they teach themselves. Come, my lord Owen, the name of the maker."

"Boethius," Owen answered. *"The Consolation of Philosophy."*

"How did he die, this Boethius?" Elutides asked.

Owen closed the book and stared down bleakly at the cover, an engraved leather one studded with jewels. "In torment," he answered. "The executioner broke all his bones before he died."

"How much consolation do you think he derived from his fine philosophy then?" Elutides asked.

Owen returned to the table and threw the book down. It landed on the boards with a loud crack. "No consolation at all," he said. "I can't imagine anything or anyone who could help a poor suffering soul in such a predicament."

"I could have," Elutides said. "I could have taught him how to ease his pain. And I can show you how to turn Ivor's very gifts against him and overthrow the berserks, if you will let me."

Owen stared down at the book on the table, deep in thought.

The berserks! The room was warm, but his skin felt cold. He'd never met one, but the tales he'd heard of them were such as to chill him to the bone.

They faced the enemy, naked or wearing the bear shirt, as living sacrifices to the battle god. Maddened by frenzy given them by the god, they possessed a strength and ferocity that struck terror into all who faced them. They knew not women, refused even to rape their female prisoners, and destroyed all captives by rope and club to the honor of their god.

A charge by even a dozen berserks might leave the hall a charred ruin. Elutides and his people would be dead, for they did not willingly leave any living thing in their wake but killed and went on killing until they themselves were cut down.

Yet Elutides was prepared to show him how to face such a charge and defeat them.

"How?" Owen asked, lifting his head.

"To the great Boethius," Elutides said, "philosophy was a beautiful maiden sitting serenely in her temple, the light of reason on her brow." He finished with the mortar and poured the mixture into a bowl. "But men are not ruled by reason. Men are driven by forces before which reason is a frail bark tossed amid the towering waves of a stormy sea.

"Come," Elutides said, and he led Owen to the door. "I have had men confess crimes to me, crimes they did not commit, trying to earn punishment they did not deserve. For most of my life, I have been the ruler of this city. I, not Ilfor or Aud, placed those heads on posts outside the city gates.

"But many I have dismissed with lesser punishments or none at all because the deeds they confessed to existed only in thought and disordered imaginings. I have come to believe over the span of my life that I am caught as tightly in the claws of unreason as they who courted death so senselessly. But all this is philosophy, and we must pass beyond such discourse now."

Elutides pointed to the statue of the fallen warrior. "Behold the tribute paid by the conqueror himself to the magnificence of the vanquished, even in defeat. Long ago men like me learned how to induce the battle frenzy and teach warriors like that how to use it."

"They failed," Owen said.

"Did they?" Elutides answered. "I think not. The armies of Gaul besieged the Romans on the rock of the Capitoline Hill. Had they not been too generous to enslave the vanquished and too greedy to pass up the opportunity for loot, the victory would have fallen to them because they controlled the forces of mind and will that transcend the flesh."

The sun had passed the zenith in the sky. The stone warrior was barred by the shadows of the Roman porch.

Owen's eyes traced the curve of the muscular shoulder, the swell of the forearm to the fingers, curved, palm up as the sword slipped from his hand. A barbarian mystery, beautiful even at the moment of destruction and return to dust.

"Were they wrong," Owen asked, "to refuse to garner the full fruits of their valor? Aren't their victories greater than the mere winning of lands and battles? If the slave is chained to the master, so the master is shackled by the slave.

"What could be greater than the conquest of freedom or the striving for self-mastery? A life of struggle and adventure lived in the bliss of liberty and choice. A search that never reaches its end in victory or defeat. I understand you, Elutides, and I yield myself your pupil, teach me what you will."

Elutides smiled joyously. He clapped Owen on the shoulder and conducted him to the table. He brushed aside some of the clutter and lit a candle.

Owen seated himself on the bench.

"We will begin now,".Elutides said. "I'll explain each step carefully and do nothing you don't understand."

The sun moved lower in the sky and the shadows in the courtyard grew longer and darker. The butterfly continued to frolic among the flowers for a time, enjoying the varied flavors of their nectar, and then departed.

When Owen and Elutides finished, fireflies danced over the herbs in the garden, and the marble of the statues glowed white against the blue twilight. The candle on the table between them had burned down to a stub in the socket of the holder.

Ceredea entered. She set torches on the walls to drive out the darkness. They lit the room warmly.

When she left Owen asked, "Is Ceredea your servant?"

"I have no servants," Elutides answered, rising from the bench by the table, "only students and friends."

"Your way is strange," Owen said, "and not as the world goes."

Elutides picked up his mantle from the chair by the wall and wrapped it around his body as the chill of evening pervaded the room. "There were never very many of us, Owen," Elutides said. "Now our order is all but extinguished, vanishing like this beautiful place. Our knowledge, all but forgotten or abandoned to baser uses, is being overtaken by the tides of time, as this villa is by the sea."

"The world grows worse as it ages," Owen said, pinching out the wick of the candle with his finger. "Order gives way to chaos. All that is beautiful perishes at the hands of Northern barbarians like Ivor."

"I don't believe that," Elutides said. "I don't give way to despair, and I hope you won't, either. Now rise," he said gently. "Take my hand one last time before we go into battle together."

At the touch of Elutides' fingers, Owen felt a great calm flow over his spirit. It was a tranquillity, quiet as the beauty of the garden in the restful twilight, simple and pure as the clear bright light from the sea.

A peace seemed to emanate from Elutides' dark eyes. Owen wondered if Elutides had reached that sublime assurance he'd only dimly grasped as he looked at the statue of the fallen warrior. It was the assurance of a life lived only for the joy of living, an absolute acceptance of both pain and pleasure as equally important parts of that human adventure, and of one who needed neither master nor a servant but met, even among his enemies, only equals, brothers, or friends.

"What are you?" Owen asked. "Who are you?"

"No," Elutides said, releasing his hand. "Ask me again at the feast tonight, and I will answer you."

"Very well," Owen said. "See you keep that promise

and the other guarantee you made me that I would live on even if I fall in battle."

"That's easy to accomplish," Elutides answered with a smile.

"I still don't see how you plan—"

"When I answer one question, I will answer the other," Elutides interrupted. "Now yield me that despair of yours. It's a burden I wouldn't have you carry into battle."

"How do I do that, old man?" Owen snapped.

"By knowing that good lives on and continues forever."

"Where?"

Elutides' hand reached out and brushed Owen's chest lightly with his fingers. "Why, here in your heart where it goes about its quiet work, through you, God's instrument on earth. And here." He touched Owen's forehead. "In your mind, through greater understanding and love."

Owen stepped back quickly, flattered but a little embarrassed. "Very uplifting," he said, "but considering we're going out to kill a man, I'm not sure the sentiment is appropriate."

"Why not?" Elutides asked with a grin. "He may kill us. Remember we're outnumbered. I've seen the man. Were he alone, we'd still be outnumbered."

"That bad?" Owen asked.

"Worse!" Elutides said.

Owen stepped away and stared at the wild miscellany on the table, at the books on the shelves against the wall. "You taught me many things, but I remain troubled. Are they reality or illusion?"

"I can't say," Elutides answered. "First, one would have to arrive at an acceptable definition of reality and illusion. I've found both of them very slippery concepts.

"It is at times like this that I envy those Greeks, Socrates, Plato, Aristotle, walking among the pleasant groves near Athens. I would have you stay with me. Find time for study, discussion and debate. Instead . . ." Elutides' eyes lingered affectionately on Owen. "I must lead my prize student into battle. I have armed you with what little knowledge I have. I can do no more."

Flanked by Cador and Casgob, Gynneth entered from the

dark garden. She wore white, a gown of silk, embroidered with violets. Her head was bare. Her flowing dark hair had a satiny sheen in the torchlight. She was crowned with flowers and herbs from Elutides' garden—flowering rosemary, blue mint blossoms, and sweetly scented chamomile twined with the delicate trumpets of fragrant scarlet sage.

She carried a golden cup in her hands. "The feast will begin within the hour," she said.

Gynneth offered the cup to Owen.

Owen looked at her and was again reminded of the goddess standing among the flowers. The statue was cold pale marble, but Gynneth's face was that of a warm, living woman. Soft pink lips trembled, eyes clear as the dew nested among the petals of a rose.

His fingers closed on the cold metal of the cup. The gold was overlaid with a scrolled motif of knots in gold wire so cunningly entwined that his eye could find neither the beginning nor the end of their journey. Pale moonstones were set around the base and rim.

He thought of Elin. She'd once offered him a cup, and he hadn't known if it held poison or not.

He'd drained that cup in a convulsion of grief that she would hate him so much. She'd wept at his trust and courage. Elutides had said he couldn't rule her, but then she'd never tried to rule him, either. They came together in freedom, and if the time came for parting, they would part in freedom also. Owen lifted the cup. "The first lesson any soldier learns is that, in love or war, one yields all or nothing. By my life and fate, I lay all at your feet now, sweet lady, and I hold back nothing."

He drained the cup and handed it back to Gynneth.

Elutides took it from her hands and turned to Gynneth. "Go now," he said, "and dress your champion."

Chapter

26

*H*AKON'S first instinct was to fight, but he restrained himself. He had given his word. They didn't hurt him. They stripped him naked. When they were finished, he was pulled to his feet. The rest kindled torches from the fires.

They led him to the plow and placed his hands on the handles. The torchbearing men surrounded him. A whip cracked and the oxen hitched to the plow began to pull.

Hakon squared his shoulders and pushed the tongue of the plow into the earth, remembering that long ago even his merciless father had never said he could not plow a straight furrow. In the torchlight, Hakon saw the black earth turn, thrust aside by the plow horn.

The bull dancer began an ecstatic dance before the plow with his head thrown back, wailing at the rising moon.

Hakon flinched and bit back a cry at the first blow of a branch from behind. It took him by surprise, since he was not one to yield to pain.

The chant began. Hakon didn't understand most of the words. He wondered if the men who surrounded him understood them, either. He was sure the words were old, old as the world perhaps, and repeated by rote memory from father to son. But the music behind the words cried out with a power words alone could never convey.

It was a cry of longing, sinking into a desert of pain, and

then leaping up into a paean of joy. The cycle repeated over and over again, and each time the cycle was repeated, another blow fell.

Hakon felt the warm blood trickling down his buttocks and his legs, entering the soil of the painful furrow he trod.

Branches of those things still green when all else is dead in the forest—oak, holly, and mistletoe—swept over his back between blows. With these, the singers surrounding the plow scattered Hakon's blood over the fields.

In some deep, cool part of his brain, a part not caught up in his struggle, a voice whispered, "They are giving you to the earth. Will they finally commit the rest of your flesh and bone to their great mother?"

No, he thought. *At least, not yet.*

The strokes to his back were not intended to maim him. His blood flowed at the touch of the light thorn canes, but no permanent harm was done. Besides, he felt only a little pain, since he was so caught up in their strange ancient song.

I have heard hints of it before, he thought. It was in the shouts of rowers at the oars of a longship, in the last cry of a woman giving birth—a cry that ends in a sigh of relief and a sob of joy—in the lonely piping of a shepherd with his sheep wandering with the wind on a high mountain meadow.

They sang of life. Not any single man or woman's life, with its unique experiences and struggles, but the journey that faces all of us, the road magnificent, sad, beautiful, and often tragic that not simply each man but every human travels from birth to death. Springtime with its hours of wild all-encompassing desire stretching from the first careless tumbles with new loves in the meadows hidden in the high grass or in the green, blossoming wood. To the tender moments of first love whence even desire fades in the heart's need to adore and be adored. To reach out and create the bonds that will mark the meaning of our lives.

The days warm and summer rises, as does the wheat. We hope our lives bear fruit even as does the ripening grain, the orchard when the blossom of springtime becomes the peach, the apple, the quince swelling on the bough. Children surround us. Our incarnate passion or sorrow, fruit of fleeting desire, duty, force, or accommodation, becomes our immortality.

Summer fades into autumn. We reap the bounty of spring's struggle, summer's toil. Whatever we have given, in love and work, is returned to grace our tables. Bonfire colors fill the trees, one last blaze of light before the end.

Winter surprises. Boughs not long ago decorated with scarlet, yellow, pale green, and brown are bare. Hoarfrost is on the grass and glitters in the weak sun. And at the edge of sleep, we hear the howling of the wind between the worlds, calling to our spirits to keep faith, turn from the table of life's bounty, and join the long procession into the dark.

Yes, Hakon thought, *I have heard it all before, but never sung as one complete whole filled with such acceptance and peace.*

At the thirteenth stroke the blows stopped. Hakon stood still and straightened up behind the plow. The chant swelled around him and ended in a shout of ecstatic joy.

Far away he heard the sound of bells.

Hakon shook his head and wiped the sweat out of his eyes. The horned dancer had guided the plow far out into the fields, then back to the threshing floor.

The torchbearing men around Hakon shepherded him onto the threshing floor. A sigh went up from around him—a sigh with a moan in it like the wind whipping through a mountain gorge.

"Behold," the bull dancer said, "the summer queen."

She was mounted on a white mule, sitting sidesaddle, dressed in white. No longer the brown-and-gray winter hag, she was crowned with wheat and barley and carried a woven sheaf as a scepter.

He didn't realize the effect her presence had on him until one of the maidens leading the mule pulled off her wheaten garland and threw it over his erection like a ring over a post.

A howl of pure laughter went up from the men on the threshing floor and the women surrounding Elspeth's mule.

For the first time in many years, Hakon found himself blushing. His organ collapsed like a withered leaf, but not before the garland tumbled down it until it reached his knees.

The bull dancer had to be helped through a fit of coughing laughter by a few slaps on the back.

"All hail the summer queen!" someone shouted.

The rest echoed the shout. "All hail the summer queen!"

Hakon took Elspeth's hand and led her to the center of the threshing floor. Around them the tinkle of the hand-bells shrilled again, louder and louder, then fell silent.

The people formed a circle around Hakon, Elspeth, and the bull dancer. They joined hands, forming circles ten deep enclosing the three in the center ring. No one spoke. No one made a sound.

Around them the fires hissed and crackled. A branch snapped, sending a cascade of embers toward the watching stars.

Hakon wasn't conscious of his nakedness. He saw only one thing . . . Elspeth.

She was not a woman, but woman. The curve of her breast under the gown was the perfect arch of a breaking wave. Her eyes had the brown gloss of acorns glowing against a rain-washed sky. The shape of her body under the gown was the shining sweep of a field of ripe wheat bending before the wind. She stood in the fire blaze like a goddess caught in a shaft of sunlight as she walked a forest floor.

It seemed to Hakon the wind might take her. She would vanish like a picture of the sky reflected in still water that shatters and disappears at a breath of breeze or a finger's touch.

My life turns on this choice, he thought. *It brings me to my glory or my doom. The three gray ladies who spin the thread of life have woven the power and pain of this moment into the tapestry of my days. 'Choose your fate, Hakon,' they say.* He looked at Elspeth. *And I have chosen you.*

"I have chosen you," he repeated thickly, aloud.

Elspeth said nothing but stepped back a little to allow the bull dancer to stand between them. Then she lifted the white sleeve of her gown above her elbow and stretched out her arm to the bull dancer.

He held a stone knife. "This is the most solemn rite," he said. "Few undertake it. Few dare. You vow yourselves by all things to one another, by all blood ties to one another. Fail the rite, fail the land, fail one another, and you are accursed."

The word "accursed" boomed in the bull's skull the dancer wore.

"I am not afraid," Elspeth said. Her eyes burned into Hakon's.

"I never saw or met the thing I feared," Hakon said. "So be it."

There was a deep sigh from those all around them, and the circle widened.

The bull dancer cut a deep chevron mark into Elspeth's arm.

Hakon's body jerked slightly when he saw blood flow, but Elspeth never moved.

"By earth," the bull dancer said, "because we all spring from her." He cut a second mark. "By air, because breath is life." The knife sliced across the skin, cutting a third mark. "By fire, because we perish without it." Again, the knife descended on Elspeth's arm. "By water because we begin in the womb bathed in the sea of life."

A little light-headed, Hakon noticed the pointed end of the chevrons were aimed at Elspeth's body.

He extended his own arm. Using the same words, the bull dancer cut the same four marks on his arm. Only this time, Hakon realized the points of the marks faced toward his hand.

Then the bull dancer joined their arms and the cuts overlapped each other perfectly.

"Toward the woman's heart," the bull dancer said, "that she may be true and fruitful. Toward the man's hand that it may be strong."

Someone handed the bull dancer a strip of linen cloth. He bound their arms together.

"Blood to blood," the bull dancer roared. "Life to life, death to death. Be one!"

Hakon stood where he was in the breathless silence. Through Elspeth's arm bound to his, he could feel her whole body shaking. Her face was almost perfectly white. He glanced around quickly and saw the bull dancer was gone. They stood alone, the center of a circle of watching faces.

"Is there more?" he whispered.

Elspeth shook her head yes.

"Have done, then," Hakon whispered. "I follow where you lead."

"Hakon, father, brother, son, husband!" Elspeth cried out, her voice silvery and clear.

"Elspeth, mother, sister, daughter, wife." His voice held a sharp note of command.

"It's done," Elspeth said as she collapsed against him, no longer a goddess but a trembling, frightened young girl.

Hakon undid the strip of linen clumsily with his left hand. He dropped it, and Elspeth clutched his body with both arms, her nails digging into his back. "Oh God," she whispered. "What have I done? Oh God." She sobbed, almost in terror. "What have I done . . . ?"

For a second Hakon thought he'd gone blind. Then he realized something had been done to the fires. They had been drenched in a few seconds. He stood in absolute darkness. The only real thing in the world was the woman in his arms.

He lifted Elspeth. She seemed featherlight in his arms. No longer blinded by the flames, he began to see in the darkness. A low cloud covered the sickle moon, its edges silvered by the light.

His feet found the furrow he had carved with the plow, and he carried her along it into ever and ever deeper darkness.

Her arms were around his neck. He felt the silken spill of her hair on his naked chest and back. Her lips were close to his ear.

"You can still run away," she whispered.

"I have run away before," he answered. "Once into a longship. Often, when I was younger, into a drunken stupor among my men. I am no longer in flight."

"You don't understand," she said.

"Oh yes, I do."

"No!" She sobbed, her tears wet on his cheeks. "It's being put to a vote among them. I lied to you! Tonight, here in the darkness, the right to choose is theirs. I tricked you."

"No!" he said. "I heard your warning in the hall. And I understood what you meant. But I came. Not because I'm a brave man and not even because I love you. Once—do you remember?—I told you I was nothing."

"Yes."

A dark cloud covered the moon, and absolute darkness descended on them. Hakon's feet moved down the deep furrow of the plow. He felt the warm, soft soil compact beneath his naked toes.

"I came because I, like them, am a son of the land. I came because in all my life I never had a home. In my youth, I was a slave on my father's steading. In my manhood, I went where the wind took me. The success of theft and killing was like ashes in my mouth. I see now all victories are not of the sword. Destruction is not the only way. This knowledge brings back my worth, my dreams of building, not destroying. My dreams of life, not death.

"To admit this to you, Elspeth, brings the deepest pain I have ever felt to my heart. The pain I feel is almost worse than death, but I will not turn away now from it or you. So speak your command."

Elspeth struck him on the shoulder with her fist. "Take me here in the furrow you made with the horn of the plow. If death comes now, the spear must pierce both our hearts."

The newly turned earth was warm under his hands and at her back. He could feel the heat at the sides of the furrow against his shoulders.

"It seems she welcomes us," he whispered.

"As I do," Elspeth returned as he came into her body.

"You are the morning," Hakon said. "Green-gold and fragrant. You are the evening filled with the tranquillity of a day's work done. The hour of sweetest pleasure worth the moment of blackest doom."

Their bodies moved together with a harmony Elspeth had never known before. "This is the dance," she murmured in his ear. "The dance before which all other dances are simply a pale illusion. The dance of life."

"Not my pleasure," he gasped out, "but your pleasure mine."

"And yours mine," Elspeth breathed.

Then they passed beyond the place of speech where even endearments were not enough. And were not two but one. They took flight together.

Hakon came to himself, his cheek against the warm earth and Elspeth's hand in his hair pressing against the scar on his forehead. He waited in the blind dark for the death stroke, thinking it fitting that her hand should be there against the mark of evil memory.

Elspeth gave a sharp cry and pointed into the distance, then collapsed with relief. "You've won," she said. "There is the token of your victory. I couldn't be sure the vote hadn't gone against you until I saw it."

Hakon raised his head and saw a wicker cage blazing against the sky at the edge of the river. Inside it were two woven straw figures consumed by the flames as they embraced.

"That could have been us?" he asked.

"Yes," she sighed as she tried to crush his big body against hers as she would a child's.

"Do you know," he mumbled as a wave of mental and physical exhaustion drowned his senses, "I'm almost sorry it isn't."

Chapter

27

GYNNETH and Casgob led Owen to the Roman baths on the other wing of the villa. A clear, blue-tiled pool filled with clean, warm water was ready for him.

Owen undressed, then sank down into the water, and looked at his battered body. *I have just allowed myself to be talked into fighting twelve berserks. I wonder what Enar will say.* He began laughing and washing at the same time.

He gave himself a thorough scrubbing and dressed quickly. He found Gynneth, Cador, and Casgob awaiting him in the antechamber of the bath.

Gynneth clothed him in a shirt of ring mail and covered it with a heavy, crimson silk dalmatic.

Owen reached for his sword.

"No," Elutides said. He stood in the doorway, a torch in his hand. "Gynneth must place the sword in your hand, then belt it around your waist."

She fetched the sword.

Between Elutides' torch and the hanging lamp in the antechamber, the light was brilliant.

"What in the world?" Elutides muttered as Gynneth passed the chains over her soft fingers.

"How lovely," she said in innocent admiration.

"Draw the sword and hand it to him," Elutides commanded.

"Accept your weapon, my lord," Gynneth said, drawing the sword and offering it to Owen.

The patterned silver of the blade shimmered like clear water against the white of her gown and the sunlit perfection of the belt and baldric. Owen seemed to see the undulant sinuousness of a thousand serpents moving in the steel.

"Your father chose one of the best swordsmiths," Elutides said.

"My father gave me the sword," Owen said. "My mother chose the smith."

"Ah," Elutides nodded, "that's as it should be. Women give weapons to a man. Woman creates man. Without her he would not exist."

"Without man, woman wouldn't exist, either," Owen said.

"I've never been sure of that," Elutides said.

Gynneth knelt at Owen's feet and fastened the sword belt at his waist. He stared down at her, naked sword in hand, a strange, helpless expression on his face.

Gynneth glanced at him. Owen looked every inch the warrior, his shoulders broadened by the mail, the long powerful arms ropy with muscle and sinew. The red of the dalmatic set off his dark skin and his big-cheekboned face. Shadowed, almost haunted, eyes stared at her.

"Ever contentious, the two of you," she said softly as Owen took her gently by the elbows and raised her to her feet. "Woman might exist without man, but I'm sure she wouldn't be happy."

She embraced him, and Owen smelled under the faint flower perfume of her herbal crown a fragrance of youth and life.

"Sweet brother," she whispered, her lips at his ear, "will you be my lover?"

Owen didn't answer. His heart wrenched by sorrow, he couldn't find the words. He wanted to push her away but couldn't find the strength.

"If you can't love me," she continued, "don't grieve. I

will know my heart's hero when he comes to me because I have known you."

Her lips brushed his as gently as the breeze caresses the petals of a flower; then she stepped back and away.

"I believe," Elutides said, his eyes scanning the group, "that we're all well prepared for what is to come."

Cador and Casgob were armed to the teeth. Studying them, Owen realized they were more particular about personal cleanliness than the Franks. Their flowing black hair and beards were freshly washed and gleamed in the lamplight. Both of their bodies gave off the same unmistakable scent of freshly washed skin Gynneth's had. Their bearskin shirts were soft. The fur shone an oily black.

Elutides' lantern-jawed face bore the nicks and scrapes of a recent shave. He wore a new tunic. Brown, split down the sides as his other robe had been, it was adorned by only a little gold at the neck and again by the same red border.

Red? Owen wondered. *Red or purple?* He pointed at the strip. "Are you . . . ?"

"Yes," Cador boomed proudly. "Our father's family is of senatorial rank."

"Senatorial rank!" Owen stammered out the words, astounded and impressed in spite of his misgivings. It was a Gaelic lineage of immense distinction, honored by the Romans themselves. Their men and women still were respected and sought after for high posts in the church because they preserved the learning of the past in the savage present. They were keepers of the flame, tutors to the barbarian kings.

"Don't you dare show me any exaggerated respect and set a bad example for my niece and my sons," Elutides thundered at Owen. "When I look in the mirror every morning, I don't see anything unusual. My ancestors, conniving bastards that they were, simply made sure the Romans found a use for them, much the same use the Gauls had for us before the Romans came.

"Here," he said. "Accompany Gynneth. I will light you to the feast."

Owen took the girl's arm. Elutides strode out along the

porch into the wind, torch in hand, leading them toward the hall. Cador and Casgob brought up the rear.

When they reached the hall, Elutides paused. The night was dark around them. The flames of the torch whipped horizontally in the endless wind. In the yellow light his eyes were shadowed hollows, his face an enigmatic mask. "Ask me at dinner the question you asked this afternoon, and I will answer you as to who and what is Elutides. I promise a satisfactory answer." Then he turned, and together they entered the hall.

Owen found the gloomy structure of wattle and daub transformed. An enormous fire of fragrant apple wood blazed in the quondam fish pond. Sweet herbs added to a fresh layer of rushes on the floor perfumed the air.

Torches were set on each pillar of the encircling colonnade. Two big curved tables followed the colonnade around the room, an upper and lower.

Cador and Casgob seated themselves on benches while Gynneth and Owen were honored by two high-backed chairs placed at the very center of the high table, facing the door.

"You're making a target of me, old man," Owen said.

"Classic misdirection," Elutides answered. He seated himself on a bench beside Owen's chair. "Ivor thinks the panoply—the trappings of power—are its reality. I want him to notice you. Not me."

For the first time Owen realized Elutides wore a sword. A rather shabby weapon with a plain unadorned iron hilt, it was encased in an oxhide scabbard. "I would think a man of your rank would carry something more imposing."

Elutides chuckled. "Look closely at the hilt."

Owen did. The iron was worked into two serpents twined around a staff. Owen felt the nape of his neck prickle. "The messenger of life carries one serpent. The messenger of death two," he said.

"Yes," Elutides answered. "My sword is certain death."

The whole town streamed in through the doors. All wore their best clothes and scrambled for a seat at the bails. The latecomers would have to sit on the floor among the rushes.

Owen smelled roses. Enar and the queen wove in, leaning on each other and laughing. They sat down on the bench next to Gynneth's chair. Owen wrinkled his nose.

Enar gave Owen a shamefaced look and hiccuped. "She overdid it," he said.

Aud shrieked with laughter. "I wanted to be able to find him in case I lost him in the dark," she said.

"I believe you would have no difficulty," Owen said. "His essence preceded him into the room."

"Aud," Elutides said in rebuke, "he stinks like a whorehouse."

"I stink worse than a whorehouse," Enar said. "I've been in a lot of them."

"Bah," Aud said. "You smell better than you did." She kissed Enar passionately, then released him and shouted, "More wine, I demand more wine."

As usual, Owen noticed, no one hurried to obey.

"Don't tell Ingund, please," Enar muttered in a low voice.

"Who is Ingund?" Aud asked.

"Aud," Elutides said, "it's better not to complicate matters unnecessarily. Don't ask too many questions."

"S'truth," she said, trying to sit up straight at Enar's side.

Owen spoke into Enar's ear. "Are you drunk?"

Aud slumped backward on the bench, falling toward the floor. Enar caught her with one hand and pushed her forward. She collapsed, glassy-eyed, over the table.

"Too much wine," Owen said.

"Too much of everything," Enar said, swaying a little. "Both of us."

"How drunk?" Owen asked.

"Moderately," Enar said, waggling his fingers. "Pleasantly. Not so drunk as the queen. Why?" He sat up straighter, obviously apprehensive.

"We're in a fight," Owen said.

Enar sat as if turned to stone. "Who?" he whispered.

"Ivor Halftroll and twelve of his ... ah, men," Owen said.

"His 'ah men'?" Enar repeated. "What kind of 'ah men'

has Ivor Halftroll got, Lord Owen, bishop of Chantalon, Christ Priest?"

"He's trying to break it to you gently," Aud said. "In a word, berserks."

"Berserks?" Enar squeaked. He cleared his throat. "You are a troublous man, Lord Christ Priest."

"When we met, you said yourself I had enemies," Owen answered.

"I didn't expect this many," Enar moaned. "Everywhere I turn it's either piss in my britches or quit your service. And I might add, your friends are no less alarming than your enemies. Very strange friends you have. They shelter in tombs among the bones of the dead. Or like this lady next to me, who knows some tricks that would cripple a young man and kill an old."

"What!" Aud shouted. "You object to being made love to?"

"A dozen times!" Enar said.

Aud slid sideways toward the empty bench on her left. Enar propped her up again.

"Eleven," Aud said. "He's ignorant. Can't count."

"I lost count," Enar said. "I was too busy to keep count."

"It wasn't you who cried for mercy at the end!" Aud said, then shouted, "More wine!"

"Now," Enar continued, "when I'm weary, sucked dry, and my few wits addled by drink, you tell me to prepare myself to fight. . . ."

Ivor Halftroll entered, followed by his men.

"Oh . . . my . . . God," Enar whispered in an awed tone.

Ivor was the largest man Owen had ever seen, and the ugliest. Close to seven feet tall and muscled in proportion, he'd been no beauty at the beginning of his life. He was big jawed, with a low sloping forehead, and his brows were a shelf of bone projecting out over his eyes. A blow sometime in the past had caved in part of his forehead and one cheekbone and cost him quite a few of his teeth. It hadn't improved Ivor's appearance at all.

He was conventionally dressed below the waist, with breeches and iron-studded leather greaves on his thighs.

He had only a bearskin thrown over his shoulder. His naked chest and arms were scored with white puckered battle scars.

His one good eye scanned the hall. The other eye was milky, blind, and oozed matter into the crater where his cheekbone had been. The eye paused for a second when it rested on Owen seated beside Gynneth at the high table, but he made no other sign of anger or surprise. He chose a seat at the high table near the door for himself and his followers.

Those already seated there made room for them—quickly.

"Satan, Lucifer, Baal, and all the lords of darkness," Enar gasped. "His men frequented the same shop where he bought his looks."

Ivor was only the most impressively savage-looking of the bunch. The rest were competitive.

One had only part of his hair; the naked bone of his skull showed through in places. Another, who lacked a left hand and part of his lower jaw, wore a necklace of dried human ears. Another had no nose, no ears, and no front teeth.

"Mutilated," Elutides commented. "Someone must have disliked him intensely. Pity they didn't kill him. Perhaps we'll have better luck tonight."

Yet another, who'd lost his right arm below the elbow, had an enormous iron hook strapped to his forearm. The rest had all their appendages, less a nose, an ear, or a few fingers here and there. None was under six feet. Every man's bare chest, like Ivor's, bore a webwork of battle scars.

Owen looked at Elutides. "I took your remark too lightly, old man. I think I may have been persuaded to commit suicide."

"I think," Enar said in stark unbelief, "that I just did piss in my britches."

"Have you also quit my service?" Owen asked.

"No," Enar answered, "but don't ask me why. For the moment I can think of no good reason not to. I have had many nightmares far, far more pleasant than this to look upon."

"Drink no more," Owen cautioned Enar. "Arm yourself. Stay sober."

Casgob rumbled, "Ivor isn't stupid. Despite his large size, he moves quickly! Beware!"

"Thank you," Enar said. "Since I am more frightened than I have ever been before in my life, your kind warnings are unnecessary. Owen, I would not call that thing a man. Why are we about to fight it? And I warn you, if the reason isn't a very good one, you're on your own. While I am faithful and courageous, I am not, I repeat, not insane. I have known for some time that your lamp has no oil in it. Your dice have a few blank sides. You ride with but one spur. However, I felt . . ."

"He serves Hakon," Owen said. "He's put a price on my head."

"He's not interested in the body?" Enar said.

"No," Owen answered. "I believe it would please him if they were separated."

"And," Aud whispered, "he wants to marry Gynneth."

Enar's mouth dropped open. He looked at Gynneth cowering in her chair, staring at Ivor and his men with the fascination of terror.

Enar shaded his eyes with his hand. "No, we will not let it happen. My fate is upon me. Lord Christ Priest, absolve me ere I depart this cruel world. If he can be persuaded to draw a little closer, I can kill him easily. I have never seen even a berserk survive when his brains are let out of his skull. And if friend Casgob will lend me an axe or two or even three, the deed is done. Three's the most I can manage. By then his friends will be upon me, and it will be all over."

"Oh no," Elutides said, "not yet. Be patient. Don't worry. Enjoy the feast. I have a plan."

Queen Aud draped both arms around Enar's neck and whispered into his ear.

Enar's eyes rolled toward Elutides. "A magnus," he muttered all but inaudibly, extending his hand to Owen.

Owen gripped Enar's hand firmly.

King Ilfor arrived, accompanied by the lady who'd thrown the garland around his neck. She was the best-endowed woman Owen had ever seen. She wore a silk dress cut so low the edges of her nipples showed.

Aud snickered. "She has a plain face."

"Has she a face?" Enar asked. "I didn't notice. It is not what draws the eyes."

Aud laughed again. "She's said to have difficulty standing up."

"I'm sure that troubles the king not at all," Enar answered.

"I understand," Aud said sweetly, "she's best appreciated lying down, on all fours, or kneeling before him. . . ."

The sounds of bells, flutes, and drums along with cheers from the people drowned out the rest of the queen's remarks.

King Ilfor's arrival evidently signaled the beginning of the feast.

To Owen's surprise, Sybilla led the procession that entered the door. Dressed in leather tights and a brief halter, with bells at her wrists and ankles, she cartwheeled around the fire. Alshan and other of the forest people followed, playing flutes and drums. Behind them came the food, more food than Owen had ever seen in his life.

There were whole roast suckling pigs, venison, pheasant, chickens, ducks, geese, gamecock, woodcock, and doves. They were prepared in every way possible to imagine—roasted, steamed, boiled, and fried. The crisp skins gleamed in sauces of pepper, cumin, wine, and bay leaf. Some had been baked into pies, crusted with fluffy pastry.

Yells of delight greeted the soup. Whole cauldrons were carried in filled with rich thick broths made of beans, ham, beef, rabbit, and chicken, swimming with dumplings, vegetables, and onions.

There were platters of steamed fish, prawns, mussels, and crabs, each accompanied by its own special sauce.

Last to be brought in was an array of breads, buns, cakes, and pastries of all kinds.

The people at the tables fell on the food with ferocity

and abandon. Table manners were optional. Eating utensils were improvised. Nearly everyone carried large sharp knives.

Elutides pulled a single-edged sax from his belt and rested the hilt on the table, licked his chops, and smiled broadly.

The platters of food started at one end of the horseshoe-shaped tables and were passed along from hand to hand. The first were soon emptied, but there were many more.

A trencher laden with bread shot past Owen. He grabbed one. A pile of wooden soup bowls followed, jiggling along. The soup came bucket-line fashion from hand to hand.

All the food was accompanied by shouts of appreciation, enthusiasm, and pure joy.

Queen Aud halted the progress of a jug of dark beer, a whole suckling pig, and a dish of prawns. Enar secured a chicken pie and a three-foot-long fish, oiled and grilled over an open fire and stuffed with crabmeat and raisins. Elutides captured the better part of a wild boar and a large quail pie.

Seeing speed was the essence of the game, Owen gathered in a bowl of crabs spiced with cumin and bay leaf, a partridge cooked in rosemary sauce, and a dish that Gynneth pointed out as being her favorite—something that looked like squirrel stuffed with pork and walnuts.

Gynneth smiled and delicately helped herself to one, eating with the trencher held under her chin so as not to spoil her gown.

"Dormice," she said to Owen.

Owen looked at the headless rodent dangling from his fingers, then shrugged and ate. It was tender, the stuffing flavorful.

A flock of wine jugs passed Owen by. He decreased their number by three, two white, one red. A flight of beer followed the wine, and Elutides pulled in several. Everyone settled down to contented mastication, interrupted only by occasional loud compliments directed at the cooks and servers.

Sybilla leaped from the floor to the first table, then

lightly to the second and, folding her legs under her, sat before Elutides.

He greeted her with a kiss and a jug of wine.

"You're a tumbler, too," Owen said.

"When I was younger," she said, glancing down shyly at her body. "Marriage and children ruin a woman's figure."

"Where is Ceredea?" Elutides asked.

Sybilla looked troubled. "She went to Elin. You should know. You sent her."

Elutides gave a self-deprecating shrug and applied himself to a thick slice of the wild boar wrapped around the stuffing of truffles cooked in wine. "No one sends Ceredea anywhere," he said. "I merely suggested . . ."

Sybilla snorted. "I know your suggestions."

Owen only half listened. He studied Ivor as he sat across the room near the door. Ivor's one eye was fixed constantly on him.

Ivor raised his cup, bared what remained of his teeth at Owen, and drank. He lifted the cup high. His fingers closed around it, and the metal crumpled into a ball in his fist.

Owen let his lip curl into a fine, delicate sneer.

Gynneth laced her fingers into his. Owen lifted his own cup, kissed the rim, and offered it to Gynneth. She drank from the spot his lips touched. As she lowered the cup, Owen leaned over the arms of the chairs, turned her face gently toward his, and kissed her. She flicked his lips lightly with her tongue.

He hadn't noticed Sybilla leave the hall until she cried from behind his chair. "Let the queen of the feast crown the king." She handed a chaplet of flowers to Gynneth.

Laughing, Owen went to one knee before her chair. She rose and placed the crown of flowers on his head.

"Elcampane," Owen whispered as he kissed Gynneth's hand, "and yarrow. Very apt. I may need them."

"How the gold and green of the crown glows against your dark skin," Gynneth said as he got to his feet. "Truly you are a beautiful youth. Ivor must hate you with all his heart, ugly thing that he is."

"A toast to the king and queen of love and beauty!" Aud shouted.

Owen kissed Gynneth. Shouts of merriment rang in his ears. A roar of joy leaped from the crowd as he embraced her.

"I wonder how we look to Ivor," Owen muttered as he gazed into her lovely face.

Gynneth brushed his cheek with her fingers and smiled up at him, but an endless ache of desolation was in her eyes. "Like everything he has not," she answered. "Youth, beauty, happiness, and love."

Owen could see Ivor's face convulse with rage. The fires of hell seemed to burn in his single eye.

"Everyone knows he's asked for my hand," Gynneth whispered. "We're humiliating him publicly. We're maddening him."

"That's dangerous for us," Owen said.

"Yes," Gynneth answered. "He wants me, but that wouldn't prevent him, once he's had his pleasure of me, from taking a rope and giving me to his god."

Owen's hand tightened on hers as they both sat down in their chairs again. "Gynneth, what and who is Elutides?"

"I see you haven't forgotten the question," Elutides said.

"No," Owen answered.

Gynneth didn't answer, and Sybilla, standing next to Owen's chair, leaped back to the table, sat down, and helped herself to some of Enar's fish. "You're about to be instructed," she said. "Ask someone else."

Owen turned to King Ilfor. The king licked his fingers and ducked his head fearfully. "I know of no one who goes by the name Elutides."

His companion placed her hand on her ample breasts and looked away, shocked, as though Owen had said something very obscene.

"The man sitting next to me," Owen said to Queen Aud. She lifted a cup of wine and took a long drink but said nothing.

Owen stared at Elutides, whose grin was growing broader by the minute.

"Is this seat empty?" Owen asked Cador and Casgob. He pointed to Elutides.

"It is," they chorused.

Owen took Gynneth by the arm. Her eyes dropped. She bit her lip and clenched her fists in her lap.

"Enar!" Owen said.

Enar was tasting some of Owen's partridge.

"My lord," he said, "you should try some of this. It's excellent."

"You, too!" Owen exclaimed.

Enar gave him a dark look. "I protest. I know nothing of these people and their customs. I prefer to be left out of this discourse entirely. One fight at a time, please, Lord Christ Priest."

"I shall be a faithful wife," Gynneth said, "and every night your arms and weapons will rest in this chair at my side while your wounds heal, my lord."

"I see."

Owen glanced back at Ivor. The rage was gone from his face, but Ivor's one eye studied him with cruel certainty. The rheum from the other snaked a path like the iridescent track of a slug down his ruined cheek.

"My wound will heal even if I take the one wound that never heals."

"Hic jacet," Elutides said. "It's been done before. I can do it."

"For a time," Owen said as he leaned toward Gynneth. He smiled at her. His eyes were dark pools of sadness. "But not for all time."

"I plight thee my troth for as long as it takes for the lord Godwin and Elin to destroy Hakon. In darkness and desolation, in battle and in death, we are one," she said.

"Hic jacet," Owen said, *"rex quondam, rex feterus."*

"The dead aren't always forgotten, Owen," Elutides said. "Some men are too important to be allowed to die right away. Some men are too important to humanity for us to ever let them die at all."

Owen glanced at Enar. The Saxon hadn't done any more drinking and had eaten lightly. There was something ugly in the big man's face.

Aud shrieked suddenly and shouted, "What! Are you a fool?"

Enar slobbered on her neck. "No," he said, "but I want Ivor to think so."

She complied, giggling. They reeled together on the bench.

"Three axes?" Casgob asked. "Can you really use three?"

"Oh yes," Enar said, tickling Aud until she boxed his ears. "Give me three axes, I'll give you three dead berserks. If I don't, you may use a fourth to cut off my head."

"Done," Cador said.

Sybilla slipped the axes and a few more edged weapons to Enar while pretending to help herself to some more of his fish.

Owen gave a start.

"What is it?" Gynneth asked.

"I don't know," Owen said, peering at the fire. "For a second I seemed to see faces in the flames."

Elutides and his sons looked at each other.

"Now," Elutides said, rising to his feet. "Bring me some water. Owen, you asked me who and what I am, did you not?"

Owen nodded.

"I'll answer your question because I'm the only one in the city who can or will answer."

He washed and dried his hands in the basin of water Casgob brought. "I am but a poor singer and teller of tales, old half-forgotten legends of love and war, the history and dreams of my people."

Cador placed the harp in his hands.

"As king of the feast," Elutides said, "the choice of songs is yours, Owen. What will be the subject, love or battle?"

Owen turned to Gynneth. Her face was pale, skin translucent under the crown of flowers. He lifted the hand that clutched him so tightly and kissed it.

"Who would sing of anything but love in your presence?" he said.

"Love it is, then," Elutides said.

"Love and the springtime," Owen said, his eyes still on Gynneth's face.

"They are the same," Elutides said.

"How many are we?" Enar asked.

"Five," Aud said.

"A little better than two to one," Enar said.

Elutides lifted the harp and began making his way around the table. "Not," he said, "when one of your companions is Elutides."

When he reached the center of the room and stood beside the fire, the whole of the great hall fell silent. The hiss and crackle of the roaring blaze in the firepit seemed suddenly loud.

Enar, having discovered a new dish, still smacked his lips over the pheasant.

"Hush," Aud whispered fiercely.

Enar looked up, surprised.

"It's not often he sings now," she said. "I wish to hear every note."

Elutides' fingers began to caress the strings. He began softly, so softly that Owen wondered at the silence of the crowd.

But as the music grew ever so gently, the melody began to compel, to draw him out of himself. Its beauty and sadness caught at his heart.

Elutides' voice twined among the fragile, ethereal sound of the strings, telling a story of two doomed and guilty lovers bound together by a black enchantment. Caught by an evil twist of fate in a trap of forbidden and tragic passion, they were held by a knot of desire neither could loose. They betrayed, one by one, all of the most sacred duties of loyalty, kinship, and wedded vows in their desperation to taste the sweetness of fulfilled desire. Over each tormented moment of their happiness hung the cruel sword of final retribution and death. And yet, in the magic circle of each other's arms, they captured a beauty beyond the dreams of common mortals.

For love is not, the music sang, the mere joining of flesh to flesh but a union of spirit and will, transcending the lives of the lovers. It is always encircled by darkness as a campfire is by the night, an everlasting darkness where all loves end.

But, the melody cried out, those who do love and take the sword of its torment freely to their breasts, those who yield their all to its grandeur, achieve a kind of glory, finding in the most fleeting of human passions an echo of eternity.

They alone reach the highest fulfillment of their humanity by realizing the utmost heights of joy and the depths of despair. Perhaps they alone know true immortality and become legend, walking forever among the dreams we weave that tell us what we are and why.

Elutides ceased to sing, and let the music speak alone to each heart in the vast silent hall.

For though lovers die, love is eternal, returning again and again, as ever renewing as the earth itself.

To Owen, the notes of the harp were as the silver rain dancing among the flowers of the earth's morning, or sunlight sifting through the new green of leaves unfolding on the bough, and the haze of newborn blossoms spread over the meadows, opening their petals in the spring sunrise. It was a spring lost to him. A doomed spring. A spring he was sure he would never see again.

The song ended as softly as it had begun. Owen realized his face was covered with tears, and they were salty in his mouth.

He moved and his muscles cramped. He'd forgotten his body for a short time and it protested his absentmindedness.

Enar sighed deeply. "No wonder it is said the singer is possessed by the spirit of a god. Such beauty is a curse and blessing both. A thing we can never quite remember and never quite forget."

Ivor raised his cup to Elutides and threw a handful of silver at Elutides' feet.

A collective gasp of horror rose from the assembled people.

"Such an insult," Aud whispered.

Ivor stood. "You do not stoop to pick them up. Is it not enough?" he asked contemptuously.

He threw another handful of coins hard at Elutides.

Some of them struck his body, scattered, and lay gleaming among the rushes at his feet.

The silence in the hall was a living thing, palpable, filled with menace.

Cador, standing beside Elutides, took the harp from his hand and replaced it in its case.

Then he lifted a log from the pile beside the hearth and tossed it into the white heat of the fire's heart.

The flames seemed to take the log instantly.

Too quickly, Owen thought.

The bonfire in the pit leaped higher. The points of the flames licked at the smoke hole in the high-domed roof.

Elutides backed away from Ivor, hand on his sword hilt.

"Do you dare to challenge me?" Ivor roared, his voice a brazen war trumpet. The wattle-and-daub roof seemed to shake with the sound.

"How dare you challenge me, poet," he spat contemptuously, "I, a warrior!" He slapped his chest with his palm. It boomed with the sound of a tabor. "What sort of creatures are the men of this place that they are ruled by singers and women?"

He raked the benches with the glare of his one eye and wiped the drool from his broken mouth with the back of his hand.

Enar sighed. "Now come the boasts."

"I am a man. Where I walk, for seven years, no grass grows. I look upon a tree and its leaves fall. I have but to glance at dry wood and it bursts into flame. I have fed the wolves and eagles with the flesh of a thousand foes."

Sybilla leaped to her feet on the table. "And a few bits and pieces of your own flesh!" she cried.

Ivor fixed the glare of his one eye on her and laughed.

"Do I hear the buzzing of a fly?" He beckoned to Sybilla. "Come here, I'll swat you like the little fly you are."

His fist crunched down on the table, splitting the oak plank in two with a loud crack.

Undaunted, Sybilla turned, leaped into the air, backflipped from the high table to the lower and from there to the floor.

"Flies have wings," she said, as she landed beside Elutides on the rushes.

"Fear me!" Ivor roared. He shook his fist at the silent people around the tables. "Because I live, a thousand mothers mourn their sons, a thousand wives their husbands."

Sybilla turned and wigwagged her behind at Ivor. "And all still rejoice that you are not either husband or son."

To Owen's surprise, Ivor laughed with the rest at Sybilla's jest.

His next move also was a surprise. Despite his size, he was nearly as agile as Sybilla.

He leaped into the air over the tables, high and low. The berserks followed, coming in one merciless wave toward Sybilla and Elutides.

Chapter

28

HAKON awoke at dawn, still lying in the furrow with Elspeth beside him. Someone had placed their clothing nearby and covered both of their bodies with his mantle. He sat up and began to dress himself.

The light was gray. The mist was so thick it blocked the stronghold from his sight.

As he was belting on his sword, Elspeth rose and draped herself in her gray mantle. Neither of them spoke. It was as though they feared to speak, to break the silence or the strange sense of peace and permanence they felt. As though no words could give utterance to the bond they felt between them. Hakon took her hand, and they began walking back together toward the hall.

When they entered the gate, Tosi leaped to his feet with a shout of joy. "Hakon! You're well. You're safe."

"Of course," Hakon answered. "When did you see the thing that could break me?"

"Oh, I don't know," Tosi said cynically. "I've seen life come close a time or two."

Hakon glanced around the yard. His men were still sleeping, draped over piles of straw. Some sprawled in the stable among the livestock. "It's a good thing we didn't have to fight this night. Have any of them awakened yet?"

"A few," Tosi said. "I sent them into the hall. I told them there was music and dancing, along with many beautiful and willing women. But the pity of it is, they can't seem to remember."

Elspeth began giggling helplessly.

"Stop it!" Hakon ordered. "Don't make fun of my men. At least not to their faces."

"Ah, yes," Tosi said, rolling his eyes. "Stalwarts all. Mighty in battle. Now they're doing battle with their skulls."

"What was in the mead?" Hakon asked Elspeth.

She shrugged. "Nothing poisonous. Only eau-de-vie. A little drink my people brew for their own use in the winter months. It's wonderfully warming."

"The water of life," Hakon said. "It has a pleasant name. I've had it before. When it went down my throat I thought I'd die. A real hell brew, but the aftereffects were paradisal. In moderation."

Tosi gazed at the Vikings scattered around the yard. "They were not moderate. Few of them will be of any use before noon."

"They'd best soak their heads well," Hakon said. "I have work for them today."

"So . . ." Tosi turned, and looked downriver toward the city.

"Yes," Hakon answered. "I'm going to do what I intended to do before Rauching's visit."

"Rauching." Elspeth said the name, then spat in the mud at her feet. "Is he still alive?"

Hakon chuckled. "No, he's dead."

"He came off second best to Godwin and the bishop's witch," Tosi said. "His mission was a failure."

"Oh no!" Hakon said. "Not a failure. I wanted him to soften up the townsfolk for me and he has. Tonight I'm preparing the death stroke. We will begin tomorrow. In the end, when I'm finished, they will open the gates to me themselves. With the bishop gone and my half promises working in their minds, victory is within my grasp." He turned away from the river and entered the hall followed by Elspeth and Tosi.

Hakon found the floor swept, the tables set up, fires lit, and fresh torches blazing on the walls. His people and

Elspeth's were gathering to break their fast. Elspeth followed him with downcast eyes.

Once in their bedroom, they both washed and dressed
for the day. At the door, Hakon took Elspeth's arm to lead
her forth as his lady, but she turned and placed one hand
on his breast.

"Those promises Rauching made to the townsfolk—
were they half promises or half lies?" she asked.

Hakon looked down at her. She saw the scar pulse red
on his forehead and then pale against his tawny skin. She
could feel his scowl in the gloom.

"Half lies," he said. "My men will take their pay from
the city."

"Then there will be nothing left. My God, my God. The
poor people," she breathed.

"Oh yes," Hakon said, "there will be something left.
And it will be mine. From your stronghold to the coast, I
will rule here." He swung the door open and led her down
the corridor into the hall.

She presided quietly at the head of the table. She was
silent and asked no more questions while they ate.

Elspeth's people ate and drank heartily. Hakon's showed
a tendency to shudder at loud noises and paid more attention to drink than they did to food. But there was color in
their cheeks, and they looked able enough when Hakon
rose to his feet to speak to them. His voice stilled the room.

"You have seen the machine I've been building at the
camp. Tomorrow we will bring it to the city. When I am
finished, they will beg us for mercy!"

He reached down and drew his sword. It slipped free of
the scabbard, but then the sword parted from the hilt and
fell with a ringing cry to the table in front of him, leaving
him standing with the hilt in his hand and staring in consternation down at the blade.

Elspeth's people rose to their feet in a body. Other than
a shuffling of feet and the scraping of benches, they made
no sound, but Hakon could see in their eyes and in the
expressions on their faces that this was a sign they had
expected. A token of his vow and his commitment.

He glared at them in fury for a second, believing himself to be the victim of some trick. *But no,* he thought, staring down at the naked tang of the sword. *This is not a trick.* The two big copper nails holding the hilt to the sword were green with verdigris. The soft metal had deteriorated over time. Strange that they had chosen this moment to part.

Then he glanced over at his own men. They were pale with fear. A few Christians made the sign of the cross. The pagans were making gestures against the evil eye.

"Fools!" he roared. Then he snatched up the sword, ignoring the pain of raw metal edges cutting into his hand. He lifted the sword and, one-handed, swung it at the edge of the table.

The blade sheared through the oak planks, and the table fell from the trestle in two parts and crashed to the floor.

"Fools!" he roared, again brandishing the sword. "Even with a broken sword I can still strike. And strike harder than any other man!"

29

*T*HEY are doing something near the forest," Denis said to Godwin as he made his rounds. It was the last thing he did to make sure the city would be secure until dawn. Denis and a dozen of his crossbowmen watched the gate.

Two torches blazed in iron baskets at the gateposts and the stars twinkled in myriads across the sky. There was no moon. Darkness circled the city. Torches glimmered like distant fireflies across the valley near the forest.

Godwin and Denis walked along the wooden palisade away from the torches, their eyes adjusting to the darkness.

"But what?" Godwin asked. "A night attack? The berserks like to fight at night, but I don't think Hakon has many of those madmen with him. If they mean to overwhelm the walls, I can't think—"

Fire flared out in the valley very near the city, then arched into the sky, passing overhead with a hissing roar to land in the square behind them.

At the very same moment, Godwin saw a bonfire spring to life in the open fields in front of the city. The firelight silhouetted Hakon's capering triumphant men and the outlines of the catapult.

Denis and his men raised their bows.

"No!" Godwin shouted. "Don't waste ammunition. They are out of range. Stay at your posts. In the confusion, they may try another assault on the city." With that he turned and raced up the street toward the square.

Screams and shouts from the household jerked Elin out of sleep. She pulled her dress over her head and ran downstairs with the rest.

When she threw open the door to the square, her sleep-numbed brain could scarcely credit what her eyes saw.

A pile of faggots burned in the center of the square. They were almost white-hot and falling to pieces in their own heat.

Someone screamed.

Elin turned and saw Routrude standing near the tavern. Infuriated, Elin strode toward the woman. Her palm landed on the gossip's cheek with a crack as sharp as breaking wood. "Stop screeching," she ordered. "Get a bucket and form a line. We are under attack and must fight back." She snatched Routrude by the wrist and dragged her toward the fountain.

Above, Elin heard a whistling hiss.

This missile struck the arcade covering the shop fronts nearest the bishop's house. The dry wood burst into flame.

Elin and the other women attacked like furies, dipping out water from the fountain and passing it hand to hand. Within seconds, the fire was out.

But above, a third bundle of fire arched across the sky. This one landed on the roof of Osbert's house near the Roman gate.

Godwin bellowed at the milling, terrified crowd in the square, "You men! There is no lack of water in the city. Spread out. Drench every roof and house front. Awaken every man in every household. Each will be responsible for his own domicile. Soak every roof and wall. Pull the thatch off the roofs if you must. We can and will defeat this attack."

The thatch on Osbert's roof still blazed.

Gunter, hammering his fist on the doors, shouted, "Wake up! You're in danger."

The doors flew open. Men and animals darted out into the square.

Helvese, Elin thought as she eyed the crowd. *Where is Osbert's wife?* The night air was freezing, and Elin's gown was wet through. Her hands were already battered and torn from pulling one bucket of water after another from the fountain. She had to do something. They couldn't keep this up.

"That fool Osbert is more concerned about his livestock than his wife," Anna said, eyeing the blazing roof of the house.

Osbert danced around among the cattle and horses, shouting for someone to come help him gather them in.

A bucking yearling colt near Elin scattered the crowd. Elin reached up, caught the bridle, and pulled him down. She began to lead him toward the corner of the square where Osbert had improvised a pen. A yell of sheer terror rose from the crowd around her.

Another flaming bundle passed overhead and struck the stone pillars supporting the church porch. It shattered into fragments and burned itself out on the church steps.

"Thank God," Anna breathed, "but Hakon won't keep missing. By morning the whole town could be in ashes."

Elin had quieted the colt's struggles and had nearly reached Osbert when she heard him shriek, "Helvese! Oh my God, Helvese!" He went to his knees on the stones.

Elin followed the direction of his gaze.

The girl stood on the topmost balcony of the burning building, backed against the rail with one hand resting on it. In the other, she held her child.

Elin's fingers slipped from the colt's bridle as she stood transfixed, staring up at her doomed friend. Osbert's house was one of the tallest in the city, and from the top floor, it was a full forty-foot drop to the square.

Flames bathed the roof and the top floor. The beams and joists of the building's frame stood out—a glowing incandescent skeleton. The windows of the floor below glowed like open doors into hell as the fire raged, eating its way downward and erupting from within.

Osbert leaped to his feet and ran for the open doors to the hell.

A half-dozen men jumped forward to pull him back, but

it was Gunter who reached him first. Elin never forgot the look of dark compassion on the smith's face as a blow of his fist put Osbert on the ground unconscious.

Helvese looked down, her hand still resting on the rail. The flames plucked at her skirt, yet her face was serene and quiet. It was as if she saw death and accepted it.

"Someone try to catch the baby," she pleaded. A section of the roof let go with a rending crash. The balcony shifted and quivered.

Godwin stepped out of the crowd into the smoke pouring from the street door and stood under the balcony. He lifted his arms. "Alfric, brace me." The little priest leaned against Godwin's back.

Godwin shouted, "Helvese, jump!"

She looked down and, seeing Godwin's open arms, turned and made the sign of the cross deliberately and slowly. Then, putting her body between the child and the stones below and clutching the child to her breast, she closed her eyes and let herself go . . . backward and down.

Godwin caught her. The weight of her body tossed Alfric clear. Godwin was bowled over, his head landing with a crack on the stony street.

In the crowd, Alfric staggered to his feet.

Helvese sat up slowly.

Godwin didn't.

Helvese began to examine the baby quickly to see if he was injured. The baby evidently wasn't, because he began to bawl lustily, adding his bit to the din in the square around Elin.

Elin forced her way through the crowd and dropped to her knees at Godwin's side. She could see he was pale, unconscious but still breathing. She wrung her hands. Godwin was her mainstay and support. With him gone, what was she to do?

A second later Edgar was beside her. "Stop it, Elin," he ordered. "You almost convince me you are a normal woman."

"I am about ready to give way to hysterics," she answered.

"Don't do that. Godwin isn't seriously hurt." Edgar

searched the older man's skull gently with his fingers. "He's just knocked out. He'll awaken none the worse."

Elin heard another hiss and roar. She clapped her hands over her ears. The crowd in the square milled like frightened sheep.

This bundle of faggots broke up in the air, scattering flaming brands all over the watching people. The crowd ran from one side of the square to the other, trying to escape the flames, but Elin's improvised brigade of women held together. They chased down and doused each burning twig.

Looking at the rooftops around the square, Elin saw the citizens were defending their property. The householders wet down the thatch roofs and wattle-and-daub walls with buckets of water.

Osbert's house burned fiercely, but men on the roof of the one next door were soaking it down so thoroughly that it didn't look as though the fire would spread.

Osbert, still half stunned by Gunter's blow, embraced his wife in desperate unbelieving joy, even as the ground floor of his house caught fire.

Elin rose to her feet. "Edgar, get Godwin into the hall. Osbert, Gunter, help him."

Together they dragged the unconscious man toward the bishop's hall. Elin hurried along behind them.

There was a crash and a yell from the direction of the tavern. By the light of the flames, Elin saw Arn the tavern keeper struggling in the grip of two men. Several others passed out flagons of beer and wine to a cheering crowd.

Cold terror clutched her heart. A drunken riot could destroy the city as surely as the raiders outside the gates.

She ran forward and snatched a bucket of water from Anna.

"Are you insane?" Anna asked as Elin wrested the bucket from her grip. "Those men are out of their minds. They'll kill you."

Ignoring her, Elin raced toward the tavern and hurled the contents of the bucket into the faces of the looters, screaming, "Dogs!"

They rounded on her, then froze when they saw they faced the sorceress.

"What are you?" she screamed again. "Dogs—to sink to this while the city burns around your ears!"

The eyes that looked back at her were cold, filled with sullen fury. She knew she couldn't reach them. In a moment, they would brush her aside, and the city would be pulled down into a whirlpool of destruction.

One of the largest men gripping Arn's tunic spoke bleakly. "My lady, get out of our way. This is the end. We cannot win. If we don't perish in the flames, we will die of hunger and cold. At least let us have a little comfort before we leave our bones in the ashes."

Elin was tempted to rail at him, but she didn't. Instead, she drew herself up on her dignity, a commanding figure in the light of Osbert's burning house. "I will not yield but try to the last. And I am but a poor, weak woman. Yet I would be ashamed to let those devils laugh at my weakness."

The man shook his head sadly. "Oh my lady, we have seen Lord Godwin fall. It is the end."

If only Owen were here, Elin thought. *A man would know how to reach other men.*

There was a rending crash behind her. She turned and saw Osbert's house had collapsed into a bonfire of burning logs. Bloody light filled the square. From above came the now familiar whistle and hiss. This one landed among the houses near the square, and the sudden flare of burning thatch brightened the sky.

One of the men around the tavern pushed Elin away roughly, saying, "Get out of here or you'll get hurt."

"Dogs!" came a voice from behind her. Gowen strode out of the smoke. A monstrous primordial figure armed for battle, he topped Elin and every man around her by a head.

"Dogs are what you are!" he raved. "Hakon greeted you with steel. You threw him back. Then he sent Rauching with smooth-tongued treachery and gold. He went his way naked on the back of a mule. Now Hakon sends fire. What! Will you get pissing, puking drunk and let him have his way? Lay hands on your lady again and I'll stop the hearts of every one of you. Any man here think I can't?"

The crowd quieted and drew back to give him room. The man holding Arn by the shirt let him go.

"I promise you," Elin cried into the sudden silence. "I promise you I will stop Hakon myself."

Gowen gave a yell of triumph. "Where are your balls and bowels? Will you have it said men cowered while women fought? After all, friends, what is a little fire? He will weary of throwing it before we weary of putting it out."

Gowen forced his way through the crowd and threw his arm over the tavern keeper's shoulder. Arn didn't look as though he found Gowen's huge arm any more comforting than the looter's grip on his tunic had been. "Our dear friend here," Gowen shouted, "will contribute a bit of beer to wet our throats. Won't you?" he asked, looking down at Arn.

There were cheers from the mutinous crowd, though a few looked unhappy when it became apparent Gowen was going to supervise the distribution of the beer.

Another fiery bundle fell out of the sky, striking the Roman gate. This time the attack on the fires was more coordinated thanks to the efforts of Gowen and the newly formed fire brigade.

Elin left Gowen in charge and hurried to the hall to see how Godwin fared.

He lay on the floor with his head in Rosamund's lap while she put cold cloths on his forehead.

"How is he?" Elin asked Edgar.

"Better," he answered. "He's beginning to mutter and moan. No doubt he will awaken soon."

"Hakon has to be stopped," Elin said.

"Oh, I quite agree," Edgar said smoothly, "but I can't think how. Have you any ideas, Lady Elin?"

"The men at the wall. Can't you lead them on an attack on that catapult?"

Edgar sighed softly. "Elin, Godwin believes your understanding is superior to most women's. Actually most men's for that matter. Sit down and I will explain."

"Explain what?" she snapped. "It's true Gowen rallied them, but he and the rest have gotten into Arn's stock. By dawn there may not be a man in the city sober enough to know fire from ashes. And Hakon will still be there, still working that dreadful machine of his."

"It's a distinct possibility," Edgar said. "Because Hakon has at least a hundred and fifty men with him, it would be suicide to take the men off the walls to attack him. He would win. The catapult would still be in action, and the city would fall."

Elin slumped down on a bench by the table and covered her face with her hands. She was suddenly aware she was cold, wet, and dirty. Her gown slopped around her ankles. Her hands were filthy, bleeding in places where the rough handle of the bucket cut them. She could feel a layer of soot on her face.

Again there was the temptation to run, to escape this city. She had the clothing of her own people in a chest upstairs. She could dress, slip out of the town. Even Hakon and his men wouldn't be much of a threat to her traveling alone in the darkness.

Behind her hands, Elin's eyes opened. "The devil!" she whispered. "We are as shadows in the night. Invisible." Her fists crashed down on the table. "I promised out there that I'd stop Hakon and I will. Damn it. I will." She turned to Edgar. "I will need some help. I need two horses. I'll take Ranulf's mare, but I need one other."

Edgar eyed Godwin still cradled in Rosamund's arms. "Take Godwin's. He is near as tough as the man who rides him. He's an iron-mouthed brute, but fast and strong."

She nodded. "Rosamund, stop mooning over Godwin and help Edgar get him to bed upstairs. Then, go fetch Judith. Ingund, go borrow some of Enar's clothes and put them on."

"What are you going to do?" Edgar asked.

"You don't want to know," she said.

Edgar nodded. "Right. It has always been my belief that there are many things a man is better off not knowing, and I believe several of those things probably pertain to you."

As Ingund hurried to dress, Edgar and Rosamund got

the still dazed and glassy-eyed Godwin to his feet and helped him up the stairs.

When Rosamund returned, Elin thrust a note into her hand. "Give this to Judith. Now. Run."

Anna confronted Elin. "What are you going to do? If you won't tell him, tell me."

"First," Elin said, "I'm going to desecrate a grave."

30

IVOR charged with his sword drawn. "Pestilent old fool!" he screamed. His first slash nearly took Elutides' head off.

Owen and Enar jumped over the tables toward the center of the hall.

Enar shouted with joy as the head of one of the berserks vanished, sheared off above the eyes. He let fly at Ivor with the second axe.

Ivor parried with his sword. The blade met the axe with a mighty clangor and hurled it into the fire. Ivor towered over them all like a giant death. His face was a twisted horror.

The people in the hall scattered, screaming as Ivor's men attacked. They bristled with weapons, terrible as the armies of hell.

Ivor faced Owen with his sword lifted high to split Owen's skull.

Owen raised his own sword, even though he knew it would be brushed aside like a twig.

Elutides threw something into the fire.

One of the berserks lunged toward him, but Elutides had his own sword in his hand. For a second the fire appeared almost quenched. The noseless berserk seemed confused by the sudden darkness. Elutides slashed him across the arm.

Nothing, Owen thought in dismay.

The berserk fell. His back arched. His heels drummed on the rushes.

Ivor brought his sword down. Owen jumped aside. A stroke that would have cleaved him to the waist swished past.

Owen lunged for Ivor's chest, aiming a straight thrust for his heart. He felt the tip enter, but Ivor only laughed. He'd caught the naked blade in his hand. Blood spurted up and around his closing fingers. He jerked Owen, still clinging to the hilt, toward him and into his next swing.

Owen's lungs emptied of breath in a whoosh. His ribs bent as Ivor's sword slammed him sideways through the smoldering fire. He let go of his sword just in time to avoid being cut in half and rolled on the rushes. As he landed, he scrambled to his feet.

Enar struggled with another berserk, the one who had a hook for a hand. Enar's axe was half deep in his chest, but the berserk fought on. His hook was buried in Enar's shoulder. Elutides slashed the berserk's leg with his sword. Finally, he, too, went down.

Enar tore free, staring at Elutides in something like horror.

"They aren't men but witches!" Ivor screamed.

The remaining berserks gathered themselves to rush Elutides.

The fire seemed almost dead. The big logs were black and sent out billows of smoke. Only torches lit the hall.

As the berserks charged him, Elutides threw something into the air, and the torches burned blue.

Ivor bared his teeth. His one evil eye stared at Owen. His face contorted into a grotesque parody of laughter. Sword raised, he started across the burned-out logs toward him.

The fire exploded.

Ivor screamed and leaped clear. He was burning. The breeches he wore, the bear skin, his hair—all were on fire.

The light was blinding as though the sun entered the hall. Even the berserks quailed before it. Elutides slashed the first to reach him across the face with the sword. The berserk fell, but another, with an expert blow, sent Elutides' sword flying out among the tables.

Enar was locked in combat. One hand was on his antagonist's throat, the other on his sword arm, bending it backward to the floor.

Casgob's foe was cut into two pieces, top and bottom. Cador, having left his sword in another, was unlimbering his axe.

Fire ran over Owen's skin. He glowed with it but didn't burn.

The fire exploded again. The flames belched white heat, licking at the smoke hole in the roof.

Owen lunged for the sword of one of the fallen berserks. His fingers closed around the hilt. He jerked it clear just in time to drive it into the berserk strangling Elutides. The man twisted on the sword. His face a dripping nightmare, he began to walk up the blade toward Owen. Elutides cut his throat and tossed something else into the fire.

This time the resulting explosion threw Owen, still clutching the sword, spinning into the tables.

Between him and the fire he saw Enar, frozen, his grip on his opponent unbroken. Another of the berserks had his axe raised to split Enar's skull.

Owen moved as if in a dream. Everything slowed down. It was as if the air in the hall were water and they fought their battle under the sea.

Three men stood between him and the sun. In the bluish light, its rays streamed out around their bodies.

Owen leaped after the one with the axe upraised over Enar's skull. He heard the butchering smack as his sword cleaved meat, the crack of breaking bone as his blade amputated the axeman's arm.

The man turned with infinite slowness, his mouth wide, screaming. The spray of blood from the stump covered Owen's face.

Casgob struggled with two berserks. Owen ran at one of them, moving at the sluggish nightmare pace, holding his sword out straight in front of him. His feet felt as though they were paddling against a dark current that dragged him down.

His lunge drove the sword through the berserk's body like a knife through soft butter. It tore him free of Casgob and sent both him and Owen into the fire and out the other side, still locked together with Owen gripping the sword hilt.

The berserk's hand slammed into Owen's chest. Both of their clothes smoldered. The iron of the mail burned Owen's skin. The sword tore free of the screaming man, taking most of his guts out in long, coiling loops. He went to his knees, clutching at them.

The berserks were all around Owen. The fire was a fountain. The embers rose in a column, falling like rain on the combatants below.

They are moving so slowly, Owen thought. *It's child's play to dodge their blows.*

One aimed an axe cut at his head. Owen watched, fascinated, as the edge grew silver, the old steel behind it pitted and scarred by craters, each reflecting light back into his eyes.

Owen dropped to one knee and felt the blade go by. It brushed his hair. He drove his sword into the groin of the man swinging it.

The arching spasm of his opponent's body, the ruby color of the blood that flowed out over his fingers, was another thing of beauty . . . and terror.

Suddenly, Ivor grabbed his arm, and Owen flew through the air. It was an exquisite freedom. He felt like a hawk drifting on the thermals high above the earth. He turned, spinning, a feather on the wind. He came to a soft landing on his feet, standing on the coals in the very heart of the fire.

Owen looked at Ivor through a curtain of flame, laughing.

Didn't the fool know water was everywhere? It filled the hall, the world. It would not let him burn.

He swam out of the fire, striking one who turned ever so slowly, trying to catch him across the back of the neck. Owen severed his spine, sending him to the floor dead, a look of surprise on his face.

The water was everywhere, blue and shot with light. A rain of gold fell slowly from the sky above.

All around Owen the ghosts of the Roman builders of the villa crowded the seats of an amphitheater, screaming for Owen's death.

Owen was a gladiator, facing Ivor and the berserk whose scalp was half scraped away so his skull showed through.

Ivor swung the sword straight down.

Owen pushed off with his toes from the floor. He let himself be brushed aside by the force of the blow. *The fool should know enough not to swing so hard underwater.*

He aimed his cut more carefully, trying for the thumb of the sword hand drifting past his face. He chopped the thumb off, sending Ivor's sword rolling free, end over end into the blueness around him.

Ivor plunged past Owen, leaping away after his sword.

Enar had the bald one. Enar's shirt hung in charred rags from his shoulders. His chest and face were mottled with burns. His hands and arms were a bloody mess. Some of his fingernails had been torn out. But he was holding the necklace of ears, throttling the berserk bare-handed.

Ivor roared. The sound filled the hall. The walls shook with the fury of his rage. The protecting water drained away, taking the ghosts of the Romans. It twisted, elongated, vanished, foaming out with it over a plain of stone.

Owen ran ahead of the breaking sea. The giant Ivor, his head touching the sky, loomed behind him. His strides shook the ground under Owen's feet. The drops of blood from his amputated thumb struck the hard ground, splattering drops that scattered ruby droplets of blood into the air.

I am dead, Owen thought. *This is Valhalla. The maidens who ride the storm will awaken me in the morning to fight again. Forever.*

Owen staggered. He gathered himself and ran on, Ivor roaring behind him. The stone under his feet cracked like the ground baked iron hard by a drought in the summer sun.

Then Owen was so tiny he had to leap from plateau to

plateau, jumping over canyons. He was no bigger than a mouse. He looked back. Ivor was a mountain looming between his eyes and the sun.

He stumbled and fell into one of the canyons, rolling down the slope into the soft dirt below. He crouched like an animal hunted by a bigger one. Ivor's shadow blotted out the sky above.

Owen pressed one hand against the wall of the crevice and clung tightly to the sword he carried with the other.

Ivor's sword stabbed down into the crack beside him. The tip filled it with steel.

Ivor's laughter rumbled like an earthquake. His words were thunder. "I will crush you like an insect!"

Owen ran along the bottom of the crevice. Grains of sand were glittering boulders, their sharp edges flashing in the sunlight. Tiny clods of dirt were cliffs to be scaled.

Everywhere, Ivor's sword stabbed savagely down. It hit inches away, sending a landslide that nearly buried Owen. A deeper crevice opened ahead. Owen plunged forward, following it. The walls grew higher and higher, and his feet splashed in a rivulet of moisture.

He stopped, crouching again. It was so silent his ears roared. His body shook as it had in the cage. He pressed his hand against his ribs. They hurt. Under them, his heart hammered, racing. He gasped for air through his open mouth, trying to be as quiet as possible lest the beast that followed hear.

His fingers tightened around the sword hilt in his hand. His mind emptied. All but one thought. He must kill Ivor or die himself.

Owen forced himself to run again. The walls of his earthen canyon grew lower, and he scrambled among the flakes of quartz and sticky granules to the top.

Ivor's heels were in front of him, only a hundred or so yards away. He methodically destroyed the broken earth before him, driving his sword straight down like a spade.

To kill him, Owen had to cross that open space. He looked down at his filthy, blood-covered hands, spat on both, and gripped the sword. He had to move now, while the giant before him was occupied. He ran, driving his legs to one manic burst of speed toward the ankles that reared like the pillars of the sky before him. A pair of feet that could crush him into a smear of red dust loomed before him.

He hewed—the way a man strikes a tree he wants to fell—at the ankle. The sword sliced through the tendon, surprising his tormented brain by the ease of its passage. Then he scrambled away as the bulk of the monster above fell backward, down and down.

Owen screamed, a full-throated howl, as the whole sky came thundering down to crush him.

Suddenly, he realized he was screaming and thrashing in Enar's arms. He looked around at the ruined hall. Ivor's body was at his feet.

"My lord," Enar panted, "it is done. Don't struggle so. Christ, how your heart beats. It will burst. Stop this!" he cried out, appealing to Elutides.

Elutides, kneeling in the rushes beside a fallen Casgob, pointed to Owen's face.

"See, even now, the drug loosens its hold on him. There is understanding in his eyes."

Enar heaved a deep sigh of relief. "Rest now. Rest my lord. Rest, please. It was a mighty battle fought this day, but it is over. We are the victors."

Aud placed a clay bottle in Enar's hand. She stood beside them. Her dress was torn, and she held a clubbed mace in her hand. She kicked Ivor in the ribs. "Behold the happy bridegroom," she said, laughing.

Owen lay gasping while Enar drank beer from the jug.

Gynneth helped Elutides with Casgob.

Others returned to the hall. They descended on the fallen men, cutting off their heads and dragging away what remained by the heels.

Two still lived—the one Owen had gutted, who lay near the fire with bloody foam around his mouth, and Ivor.

Elutides looked up from Casgob's wound, studied the gutted man for a second, then said, "Cut his throat."

Owen looked away.

Enar took a long pull at the jug of beer. "I will never understand you, Lord Christ Priest."

"For the moment," Owen said, "I have had enough of slaughter. I cannot even tell if I am whole."

"You are," Enar answered. "All the parts are present and they move as they should. I know because you clawed savagely at me after you hamstrung Ivor."

"I'm sorry," Owen said. "I didn't know you."

"I could tell," Enar said. "Your eyes stared like a madman's. But I was not afraid since, after Ivor fell, you dropped your sword. I held you lest you do yourself some harm. I have some experience with men taking leave of their senses. My uncle Wilderbrand was overfond of drink and saw dragons. This failing of his, you understand, would have caused but little remark had he not taken to chasing them with axe and sword."

"Unnerving," Owen said.

"Very," Enar answered, "especially for his wife. She left him after he saw one sitting on her shoulder. It is well she was fleet of foot. He chased her down the road past our house with all the neighbors running full tilt after them, trying to catch him. It was his misfortune my mother was the one who did. After his ribs healed and the broken arm mended, he was much easier to get along with."

"Your mother had that effect on people?" Owen said.

"Frequently she did," Enar said with a grin.

"Did he continue to see dragons?" Owen asked.

"Oh yes," Enar answered. "Sometimes, if asked, he described them. But they were very conventional creatures and not unusual at all."

Owen mulled this over. "Conventional dragons?"

"Snakes with legs and teeth," Enar said, "pink-and-green scales."

"They didn't breathe fire?" Owen asked.

"Nay," Enar said. "They were average Saxon dragons. Only foreign dragons breathe flame."

Elutides left Casgob and knelt beside Owen. "How is he now?" he asked.

"Very well," Owen said. "We were discussing the nationality of dragons."

"Indeed!" Elutides said as he peered into Owen's eyes and turned his head from side to side. "Dragons? Were you struck on the skull?"

"Likely not since infancy," Enar said.

"I'm disappointed they did not breathe fire," Owen said. "But then," he added, "what can you expect of a Saxon dragon?"

"It's true," Enar said dolefully. "We are a plain, down-to-earth, unimaginative people. It follows that our dragons would be also."

"Do you see these dragons now?" Elutides asked.

"I do not," Owen said, "but no thanks to you."

"We were discussing the dragons of my uncle Wilderbrand," Enar said.

"Ah!" Elutides said, "those that crawl out of the cup."

"They were conventional dragons," Owen said. He rolled on his side and began to cry.

"Oh no!" Enar cried. Setting down the beer jug, he reached toward Owen.

"It's nothing," Elutides said. "Many are taken this way after the close approach of death."

"It never happens to me," Enar said.

"No," Elutides snapped, "instead you babble of dragons. Get him to the bench. Fill him with food and drink, especially with drink. He'll be fine in the morning."

Gynneth left Casgob, who was sitting up. His thigh was bandaged.

She took one of Owen's arms, Enar the other. With their help, he got to his knees but feared he could get no further. His legs refused him.

Ivor moaned.

Owen leaped to his feet.

Aud raised the mace, with both hands, over her head. "I didn't hit him hard enough."

"No," Owen said.

Aud dropped the mace to her side. "He's a monster. The mice running about in the rushes deserve mercy more than he," she said.

"I wonder," Owen said, "how many have thought so?"

"He won't thank you," Enar said, staggering back toward his table. "He'll take it as an insult if you don't kill him."

"I don't have it in me!" Owen answered.

Gynneth offered Owen some mead. He kissed her on the forehead and leaned on her shoulder while he drank.

"Elutides!" Aud said. Exasperated, she stamped her foot.

Elutides dropped to his knees beside Ivor. He examined the giant's wounded foot.

"He will never walk again. Not as a normal man does, at any rate." He lifted the lid of his one eye. "He will awaken in time, not soon I think."

He placed one hand on Ivor's chest, palm down, and closed his eyes. A shadow crept over his face. It hardened, then paled. His mouth twisted like that of a man in pain. Then he pulled away quickly, sat back on his heels, and looked at Owen.

"You're right," he said. "I don't want his blood on my hands. Neither of us is his destiny. I cannot tell what his fate will be. Bind him. When morning comes, lead him to the border of our land. Drive him away never to return on pain of death."

Aud shrugged, lifted the wine jar to her lips, then wandered away.

The hall was nearly full again, and everyone seemed to be talking at once.

Since the battle had taken place in the center, most of the food remained on the tables. The townsfolk milled around trying to find their former places.

A fistfight broke out between two men over the seating arrangements. Aud strolled over, still trailing the mace, to join the spectators and be entertained.

One of the combatants floored the other. He lay prone until revived by a jug of beer poured over his head.

Ivor was removed by Cador and several men, one on each limb, as Owen and Gynneth returned to their chairs.

"I warned him," King Ilfor said.

"Did you?" Elutides said, taking his seat beside Owen.

The king was still eating, his well-endowed friend beside him.

"No one ever pays any attention to what I say about you, Elutides. I wondered what you would do about Ivor. I must say, this has been one of your more entertaining—"

His companion turned and smacked him over the head with a roast chicken. "Stop talking about it or you will bring a perfect plague of misfortune down on us."

Aud pulled Enar's head down into her lap and began peeling prawns and feeding them to him.

"You are the king?" Owen asked.

"Yes," Ilfor answered, "I am, but Elutides . . ."

His friend hit him on the head with the remains of the chicken and silenced him again.

"Aud is your queen?" Owen asked.

Aud pushed a platter of pork in wine sauce in front of Owen. "Here, eat," she said. "You must be famished. I am not his queen. I am Queen."

"You are not husband and wife?" Enar asked cautiously.

"No," Aud answered, shelling another prawn, dipping it in sauce, and popping it into Enar's mouth. "You insult me. That tub of lard?"

"Tub of lard?" Ilfor yelled.

"Be quiet," Elutides said. "It's unseemly to shout insults at each other in public. Besides, it disturbs my digestion, and I've had enough of that for one night."

"Thank you for granting me Ivor's life," Owen said.

"Surely," Elutides said, "you know I would refuse you nothing."

"You used me, old man!"

"That I did," Elutides answered smoothly. "You shall have the reward of your valor."

"I want no reward," Owen said. He ate the pork without tasting it. Now that the rage in his flesh was fading, his stomach cramped agonizingly. He shook all over with weakness. The high-domed roof above had a tendency to spin when he looked at it. He felt disgusted with Elutides, Enar, and everyone around him for joining again so quickly in the revelry. For forgetting the horrors that lately assailed him.

"I want to go home," he whispered. "Home. Home."

He stared hollow-eyed at the floor of the firepit, at the flames consuming the high mass of blackened faggots, at the figures leaping and dancing, led by Sybilla and piped by Alshan, in a ring dance around the blaze.

"Men died here not an hour ago," Owen said, "and they dance on the killing ground."

"My lord," Enar said in a soothing tone, "men die everywhere. If laughter and feasting departed from the world because of death, we would all be . . . gloomy forever."

Owen turned on Enar in fury. "And would you have laughed and feasted if I had fallen instead of Ivor?"

Enar leaped to his feet. "Lord Christ Priest, I have fought for you, to defend you, and beside you since this adventure began. But one thing I will not do is join you in mourning Ivor. Yes, I would have laughed had you died. I laugh at death, in spite of death, and perhaps because of death. Why not, eh, Lord Christ Priest? Death laughs at us and has a much longer time for laughter than we do."

Owen leaped to his feet and gave Enar a stare of pure hatred. Then he turned and stalked out of the hall. He went through the deserted palace, the sounds of the feast fading behind him, until he reached the long porch overlooking the ocean.

The sky was clear. The stars hung in myriads above him. He couldn't see the black roll of water below him, but he could hear the endless voice of the waves and see the glimmer of brief threads of foam as the seas crested and fell against the rocks.

Owen rested his head against one of the cool marble columns and let the rhythmic sound fill first his ears and then his mind, until at last his jumping, cringing nerves quieted. He felt someone behind him.

"Who is it?" he asked.

"Elutides. I see you have that, too."

"Have what?" Owen asked dully.

"The ability to perceive the nearness of others," Elutides said.

"Is it unusual?"

"No," Elutides said, "but it's valuable."

Owen nodded.

"The Northman loves you," Elutides said, "but he won't let you trouble his heart or break his spirit."

Owen sighed. "I wouldn't want to do either one. Tell him. Tell him I'm sorry."

"He knows," Elutides answered. "Your friend is a philosopher."

"Enar?" Owen laughed. "Enar a philosopher? How so?"

"He perceives," Elutides said, "a profound truth even Pythagoras had difficulty elucidating. The gods grant man neither time nor eternity. Only ..." Elutides stopped speaking and Owen turned to face him.

"Only what?" Owen asked.

"Only the moment," Elutides said.

The star blaze gleamed on Elutides' face, turning the eye sockets to hollows. He reminded Owen so strongly of the king in the tomb that Owen looked quickly away.

"I'm not Enar," he said.

"I know," Elutides said.

He said no more, only stood and waited with his death's-head face in the shadows.

"I must save my city," Owen said.

"Yes," Elutides answered.

"Even if it costs me my own soul?" Owen asked.

"The welfare of his people is a ruler's highest duty. He has no other," Elutides said.

"These things have the smoke of damnation on them!" Owen cried to the night and the stars.

"Go and bathe," Elutides said. "Gynneth awaits you."

Owen paid no attention.

"We didn't fight in this world," he said, "but in another."

"I didn't see you depart for anywhere else," Elutides said. "I watched you fight. Saw you strike him down. The swordplay was so quick, my eyes almost couldn't follow it. Never have I seen such speed on the part of two men. I thought his last lunge would finish you. But then in one of the boldest strokes I've ever seen, you went to one knee. His speed sent him past you, almost tripping over your body. Your blade sliced the tendon and he went down. Aud used her mace on his head."

"That's not what I remember," Owen said.

"What do you remember?" Elutides asked.

Owen swung around and stared out at the sea.

"We fought on a broken desert. I was alone. I had no help."

"The drug gives you strength and speed but sometimes does other things to the minds of those who take it," Elutides said.

"He filled the sky," Owen shouted. "I can't escape the memory."

"Then don't escape it," Elutides flared back at him. "Conquer your terror. If you would learn to use such weapons, don't complain if you sometimes feel their teeth."

Owen was silent, partly because he felt he had no answer and partly because he could hear the whine in his voice. He despised himself for being so craven.

"This has cost you little, old man," Owen said bitterly.

"A wound in the body of one of my sons. That is much to me," Elutides said, turning away. "Go bathe. Gynneth awaits you."

Cador stepped out of the shadows. "Come," he said quietly.

Owen followed.

For the second time that day he found himself sitting in warm water.

A purpling bruise on one side covered six of his ribs. His hands were in the worst condition he had ever seen. In places on his chest and back, the pattern of the ring mail was branded into his flesh.

The bath eased the stiffness out of his muscles and joints. He decided he might not be as sore in the morning as he had been when he awakened in the tomb.

"I've grown soft as a bishop," he said.

The ceiling of the bath, inlaid with marble and porphyry, danced with the bright reflections of light in the water.

"Gynneth awaits you," Elutides said.

Owen drowsed. His neck rested against the alabaster edging of the pool as he watched the play of light on the ceiling and tried to make a decision about Gynneth.

He thought of Elin. Her face rose before him as it had in the cage. He knew instinctively his fidelity would mean nothing to her measured against his chances of survival. She'd want him to do anything necessary to save the city and stay alive.

When he rose from the bath and dried off, Cador handed him a long white linen gown and led him to Gynneth's chamber.

Gynneth's bedroom looked out over the sea. One wall, made of columns and arches, led to a small porch. Beyond, Owen heard the whisper and hiss of the waves.

A mosaic of leaping dolphins circled the bed in the center of the floor.

The other three walls were painted. The one near the door was of women. They were crowned with laurel and carried dark garlands. All were weeping and bowed with grief.

On the wall behind the bed was pictured a procession. Shadowed figures, wearing the heads of beasts, escorted one whose face was half obscured by the rest. He, alone, had a human face.

On the wall facing the foot of the bed were painted panels of four colors. One red, one white, one blue, one black. In the center of each panel was a flower.

The room was lit by only one lamp. The light was set within a crystal bowl bound with gold.

The facets of the crystal shattered the flames into thousands of flashes of prismatic brilliance that spattered the walls and the domed ceiling with rainbows.

In the strange changing light, the paintings on the walls seemed to move. The draperies on the figures appeared to stir and flutter in the unending sea breeze flowing through the wide portico to the ocean.

On the bed Gynneth lay sleeping. She wore an almost transparent gown of silk and lace.

Owen felt desire rise through his body. His blood was molten gold in his veins.

He stared up at the painting behind the bed. The one human-faced creature in it looked out, pale, from among the beast-masked men surrounding him.

The head was turned to one side. The large, dark eyes gazed at Owen with a strangely alert and knowing look.

The clinging silk that outlined the beautiful form and the lace foaming at Gynneth's breasts were more tantalizing than naked flesh.

Owen longed to tear away the silk and possess the warm, sweet flesh under it. He closed his eyes. He was dizzy with the storm raging in his body.

"She is a virgin." Elutides spoke from the shadows behind him.

"I know," Owen answered. "Why do you offer her to me?"

"Because," Elutides said, "you will be a great king. Only let me guide you."

"No," Owen said. "My flesh is in torment. I desire her more than food, more than joy, more than hope, almost more than life itself, but I cannot take her."

The sword and the shirt of ring mail rested on the foot of the bed.

Owen's trembling fingers found the hilt. He drew it, then held it high, his fists around the hand guard. He turned and raised it, cross hilt up, between himself and Elutides.

The old man had the same golden cup in his hand.

Owen recognized the serpentine designs that covered it.

Elutides lifted the cup with both hands, the way a priest raises the mass chalice, but outward, toward Owen. "Take and drink."

"What drugs will you give me now, old man?" Owen asked between his teeth.

"Those of love, perfect and everlasting. Drink and awaken her. I will refill the cup. Drink and taste the ecstasy of paradise together."

"Is this what the lovers drank in your song?"

"Yes," Elutides answered, "but its keeper failed in her

trust. The lovers were ignorant of its powers. All three paid dearly. But this is a lawful union, honestly sanctioned. Drink!"

"No!" Owen shouted.

"You risk your life by refusing."

"All the more reason why I should refuse."

"The paintings around you, had you eyes for them, would instruct you on what you risk if you refuse me." Elutides pushed the cup toward Owen. "Drink!"

"I have seen them and I understand," Owen said. "It is the wild hunt when the beasts hunt men. I had thought it only an old legend till now."

"It is how we choose a king," Elutides said.

"You survived it. So can I," Owen said.

Elutides' teeth gleamed in the lantern jaw. "If I wish, you won't survive," he said. "I have no desire to be supplanted."

"And I have no desire to supplant you," Owen said.

"Yet you challenge me as Ivor did. Not in the same way, but just as surely."

"The challenge is in your reading," Owen said. "Make no mistake. I will belong to no one, not you, not the god, not Gynneth, but to myself. If I am to be a king, I will be one in fact."

Owen turned toward the sleeping girl on the bed. The point of the sword in his hand hung suspended over her breasts.

Owen met Elutides' eyes and knew that were he to plunge it down into her helpless body, Elutides would make no move to stay his hand. But he had no wish to do this. He set it gently beside her in the place where he might have lain, saying, "Let any tie between us be severed forever."

As he did, the raging desire he felt burst its bounds. He snapped upright, back arched, crying out hoarsely, as his seed spurted hot on the linen gown and ran down his legs.

Elutides let out a long, slow, weary breath. "You have chosen. Events have gone beyond me. Now you face the ordeal. Because of all you've done for me, I'll give you the opportunity to prevail, a fair chance. I can do no less. But I will do no more. You go to face the great darkness. Alone."

Chapter
31

J UDITH arrived a few minutes later. She found Elin
and Ingund, both dressed as men, waiting for her. In
truth, Elin was only dressed as a woman of her people, in loose dalmatic and leather trousers.

Judith looked completely scandalized. "Ingund, I
might almost be looking at your husband. Surely the holy
church . . ."

"I don't think you should quote the church fathers,"
Anna said.

"Very well." Judith placed her hands on her hips. "Elin,
I have always felt war is best left to men."

"I have no time for this, Judith," Elin said. "Get a torch
and follow me."

The women followed her into the church crypt.

"I don't like this," Judith whispered.

"What?" Ingund answered. "You like the city burning
down over your head? Soon Gowen and his men will be
too drunk to fight the fires. What then?"

"Lady Elin, do you think I could change my life? Become
a virtuous woman, I mean?" Rosamund asked.

Judith held the torch while Elin examined the dates on
the tombs. "We don't want anyone too recently buried,"
Elin murmured. "He might be a bit too ripe."

Anna answered Rosamund's question. "Girl, you are

well established in your profession. Why would you want to become virtuous now?"

"Alfric has been telling me about Mary Magdalene," Rosamund said. "She was converted from her evil ways by Christ himself."

Elin flitted forward toward the oldest part of the crypt.

"Heavens above, it's dark down here," Judith said.

"Mary Magdalene," Anna snorted. "First, those priests go on about the holy Virgin. Then, when a girl does the sensible thing and starts to take presents, the idiots enlarge on the subject of Mary Magdalene. Girl, it's my belief that Magdalene either starved to death or went back to her trade the night Jesus left town."

"My knees are knocking together," Judith said. "I'm about to piss on myself. Why are we standing here talking about Mary Magdalene?"

Ingund chuckled. "Because Rosamund is falling in love with Godwin."

They all paused and looked at the young girl. She blushed.

"Love," Anna cackled. "Oh my, that's another matter."

"Yes," Elin said. "I suppose you should start behaving yourself. Stay in Anna's room at night. I'll give the knights some excuse."

"He's a good catch," Judith said.

"He's a rotten catch," Ingund retorted. "He'll likely be run through in the next battle he fights, but he'll leave you a noble name and probably some wealth. Your prospects for remarriage will be excellent."

Rosamund sat down on a low tomb and began to cry.

Elin gritted her teeth. "Stop bawling, Rosamund."

"Yes," Anna snapped. "Ingund, leave off tormenting her. Godwin is an old wolf, but his teeth are still as long and sharp as they ever were. He will not fall easily. He has buried a lot of men who thought they could bury him."

"Yes," Rosamund said, rising reassured. "But could he love me?"

Elin paused next to one of the tombs. "Help me get the lid off this one."

They all pushed. There was a grinding sound of marble against marble. Judith wouldn't look. She thrust the torch into the tomb and averted her face.

"Moldering bones," Elin said. "No good."

They pushed the slab back into place and went on.

"Could he love me?" Rosamund repeated.

All five women gathered at the next sarcophagus.

"What are we talking about here?" Judith asked. "Love or marriage?"

"Doesn't matter," Anna said. "Rosamund will definitely gain by the connection. He is not a man to pick up a woman and put her down like a loaf of bread after taking only one bite."

"True," Judith mused.

"As I said," Anna continued, "he is a very old wolf and will not easily be trapped, but I have reason to believe he is eyeing the bait."

"Really?" Rosamund asked excitedly, and started to blow her nose in her apron.

Anna slapped the apron out of her hand. "Don't be disgusting."

Rosamund sniveled.

Judith handed her a handkerchief.

"We must make a lady of her," Anna told Judith. "I have not done badly so far. First, I got her to wash off that filthy paint. Now we have gotten her out of the knights' room. She no longer blows her nose with her fingers. Her table manners are improving. I cannot remember the last time she wiped her fingers on her dress or spit out gristle on the floor."

"The men . . ." Rosamund began mutinously.

Anna clouted her. "You are not a man," she said, ignoring the girl's wail. "Remember that at all times. Godwin does not care to couple with those vile knights of his. I think they even turn Edgar's stomach a bit, and he's inclined toward the male sex. Godwin would not care for their manners in a consort."

"A consort." Rosamund drew herself up.

"Yes," Anna said, "think of yourself that way and you cannot fail."

In the darkness beyond the circle of torchlight, something scurried and fled. Judith moaned and pressed her hand to her breast.

"Only a rat," Anna said dismissingly.

"Don't be so nice, Judith. You have seen rats before," Ingund said.

Judith ignored her taunt and turned to Elin. "What are we doing here?"

"I'm looking for a corpse," Elin answered, peering at the dates on yet another tomb. "Apparently the rest of you are marrying off Rosamund."

"What kind of spell could you need a corpse for?" Judith grumbled. "Besides, we've found several perfectly good ones, and you've turned them all down."

Elin bypassed several graves, mumbling to herself. At last, she paused before an obviously expensive and elaborately carved sarcophagus.

"Don't even think about it," Judith warned. "This is Bishop Calexties."

Even deep in the church crypt, Elin heard the hideously familiar whoosh and roar followed by loud panicked crowd noise from the square.

The women drew closer together.

"Bishop Calexties, eh?" Elin said. "Help me get the top off. All of you pull together now."

The big stone cover of the tomb grated and scraped but finally yielded. This time, Judith's curiosity got the better of her. She tilted the torch and sneaked a quick look into the tomb.

"Eeeeeee!" she yelled.

Elin snatched the torch from her hand and peered down at the earthly relics there. "Perfect. Now, if he will only hold together."

"No!" Judith screeched, then repeated the word about fifteen or twenty times as she collapsed on the floor.

Anna looked and paled.

Rosamund drew back, staring at Elin in horror.

Judith threw herself at Elin's knees.

Ingund poked her torch into the tomb. "How wonderful. I believe he may even be a little bit bowlegged."

"Judith, stop making those horrible noises," Elin ordered. "What's the matter with you? I need your help."

Anna sat down on a low tomb and began fanning herself with her skirt. "We don't want to be there when you reanimate him."

"I'm not going to reanimate him," Elin said.

Judith struggled away from Elin and sat down on the tomb next to Anna. "Thank God," she breathed.

Ingund reached into the tomb. "See," she said. "He is dry as a stick and very stiff. I can lift him with one hand."

Elin met Edgar as she was leaving through the back door to the hall. She carried two large bottles, one in each hand. Ingund followed her wearing all her weapons, including her boar-tusk helmet. She carried Bishop Calexties, rather inadequately covered with a black mantle, over her shoulder like a log of stove wood.

Edgar got a partial look at Bishop Calexties by the dim glow of the hearth fire. He was immediately glad he did not get a better one. "Holy Virgin Mary, mother of God," he said. "Elin, may I ask what you think you're doing?"

"No," Elin replied. "You may not ask. Hold the door for Ingund. We don't want to break Bishop Calexties."

Elin and Ingund led the horses quickly through the dark streets toward the spot where the wooden palisade stopped at the river. Bishop Calexties was mounted while the two women were afoot.

"Indeed he is brittle," Ingund said. "It's as well he is bowlegged, otherwise we would not have gotten him on the horse. I hope this works."

Elin shivered and looked up at the stars. Against their blaze she could see the light of at least two fires burning in the stricken town. "Whatever happens, Ingund, don't let yourself be taken alive," she said.

"What about you?" Ingund asked.

"I know how to die when I want to, when I have to. I'm more worried about you."

"I have a dagger," Ingund said. "I know how to use it. On myself if necessary or another if possible."

They reached the end of the palisade. It stretched out through thorny undergrowth into the river.

The two women waded into the river and turned the corner of the wooden wall. They found themselves forcing their way through a thick screen of willows and poplars that choked the water's edge. The branches of the trees were bare, but the wandlike branches formed a nearly impenetrable barrier. Ingund broke trail for Elin and the two horses, forcing the heavy canes aside until they were opposite the point where the catapult was located.

They moved cautiously through the trees until they looked out across the open field.

A ring of fires surrounded the catapult. Inside the ring, a holiday atmosphere prevailed. The Vikings had come prepared to enjoy themselves. They lounged around drinking from plentiful casks of beer and wine. Several whole oxen were spitted and roasting over the many fires.

Hakon, a glittering figure in a golden helmet and cuirass, supervised the loading of the iron basket himself. He lit the pitch-smeared bundles with a flaming brand from one of the fires surrounding the terrible engine of destruction.

Then, backing his white stallion away from the catapult, he watched as the ball of fire lifted into the air, arching up to fall among the homes of those so bold as to defy his will.

Elin knelt in the mud and looked at him. "Hakon the magnificent," she whispered.

"That he is," Ingund agreed.

Elin heard shouts and cheers. A thud rang out and another ball of fire followed the first.

Her gaze followed the packet of fire across the sky. Tears of rage and grief burned in her eyes. Despite the best efforts of Gowen and the townspeople, two fires raged out of control, one near the square and another close to the river.

She hunkered down in the mud, turning her gaze away from the firelight where Hakon and his men took their ease. She let her eyes get used to the darkness. "What happens to me doesn't matter," she told Ingund. "I'm there to frighten them. You go in for the kill."

Above them the wind moaned in the bare branches of

the trees. It rose to a high keening whistle, then died to a rattle. The winter-stripped boughs clattered like bones.

The wind carried Hakon's shout to Elin's ears. "Faster!" he bellowed. "Faster, you lazy fools. The wind is rising. Before dawn the whole city will be one sea of flame."

"Bastard!" Ingund whispered, then spat in the mud at her feet.

"Be quiet," Elin ordered. "Stop looking at them. The firelight will blind you." As she spoke she lighted a horn-shielded lantern hooked in between the late prelate's ribs. The bishop was mounted on Godwin's bay.

"Ooh," Ingund shuddered. "He is horrible enough to frighten me. If I didn't know the trick of it, I would run screaming."

Elin drew back a little and tried to judge what effect the figure in the saddle would have on the unsuspecting Vikings. "It will work, if it does not fall to pieces at a gallop."

The late bishop, sealed in his expensive airtight coffin, had not so much decomposed as mummified. His long hair was intact and flowed down from his ivory brow. It framed the staring eye sockets and gleaming teeth of his skull. The rest of his skin was reduced to parchment stretched over shriveled muscle and bone.

The lantern hung where it was nearly invisible. It cast a dim but ghastly light between the ribs. Enough of the dried skin clung to them to render the source of the light invisible, but it was thin enough to highlight the bishop's face.

Elin straightened her belt and checked the position of her knife. One of Anna's kitchen utensils, it had a dirty gray-black iron blade. The weapon was longer than her forearm, ragged, and razor sharp. "Remember, nothing matters but that catapult," she hissed at Ingund.

Ingund stretched out her hand and grasped Elin's. "Good fortune, my lady. Give the bastards hell."

Elin swung herself into the saddle behind the incarnate death. She tightened the reins to see if she could properly control Godwin's warhorse. To her surprise, the bay stallion answered easily to the bit. His head came down and he stamped his feet.

Beside Elin, Ingund also was in the saddle. "Give me the signal," she said.

Elin looked up. The moon was a sickle of ghostly light seen through the high, drifting clouds. She waited until one thick cloud covered it completely, plunging everything around them into darkness. She loosed the reins and drove her heels into the stallion's flanks as she spat out one savage whisper. "Let's ride!"

Together, Ingund's mount and the stallion lunged forward into the blackness.

Hakon had surrounded the catapult with a double ring of fires. Elin held the stallion at a gallop until she reached the first ring; then she slowed to a canter.

Sentries were posted all along the outer perimeter. One, standing only a few feet away from Elin, lifted a drinking horn to his lips.

Elin pulled back on the reins, almost bringing the stallion to a halt. The horse slowed, tossed his head in protest of having his enjoyable run interrupted, and whickered loudly.

Drinking horn still at his lips, the sentry looked up at what loomed before him. The bay horse seemed almost blue in the faint moonlight. From its back, a horror looked down on the guard. The wind whipped the dead man's long hair across the bony face. The teeth grinned down at the Northman, and the empty eye sockets glared at him.

He screamed. The drinking horn went one way, the sentry the other at a dead run, still screaming.

Well, Elin thought. *Now I have their attention.* She jerked back on the bit and brought the stallion to a rearing halt. She gave a long wailing cry, a cry that to the men lounging around the fires seemed to issue from a dead man's fleshless lips.

Towering over them, the stallion seemed to stand still in the air while death incarnate looked down and cried out to them.

Elin moaned, loosed the reins, hammered the stallion's

flanks with her heels, and launched him directly toward Hakon.

She saw the Viking chief's eyes widen in shock, but he gathered the reins of his horse in one hand and jerked his sword from the scabbard with the other.

Hakon's men thought they saw death itself riding in to take their chieftain. They scattered, howling.

"Stupid bastards!" Hakon roared. "Come back, you jackasses. It's nothing but a trick."

"Damn him!" Elin cursed. "He is too brave." She crouched down behind the corpse. In front of her she saw the glittering flash of Hakon's sword blade.

They were on a collision course. There was nothing more she could do except hope she had created a sufficient diversion for Ingund. Even she didn't dare brave Hakon's sword.

Elin dropped the reins and picked up the late bishop by the backbone. She hurled him into Hakon's face. The corpse was light, but its forehead crashed against Hakon and its face pressed against his own.

Hakon jerked back in terror and sheer disgust. He lost his horse's reins but struck out two-handed with his sword. What was left of the bishop disintegrated in a shower of bones around him.

What seemed to be a piece of the night whipped past Hakon. The terrorized sentries didn't even see the intruder. With a loud crack, something exploded against the arm of the catapult. All around Hakon the night roared into white brilliance.

Hakon was desperately trying to regain the reins and control his terrified mount. The fleeing Vikings stopped, mouths agape, staring.

The naphtha Elin had gotten from Judith spread over Hakon's catapult, and inextinguishable flames roared toward the sky.

Elin was caught between the blazing catapult and the terrified Vikings. She'd lost the horse's reins when she threw the corpse at Hakon, so when the stallion reared, she clutched the pommel and held on.

Hakon pointed at her. "The witch!" he shouted. "God curse

you." He screamed at his men, "May all the gods curse you! We have her now. Kill her! The weight of her head in gold to the man who takes it."

Frightened at the brilliance of the flames erupting from the doomed catapult, the stallion plunged, then tore out across the plowed fields, away from the smell of human rage and the stench of naphtha.

Elin hunkered down, fingers tightening on the pommel. The coarse mane whipped her face, blinding her in the darkness. She couldn't even tell which way the horse was running. She felt the horse slow, then stumble as his hooves struck the soft earth of a freshly plowed area.

No, Elin thought. *No.* She felt the beast fall away under her. Her last thought as she was flung forward into nothingness was *So this is death.*

Leaving the burning catapult behind her, Ingund rode like mad for the city. As she approached the gates she shouted, "Don't shoot! Don't shoot. It's me, Ingund."

To her surprise, when she was within bowshot of the gate, it began to open. The horse darted through, and she pulled him to a rearing halt. The men behind the gate slammed it shut, then sent a few crossbow bolts into the darkness to deter any pursuit.

From the back of the horse, Ingund looked anxiously out over the gate. "Where is Elin?"

Standing beside Ingund's horse, Edgar stared at the blinding mass of flame that had been the catapult. "I saw her horse fall."

"No!" Ingund cried. She reached down and snatched at the gate bar, but she was too late. Edgar had her horse by the bridle and Ranulf grabbed her by the belt, pulling her from the saddle. She flailed wildly at the two men.

"Ingund!" Edgar roared. "Show some sense. If Hakon catches you, he will kill you. What good will your death do Elin?"

Rosamund stood among the archers holding a lantern. "I'm going to get Godwin!" she shouted as she turned and ran up the street. "He'll know what to do."

* * *

Godwin woke with one candle burning at his feet and another at his head. He was still slightly addled from the blow he had received to the skull. He spent several minutes wondering if he was dead.

On the whole, he was relieved to have gotten it over with in a relatively painless manner. Then he passed from relief to puzzlement. What exactly had killed him? He began to take inventory.

My, he thought, *I'm laid out nicely. Clothing straightened, head on a pillow, my hands folded.* He scratched the back of his right hand with his left. *If I am dead, I have no business to be moving.* He began feeling around with his right hand. No major wounds to his torso. Then his fingers explored his scalp. In the front, not bad. Then the back. "Jesus, that hurts!"

Just then, Rosamund charged into his room. She stopped, gasping for breath, winded by the run from the gates.

Godwin's eyes swiveled toward her. He was certain he was not dead. He felt annoyed and slightly disappointed.

Rosamund approached him cautiously. "Are you awake?"

"I'm no longer unconscious," he replied.

"Oh, good," she breathed. "Lady Elin needs your help badly. Her life is in danger."

"Why is Lady Elin's life in danger?"

"Because she's out alone in the dark with Bishop Calexties."

A few moments later Godwin arrived at the gate with Rosamund in tow. Threats of death or grievous bodily harm had elicited an explanation of events from Rosamund on the way there. Now he surveyed the situation with Edgar, Ranulf, and Ingund.

"Your horse arrived shortly after Ingund," Edgar said. "The saddle was empty."

"Have they found her?" Godwin asked.

"I don't think so," Ranulf said.

Godwin nodded cautiously. His head still pounded. He turned to the archers clustered behind him. "I need five brave men."

"What are you going to do?" Ingund asked.

"I'm going to go play hide-and-seek with the Vikings."

* * *

Hakon stood looking at the catapult. He was not even conscious of swearing. The thing was a mass of brightly glowing embers now. Utterly destroyed. On the ground near it lay a scattering of bones. Hakon walked over and picked up the corpse's skull and swung it by its long hair.

"Tricked," he roared. "Tricked by a woman!" He flung the skull away into the darkness.

The wind was blowing very hard, whipping the flames of the fires that had surrounded the catapult. The flames seemed almost to be crawling along the ground.

Hakon turned toward the city. Most of the conflagrations started by the catapult seemed to be out with the exception of a dull glow near the docks. The only lights coming from the city were the two torches blazing at the gates.

Hakon wanted to cry. He could not think of a curse word dreadful enough to aim at Elin. He wanted to kill something. He felt the next man to approach him would die.

Seeing murder in his face, the men hung back until Tosi strode into the ring of fires. Even he quailed a little at the expression in Hakon's eyes, but without hesitating, he went toward him. When he was but a few feet away, he paused and whispered, "Hakon, are you mad to let the men see you like this? What are you to allow yourself to be so stricken by misfortune—a woman?"

Hakon froze. He brought himself under control.

"The witch is lost in the plowed land before the city. I saw her horse fall," Tosi said. "Likely she lies in a ditch somewhere, unconscious. She is waiting for the man who will find her and claim the fortune in gold offered for her head."

His words sent Hakon's men into action. They kindled torches and, shouting, raced out into the open fields to find Elin.

Elin woke with her cheek in the mud. Her eyes opened to darkness. The only thing she could see were sparks of light moving back and forth in the distance, and she heard voices. "She is here somewhere," someone shouted.

She lay still, afraid to move. *Oh God, no,* she thought, and rolled over on her stomach. Nauseated and half blinded by the blood and mud in her eyes, she realized the men were hunting her.

They had set themselves out in a pattern like beaters trying to drive wild animals. Each carried a torch, and they were spread just wide enough so that nothing could slip past the band of illuminating torches.

A quick glance at the city was enough to tell her she was not nearly close enough to run toward the shelter of the walls. She was at least a hundred yards beyond the range of the crossbowmen on the palisade. The shallow ditch she lay in formed the boundary between two fields.

She had only two choices. One was to chance a run for it, but in her present condition, she decided reluctantly she probably wouldn't make it. The nausea and dizziness from her rough landing still dogged her. The other was to lie still and pretend to be another clod of earth. She was dressed in dark clothing and probably covered with mud, so it wouldn't be difficult to mistake her for part of the ground.

The line of searchers came closer and closer. She could hear the squelch and pop of their boots in the newly turned soil. The ditch was faintly illuminated by the torchlight.

Trembling, she risked a small movement. She got her hand on the hilt of the knife in her belt and loosened it in the sheath. Behind her she heard the thud and plop of a walking horse. Hakon's voice called out to the cordon of torchmen. "Look you," he shouted. "Be careful you don't miss her in the darkness. Kick every odd-looking clod of mud you see."

Elin shivered. They were very close.

One of the men shouted to Hakon, "When we catch her will we let her live for a little time?"

"Do as you like," Hakon answered laconically. "I want only her head, and that is all I will take. I saw her face at the walls when we attacked the city. I have seen those eyes before. They are difficult to forget. I want her dead."

The torchmen reached the edge of the ditch. The torch flashed in her eyes and blinded her. A Viking stepped on her leg. He reached down and pulled her to her knees by her hair. He was silent as he dropped the torch. It hissed out in the damp earth. Keeping a firm grip on her hair, he went for his sword.

Still on her knees, Elin drew the knife as he drew his sword. She knew she would never live to get to her feet. She understood why the man was so silent. In a second, he would have her head off and the reward would be all his. Elin slashed at his legs and knew absolute despair when the edge of the knife grated against leather greaves.

He pulled her head up, stretching her neck for the sword cut, when over his shoulder she saw bared white teeth and hollow eye sockets.

She knew one moment of stark terror, thinking Bishop Calexties had returned to claim his revenge. A knife appeared in the darkness and slit the man's throat from ear to ear. He fell back without a sound, and Elin realized she'd looked into Godwin's naked killing smile. He pulled her to her feet and held her tightly in his embrace.

The line of torchmen passed on, out of the ditch toward the city. Hakon rode behind them.

Elin could see now that Godwin had two or three men with him. To her eyes they were simply shapes in the darkness, but she could see enough to be aware they all carried crossbows.

"Hush," Godwin whispered. "Give them a moment to move away, then we will . . ."

She never found out what Godwin wanted to do. She tested her legs and found them firm. She could stand without being dizzy. She stared at Hakon, still a figure of splendor as the torches reflected off his armor.

"Damn you," she whispered. "You know my eyes, do you? I will give you a reason never to forget them."

That same moment Hakon pulled his horse to a halt. "A man is missing!" he shouted. The line of men stopped, broke ranks, and began milling around in confusion.

Elin pulled free of Godwin's grasp, snatched a crossbow from the nearest man, and ran toward Hakon.

He looked down and saw her face appear out of the darkness. Her eyes were blue flames against her dead-white skin. She drove her knife to the hilt behind and above the horse's front leg.

The horse reared, venting a sound of agony and terror. Hakon went for his sword, but Elin lifted the crossbow, pointed it at his chest, and fired.

The force of the bolt took Hakon over the crupper of his saddle and down. Elin turned as Hakon's men rushed toward her. Two had almost reached her when they died with crossbow bolts in their chests. The next died with Godwin's sword in his throat.

Godwin spun Elin around and flung her toward the city gates. "Die on your own," he roared. "I don't plan to go with you. Run!"

Elin staggered. "Faster," Godwin roared, bringing the flat of his sword down across her back. Elin choked back a scream. "Run!" Godwin commanded, and Elin ran like the wind.

*E*NAR awakened with a mouth that tasted like the floor of a cave, a head that felt delicate, and a number of very intriguing memories.

Owen stood by the window, watching the beautiful play of light and color as the sun rose over the ocean.

Enar experimented with moving his head. "Oh God," he whispered. The head proved no longer delicate but painful.

Without turning, Owen said, "There is mead in a jug on the table beside you, and you had best mention Christ's name so he will know you are properly honoring him."

Enar sat up holding his head with both hands. "You are a most vindictive man, Lord Christ Priest, and never forget a slight." He opened his eyes, and the morning sun shone directly into them. He closed them quickly. "Oh Christ!" He opened his eyes again, fumbled for the jug, and drank some mead.

The sea outside was quiet and the tide at its ebb. The waves caressed, rather than thundered against the rocks below, whispering quietly.

Enar shook his head very gently from side to side. "The queen is a strange woman," he said. "Would you not agree, Lord Christ Priest, that I am a man well versed in all the carnal sins? For me, these are well-trodden paths."

Owen nodded, still staring out at the ocean. "There are few new variations," he agreed.

Enar sucked down some more of the mead. "She has invented at least one."

Owen turned away from the window. "I must hear this!"

"We did it on the back of a horse."

"No!"

"Yes!" Enar moaned, clutching his skull. "Don't laugh."

"May I smile?" Owen asked.

Enar peered up at him, eyes slitted against the light. "You are not only vindictive," he said, "you are cruel."

Owen tipped the jug and poured him some more mead. Enar sighed and drank gratefully. "I forgive you," he said at length. "I even begin to love you again. When you left the feast, I felt rebuffed, so I turned my attention to Queen Aud."

"I seem to remember you were not indifferent to her," Owen said.

"Her caresses do not inspire indifference," Enar answered. "Having eaten our fill, we departed together and went to her chamber. These people understand the magic of love. She had some mead . . ." Enar looked down at the cup in his hand and frowned. "Not like this. It had a very peculiar fragrance. Having partaken of it, she told me not to be surprised at anything I would see or hear because we would leave this world and journey through another."

"And did you?" Owen asked.

"The scenery did change a lot," Enar said, "but more changes were, I think, worked within me. It was then she suggested we try it on horseback. So we wandered out into the fields. She chose a big horse with a strong back. We sat facing each other." Enar shook his head again. "I cannot think what made me do such a mad thing. We were both, no all three bare, she, I, and the horse."

"I would not think that even a very big saddle could contain this type of activity."

"No," Enar said. "We quarreled at first. I remember it dimly. I refused to sit facing the creature's rump, so she took that position. I faced forward. She slapped the horse on the rear. He began to walk. That was not so bad. I embraced Aud and grabbed the mane. We coupled. She lifted a huntsman's horn and blew a call. The blasted horse began to trot. We went everywhere, up and down, back and forth, jouncing around.

"This must have pleased her. I hope it did. Nothing pleased me. Lord Christ Priest, the backbone of a horse is sharp; it cut me cruelly in the place where I sit down. Moreover, horsehair, however sleek it looks, is rough." Enar sighed. "She seemed to enjoy it and blew another loud note on the horn. The thing began to gallop. The earth and sky flew past all around me. I wanted to close my eyes, but I feared death might come to me in the darkness. I clung to the creature's mane with both hands. We were approaching a small stream. She blew the horn again and the horse jumped." Enar became silent, a look of jaundiced disgust on his face.

"And?" Owen prompted.

"And," Enar continued, "I found myself lying in a rosebush. I cannot say how it happened. One minute I was on the horse, the next I wiggled howling among the thorns."

"What of Aud?" Owen asked.

"She thought it was funny," Enar said. "I screamed with pain, trying to free myself. She stood over me screaming with laughter."

Owen sucked in hard on his cheeks.

"Don't strain yourself, Lord Christ Priest!" Enar said. "A man can give himself a rupture trying not to laugh."

Owen smiled. "Do the scratches still pain you?"

Enar helped himself to the jug of mead this time. "I didn't get very many. My screams brought help—Elutides and a dozen men with torches. They cut me out of the rosebush and gave me clothing. I can't remember much else except that I resisted being put back on a horse, but Elutides had it done anyway."

Enar looked around the room. It held two beds and one table. A few silver dishes on the table contained the remains of a meal. "I need to go outside," Enar said.

"In the corner," Owen said, pointing to a pot.

"I would prefer to go outside," Enar said. "Drink troubles my bowels."

"That isn't possible," Owen said, returning to the window.

Enar groped for the jug and took a hearty swig of mead. "I will contain myself and wait until later," he said. "But, Lord Owen, son of Gestric, bishop of Chantalon, prince of the church, binder and looser of magics, Christ Priest, why are we locked in?"

"I quarreled with Elutides."

Enar swallowed the rest of the mead, then lay down and covered his face. "I hope they kill me soon. The way my head feels, it will be a relief to die."

"I don't think they'll harm you," Owen said.

"Why did you quarrel with Elutides?" Enar asked, his voice muffled by the covers.

"He wished me to marry Gynneth," Owen answered.

Enar uncovered his face. "I cannot berate you; I have not the strength. But if I must sacrifice my virtue to Queen Aud, could you not sacrifice a little of yours? This Elutides is a great man."

"It wasn't the wedding I objected to," Owen said, "but the manner of its celebration. Now I must survive the wild hunt."

Enar covered his face again. "I ask leave to quit your service."

"You've always had that," Owen answered, "and my thanks for all your good offices." He lifted his sword, sheath belt and baldric attached, and finding Enar's hands under the covers, placed his fingers around it.

Enar let the blanket slip down until it uncovered his two gray eyes. He stared up at Owen sadly.

"Take this," Owen said. "It is the purchase of one manor at least. Find some lord who loves your merry tales as I do. I would not go into death thinking of you lost along the roads begging your bread."

Even as he spoke there was a sound of bolts being drawn and locks turning. The door flew open, and Elutides stepped into the room.

Enar's hand found the sword hilt. He drew even as he

rose, pushing Owen aside, shouting, "Death to the first who touches my lord!" The net left Elutides' hand like a black shadow. It wrapped itself around Enar's upper body; then he was pinned down by four men.

Elutides wore the mask of a wolf. His face stared at Owen through the mouth past the sharp teeth. The yellow eyes glared out above his head; pointed ears stuck up through the ruff surrounding his face.

Ilfor was arrayed as a bear. The muzzle covered his face. He wore the whole skin down over his shoulders and back. The long claws were sewn into gloves on his hands. Aud was a fox, the red fur covering her shoulders and arms. Enar stopped struggling. "They run mad!" he whispered.

Owen approached Elutides open-handed. "Don't harm him. I am yours to do with as you like, but let him go. He has no part in this."

"In two days' time," Elutides answered, "we will lead him to the border and send him on his way."

Owen went with them. The door closed behind him. Enar lay bound on the floor. He sighed deeply and closed his eyes again. In the distance, he could hear the endless chant of the sea. "I would have a sore head," he muttered. "I am always overtaken by misfortune when I have a sore head. It should teach me to give up drunkenness."

He opened his eyes to find the rising sun had cleared the windowsill. It caught him full in the face. He closed his eyes again tightly, but not before he caught sight of the sword, lying where it had fallen next to one of the cots. He began using his shoulders and heels to inch his way toward the unsheathed blade, murmuring, "No. It's sobriety I should renounce. Nothing good," he panted between his teeth, "ever happens to me when I am sober."

Owen followed Elutides into the corridor. It resounded with the wailing and shrieking of women. They were dressed in black as the women in the wall paintings had been, and they carried dark garlands.

Gynneth stood among them, her face covered by a thin black silk veil. She carried an earthenware pitcher in her hand. Even through the dark gauze covering her features

Owen could see her expression was somber. She stepped before him. "It is given to us to conduct you to your fate," she said, and shattered the pitcher at his feet.

Owen looked down at the fragments, then up again at her. "I'm sorry he's made you a part of this."

Gynneth didn't reply and the crowd of women surrounded Owen. Cador and Casgob were on either side. Cador was attired as an eagle, the open beak rearing above his head, the wing feathers spreading over his shoulders. Casgob was a wild boar, the snout dipped low in front of his forehead, the tusks curled at his cheeks.

The two of them took hold of Owen's arms, but he shook them off angrily. "Whatever my fate, I can walk to it alone."

The women raised a shout, a howl, scratching their faces and moaning. But the worst terror was that none of them would meet his eyes, not even Gynneth, except for the one second when she smashed the pitcher.

Owen remembered the one human-faced captive in the painting and knew why the eyes sought his own beyond the shadows of the wall. He, too, was alone.

Gynneth led him to the hall. It was dark, as it had been on the day Owen first entered. The crowd surrounding Owen drew back, leaving him standing near the smoke hole beside the banked hearth. The fire was a heap of pale ash in the gloom, but deep in its heart a few coals smoldered. Wisps of smoke rose through the rays of blue daylight streaming in from above.

Alone, Owen thought, sending a raking glance at those crowded around him, at faces whose eyes still refused to meet his until he came to Gynneth.

She met his stare. Her eyes not only met his, but her gaze locked with his and held him. Even through the veil, he could see her expression wasn't just somber but tragic. "Why would you not love me?" she asked.

"Lady," Owen answered sadly, "any love I offered you would be a lie."

A low sigh ran through the gathering around him. They drew further away from him into the gloom.

"I am the loser in this," she said. "Your victory in this brings my uncle death, his victory, yours."

Ilfor the bear shambled forward into the clear space around Owen, moving toward him, claws raised. Owen backed away. As he moved, the boar Casgob stepped forward and shoved him toward the bear's menacing claws.

One paw swept down across Owen's chest, ripping the fabric of his linen shirt and scouring five bloody lines across his chest.

A second later he was in the bear's embrace, smelling the musky animal stench of half-tanned hide while the ivory hooks scored themselves deeply into his back.

Owen screamed and hit out with his fists. He felt Ilfor's paunch give behind the bear skin. The bear staggered back, releasing him. Owen saw drops of his blood dripping down from Ilfor's claws on the filthy carpet of rushes at his feet. Inside the cage of teeth at the bear's muzzle Owen caught a glimpse of Ilfor's face, pale and seemingly sickened by what he'd just done.

Then Owen stood alone again near the fire pit.

"Did you think we jested with you?" Elutides' voice snarled behind the wolf's muzzle. He extended his hands to Owen. He held a cup, but not the golden one of the night before. This one was earthenware. The liquid in it was black. "Take it and drink."

The beast-masked men and women had spread out around Owen. They stood in the forefront of the crowd. In the dim light they truly did seem to be animals. There were others besides Elutides, Casgob, Cador, and Aud. In the shadows, Owen saw the long snout of a badger, the high antlers of a stag, and the yellow beak and glossy feathers of a crow. Near them were the ghastly vestiges of a few more wolves and the pale glimmer of the weapons belonging to the most ferocious and merciless of all wild creatures, the tusked boar.

"You knew what you were doing when you refused Gynneth," Elutides said. "Now cry for mercy if you will to the storm, to the lightning striking at a mountain peak, to a cresting river or a falling tree. You will gain it more quickly than from these, my companions."

Owen took the cup and cradled it in his hands. The crowd and the beast masks in the forefront were silent, silent the way the stone that begins a landslide is silent as it trembles on the brink of falling. Owen could feel the tension in the darkened hall building, the tug of wills between himself and Elutides.

He looked down at the black liquid in the cup and saw his own face mirrored in it. It gave him a shock because it was the face of a stranger—pale, tight-lipped, the eyes two dim hollows haunted by a glimmer of light—a face that said, I do yield, I must yield but I won't, I won't and I never will—himself.

He stared at the wolf, at the shadowed face behind the mask, at the eyes black and unfathomable, nearly lost in the wolf's fur.

"Yield and be ruled. Drink and stand alone."

Owen didn't know if he spoke the words or Elutides did. He only knew he heard them ringing out, echoing in his ears, in his brain, part of his consciousness.

And Owen prayed as he had prayed when he'd been captured by Osric and Hakon. *Let me die well.* And so praying, he drained the cup to the dregs.

The stuff had a vile smell and an even viler taste. Owen spun around and went to one knee trying not to vomit. Sweat broke out all over his skin.

"Begin you now," Elutides shouted, "the king's journey. From this moment, from this hour, hated by all mankind, expelled by all creation, despised by every living thing, go forth. . . ."

Owen staggered to his feet. His back was to Elutides. Gynneth was in front of him. Her face was turned away, covered by both one arm and the black veil, as though he were something unclean she didn't wish to look upon. With one outstretched arm, she pointed toward the doorway. Behind him, Owen heard a howl of rage rise from all those assembled in the hall—a scream of fury and hatred.

"Oh, you beasts, now crowned with the world's power," Elutides shouted, "hunt the man down!"

Owen lurched into a staggering run toward the doorway, toward the light. It seemed only seconds before he was across the square and flying down the muddy street toward the gates. The few people he met fled from him, diving back into the houses, covering their faces, turning away as if his very glance could kill, as if his touch were unbearable contamination.

He passed the gates into the morning. His run took him across the plowed fields into the pastureland toward the forest. As he neared the trees, he realized his sprint had almost exhausted him. His boots were encrusted with mud. He slowed near a woodcutter's hut, looked back, and realized nothing was chasing him. Looking back over his shoulder, he saw the city gates were open and the streets seemed deserted.

He dropped from a run into a fast walk. Near the hut was a hollow tree that served as a horse trough. Owen stopped and, bending over it, washed his face and drank.

The farm wife ran out of the hut screaming and hurling clods of mud at him. Owen cringed but he was still thirsty. He tried to stand his ground. Then a man, evidently the woman's husband, joined her and began throwing firewood in his direction. A heavy log bounced off Owen's shoulder. He gave up and ran out of the yard.

Once safe from the shower of missiles, he turned and stared back at them. They both covered their faces and turned their backs on him. The worst to Owen's mind was the goodwife; she collapsed sobbing into her husband's arms, covering her face with her apron.

Of course, Owen thought. Hospitality was a sacred duty, a courtesy accorded even to the humble, the hunted, the lost. She had breached it by driving Owen away.

He looked back toward the city. The hunt was issuing from the gates—dark mounted figures. In the distance, Owen heard hounds bellowing.

Dogs! Christ, how could he ever outrun dogs! Owen turned and bolted toward the forest.

Enar was making no progress at all with the sword when Gynneth and Sybilla walked in, accompanied by Queen Aud. The queen had an odd look in her eyes; she was shaking her head and muttering to herself. Gynneth, still dressed in black, was holding a knife in her hand.

"Gentle lady?" Enar said.

"You are hoping she is a gentle lady," Sybilla said.

"Whenever we meet," Enar replied, "you always seem to have me at a disadvantage."

"Roll over," Gynneth said.

Since he was bound hand and foot and was completely helpless, Enar felt he might as well, so he did. Gynneth cut him free.

"Come," she said.

Enar followed. "What have they done with him?"

Gynneth walked ahead of Enar toward the hall. "The hunt has begun. They are on his track, but I won two concessions for him from my uncle. I'll send you and the stallion after him, and he may have his sword."

"The sword!" Enar exclaimed, and spun around.

Sybilla carried the sword. Enar reached for it, but she jumped away. "No," she said. "I'll be able to find him first." She slung the golden chained belt over her shoulder.

"She's right," Aud told Enar. "Her people belong to the forest as much as the deer do. If anyone can track him, she can."

To Enar the queen seemed preoccupied. Even while she was speaking to him, her eyes roved all over the corridor.

"Come," Gynneth said impatiently. "We must hurry. The horse is in the hall."

As they entered the hall, the queen said, "Eeeeeeee!" and pointed a shaking finger toward the dim colonnade surrounding them. "Did you see that?"

Enar peered suspiciously into the darkness near the colonnade. "No," he replied. "I don't see anything."

"Thank God." The queen breathed a shaky sigh of relief. "I was hoping it wasn't there."

"It isn't," Enar said. "At least, whatever it was, I hope it isn't." He turned and appealed to Gynneth. "What's wrong with her?"

"She's part of the hunt and has taken a potion."

Enar stopped walking and his shoulders sagged. He almost sat down where he was on the rushes. "I must find something to give Christ. He has certainly served us well on this journey."

Gynneth paused. "How so?"

"Sweet lady," Enar replied, "if the hunters have taken any of the potions Elutides hands out, it's my belief they'll soon have difficulty finding each other. And so far as recognizing my lord, they'll like as not pass him by thinking him a tree stump or some such thing. Come dusk, our big problem may be rounding them up before they fall over cliffs or wander out to sea and drown."

"Oh," Gynneth said, "you think, then, my uncle's rite has no meaning."

Enar looked down away from her face very quickly. "I didn't say . . ." he tried to answer.

"I am taken strangely with the potion," Aud said. "It doesn't work its spell completely on me. But those on his track believe they are the beasts whose skins they wear, and should they catch up to him . . ."

"Of those who attempt what he attempts this day," Sybilla said, "more die than not."

Enar spread his hands in complete exasperation. "Then why attempt it?"

"Sovereignty!" Gynneth said. "Knowledge!"

"Love would not content him," Aud intoned.

"Power would not content him," Gynneth whispered.

"Honors would not satisfy, pleasure stales," Sybilla said.

Enar felt cold run over his skin in a wave. "You are all mad, mad as Owen is and Elutides. Fetch the horse!" he shouted. "I'll go after him, try to rescue him."

"If we are mad," Gynneth asked, "why are you here, Saxon?"

Enar's eyes searched the vast dim hall. He stared at the three women standing near the fire pit, at the sword over Sybilla's shoulder, glimmering in the half darkness. "I have never given my hand or my oath to a man, then withdrawn it," he answered. "It is all I have left. All else have I betrayed. My honor alone remains."

"And has honor clothing? Does it walk the earth?" Gynneth asked. "Has it strong arms? A sword? How can it constrain you?"

Enar pondered this for a moment, then answered. "It is sufficient for me that it does. You are what I would expect of Elutides' niece, a very strange girl."

"I was born to be a queen," she answered, then snapped, "Aud, go fetch the horse!"

"I'll bring him the sword," Sybilla said, and darted through the door running.

Owen was running also, but slowly, holding a steady pace and trying to save his strength. He didn't know how long or how far he would have to go today. He'd reached the forest, but it offered little cover. The tall trees shut out most of the light, and the ground under them was clear, brown leaf loam that supported very little growth besides the giant oaks. In the distance, he could hear the hounds in full cry. He knew he must find a hiding place soon or be caught. The only place Owen could think of was the tomb, so he ran in the direction of the shore.

Sybilla stepped out from behind a tree holding his sword. Owen stumbled to a halt. The trees around him blurred away. He wiped his face and was able to see clearly again. Was it the effect of the drug Elutides had given him or just the sweat running into his eyes?

"Follow me," Sybilla whispered. "Hurry! I'll lead you to a safe place."

"The tomb?" Owen asked.

"No," she said, shaking her head. "He knows about the tomb. Not many do, but he does. He knows about this one, too, but it will take him longer to think of it."

Then she turned, leading Owen deeper and deeper into the forest. Owen followed until ahead of him he saw the blasted forest giant, the shattered oak where the horse had been stabled.

When Sybilla entered the vine-covered tunnel leading to the tree, the hounds' voices were only a faint murmur in the distance. Near the tree trunk she turned and handed him his sword.

Holding it in his hands, Owen felt an unspeakable sense of assurance, relief, and new confidence. The fingers of his right hand closed around the hilt, his left around the golden scabbard.

"A man's weapon is his life," he told Sybilla.

Sybilla pointed to the hollow in the tree trunk. "Hide there," she said. "He won't be able to find you."

"Hide there and be trapped, you mean."

"No," Sybilla said. "For the present, the huntsmen are beasts. They can't think. They would have to face you one by one. The tree would be your back and sides. It may be they won't find you at all, and you have your sword. Inside, we made a bed of sweet grasses for the horse. You can rest there."

Owen studied the ruined tree. The hollow was a big one. Across the thick, twisted roots that gripped the earth like a hawk's talons, it lay shadowed and dark, cushioned with the thick piles of hay where they'd bedded the horse. The clearing was silent now, and Owen realized the hunt must have gone in another direction.

He was suddenly aware of how tired he was. The thought of sinking down into the soft straw drew him almost hypnotically forward.

Sybilla stood beside him, still pointing to the hollow tree. Owen stumbled forward following the direction her finger pointed. As he entered the tree, the ground gave way beneath his feet and he was falling. He let go of the sword to clutch at the earth slipping past and screamed, "Sybilla!"

He heard her voice coming from far away in the darkness. "You should have listened to Elutides, Owen. For the time of the hunt, we are all your enemies."

He slid faster and faster. The earth he clawed at slipped away, crumbling beneath his fingers. Light vanished, then the distant, soft sounds of the oak forest. He landed hard on his back, on stone, enveloped in silence and utter primordial blackness.

Owen got to his knees; his whole body shook. He wanted to shriek but wouldn't let himself. He bit down hard on his lip until he tasted blood. He'd heard his sword clatter as it, too, fell, joining him in darkness. He groped for it and felt something crawl over his ankle.

This time he did scream. His scream echoed back at him from distant walls like maniacal laughter.

He could hear them now, the slithering reptilian movement, a soft almost imperceptible rustling in the darkness. He was afraid to move, afraid to reach out and search for the sword. The long smooth coil of a body brushed against his knee. He felt it slide past ever so slowly until the serpent's movements took it away toward the other pools of cold life inhabiting this stygian domain.

His gorge rose. He could smell them, the dank, thick reptilian smell. Owen vomited, a hard, cruel retching that shook his body with savage spasms, leaving his stomach empty, his skin slimy with sweat. The rustling around him grew louder.

Christ, he thought. *Christ God, where is my sword. I mustn't disturb them.* "Mustn't disturb them," he muttered between his teeth.

Slowly he began moving his hands. First the right, then the left, in circles over the stone floor. He touched something. His fingers explored. It moved, muscular and slow but away from him.

He retched again, but his hands continued to grope, his half-paralyzed consciousness struggling to remember where the sword had landed. Finally, his fingers closed over the hilt. He drew the sword to him, folded both arms around it, and held it against his body. Sobbing with relief, his eyes searched the blackness.

Ahead of him he seemed to see a point of light. He began using the sheathed weapon as a sweep to clear the floor ahead of him and to crawl forward toward the light. He was blind . . . blind as a plant root groping in the soil toward water, toward life.

At times he seemed only to encounter a few snakes. They allowed themselves to be moved aside, though sometimes they came back and he could feel the brief, hard pressures in the dark as they flowed like ribbons past his knees, along his calves, and around his feet.

At other times the scabbard shoved whole knots of them aside, big clots of withering life. Some hissed and struck at the sword. He heard the blunt, dull bank of their heads against the gold overlay.

Is this what the damned feel? Owen wondered in blackness and silence. *There is no time, or is it simply that time becomes eternity?*

Owen's stomach cramped. His knees felt raw, bruised by their sliding progress along the stone floor. The strain of sweeping the sword back and forth to keep these denizens of darkness away told on his arms and back. The distant point of light appeared to come no nearer.

Owen gritted his teeth and told himself, *I will endure.* He was tortured by the thought, the fear that he might be dead. *Would He judge me without giving me a chance to defend myself?* he wondered. Elutides' cup might have been poison. This hole, the serpents, could be his final punishment, and Sybilla the messenger of his condemnation. Was he to be alone, trapped with these horrors forever?

He wanted to curl up on his side, seal his eyelids against the blackness, let his mind snap, hurl him away from this hideous reality forever, but he didn't.

Hell or no hell, he would struggle on, even as he had in Bertrand's hole, drowned in the blind whirlpool of madness.

Then abruptly he realized the sword touched nothing. The floor was clear around him, and the light was drawing closer. Owen stood up and began to walk toward the light. It resolved itself into a woman, the light a nimbus surrounding her.

"Elin!" Owen called out, for the woman appeared to be Elin. "How did you find me, Elin?" he asked.

She glided toward him. She was simply dressed as he'd always seen her, wearing only a coarse gray linen gown with a blue mantle thrown over her shoulders. Her hair hung down around her face, cloaking her throat and shoulders with its blue-black sheen, gleaming in the brilliance she carried with her.

"Elin?" Owen said again. "How did you find me?"

"Do you wish me to be Elin?" the woman asked. "Well

then, since you wish it, I will be Elin. I didn't find you. You found me. Haven't you always searched for me?"

"No," Owen answered, but he was stretching out his hand to touch her cheek, to brush it lightly with his fingertips, to run them gently over downy, velvet flesh, across lips pink and moist as cherry blossoms.

"No," Owen said. "I wouldn't search you out to bring you here into this tomb, to be condemned to this eyeless place with me. I don't know for what it is I search, and I cannot understand the road I take to find it."

"Then you will find it," she said, twining her fingers with his and clasping them to her breast. "Only those who don't know the way are the ones who reach their goal. Only those who cannot understand will ever come to knowledge."

He could feel her fingers, warm around his. Feel the heat radiating from her flesh, pierce the cold, the loneliness surrounding him.

Remembering Elutides' warning, Owen wanted to pull away but couldn't bring himself to do it.

He searched her face with his eyes, met the blue azure, pure as the open vastness of the summer sky. She brought the azure splendor of a spring morning to him, down to him, down even into this evil prison, down even into the earth piled over his tomb. "Are you my enemy, as Elutides said? Are you here to make me suffer as the rest?"

Slowly, ever so slowly, she nodded. "Only those we love," she said, "can ever make us suffer. Our suffering is the measure of our love and trust. Everything here is suffering, even love."

"I will not forsake it," Owen answered. "Though God use you to torture me, yet I will love you still, forever, even in this . . . wasteland."

Elin smiled, a beautiful smile, a smile like a reflection of sunlight on still water, blinding in its brightness. She drew him toward her. Their lips met. He kissed the teeth of a grinning skull.

No time. Time is a flash of light. He was plunging, racked by horror, into infinity.

He came to rest standing. Standing with others on the grass beside the tomb, the green mound where his journey in this strange land had begun. *A life* . . . he had time to think, *a life . . . but not mine.*

The rain was falling. He could feel the drops striking his unprotected head, slapping at his shoulders, running down his face.

The very skies weep for her, he thought. *The very skies weep that they carry her to her tomb.* The door to the tomb was open and the one he had loved, loved more. than life, lay on the bier being borne past him.

Oh, she had been young, too young to have a child some said, no more than a child herself. But the passion that to him seemed the consummation of his life had planted the child in her womb and brought her to her death.

Grief and guilt were a sickness in his body, thick as the stench in his nostrils, and he knew the stench he smelled was himself, the stink of his own foulness, the rot inside him.

In the tomb, decay might consume her flesh. Outside, his soul would rot inside his body, self-loathing and guilt eat away his life.

He lunged forward, screaming "No!" Catching the poles of the bier, he pulled it down and fell beside it. He looked upon her for the last time, the last time in the cold, in the rain, with the sea thunderously crying out in rage, on the rocks behind him.

He looked on pale skin, icy as the rain to his touch, skin that would never be warm again. On stiff, dark lips that would never answer his own in a loving kiss. On folded hands that would never reach out to him. On a body that would never leap and dance and run again.

Then the bier was torn from his hands. He left his flesh on the carrying poles. And they held him. His companions held him tightly pressed against the earth while the stony entrance to the green mound was pushed aside and the white figure on the bier—all his life, all he ever loved—disappeared within.

Owen was wrenched away, sobbing with pain. He stood on the swaying deck of a ship. This time there was no rain, but the clouds rolled above, sodden, gray as the churning waves, boiling around the wooden hull.

She clutched an infant to one sagging breast. It moved weakly and suckled, but she knew it got nothing. Journey's end. The baby gave a thin cry and dragged on her nipple with a strength born of desperation, then wailed again. Journey's end. The woman knew in her despair that it had been a long time since her breasts had had any milk to give it. None of the rest of the people on the ship were in any better condition than she was.

Men and women both slumped against the wooden sides of the gunwales or sprawled on the narrow decks unmoving, resigned to their fate. Crouching around and among them were children too weak now to even cry any longer and beg for food.

They waited as she waited, the starving child at her breasts, to be broken on the rocks of the headland she saw approaching or to be claimed by the endless cold gray waves.

Oh, she thought, *oh, to stand on dry firm earth again, to set my feet on something that doesn't shift and move with every step.* A man lay near her, his body rolled with the motion of the ship. He lay facedown, head and face covered by bilge water.

Dead, and no one has the strength to toss him overboard. "Row!" she screamed at them. "Row! Try to find a cove."

"Lady, lady," someone replied from among the living corpses lying at her feet, "lady, the gods have forsaken us."

She walked toward the bow of the ship. "Then I . . . I will bring them back!"

She reached the prow post, and the spindrift hit her in the face, half blinding her.

She paused for a moment wishing for warmth, trying to remember the life-giving heat of a fire, the yellow, blue, and gold flames shifting, fluttering above logs and turf.

The sun. The hot, bright sun on her back. Bright, so bright she could feel it on her face, see its light through her closed eyelids. Then her eyes opened and she stared out at the leaping sea.

Journey's end.

She tossed the child away from her first. It landed on its back, twitching once convulsively as it struck the icy water. The sea swirled and poured over its face; then it was only a glimmer of pink flesh as it vanished into the deep.

She followed, turning as she fell, turning for one last glimpse of even a gray sky. The water closed over her open, staring eyes. The breath left her lungs, silver bubbles drifting up and up, floating toward a sky of water. A thousand knives stabbed her lungs. Her body jerked, heavy against the water as she tried to struggle and a red light flooded her brain.

She floated down, seeing above the world she'd left, no longer fighting against the blanketing dark. But before the last light left her eyes, she saw above her the oars rise and fall.

Owen was running, running and knowing he could run no longer, running down a muddy road in the rain. The city was behind him, no life in it and no safety. There seemed to be lights in the windows, and from a distance they were almost comforting. They would have been comforting if he hadn't known they were devouring flames and, even now, his people were being dragged out, screaming, into the rain, to be slaughtered where they stood or carried off into slavery in some unimaginable land.

He stumbled to a stop, breathing in gasps that seemed to rise shuddering from his toes. There were others with him, others nearly as done in as he was.

"We have lost!" He gasped out the words. Not one of them answered. None of them had the strength to reply, and the truth of his words was self-evident.

Again, as at the beginning of his vision, the rain poured down, almost blinding him. He accepted his fate.

His companions hurried on, away from the doomed town. He was alone.

No poets would sing of him. His parents would, if they lived long enough, only curse him, curse him for not doing enough. And no one would remember a boy dying before a nameless town, in a dirty dying because his legs and lungs failed him, dying because he could run no longer.

They were on him almost before he saw them, and the sword was in deep, tearing his guts out before he could parry. He wasn't quite dead when the feet on his back trampled his body into the mud.

Owen came to himself standing before Elin. The darkness was all around them. "Those things were real, were they?" he asked.

She nodded and smiled sadly. "They were once and perhaps still are," she replied.

"Elin . . . Elin!" he cried. "How many deaths will you make me die?"

"How many deaths are there?" she asked in return.

"As many as there are lives that have been lived," Owen answered. "And not all of them will ever make me stop loving you. Nothing will ever make me let you go." He took her hand.

"If you love me," she whispered, "kiss me again."

And in an act of courage that was perhaps the greatest he had ever performed, he drew her toward him and pressed his lips to hers. This time they were soft, warm, and human.

"Elin," he sighed.

But she pulled away. "I'm not Elin."

"What . . . who are you then?"

In answer, she thrust her fist at him. A fist, fingers clinched, palm up. Slowly she opened her hand. Cradled in her palm she held a wheat seed.

As he watched, it grew. First the tiny shoot, the green spike lengthening, brown roots curling around her fingers. Taller and taller it grew, the spiked glumes at the tip of the stalk filling and ripening. Then time stuck and it filled with the richness of life. As he watched, it browned; the satiny kernels bowed down into her other hand and shed their abundance into her cupped fingers.

"What are you?" he asked again. "Who are you?"

"Woman," she said, "and whatever a man's foolish pride will let her be to him."

The wheat stalk vanished, and she flung the wheat

upward, and the wheat grains were faraway points of light. They shone against the darkness, bright stars among a thousand others.

They were above him, behind him, below him, all around him. There was no up, no down, no east, no west, only an infinity of lights. The stars were everywhere.

Or was he walking across a vast polished floor? He didn't know. Were they only reflections like the sparkle of stars in a pool by night?

Caped and hooded, it was before him. Then the hood fell back. He looked into empty eyes and the fleshless grin. Owen drew his sword and raised it. *Against this adversary,* he thought, *no man prevails.*

Steel met steel and he fought across a moonless midnight sky, face-to-face with death. At first his opponent was no stronger than he, until he began to fail.

There is no time, he thought, looking into the unchanging grin. *No time but what time takes from us, our youth, our strength, our will.*

Steel met steel again and again. His arms became leaden, the sweat poured from his body, but he raised his arms again and again, until every breath was fire in his lungs, until every time he raised the sword his arms were bound together by raw ropes of agony. He could hear his own ragged breath rattle in his chest. The skull-faced thing before him was inexorable. That was half its terror. It shows us nothing but an empty grin.

All our torments, our defiance, our vaunting pride mean nothing to it. Still it comes, like the rising tide or like the endless waves breaking a ship to pieces against a rocky shore.

He couldn't feel his arms any longer, couldn't be sure each time he raised them that they would obey. The sweat ran into his eyes and all he could see before him was a gray-black shadow moving against a star-filled sky. Their swords locked, hilt to hilt, and he saw the ivory smile approach closer and closer to his face.

This will kill me, he thought. *I will die standing toe to toe, locked in combat with this horror.* His arms and shoulders felt on fire; the breath he gulped into his lungs rasped like a knife drawn across burned flesh. He no longer had the strength to jerk his sword's hand guard free. Blood from his overstrained lungs clotted in his mouth and ran down his chin.

Die. I will die, he thought. *My body can't take much more.*

The black orbits of the sockets were only inches from his own. The obscene blank nose triangle and the curving row of teeth were all he could see. The sword pressed against his harder and harder, forcing him down.

"No," Owen gasped. The word bubbled out of his throat through the bloody froth on his lips. "No, I will hold until my heart bursts."

Abruptly it was gone, a shadow fading, thinning, a wisp of smoke among the million dreaming stars.

Owen staggered forward, the whole universe reeling, spinning around him, falling through the night sky. His body crashed down hard. The breath was driven out of his lungs and consciousness from his brain.

33

GODWIN, Elin, and the men with them stopped running when they reached the cover provided by the crossbowmen at the city gates.

Elin was angry about the blow across her back, but her pride would not let her admit it. She tossed her head. Her cap was gone and her long hair trailed down around her shoulders in a fall of blackness.

Godwin wasn't in a mood for her pride. "You were out of control," he said. "I believed Owen was headlong and a madman in his rage. I can see you're a piece of work also. In another second, you'd have been after Hakon on the ground. I wouldn't have been able to save your life."

"Do you think I killed him?" she asked.

"No," he answered. "I've noticed lately he goes double armored. He wears a breastplate over scale mail. Besides, Hakon is incredibly strong and tough. He's not a man to fall to one blow. However, you may have put him out of action for a time."

Then the gates opened and a cheer rang out. "Come," Godwin said. "Take the homage you deserve."

Elin paused for a moment and turned to look back over the plain. The ring of fires that had surrounded the catapult were going out. In the circle where the engine of destruction had been lay only darkness. Even the embers were quenched.

The shouts of acclaim behind her drew her attention. "Ingund?" she asked in some alarm.

The woman pushed through the crowd and came to her side. "The fires are out. No one was killed," she said. "A large number of people are getting drunk, and you are universally admired. For the moment, we have won."

Hakon's men carried him straight to Elspeth. They placed him on a horse litter and rushed him to her stronghold.

They placed him tenderly on a bear skin in the center of the hall. The fletchings and shaft of the crossbow bolt protruded from the metal breastplate he wore. His face was the color of ash, highlighted in blue shadow. He struggled for every breath he took.

His men gathered around the stretcher cursing and moaning. The women of the household wept and rent their garments, scratched their faces, and generally called on heaven, both Christian and pagan.

Nausea flowed over Elspeth in a wave. *He will die,* she thought. In the distance, she could hear her daughters screaming and laughing as they played around the feet of the trestle tables. Dread seemed to have replaced her heart with a stone.

As she pushed her way between the people crowded around Hakon's prone body, she felt a tug on her skirt. She looked down and saw Eric, her son. His eyes were wide and frightened. Elspeth reached down and gathered him into her arms, then said, "Make way. I would stand beside my lord."

Hakon's eyes were closed; the wheezing from his chest was loud.

Tosi knelt next to his chief. He looked panic stricken. He glanced up at Elspeth. A light sheen of sweat covered his face. "I think the bolt is in his lungs. He's dying. Ah, God, when we pull it out, he will be gone. My lady Elspeth, I can't bear it. We have been friends so long."

Elspeth didn't answer, but Eric pointed down. "The plate is bent. It's keeping him from breathing easily," the boy said.

"He's right," Elspeth said. "Cut the cuirass free, Tosi."

Tosi did. As the steel plate clattered away and took the crossbow bolt with it, they could see the bolt had split the cuirass and rested against the scale mail covering Hakon's chest.

"Through the armor, by all the gods, but not the man!" Tosi cried. "I have often heard it said that good luck is better than strength, wealth, or fame. And you were ever a lucky bastard, Hakon."

Freed from the constraints of the armor, the chieftain began to breathe more easily, and color started reentering his cheeks. When it became clear that Hakon was not to die immediately, the hubbub in the hall began to calm down. Elspeth had him carried to her bedroom.

When Hakon awoke, he was lying in the big bed they shared. A large bandage was wrapped around his ribs, and Eric sat cross-legged beside him.

"Does it hurt?" Eric asked.

"Yes," Hakon replied.

Elspeth was mixing a potion. She glanced quickly at Hakon. "The witch almost got you."

"Indeed," he answered. "She came very close." Then, indicating Eric, he asked, "What's he doing here? I told you to keep the child out of my way." His words brought instant hurt to Eric's eyes.

"You had best show at least some small gratitude to Eric," Elspeth said. "It was he who told us what was causing you to have trouble breathing."

Hakon's cold gaze flashed toward Eric again. This time his glance acknowledged the boy's existence. Any debt, even a small one, commanded a response from him. "Well?" he asked.

"Who are you to me?" Eric asked in return. "Are you my father?"

"No," Hakon said. "I have no sons and want none. Reynald was your father. He is dead."

"The men in the hall say that if Mother becomes pregnant by you, I will be sent away," Eric said.

"Eric!" Elspeth gasped. "Who has—"

Hakon made an impatient sign to Elspeth to be silent. "No, you will not be sent away, though I have heard that is your custom. You will be trained to the craft of arms here. When you stand before me as a man, you may claim gold to the value of a longship, the ship itself, or your own stronghold. In the interim you must learn to care for all three. A fool would quickly lose gold, a ship, or lands. They require some management. At present, you don't even know what the plowman knows."

Eric nodded. He slid off the bed, satisfied that his place in the household was secure. Before he left the room, he turned to Hakon with one last question. "What does the plowman know?"

"A lot," Hakon said. "First, he knows everything begins and ends with the plow. He can take off his shoes, feel the damp earth between his toes, and know if it is wet enough to turn easily but not so damp as to bog oxen and plow in the mud. He knows when the soil is warm enough for final harrowing and planting. That is only a little of what he knows and what you must learn if you will learn to rule lands and men."

"Are you content?" Elspeth asked Eric.

"Yes," the child answered.

"Very well," Elspeth said. "It's past your bedtime, so find Bettena and have her ready you for sleep."

Eric scurried out of the room.

"Long headed for such a little one," Hakon commented.

"He has been frightened since you came here," Elspeth said. "Afraid, I think, that he would be supplanted in my affections."

"Yes, also the men in the hall chatter worse than women," Hakon said. "And they probably don't pay attention to what the child hears. Better to deal honestly with him now. I would not want to look up from my meat one day and find myself staring into the eyes of an enemy."

Elspeth finished mixing the potion. "I think this will ease your pain."

"Only ease it?" he asked sarcastically. "Not put me out of my misery permanently?"

Elspeth looked faintly exasperated. She set the cup down hard on the table near the bed. "If you're suspicious or dissatisfied with my skills, I'll drink part of the mixture. Then you'll see it's safe."

Hakon sighed. His frosty eyes slid away from her face. He stared into the distance. "Sorry, don't bother. You're not the one who needs to be drugged. I do. Every breath I take pains me."

"If it's any consolation, I don't think your ribs are broken."

"I know," Hakon said. "It's just a bad bruise. I've had them before. It prevents me from doing what I want to do. It would hurt too much."

"What's that?" Elspeth asked.

"First," Hakon said gravely, "I would like to get up and break all the furniture in this room. Then terrorize you with my cursing and shouting until you fled weeping and went to sleep among your women. After that, I would go into the hall and gulp down enough wine to put myself into a drunken rage and pick out at least three fights with my men, taking on those who are even more sodden than I am. I would hurt them, probably not seriously, but painfully. This done, I would complete the process of drinking myself into a stupor.

"In the morning, I would awaken with a horrible pain in my head and a worse taste in my mouth. I would then crawl to you where you sat among your women sewing and whine and beg for forgiveness and comfort."

Elspeth's lips twitched. "Drink the potion," she said. "In the morning when you awake and the first stiffness works itself out, you will be better."

Hakon reached over, picked up the cup, and emptied it. "Syrup of poppies. I recognize the bitter taste." Elspeth nodded. He paused. "What am I going to do about the city?"

Elspeth began undressing. She cocked her head to one side for a moment, listening. "Do you hear it?" she asked.

"Hear what?"

"The silence," she answered. She went to the window and gazed out at the winter stars.

Two of Hakon's men and one of her own lounged near the gate. Their small fire was the only light. The big gates into the bailey were shut and barred. The lake surrounding the fortress was deep, over a man's head, so there was no need for a larger number of guards.

The cold air of midnight flowed over Elspeth's face and hands. She closed the wooden casement and turned back to Hakon. "The household is at peace. They know their lord is well. Every day you remain here, you become more and more one of us. Sleep now. I'll be beside you. If you want anything, wake me. In the morning we will put our heads together and think of what to do. I'll wager we come up with something."

She was awakened by his muttering only a few hours later. The room was very dark. She'd blown out the candle before she went to sleep, but a lamp burned at her bedside.

She sat up. Elspeth was well acquainted with the effects of the poppy on the taker's breathing. She'd propped Hakon high on a big pillow and covered him warmly.

She looked over and was reassured. His eyes were open. She turned on her side and propped herself on an elbow. "Are you in pain?" she asked.

He chuckled. "No. I'm not in any kind of pain, but I dreamed . . . I dreamed that . . . someone . . . had come into the room. Someone . . . she spoke to me, but I didn't want to answer. . . . No! Tosi knows the story . . . how I got the scar . . . on my face. Long ago."

Elspeth studied his eyes carefully. What she saw frightened her. His pupils were tiny; she could barely see them. In the dark room, they should be wider, even after taking the drug. He was deep in a drugged dream. She was afraid to let him go back to sleep. "Tell me about it."

"What?"

"How you got the scar on your face." She expected some boast of battle or conquest and adventure.

Hakon huffed. His breath steamed in the cold air. Then he coughed. The room was icy, but the bed, warmed by padded bricks, was comfortable enough.

He needs to talk a bit, she thought. *Till the drug clears out of his body. He's big. Bettena mixed a strong draught, but he rarely takes medicine. He has no resistance.* "Tell me." She was insistent.

"Yes, I'll tell you." His voice was flat, detached. "I'm not in any pain, so I can tell you how it was. How it happened.

"My father and I quarreled. One of the horses intended for the horse fight strayed. I took out on foot after him. My boots were worn. After I caught the animal, it turned cold and began to snow. When I returned to my father's hall, I stripped off my boots. I saw two toes were frostbitten. This is painful, Elspeth. Frostbite is when the blood comes back into the toe or finger caught by the chill.

"As I was rubbing the life back into my toes before the fire, he came in and struck me across the back with his riding whip. He called me a lazy piece of dung to be lounging at the hearth when the farm needed to be secured against the storm.

"I cannot think how it happened." Hakon's voice was plaintive. "I don't remember how it happened. One moment he was hitting me with the whip, cursing me, the next he lay on the floor and I was standing over him, looking down. My fist lifted to hit him again. I remember the expression on his face. If you can combine respect, fear, and cold hatred in a word, it would describe what I saw in his face perfectly. I found myself a pair of better boots and left."

"That doesn't sound so terrible," Elspeth said. "No real harm was done."

"Yes, indeed. I thought as you do. At first. I was seventeen. It was time I left to take up my life. We need not share the same house again. In time, we could be peacefully reconciled. Though the occasional winter storm still troubled us, it was spring and the first freshets were flowing.

"I journeyed toward the mountains where a cousin of mine grazed cattle in the high pastures. He had a standing near the peaks, set among tall firs and pines, a wild lonely place near a river fed by snowmelt that emptied into a fjord. He had no near neighbors. Summer was brief so high up. Few crops could be grown.

"Thorhold—that was his name—and his family lived on what his cattle produced—milk, butter, and cheese—half-wild pigs that foraged in the dense undergrowth among the trees, and such game as he and his sons hunted and killed during the winter. He had a daughter, Thora by name, and three sons.

"They gave me fair welcome, and I sat down to meat among them. When the talk came round to my father, I explained the trouble that had arisen between us and asked Thorhold if I could stay with him until both our tempers cooled.

"Now, I had more to offer Thorhold than my good wishes. He was a hard and grasping man, tightfisted with even his closest kin. I didn't think he loved my father enough to turn away a strong and willing worker. A strong back he could use to carry his burdens. I was right. He drove me hard, but then so had my father. I was not yet twenty and could outwork a plow horse. I didn't care. I was, by then, thinking of other things.

"I did notice Thorhold's three sons did little but eat, drink, and lie around jeering at me for letting their father squeeze me. Except for Thora, they were all lazy. I went to work with a will, and I could see, in the hands of a better man, a lot could be made of the place. I hunted down and rooted out bears and wolves. Those, at any rate, who showed a taste for beef or troubled the calves. I kept a sharp eye on the herdsmen, a band of feckless hirelings who drifted up from the lowlands every year to take Thorhold's coin and do as little as possible for it. I saw, too, that the cattle grazed no pasture down to its roots and no beast strayed.

"Thora was equally energetic. She had a few maids to help her, but the main burden of the cheese making fell on her. And cheeses sent to market and sold were the chief source of sustenance for the family. Money from them bought grain to make bread and beer for those lazy sots, her brothers and father, and went to purchase the different-colored wools she used to make clothing and the heavy blankets and wall hangings that helped keep out the winter cold. She spent all winter at the loom. She had no women to help her. The maids were only hired for the summer, the way the men were."

Hakon's eyes closed and he seemed to drift away for a time.

Elspeth got to her feet and threw on a heavy woolen long-sleeved shift. She hurried around to Hakon's side of the bed. His breathing was shallow. The pillows she'd propped him on had compressed under his weight. She went to the corner and added more coals to the brazier. The air in the room was like ice. She took a big, brocaded pillow from a chair, then checked the bed around Hakon. It was warm, overwarm really. He was feverish. He cried out in pain when she awakened him to shove the brocade pillow under the rest to hold him up higher.

Then she went to the chest that held her pharmaceuticals. She found a silver flask of elderflower wine and a crystal-and-silver cup. She added a bit of the wine to some water and brought the cup to Hakon. He drank greedily, then looked at the cup. "Beautiful." Elspeth brushed a strand of hair from his forehead. Her fingers touched the scar.

His hand moved like lightning and snapped like a fetter around her wrist. His eyes opened. He let her go. "I was talking about her, wasn't I? Thora?"

"Yes," Elspeth said. "Finish telling me about her." Elspeth really wasn't sure she wanted to hear any more. A deep sense of unease was creeping over her, but she needed to keep him talking for a little while longer. Keep him conscious until his fever broke and more of the drug burned its way out of his body. "You told me she wasn't like her brothers," Elspeth prompted.

"No," he answered. "She wasn't like her brothers." Then he paused. "Why?" he continued, sounding like a troubled child. "Why, after so many years, does it bring me so much pain to speak of her?"

"You liked her?" Elspeth asked.

"Oh yes, we liked each other entirely too well. So well, in fact, that by winter she was pregnant by me. I have thought long about my guilt in the matter. If I had been more of a man of honor, what happened later would not have come to pass. But then, at other times, I think, well . . . we had done no worse than many another couple who lived long, happy wedded lives.

"Thora wasn't the daughter of a jarl who could look

high for a match. I might have even ranked a bit above her. I was the freeborn son of a wealthy and respected family. Even if I was on the outs with my father, I could still stand before him and demand a sum in coin to help me begin my life.

"There was no reason in what happened next. Even if my father denied me my rights, I still brought Thorhold a thing of great value—myself. The lazy fool and his even more shiftless sons scratched for a living where I would have prospered or even grown wealthy. I'd have made them all a fat living. The stupid bastard couldn't even see when he was on to a good thing."

Something terrible came into Hakon's face. She'd heard Tosi speak of the way he looked in a killing rage. She could see even in the pale lamplight that his eyes were glacial, clear frozen into a terrible, eternal stillness.

He continued speaking, but Elspeth suddenly had the sickening sensation that the empty eyes were turned inward and he was alone with his memories.

"Yearly, Thorhold drove his surplus livestock and wagons filled with fine cheeses to Hideaby to sell them at the fair. He returned all smiles and singing my praises, saying never had he enjoyed a more prosperous summer. That night we had a feast. My sister, Asa, had heard about the trouble with my father. Tosi, my nephew, had been visiting all summer, off and on, though a certain coldness had arisen between us. I felt he had his eye on Thora, too. But this night, I could feel no malice toward anyone in the world.

"Thora and I had a trysting place high above the fjord. It was on a rock overlooking the water, surrounded by the forest. Oh, Elspeth, you have never known beauty until you hear the cry of a mountain forest as it answers the caress of the wind. Or see the great slash of water that is a fjord glowing silver in the full sun of our long northern nights. Or looked down the steep, rocky slopes mantled in stately trees, thick-trunked giants, seeming older than the world.

"We lay together on a soft bed of fragrant needles

fallen from the encircling trees and made love. She told me she carried my child. I was so happy."

The lamp on Elspeth's side of the bed began to gutter, flaring and sinking, sending strange shadows chasing each other round and round the room. Elspeth shivered violently and pulled the covers up over her.

"No matter what other joys life may hold, that kind of happiness comes but once to a man, once only, and however fleeting, remains pure as the light of a star, a guiding star that steadies the helmsman on his journey across a treacherous sea. We lay in each other's arms, listening to the song of the forest bowing before the autumn wind, and planned our lives.

"Thora hadn't been afraid to tell me she was with child. She was sure of me, my good faith, my honor. Indeed, she had no reason to doubt me. I thought to make my home in her mountains. Their beauty won my heart, as she had.

"The high pastures were always cool, even in the hottest summers, lush with grass so rich, even the turf taken to roof the houses, untroubled by being separated from the earth, continued to grow, crowning the gray stone dwellings of men with living green. Even the dark wilderness haunt of wolf and bear challenged my spirit, my youthful strength. I would pit myself against it. Plumb the steep, dangerous depths, let its silences sink deep within my soul. I had the strength to force my way into its deepest ravines where the trunks of tall trees contended together in their struggle toward the light. And I would fell the tallest, oldest of the forest giants to be the roof tree of the hall I would build for her.

"She would never fear the cold as my wife. She would go warm, draped in the skins of wolverine, wolf, bear, ermine, and sable. All these things I promised her as she lay in my arms and we looked down on the placid water of the fjord. Water that seemed to stretch before us, as our future, a clean and shining path into the haze of distance when the eye reaches the horizon where sky and water become one."

Hakon coughed again. This time he showed more pain than he had earlier. "My wounds have stiffened," he complained. "It hurts when I breathe." He was beginning to perspire. Elspeth filled the crystal cup. He drank thirstily, deeply. "Cold water," he said.

"Only partially. I put some elderflower wine in it to purify it." She took the empty cup from his hand. "Finish the story?" she asked.

"Finish the story," he echoed. "Yes, if only I could. That night, as I told you, we feasted together in the hall. It would have seemed a wretched place to you—a farm-house, walls and roof of split logs with a louvered hole in the roof our chimney. I never saw a fireplace till I came among the Franks. We had but little iron, and that only in the form of tools and weapons. We dined at bare tables whose surfaces still showed the mark of adze and saw. Drank our beer from leather tankards.

"But, oh, how the fire blazed on the hearth. The room was warm with our merriment, the air rich with the smell of beef, venison, and ruddy salmon. I sat beside Thora, holding her hand under the table, feeling near godlike happiness as her fingers twined with mine.

"Tosi sat beside us and, noticing where her hand was, rolled his eyes and laughed. Tosi, then as now, was a good-natured fellow and accepted my success without malice. Thora and I smiled at his eye rolling and teased him about his stories. For Tosi managed to sign on to a trade voyage to Byzantium. He brought back a thousand tales we only half believed.

"You see, Thora and I were both mired in our daily round. It began before sunrise and ended with darkness. When we finished one task, another always beckoned instantly. She had to see to the cleaning, brewing, and baking with one hand while with the other she tended a herdsman gored by a bull or brought up a calf orphaned by a bear. At night, she wove by candlelight until she was too weary to see the pattern in the threads.

"My hunts were no lighthearted affair, a day in the saddle ending with a feast. Instead, I had to track some cattle-killing beast night and day through the rugged mountain woods, across bare slopes of scree and windblown rock. Then bring a wolf or bear to bay, and alone, on foot, brave fang and claw to bring him down.

"How could we, living such a life, believe the wonders Tosi said he had seen? He spoke of cities where men thronged together so tightly packed that they piled rooms on top of one another, kings who went robed in gold, lords and ladies so rich they loaded their arms and necks with precious stones and never allowed their feet to touch the ground. Instead, they were carried on litters set on the backs of their slaves. Cities where even the courtesans robed themselves in brocade and embraced their lovers on silk.

"He spun a shining vision of lands set in a warm, blue sea. Kingdoms of eternal springtime, where flowers bloomed through the winter and snow fell only on the mountaintops. He told us of churches decorated by paintings made with splinters of glass and illuminated by the priests when they worshiped with a thousand candles.

"Nearer at hand, Tosi told us, were the forests of Gaul. Even there, he claimed, winter was but a passing fancy of nature. It troubled the farmers little. The soil was rich and readily yielded two crops a year to the enterprising husbandman.

"But to Thora and me sitting in the narrow farmhouse, its heavy beamed roof steeply pitched so that the sheer weight of winter snow wouldn't crush it in, how could such fantastic things be real?

"Besides, whatever riches lay beyond the fjord and the perils of the cold gray sea, how could they compare with the delight we had in the strength of our youth, the joys of first love? All the wealth either of us wanted we'd found in each other, in the child to be born in the winter, and the future we planned together. And who is to say we were wrong? I cannot ever again remember being so happy.

"I can still feel her hand in mine. It was not a soft hand as yours is, but long-fingered, hard, and strong. Even when age dims my sight and the sounds of the world are but an echo of their former selves in my ears, I think I will still feel her touch, the pressure of her warm fingers on mine. So she remains beside me forever and will never leave me. The gods are cruel, Elspeth. The only mercy they show mankind is to hide the future from us. So we sat and begged Tosi for one tale after another. And he, warmed by Thora's rich, dark brew, obliged us."

"Thorhold presided over the table, looking very pleased with himself, very much as though he'd concluded some profitable bargain. And even Thora's three brothers, usually grim, jeering, savage men, seemed . . . tonight . . . easy to amuse. They laughed loud and long at Tosi's stories, telling him if he was not the boldest liar in the mountains, he was at least the most entertaining one.

"I, in my stupidity, believed the good fellowship that reigned among us was because Thorhold guessed he'd won a strong son-in-law and was pleased with the match.

"My bed was in the stable, the loft above the cattle we'd brought down from the mountain meadows. Thora followed me out into the night. Oh, the air of an autumn night. It held the purity of the earth's first morning, and the stars! There was no moon, but we could see each other's faces by their light as they hung a curtain of splendor across the sky. We might have found a stall where we could embrace in the warm straw, but we didn't. We only reaffirmed our vows, our love for one another."

Hakon was perspiring freely. His fever was breaking. He was breathing more strongly now. The lamp chose that moment to exhaust its oil and expire. The flame burned blue for a few seconds, then died, leaving the room in darkness.

Elspeth could still see fairly well. Faint light from the moon and stars entered the room. She got up and made him change his shirt, then tucked him in, making sure he was well covered and warm. Then she returned to bed, cuddled up next to him, and took him in her arms. "Finish this, Hakon," she told him. "I must know. I think I need to know."

He pulled himself free of her arms. The pillows held him at a high angle. "My chest hurts. The drug is wearing off. I'm sorry I began this with you, but . . .

"There, as here, pigs were allowed to run free in the

woods, to fatten during the summer. So I wasn't surprised when, the next morning, Hoskold, Thorhold's eldest, awakened me, saying we must go down to the river valley, kill a few, and smoke the hams for winter. I got my spear and followed.

"The going was rough. The river, a mountain torrent, followed land that sloped steeply down to the fjord. The narrow gorge the river cut in the mountainside was choked with boulders, brush, fallen trees. All manner of debris washed down from the heights, and the banks were rocky and deeply cut by crevices and ravines.

"The pigs usually congregated near the river mouth. I should have known. . . . Thora's brothers were too merry. They smiled too much, seemingly laughing at some jest I didn't share. But I was young . . . foolish . . . yet even so, when we had gone a little way following the river, I began to feel very uneasy. I felt they were up to no good.

"I knew it when Skleg, the youngest brother, got my spear away from me. He snatched it from my hand as we forded a brook, saying, 'Jump across, Hakon. I'll throw the spear to you when you're on the other side.'

"A huge fallen oak lay parallel to the stream on the other side. I cleared both stream and tree trunk in one leap and landed sheltered behind the thick tree. The oak was yet green, leaves unfallen. I snapped off a branch nearly as thick as a man's thigh and shouted back at Skleg, 'I think I can do as much damage to the pigs with this as you can with my spear.' The brothers laughed and Hoskold shouted, 'I think I hear the pigs just ahead. Go forward, Hakon, and see what damage you can do with that club.'

"The pigs were only a little way beyond where we stood, grunting and squealing as they do when they feed. They were gathered in a steep cut scooped out of the bank when the river rises and eddies there in spring. A pleasant place, green till snow flies. Thora and I had gathered cress and cattail root there in summer.

"I hurried over the lip of the cut through bushes and sapling trees thinking to head back up the mountain. I had hidden in the stable an axe and sword given me by Tosi.

Neither he nor my sister, Asa, liked or trusted Thorhold and his sons.

"Then, ahead of me I saw the pigs grouped near the water. I drew closer and saw the pigs fed on flesh. And the flesh the pigs fed on was . . . Thora."

Elspeth jumped from the bed. She had, among her medicines, a flask of oil. It took only a few seconds to refill the lamp and light it. Because, for a second, Elspeth had felt a chill as though a breath of icy air wafted through the room. As though something or someone had entered from the cold darkness outside, and now stood, listening in the shadows, just beyond the reach of the lamplight.

Hakon's face seemed no longer human, his eyes frozen, his mouth a bloodless slash, flesh drawn tight over the bones. He continued. "The pigs had, as beasts will, eaten the soft parts first, so she was a shell, but a shell with the head, hands and feet of a woman. I had thought of running, but now I no longer thought of anything.

"Skleg reached the edge of the cut above me. He laughed and shouted down, 'Flee, Hakon. Go fast, go far. Maybe you will escape us.'

"I answered, 'Come down, Skleg. A man may do no more than die. And I see now that's not the worst thing he must face in life, only the last.' He jumped down and ran at me with his axe raised.

"I stood still as a post and made no move to dodge or step away. The axe struck my skull. I felt the edge bite bone. Perhaps he'd been too eager and hadn't set himself for the blow, because the blade skidded, slicing my forehead and face as you see the scar now. Or perhaps he'd been too neglectful to sharpen his weapons and was killed by his lazy ways.

"For killed he was. When the blade passed my face, I swung the club. There was no need for second blows or even second looks. Most of his head just disappeared. I had not known I was so strong.

"Hesveg, the middle brother, arrived. He had my spear. He cast it. I don't know why it didn't hit me. Perhaps he was unnerved by seeing Skleg dead so quickly or because

I was already running at him with Skleg's axe in my hand. Hesveg still had his axe, but it didn't do him much good. His body hit the ground in two different places.

"Hoskold didn't care much for fighting me then. You see, they thought to overpower and kill me quickly. To them, I was but a boy, not much better than the hirelings who tended their cattle. My father had never allowed me to go armed or given me weapons.

"Hoskold still stood above me, high on the bank. As he turned to run, I shouted at him, 'Your brothers died too quickly for my taste. You will wish you had their good luck when I catch you.' And catch him I did in no long time.

"I had the truth from him before he died. They never meant to kill Thora. But in the night after the feast, they brought her to an old woman in the business of saving young girls' reputations. The old woman used her strong hand to crush the child in the womb. When Thora saw where they were taking her and found out what they meant to do, she struggled so violently that the old woman used too much force. Thora bled and was delivered of a still-born child. The bleeding grew worse and worse until she died.

"It seems when Thorhold went to the fair, he met my father. He knew we were lovers. Only a greater fool than he would not have known. He proposed a match. My father grew angry and told Thorhold I would get nothing from him. Moreover, he bribed Thorhold to put an end to the child and drive me away.

"Thorhold promised to do as my father wished. But when Thora died, Thorhold realized matters had gone too far. He was angry because he had hoped to give her to Tosi for a fat price. So angered at the failure of all his plans, he said to his sons, 'Throw her down among the pigs. Take him there to see what he has done, then kill him. Let the pigs eat their fill and throw what remains into the fjord.'

"When I finished beating the truth out of Hoskold, I sent him to join his brothers. I cannot say if the pigs began their meal before or after he died, but his screams followed me a long way on the path back to the house. He would not have lived long in any case. I broke both his arms and legs.

"When I entered the hall, Tosi was sitting at the board with Thorhold. Unlike me, he had been drunk the night before and was just waking up. Thorhold was horrified. He snatched up his axe. I imagine I was the last person he expected to see. Tosi jumped up, not understanding. He tried to hinder me. I knocked him down.

"Thorhold made as if to run. I said, 'It offends me that you yet live, Thorhold.' I caught him by the shirt, threw him down, and struck off his head. He died on his own threshold.

"Tosi faced me. 'Hakon, why was this done?'

"Follow the river, I told him, to where it joins the fjord and look at what you find there. After a time, he returned, carrying what remained of Thora in his mantle. He set the sad bundle on the ground. 'What happened?' he asked. I told him what Hoskold told me.

"We fed what remained of Thorhold to the pigs, too. Tosi approved, saying, 'He smiled too much last night.' Thorhold had more wealth than he admitted to, some gold and jewels besides the silver he had from my father.

"We wrapped her body in the woolen wall hangings that once brightened her hall and scattered Thorhold's wealth over her body. I buried Skleg's axe in the skull of the best stallion and bull Thorhold owned and placed them beside her. Then we put Thora in the hall on the table where we'd banqueted the night before. We sent her spirit skyward in a cloud of fire. I wanted her to be welcomed and treated with honor . . . among the dead.

"We turned his beasts, fine dairy cattle and some sheep and goats, loose in the woods, free to any takers. We watched the hall burn for a time until we were sure of its utter destruction. It soon was a roaring cauldron of flame, since we left Thorhold's stores within and they included much butter and oil. It burned white-hot once they caught. Then, Tosi and I left with our weapons, the clothes we were standing in, and nothing else. We didn't stop to see what the pigs made of Thorhold and his sons. We traveled until we reached my sister's home. She knew I would return to my father's house and kill him. So she and Tosi tricked me.

"One morning after a bout of heavy drinking—I spent all my nights that way then—I found myself on a dragon ship bound for raids in Wessex, in England. Tosi was with me. We have been together ever since. I have been told that some neighbors took the cattle. What remains of Thorhold's steading is only a low mound covered by grass, the saplings already sprouting on it."

Elspeth felt the presence press closer. Deliberately, she blew out the lamp.

"Do you know, Elspeth . . ." Hakon's voice was hoarse, as the rasp of files on steel. "I have never told this to a living soul, not even Tosi. Hoskold said she died cursing me."

The presence waited, as though asking for justice. As though drawn by Hakon's pain.

"No," Elspeth replied. "She loved you." For a moment, the weight of an immense responsibility rested on her shoulders. "Oh no, my love. Believe me. She didn't die cursing you, no matter what her cruel brother said. One woman knows the heart of another. Hoskold knew he would never go living out of your hands. He and his brothers and father were petty in their cruelty and greed. And he was also petty in the only revenge he could take."

"Come here. Keep me warm." Hakon pulled her into his embrace. She could feel his long, strong body; feel his temperature was down, his breathing normal. She sensed its change as he drifted into an ordinary sleep. The fever was gone, the drug worn off, the worst of his pain over. He would rest peacefully till morning. He was no longer in danger.

Still, the presence lingered.

"No," Elspeth whispered softly into the darkness, the silence. "Hoskold didn't lie, not really. He was simply mistaken. While I cannot believe she cursed you, I can well believe she died calling your name. Is that the justice you seek?"

She found she asked her question of the empty night. The presence was gone. Elspeth drifted away to join Hakon in slumber, slipping into the dark pageantry of her dreams.

Chapter
34

*T*OSI woke her before dawn. She trusted her household but met him at the door with her dagger drawn.

He stared at the weapon in her hand with distaste. "I have been his friend for many years," he said. "I've slept beside him more often than you have. He has never had anything to fear from me."

"Well and good," Elspeth said, sheathing her dagger. "And are all the men as loyal as you?"

The room was very dim; only a candle flickered on a clothes chest in the corner. As they approached the bed, they saw Hakon was awake, his sword in his hand.

"Ivor is back," Tosi whispered. "He wants to see you."

Elspeth was mystified. "Ivor?"

Tosi chuckled. "I would not want my fair lady to confront Ivor. His face has frightened many men."

"I've seen the results of wounds before," Elspeth said.

"Why need she see him at all?" Hakon whispered.

Tosi spread his hands in a gesture of futility. "Hakon, he is badly injured. All his men are dead. It seems he encountered Owen and came off second best. The bishop was aided by a magus of great power. More than that he wouldn't tell me. He insists on talking to you."

Hakon tried to get up, but Elspeth pushed him back down. "You will catch your death in the winter woods."

"The devil I will," Hakon said, sitting up again.

"Lie still," Tosi said. "I think she's right. The gray ladies have greatly favored you of late. I would not ask too much of them. Ivor will tell her what you want to know." He grinned. "You would never ever believe it to look at him, but Ivor has a real weakness for women."

Elspeth, wrapped in a dark cloak, went with Tosi to the grove of aspens where Ivor lay. A torch was pushed into the soft earth beside him. Elspeth was able to control her expression when she saw his face. He accepted her as a messenger to Hakon.

As Tosi led the guard away out of earshot, Elspeth sat down on a log at Ivor's side. She drew the cloak around her against the cold and listened to his tale. She wasn't surprised when he wept with rage and frustration. Neither he nor Hakon understood mercy or compassion. They took it for derision, and neither could bear the thought of anyone making fun of them. However, she demurred when Ivor expressed the intention of refusing food until he died.

"No," she said. "I promise you vengeance. Eat, drink what Tosi brings you. I will return shortly." She was so deep in thought when she got up to return to the hall, she almost forgot to call her escort. Even so, she outpaced Tosi and the rest of the men. They blundered around among the ravines leading down to the river, but she knew the way.

When she came close to the stronghold, Elspeth sent Tosi on ahead. She paused and watched the sun rise over the river. She was sure she knew how to give Hakon the city. Now the only thing left to do was to convince him she could.

Ivor hardly noticed his suffering. Pain had been a part of his life for so long, a background to everything he did, that he felt almost lost in the rare moments when it was absent.

Elspeth sewed his heel back to his foot. Then she softened untanned leather with water and cradled his ankle in it, binding it to his foot with more strips of hide. Ivor found he could walk again after a fashion. He limped badly and the pain in his leg was intense, but he was mobile.

As for the right thumb, there was little Elspeth could do about that, but he was a good left-handed swordsman.

Killing was Ivor's trade and he loved it. It was power and he had been born among the powerless. His mother was a slave. In all his life, she alone had loved him. And the company of battle shamans, the berserks, were the only friends he had ever known. All others turned from him in revulsion and terror.

He was his mother's good fortune, though she did not know it as she suckled the big baby near the hearth of the farmhouse kitchen after he was born. She swore in terror that she had never known a man. The truth was she went in mortal fear of her mistress, the farmer's wife, a hardhanded, hell-raising woman who bullied everyone, including her husband. She only half believed the wretched protestations of the cowering girl clutching the baby to her breast.

And as a result, Ivor was banished to the stables as soon as he was able to fend for himself. He grew up among the animals, more or less treated like one himself. No one noticed that the brooding dark eyes under the overhanging brows were intelligent or that his ugly features reflected pain and loneliness. His head was usually bowed.

The farmstead was his only narrow hellish world. The land was marginal at best. The few years of prosperity the farmer enjoyed after Ivor was born soon gave way to leaner and leaner ones. In the last year Ivor lived there, life for the slaves became a nightmare of abuse and starvation.

He was twelve and larger than most of the grown men. He killed the farmer's wife one night after she nearly beat his mother to death. She was his first killing, and in doing it, he learned the full sweetness of power and revenge.

His mother had been stealing food for him. His big body needed more nourishment than it was being given. He was kneeling in the straw of a stall wolfing the bread and few meat scraps his mother had managed to conceal for him when the farmer's wife burst in on them.

He remembered his mother's face, the look of mute despair in her eyes as she folded her body into a ball, one arm over her eyes to shield them from the strap in the other woman's hand. Surprise and fear distorted by madness framed the farmer's wife's face.

Neither woman paid any attention to him. He might as well have been one of the horses standing in the manger. He watched nearly hypnotized by fear as the strap rose and fell endlessly. Ribbons of scarlet appeared, crisscrossing the back of his mother's dress. She began to whimper and then scream, each scream a shrill wail that burst from her lips.

He watched as her body twisted and turned, writhing away from the blows. Her blood dripped down, smearing the straw and the fragments of bread and meat she'd stolen for him.

Finally, he reached out and caught the old woman around the body, pinning her arms to her sides and lifting her from her feet. She screeched with an insane fury and began kicking and lashing his calves and thighs with the strap.

He carried her outside where a snowstorm raged. A few steps beyond the barn door and he was ankle deep in snow. The wind hit him, howling louder than the half-insane bundle of bones and fury in his arms. Beyond the barn, the house was a nearly invisible black shape in the blowing ice.

Ivor turned his face to the blast, laughing, holding the old woman full into it. He simply stood there. The blizzard did the rest.

When she no longer struggled, he dropped her, then looked down carefully at her face. A film of ice was beginning to form across the open, glaring eyes. Then he turned and walked back into the barn to do what he could to comfort his mother.

After that, things became better. The farmer freed them. Ivor was his son. Unwanted, unloved, and unacknowledged, but still his son.

There were no marks on the farmer's wife. The farmer said nervously that she must have left the house going to the barn, been caught by the blizzard, and lost her way. No one else on the farmstead said anything at all. She had been well and truly hated.

The farmer gave up the unequal struggle with land that would not yield and moved to the coast to a trading settlement.

Ivor found work enough to keep him and his mother well. His giant strength stood him in good stead. He sailed on his first raid when he was fourteen. It was there he met the group of warriors who devoted themselves to the battle training of the berserks.

He became one of them when the hand of the god struck his face. He became rich on that raid, too. With the booty he brought back, he saw his mother settled with a house and farm of her own. The year she died, he sailed with Hakon.

If she was the only thing he loved, he was sure she was one of the many things he did not understand. Goswentha was kind. Many times, away from the hideous farmstead over which starvation seemed to hover like a specter, he was sure his dour strength was only tolerated for her sake. All in trouble turned to her. The periods of hunger in her youth marked her deeply. She fed all the beggars who came to her door. Her kitchen was always filled with women visiting, complaining, chattering.

Because his loyalty to Goswentha was as much a part of him as his heart, he accepted this. But he hated remembering his brutal childhood. A fiercer woman might have protected him, but she could only give him her gentle love. In some sad way she seemed to understand this, and died with his big hand in hers, begging for his forgiveness. But he had not given it. He had never forgiven anyone who injured him and did not understand the meaning of the word.

The boy who defeated him—Owen—reminded him of her. He had that same strange combination of constant strength and sniveling weakness. He wanted to destroy it. So he limped toward the trees by the riverbank and promised the god his own life if he could kill Owen.

Owen had not thought him worth the killing, but he would realize his mistake.

Ivor sat on the riverbank and sought the trance. Death and the stench of battle were his pleasure. He dreamed of climbing the green hills with the sun scalding the back of his neck, the sword, a blaze of light in his hand, as he waded through the long grass of the raiders' springtime. The farm lay below him, very like where he had been born. The thatched roofs of the main hall, the scattering of outbuildings were no different from the ones where he'd been kenneled like a beast. All were surrounded by a rude wooden palisade.

He dreamed of the frantic terror as the surprised inhabitants tried to flee. He gloried in the knowledge that they had no chance. He and his men were invincible death under the white clear light of the noonday sky.

He went through the half-rotted fence himself. Nothing could stand against the power of the god coursing through his veins. It was sweeter than the love of women, food, or the filled cup.

His hands tore apart the stakes like twigs and his sword drank blood. And he killed everything that stood before him as he had vowed. All the men at the wall and then the women and children, dragged screaming from the flaming longhouse to be slaughtered in the yard. Everything his hands touched died, and that was power. They chopped down even the beasts in their stalls—the cattle, horses, sheep, and even the dogs. They took what they wanted and destroyed what they did not. That was power.

And the god-given madness, the hate set him free of pain. It left the ruined side of his face, the burning cut in the heel, and his hand. He walked to the stronghold and asked Elspeth what he must do.

The marshy wooded land that protected the city's flanks from attack lent cover to the man moving quietly by night. The palisade terminated in an earthen bank and then the river. Ivor simply waded around it as Elin had. No large force or even a small raiding party could clip past because the dock was guarded. Most of the merchants, like Judith's father, had their own armed retainers to keep watch. Torches lighted the small bay and the dock where the ships dropped anchor.

Ivor wore a heavy woolen mantle, carried a wooden staff, and was almost invisible in the darkness. It was child's play.

The night was cold and the guards were gathered around their fires. Ivor simply walked by them. Only one challenged him, and Ivor dropped to a crouch and in a whining tone begged alms of the man.

The soldier caught a glimpse of his ruined face, half hidden by the folds of the mantle, and whispered, "By the holy Christ." He threw him a coin and said, "Get away from here, foul one. The bishop feeds all on the cathedral porch every morning. Hurry or you'll get nothing." Ivor scrambled convincingly for the coin, then bent and, leaning on the staff, went limping on his way.

The first light was in the sky when he reached the cathedral. The beggars were gathered in one corner out of the wind, huddled in a ragged group near the door of the bishop's house. Ivor took a position by one of the pillars and studied his companions covertly.

One was a toothless graybeard with a mane of white hair whose faded blue eyes stared into emptiness. His lips moved constantly as he spoke to someone only he could see. Ivor dismissed him.

Fortunatas, the drunkard, crouched next to the old man. He was filthy as usual, but bright-eyed and alert. Two women, both ragged, stood a little apart from the men. One woman had a baby at her breast. Fortunatas said something to the nearest, and she drew her skirts away from him disdainfully and turned her back.

The drunkard scooted himself along on his backside until he sat next to Ivor and shouted at the woman, "You loved me when I had money."

"No," she replied. "I loved the money."

Fortunatas got a good look at Ivor's face under the hood of his mantle. "Felicitations, friend. I have not seen you here before."

"No," Ivor said shortly.

"That face of yours is a wonderful thing. Is it real or a

trick designed to squeeze the silver from pious folks' pockets?"

Ivor had lived with his face a long time, but time had not made it easier to bear. He glared at Fortunatas with one eye. "Is my face, then, a beggar's fortune?"

"It is indeed of most monstrous ugliness," Fortunatas said cheerfully. "But I have seen as much done with a little paint and putty."

Ivor's voice was a basso profundo, disturbing as a small earthquake. "No paint and putty made this," he said, pointing to his one dead eye, "but the hard end of a mace."

Fortunatas sighed. "I had hoped you were a master trickster and I might learn a few new ones."

"Indeed," Ivor said. "I do know a few tricks. One is to place my thumbs below eyes that see too much and pop them out of their sockets."

Fortunatas hopped his backside quickly away from Ivor in the direction of the muttering graybeard.

"Another similar feat of legerdemain may be performed on the tongues of those who talk too much. The root of that organ that gives us speech is particularly soft and mushy. Pull it out, then aim a well-directed blow at the chin of the offender. I," Ivor boasted, "have deprived two or three prattling bastards of . . ." He broke off as Fortunatas moved out of earshot on the other side of the old man.

Ivor found himself alone again. He pulled the mantle more tightly around him and bent his head to shield his face from any casual scrutiny. Hakon had promised him a diversion, and he set himself to wait for it.

It was going to be a gray cold day. The light grew brighter, but the overcast above remained unbroken. Still, Ivor decided there would be no more rain. The clouds were high and furrowed and showed none of the threatening plumpness of storm clouds.

The wind was harsh and blew constantly, funneled by the narrow streets into the square, whistling and moaning around the pillars of the cathedral porch. Even Ivor, big as he was, felt its bite through the heavy wool. The two women turned their backs to it miserably. Fortunatas and the old man contrived to squeeze themselves into the narrow alcove where the cathedral wall jutted out from the bishop's residence.

Finally, Anna and Alfric came out to feed the beggars. She went to the two women first, giving them bread, cheese, and some hot cereal from the kitchen. Then the old man took his portion and limped into the cathedral to eat where it was warmer and out of the wind.

Fortunatas came forward and crouched at her feet. Anna set a bowl before him. He grabbed the food and ran into the church laughing.

Alfric walked toward Ivor asking, "Are you in need, friend?"

Anna eyed Ivor suspiciously. Something about him disturbed her. "He hasn't applied to us."

Ivor inwardly cursed the priest's nosiness. The last thing he wanted to do was attract any attention to himself, and he wanted no part of the bread and salt of the man he was going to do his best to destroy.

He went to his knees, head bowed, not wanting Alfric to see his face. "No," he said, moderating the steel trumpet of his voice as much as possible. "I was wounded and thought, being on the mend, simply to take the air."

"A blessing then," Alfric said, "that you may be whole soon and comforted by good health. But it is strange. I assisted many after the fighting, but I don't remember you."

Ivor raised his face, keeping the ruined cheek covered by the mantle, and met Alfric's eyes. He felt a shock of recognition, for the face was Goswentha's. Or rather it had the same thing shining in it as hers had. And he felt sometimes as he had felt when he saw her among her friends—like an outcast standing in the cold and darkness peering into a warm, bright room filled with laughter and love. It was a place he did not understand, and from which he was forever barred.

Alfric's eyes were brown but clear and reminded Ivor of a forest well whose depths are dark but filled with sweet water transparent in the sunlight. The round face of the little priest was very ordinary, yet the corners of his mouth turned up slightly, seemingly always about to smile or laugh. It almost made even Ivor's lips twitch with good humor.

Ivor felt a wave of defeat flow through him, bitter defeat and then anger. Those eyes might, like his mother's, fill with pain or sorrow, but they would never glare at him with hatred or rage, even if he killed the little man standing before him, something he could easily do, even in his present crippled state. All he would see in those clear, dark eyes would be a look of pained surprise.

Then Alfric smiled radiantly and raised his hand over Ivor's head. "No matter that we have not met. I am a gossipy old fool who wants to know everyone. May the Lord Christ bring you the consolation of His love in sickness or in suffering." His lips moved slightly in the Latin of the blessing.

Ivor eased himself back against the pillar. He was, as Enar had been warned not long ago, not a stupid man. He tried to analyze the effect Alfric had on him but found he didn't want to. Sufficient that whatever he saw in Alfric's face spoiled the pleasure of revenge. No one else paid any attention to him. As he crouched against the pillar, trying to make himself small, he began to seethe with fury. Where was Hakon's diversion?

Judith came clattering up the stone street on a horse. She was accompanied by three of her men. She jumped off, cursed horses in general as a means of transportation, and ran into the hall, rubbing her backside. The three men of her escort stood near the door trying to look casual. No one who had seen Judith's rapid progress tried any acting at all.

Within a few minutes, a crowd had gathered around the bishop's place. The widow and her ladies nearly knocked Ivor from his seat on the church steps in their haste to cross the porch and reach the bishop's door.

The news spread the way ripples fly outward in a circle from a stone thrown into the water. Men ran home to tell their wives, wives to bring the news to their husbands. The shops closed. The food sellers vanished. The benches in front of the tavern emptied as people rushed away to spread the story.

Ivor got it from the widow. He plucked at her mantle as she ran past. "Hakon, the raider chief, wants to parley."

Ivor settled back. The perfect thing, it would give him the time he needed. Everyone would be at the wall.

He watched the household file out an hour later. Elin had taken care that all were dressed in their best clothing so as to make the most impressive show possible.

Alfric led the procession off, holding up the big silver cross. Elin followed, escorted, as was proper, by Godwin and her ladies. Godwin wore a rather magnificent old garment of red velvet with golden embroidery. It made a brave show. However, as Judith noted on closer examination, it had seen much better days.

"Good heavens," she remarked as they walked past. "This was once trimmed with fur. What happened to it?"

Godwin sighed. "When I took ship for Francia, I passed through London. King Alfred and I were no longer on speaking terms. I had to get some money to feed my horses."

"Hush, Judith," Elin said. "Cease troubling Godwin. Let us go and speak to Hakon. Futile though it may be."

Elin wore a simple blue gown with a white veil. Judith had managed to belt this with a ring of golden plates and press a diadem of rubies on her head. Rosamund and Ingund were by her side. Elfwine and Anna followed, with Anna carrying the baby. Ranulf remained behind alone to guard the square.

Ivor stood up slowly, trying to give the impression of age and decrepitude. He approached Ranulf with shuffling steps, leaning heavily on the staff. But for the two of them, the square was empty. The only sound beside Ivor's scraping footfalls was the high, shrill whistling of the wind.

Ranulf was jumpy and preoccupied. Before he left, Godwin had warned him to be on his guard. He was sure Hakon's offer was a ruse.

Ivor was only a few feet away when Ranulf realized he was there. "Sir," Ivor said, "I would have speech with you."

Ranulf turned, alarmed, and his hand fell to his sword hilt. Ivor swung the staff in a whistling arc at his head. It connected with a crack on Ranulf's temple and cheek-bone. Ranulf went to his knees, stunned but still trying to draw the sword.

Ivor scrambled awkwardly up the last few steps to reach him. This time he used his fist and Ranulf lay quietly, his cheek in a spreading pool of blood. Ivor stood listening, but there was no sign that the archers had heard anything. Ranulf had fallen without a sound. Ivor limped down the steps in front of the door and into the alleyway that led to the back garden.

Chapter

35

*A*LFRIC stood at the palisade beside Elin. He, too, wondered why the raider chief was paying them a visit. Hakon seemed to have little new to say, and Alfric felt bluster and threats would have little effect on the city's now battle-hardened citizens. He became aware of a tug on his mantle. He looked down and saw Fortunatas trying to get his attention. He jumped down, a little frightened by the alarm in the beggar's face. "What's wrong?" he asked.

Behind him he could hear Elin's halting speech as she laboriously tried to take the path of reason with Hakon.

"The large man," Fortunatas gasped. "The one who said he was not a beggar."

"Yes," Alfric prompted.

"He is a most fierce, dangerous man," Fortunatas stammered. "He did not leave the square with the rest."

Alfric's head snapped back and he looked around. The whole city must be at the walls. "Oh," he whispered to himself. "Oh sweet merciful God, I am a fool." He realized there was no need to answer Hakon. He was only here to draw them away from the fortress and the hall.

Alfric turned to Godwin standing above him and hissed, "This is a trap. A trick of some kind. Come." The little priest ran up the street in the direction of the inner

keep. Godwin had too much respect for his judgment not
to follow.

Rosamund ran after him. She had been watching his face.
He puzzled her. She had never been treated so strangely by
a man. Usually they took what they wanted and were gone,
but he had spoken to her pleasantly of many things she
didn't really understand and then dismissed her. She wasn't
used to kindness and consideration, but he had shown her
both. So when he went flying up the street behind Alfric,
she followed. Hampered by her skirts, she wasn't as fast as
the men.

Alfric, despite his smaller size, had a head start on
Godwin, so he reached the top of the street first. He saw
Ranulf lying on the top step of the hall. When both men
reached the fallen boy, Alfric knelt down and touched his
cheek. "He still breathes," he said.

"But for how long?" Godwin asked. "I should never
have dubbed him or accepted him into my service." Then
he looked quickly around the empty, silent square. "Who?
And why?"

"The food stores," Alfric said, pointing at the big doors
in front of them, "at the back."

Godwin threw open the door and went flying across the
big room followed by Alfric and Rosamund. They all
smelled the smoke before they got the back doors open.

Ivor stood in the yard by the cellar entrance, smoke
pouring out behind him. When he saw Godwin's drawn
sword, he knew he could get no farther. He threw the
mantle aside and drew his own blade.

"The devil," Godwin said, looking at Ivor's shattered
face. He leaped from the low porch into the yard, yelling
at Alfric, "Sound the alarm! Get someone here to fight the
fire."

Ivor planted himself in front of the cellar door and
cried, "Come, Jarl Godwin! You must get me away first."

Something inside the cellar exploded, and flames leaped
from the open door at Ivor's back.

"It's too late," Alfric said in an agonized voice. "Too
late."

"We don't know that," Godwin snarled. "Sound the

alarm." As he crossed swords with Ivor, steel rang on steel. Godwin struck, but Ivor parried. The force of his blow threw Godwin back a few paces. Godwin looked surprised at the strength of the man, but he was frantic to get him out of the doorway.

He crouched and came in low, aiming a vicious slash at Ivor's leg. He underestimated both the Viking's strength and speed. Ivor caught Godwin's blade with his own, and his crippled right hand slammed into Godwin's left temple.

Godwin went down as Ranulf had, stunned. He hit the cobbles of the yard, and Ivor pinned his sword arm with his good foot and raised his weapon for the killing stroke.

It never landed. Rosamund, standing beside Alfric on the steps, seemed to take wing. She leaped on Ivor's back, viciously clawing at his one good eye. Instead of killing Godwin, Ivor slammed backward with the sword. It connected with a slapping sound on the side of Rosamund's head, but miraculously she still clung to him. Ultimately, her fingers found the eye.

Ivor, blinded not by Rosamund's fingers but by his own protective reflex, staggered away from Godwin and the door and bucked like an infuriated horse. Rosamund landed in a limp and bloody heap in one corner of the yard.

Alfric still held the processional cross. He slammed it down on Ivor's back and realized that he was not dealing with a crippled, slow-moving man. Ivor turned and slashed at him savagely with the sword.

Alfric leaped back. Their eyes met again. "Still taking the air?" Alfric smiled.

Ivor felt again that same shock of recognition. He roared with fury and swung. Alfric lifted the cross, and sparks flew from it as the top above the Christus was sheared off by Ivor's sword.

He danced away behind Ivor and smashed him across the kidneys with the cross's iron probe. Ivor screamed, partly in rage, partly in pain. Alfric kept turning, moving, slowly easing Ivor away from Godwin.

There were more explosions from the cellar, and men were running into the yard from the square. Godwin had recovered and was more interested in fighting the fire than in downing Ivor. The crowd gathered around them, none bold enough to approach closely.

But Alfric and Ivor concentrated on each other. Somehow both knew it was between them now. Ivor glared at the little priest with insane rage. The ruined face was a distorted mask of hatred.

Alfric slowly circled Ivor, the cross held low in front of him. His eyes locked with Ivor's. The hatred, the impotent rage he saw in them sickened his soul.

Suddenly, Ivor raised the sword in his hand over his head. He swung it around and threw it at Alfric, point first. The men in the crowd scattered and the priest leaped back, raising the cross in front of his face in what seemed a futile effort to save himself as the blade flashed at his chest.

The point struck the body of the figure on the cross. It hit the chest, and the silver of the image dented and gave, sending the sword spinning harmlessly away into the air. It landed on the stone of the yard with a final metallic cry as though stricken by Ivor's defeat. Alfric looked down at the cross in disbelief, saying softly, "I never thought you would take it so personally."

Ivor drew his knife and staggered down the alley toward the square. People made way for him, staying well out of Ivor's reach as he slashed out with the knife. Alfric plunged after him.

Ivor was too slow, and the wrappings on the brace of hardened leather on his heel were beginning to loosen. As he reached the square, Alfric tripped him with the cross, and he went down with a crash. He rolled but found he couldn't rise again. His foot wouldn't hold him.

Alfric chopped down with one arm of the cross and knocked the wind out of him. Then he pinned his throat with the top and crosspiece the way the head of a serpent is pinned by a forked stick. Ivor tried to strike at his own heart with the knife, but the ring mail he wore defeated the first stroke and he only sliced his own ribs. Then three men fell on his good arm and wrestled away the knife.

Godwin and Edgar fought the fire from below. Godwin ran down the steps throwing bucket after bucket of water on the flames. The fire raged around him in the darkness, consuming the sacks of wheat, the dried meats, fruit and vegetables that were the town's safety. He fought the flames in murk and darkness, in the stifling ovenlike heat.

The smoke was so thick it was impossible to see, but he staggered into it again and again until his knees began to give way and he was so nauseated he fell at the blacksmith's feet retching violently.

Gunter pulled him out of the way and joined Edgar down below.

When Elin reached the hall, Elfwine was crouched over Ranulf, screaming, and smoke was pouring from the open door. Elin shoved Ingund toward the well. She had no time for the fallen boy.

"We must flood the place," Anna said. She ran into the smoke, got a spear, and began poking holes through the mortar between the flagstones to let the water rain down on the fire below. Elin and Anna poured water over the floors and soaked down the lower walls and beams.

But the fire was winning, at least near the door. The oil was stored there and it burned on, untouched by the water. The heat of the stones seared Elin's feet as she ran carrying bucket after bucket into the room, but when the flags shifted under her, she grabbed Anna and screeched at Ingund near the door to back away.

Ingund looked down and saw tongues of flame poking up between the stones and fled. The front part of the flooring nearest the door let go, sending blocks of stone and broken wood into the inferno below. The flames leaped through the whole, charring the door and threatening the whole building.

Elin screamed, "No!" but Anna said, "Earth. Such a fire needs earth, not water." She began snatching up every container she could find and handing them out to the men and women in the yard to fill from the garden.

And that was how they won.

The heat near the oil jars was so intense, the smoke so thick, that none could remain there long, but they took turns. The women from above, the men below, heaved the baskets and pots of dirt and sand on the flaming oil.

Godwin and Edgar wet their mantles and ran at the fire, any uncovered skin on the backs of their hands and faces blistering in the radiant heat. Siefert brought hides from his tannery, and they threw them on the flaming oil that lay in pools between the broken jars. Those still intact they stoppered with hides covered by dirt and gravel, until at last they staggered from the reeking darkness as the victors. No more flames glowed anywhere.

Elin sat on the back steps of the hall, sobbing wildly with her fist pounding on her knee. Her gown was blackened by soot. The belt of golden plates was gone. A half dozen of the other women surrounded the fallen Rosamund. Godwin retched and coughed. "How is she?" he asked of Rosamund.

Ingund walked toward them, wringing out a wet cloth. She began to wash Elin's face roughly. "Stop wailing and be still," she commanded Elin. "You and Godwin have lordship here now. You must speak to the people. As for Rosamund, she is bereft of her wits. She hit her head hard. We must wait until they return."

"Oh, sweet savior," Godwin moaned. "Imagine the likes of her defending me. Who could have thought it?"

"Indeed," Ingund said. "It was the most foolish day of Rosamund's life when she got between you and that thing. He is a prisoner in the square. Alfric is holding him, trapped like a snake, by what remains of the cross. His name is said to be Ivor Halfdemon or some such."

When she had control of herself again, Elin got to her feet. Godwin followed and together they strode toward the square where Ivor lay waiting. Alfric, his chest heaving with exertion, held Ivor beside the fountain. All the townspeople surrounded them, staring in despair at the thinning smoke still streaming from the doors of the hall.

Elin paused when she reached the square and met the people's eyes. She felt a sense of shock run through her. They were not the same people who had gawked at her when she rode into town beside Owen what seemed like ages ago. They had fought first the count, then the Vikings. Both engagements they'd won. They were not to be patronized or even led. They were ready now to face the ultimate with her.

Ivor glared up at her furiously with one eye. "They told me of you, witch woman. All said you were deep in the bishop's councils."

"Yes," Elin answered.

Ivor laughed. The deep coarse rasp of his voice echoed through the square. "Your day is over, witch, over as mine is. You are doomed. You and all the people who follow you. He is captured forever by the Bretons, the magus Elutides, and he will be husband to the girl, Gynneth. Their kingdom comes with her, and he has proven himself worthy to be her husband."

Elin's summer twilight eyes burned blue. Her face went white.

"You know the names?" Godwin murmured to Elin.

"Yes," she replied. "Elutides is indeed a great man, and if he wants Owen for his niece, likely he will win him."

"Perhaps you underestimate Owen," Godwin said.

"This will cost you your life. Do you so willingly lay it down for Hakon?" Elin asked Ivor.

"Not for Hakon," Ivor roared, "but for the bishop. My curse I lay on him to take all he loves!" He shouted and struggled against the heavy silver cross that held him to the stones. He kicked and thrashed, hammering his one good hand against the cobbles. So obvious was the sheer physical might of the man, even in defeat, that the people nearest backed away, still frightened that he might yet find a way to break free.

Ingund and her father, Gunter the blacksmith, had separated themselves from the crowd and stared down at Ivor. "We are done," Gunter said. "We have no choice but to fight now."

"My life," Ivor cried out in anguish. "The bishop Owen gave me my life. My life to live a cripple, scorned by all." He spat at Elin. "Truth to tell, he didn't think me worth killing. When he hears of his love's fate and the city's, he will know how much of a mistake he made."

In her heart, Elin felt the darkest despair she had ever known. All was lost—Owen and the city both. "I believe . . .

I believe that Owen would return if he could, but he can't, and we must stand alone." She stared at Ivor. "You have your revenge," she said in a matter-of-fact voice.

He looked away from her up at the gray sky. He felt the cold wind on his face and the stone under his back. "I am avenged and content with things as they are. You will walk one and all in the bishop's dreams. Each one marking his failure. He, Owen, will wither and die in the Breton girl's arms."

"I think not," Elin answered ringingly. "Your words are thistledown to be swept away by the winds of morning. They are written in dew and vanish with the sunlight. My geas is stronger than yours, Ivor Halfdemon. Die now." Then she turned her red-rimmed eyes to the people in the square. "He is yours. Take him."

Godwin walked over to Ivor and put his foot down on his good wrist, grinding it into the cobbles. He seized Ivor by the hair and jerked his head back.

It looked as though Godwin was going to cut his throat, and a voice from the crowd cried, "Not so quickly." Godwin looked up at the speaker and smiled. Actually, he bared his teeth. "No, not quickly at all." He slit Ivor's nose, slicing from the bridge down the nostril and pulled Ivor's head further back.

Alfric looked away. He'd seen this done before. The blood would run down inside the nose and throat, slowly strangling the victim to death.

As that began to happen to Ivor, he started to struggle, this time desperately. He tried to cough the blood out of his lungs. It sprayed from his mouth, reddening his lips and tongue. He tried to club savagely at Godwin with his free hand.

Godwin smiled and jerked his head back even further. Ivor's face turned blue. He gurgled, his body heaving spasmodically as he struggled to get air past the blood in his lungs.

Alfric couldn't stand any more. Still holding Ivor pinned, he kicked out, catching Godwin's shoulder with his heel, and sent him sprawling.

Ivor raised his head, spewing blood from his mouth and

drew one gasping, whistling breath after another, sobbing with the relief of being able to breathe.

Godwin, no sooner down, was up again, knife in hand facing Alfric. His face was chalk white under the fury in his eyes.

Alfric's stare locked with his. "No, damn your own soul if you must, but not mine for helping you."

"Priest," Godwin hissed, "interfere with me again and you're a dead man."

Alfric's gaze remained steady. "Confront me with something I fear," he said quietly. "I am an old man. You will not have much satisfaction of the deed. Only send me to my maker a little sooner. I will go clean. Not with blood on my hands."

Godwin's fingers tightened on the knife, but his attention was diverted by a woman who pushed her way through the crowd. The rage in his face was so palpable that she quailed from him. "Lord Godwin, the girl, Rosamund . . . she asks for you," the woman stammered. "I think she is dying."

"You owe Rosamund your life," Alfric said, his stance still calm.

Godwin's chest heaved twice as he mastered himself and his anger. Then he sheathed the knife and followed where the woman led. Rosamund still lay where she had fallen but appeared composed with her dress down and her hands folded on her breast. He knelt down beside her.

She looked up at him. "My neck is broken," she said. "I can't feel my body at all, but they won't move my head and let me die. I asked for you because I knew you would have the courage to do it. I want it done before I have time to think about it too much and become afraid. Do you understand?"

He did understand and the girl was right. She couldn't live in this state. "Yes," he answered. "I will do it."

"Thank you," Rosamund said. She bit her lip. "I've ruined my nice dress. Will the Lady Elin think me ungrateful?"

Elin moved to Godwin's elbow. "No," she said softly. "I don't think you ungrateful."

Godwin placed the palms of his hands on either side of Rosamund's face. Elin turned away as Rosamund's eyes widened and her lips quivered.

Godwin knew she was very much afraid, and he cursed himself for not being able to alleviate the pain at least a little. "Rosamund . . ." he began.

"Give my gold to the poor, for that is where a whore's money should go," she said quickly. "All but my earrings. Please let me keep them. Bury me with them. Promise."

"You have my word," Godwin said.

Her eyes swam with tears. "Now. Please hurry," she pleaded.

Godwin felt someone holding his wrists. He tore his eyes from Rosamund's face to see who stopped him. Rosamund's own hands clutched his. The reprieve made him laugh, and he raised his hands, palms joined, before Rosamund's eyes so she could see where her fingers were.

"Oh God," she whispered. "Oh God be praised." A radiance came into her eyes.

"You will not die," Godwin said. "At least I do not think so. You only landed on your neck. Here, rise to your knees."

She did. "I still can't feel them, only tingling."

He began examining her neck with careful fingers. It was swollen but supple. He was more concerned about the blood in her hair above the ear. He searched with his fingers and found a long cut on her scalp. He helped Rosamund sit up. "Can you feel your body now?"

"Yes," she said as she tried to stand with his help. "Everything is spinning."

The woman who had called Godwin earlier ran back into the yard and pulled Elin away. A few seconds later, Godwin heard Elin calling him. He scooped Rosamund up because he didn't want to leave her alone just then, though he couldn't have given a good reason why not.

Elin stood at the entrance of the alley, looking out at the square. "Ranulf was struck hard. He also is alive, but wandering in his wits. Elfwine is with him. Look." Alfric and Ivor had remained at the fountain with Ivor lying against the marble basin and Alfric threatening the mob around him with the battered head of the cross. "Oh Lord," Elin whispered in horror, "he is preaching to them about Christian charity."

"And they are not in a receptive mood," Godwin said.

"He will be killed. Help him. Please, Godwin."

"Help him do what, Elin?" Godwin snarled. "Commit suicide? Those people want blood, and they have a right to it."

The crowd closing slowly in around Alfric wasn't noisy. They were silent, ominously so. Godwin noticed them picking up things—stones, pieces of wood, any refuse they could find. As he watched, a man began to pry up one of the cobbles in the square. A woman nearby turned and began helping him. The idea spread with such speed that it raised the hackles on the back of Godwin's neck.

Ivor lay watching them, his back against the basin of the fountain, arms spread out over the rim on either side. He seemed indifferent to his fate. It was no longer possible for him to run or fight. His good hand was swollen and purple where Godwin had crushed it with his heel. The wrappings around the wounded ankle were completely off now. It drooped forward, leaking still more blood around Elspeth's stitches. The dressings on his thumbless right hand were a gory mess since those wounds had opened in the struggle with Godwin. Someone hurled a piece of roof tile at Ivor. He flinched as it bounced off his chest.

That is how it will go, Godwin thought. He had seen men stoned before. They lived longer than he had believed possible under the savage rain of missiles. This particular one would live longer than most.

Alfric shouted and swung the cross around in a circle driving the crowd back. "He is mine. I defeated him in battle. He is my prisoner. Will you defy the cross of Christ?"

Godwin looked wildly around for help and found it. Ranulf lay on a bench in front of the tavern, his bandaged head in Elfwine's lap, flanked by Gowen and Wolf the Short. In one hand, Gowen had a full pitcher of beer, in the other he tore the meat from the bone of some animal.

Wolf the Short was courteously helping a sweet-faced old woman pry up one of the stones near the bench.

Godwin drew his sword and shouted, "You two, here to me." They came at a run. He set Rosamund on her feet and thrust her into Elin's arms. "Follow me," he ordered the knights. "We must help Alfric."

Gowen stared at him, incredulous. "Were you struck on the head in the fighting?" Wolf the Short took the pitcher of beer from Gowen, emptied it, slapped his stomach, and gave a resigned belch. Edgar appeared at his elbow, and they pushed their way through the mass of people crowded around Alfric.

The mob backed away, particularly far away from Gowen, who stared at them and continued to tear the meat from the bone. Godwin took a position next to the panting Alfric. He raised his arms in a gesture to command silence. "The priest speaks the truth. He conquered the raider and the man belongs to him."

An inarticulate snarl of rage rose from every throat in the crowd. Godwin felt cold fear in his belly. If the mob decided they wanted the pirate, not even the strength of his men would prevail.

"Wait!" he shouted. "Many of you know Alfric. He is a true and loving servant of God and God's people."

The old woman whom Wolf the Short had been assisting stepped forward, clutching the cobblestone in her hands. "It is only the love we feel for him that has saved that creature till now." She pointed at Ivor. "Kill him!" she screeched. She heaved the stone and it landed near him with a crack.

"No." Alfric stretched out his arms in a gesture of supplication. "Would you send a man like yourselves to face the justice of God in his sins, unbaptized? Unshriven?"

Another cry of fury rose from the people around. "Have done," someone shouted. "Give him to us. The lady gave him to us." A dozen voices, then a hundred took up the cry, and the front rank began to advance on Godwin and the knights.

Gowen threw the bone aside, drew his sword in a leisurely manner, and roared above the noise of the mob.

"Stop." He pointed at Alfric. "He is going to baptize that." His arm swung to Ivor. "I must see this."

Silence fell. It seemed others were of the same mind as Gowen. The spectacle might be even more entertaining than stoning the raider to death.

Godwin turned to Ivor. "Can you walk?"

"No," Ivor rumbled. "Use that sword and kill me, Jarl Godwin. I can go nowhere."

"Killing is too good for you," Godwin answered. He jerked Ivor forward by the hair to rest on his hands and knees. He brought the flat of the sword down on his back. It landed with a vicious smack, and blood wealed through the coarse rings of the pirate's mail shirt. Again, Godwin lifted the sword and, swinging it two-handed, brought it down with even more force. "If you cannot walk, sow's bastard, crawl."

Ivor shook his head like a tormented beast but didn't move. Godwin raised the sword twice more, bringing it down on Ivor's back. The covering of ring mail was a mass of blood.

"Someone fetch a torch," Gowen suggested cheerfully. "Even a beast will crawl away from fire."

Something seemed to go out of Ivor. The pain was almost too much for him. He no longer felt defiance. All he had left was a kind of brute endurance. He began to move forward, slowly, painfully on his hands and knees. The crowd cleared a path for him.

"To the church," Godwin commanded, smacking him on the shoulder.

For the first time Ivor flinched and turned, crawling slowly toward the portals of the cathedral. If there had been some pleasure in the sport for Godwin at first, it was gone now. He didn't hit the big man again. Missiles, this time small ones, began to rain down on Ivor as he continued his snail's progress toward the church. Bones, spoiled food, and offal of all kinds struck his body. Curses, insults, and taunts rang in his ears.

Gowen got his torch and played at thrusting it at Ivor's face. He cringed away from the flames. This amused the crowd no end and they applauded Gowen, egging him on.

"Well," Godwin said, turning to a white-faced Alfric walking beside him, "you have saved his life and for what? This. I think he might have preferred to die."

The walk behind Ivor was an eternal ordeal for Alfric. All he could do was pray.

At length they reached the baptistry. It was on the church porch protected by double doors. With these thrown open, it was visible to all the square beyond. It was simply a stone basin, rather like the fountain with a thick earthenware pipe in the center, but it possessed its own spring and sweet water flowed down the pipe, filling the basin until it trickled away through a drain below. Ivor collapsed beside the basin on his face.

Gowen coveted his mail shirt. It was a big one, and despite his captures on the battlefield, he had few that would fit him. He stripped it off the unresisting man, then thrust the torch at the good side of Ivor's face. "Get in." He pointed to the basin, shoving the torch so close it singed Ivor's hair.

Ivor crawled over the lip and fell into the water. Alfric stepped forward and helped him lever his body upright against the pipe. The water went scarlet with Ivor's blood, but then as the flow ran down his face and over his bare shoulders, it began to clear. It washed him, cleansing the wounds, taking away the filth down the drains at the foot of the basin and into the river.

Ivor leaned back, eyes closed. A hush fell over the crowd. There was a strange dignity about the giant, and the water itself seemed to befriend him, as though he found in a simple blind force of nature the mercy denied him by men.

He was dreadfully scarred. New wounds and old seamed his body. The pulsing water bared those scars and emphasized them, making some of those nearest wonder how one could live so long and bear such suffering as those white scars proclaimed.

Alfric picked up the silver ewer used for baptisms, filled it at the top of the pipe, and held it to Ivor's lips. He drank greedily.

"I am your friend," Alfric whispered. "I would save both your soul and body if I could."

Ivor looked up into Alfric's face and knew it was true. He took Alfric's right hand with his own mutilated one and closed his fingers around it, bowing his head.

Godwin, who had heard the exchange, said smoothly, "I would not count too much on Alfric's friendship if I were you. It is very cheap. He is the friend of all men."

Ivor raised his head and looked slowly around at the crowd. The faces staring at him seemed to display one degree or another of mirth and savagery. They, Godwin with drawn sword, and Gowen with the torch were what he had always seen. Then he looked back at Alfric, at the compassion and distress in the priest's face. "Is it cheap and easy to be the friend of all men? I do not believe this. I have not found it easy or cheap to be the enemy of all. Very well," he said to Alfric, "yours is the victory, but is your God so strong that He can take away my sins?"

Alfric straightened up, filling the silver vessel again at the top of the pipe. It gleamed and he turned, looking up at the sky. The overcast was blowing away, and through a rift in the clouds the benediction of the sun shone down on the baptismal font and the people around it. He felt the blessing of its warmth on his back.

"Can He wash away my sins?" Ivor repeated.

"Yes," Alfric answered strongly. "There is no spirit He cannot heal. No grief He cannot mend if you have but the heart to let Him." His voice echoed over the silent crowd with the sound of a trumpet, clear and utterly pure in its love and courage. "Say after me," he told Ivor, and he began the beautiful litany of baptism. "I renounce the devil and all his works. Answer 'I do renounce him.' "

Ivor swayed on his knees in the basin of the font and clutched at Alfric's hand now with both of his own. He bowed his head, then raised it and looked helplessly into Alfric's face. "I do renounce him." The words seemed torn from him by some power he saw there.

Alfric continued and the staring people knew now that something was at work that was greater than Alfric, greater than the world, and infinitely greater than death and pain. Ivor's responses grew louder, carrying with them such a freight of conviction and absolute belief that Godwin crossed himself and backed away from what was happening. Gowen extinguished the flames of the torch, rolling it under his foot, not wanting to be caught by the eye of God in his cruelty.

Alfric raised the silver vessel and poured the water saying, "I baptize thee in the name of the Father, Son, and Holy Spirit." And it was ended. The sun went behind the clouds and gloom descended. Ivor withdrew his hands from Alfric's. "Stand back, priest, and let the knight take what is due and that I owe."

Godwin stepped forward, raising his naked sword for the killing stroke, one that would behead Ivor with one blow. He could not do it. His arm froze. The cramp ran in a wave from shoulder to wrist in an instant. Muscles knotted and tendons tightened holding the limb aloft, sword raised above Ivor's bent neck. Godwin's face twisted and darkened. The veins on his forehead distended as he tried with all his strength to break the cramp and send the blade into its lethal descent.

A sound of awe rose from the crowd. People began to fall to their knees. Someone shouted, "A miracle!"

But Alfric was only afraid for Godwin and the torment and effort he saw in his face. He stepped between Ivor and Godwin and caught the upraised arm with both hands. The cramp let go and Godwin's arm relaxed, trembling as he backed away from Alfric and Ivor. He looked at the sword like it was an unclean thing, then sheathed it quickly. "He is, indeed, yours, priest. God wills it."

OWEN woke, sword still in his hand, looking at faint sunlight through a wavering silver curtain. He was lying in a shallow cave behind a waterfall. He twisted himself to his knees and screamed. The scream resounded in the tiny grotto, the echoes falling around him like stones. He howled again, sucking, dragging the breath into his lungs to do so. Even as he did, he realized he wasn't alone.

Sybilla was crouched in one corner. Her small body was curled into a ball. Her pale eyes stared at him desperately.

Owen leaped to his feet. He spat out blood on the stone floor. He turned his burning gaze on her, hating her, hating all living things. "After that awful night," he shrieked, "how can I ever believe in the day again?"

She only stared up at him, uncomprehending.

"Why did you betray me," he screamed at her, "betray me into that darkness?"

"What darkness?" she whimpered. "You wouldn't enter the tree or lie down to rest; you ran through the forest. I followed. I have heard tell of the king's madness, but until I saw you, I didn't understand, didn't know there could be such frenzy."

Owen's frantic eyes darted away from Sybilla and took in the grotto. He realized she was telling the truth. It was nothing but a shallow cave. No passage led away into deeper regions. Owen lurched where he stood, the rage draining out of his body, leaving exhaustion in its wake. He stepped hesitantly toward the rippling, shimmering curtain of water, toward the sunlight he saw shining through it, comprehending, as he did, the mystery. "I am," he said, "betrayed and betrayer at one."

He looked down at his body. His breeches and leggings were slimed with mud and splattered with blood. The blood was his own, dripping from dozens of cuts and gashes inflicted by the thorny undergrowth through which he'd plunged without regard for his skin. His shirt hung in bloody rags from his shoulders.

He stepped forward toward the water, wanting to leave his hurts in its coolness, feel the flowing sweetness wash away the sweat, mud, and blood clinging to his body, longing for its touch to cleanse the wounds in his soul and bring him peace.

"No," Sybilla said, rising to her feet. "They're outside. They followed you. All you need do is remain here."

Owen felt fury rise in his soul again, galvanizing him. "So," he shouted, "they wait for me—the wolf and his cohorts." He lunged forward through the hissing curtain of water, passed through, and found himself standing in a muddy pool. Thick water lily pads clustered at his feet.

The pool lay in a shadowed dell; the waterfall began high above him on the cliff at his back. It meandered down from rock to rock, its mossy, green velvet path encrusted with ferns, the lacy fronds shivering in the moisture of the falls. The ground in front of him sloped upward gradually into a lightly forested amphitheater.

They waited for him in the shadow of the trees, dark figures melting into the deep brown of oak trunks or standing out against the pale shells of aspen and birch. The dogs—a writhing pack of varicolored bodies—plunged toward him first.

Owen's hand tightened around the sword for a second. Then the first hound reached his feet, and he realized they only wanted to fall down and worship him. These weren't fighting dogs, not mastiffs but only hounds. No human could ever be a quarry to them. They bid fair to drown him with their affection as he waded through the pond to shore. They fell fawning at his feet, leaped to lick his hands and face, and pressed against his legs in an ecstasy of devotion.

To real beasts, he thought sadly, a man is ever a god, and, God, how we make them pay for their innocence. Then he had no further time for thought because the beast-men were upon him.

The first to come was a wild boar. Boar, Owen wondered, or Casgob? He had a moment to take in the low ugly snout, the vicious curving tusks. Owen was sick with madness, of madness. The tusks just missed carving him from ankle to groin. The boar gave a quick serpentine turn and lunged toward him again.

You were my brother, Owen thought with a mortal horror clawing at his heart. *I loved you. We fought the berserks together.* His sword was in his hand, and the fighting ferocity of the drug burned in his veins. It deceived his eyes, but in return it gave the blinding speed, the lightning ability to perceive weakness.

He danced lightly away and swung the sword down hard. The flat blade slapped the boar, catching him a stinging blow across the thick haunches. Clutching at his backside, a howling Casgob rolled on the grass before Owen. Owen plunged forward, shouting, waving the sword as a challenge. "I am the master of the battle spell! When have beasts ever been a match for man? I hunt you now!" he screamed exultantly.

The fox and the deer sprang toward him: the deer, with its antlers lowered, the sharp black prongs like so many knives aimed at his belly; the fox, her small sharp teeth snapping at his heels.

Owen ran up the slope toward a thicket of brambles. The splayed menacing stems were armored in long thorns. The deer charged, still seeming to Owen's half-dazed mind to be a deer. The delicate muzzle, the mild eyes belied the cruelty of the lowered antlers, the oncoming weapons.

At the last second Owen dodged to one side. His fist landed like a hammer on the furred shoulder. A second

later a half-naked man tore free of the brambles, screaming, the heavy antlered mask caught among the thorny
stems.

The fox still darted at him, and beyond the brambles the
bear reared, red-eyed, maddened, roaring, his fangs dripping, claws outstretched to take Owen into his embrace.
Owen vaulted a deadfall, putting the thick tree trunk
between himself and the bear.

The bear's claws scratched at his chest. He jumped
aside, away from the reaching claws, and brought the flat
of his sword down hard across the bear's back. Ilfor
screamed and staggered into the brambles. Then he tumbled over and over, down the gentle slope toward the pool
at the foot of the falls. "Unmask!" Owen shrieked at him.
"Drunkard, buffoon, you have no real power."

"I know," the erstwhile bear said as he sat weeping
beside the pool, the useless claws dangling grotesquely at
the end of his arms. "I know, but I think throwing it in my
face is most unkind of you."

The fox was still snapping at him, dodging back into
the bushes or under the brambles. Owen aimed a back-
handed slap at her and sent her sprawling. The fox was
gone and Aud lay on the grass. The russet fox skin lay in a
tangled heap by her face.

"Vixen," Owen said in a voice edged with cold hatred.
"Bitch," he whispered. "The queen has many lovers, but
where are your sons, vixen? The fox is a fine mother to
her cubs, protecting and teaching them. You have neither
cub nor child. Discard your mask, too," he said as she
turned her stricken eyes from his face.

"The wolf is your master."

"Where is the wolf?" Owen shouted.

And the wolf glided out of the trees. While Owen had
struggled with his own darkness, the day was wearing
toward its end. The sun was low and no longer shone
down into these narrow defiles by the sea. From beyond
the hills its last rays flashed on the waterfall, and the
black rocks seemed to be wearing a silken veil. Below, all
lay in shadow.

The wolf paused close to Ilfor where he wept silently at

the edge of the pool that seemed a midnight mirror, the
only light the pale foam bubbling at the base of the
cataract. Owen strode down the slope toward the pool to
confront the wolf, Elutides. He held his sword two-
handed, at the ready in front of him. The giant gray beast
snarled, the wrinkling muzzle drawing back over fangs as
if to say, Now unmask me!

"You tried to make me doubt Elin," Owen said. "Tried
to make me forsake her. But, old man . . ." His voice trembled with the rage in it as he stared at the thing before him
trying, trying desperately to see it as a man and break its
power over his senses and his will. "What have you
loved?" he asked. "I see your sons, but where is your wife?
What have you loved?"

Elutides stood before him, the wolf mask on the ground
at his feet. Of all the beast-men, he alone was armed. He
carried the sword he'd used to fight the berserks. It was in
his hand, his fingers gripping the serpent coils at the hilt.
"I think you may have been foolish to unmask me," he
said. "I was much less dangerous as a wolf."

Owen raised his sword slightly. "Wolf or man," he
said, "I don't fear you as either one. Who did you love?"
he repeated.

A flicker of almost intolerable pain crossed Elutides'
face. "She had red-gold hair," he said. "My sons and I are
dark. They took after me. She didn't even leave that
behind. My happiest dreams are when I dream that I wake
to find that red-gold hair beside me on my pillow, that
morning-fair face, that hair the color of a cloudless sunrise. But they are only dreams. I wake to silence, alone—
as you will one day wake alone. They cannot be captured;
they cannot be held. To clutch them too tightly is to kill
them, to drench the fire of the magnificent dark passion
between you. Yes, I loved a witch. My love was like
yours, given to a lady of the wood, a forbidden sorceress,
and she has spoiled me for all other women."

In the green gloom, the hatred flowed like an icy current between Owen and Elutides. The still air of the
narrow valley was thick with it. "Whining young whelp,"
Elutides whispered. "I will make you pay and pay dearly

for so cruel an unmasking. I will make you pay for so nakedly baring my pain."

"Wise, so wise," Owen said contemptuously, "telling me to be faithless to what I loved so you could use me. 'You will be a great king,' " Owen repeated Elutides' words jeeringly, " 'only let me guide you.' Of what use is the counsel of a liar, a liar playing a cruel farce with a helpless man?"

As Owen brandished the sword, his glance raked them— Ilfor sobbing by the pool, Casgob rubbing his backside, Cador still attired as an eagle but plainly a man, the others still masked, hovering like strange shadows among the trees.

"A pity," Elutides said, "a tremendous pity." He smiled a brief wry smile of satisfaction. "You almost won."

The first missile cracked against the side of Owen's head. Aud threw the second, and the sharp flint gashed Owen's chest. "A curse on you!" she screeched. "A curse on you for reminding me of my barren womb."

"Run, my hero," Elutides taunted. "It is given to the king to see beneath men's masks, but only a fool strips them away."

Owen edged back, retreating from their fury, raising one arm to protect his face against the objects raining down around him. Elutides lifted his sword and advanced toward him.

Owen glanced over his shoulder. Behind him the valley narrowed into a passage between two giant boulders. The ground between them sloped down to the beach. Beyond the rocks, Owen could hear the wash of the sea.

Ahead of him, Elutides and his companions had drawn together in a black knot and were throwing everything they could lay their hands on at him. Rocks, branches, and mud flew at Owen, battering his chest, arms, and legs.

Owen, still half blind with fury, backed up, brandishing his sword. He could do nothing against so many, and he'd seen how quickly Elutides' odd weapon could kill. Almost before he realized where he was, he was on the slope to the beach and his feet were sliding. He looked behind him, and a shock of absolute terror tore through his whole being.

Set below him in the sand was a serried rank of spears, six deep, set at an angle; their glimmering razor-sharp heads awaited his falling body. Owen screamed a full-throated cry of agony and terror. He dropped his sword as he fell, trying to clutch at the grass with his fingers. But the grass, wet with the forest dampness, slid through his clawing fingers. It was no use. He was falling, sliding down faster and faster toward the waiting spearheads.

He howled when he reached them, arching, twisting, trying to pull his flesh away from death. Then he was among them. They broke, scattering around him like the painted willow wands they were. Owen lay perfectly still for a moment, his mind empty of everything but terror and raw shock. It took almost a full minute for his full humiliation to dawn on him as he dragged himself to his feet. It took almost a full minute for the laughter from above to penetrate his shattered consciousness.

He staggered among the broken wands, hands groping for his sword, red murder raging in his brain. He no longer thought. He was as he had been in the square when Gerlos taunted him. Beyond thought, beyond reason. Dimly he realized he was where his journey into this strange land had begun, near the green mound, the king's tomb by the sea.

Elutides stood at the top of the mound, sword in hand, waiting. Owen charged him, bounding up over the grassy surface of the mound, hatred driving him like the wind. He confronted Elutides at the very top. Elutides raised his sword. "My sword is certain death," he said, but there was a strange emptiness in his eyes, a weird, lonely sadness.

Owen didn't answer. His mind had no room for anything but rage. He'd struck no more than two blows when he realized he was stronger than Elutides. Stronger than anything.

He drew that strength from within. He knew what punishment he'd suffered that day. He understood his heedless, headlong attack might finish him, but he knew also he would never yield this side of death. He foresaw the end of this battle even as it began and knew Elutides foresaw it, too. He had loosed something in Owen even he could not contain, and it would destroy him.

Elutides was a fine swordsman. In some corner of Owen's maddened brain, he admired that skill. His sword was quick as the flicker of a serpent's tongue, but Owen's was summer lightning. Elutides couldn't break through Owen's guard. Not the slightest scratch could he give him.

Faster and faster Owen struck, until the crash of iron on iron was a constant resounding din in both their ears and Elutides was beaten back toward the center of the green mound, toward a gray stone, a strange thing carved with spirals and flowers.

Elutides staggered back under the unending savagery of Owen's blows. His heel hit the stone, and Owen's flashing blade hooked the hand guard of his sword and tore it free, sending it spinning up into the air and away, to fall into the foliage of the greenwood surrounding the mound.

Elutides fell. His head struck the stone and he collapsed unconscious, one side of his head smeared with blood, at Owen's feet.

Owen stared down at him. His mouth gulped air into his lungs, his whole body quivering, taut with rage. One word, "death," was all his consciousness. *How many times did I die?* he wondered. *Four times? Five? Once in Osric's cage, three times in darkness at Elin's hands, and once on Elutides' spears. Each time in terror.*

Memory flooded in on him. The pain of his body in the cage. The guilt in his soul as he destroyed what he loved. Again, water filled his lungs as he drowned. Again, he felt the sword in his guts, letting out his life in a scarlet rush, the iron in his body, the final violation. The images he'd seen as he fled through the cave of his own desolation returned. The images of pain, bitterness, shame, and defeat, of a victory that was an agonizing loss, the raw open bleeding wound that was the suffering of all mankind. Mankind—a splinter of awareness among the stars, a brief moment of thought in eternity.

He turned away from Elutides' prostrate body, looking for something—anything—and saw an oak sapling with clean, smooth, gray bark and the shiny, crisp leaves, leaves so deep a green they were almost black. The sword in his hand came whistling down, and the sapling fell, the high green crown separated by one cut at the tiny trunk.

The tree bleeds, Owen thought, his first clear, coherent thought in what seemed like an eternity. *Oh God, the tree bleeds like a man.* And it did, the pale sap oozing from the severed trunk and trickling down to the grass at his feet.

Owen cast his sword down to the ground beside the fallen Elutides and ran for the sea. He felt unclean, filthy, befouled beyond words. God, he could smell the stench of his shame on his own body, in the effluvia of vomit, sweat, and excrement that soiled every inch of his skin.

As it had before, the sea cleansed him, dealing quick thrusts of pain to his cuts and scratches, then a healing numbness. It welcomed with a bitter, icy embrace, then warmed him.

His mind was a jumble of images. Images of destruction—the grinning thing in the cave, Elutides lying bleeding in the grass, Elin's face turning into a skull, the darkness, the darkness all around him. Elutides had shown him the pit that lay at the bottom of his own mind—the sewer, the swamp, the very cloaca of night.

The king's journey. Journey to what? To where? His mind struggled furiously with it as he stared out over the ocean. He need not have finished the journey; he knew that. Despite his rage at Elutides for tormenting him, he might have remained in the grotto with Sybilla, might have escaped this last and worst, might have escaped and still be proclaimed the victor.

The sea around him was silent, the only sound a soft whistling, the endless cry of the wind in his ears. The sky was tiled with clouds. Their edges glowed as the sun struck down long shafts of light between them. The billows were calm, rolling in long, smooth, shallow swells, the water gleaming with the luminescent polish of old silver.

Tell me, he implored. *Tell me. Is this all? I want to*

know. His mind screamed in wild rebellion at the empty, silent sea and sky, the empty, silent universe. *Tell me. I want to know.*

It took him by surprise because it came so quietly. Not a vast fiery light, but an illumination. It came and was upon him before his stunned mind could grasp that it was upon him, and he understood at last the full meaning of the words "Be still and know that I am God."

Love is the light of the heart.

Thought is the light of the mind.

They were both unveiled to him then by a mind vast enough to create the manifold complexities of the universe, illumined by the glory of an infinite and everlasting love, and the love was handed to him like a gift.

Is there any sound that can suggest a silence? If so, that sound should be placed here, because God is known in silence. Not an empty silence, but a living silence like that of a great tree or a forest, beautiful under the benediction of the morning light, the silence of the sea moving beneath the stars, the silence that accompanies a kiss of love, the silence of an infant's first leap in the womb, the first stirring as it begins its journey toward life and light, the silence of a heart's passionate quest transcending all words.

Words tumble after one another, their sound meaningless as the clatter of stones in a landslip. Words as meaningless as is the darting of minnows in a pond, the sparkle of God's delight in the sun. For speech is shared meaning, and Owen knew no one who had ever experienced what he was experiencing could truly share or even understand it.

Elutides had said it is given to the king to see beneath the mask, and he had. He had looked through the mask the world wears and seen that it was a song of praise—praise to a maker whose love was boundless enough to reduce the sea he stood in to a teardrop in the eye of time, a love boundless enough to reduce all human suffering, all human evil to pale shadow. And when the noon sun shines, even those shadows disappear.

Thought is the light of the mind.

Love is the light of the heart.

Pure light shown on him, in him and through him, and

he was transparent to it. As transparent as pure water is to sunlight, translucent as the fragile petals of a flower are to the glory of the day, and all of creation is but a magnificent stained glass, a jeweled window to the sight, to the light of God.

Then slowly, as quietly as a sun disappears behind a cloud, it left him. Left him not anguished or grief stricken, not emptied but filled, brimming with that unutterable tranquillity that is the peace of God. Owen stood in silence, within and without, his mind emptied of all visions but his vision of absolute glory, his heart at peace, his troubled, tumultuous spirit at last at rest.

There was a sadness in him as there had been in the cathedral when he had reached so high before, because he knew one day he would speak of this to others and try to tell them what he had seen, what he had known. But he knew no words would ever convey it. Words would not come to the end of it—they would not even reach the beginning—and so he would fail. If he could bring to their hearts, their minds, their lives, even a glimmer, a touch of that transcendent grandeur, he would count his life, his priesthood, himself fulfilled. So his heart was at peace.

When at length he turned toward the shore, Elutides stood waiting for him. There was blood on his face and clean clothing over his arm. Alshan was beside him. The look in Elutides' eyes as he gazed at Owen was one of simple kindness, the look one gives to a beloved friend who has endured some suffering and at last, at long last, triumphed.

Alshan handed Owen his sword. Owen sheathed it, then looked down at the glowing ruby hilt resting in its scabbard. "It's heavy," he said.

"The weight of manhood," Elutides said, "the weight of responsibility."

Owen turned toward Elutides. "Weren't you afraid I'd kill you?" he asked.

A shadow of pride and suffering crossed Elutides' face. "Owen," he said, "the journey is real, real as is the journey of life. Despite some mummery, the pain must be real and the death, if it comes, must be real also."

"By the time I was halfway through the journey, I'd forgotten why I wanted the victory," Owen said.

"And by the time you finished it," Elutides said, "you understood what victory really is."

"Yes," Owen said softly, "I do. I can't tell what else I know, but I know that."

"You know many things," Elutides said. "Real knowledge is like a tree. It has small beginnings but grows larger and larger until it is always with us, our life's companion. Few have the courage to take the journey you took, fewer still the courage to complete it. So I cannot tell you what you know, only that it will follow you, guide you all the days of your life." He extended the clothing to Owen. "Here, bathe in the sea and then dress."

"Here?" Owen asked, because he saw Ilfor, Aud, and the others. They rested a little beyond the beach. A cloth was spread on the grass and they shared bread, cheese, and wine. The discarded masks lay in a scatter around them.

Alshan shook his head. "No one will see the king or even acknowledge he exists until he is ready. Wash yourself in the healing waters that lap at the world's margins. Be at peace."

Owen stared at Alshan as if seeing him for the first time. In a way he was, for the power of his awesome experience hadn't completely left him. He saw beneath the simple clothing that leader who had had the courage to search out an alliance with a lord alien to his own people, a lord he knew must have at times despised him and his timid kind. Alshan, whose wisdom succored and protected him throughout his long journey. Alshan, a friend.

It made what he had to say even more difficult. "A king?" Owen said. "And of what am I king?"

Alshan smiled and Owen saw in the brown wrinkled face, in the gentle eyes, a glimmer of the eternal light he had seen as he stood in the sea. "From beyond words," Alshan said, "is the word made manifest, and a king's words are always heeded."

"Very well," Owen answered. "The child, Elin's child is mine. I will not allow it to be fostered among you."

"It will be as you say," Alshan answered, "for who can deny the king, but . . ." The little man fingered the jewel at his breast. "You should know, because Elin's father feared us so much . . . he lost her. Had he allowed us a share in her rearing, she would never have felt the need to flee to us, to learn our secrets. For be this child boy or girl, we can be its allies as we have been yours and can teach it many useful things."

Owen took the rebuke in good part.

"Don't answer now," Alshan continued. "When the child is born and when it has reached an age to be fostered we will speak again."

"Very well." Owen smiled. "We will decide the child's future together." Then he turned and gave himself to the sea. He'd washed and almost finished dressing himself when he saw Enar coming, mounted on the stallion. The big red horse cantered along the beach and came to a stop at Owen's side.

Enar sat in the saddle, his fingers locked around the pommel, a glassy stare in his eyes. The stallion shook his head and waited.

Owen pulled his tunic over the linen shirt and studied Enar carefully. "Aren't you going to get down?" he asked.

"No," Enar answered in a distant voice. "I'm waiting for permission to dismount." The stallion nuzzled Enar's foot gently. Enar leaped from the saddle and staggered away. "My legs ache at the groin," he said, "and I am rubbed raw in some very tender places. And how do I find you? Taking the air by the sea. No doubt . . ." He shot a glance at Elutides and his companions seated near the mound. "No doubt," he continued wrathfully, "walking off the comfortable dinner you shared with your friends."

"You're a bit late," Owen said, belting on his sword.

"What happened?" Enar asked, eyeing the masks spread out on the ground around Elutides and his friends.

"Nothing so terrible," Owen said. "Someday . . . someday I'll tell you, but not now."

Enar looked at Owen and then quickly away. There was something in his eyes that reminded him of Elutides' music, a serenity, a beauty so profound they were almost frightening.

"I have heard of such rites," Enar said haltingly. "And you are still alive?"

"Sometime," Owen said.

"No," Enar said. "No man who endures such a thing and lives to tell the tale ever does. Not really."

Owen smiled.

Enar found he didn't want to look at that smile at all. He didn't want to believe such things existed.

Owen looked around quickly for the horse and saw him cropping grass near the mound. "He's not wearing a bit."

"No," Enar said. "He disliked it, so I removed it."

"Indeed," Owen said. "He is a horse; you are a man none would expect . . ."

"He is a horse," Enar said, "who can turn himself into a flying serpent. When I came to my senses for the fourth time, with my belly in the mud and my face in a bog, I undertook to see things from his point of view. After all, I wouldn't want a bit in my mouth, either."

"You are," Owen said, "as usual, unique. I have seen many horses broken by men, but only once have I seen a man broken by a horse."

"Thank you," Enar said, "for the compliment. I will ignore the rest. Now I feel the need of something to eat." He and Owen walked over to Elutides and his companions.

Owen greeted them all quietly by name until he came to Aud. "My lady . . ." he said.

"Don't speak of it," she said. "Did you think you were alone? We all meet our secret sorrows there."

"No," Enar said firmly. He was on his knees on the turf reaching for the wine. "I will not ask."

"Just as well," a voice spoke behind Enar. The voice was Ceredea's. "They couldn't tell you." She had come on them without their being aware of her, slipping out of the shadowed evening forest. "I bring news," she said. "Lord Owen, the Vikings are at your gates."

Owen was on his feet in an instant, facing her. "The

city?" he asked. "What of Elin? What of my kinsman, Godwin?"

"They live," she proclaimed triumphantly. "Hakon tried to murder Elin twice. Twice her cleverness defeated him, but then Elspeth took a hand."

"Elspeth!" Owen exclaimed.

"Indeed." Ceredea smiled. "She dotes on the Northman. You were mad not to kill Ivor. Just when Hakon was at his wit's end not knowing how to defeat your lady, Elspeth found Ivor, a tool ready and willing. One that fitted his hand better than an axe or sword."

Owen felt his skin grow cold. "What did Ivor do?"

"He burned the stores. Those in your hall. The city's guarantee against starvation. Tomorrow, the lord Godwin rides against Hakon."

"So soon?" Owen asked.

"This Godwin," Elutides said, "is a mighty man of war. He understands the hearts of his people well. He knows that though the city might hold out for a few weeks longer, hunger will bite deep and fear even deeper into the hearts of the citizens. Better strike now before they feel the rumbling of their empty bellies and have long nights to lie awake and consider the odds against them. No, he will lead them out while their hearts are high and filled with righteous rage."

"He could wait for me to return," Owen insisted. "He promised. . . ."

"He does not think you will ever return," Ceredea said. "I was in the crowd when Ivor spoke to Elin. I read the doom in her eyes. They both believe you faithless. It is left to them to pay the forfeit."

"Ah," Elutides purred, "who will not believe you foresworn?" He put his hand on Owen's shoulder, speaking into his ear. "Come back to the city with me. Embrace Gynneth. You will rule. I will be your counselor. They are riding to their destruction. What will you do? Go lay your bones beside Godwin as an uninvited guest?"

For a second, Owen tried to find anger in his heart and then fear. But he could find neither—only laughter, clear and fresh as a new spring bubbling from the earth. He threw back his head and howled.

Elutides stepped away from him. "God bless. It finds neither insult nor temptation, only a jest even in the most evil of counsel."

"To be sure," Owen said, turning to Enar. "Well, you may now lecture me on my foolishness."

"No," he answered. "I am an ignorant man. I do not know *a* from *b* were they together on a page. But I do understand honor. None of my father's get or my mother's ever left the field except at his lord's back. None ever lived beyond the hour his lord fell. If my mother ever heard such a tale of me, she would whip me from her hearth saying I was such an unnatural child she must have mistaken herself while in her cups and coupled with a serpent."

Elutides shouted at the people eating beside the green mound. "Bring me the war horn! I will muster all the able-bodied men I can. We must ride to the city now. I, Aud, and my sons will accompany you. Not much help I admit, but all I can give."

"Bring that sword of yours," Owen said. "You may need it." The sword lay on the ground near the food.

"Not my sword but yours, Owen. You won it and are wise enough to wield it."

Elutides picked up the weapon. Enar peered curiously at the thing. "It's magic if I ever saw magic," he said. "He no more than touched three men with it and they died."

Elutides was vastly amused. He threw back his head and began laughing. "Sweet credulity," he said, "is the secret of all wise men, wizards, and magi from the beginning of time. The sword is nothing but a trick." He handed the sword to Owen, who drew it cautiously. "Don't worry," Elutides said. "It's perfectly safe."

Owen examined the blunt, tapered blade and the iron serpent-crowned hilt. "It doesn't look as though it could cut butter," he said.

"The serpents are twined around a staff at the hilt," Elutides said. "Press down on the staff."

Owen did and heard a click.

"Now," Elutides directed, "tighten your fingers on the hilt."

Two blades sprang out from their place of concealment within. The blunt blade was suddenly edged with razor-sharp steel. Enar jumped back. Owen gave a start and almost dropped the sword. His fingers loosened on the hilt, and the sharp blades sprang back into their place and within the blunt one.

"The inner blades are anointed with poison," Elutides said, "but don't be afraid. At present they are clean."

Owen put the sword through its paces a few more times to see how it worked, then replaced it in the scabbard.

"A trick," Enar said, drawing closer, "but still a fearful weapon."

"No, my friend," Elutides said, turning to him, "only if the wielder understands its limitations. It's only good for about three men; after that the poison is worn off the blade. That's why I wasn't greatly troubled about losing it. It's my gift to you, Owen. Carrying it, you can never be defeated in single combat."

"A greater gift is the knowledge that when you fought me the blade was clean."

The evening was upon them and the night grew cold. Elutides wrapped his mantle around his shoulders and met Owen's eyes. There was a look of faint regret in his face. "There are men," he said finally, "for whom I would have set real spears and anointed the blade, but not for you. I would have been glad to leave my kingdom in your hands, but you chose not to take it. Firstly by not lying with Gynneth and then by not killing me when you had the opportunity. So you have chosen your city. The least I can do is offer you what help I can give you to defend it. The ride will be a long, hard one, but we can reach the city before sunset."

Owen looked up at the green mound for a moment, then out at the sea. "There is one more thing I have to do," he said, and began climbing the sloping hill. He reached the top of the mound and began walking toward the gray stone where Elutides had fallen. He stopped beside the sapling tree he'd destroyed.

"I'm sorry," he said, stroking the sliced-off trunk gently with his fingers. "Into what cruel paths does our rage lead us," he said. "It might have become something beautiful."

Elutides' hand reached down and guided Owen's fingers toward a small twig that bore only one green leaf. In a flash Owen saw the tree and knew the long strong roots would give rise to new branches, and it stood before him tall, joyously bearing its regal green burden of life, growing anew and looking into the sun. Then the vision faded, and he stood staring into Elutides' face.

"Can you see, Owen," Elutides said, "can you understand how difficult it is to kill anything?"

"No," Enar said. "What game of words and dreams is this? All I have ever seen is that it is only too easy for men to destroy, only too easy for them to lay waste the beautiful, the good.

"The father of lies is he who tells us our actions mean nothing and the consequences don't exist."

Owen unbuckled his sword belt. "Come," Owen said to Enar, "stand at my right hand." Enar stepped forward.

"Once kings were crowned here," Elutides said.

"Were I a real king," Owen said to Enar, "I could offer you lands and honors. As it is, all I can give you is my friendship and a seat at my hearth that you may ever call your home."

Enar didn't answer for a moment. He turned his face slightly away from Owen so he couldn't see his eyes.

"Wargus. Wanderer," he said. "So I have been called; so I am. I have stumbled down many a strange path, but the strangest of all journeys is the journey into the heart of another. I cannot think I am worthy, but I accept with a full heart."

Owen stared out over the ocean at the sun, now far in the west signaling the end of day. Its face was covered by rising thunderheads, but the last rays shone out around them, a corona that glanced back from the ever moving waters, forming in the distance a crown of light. He raised his sheathed sword hilt up, lifting it to the heavens as a vassal offers it to his king.

The sea breeze was a soft whisper in his ears, and the long grass moved under its touch brushing his legs. The distant sun crowned the ocean with a diadem of light.

He lowered the sword and turned. "To Chantalon."

Chapter
37

GODWIN walked through the square thinking the town was very quiet. He had just been to Siefert's house to talk with the town's leading men. The worst was upon them. Ivor, whatever his penitence now, had done only too good a job of destroying their stores. While many things had survived, the all-important oil and wheat had been totally ruined.

Ranulf and Denis reported Hakon was already beginning to mass his forces near the forest way to his lady's hall.

Godwin had found the townsfolk refreshingly calm, but then, he thought, they were no longer the same people Owen had rallied so long ago to take the first assault. They had been tried both by battle and fire and not found wanting. They were quiet now, no longer even defiant. They glowed with an unthinking resolution, an assurance greater than defiance or hatred that they would prevail.

Godwin paused in front of the church steps. The sun was westering. Big, dark shadows filled the square. The gray clouds of yesterday had been swept away by a night's cold wind. The sky was a bright, clear winter blue with not a cloud in sight. He removed his helmet.

"The god Win is a friend to man," a grating voice near him spoke.

Godwin, fully aware of Ivor's proximity, hadn't given any indication of awareness, but he didn't startle. "So I was called by Alfred, king of Wessex long ago," Godwin replied.

"He brought fire and the arts to mankind," Ivor said, "but belike Alfred a Christian wouldn't know who the god Win was."

"I believe he may have known," Godwin said.

"Run away," Ivor urged. "Before his death Rauching had asked that you be crucified on the city gates."

It was Godwin's turn to laugh. "Damnation, what an imaginative idea. Not pleasant, but quite imaginative. Tell me, has Hakon promised he will do it?"

"No," Ivor said. "He despised Rauching and I cannot believe he would do anything the false one asked, but if he catches you, he will certainly kill you."

Godwin turned around and sat down next to Ivor on the cathedral steps. "He will need to get in line," Godwin said. "There are many ahead of him. If no one were trying to kill me, I would feel lost and neglected."

"Yes," Ivor said in a bass voice. "Likely you would fall into a decline and be overtaken by illness and have to go pick a fight with several large families in order to return to your usual state of health."

Surprised, Godwin chuckled. He hadn't expected to find a sense of humor in such as Ivor. "What are you doing here?"

"Waiting for Alfric. He is trying to find someone who will take me into their household. He is not having much success. They are all afraid of me. The only one who would take me will have me wear chains night and day."

"No!" Godwin said. "Christ, is it worth the agony to live on Alfric's terms? I will give you a horse and free passage out of the city. All you need do is promise not to return and burn anything else. Run away."

"No," Ivor said. "I will remain even if I must live a beggar stretching out my open hands for alms at the church door. I am an oath man of the Christ. He stretched out his hand to me. Forgave my sins. I will not show Him my back, nor be false to my oath."

"Ivor, I perceive you are a man of discernment. Do you really believe anyone can forgive our sins?"

"Yes."

Godwin bowed his head. He sat quietly for a moment, his fingers caressing the filigreed scrollwork on his helmet. "Very well," he said quietly. "First, Hakon sent a man armed with lies to destroy us. Now he sends a man armed with truth, even if the truth be his own hatred and rage. Lies fail, but we have fallen to truth. We stand now between God and the devil. I cannot think which one will claim us. I cannot think which one to pray to for aid. Last night, I would have said it didn't matter, but today, having seen you and Alfric, for a moment I actually believed there might be something more on the altar of the church behind us than wood, bone, and self-delusion. For this reason . . ." Godwin hesitated, his brow furrowed in thought. "For this reason, if you are willing, I will take your hand."

Ivor turned toward him, his brutally scarred face stiff with astonishment. "What? You? A hater of all Vikings? A man renowned for his merciless treatment of our breed? You took the wild Picts to your bosom before you would take us. And you would accept me? I cannot believe it. Or is it that you wish to point to me and say here is the worshiper of Odin conquered?"

"No," Godwin said. "I do not. Anyone whose hand I take becomes one of mine and has no past. My people belong to me at table, in battle, and in the hall. Even when I stand before kings, they are with me. Choose and speak."

Ivor stretched out his left hand and Godwin took it. The Viking's right hand was still swollen and heavily bandaged.

"Besides," Godwin said quietly, "all other considerations aside, I have reason to believe a man knows where he stands with you."

Ivor nodded. "I have never been false."

Godwin threw back his head and laughed. "So truth stands among us. Even if it is only the truth of cruelty and pain."

"More than cruelty and pain," said a voice behind them.

"The truth of repentance and peace." Alfric stood there quietly. He had been listening all the while.

Godwin heard voices on the ramp leading down from the fortress. He turned and saw Elin accompanied by Judith. "The walkway will be finished by tomorrow," Judith said as she mounted her mule and turned toward the docks.

Elin continued toward the men. She was barefoot and without a mantle. Her skirts were pulled up into her belt so they would not brush the ground. Her hair was tied up in a fillet at the back of her neck. She walked alone, arms swinging at her sides.

"The greenwood queen," Ivor whispered. He made the sign against the evil eye.

"Elin," Godwin called, "were you and Judith doing as I asked?"

Elin nodded. "The carpenters will work all night. By tomorrow the fortress will be ready as a last refuge, if necessary."

Godwin nodded. "If we fall, the walls will be breached. They cannot be held because I will take most of the able-bodied defenders with me. You, the women, and children will retreat to the fortress." He turned to Ivor. "This is my first charge to you and perhaps my last. Stand with Lady Elin. Cut the throats of those too badly injured to fight, then lead the rest into the fortress to defend the women."

"Christ," Alfric broke in, "the wounded . . ."

"Must all be dead," Godwin finished the sentence for him. "I want no bungling, Ivor. All dead. Beyond terror, beyond suffering, beyond any act able to weaken the resolve of those in the fortress. And should any be unfortunate enough to be taken prisoner, harden your heart and turn your eyes away. Don't open the gates for anything but a promise of safe conduct from Hakon. Likely he will offer it in return for treasure and to avoid a costly assault."

"Can he be trusted?" Alfric asked Ivor.

Ivor nodded. "What he promises, he will perform. In spirit and in fact."

"My last chore, if all else fails," Elin said. "Judith will be at my side. She will handle the negotiations."

Godwin chuckled. "I wish I could be there to witness that encounter. She will probably have him grinding his teeth within an hour and regretting his victory by sundown. Now, have I your word, Elin?"

"Yes," she said.

Godwin turned to Ivor. "And yours?"

"It is given, so I am bound." He placed both his maimed and whole hands between Godwin's palms.

Godwin gave them a squeeze, then rose to his feet. "I suppose there's nothing more to be said."

"No!" Elin exclaimed. "Stay a while. I need you." Ivor was seated slightly above Elin on the cathedral steps. She had to tilt her head slightly to see his face. He remained, as always, hooded, and she could see only his one good eye. The nest of scars surrounding his other eye and mouth were in shadow. "Ivor half demon, Ivor half troll, Ivor half thing of waste and darkness, did one of those banished from forest, orchards, plowed land, or any fair place find your mother before you were born? Tell me truly."

Ivor bowed his head slightly. "Greenwood queen, I am born of man and woman only. My mother, a slave, embraced her owner, a farmer. They both feared the farmer's wife, who was a cruel hag and a shrew. I fitted the lie and the lie described me. Such things impress other fighting men. What care I what a warrior who wants to put a sword in my guts or an axe in my skull thinks of my family?"

Elin moved closer out of the shadowed square and into a ray of red-gold light. Godwin was horrified. Her eyes were red-rimmed and swollen. Her face was lined and tight with strain. She looked as though she'd aged ten years overnight.

"Tell me, Ivor," Elin asked in a low voice, "is she young?"

"Elin, don't do this," Godwin pleaded. "Have a little faith. He may yet return."

"Don't interfere with me, Godwin. I want the truth. I will have no other. His life and hers depend on it. If my spirit runs amok, I will destroy them both. I must seal my soul now."

"Elin," Alfric said. "Accept Christ. Turn away. Don't . . ."

"Little priest," Elin said. "The covenant between God and man is a covenant of choice. I have chosen. You have no right to interfere with me."

"As you will," Alfric said, his face hardening. He turned to Ivor. "On your life, on your soul, answer her truly."

"Is she young?" Elin asked.

"Yes, not yet twenty."

"Is she beautiful?"

"As those nymphs that haunt the sleep of young men just learning about love."

"Is she virgin?"

"Guarded by the wisest and most dangerous of magi, Elutides. I think almost certainly yes."

Elin turned around. It was nearly sunset, and the last rays gilded the rooftops and the church steeple. All around them blue shadows gathered. The air was turning cold. Lights were beginning to appear in windows overlooking the square. The tavern door opened, and Elin caught a glimpse of the hearth fire blazing within. She swung around and faced the three men again. "Come with me to the hall."

The big room was a ruin. The walls were scarred by fire and darkened by soot. They had to walk carefully. The floor was shattered and had fallen in here and there. The furniture was a pile of broken planking in the corner. The hearth was dark and dead. No fire burned on the stones. Alfric kindled two wax lights.

"You know what I can do?" Elin asked.

"Yes, I do," Alfric said evenly.

"I can haunt his sleep," Elin said. "I can trouble his dreams, stretching out my arms to him, draining his manhood until he turns from her in revulsion. Goes soft, not hard when he sees her. This I will not do."

The night wind moaned in the chimney. The pile of dead ash on the hearth stirred in the icy draft.

"However carefully she eats or drinks, I can make her first careless cup, her first thoughtless taste of a sweetmeat her last," Elin whispered into the cold stillness. "But this I will not do. She is safe from me. I can make her womb barren or worse. Curse it with a seed that will not come to fruition so that she loses child after child in blood and pain. But this I will not do. May his seed and hers prosper as wheat in the soft summer rain.

"She may walk the forest and meadow. I will not wait beneath a tree with an apple in my hand tempting her to taste the first fruits of autumn. I so vow."

Alfric brought the processional cross he had used to conquer Ivor. Godwin drew his sword. Elin knelt before the dead hearth. And by the wavering light of Alfric's taper, one hand on the cross, the other on the hilt of Godwin's sword, she swore an oath binding her soul. On pain of her own death.

When she was finished, she took the wax light from Alfric. "Now leave me. The rest of the household is with Judith." Elin turned and walked toward the passage into the church.

Godwin, Ivor, and Alfric stood together in the darkened hall. Godwin walked to the door. Through the panels he heard a cry of agony so despairing and so terrible it raised the hair on his arms and on the back of his neck. He shivered. "Alfric, maybe we should go to her."

"No," Alfric replied. "This is between Elin and God."

Godwin snorted despairingly. "What god can Elin possibly believe in who has anything to do with yours?"

"Godwin, it matters nothing how many names are cast over the everlasting mystery. There is only one God. Elin prays to Him. You ponder His motives. I worship Him. None of us understands Him."

"I'm going upstairs," Godwin said. "When you see Ranulf, send him to me. I have things to do."

Godwin went to his room. It was narrow and very spartan. Elin had tried to make him take a better one, but he had refused. It faced the ramparts overlooking the river, but no part of the town could be seen, only the river, the forest, and the wide and empty sky. It was a view he enjoyed, one he feared he wouldn't live to enjoy very much longer.

The room contained only a bed and a cushioned chest for his clothes that doubled as a window seat. He opened the chest, lifted a box, and set it on the bed. He unlocked it, lifted an item out, and sent for Ranulf.

The young man arrived immediately and began excusing himself.

"Be quiet," Godwin said, unwrapping the cloth from around the scabbard of a sword. The hilt gleamed with gold and enamel work. The scabbard itself was plain but had three rich golden rosettes decorating its length. He showed it to Ranulf. "What is this?"

Ranulf stepped closer as Godwin drew the blade slowly from its sheath. "A sword," he answered.

"Only a sword?"

Ranulf shook his head. Looking down at the exposed length of blade he said, "No. It is one of the very best kind. The kind it takes a very skilled smith half a year or more to make. May I touch it?"

Godwin finished drawing the blade and handed it hilt first to him. The boy's fingers closed around the golden grip. The window caught the last rays of the sun, filling the room with light. Ranulf turned the sword slowly and tried the edge with his thumb.

"Be careful," Godwin warned. A second later Ranulf jerked his thumb away and licked it. "Sharp as a razor," Godwin laughed.

The blade flashed the sunlight into Ranulf's eyes like a mirror, covering his face with rainbows. "Sharp and strong, yet light," Ranulf said, his voice filled with awe. He turned the blade slowly and studied the play of light over its surface. "You can see the work of the smith."

Godwin nodded. "All the men of that family give the same twist to the iron when it is lifted glowing white from the forge."

Ranulf spoke the name of a famous family of armorers.

"Close, but older," Godwin said. "His grandsire. This is from the time of Charlemagne. Charles the Great. The house of our last glory. We are the lesser sons of greater fathers, but we have some courage and honor yet."

The sun sank below the rim of the world and the room darkened, but the blade seemed to shimmer just as brightly as though the fire of the daystar still burned in the steel, but now as moonglow.

"Swing it through the air," Godwin said. Ranulf's first swing was weak and tentative. "No," Godwin commanded. "Harder, as though you struck at an enemy." Ranulf's second swing was all that could be desired. The blade moaned softly.

"They say of the smith that made these swords that if the blade did not cry out for joy on the first strike, he melted it down and used the steel for baser objects," Godwin said. "It is light, but it will cleave a helmet and the head beneath it at one stroke, slice through a shield as though it were made of soft butter, not wood and hide. And yet so strong and flexible that it will yield to the hardest parry and not break. Now sheathe it."

Ranulf took the scabbard from him and obeyed. The magnificent blade seemed to give a faint sigh of regret as it slid into the soft padding.

"Now take it and be ready to unsheathe it at my command tomorrow," Godwin said.

"It is too fine to wear in battle. Something might happen to it," Ranulf protested.

For a second, Godwin looked shocked, then began to laugh. "That is its purpose. It is my gift to you."

Ranulf stared at the sword, turning the worked leather of the scabbard in his hands. "I can't. It is too fine—the value of two manors at least. I have done nothing to deserve . . ."

"Stop babbling," Godwin said sharply, "and repeat after me. 'It is a princely gift.' "

"It is that," Ranulf said.

"I accept and will wear it proudly."

Ranulf stood silent.

As Godwin looked at the boy, he realized he was beginning to attain his growth. Always tall, his frame was beginning to fill out now. While he would never be an ox like Gowen or Wolf the Short, he would be a handsome man, well-set, broad-shouldered, and strong. A credit to the sword and it a credit to him. The boy's face was intelligent, the eyes wide and clear.

"It is a princely gift, and I will wear it proudly," Ranulf said, his eyes meeting Godwin's. He could barely see the old man's face in the gathering dusk.

"Good. Now go fetch Judith for me."

Ranulf lingered. He wanted to say something more to the tall figure in the gloom. Finally, he got the words out. "A princely gift and from the hand of one great enough to be a king."

He didn't see Godwin smile in the darkness but felt it in the warmth of his reply. "You do me great honor and I thank you."

Judith came with a lamp and set it on the windowsill. "All in the dark, Godwin," she said.

"It closes over me, Judith, but the winter night is brilliant with stars." Godwin upended the chest on the bed. A pile of jeweled ornaments, gold and silver, glittered in the flickering light of the lamp. "Make me a price, a fair one. I have no time to haggle."

She examined the hoard for a few moments and complied with his request. He nodded his acceptance. "Half is for the ladies of this household—Anna, Ingund, and Elfwine and Ranulf's child—so that they may never know want. You are famed far and wide as a clever woman of business. You will associate Alfric with you and see that they are cared for. The other half is for Rosamund so that she need never ply her trade as a woman of the town unless she so wishes."

"Rosamund is a child," Judith said. "For all her hard life, in some ways she is still very innocent."

Godwin looked up from the pile of gold. "Rosamund will grow into a fine woman. Nothing I do will hinder that. I give you my word."

* * *

Judith watched as her maids bustled about the kitchen. Rosamund sat in a bath with one maid scrubbing her back and another washing her hair. Two others consulted with Judith about the girl's appearance.

"No paint. At her age nature is enough," said the first maid.

"Just a bit on the lips, a pink shade," the other insisted. "I know just the color I will mix."

Judith nodded judiciously in the direction of the second maid. "I agree. She needs but little, and yet some on the lips always helps. What perfume?"

"Jasmine?" suggested one.

Judith shook her head negatively. A bubbling sound from Rosamund interrupted their considerations.

She had been ducked underwater to rinse her hair and came up protesting. "I know something of men."

"Pah!" Judith answered in disgust. "What did the widow ever teach you except to spread your legs quickly and often. There is more to it than that."

Rosamund surfaced again. "Truly, I cannot see what more . . ."

"He has married you, foolish girl," Judith snapped. "We are preparing you for your wedding night."

"Married!" Rosamund cried. "He would not marry me. I am not the sort of woman . . . a man marries."

"Oh, stuff a rag in her mouth and finish washing her hair," Judith said. "He has settled property on you, girl. That is marriage to me. I am already planning how I will invest your money. I have picked out five fine houses. All have gardens and orchards. And there is yet some left over to make you a partner in some enterprise. I will look about—" She broke off. "What's wrong, girl? Has the water grown too cold?"

Rosamund was white, her skin covered with goose-flesh. "He really believes he is going to die," she whispered, her eyes wide with terror. She had heard his words in the hall, but she had been unable or unwilling to fully comprehend them. Now the full realization struck her.

"Fetch some more hot water," Judith commanded a maid. "This kitchen is drafty." She turned again to Rosamund.

"He marries a young wife today. How does it follow that he will die tomorrow?"

"The battle," Rosamund said.

Judith snapped her fingers. "That for the battle. He has survived fifty battles and will live through fifty more. Live till you weary of him and he becomes just another husband."

"Do you really think so?" Rosamund's desperate young eyes probed Judith's face.

"Yes," she said, and smiled. She never showed what the smile cost her. "Now stop fretting and make yourself beautiful for him. The last thing a soldier needs is a woman who hangs about his neck and weeps." She nodded decisively. "What kind of perfume did we pick?"

They settled on a flower scent, a white shift, and a blue gown. Judith led Rosamund to the solar of one of the houses she planned to buy with Godwin's money. She opened the door unceremoniously, pushed her in, and closed it behind her.

Rosamund tried to curtsy to Godwin but lost her balance and nearly fell. Godwin caught her hand, steadied her, then brought her hand to his lips in one smooth movement and kissed it gallantly.

Rosamund's eyes shone. "Oh," she whispered, delighted. "Judith said I should curtsy to show proper respect."

"I am properly respected, then," Godwin said. "I don't want you to break your neck." He led her to the table. It was set for a feast. Sweet wine, sliced chicken, venison, partridge, and veal vied for space with crystallized fruits, cakes, and apples cooked with cloves and other spices.

"No wonder Judith wouldn't let me eat anything," Rosamund said. She looked around the room. "But there is no bed."

Godwin filled her cup with wine. "There are beds aplenty if we . . . if you want one. You wished to be a lady. Well, a lady calls the tune. What would you like to do first?"

"Eat," Rosamund said with a radiant smile. "I'm starving. Lady Elin worked us all day without hardly a bite.

Then Judith came and plunged me into a tub, and I was scrubbed all over, even my hair. Then it was 'try this, do that, turn this way, turn that, I like this, no, then again, I don't.' After that, I was given more instruction than I can remember. 'Don't be a chatterbox, show proper respect, mind your table manners.' " She paused and sipped the wine. "Oh, that is good."

Godwin lifted the cup and drank from the same spot her lips had touched.

"That was the other thing they told me," Rosamund continued. " 'Don't drink too deeply and don't eat too much. Don't wave knives at him.' The whole town knows that."

"What a lot of don'ts," Godwin chuckled.

"I am well instructed."

"I hope you will forget it all."

"I must," she answered between bites. "It was so contradictory. When Judith said don't drink too deeply, I was all anxiety. I asked how much. She said one cup of wine. One maid said two; the other thought I should be allowed three. Then they fell to quarreling among themselves about whether I should take the wine before or after dinner or just with the meal. I gave up asking questions and just listened."

"Knowing Judith, that was probably wise. Had you continued to dispute them, I might still be sitting here waiting while they squabbled about etiquette."

"Yes, I know."

She is very beautiful, no, radiant, Godwin thought as he watched her eat. Judith had chosen a high-necked shift of linen woven with silk. It was very soft and fine. The overdress of blue silk was cut with flowing sleeves. She'd belted it with a simple braided golden cord wound around Rosamund several times and tied in the front. It emphasized the slenderness of the girl's waist and the swell of her hips. The soft shift outlined the two small, high breasts, rising and falling gently with each breath. The filigreed earrings she had worn earlier were missing. Instead there were two confections of silver wire and sapphires. A silver fillet held her golden hair high on her head. Judith had resisted the temptation to dress it elaborately. Instead she had coiled it on the top of Rosamund's head, a golden aureole that framed her face, with its creamy skin and sparkling blue eyes.

Rigged out in his best red velvet tunic with the neck and sleeves trimmed in sable, Godwin seemed handsome to her. The scarlet set off his dark hair and eyes, his hawk's nose and strong mouth. He wore a golden sword belt and baldric that fell across the ruby tunic in a slash of sunlight. The man and the warrior in one; his face had a brooding beauty in the candlelight.

He smiled indulgently on Rosamund as she stuffed herself with unaccustomed delicacies. Her fingers moved from plate to plate, tasting and trying a different one each time.

"Oh, but this is strange yet very good," she said as she tasted the fruit of a Seville orange preserved in honey, then some cherries sparkling with sugar. She finished with an apple cooked in wine and spiced with cinnamon and cloves. "How wonderful," she said as she sank back in the chair. "Oh, I wish I could eat more, but I will make myself sick. I would not want to spend the rest of this beautiful night with my head over a basin."

"It is a pretty head," Godwin said. "I wouldn't mind holding it. Have some more wine." He lifted the jug to her cup.

"No, not that, either. I have had enough. I never drink it unwatered. My head is spinning and the whole world sparkles." To her surprise, one of Judith's servants entered with water and a towel so that she could wash her hands.

"What now?" Godwin asked.

Emboldened by the wine and the kindness of his face, she smiled. "Could we go to the square? They say there will be music and dancing there. I love music, and at the widow's, I always used to be the first to the window when the tumblers came." Then she shook her head. "I shouldn't have said that."

"Why?" Godwin asked as he led her to the door. "I know about the widow's."

"Yes, but Judith said not to remind you."

"The widow and her business are not important to me."

As he said the words, he realized they were true. "Though a gem be buried in filth, yet it will retain its luster and shine just as brightly when cleaned." She was lightly clad for the chill night, so he wrapped her in his mantle. "We'll take my horse, even though it is only a short walk to the square."

He lifted her into the saddle. She curled one leg over the pommel and gave a small gasp of fear. The big war horse stamped his feet and blew his breath. Frost crystals formed in the icy air. She clutched the saddle. "What's this?" Godwin asked. "You rode him well enough the other night."

"But you were with me. This is the first time I've ever been on a horse alone."

He took the animal's bridle. "Never fear. You will ride safely. I will be your footman."

Judith's servant went before them carrying a torch. The night air was still, and above the narrow street, a million stars arched in a canopy of jewels. A meteor shot its lance of fire across the sky. Rosamund gave a soft exclamation of wonder and pointed upward. "Look! A falling star. You are a learned man and can read; do stars really fall?"

Godwin tilted his head back and stared up at the splendid loneliness. "I cannot think it, Rosamund, for though I have seen these flights all my life, the stars remain undiminished in number and brilliance." He shrugged. "Then again, no man knows."

Two more trailed their fire across the sky. "Do they grant wishes?" she whispered.

"So it is said."

"Then all my wishes are for you, that you may be safe tomorrow." She clutched his hand where it rested on her knee. His other arm steadied her in the saddle.

He laughed. "I will be safe."

"Don't make promises you can't keep," Rosamund said.

Strange, he thought, *Richilda, my unfaithful wife, looked very much the woman, but her soul was that of a petulant child. This girl who looks so much the child is more of a woman than Richilda could ever be.* "Very well," he answered. "Honesty to honesty. I cannot tell if I will live or die, for no man can predict the chances of war any more than one can truly say if stars fall, but I will try to live for your sake if none other. Does that content you?"

She leaned down in the darkness, and he felt her lips brush his in a petal-soft kiss. "So it is sealed with a kiss," he said.

The horse had stopped, and Godwin pulled on the bridle to get him moving again. The torchman was far ahead in the narrow street. To Godwin's eye, the stars above seemed very cold and far away, while the enveloping darkness was overwhelmingly real and present.

The celebration seemed very subdued. The older women gathered by the fountain or with the men in front of the tavern. The young danced a round dance to the piper's tune. Under the arcades, families wandered about, embracing and greeting in what they knew might be a hail and farewell.

Rosamund joined the young people in the dance, but she could feel Godwin's eyes on her like an invisible tether that might let her run free to the far corners of the earth yet bring her back to him with a glance.

Godwin stood beside Alfric. "Should we not be better employed in fasting and prayer?" he asked the priest.

"No." Alfric smiled. "It is well that Hakon should hear the sounds of merriment, laughter, and song, and know we do not fear him."

Judith caught his last comment. "Then tread the measure with me, Alfric. My menfolk are away, and I have no one to dance with."

They danced a roundelay before the bonfire that lit up the sky. It was surrounded by a circle of laughter and clapping hands; laughter because the little man looked so funny capering around the tall, beautifully dressed woman, and clapping hands because Alfric joined in the jest with them and his merriment was contagious.

Godwin felt Edgar come stand by his side. "We will gather at the cathedral just before dawn," Godwin told him before draining his cup and looking for Rosamund.

Her eyes met his, and she drifted toward him as if in a

dream. When she reached him, she took his hand. Outlined against the tapestry of torch fire, his head was like a Caesarean Roman coin, princely and beautiful. "Take me home," she said.

He lifted her to the saddle and, this time, mounted behind her. It seemed as though they were but a moment in the street; then he was carrying her up the stair to their room.

She started to undress herself, but he refused to let her, slipping the blue dress away. Her shift was indeed beautiful, more so with her body in it. It outlined her small curvaceous form, gently molding to the smooth curve of breast, down the ribs, lying across the mound of her belly, and draping the shapely silken thighs.

He loosed the silver fillet, and her hair fell over her shoulders in a golden cascade. Bending down, he embraced and kissed her, luxuriating in the softness of her lips.

She threw her arms around his chest and rested her cheek against his breast. "Oh God," she whispered, "I desire you so. My whole body burns for you as the parched earth cries for rain and the rivers dream of the sea." She felt him tremble with an answering desire as he drew the shift away and discarded his own tunic.

"I am yours," he said softly in return, "for this night and all the days of my life." He felt her heart beating against his own, racing like a captured bird.

"I am not fit for such a thing. It has never happened to me before," she said in wonder, grief, and delight. She drew away and looked up at him. The dim lamplight shadowed her body while her face was a pale oval. "Will you make me love you and then die?"

Godwin paused, then touched her cheek gently with his fingers as softly as someone touches the wing of a bird or a butterfly. "Never fear. No love is born in one night. I only want you to know that it is possible to love and be loved. I want you to see what tenderness can be like between a man and a woman. Tenderness and trust. All my wealth is but a small gift if you cannot learn to value yourself as a pearl beyond price. It is my gift to you as the sword was to Ranulf. Poor enough, but all I have."

She wrapped her arms around his tall, lean frame. "And if you fall?"

"Nothing is ever a certainty in this life." His strong, long-fingered hands caressed her body.

"Except death," she said.

He lifted her to the bed and rested one knee on it, kissing her on the neck, the ear, and the lips. "Since meeting Alfric, I'm not even sure about that," he replied.

Rosamund felt the tears start in her eyes, but his lips were on hers and his hands—the gentlest yet the most expert she had ever known—were drawing fire from her loins.

He kissed her earlobe, nibbled it, and whispered, "This night is for you, Rosamund. I am here for you. Your joy, girl, your pleasure, so let us forget death, battles, and war. Come to me. Let me love you."

And she did.

He took her as a wise man takes a virgin, gently, slowly, careful to rouse her to the highest pitch of delight. She was not used to seeking her own enjoyment in men's arms but found herself seeking it in his. She was enraptured by the wonderful things he did with his fingers, his lips, his tongue and the controlled movements of his lean, powerful body.

He lifted her on wild flights of ecstasy among the stars until she felt in her own body the consuming flash of the star fall. She descended from the dream of passion and found herself lying in his arms.

Her cheek rested near his lips, her legs twined around his, warmed and spent from his lovemaking. After a time of glorious contentment to Rosamund, he eased himself up, slipping his arm from under her head. He left for a few moments, returning with meat and wine.

She fell on the food ravenously, sitting up cross-legged beside him. "It leaves me hungry," she said, "but I'm going to get crumbs in the bed. The widow . . ." She lowered her lashes and looked abashed. "I can't seem to remember. . . ."

He was about to drink but stopped the cup near his lips

to finish her sentence for her. "The widow didn't like you to get crumbs in the bed."

She shook her bowed head.

"Don't worry. I'll still love you if you get crumbs in the bed. I consider it only a minor flaw."

"A minor flaw? What would be a major flaw?"

Godwin rescued her cup as it tilted precariously. "Spilling wine on the bed. I believe I could put up with drunkenness, shrewishness, and even infidelity, but I couldn't stand a woman who spilled wine in my bed."

Rosamund's face was solemn even though she chewed a big bite of bread and beef. "I'm serious. I have many flaws."

"So do I," Godwin answered. "It is the minor annoyances of life that drive husbands to desertion and divorce, not the major calamities. Tell me about your flaws, and I will see if I can endure them patiently."

She swallowed the food and lifted the cup to her lips. "I'm serious," she repeated.

"So am I."

She studied his face in the yellow lamplight. His eyes were flat black stones, his mouth a hard line. He seemed to have withdrawn from her to some far place of his own, alone. "I'm lecherous," she said timidly.

He did laugh then. Lightninglike good humor flared on his features and the hardness vanished. "That's not a flaw but a titillation." He reached out and stroked one of her breasts, gently running a finger around the velvet curve until it reached the satin of her nipple. Rosamund quickened at his touch. Unexpected pleasure flared in her body. "More than a titillation, an invitation. A promise that you will invite me in often."

She ignored his hint, instead determined to make him see reason. "I am greedy."

"Excellent. The young should be greedy for all life can give them: love, laughter, the joys of the world, even drunkenness and desire. For life is a thing more fragile than a tiny flicker of light amid a great darkness. Fierce winds blow out of that storm of darkness that extinguish life all too soon."

He was shaken by his passion. She could see the harshness of it in his eyes, the force of it driving his heart against his ribs, the flying pulsations in his throat. She bowed her head over the wine cup. The red of the wine looked black in the shadow of the cup. She spoke softly. "Judith said that property was marriage. I cannot think it, but if you want me, there is something very important you should know."

She raised her blue eyes and met the flat darkness of his. "Do not laugh because it is not funny."

He saw the sorrow in her face and nodded as if insisting she continue.

"I do not think I can ever bear a child. I was hurt too badly when I was captured." Her eyes fell again to the black pool in the cup, and the bitterness in her voice was as ragged as the edge of a badly sharpened knife. "There is the widow, Godwin. That will follow me all my life, and you know it, and I know it, and . . ."

He reached out and took the cup from her hand, setting it on the floor beside his. His fingers shot back and closed around the sword hilt hanging from the belt and baldric on the bedpost. His voice quivered with rage. "See, Rosamund. Look how close this is to my hand. I can reach it always, and always I have drawn it. There is no day in my life when I have not drawn it to strike at my enemies, avenge my friends, defend myself. Christ, I have often had to use it to control those wolves who follow me, for they must constantly be reminded that I am an older, stronger killer than they. I will tell you a terrible thing. To me, tomorrow is only another day. A day like all the rest. A day when other men will try to kill me. I was with Eudes at Paris, beside Gestric when he faced Rollo's men. Now I meet Hakon. The Normans have blown like summer storms over this land all my life, and all of that life I have fought them. Every day I have felt the bony hand of death on my shoulder, walked with its shadow near me."

His hand slipped away from the hilt. He caught Rosamund by both arms and drew her toward him. "You would be surprised how many things, seemingly important things, fade into triviality in that cold shadow. I cannot bring myself to care, to even waste a moment's worry on what the world will think of you and I. I do not want the tree of autumn in my arms no matter how beautiful it is. I want you, laden with the promise of beauty's blossoming spring-time. That look in your eyes now, the way you look at me this moment, melts the winter in my heart. If it grieves you to be childless, then it will grieve me, but only because of you."

His fingers tightened almost painfully on her arms, but her hands softly stroked over his chest, then down, embracing him.

"I care nothing for the opinion of God, and that of man is less than nothing to me." He drew her lips toward his. "Only you, my Rose of paradise. Only you."

He was the sun and his fire flowed through her veins, light and heat at once. She was carried upward, triumphant as the cresting sea, an Aphrodite, born of foam and pure light. She broke as a wave breaks, spilling into brilliance, over and over again until the ninth wave carried her to rest, warm and complete beside him.

Judith came to rouse them near dawn. She found God-win already awake, arming himself. "I'm an old man who sleeps lightly," he explained.

She lifted the lantern and studied Rosamund, who was a sweet sprawl of limbs in bed, sleeping the sleep of the weary young. "Not that old," she said with a raised eyebrow.

"I hope I will never live to grow that old." He lifted Judith's hand. "Take care of my wife."

When the door closed behind him, Rosamund's eyes opened. "Is he gone?" she asked.

"Yes."

Rosamund sat up. "Good. I was afraid to open my eyes and say good-bye." She wrapped herself in the quilt, ran to the window, and looked down on the narrow street. Judith moved to stand beside her.

Rosamund took a deep breath. "You said a soldier didn't need a woman who hung about his neck and wept. I was afraid I would weep and beg him not to go." As they watched, Godwin left the gate, a tall, lonely figure riding out in the faint gray light to meet his fate.

"He would have gone, though," Judith said.

"Yes, I know," Rosamund answered. The tall horseman blurred before her eyes as they flooded with tears. "He said . . . he told me, Judith, that no love could be born in one night, but I think it can. Oh God, I think it can," she cried as she turned blindly into Judith's arms.

Chapter
38

G ODWIN rode toward the square in the gray, almost shadowless light of the predawn. Many men passed him, some on foot, others mounted. All carried weapons on their way to the square. A few raised their hands in greeting. Others simply trudged by. None looked very fearful or very eager.

Yes, Godwin thought, *here at last was a thing that must be done. They only hope it will be done well. We will not whine or whimper if the fates turn against us.* He reined in his horse at the hall.

Elin, Judith, and Gynnor, Siefert's stout wife, waited within. They sat together quietly before the dead hearth. Elin wore gray and her face had been painted.

"At least we will make a brave show, won't we?" he asked.

"Yes," Elin answered, rising slowly.

"By dawn we must ride out."

There were no tears, no shouts, and no speeches. Godwin and the men massed at the gates, carrying every weapon they could muster. Far off, near the forest, Godwin could see Hakon forming his warriors into a boar's head. The formation was a deceptively simple weapon. The men in it formed a wall with their overlapping shields. The wall folded back into a wedge, flat at the apex. Besides being simple, it also was hideously dangerous.

The Vikings had used it to soundly trounce the irregular infantry of the Anglo-Saxons and the Franks. Their lack of coordination allowed them to be rolled up in flank attacks or butchered one by one as they hurled themselves at the massed shields of their enemies. The shield wall could be broken by heavy cavalry, but Godwin knew he did not have enough men for such a charge.

He had no hope of pulling any fancy tricks such as a feigned retreat with the men he had. Although they were blooded, they still were inexperienced. Their retreats would be real ones. Godwin only hoped that after the first charge at the shield wall was broken, his green troops could be persuaded to undertake another.

As he watched and swore inwardly, the shield wall completed itself and began its slow movement toward the city. "He is offering battle," Godwin said. There was a murmur of assent from the mounted men around him.

"Very well," Godwin said. "We will accept his offer." A horse stamped restively. Saddles creaked and bridles jingled. Then silence descended. No one prayed or wept; not even the sound of a sigh broke the stillness around Godwin.

He looked up and saw in the growing light that furrowed gray clouds covered the sky. The wind fanning his face smelled of the ocean rolling at the river mouth. It slashed at his cheeks and was bitterly cold.

No one ventured to unbar the gate in front of them. Godwin reached down and lifted it himself, then kicked his horse and rode out without looking back. The rest followed.

Elin, along with those left behind, stood at the wall and watched. At first, nothing much happened. It was as though the two armies had to get used to the idea that some on one side and some on the other would not survive the day. They stalked each other in the open field, silently jockeying for position. Godwin tried vainly to turn Hakon's flank, while Hakon tried to draw Godwin into a foolish charge at his main strength. Neither was completely successful.

Godwin and his men feinted half a dozen times at Hakon's left. Each time the shield men turned to meet them. Godwin swore. His men and horses only had so much stamina. He couldn't keep this game up as long as Hakon could.

Then he spotted the weakness on the right. While Hakon was occupied to his left, some of his men had let the shield wall slip to the right. Godwin drew his men back and charged the carelessness he saw. The two armies struck each other the way the hammer strikes the anvil. They slammed together with the clang of iron on iron, but almost in silence. It was as though every man saved each precious breath so he might strike an extra blow or reach out those few more inches to bring his enemies down.

Hakon's line bowed but held, and Godwin drew his men back. They began stalking each other again. The day seemed to grow darker, not lighter as more clouds rolled in. Charge after charge was repelled by Hakon's warriors.

Near noon, a fine misty rain began to fall, not enough to stop the battle but sufficient to assure every man's cup of misery would be filled to the brim. Exhaustion began to set in.

Godwin couldn't remember how many times he had ridden forward in the charge. Six, seven times? He was sure if he had given an order to charge instead of simply feinting at Hakon, the men around him would have been routed long ago. Still, the terrible silence prevailed. Steel crashed together with steel, but the horses died without a scream. Men died the same way.

From the walls, Elin could see the long snake's trace of the battle. It was marked by bloody, trampled ground and the scattered bodies of the wounded and dying. Sometimes one of the bodies moved, lifted an arm or leg, and tried to rise, showing they were living still. Most did not.

The people around Elin watched as if hypnotized by the slaughter. Judith's head was bowed, her lips moving in silent prayer. Rosamund's eyes were fixed on Godwin, the expression on her face bleak. Anna held the baby while Elfwine knelt, her mantle covering her face. She was sure she had seen Ranulf fall. Cynically, Elin wondered what the cloth hid.

Elin stood between Alfric and Ivor. Perhaps Ivor alone studied the battle he saw with a cold, analytical eye. "This will be his last charge," he said to Elin.

Her face was numb with fear. Godwin was going to fail. Beyond this she could not think or see. *I suppose I must lead a retreat into the fortress,* she thought.

"The jarl Godwin, all honor to his name," Ivor continued. "He has accomplished his desire. Hakon is defeated. The jarl Godwin will stand with honor among the dead. I think even Hakon will build him a pyre."

"Yes," Elin said, "were Godwin my enemy, I, too, would go in dread of his ghost."

Alfric turned to the grim woman beside him. In the gown and mantle she looked as stern as Atropos, the last Fate who cuts the thread. Beside her, Ivor towered, stark and ugly as some primitive monument. Alfric looked back at Hakon's shield wall. They staggered with weariness. Godwin's scattered forces slowly regrouped and readied for their final assault. Alfric lifted his hand in absolution.

"The jarl Godwin began with one hundred men," Ivor said. "I doubt if he has thirty left. Hakon began with three hundred. Of those, he has two hundred left, and many are wounded and exhausted. They will have no stomach for attacking the walls and capturing the city."

His words took Elin with the force of a blow. "Christ Jesus God! What am I? Asleep? Awake? Judith!" she shouted.

"Have you gone mad?" Judith snapped.

"No, sane," Elin replied hurriedly. "Godwin will fall, but we will still win. Everyone! Search everywhere. Find any weapon you can and come back. We will hold the walls yet. The city will stand. If you cannot find anything that has an edge, take the furniture. Break a chair or table leg and use it as a club. Return well armed and ready to fight!"

Shouting, the people around her scattered into the streets.

* * *

In the field Godwin pulled his horse's head up. The beast was dying. *Simply floundered,* Godwin thought, but as he leaned forward he saw the deep axe gouge in the animal's chest and the bloody foam from the mouth and nostrils. Godwin patted one steaming flank softly. "Well, old friend, no matter. We will go down together."

He glanced around taking stock of what forces he had left. Edgar was still in the saddle, but his left hand was gone. A strip of leather was tied at the stump to stop the bleeding. Gowen was a bloody mess. He had a sword cut across his face from bow to chin and another cut through his thigh. His leg dangled as though the tendons were cut. Gowen held himself upright in the saddle with one leg. Ranulf alone appeared not too badly hurt, though he had half a dozen superficial wounds and was missing some fingers. Of the rest, no one was without a wound.

"We are done," Godwin said to the men around him. "If we charge again, we will fall. All the horses are floundered or dying. If we run, Hakon's men will pursue and kill us. Either way, we die."

Gowen reeled in the saddle. He spat blood on the ground. "What is life, but coin for the spending," he roared. "When I fall, no one will find a wound in my back."

Godwin smiled grimly and slammed his heels into his dying horse, managing to get it into a shambling trot. "Now!" he screamed. "Now for ruin and red nightfall!" He heard the first and last faint cheer from his men.

Ahead of him, he saw Hakon leave the sanctuary of the boar's head. The wings of the wedge-shaped formation began to move forward to encircle Godwin and his men.

Hakon rode toward him, sword drawn, to run him through. Godwin's horse died, folding up on its haunches. Hakon's sword tore across his belly, and Godwin went down with one leg under his fallen horse. Pinned and waiting to die, he thought he heard the bellow of a war horn far away. *My mind must be playing tricks,* he thought. *I heard the same sound when the Picts came raiding into Scotland. But that was a long time ago, and there are no Picts here.*

The formation broke at last as the defeated warriors

were surrounded. They gathered in a knot around God-win. Ranulf stood astride his fallen captain.

Hakon's men paused, perhaps to gloat over the defeated, perhaps in simple weariness. The day had been a long one for them, too.

"Hey, pretty boy!" one of them shouted at Ranulf. "Give me that beautiful sword and I will let you go. Drop it and be off. That blade is fine enough to buy a life or two." Hakon's men laughed at the sally.

Ranulf raised the weapon. "No, the price you ask is too high." He didn't see Godwin smile.

A war horn bellowed again, this time closer. Hakon's men looked around uneasily.

Ranulf heard the sound. It was like nothing on God's earth he had ever heard before. The sound was a scream, coming toward him, louder and louder. He saw the faces of the Vikings closing in on him go pale as they drew back in awe and terror. He swung around.

They were coming fast, screaming with rage—unbounded, maddening rage—as they flowed from the gates of the city across the field. Ranulf's jaw dropped and he crouched over Godwin's body to protect him. Not from the Vikings. They were already in flight. But from the people of Chantalon. The city had emptied itself in one unspeakable burst of absolute fury. They came screaming like demons of hell. They came killing.

Judith flashed past Ranulf waving a double-bladed axe. Mud coated her skirts to her thighs. She crushed one fleeing warrior's skull without pausing and kept on coming.

Then, the gigantic living wave engulfed Ranulf. The people of Chantalon. The women of Chantalon. They carried knives, fire irons, kitchen spits, warming pans, and clubs. Every kind of club made from bedsteads, chairs, tables, and stove wood. Nail-studded clubs, stone-studded clubs.

The people were fresh. They were strong. They were enraged and they fell on Hakon's weary men like an invasion from hell. But there was fight in the Vikings yet. They were professionals used to nasty surprises. They formed into the boar's-head wall again.

The sound of roaring war horns drew Ranulf's gaze toward the river. As the sun dipped below the clouds, he saw Owen riding the red stallion, leading a moderate-size force. They looked well armed and dangerous.

Owen's men crashed into Hakon's rear, and Hakon's exhausted followers could do no more. The boar's head dissolved into a screaming, raging whirlpool of destruction. The women of Chantalon fell on the Vikings like Furies on a damned soul. Many of their men were dead, but the women killed and killed and killed until they were red to the armpits with blood.

Elin was not far from Judith as she led the charge, but drew back at the end. The child in her womb kicked. She felt it quicken. She couldn't pollute herself with death now.

Above, the clouds swept past, driven by the wild north sea wind. The dying sun shone red on the stricken field. Owen also turned away from the slaughter. He sent his men in to mop up and sat watching, Elutides at his side. The old man glanced over and saw Elin. Their eyes met.

Owen was with the Bretons. He led their men and was dressed as a nobleman, accompanied by the most powerful of their magi. *My soul is sealed,* she thought. *He has bedded the girl. Likely his seed is already sprouting in her womb.*

Owen turned and saw her. In the dying rays of the setting sun, she looked like a woodland being—dark-haired and -eyed, but robed in scarlet as an autumn tree.

From the first moment he saw her, Owen thought of nothing else. He spurred his horse and galloped hard toward her. She turned and ran. The stallion stumbled and slowed. Owen had no whip, so he had to slam his heels into the stallion's flanks again.

He realized that in a few seconds Elin would be under the dark boughs. He would never be able to catch her in the blackness of the twilight forest.

Elutides and Alshan drew near Owen. "Even the horse knows," Alshan said.

Owen leaped from the saddle and began to pursue Elin on foot. But she vanished into the shadow of the trees and was seen no more.

* * *

Somehow he had known she would go. She'd always felt light in his arms like a hawk riding a fist. Spreading its wings to keep its balance. Imprisoned only by the falconer's fist and hand. He hadn't been able to hold Elin. Or tame her. Now she had flown.

Owen turned back to the red horse, mounted, and rode toward the town. He felt sick with the nightmare horror around him.

Men lay dead and dying everywhere. Some of the dead were horribly mutilated. Others looked as though they had never taken a blow.

The living wounded screamed, some in agony, others in terror because the townspeople were still mindlessly slaughtering every living Viking they could find.

Owen rode to where he had last seen Godwin, wondering as he picked his way across the field if the old man was still alive.

Godwin was alive. Just alive, not much more. Rosamund cradled his head in her lap. Owen wondered at the young girl's calm until he looked at her face. Her skin was clammy. The long strands of blond hair stuck to her cheeks. Her eyes had the blind, unfocused stare of shock.

Owen glanced once at the grisly wound in Godwin's midsection, then looked away. The gash had opened him from the groin to the rib cage. Owen dismounted and knelt at his cousin's side.

Godwin's eyes were closed, his face pale. Only the slow, regular movement of his chest showed he was still alive.

"A strong man," Elutides commented as he dismounted. "He should be dead."

Godwin's eyes opened. He didn't see Owen or Elutides, only Ranulf. The boy stood at his feet. He held the sword Godwin had given him by the blade on either side like a cross. Light from the blade and hilt, bloody with the setting sun, flashed in his eyes. It looked like a cross of fire in the air.

"Did we win?" he asked.

"Yes," said Ranulf. "We did."

"What are the cries I hear?"

"They're killing the wounded," the boy answered.

"Stop them," Godwin ordered.

"How?" Ranulf looked bewildered. The maddened townsfolk were taking revenge for months of terror. Their repressed fear and fury gushed out in an orgy of violence and cruelty. The people rioting in the field stripping the dead and murdering the wounded were both frenzied and fearsome. Their rage would not lightly be turned aside.

Godwin grinned, perhaps for the last time, and said, "Tell them the prisoners are worth money. Since they intended to sell us, we can sell them. This is my last order. It's time the killing ended." Even as he spoke, the melee was fading as sheer exhaustion overtook the townspeople.

Ranulf nodded and sheathed his sword. His eyes hurt. He stumbled across the field, relaying Godwin's order. One corner of his mind felt mild astonishment at the looks he was receiving until he realized he was crying.

The tears were painful and caused his eyes to sting. He was doing his best to wipe them with his shirt when he stumbled over something. He finally managed to clear his eyes and looked down.

The thing that had caught his boot was the side of Edgar's body. The Northumbrian knight lay slightly curved, his beautiful sword still in his hand. No one had ventured to touch it.

Early in the fighting, his left hand had been nearly severed. He had lost a great deal of blood from the wrist. His clothing was still where the sanguinary flow clotted and dried. An axe cut to the side of his neck delivered in the final melee had finished him.

Ranulf went to his knees beside the body. The fierce tears began again as he realized there are things that are simply unbearable. The sense of utter loss darkened his mind so deeply that he didn't hear his name being called.

Finally, he looked up, cleared his eyes, and found himself staring at Gunter and several of the townsfolk. They had a prisoner—Tosi, Hakon's right-hand man.

Gunter spoke quietly. "We are penning the rest of the Vikings. We will do as the lord Godwin directs and sell them. But this one," he pointed at Tosi, "all, even the prisoners, say if he is sold, Hakon will ransom him. We took council among ourselves and decided it might be best to deprive Hakon of his company forever by hanging him."

Ranulf looked down at Edgar again. He was at once sorry. His eyes filled with the same burning, painful tears they had before. *My eyes seem to live of their own today,* he thought. They looked at certain sights, and tears fell from them the same way blood gushes from an open wound. He knew he would carry the grief of this day like a hidden wound on his soul all the days of his life.

He stared at Tosi through the mist of tears and hoped Tosi wouldn't beg for his life. Then, he realized Tosi was grim and tight-lipped, determined to endure whatever fate visited on him without whining.

Ranulf glanced over to where Godwin lay. It was almost night. The sun was on the hills above the river. The last fitful rays reddened the earth around the battlefield and turned the gray stones of Chantalon to molten gold.

Morning, Ranulf thought. *Had it ever been morning?* This day seemed to have lasted a thousand years.

They had placed Godwin on a long pole litter. Even at this distance, Ranulf couldn't tell if he was living or dead. Perhaps he was already gone and the litter his bier. Four men took up positions at each corner of the stretcher with torchbearers alongside them to light their way. At a single command, they lifted the litter from the ground.

Owen walked ahead of the litter, leading the stallion, Rosamund beside it with Godwin's hand in hers. From this, Ranulf surmised the old warrior must still be alive.

As the litter passed Ranulf, the townspeople fell in behind it. Then the sorrowful procession went on until it became four stars in the distance to his eyes. The torches blazed against the velvet black covering the valley, moving ever so slowly toward the city gates.

Ranulf suddenly realized he was alone with Tosi.

"I will sit, if I may, while you determine how to kill me," Tosi said.

Ranulf glanced at Tosi's leg and saw the man had taken a terrific sword cut across the thigh. He'd bound it with cloth and leather to put pressure on it, but blood still leaked out around the edges. Ranulf knew that, like the dead scattered around them, Tosi was no threat to anyone.

Just then he heard a harsh clicking sound behind him. He started and found the act of tightening his sore muscles almost unbearably painful.

"It's only your horse, brave warrior," Tosi jeered. "A most manly steed. A mare in foal."

The mare gave Ranulf a sharp poke in the back with her nose, shoving him several feet forward. Ranulf turned and caught her by the reins. Alone of all the things around him the little strawberry mare seemed unhurt. She was heavily lathered and weary, but she was unwounded and whole.

"Is she in foal?" Ranulf asked innocently.

"Look at her belly, youngster," Tosi directed.

Ranulf saw the low gentle curve of the abdomen. "I thought . . . I thought she was just getting fat," he said.

Tosi made a choking sound, then gave an exclamation of pain. "Don't make me laugh, boy. My leg hurts when I laugh. If you are going to kill me, do it now before the scavengers creep out of the woods to finish the wounded."

In the distance, something howled. Dog or wolf? Ranulf wondered. But then perhaps to those who lay dying, one set of fangs was the same as another.

"And be kind to that mare," Tosi continued. "She carried you as well as her little one through this long, bitter day. She's a game little wench, and you will get a fine foal of her."

Ranulf made his decision and acted on it with a speed that astonished even Tosi. With one quick movement, he cut Tosi free and pulled him toward the strawberry mare.

"What are you doing?" Tosi asked.

"Putting you on the horse," Ranulf said.

Tosi's leg was so badly injured that getting him into the saddle was quite a struggle. At the last, he had to hold Tosi's belt and give him a final hard boost to help him get his injured leg over the horse's back.

Tosi seemed in no hurry to leave. He stared down at Ranulf, puzzled.

Ranulf looked up at the sky. The sunset had reached

that magical moment when the whole earth is dark but the sky is suffused with a crystalline blue light.

"Godwin would probably hang you," Ranulf said. "I cannot think what Owen would do, but I don't think he would show you any mercy, either. I believed I had abandoned hope today, but then you spoke and told me the mare was in foal. I saw life hides under the very mantle of death. Sometimes a man born to his duty may not choose life over death, but from this day forward, I will, whenever I can." He looked at Tosi. "Go now. Tell Hakon to trouble us no more. As to the mare, I ask only that you treat her with the kindness she deserves."

"You have my word," Tosi said. Then he clucked softly to the mare and began to wend his way slowly toward the forest.

Ranulf saw torches on the road and walked toward them. He met Judith driving two dappled gray mules. Several outriders accompanied her.

Ranulf told Judith about Edgar's body. She sent her men and refused to let Ranulf show them the way. Instead, she seated him in the cart and gave him some wine.

When Judith's men returned with the dark cloth-wrapped bundle, their leader removed his helmet and spoke softly to Judith and Ranulf. "We did our best with him, but his flesh had stiffened, and we could not free the sword from his hand."

To his own horror, Ranulf's tears began to flow again, and however comforted, he could not get them to stop.

Darkness had begun to gather at the edges of Godwin's mind. He couldn't seem to organize his awareness into one clear coherent train of thought. He drifted away before he could finish the sentences his mind forged.

Near the city, the stretcher lurched as one of the bearers stumbled. Godwin cried out in pain and was brought to full consciousness by his own shout. He felt instantly ashamed. He heard Owen close by, admonishing the litter bearers to be more careful.

Near him, someone wept. The sound was one of utter

desolation and bottomless pain. *Who?* he thought, then realized to his irritation that his eyes were closed.

He opened his eyes, afraid he would see only darkness, the harbinger of eternal night. However, he was profoundly relieved to realize he could see at least dimly by the light of the torches surrounding the litter. The weeping one was Rosamund.

"Stop caterwauling!" he snarled.

Rosamund hiccupped, gasped, and stopped.

"Take my hand," he said.

She did. He could feel her small damp fingers lost in his own large, dry ones. Godwin glanced toward her. She walked facing forward, striding along beside the litter. Her expression suggested her feelings were a little bit hurt.

He turned his eyes from her and looked toward the sky. Above him and on either side the burned-out house fronts of the lower town passed by. He knew in a few minutes he would be in the square.

He tightened his fingers around Rosamund's. She turned toward him, the expression on her face remote, hurt, and puzzled at the same time.

"Listen to me," he whispered. "I have only a few moments to give you. Then I must die as a man like me is supposed to die—without whining or moaning and with the proper words on my lips. I will tell you presently what I wish you to publish as my last words.

"Now pay attention! You have property. Judith has it here with her. She will know how to invest it to get you a good living. You need never ply your trade as a woman of the town again."

Rosamund nodded in a dazed fashion.

"I will not caution you *not* to marry the first handsome young man who smiles upon you," Godwin continued. "I believe you are already smarter than that. If you do marry, let it be someone of substance. And make sure Judith and Owen examine the contract before you sign it. Should you ever need help, apply to Judith and Owen at once. However much they may deny it, they both love you."

"Lady Elin is gone," Rosamund whispered.

"Yes," Godwin muttered almost to himself. "I thought

as much." His eyes closed and Elin was before him with her dark hair and blue eyes. In his mind's eye he could see her moving swiftly under the trees, as much a part of the forest as a black shadow or the wind-driven clouds flying past the dim moon.

God go with you, kinswoman, he thought. *Your sorrow ransoms the city. When you see the mountains at last and they catch the first of morning on their snow-clad peaks, think of me and my soul will ride beside you for a moment into the light.*

Pain and exhaustion began to overwhelm him. "Cover your head with your veil," he told Rosamund. She obeyed, wrapping it around her face.

"No doubt," he said softly, "the other women will screech and howl as though they are taken in travail, but from you I shall expect the discretion of a wife."

He heard the shout that went up as he was carried into the square and endured the jolts as the litter was placed on trestles near the fountain so all the city could look on him. He let his mind drift.

After all . . . he thought, *there is nothing left for me to do . . . except be mourned.* He knew what they could give him, and it would end his pain.

The women were wailing around him. Alfric lifted the blanket covering him, looked at the wound in his belly, then turned away with a shiver. He let the blanket fall back. Something like a tree blotted out the light at Godwin's left hand. He looked up and recognized Ivor.

"Jarl Godwin," Ivor said with an inclination of his head. The berserk, as was his custom, was robed and hooded in black, his maimed face hidden from the crowd.

"You will, of all men, understand," Godwin told him, "that I do not want to be a pile of rotting flesh, to be shoved into a coffin by veiled men covering their faces with cloths soaked in spirits to kill the stench. I wish to die clean. I wish to die with brave words on my lips as a proper man of my rank does. Alfric, you will invent proper last words for me."

Alfric and Owen, standing at his feet, glanced at each other, a bit of consternation in their faces.

Elutides stroked his lantern jaw. "Memorable, you say," he commented. "How about 'I failed the honor of my name for love, but in war I stand forever unconquered' or 'In desire I embraced my doom, but stride out among men of war . . . invincible.' "

Godwin smiled. Not the terrible smile of his rage and destruction but the amused, ironic laughter he showed Rosamund or his friends. "Each or both, if you like," he whispered. "A very intelligent and inventive man. I believe I would like you, had I time to get to make your acquaintance."

Gowen was carried by in a litter; he was howling. A dozen women followed him, weeping.

"What?" Godwin asked.

"Gowen," Owen explained. "They are taking him to the hall."

"I hate it," Godwin whispered. "The big son of a bitch will probably survive."

"Look at her," Routrude shouted, pointing at Rosamund. "Not a tear in her eye. I'll bet she can't wait to get her hands on his property." There was a growl of fury from the crowd, and a shower of missiles descended on Rosamund.

She screamed and began sobbing as though this last attack were simply too much for her. "No," she moaned. "No, I won't lose you and remain behind. I won't and you can't make me!" Then she shrieked and fell to her knees beside the litter.

Godwin cried, "Owen! You are the lord here! See to her protection." Then he made as if to rise. He was only able to lift himself a few inches from the pillow. Then he whimpered and fell back, his eyes half open, set; his face pale, looking like a dead man. For a long half minute, he didn't breathe until Ivor turned his head to one side, and he took a deep breath and sank into even deeper unconsciousness.

Judith pushed her way through the crowd followed by Gynnor. They were the women in the town with the most medical knowledge. Judith lifted the blanket and they both studied the wound. Fresh blood was oozing from the edges. "Ivor, what do you think?" Judith asked. "Shall we prepare the cup?"

Ivor studied Rosamund. She was still kneeling, forehead against the edge of the litter, her hands clutching the poles. Her face was hidden from his eyes. The crowd pressed in all around. For the most part, they were silent. Gowen's howling was still coming from the cathedral, where he and many of the other wounded had been carried. The torches hissed in the still air.

Everyone knew what the cup was. Both Gynnor and Judith could put together the mixture: eau-de-vie with a large dose of opium dissolved in it. Sometimes, if the patient didn't know he was dying, syrup of violets was added to cut the bitter taste of so much opiate. Sometimes, a sedative dose of valerian was added. This relaxed the dying one, sending him or her into a deep sleep before opium stilled the breath. But usually the patient knew what was offered and welcomed it. It was given to women who were dying in childbirth, men wounded in the gut, their insides rotting out, and others with infected wounds that wouldn't heal who slowly wasted away until only a shell or a shadow remained.

"Owen, you make the decision," Judith said. "You are lord here now. All the rest are gone. The count, Reynald, now even Godwin. You rule here. Speak!"

Owen looked up, then around. The torch fires wavered, then guttered in the winter wind, the sound of flames the only noise. No one would meet his eyes, not even Elutides. Only Rosamund.

She lifted her head and looked up. "I understand his wishes," she said. "I think he was afraid of death, but never a man to yield his dignity to fear. Yet, I think we must try this one last time before we lose him. If I see him unmanned, I will yield him to you. As for me . . ." She looked away from Owen into Ivor's face. "You are not from here, and I think you understand what must be done if he dies."

Ivor nodded gravely.

"I will deck myself in all my jewels," she whispered.

"And I will strangle you with my own hands and send you with him. I will place your body beside him. I promise you," Ivor said. "And," he continued, "you will stand before him in those halls where the dead sit and be ranked with him. He will take the cup of immortality from your hands, both of you forever honored among the brave."

A gasp of horror rose from the crowd.

"No," Judith said. "Don't be a fool."

"Be quiet," Owen said. "Wife he called her and wife she is. Nor will I hear her spoken of as less than wife without punishing the speaker. If he dies, and she still wishes to follow him, then she may do so even as she has promised. Now, while he remains senseless, carry him into the hall."

For a time, Godwin didn't really become conscious again.

Rosamund gave everyone cause to admire her.

Elutides, Anna, Judith, and Gynnor put their heads together over Godwin's wound. Judith departed and returned with gold wire, an awl, and a wire cutter. Gynnor busied herself mixing a cup. Not the death cup, but one heavily laced with opium, syrup of valerian, and a mild, white wine steeped in chamomile. Rosamund managed to awaken Godwin long enough to drink it.

His eyes opened and he looked up at her face. It was close to his, and he felt mildly grateful, gazing out as he now did from the halls of darkness, that she would be his last sight. She seemed, in the candlelit shadows of his bedroom, to be a perfect incarnation of springtime. Even yellowed by lamplight, her skin reminded him of apple blossoms dipped in cream, and the greatest painters and sculptors couldn't for one moment duplicate the curve of her rose-petal lips. Her eyes were blue, not the almost cruel sapphire blue of Elin's eyes, but warm, silken blue like a harebell in a wind-tossed meadow. Godwin drained the cup to the dregs, thinking such a vision might be a happy beginning to an eternal sleep.

He woke twice while they were putting him back

together. Ivor held his arms, Elutides his feet. Alfric tied his belly muscles together with the gold wire. "It is an alloy," Judith had explained as she handed the wire to Alfric. "Pure gold wire would be too soft."

The opium in the cup kept Godwin from feeling anything. The first time he wondered if he was dying and the embalmers had somehow begun their work before he was dead. He looked down carefully at what Alfric was doing and felt he'd been wrong. He must be dead already, eviscerated and being prepared for laying out in state at the cathedral altar.

He drifted into darkness again, hoping these vagrant returns to consciousness wouldn't continue for too long. When he woke again, he was annoyed by the realization that he was still alive. Ivor was holding his naked body in his arms. Rosamund was arranging a poultice on the sword cut, then bandaging him from groin to chest with clean dressings. "I find this humiliating," he told them. "Cover me."

"Presently," Ivor promised.

Presently, they dressed him in a clean linen shift and put him to bed. He rested for a time uncomfortably, neither asleep nor awake, unable, because of the drug, to reach full consciousness, unable, because of the growing pain in his wounds, to reach the full darkness of sleep. Then, at dawn, he was plunged into the maelstrom of fever.

Everyone in the city was hard at work. There were many wounded. The battlefield had to be cleaned up. The dead were either buried or, in the case of the Vikings, thrown into the river before the stench of decay poisoned air and water, and caused plague. Loot was gathered, shared out among the citizens.

Owen adjudicated quarrels for days.

Rosamund and Ivor cared for Godwin. He chilled, shivering violently. They piled on blankets and kept him warm until he threw them off, his body burning with fever.

Rosamund ran to the cellar and mixed draughts that brought his temperature down and at least allowed him to drink the mixture of white wine and water, which was all his stomach would hold. Then he would manage a few hours' rest until the next chill struck him.

Daily, she washed his clothing and bed linens, there being no one else to share the task. Daily, she and Ivor sponged him when the chills ended and the fever reached its apogee, then doused him until it broke and he soaked his bedding with perspiration. Then Ivor held him in his arms while Rosamund changed bed, bandages, poultice, and Godwin's woolen nightshirt.

Ivor noticed two things. The wound was healing clean under the poultice. The chills were growing shorter and shorter, the fever less intense. Godwin was recovering.

After about four days, near the end of the week, Godwin furnished everyone proof that he was going to survive and the crisis was past. He woke in the night lucid, without fever.

Rosamund and Ivor had worked out a rough nursing schedule between them. She cared for Godwin by day; he took the long, dark night watch. This was a fair division. There was more work to be done by day, but the nights depressed Rosamund and she spent her precious energies weeping over Godwin.

Now she slept in a cot against the wall. She was exhausted, her hands swollen, cuticles cracked and bleeding after her efforts with the washing.

Ivor sat beside Godwin's bed, a rush light burning on the table beside him.

Godwin glanced over at him, then up at the stars beyond the window. They were all he could see. They sparkled in the clear, cold winter sky, a haze of light across the darkness.

"What are they?" Godwin asked. "Did you ever wonder?"

"Often," Ivor said. "I have heard all of the explanations men gave for them. I believe none of them."

"Yes." Godwin's brow wrinkled. "Rosamund asked me a question about them once. I had no satisfactory answer for her, either."

"I believe," Ivor said, "that the explanations even philosophers give are only children's stories, tales we tell one another so we can believe we know about the world when, in fact, we are surrounded by a vast unknown, and each night it arches over us, the rafters of God's immense hall. They wheel in their predetermined dance steps. I have seen them from the sea, where they stretch from horizon's rim to horizon's rim, and any man who knows them well can tell the day of the year, the hour, and even where on the whale road the ship is placed and how soon she will reach land. I have seen them from the mountains, peaks so high neither trees nor even grass will grow, where blood bursts from men's noses and hammers in their ears. In the thin, bitter air, they seem as far away as they are here, only there are many more, and they rule heaven's darkness."

Godwin nodded. "I am alive."

"Yes," Ivor said. "I believe she needed you." He looked over at the dark sprawl of a very weary Rosamund. "And so did I."

"You?" Godwin exclaimed. "Why?"

"Alfric taught me the meaning of the word 'forgiveness,' but you taught me the meaning of the word 'friend.' No man has ever freely taken my hand in generosity as you did. We could not let you go."

Godwin shifted in the bed. "I have a problem."

"What?" Ivor asked.

"I must move my bowels and I believe . . . I believe . . . I could drink one of Judith's possets."

A few minutes later, a bright-eyed Rosamund hurried down the stair.

Ine crawled out from under the table.

"He is . . . he is . . ." Rosamund started. "Call Owen."

Ine charged upstairs.

The entire household arrived in the hall within one minute. Before Owen could get downstairs, Routrude, the widow Clea, and three of her ladies were pushing through the door.

"What is it?" Owen asked.

They were all gummy-eyed and clad in early morning dishabille.

"Godwin has asked for the pot and one of Judith's possets."

A violent battle immediately broke out between those believing Godwin was to be despaired of and those thinking he was much improved. The war of words hinged on Judith's posset.

They were far famed. Several of the injured in the church demonstrated exceptionally rapid recovery from their wounds after drinking one. The other party was of the opinion that not a few men died in an effort to escape being given another.

Once, having tasted one, Enar expressed the opinion loudly that since Judith's recipe was a secret, it would be just as well if she did not communicate the ingredients to any third party, the interests of humanity being best served if this particular concoction perished with Judith.

Anna, Rosamund, and Elfwine took issue with this. Routrude took Enar's part, as did the widow and one of her girls. The other felt the posset in question was a help to her during her monthly. A recuperating Gowen, Denis, and Ranulf jumped in on the side of Routrude. Gowen, who had consumed ten of the things, began to wax descriptive about the taste.

Owen put an end to the uproar with a short "Silence."

It worked. Silence fell.

"If Godwin wants a posset, get him one at once." He pointed to Enar, who charged out of the house wearing a nightshirt and a pair of knee-length drawers. "I assume Ivor is giving him the pot?" Owen asked Rosamund.

"Yes." She shook her head so violently her curls tossed everywhere.

A few minutes later, Enar was hammering on Judith's door. The citizens, alarmed by loud noises at this early hour of the morning, charged out into the street bearing swords, axes, clubs, spears, pitch (in case something needed to be burned), and torches. Enar narrowly escaped death at their hands. The only thing that saved him was that he was plainly unarmed, and he made voluble and fluent explanations in four languages.

Judith woke all her servants, whether she needed them or not, to make the posset. She evidently wanted company.

A short time later, Owen was pleased to note Ivor

coming downstairs, covered clay pot in his hands, and Enar returning, posset in hand, with an escort of Judith, her servants, men at arms, and about forty armed men. Every light in the city was burning; every citizen except children not old enough to talk knew Godwin had used the pot and asked for a posset. And they were as divided on the issue as those in the bishop's hall.

Ivor had helped Godwin back to bed. Despite Godwin's protests, he cleaned him and pulled the covers up around his shoulders.

Rosamund entered with the posset. Godwin drank the posset down. He frowned. "Do you know, it's been a long time since I ate, but I do not find the taste of that at all bad. Do you think she would consider making me another one for breakfast?"

"I'm sure she would," Rosamund promised.

Godwin stretched out, albeit slowly, pulled the blankets up to his chin, and drifted away into a deep, dreamless sleep.

OWEN was successful. Elin was gone, but he was successful. Everyone in the city called him lord. And it appeared they conspired among themselves to drive him crazy.

The women arrived at his hall before dawn. Normally it began with Routrude. She came to visit Anna. Clea the widow and one or two of her girls usually followed. Anna and Ingund arrived from upstairs. Elfwine followed. She was still often sullen and quiet, but more and more she joined in the chatter around the hearth that went on day and night.

The men were not much better. For a time, Alfric kept Enar occupied with the wounded. He found Enar's nursing care accelerated recovery in those he suspected liked the free meals and warm beds in the cathedral. And as Godwin's health improved, Ivor joined Enar in emptying the church. A mere glance at Ivor caused several who clung, in spite of Enar's best efforts, to find their health much improved and to take their departure. Alfric carefully avoided giving either man anyone critically injured. He felt their attentions might speed those individuals in the opposite direction.

Ranulf, Denis, and the "boys," Seifert the tanner, and Osbert the stock dealer, arrived for meals. Ine was underfoot at all times, this quite literally, since he spent a lot of time under the table devouring whatever leftovers he could find.

Judith came frequently, bringing Rieulf and her men at arms. She usually managed to spare the time—between exchanging gossip with Anna and the other ladies who chattered like magpies around the hearth—to lecture Owen on his health.

Half the city treated Owen's hall like their backyard, the other half like the front. They brought him every quarrel that arose between themselves to settle and consulted him frequently on the many marriage negotiations going on throughout the city. They ate like locusts, drank like thirsty cattle, and asked every favor they possibly could of him.

To cap the commotion and confusion, Godwin decided to become the most irritable and querulous invalid in the entire history of the world. He treated Rosamund like a combination companion, scullion, maid, and body servant. He ordered her all over the house. Every time Owen looked up, she was dashing by on some errand Godwin had sent her to carry out. In the evening, when Ivor came to do his stint, she usually collapsed with exhaustion. She was remarkably submissive with one small exception.

The problem arose when Godwin began to take solid food. Over the toast. Rosamund firmly believed toasted bread should be a brown color and crisp. Godwin felt it should be a light, golden color, just slightly crunchy.

Every morning, Rosamund fixed his breakfast. Poached eggs, two, only just lightly cooked, the whites congealed, the yolks runny; a bit of the local pork sausage with sage, lightly fried; and the *toast*.

On the first day, Godwin grumbled a bit. On the second, his comments were sarcastic, but not overloud. By the third day, everyone was waiting for the explosion. Rosamund knew what she was doing but was so annoyed with him that she was unable to keep herself from this one small rebellion.

Owen came down early. Anna was at the fire as usual. "Toast Godwin's bread, please," Owen asked her. "I am afraid if she brings him dark toast again, he will do himself some mortal injury."

"Pha!" Anna exclaimed. "Let him. She worked day and night to save him, pitting her youth and strength against the worst of his illness. She would have died for him. She would have died with him. And how has he behaved toward her since he began to recover? Like a perfect beast. He has not one kind or loving word for her. She has poured out at his feet all her tiny, generous heart and soul, and he spurns her!"

"Ah, well," Owen sighed sadly, "perhaps you're right. I haven't the energy to worry about lovers. They will solve it themselves or not. I think that's the problem. She thinks he doesn't love or want her. Not any longer, and the sad thing is, she may be right. Rosamund isn't much. I don't think she ever was from an important family even when she was a free woman, whereas he was once a great nobleman."

Rosamund marched downstairs and picked up the toasting tongs. Her head was bowed; she looked angry. Anna broke two eggs into wine and butter in a long-handled pan and stretched them out over the rising fire. Rosamund toasted the bread.

"He will be angry," Anna said when she noted the color.

Rosamund didn't reply. The pink flush in her cheeks deepened. Somehow she managed to look like a small thundercloud as she stalked up the stairs carrying Godwin's breakfast on a pewter tray.

Crash!

Godwin's yell of rage was audible in the square outside. Rosamund exited Godwin's room, face contorted with rage and sorrow. She slammed his door behind her with a whack that lifted Owen almost completely out of his chair and shook the entire house. Then she ran downstairs weeping—into Anna's arms.

The entire household arrived as they had in the matter of the posset. Routrude heard the yell. Routrude, Clea, and Wolf the Short, who'd been at the widow's house, streamed in, followed by assorted drunks, tavern lice, or just anyone who happened to be passing by. Again, as in the matter of the posset, everyone took sides.

Crash! The front door opened and Ivor entered. Silence fell in the hall. Ivor shambled past, up the stairs, and into Godwin's room.

Everyone—Enar, Ranulf, Denis, Routrude, Clea, Wolf the Short, even Gowen, with his bevy of females, and Ine, who crawled out from under the table, migrated to the foot of the stair and tried to hear what was being said in Godwin's room.

A few moments later, Ivor exited. He was carrying the tray filled with broken dishes and spilled food. He descended the steps and paused next to Rosamund.

She dried her eyes.

"Go up, girl," Ivor said. "He wants to see you."

"I don't believe I want to see him," Rosamund snapped back.

"Don't be foolish. He wants to apologize. Be kind."

Rosamund's tears were forgotten. An expression so beautiful transfigured her face that it shook every one of the watchers to the deepest part of their souls. In a moment, she was flying up the stair, taking the risers three at a time.

As for Owen, he moved away with an expression of terrible desolation on his face. Everyone turned to watch him. He took a few steps toward the table, stumbling a little, eyes unseeing like a blind man. Then he burst into tears.

Enar, Alfric, Judith, and Ranulf met in the cathedral the next day. They held their little conclave under the eyes of a very old wooden statue of Christ. It stood near a door that led from the church to Owen's house.

The side of the cathedral with windows that let in the light was a high-domed building with a basilica look. Something of the Roman classical grace and power was remembered in it. The aisle nearest the bishop's residence hovered in a sort of Merovingian stolidity. The ceiling was lower, and even the squat pillars supporting the graceful, if somewhat flattened arches, managed to suggest the tree trunks of some dark, German forest.

It was called the old statue of Christ just because no one could remember who had carried the thing or brought it to the city, only that it was long ago, even before the sacred oak was felled and the bishop's chair made from the seasoned wood. Some said the statue had been there when the last Romans marched away, leaving the fortress gates open and the empty basilica inhabited only by rats and bats, its broken roof open to the rain.

Now the church stood where the basilica had, incorporating parts of its ancient Roman stonework. This Christ resided comfortably within.

He stood quietly. The wood carver had portrayed Him as a beardless youth, long hair parted in the middle and held back by a leather fillet. He faced the world, a half smile on His lips, eyes wide, looking out with evident enjoyment on all He surveyed. He wore only the rough tunic and mantle of a peasant or laborer. The mantle fastened at the right shoulder with a simple fibula. He made a fifth to their conversation.

"Is he brainsick?" Ranulf asked despairingly. "Elfwine managed to suggest he was last night after we went to bed. She told me the women, led by Routrude, believe Elin put a curse on him because he lay with the magus Elutides' niece in Amajorkia, and he will sink into despair and die as Reynald did."

Judith pushed him back into a beam of light from one of the windows and studied his face. His eyes were red-rimmed and bloodshot. He looked as though he'd been crying. "Ye gods, that woman of yours had turned into a troublemaker—little painted snake that she is. Tell her if you catch her carrying such tales again, you'll send her down to Anna. That terrible hag won't scruple to take a horsewhip to her. When she's nursing a sore behind and must take her meals standing, she won't be so ready to pour every bit of nasty gossip she hears into your ears."

"I don't think she meant any harm," Alfric interjected quietly. "She simply told us what people were saying and we need to know."

Ranulf nodded. "She seemed as worried and frightened by it as I was. We clung together for a long time. After all, Judith, what would we do if we lost him? He first united us, then—or so it is said—his penance and prayer saved us."

Enar nodded gravely. "No, I cannot think he is brain-sick, but I do believe him womansick."

"What is womansick?" Judith asked. "Your name for love?"

Enar looked injured. "No, love is what Ingund and I have. By day we smile on each other, by night . . ."

"We know what you do by night," Judith interrupted impatiently. "Anna tells me this makes the fourth feather tick she's sewn for you. She despairs of keeping you two in mattresses. She says she cannot understand how you can punch out the stuffing, but apparently you . . ."

"Lord!" Alfric cried. "And they say Routrude is a gossip."

Enar's face was a dull red. "He is womansick, I tell you," he repeated. "And that is very dangerous."

"All right, what is womansick?" Judith asked.

"Womansick is when a man follows and looks too long on one who will not look on him. Womansick is when a man sickens with desire for one belonging to another, often another very powerful and dangerous. But the worst womansickness comes to those who follow the dead, for virgins lie in their graves and dream of love and some-times rise with the quicksilver mist to seek it. The never born prowl when the moon is low or on nights when she hides her light and the ground mist thickens on the meadows. And they . . ."

"Pah!" Judith made a sound of total disgust. "You and Routrude are soul mates. Have none of you a brain in your head? Ranulf is frightened by his wife's fancies; you are frightened by your own. Is there no one here with sense?"

"Yes," Alfric said, "me!"

Judith subsided. "And?"

The little monk held up his hands—ink-stained and dusty. "I have been seeing to his papers. And you can learn much about a man by how he conducts his affairs.

Owen is not the meticulous, self-regarding, cautious sort. For that matter, neither was she."

"True," Ranulf said. "Had they been, Hakon would rule here now."

"His accounts are messy to the point of chaos, but he was a good lord unto his people. He knew their poverty when they were suffering the Viking raids and the count's exactions. He canceled most of their debts and, at times, demanded no tithes, not even market fees. Yet he prospered. Much may be accomplished by hard work, and he was an impressively energetic man. He planted orchards, quince, apple, pear, and other fruits. Honey is always in demand, even in times of scarcity. If vermin and other animal and human predators are kept away from the hives, bees keep themselves. He managed every year to produce a large supply of this very expensive commodity. He was, in short, an able man of his hands and thinks well on his feet. He is *not* good at keeping the importunate from driving him into an early grave, so we must take over and free him to protect us and make the city rich."

"Elin made sure he had clean clothes, that he ate, a thing he is wont to forget to do unless reminded," Enar said sadly. "And that a fire was lit on the hearth at night, so he did not wake in darkness. We must do these things."

"Very well," Alfric said. "I will handle the petitioners and decide who he needs to see."

"You!" Enar exclaimed.

"Ivor will stand behind my chair," the little monk said sweetly.

Judith began to laugh.

"Marriages?" Alfric asked. "Who will do the marriages?" Then he added twelve names in rapid succession.

Judith thought for a moment. "Suitable, suitable, a good match, ridiculous, since she is fifteen years older than he, but it will probably work out. He is hardworking and ambitious, she has good land, and the women in her family drop a baby every nine months until they drop dead. As to the last, the woman is a fool. His brothers are tavern lice. They will gamble away her money, her land, and then her. She will wind up working for the widow. Send her to me; I'll put a flea in her ear. If she won't listen, I'll have that nasty curmudgeon of a brother of hers take a stick to her. Unpleasant, but better than being delivered to that fool and his scoundrel family."

"You do the marriages," Ranulf, Enar, and Alfric chorused.

"Certainly," Judith replied. "Elin consulted me on all of them. Who better? And each night at dinner, Alfric, you sit on his right hand. Enar, you sit at his left. Between you two you know every off-color story, every jest that ever brought a blush to the devil's cheek, and every folly ever penned or spoken by the hand or tongue of man. Keep him entertained!"

Suddenly Owen found things much more peaceful. He heard a stated number of petitioners every morning with Alfric and Ivor standing beside him. Then, for the rest of the day, he was free to ride out and hunt. This was necessary. It helped feed his people. Much domestic livestock had been lost to the Vikings. He was able to see to the church's lands and his own, to rescue his orchards and sheep where possible.

The whole valley buzzed with activity. New houses were rising in the villages. The land was being plowed to put in the winter crop. Young trees were being dug up in the forest and planted as windbreaks around the farms.

Godwin was soon up, first on his feet, then able to ride. He, Enar, and Ranulf started to lay out plans to dike a section of the marsh. It turned out that Enar really knew something about reclaiming land from water by using earthworks. And soon the soil was being turned and shoveled into baskets by those promised some of the farms newly freed from swamp and sea.

Wolf the Short finally married Clea the widow. No one was surprised. Gowen started a quarrel with a large and malevolent family by seducing the exceptionally beautiful daughter of the clan's worst troublemaker. No one was surprised by that, either. Owen settled the dispute by paying off the girl's father and threatening to hang all concerned if it went further. Owen was surprised at how readily he was obeyed.

Godwin chuckled when he confessed his doubts. "They are used to you," he said. "Used to obeying you. You will rule here now. So will I."

"I'm not sure what we're doing is legal," Owen mused.

Godwin, standing with his back to the fire on the chilly evening, broke into a roar of laughter. "Stop! It hurts my stomach. Legal! Who gives a damn about legal? What they want to feel is what poor, stupid, little Elfwine wanted to feel when she embraced Rauching. They want to feel safe. You have given them that, and they will cling to you all the days of your life."

"Yes," Owen answered, and knew that Godwin spoke the truth.

In fact, an air of cheerful bustle pervaded the city, and everyone felt a new sense of security. Indeed, a deeper sense of security and optimism than had ever existed in the living memory of even the oldest inhabitant brought new life and energy to every enterprise the citizens began.

No one could remember when there had been no raids, no war. The city had been first attacked almost one hundred years ago. There had been no wooden wall, no palisade then. The Vikings had raped, looted, and burned up to the Roman wall. There had been no defense. This wave of invasion had carried Owen's grandfather to settle on these shores.

Now Owen and the raider chief, Hakon, had squared off to settle matters. In their way, they'd each won. Upriver, Hakon had burned the fortress on the island. He'd invited his men to either settle on Elspeth's land or depart. Most chose to remain. Depending on their wealth and rank, they either took up farming or bought slaves to settle on their lands as tenants. Those had little enough time for fighting, being as much involved in farming as those who walked behind a plow.

When another group of marauders attempted to reoccupy and refortify the island, Owen was gratified to learn Hakon treated them far more brutally than he or Godwin would have. Hakon killed almost all of them out of hand, then crucified the few survivors on the remnants of the palisade. Some months later, when the bodies had begun to fall to pieces, he had Tosi take a party of men and drive new nails through skull and bone so that the skeletons remained as a warning to any who cared to try encroaching on what Hakon considered his land.

The grinning corpses, rags of skin and remnants of clothing flapping in the river breeze, must have discouraged other ambitious thieves because no one tried again. The river and the valley were left in peace.

So Owen thought, *I am a success and she is gone. I am a success and I am alone.*

Enar and Alfric did as Judith told them. One sat at his right hand, the other at his left. They worked so hard at keeping him amused, that he was sometimes embarrassed on nights when even their best efforts seemed fruitless, when he sat late over his wine, staring into the distance, not seeming to hear what was said around him.

He found himself more and more alone. Some days he would ride in early. At times, the hall was empty, both doors open (this would never have happened in the old days) to create a crossbreeze. He would sit in the cool gloom and watch dust motes dancing in the shaft of afternoon sunlight falling through the open door.

One day, several men were brought to him at daggers drawn over some seed grain, but they wouldn't explain why it was so important. Godwin dismissed them, promising to settle the dispute.

Later that night, Godwin explained. "Don't you remember the day when Anna caught the two of you playing about on the seed corn? You were tumbling her, I believe."

"Yes," Owen whispered. "We hadn't been together long. God!" His voice broke. "It seems a thousand years ago." Then he brought himself under control. "But why do they care about that?"

Godwin stared down into his wine cup and wouldn't meet Owen's eyes. "I'm not sure they think she's human or that they ever did. But one thing they do believe is that when such as you and she join in love on . . . well, you know. They half believe seed grain is magical anyway. To them, this has a special blessing."

"Just so," Owen replied. His dark eyes were luminous in the half-light as they sought and met Godwin's. "Do you think she will ever return?"

Godwin shaded his face with his hand so he didn't have to look at Owen any longer. It was simply too painful. "Cousin, I wish I could give you hope, but I don't know. But one thing I do know is that she finds this separation as painful as you do. She loves you to distraction. I knew when I saw her forswear revenge. She would rather see you living and happy in the arms of another than seek your death. And Owen, to place the good of another before all else is the purest love."

"Share out the seed corn as fairly as possible," Owen said as he rose from his chair. "Will you do that for me?"

"Yes," Godwin replied. Then he watched Owen turn hurriedly toward the stair to his room. But the boy hadn't been quick enough, and Godwin saw the tears on his cheeks.

The weather grew warmer. The seed corn was given out. Every farmer took a cup to mix with his own. Owen and other landowners trooped out into the fields to work. While most of the heavy labor was carried out by serfs and free tenants, Owen himself had to be involved as a supervisor and decision maker.

The period of disorder had continued so long that once productive manors had been allowed to return to waste. Fences were broken down, boundaries were doubtful, and whole families had lost track of land they had cultivated for both the church and themselves.

Owen's presence reassured his people, and his decisions helped move the work along. Thus, he was there when the cart made its rounds through the fields. It was piled high with meat, bread, wine, and beer. A procession of wild revelers followed it. "She" rode in it.

Who was she? There were those, even among his priests, who told him with almost straight faces "she" was the Blessed Virgin. There were other stories. He'd heard them all and believed none of them.

But whoever "she" was, "she" did not brook interference with *her* procession over *her* demesne. Long ago, a bishop had tried to ban her. The harvest failed. No one would say what happened to the bishop. But a year later the see fell vacant. The next bishop wisely let her alone, as had all subsequent churchmen.

The wooden image the cart bore was so old and worn, no one could make much of it. But the exaggerated sexual features left no doubt that a woman was represented. Normally these attributes were covered by a silk tunic, but this year an extra garment had been added—an azure mantle held in place on the right shoulder by a brooch set with clear, blue aquamarines. He recognized it. Long ago both had belonged to Elin. She had given them to Rosamund in return for some favor the girl had done her.

Normally, no one would have brought the cart near him, but Owen was dressed as simply as the plowman laboring in the next field, wearing an old, brown tunic and helping to mend the coping on a broken stone wall. When he looked up, the cart was almost in front of him.

The cart driver was aghast. The revelers fell silent as though caught in a frozen tableau. No one could think what to say or do.

Owen gazed at the mantle and brooch. Then he smiled, a strange sad half-smile, and looked away toward the river.

The sky was a hazy blue. The force of the winter sun was broken by hundreds of soft mare's-tail clouds. The wind was from the woodland, filled with the first promise of the new season, damp earth, oak bark, and a fresh tang of pine.

Owen glanced back toward the cart, and for one heartbreaking moment, he seemed to see her standing there. She would have been just as ready to join in the work as he was. Skirts pulled up above her ankles, feet bare, her slender waist and high breasts giving her dress something to do to hold back those beauties. Her face with the well-remembered smile, blue eyes, and long, iridescent black hair floated before him. Then the image faded. *Ah, love,* he thought. *Ah, my love, Elin. Where are you?* "Where are you?" he whispered. But there was no answer. Nothing but his strangely abashed people looking at him both in sorrow and fear.

Just when the silence seemed to become unbearable, he spoke. "What?" Owen asked, still smiling. "Will no one give me a drink that I may raise a cup to my lady?"

A woman brought him a cup. He lifted it. It was filled with a fine white wine. He drained it; then the cart passed on with its laughter and bawdy jests, receding in the distance and leaving silence behind.

The men who'd been working with Owen eased away from him. They spoke quietly among themselves but didn't address any further questions or requests to him that day. And he, in his turn, was thankful to be left leaning against the wall, gazing into the distance, watching the day turn to evening gold, feeling the wind on his face, along with the wind, the river, and the wide and empty sky.

From Amajorkia, Elutides sent a sort of crown of honor. A laurel victor's crown, not of the fresh plant, but worked in a very soft old silver with gold ribbons. Owen called on Martin, the priest from the fishing village, and Alfric to sing a mass. After the mass, he had them make an offering of the crown to the church. Thereafter, it hung over the altar by several fine chains from the roof.

The food and wine he received from the Bretons in return for his services he had distributed to the needy. And more and more, as the weather warmed and the field burgeoned with new life, he could be found sitting over an untouched cup of wine in an empty hall watching the play of dust motes in the air and the movement of sun on the floor.

Hakon was also successful. Though he was less unhappy than Owen and less surprised than Godwin, he was equally in love.

True, he'd been defeated, and this defeat was final, but he still retained all of Elspeth's lands and much other heavily forested acreage all along and on both sides of the river. Most had been abandoned by settlers at the very beginning of the Viking raids, almost a hundred years ago, long before he'd come to the valley. He wasn't slow in seizing control of it. The few still clinging to homesteads in what was now called a waste hurried to pledge him fealty. He accepted quickly and, seeing their loyalty much to his advantage, offered them generous terms to remain. The agricultural villages of the region could become tightly closed corporations that would not admit an outsider and would even expel young people who married, without permission, someone not a member of the controlling group. These outlyers, on the contrary, were not jealous and had land to spare. He could use them as a nucleus for new settlements.

He was also careful to distinguish between actual scofflaws, brigands, and Viking marauders and those frequent sojourners who came asking for honest work. He was quick to find ingenious ways to fit them in without offending Elspeth's people, and while a few proved dishonest and had to be executed or expelled, most were useful adjuncts to the community.

He also was pleased to note Owen could be as remorseless as he in dealing with those who would not keep the peace. Five men who escaped his hand when he chased the new Viking band out of the fortress reached Owen's lands. There, they made the grisly mistake of murdering a smallholder and his wife who lived at the edge of the forest.

These were the lowest of the low, slaves belonging to a serf tenant of Owen's, a man higher in status than they, though not even free himself. They had survived by keeping their owner's few sheep, catching the occasional pig in the wood, and gathering firewood, honey, and wild mushrooms in spring and autumn. Slaves, and not even very valuable ones at that. So base as to barely be considered human.

Owen captured the five within hours. His force was now the most formidable for some hundreds of miles around: one hundred men who could fight mounted or on foot, fully armed with swords and axes besides carrying the magnificent crossbows Denis made. Owen kept another hundred in reserve.

Very privately, Hakon reckoned he would rather kiss a viper than take Owen on now.

Many of the townsfolk were willing to shrug such a killing off. The leader swaggered before Owen and offered him the same kind of bribe they'd once offered Count Anton—a part of their takings when they robbed Hakon's people. They would, in short, plunder among Hakon's out-lying villages in return for Owen's protection.

Death, no doubt, Hakon thought, came as a shock to them, because within ten minutes they were all dead. Hakon's informant told him Owen's rage had to be seen to be believed. Their heads were spiked on the Roman wall, bodies hung by the heels beneath them.

Summary justice. Public opinion was in favor of it. Owen was cheered in the city streets and openly spoken of with approval even among Hakon's men. Elspeth's short "About time!" was as close to defiance of him as she'd ever come.

Owen's fame spread as a lord who did justice and would tolerate no rowdies, even when they were a nuisance to an enemy. Owen also acquired a reputation for generosity because he gave the murdered pair a decent funeral and gravesite in one of the churchyards near the city.

Hakon knew something about Owen. It wasn't a thing he wanted to know about a friend, much less an enemy. He knew the pair who perished at the brigands' hands had not been only lowly unregarded objects to Owen. They had been people, human beings he felt he should have protected, to whom he believed he owed protection by virtue of what he was—the bishop of Chantalon. Owen bowed the knee to a God who called all men brothers, and believed in his teachings.

At times Hakon sat at table and he glanced over at Bertrand, his brother-in-law. He knew him to be cruel, a man who was sure the church's authority allowed him to persecute others. And he knew there would always be Bertrands, stiff-necked, angry men who wrapped love and compassion in an armor of self-righteousness.

But then, there would always be men like Owen who believed in and acted on duty, charity, and love. Overall, the message they heard and preached offered more hope to the world than the dark northern gods sitting in their smoky halls, ready to drink the blood of sacrifices, animal and human, and offer the highest rewards to the violent.

Because of this, one day—he was putting off the time—he would bend his neck and enter the baptismal water. Some of the things he'd captured were Christian books. And Elspeth had been surprised to learn he could read all of them and that, from time to time, he would sit with one open on his lap, staring into space, a puzzled expression on his face.

At times, he asked her questions which she answered as best she could. As far as the earth and its needs, she was more than half pagan. But in some ways, such as in faith, in the sacraments, and attendance at mass, she was a good Christian. Indeed, women like her puzzled him. They refused to give up pagan roots but were devout in church attendance. But then he didn't care. Like most of the human beings he'd known, women mostly didn't feel an obligation to be consistent. And as far as he was concerned, she was one deeply loved and free to be anything she chose.

Only one thing still bothered Hakon. The boy, Eric. He was all the more anxious because Elspeth doted on the boy. At first, he'd felt this was simply a woman's preference for a male child, but after a time, he came to believe her sense of closeness was routed differently than her feelings for the girls.

They were plainly Reynald's offspring, but they'd inherited the sunny side of his nature, not the dark, brooding, treacherous one, though Hakon thought once, as he watched them scuffle savagely over a toy, that they might easily slide off in that direction.

He would see they married well, but not to doting old men. He would find young, vigorous husbands for both. He was fairly sure they would inherit the lusty side of Reynald's nature, also. They would need men who put them through their paces frequently and satisfactorily.

Eric was a different matter. The boy shared his mother's complex character. He watched the procession of life as it passed him by with wide, dark eyes. He sometimes seemed what the girls never were—intimidated. Hakon had unpleasant visions of the boy growing into the same type of young man he had been. Hakon reckoned his father and a few of his father's friends who singled him out for abuse had been lucky. Remembering what happened when his rage finally exploded still gave him chills. He wanted no brooding presence at his table, sitting next to Elspeth, totaling up his weaknesses as he aged. Now the boy stalked him, watching everything he did. The kind of cool intelligence he found in Elspeth was well and good in a woman, especially a woman who loved him, but it frightened him in a man.

At least it did until a day in early spring. One morning he awoke hearing the women shushing each other. His suspicions were immediately aroused. "What's going on?" he asked, sitting up and reaching for his sword. It hung at the bedstead.

"I didn't mean for them to awaken you," Elspeth said. She was standing at their chamber door. He noticed she wore a silken nightdress under a heavy woolen mantle trimmed with wolf fur. Incongruously, she was booted. Several of her women were gathered around her. They were also partly clad in night wear. They were frightened. She looked distraught.

"What's wrong?"

"It's Eric." One of the women he recognized as the children's nurse spoke. "He's gone." Then she burst into tears. "I swear, I never heard him sneak out. I can't imagine why he would do such a thing to terrify his mother. . . ."

"Maybe he didn't." Hakon was growing impatient. "Maybe he was taken."

Elspeth went white under the impact of his words. The rest of the women looked ready to fly into hysterics.

As though that would do any good, he thought gloomily. But he wasn't about to suffer this tamely. "Elspeth, come here!" he ordered. "As for the rest of you, go! Now, unless you're prepared to watch me relieve myself and dress, for I'm naked under this bedcover."

They departed quickly. He rose and pulled the pot from under the bed.

"You don't really believe he's been carried off, do you?" Elspeth asked.

"No!" He covered the pot and donned his clothes quickly. "Belike he is about some child's trick. Elspeth, I wouldn't worry. I and my men will find him quickly enough. I only spoke the way I did because their cater-wauling annoyed me."

She spun around and walked to one of the narrow slits that served as windows. She shivered. "It's not yet dawn. The light is gray. But he's a strong boy. He could go far in a short time. Who knows what wanders those woods at night. He's been very troubled of late. I've felt it. But he wouldn't confide in me."

"Elspeth"—Hakon spread his hands helplessly—"I can probably find the boy, but I told you once, as a father . . . as for taking a belt to him, well, I'm a good judge of character . . . that would earn me his hatred and you no better obedience than before."

"Only find him." She lifted her fist and pressed her forehead down on her knuckles. "Hakon, please, please find him."

He nodded and was reaching for his heavy mantle when the door burst open.

One of Hakon's men entered towing a rebellious-looking Eric by one arm. The man was a giant. He wore a boar-tooth cuirass and bear skins. "He was following me as I was plowing," the big man told Hakon.

Hakon saw a few bruises purpling on Eric's biceps. "Llwyd, go easy. He's a son of the house, not a runaway slave."

"Aye," Llwyd answered, "and just as well because he has tried to bite me three times and succeeded once. I will accept compensation, not take revenge."

"You didn't tell me where you were taking me." Eric stared up at the big man with furious eyes.

Llwyd chuckled. "An oversight on my part." He looked

down appraisingly at Eric. "I had to chase him nearly a mile. He shin kicks, climbs trees, and, as I said, bites really well. He is slender after the manner of the bishop, but like the bishop, will answer to neither God nor the devil when he is a man." Then Llwyd turned and was gone.

"Thank God!" Elspeth was on her knees embracing Eric. He stiffened. "I'm muddy, Mother."

"Who was that?" she gestured at the door.

"The Welshman," Hakon answered. "A law unto himself. But none better to bring him home safe." He scooped Eric up, noting that the women had done a useful thing at least: brought him his shaving water. Eric was, as he had said, mud to the knees.

Holding Eric in the crook of one arm, he began to wash his feet with the other hand. For a second he was a bit shocked by his sensations. *How long has it been since I held a child in my arms?* Eric was warm, though the small fingers and toes were chilled. He was fragrant, smelling of fresh, cold air and damp earth.

"Will he want much compensation?" Eric asked.

"Who?" Hakon had forgotten.

"Llwyd!" Eric prompted.

"No, that's his idea of a joke."

"Oh." Eric looked thoughtful. "I really didn't need to be afraid of him."

"No. Despite his looks, he's very kind." Hakon finished with the feet and began drying them on a towel. "But don't let on to him that you were afraid. You won him over by being brave. He didn't think you were frightened. He believed you were up to some kind of mischief."

"No." Eric was emphatic and shook his head.

Elspeth watched them in silence, delighted, afraid to move or speak lest she interrupt something she hadn't believed could ever happen.

"Well," Hakon asked, "what were you doing, then? You frightened your lady mother. That's undutiful and unkind."

Eric looked stricken. "I only wanted you to be proud of me. All the men said Llwyd was the best farmer. You said I needed to know what the plowman knows. I got up in the cold and dark the way the plowmen do and followed him a long way, but I didn't learn anything. It's time I began my preparation for manhood, but there's no one to teach me."

Hakon picked up his heavy mantle, decorated by black fox and wolf. He wrapped it around both of them. The boy's feet and hands were thoroughly chilled. Odd, he felt as he had when he'd first seen Elspeth, as though something momentous was happening, but he couldn't think what.

Then he understood. He was being offered something. Something he wasn't sure he wanted. He studied Eric for a long moment. He was a child handsome as his mother was beautiful. And as intelligent and steadfast as she. Yes, Llwyd had been right. He was slender, but he would one day be tall, graceful, quick, and strong. A son to be proud of. A good friend but a dangerous enemy.

For the first time in a long time, Hakon felt the mountain ice that even high summer doesn't melt enter his soul. He saw the sadness in Eric's eyes mirror the chill in his. But just then, the fell truth was borne upon him.

His father had thrown him away. He remembered his rage. In the end, that rage would have brought him killing to his father's hall. If Tosi and Asa hadn't drugged him and loaded him on a boat for Wessex, he would certainly have confronted his father and not stopped until he or everything in front of him was dead.

But however deep and pitiless that rage had been, it only mirrored the love he might have felt if his love had been returned.

Now he was standing where his father once stood. He was being offered such a love, and it was up to him to accept or reject it. And what had stubborn hatred ever won that evil old man? Nothing, he was certain now.

No, he wouldn't emulate his sire's folly. No, he would not throw this away.

"Come," he said to Eric. "I'll bring you to the hall. We need to get some warm food in you."

"But I didn't learn anything," Eric repeated disconsolately.

"Didn't you?" Hakon asked. "Did you walk the furrow?"

"Yes."

"And how did the earth feel?"

"Wet."

"How wet? Squishy like the river?"

"No. Crumbly moist, but not dry like in summer."

Hakon nodded. "An apt description. Very good."

"It was warm," Eric added.

"See, you did learn," Hakon said. "This is the beginning of what the plowman must know. When the earth is ready to turn. When she is ready to receive seed. We will begin your training now. You are ready to become a man." Hakon frowned.

"What's wrong?" Elspeth asked.

"I can't think I'll trust myself as a father."

"How about as a brother?" she suggested impatiently.

Hakon laughed.

Eric looked delighted. "Can we do it now?"

"No," Hakon said, "but we will." He walked toward the hall, still holding Eric. "First, we must build a turf arch, then have a feast. . . ."

Elspeth relaxed her shoulder against the door frame, looking after them, eyes filled with purest love.

40

*B*Y late spring, happiness as well as the river seemed to flow through the entire valley. The crop was green in the fields. Everywhere orchards were in bloom. Cattle and sheep fattened in pastures thick with new, green grass dotted with red, wild poppies and yellow and white daisies. Wild violets, purple, white, yellow, and every shade between, bloomed on every damp and sheltered spot throughout the woodland and valley.

The cold, gray, or brittle blue skies of winter departed and, when soft, warm spring rain didn't bathe cropland, pasture, and forest, the sun shone among puffy white clouds in an azure sky.

Winter lingered only in Owen's heart. He knew Elin must be near her time and felt all the more sorrow for not being able to be with her at this moment. Childbirth was hideously dangerous. Few men cared to look at the matter straight on; some laughed off the hazards their wives faced, but most, when they brought up the matter, privately admitted they viewed it with fear and trembling.

If men felt that way, what did women feel? In his younger days, he'd been brash enough to ask a few. Mostly they laughed it off. One or two played the martyr, but his mother, Clotild, had been simple and direct.

They had ridden together to Reims to make an offering.

Clotild had reached her climacteric safely and was grateful. She told him with stark objectivity that most of the women she'd known died in or after childbirth of direct complications or of some lingering problem related to the act. She could recall, of all the women she'd known in a long life, only a few whose deaths hadn't been connected somehow to childbirth.

He was sick with fear for Elin when Ilo appeared on a beam over the table in the hall.

"My Lord Owen," she called in her piping, little girl's voice.

Owen was so startled he dumped his chair on the floor behind him.

Ilo dropped to the table in front of him. "Go to the church quickly. Alshan wants to talk to you," she said.

Owen left on the run.

He found Alshan standing near the wooden statue of Christ. The old man's eyes and cheeks looked sunken. He was clutching the amber jewel at his breast. "She is taken!" he told Owen.

"What?" Owen gasped. "When? Where? By who? What is she doing here?" he cried out frantically. "Why wasn't I told? Why didn't I know?"

Alshan raised both hands in a temporizing gesture and backed away from Owen. The bishop looked dangerous. "Sybilla was escorting her back to the city. She asked to see Ranulf and Alfric. She asked them to meet her at the giant spider oak."

"Ranulf and Alfric!" Owen exclaimed. "What was she thinking? I could have been there, brought a party of bowmen along. She'd have been safe!"

"She wished to ask if you still wanted her."

"Still wanted her!" Owen cried out in agony. "Oh my God! Oh Christ, I think I will never want anyone else. What happened? How were they captured?"

"If 'capture' is the right word," Alshan said sadly. "Hakon was on the hunt. The dogs found them."

"The dogs!" Owen cried in agony.

"No, no," Alshan stammered. "Don't think such terrible things. Ranulf rode out full armed head to toe. He killed the boar hounds with his sword. The rest of the pack were glad to fall back, whining. But then Hakon, his men, and Elspeth rode up . . ."

In the dim light Alshan saw Owen's face was set.

"And?" he asked.

Alshan backed further away. "Hakon was heard to say 'Hang her! It is the witch. Hang her!'" Seeing Owen didn't move, Alshan continued. "Then Sybilla had to run away. Hakon's men were beating the bushes. She came to me. She was afraid you'd kill her."

"And she was right." Owen spoke with terrible calm. "If ever she comes near me again . . . I will." Then Owen turned. He rested his forehead against the wooden statue, clutching it with both hands.

Godwin had come in time to hear the last part of the message.

"Are you here to tell me to bear up under my loss?" Owen asked. "That I will live to love life again?"

"No, Owen," the old man said. "Some griefs never pass. And I have seen men and women who walk in the light but who put the best and most important part of themselves into a grave. They but keep a vigil, waiting for the dark messenger to invite them down the same road traveled by those they loved. Having watched you for the last months, I can believe you may be one of those faithful unto death and beyond. But even among the dead one may play the man. Do so now. Deal finally with that serpent Hakon. You should never have suffered him so long."

"Oh yes." Owen's voice still held the steely calm. "I will kill Hakon and as many of his men as I can catch. And perhaps Elspeth also, and anyone else who gets in my way."

"Well enough," Godwin said, "but how?"

"I've known how for a long time. The plans are in place. The men are trained. Simply summon Denis. It's child's play. By dawn his stronghold is a pile of smoking embers, and any who gainsay me, charred corpses within."

Owen was surprised by Alshan's voice. "She was one of ours. We also . . . will mourn her. And don't blame Sybilla. She only did what Elin asked of her."

Owen looked up at the beardless Christ. The benign face spoke wordlessly to his own. "Yes," he replied, "please forgive me. You have done us much service. She was always willful and did as she wished." Then he couldn't see the face any longer. His eyes were filled with tears.

Ranulf stood in front of Elin. She was backed up to the broad trunk of the tree. She stood silent, hand on her belly, cursing not her pregnancy but her temporary helpless state. Once, she would have been around the tree trunk and gone. But now . . . both she and the child might die tonight because she was trapped by her coming child.

Tosi stood in front of Ranulf holding the wrist of his sword arm. "Don't," Tosi said. His shoulder was grinding into Ranulf's chest. "Sheathe it! Surrender!"

"He's talking of hanging," Ranulf said shortly.

"Trust me," Tosi said between his teeth. "No one is going to be hanged."

One man rode toward Ranulf, axe upraised. Tosi let go of Ranulf and deliberately turned his back on him.

The axe wielder snarled, "Out of the way." The next moment he lay on the ground, his face bloody.

Ranulf realized Tosi had a short, iron-clubbed mace in his hands. Such things were usually used to give the coup de grâce to large quarry—boar, bear, or bull. Tosi had used it on the man, which meant he could easily have dropped Ranulf. He hadn't wanted to.

"Hang her and do it now!" Hakon ordered. He'd been enraged at first, but now his voice was cold, firm.

Alfric spoke up for the first time. He was standing near Hakon. No one had taken any note of him since he was unarmed and, moreover, a very small man. "Hakon," he piped, "haven't you already enough enemies?"

Hakon pulled his foot free of the stirrup and kicked out. The toe of his heavy riding boot caught Alfric on one cheekbone, sending him sprawling to the ground, blood oozing from his nose.

But Alfric was made of sterner stuff than Hakon supposed. He scrambled to his feet, putting himself in front of Hakon's horse, between the line of Vikings and Elin. Alfric raised his hands in supplication. His large, dark eyes had something of the same effect on Hakon they'd once had on Ivor. "I suppose I'm an easy target, being as I am old, small, and unarmed. If you like, take out your rage on me. Spare the lady Elin . . . at least long enough to bear her child."

Hakon used his horse's bulk to shove Alfric aside. "What is it, Elin?" Hakon taunted. "Hiding behind a boy and a priest?"

Suddenly, Elin pushed Ranulf, who was still in a shoving match with Tosi, aside. She strode into the center of the clearing and stood squarely in front of Hakon's horse.

"Oh God!" Alfric cried frantically. "Elin, you're not helping me."

Hakon's sword left the sheath with a hiss like an angry serpent. The clearing was silent as everyone watched the pair.

By now there was only a faint light in the sky, the dark opal color of deep twilight. Hakon's men were gathered in a semicircle at his back. Their torches lighted the area under the enormous oak. One huge tree, at least as wide as a man is long, dominated the clearing. The limbs stretched out far from the trunk and were so low to the ground, they could be used as benches.

Hakon shivered with the quick, uncontrollable twitching of one taken with a chill. He remembered why. This was the clearing where he'd received Owen from Reynald. Where Osric of evil memory tried to blind his prisoner. That night all his instincts had told him to kill Owen out of hand or . . . let him go. He'd ignored the promptings of instinct, to his cost.

He felt the same about the woman standing before him: kill her or let her go. He remembered her from the camp. Like the rest, he'd thought her mad, but she'd escaped and made mighty war against him. No half measures would do with her.

She was wearing the leather clothing of her people, the deer-hide dalmatic, trousers, and leggings, soft boots on her feet. She was heavily pregnant.

"What?" he asked, mockingly flourishing the sword. "Does the witch plead her belly?"

"I plead nothing. I deny nothing. I regret nothing and . . . I fear nothing," she spat hoarsely.

Elspeth sat beside him watching her world fall apart. She watched Hakon's wrist bend, knowing the sword would take Elin's head off the way a stick snaps off the top of a roadside weed. Hakon needn't even put his arm into the swing.

She leaped down from the horse and flung herself at Elin, embracing her, wrapping her arms around her body and pressing her cheek to Elin's face.

Elin tried to thrust her away. "Elspeth, you'll be killed!" She could feel Elspeth trembling.

"Tosi, help me!" Elspeth shrieked.

Tosi snatched Elin's dalmatic and then, covering her body with their own, both of them wrestled her back toward the tree.

"Are you mad?" Hakon asked. His voice was still quiet.

"Hakon," Tosi said, "admit it. Once before, I took the sword from your hand. I was right then, and I'm right now. Owen loves this forest woman to distraction. The bishop will kill you."

"Oh, will he?"

Elin saw the skin on Hakon's face pulse red around the scar; then it went white, ice color against the snow of his lips and cheeks. His lips drew back in the rictus, the killing smile Elin had seen on Godwin's face. Hakon jerked the horse's head aside and smashed his fist, still wrapped about the sword hilt, into the side of Tosi's head.

He lifted Tosi's body from the ground. After a second in the air, he fell bonelessly into the leaf litter around the tree trunk.

"God!" Elspeth whispered. "He was your brother. He shared the same breast, the same blood you did."

"Elspeth." Hakon flourished the sword. His knuckles were bleeding with the force of his blow to Tosi's skull. "I brook such defiance from no man and no woman, either. Get out of my way or I swear by Christ and the horned one both, I'll send you with the witch to whatever paradise or hell her people's souls inhabit. Now, choose, for I will wait only a few heartbeats till I strike."

"Hakon! Back away!"

There was such urgency in the voice that Hakon pulled the horse back. Ranulf's sword stroke missed by inches.

This left Ranulf standing in front of Elin and Elspeth, drawn sword in hand.

"Don't be a fool, boy," Hakon said, gesturing toward Tosi's prone body. "You won't last any longer than he did."

"Alfric!" Ranulf yelled. "Why did you warn him?"

"Because he must live," Alfric said. "His men are a mob of fools without a head. They would kill us all. Also, I thought him a man who could be reasoned with. Am I wrong, raider?"

"No." Alfric was behind him, but Hakon didn't want to turn. He'd heard enough of Ranulf to be wary of him. The boy had almost taken advantage of his distraction to kill him. This roused his respect as well as his anger. His rage was cooling now. He was beginning to be frightened about what he'd done to Tosi.

"Grant me one favor?" Alfric asked.

"What?"

"Ask your wife why she's so afraid . . . of killing Elin."

"She also believes in Owen's invincibility," Hakon snarled.

"No," Elspeth sobbed. "No! Hakon, they will take my children. I'd rather die than see them take my children."

"Who would take our children, Elspeth? Even the worst of men don't avenge themselves on little ones. You are frightened of old wives' tales."

"No—she's—not." Alfric's voice was clear, crisp, and rational. "Elin's people believe in a life for a life, but not in the sense we do. When one of them dies as the result of something done by an outsider, they feel they have a right to a replacement. The child wouldn't be harmed or even badly treated. They would cherish him or her as one of their own. But the little one would be sent so far as never to be able to find the way back home. Tell me, Elin, how many would they take . . . how many *will* they take? One or two?"

"Two—one for me, one for the child in my womb. Probably the boy and one of the girls," she answered.

Hakon drew back, a stunned expression on his face. He could see Elspeth was in agony.

"Please . . . please . . ." she pleaded brokenly. "Don't let them take my children. I lost the first I ever carried. It was stillborn. I believe there is no worse pain."

"No!" He sheathed his sword, walked over, and embraced her, leading her away from Elin.

Ranulf was helping Tosi to his feet. He was up and aware, but the glance he directed at Hakon was hot with anger. "I believe," he commented bitingly, "Owen would accept a man who came and offered him honest service."

"I would speak for you," Ranulf assured him.

Hakon, his arm around Elspeth, looked shamefaced and sad.

It took some time for the party to get underway. A mount had to be fetched for Elin. Ranulf had a horse, and Alfric was mounted on Enar's mule. Ranulf and Tosi sat on a log and talked horses while Elin's mount was brought to her.

"I'm sure that stallion of Owen's is the sire," he told Ranulf excitedly. "He is a dark, blood bay, not a white mark on him. The little mare is a perfect mother. I'll take you to see them when we get to the hall."

"You told me I'd get a good foal of her," Ranulf said. "I see I bestowed her well."

Elin sat on one of the low tree limbs. Alfric remained with her when he wasn't reassuring Hakon that he would receive a good ransom from Owen for Elin's safe return.

Elspeth dried her tears and continued to watch Elin

anxiously. Elin's hand was on her back in a way Elspeth recognized only too well. Finally, she walked over to her. "Are you in pain?" she asked.

Elin grimaced. "I've been in pain off and on for the last several days."

Elspeth felt a pang of fear. "We'll get you to the hall as quickly as possible."

It was late when Hakon and his party left the woods and turned into the cart trace through the plowed land. There was no moon, the only light the links Hakon's people carried and the distant torches at the gates to Elspeth's stronghold. Elin's condition held the horses to a walk.

It didn't take any great wisdom to know she couldn't bear any speed above a walk and must be within hours of her time. Hakon ignored everyone because he knew he was inches from a blistering fury. What a mess! Elin might still die in childbirth, and Owen would certainly blame him. He also realized bitterly that Alfric had saved him from Ranulf's attack because the little priest had known his man.

In Hakon's view, honor and reputation mandated certain basic decencies. Once having decided to take Elin prisoner, he was incapable of treating her badly.

Single file, Hakon leading, they reached the earthen causeway to the stronghold. It led across the pond that served as a small moat surrounding the palisade fence and the bailey yard where the hall stood.

When he reached the bailey gate, he pounded on it with his fist. He was a bit surprised. Usually his men opened the gate before he reached it, but they had been on the hunt since before dawn, and he was too preoccupied by his irritation and weariness to notice the strangeness, the silence around him.

Except for the torches by the gate and a fire burning in the center of the bailey yard, it was very dark. This was uncommon. Usually on good nights a few of his men would gather around the fire to dice, drink, and tell stories.

But tonight the yard was empty. The fire burned high but alone. The stables on his right were in darkness.

Hakon turned as he entered the gate and spoke to Elspeth. "See to my supper!"

She answered in a voice tight with fear. "Elin's horse is restive. It's not used to the causeway. I must see to her safety and find a midwife. Her time is upon her!"

"Very well, do what seems best to you," he replied furiously, then dismounted and stalked off to the stables leading his big, gray hunter.

Owen was waiting in the darkness just inside the stable door. He hadn't expected it to be this easy, he thought, as he watched Hakon walking toward him. He felt for the knife in his belt. Godwin had given it to him, saying, "Best silent killer I know. Mostly it's used to slaughter cattle and large pigs, but I've used it on a few men. You'll be amazed how quietly he dies." The dirk was only four inches long, but it was three inches wide, and thick, with razor-sharp edges. "It goes into the neck, between the skull and the spine, as close to the skull as possible," Godwin finished.

Owen retreated slightly into even deeper darkness. He meant to draw Hakon in.

Hakon entered the stable and thrust the reins into Owen's hand, saying harshly, "Don't just unsaddle him and shove him into a stall. See he's watered, fed, curried, rubbed down, and given clean straw for bedding. If I don't find him dry and his coat smooth in the morning, I'll have your hide." Then he turned and started out into the yard.

Someone, a heavyset man Hakon couldn't place, stepped out and threw another log on the fire burning in the center of the yard. The flames leaped up, flaring brightly. Hakon glanced up at the sky. It was becoming overcast. *Rain tonight,* he thought. *Fine. It was very dry last month. The crops need it.*

He was worried about Elspeth. She was taking a long time. He wondered if she was having problems with Elin's horse. Maybe he had best go help her.

Behind him, Owen was keeping a grip on the reins with

one hand while he quietly freed the knife from its sheath
with the other. He'd killed a great many men, but he'd
never really had time to think about it. Now he did. There
was nothing good about it. It might be necessary, but no,
it couldn't be good.

His hand tightened on the knife hilt. He dropped the
horse's reins. The right hand would position the blade, the
left would act as a hammer helping drive it home. His
eyes were fixed on the spot where Hakon's spine joined
his skull.

And . . . Elin rode into the yard.

For Owen, time stood still. The blade slipped from his
hand and, cushioned by the straw, fell silently to the floor.

Hatred, anger, and grief are the three most terrible burdens the soul bears. We never realize their weight while
we stagger under them. It is only when the struggling
spirit lifts its face toward the light and its burden drops
free that we truly know its cost, how much we suffered
under that sorrow.

So it was with Owen.

He no longer wanted Hakon's life. And he no longer
felt the same bitter resentment and anger that had poisoned his grief over Elin's desertion. She had run far, far
into the northern forests trying to escape him, Alshan had
told him, but then she'd decided a life without him was no
life at all. So she walked across half the world to return
to him.

Yes, he was still frightened for her. She must be drained
by such a long journey while she was with child. But
whatever happened, she would be beside him, and it would
happen in his arms.

He was jerked out of his reverie by Hakon's voice.
"What? Why are you peering and prying? Put that horse
up and do it now! Lest you stand before me in the hall
tomorrow and answer for your dereliction."

"Yes, sir," Owen stammered, hoping he sounded appropriately servile. "The lady . . ."

"Busybody, eh?" Hakon was standing half in and half
out of the stable door, one eye on Elspeth, who was

helping Elin to dismount, the other on the dark shape that was all he could see of Owen. "You'd best mind your own business. The lady will be a guest for a few days until she returns to her husband. Put up that horse. Now!" Then Hakon strode toward Elspeth. Elin's mount was a skittish animal and looked like giving more trouble.

Enar emerged from a stall near where Owen was standing. "Let's care for the horse properly or Hakon may come back and give us a flogging." He was wearing a wide grin and enjoying the joke hugely.

"She's alive. He didn't kill her. Thank God, he didn't kill her," Owen whispered.

"Yes," Enar replied, "thank God." And he sounded to Owen as though for one of the few times in his reckless life, he was sincerely thankful.

Once Elin was out of the saddle, Elspeth managed to quiet Elin's mount without Hakon's assistance. Elin marched into the hall like a queen in procession. A serving girl lit her way carrying a torch, Alfric and Ranulf on either side and Tosi bringing up the rear.

The hunt had been a success—two boars, three deer, a dozen hares from the snares Hakon set in the burn. The men would do the butchering (what hadn't been done in the field). But even so, Elspeth would have her hands full. The meat that wouldn't be consumed in the next few days would need salting or smoking. This had to be done by the women. They would also undertake the considerable task of sausage making. The men Hakon brought with him on the hunt would be occupied with butchering until late at night. They were already building a fire in the corner of the yard and setting to work on the carcasses.

She began gathering up the horses. One of Hakon's men came to help her, or at least she surmised he was one of Hakon's men. He was big, with long, dark hair, and looked well able to take care of himself in a fight. He wore an axe in his belt, but he had a respectful manner and a cheerful countenance.

Together they led the horses to the stable. As they reached the door, she glanced over and saw one of the grooms currying Hakon's mount. For a moment he paused as he checked the straps on the horse blanket.

The stable was a rather open building, and she saw the young groom's profile against the firelight.

Then, the one with the axe got between her and the stableman. Taking the reins from her hands, he reassured her that the horses would be well cared for. Elspeth took him at his word and left for the hall.

Enar began unsaddling the horses. "Lord Christ Priest," he said with some alarm in his voice, "Elspeth got a good look at you."

Owen, finished with Hakon's mount, came over to help Enar. "Did she know what she saw?"

"I don't think so, but she knew you well and may remember."

Owen leaned down and loosened the girth on the horse Enar was holding. As he was about to remove the saddle, Enar seized it and stopped him. They stood on either side of the horse. Enar spoke to him over the saddle: "My lord, why are you behaving as though you really were Hakon's stableboy? You have had three favors from the goddess of luck tonight: Elin is alive, Hakon didn't recognize you, and Elspeth didn't, either. I would not push the lady luck too far. She is known to be, at best, an inconstant patroness. Whatever you are going to do, you had best act quickly while you have the advantage."

Owen froze, his hand on the saddle. His plans had been formulated when he attacked. He and his men—he took Enar and about thirty archers with him—had waded the lake around the stronghold. It looked like a firm defense, but he and Godwin had known there were areas where the water was only knee deep at best.

He and Godwin had been the only ones who'd known. To everyone else, the little lake with its stronghold in the center looked impregnable. Hakon, Elspeth, and the rest of the world had believed an attacker would have to come by the earthen causeway to the gates. Hakon kept those well guarded, believing any others approaching through the water would drown.

Just after dark, Owen had led his men into the lake. He

found the route he picked even shallower than he remembered, and the rest reached the palisade almost dry shod. In seconds, they were up and over; in minutes they held the fortress. Hakon's men at the gate threw down their weapons when they turned and found crossbows pointed at their hearts.

They were a small force, only about a dozen, but Owen believed that even had they outnumbered his men, the shock of seeing what they believed impossible, so quickly and easily done, would have stunned them into quick surrender.

The rest of Hakon's men were on the hunt or at their farms and manors. The hall was peopled only by unarmed servants and women. They yielded without even the semblance of a struggle. No one was killed; in fact, not even one drop of blood was shed. Owen's men were capable and very well disciplined.

Hakon and Elspeth's people were loyal, but in a cleft stick. Owen had the men gathered in the hall; his men joined them at the tables, weapons and crossbows at the ready.

The women continued their work in the kitchen, storerooms, and weaving rooms. Most were married to the men servants. They were hostage for each other's behavior.

Owen's plan had been simple—when Hakon returned, Owen would kill him. As for Elspeth and her children, she would either marry the husband of his choice or go, taking her children with her. As for the men Hakon had settled on his lands, Owen was fairly sure he could reach an accommodation with the small farmers. They would, in the end, swear fealty to him. As for the more powerful of Hakon's chieftains, he didn't plan to suffer them. He would offer them a choice—leave, or be burned out, killed, or driven away. And he was also sure they would obey him. They now had no leader and no fortified position to retreat to.

When he had told these plans to Godwin, the old devil had given him something more precious than rubies—a look of absolute approval. "You are no longer the boy who once rode out with a man he thought his friend, into treachery and ambush, are you?"

Owen realized he was referring to a day long past when he'd ridden out with Reynald and had been treacherously sold to Hakon. "No," he replied. "I've learned a thing or two since, to my sorrow. Was that this winter? It seems a thousand years ago."

It wasn't a happy solution, though, and Owen knew it. Elspeth's family had dwelt in this valley time out of mind. Some said since before the Romans. Her people would hate him bitterly. At some time in the future, he might even have to crush a revolt. They suffered Reynald for her sake, and Hakon had reached out and tried to win their love and, in a measure, had succeeded.

"Lord Christ Priest!" Enar broke in on his thoughts. "Will you hang on to that saddle all day?"

"No." Owen pulled it off the horse's back. "Get the horses unsaddled and remove their bridles. Someone may notice they haven't been tended to and become suspicious. As to what I will do, I was going to do my worst. Now I'm going to do my best."

Elspeth was prey to so many fears, the worst didn't strike her until she was hurrying through a shadowy hall on what was the men's side of the house.

That man, the one stalling Hakon's horse, was Owen. She staggered; her head spun for a moment. She leaned against the wall. Ahead in the guest quarters where she'd installed Elin, she heard the sounds of chatter and water splashing as her maids helped Elin to bathe and freshen up. Elspeth collected herself with difficulty and hurried toward the kitchen.

The big room was dark except for the cook fire. Bettena was tending a beef haunch roasting slowly in the smoke. When she heard Elspeth's footsteps, she turned, and Elspeth saw the stark terror in her eyes. Then she sighed with relief when she recognized Elspeth.

"The children," Elspeth managed to stammer. Her face was stiff with fear.

"The girls are in their rooms. Some of the weaving women are preparing them for bed."

From where she stood, Elspeth could see into the weaving hall. The women were still there, working by lamplight. This wasn't customary.

"Eric is with the farmer, Llwyd. I sent word for him to stay the night and told the women not to bring the girls to supper. The men . . ." Bettena stared at Elspeth and licked dry lips. "The men are in the hall." Her expression spoke whole volumes.

"Does Hakon know?"

Bettena shook her head. "He's bathing. Corwin and some of the men are attending him."

"How could this happen? How did they get in?"

"My lady, the bishop is the lord of the forest and the sewn. The witch queen, Elin, brought the small people to him. They are her dowry. But he rules in his own right, also. He traveled in the lower world among the dead, drank the cup of life, and looked on the nameless mystery. We had no chance. Even Hakon's men had no chance. Ere we knew, they were among us. We were taken."

"My love and my lord," Elspeth whispered.

"And the bishop wishes your love and lord a dead man," Bettena said as she turned back to the fire.

For a few moments, Elspeth stood trying to collect her wits. "I will need a supper for Elin," she said abruptly. "I don't think she can eat a heavy meal."

"Her people don't believe in much," Bettena said as she fixed a tray for Elin. "But they do answer to the laws of hospitality. Bind her with them. At least she won't be able to call for his death." Bettena carved a larded capon breast into a dozen thin slices and added fresh, sweet bread, the white honey loaf Elspeth favored; a pale, golden wine from an earthenware jug; and a bowl of clear chicken broth with arugula greens floating in it. She added small bowls of salt and expensive pepper on the side.

Elspeth carried the tray to Elin. Her women had finished with her, and Elspeth was pleased to note they'd done a good job. Considering her importance at present, it was likely they'd been afraid not to.

The browned, soot-stained forest woman was gone and a great lady remained in her place. Elin was wearing a heavy, warm woolen and silk gown she'd worn when she carried the twins. God, but that had been a miserable pregnancy. Purchasing the gown had been the only considerate thing Reynald had done for her. It was both beautiful and comfortable. It was a rich, red brown embroidered in gold at the neck and sleeves. They'd also found Elin a wide carven armchair and padded it with emerald velvet cushions. Elin was leaning back, her eyes closed. Her face was clean, her hair combed, braided, and pinned around her head like a coronet.

Elspeth placed the tray on a low table beside her.

Elin opened her eyes and smiled quietly at Elspeth and the food. "Thank you. I hope you didn't go to a great deal of trouble. I don't know if I can eat anything."

Elspeth turned away from Elin. "You must."

Suddenly, Elin gasped. She came out of the chair. Elspeth could see, even under the gown, her belly tighten as the pain hit her. Elspeth leaped toward her and supported her body in a semi-upright position. She could feel, in the bite of Elin's fingers on her upper arms, the intensity of the contraction. It passed, and Elin sank back panting.

"Is that what a real labor pain feels like?" Elin asked.

Elspeth nodded. "I forgot. This is your first. You don't have any direct personal experience with labor."

"No." Elin shook her head. "But I had some pains like this earlier this evening. One almost caused me to fall from the horse. I had another before you came in. They are, as yet, very far apart."

"Yes." Elspeth helped her settle herself in the chair.

Elin shook her head. "I don't believe I want to eat, Elspeth. And I know Hakon has invited me to dinner. Your maids told me so, but I don't believe I want to enter the hall. Make my excuses."

"But you must, Elin! You must!" Elspeth cried.

"Why?" Elin asked. She was completely mystified. Elspeth was obviously frantic. She looked haggard. There were traces of tears on her cheeks. "Why?" she repeated.

"Because if you don't appear in the hall, well and in the guise of an honored guest, Owen will kill my husband."

Owen sat with the rest at one of the benches in the hall at the low table. Hakon kept the same state Reynald had. The benches formed an inverted υ. The high table at one end of the room facing the doors. It was raised on a low dais. The two long, low tables ran the length of the hall near each wall to the door.

Owen's men sat on one side of each low table, Hakon's on the other. He, Godwin, wrapped in his dark fur-trimmed mantle, and Enar sat with the rest. Enar was armed with his axe. Owen wore only his sword and the clothing of the forest people. Godwin was fully armed, but covered with his dark mantle, he was only a shadowy figure in the gloom near the door. The lower tables were all poorly lit. Only a few smoky torches illuminated each one. The high table was well lit by several torches and the big, multimouthed dragon lamp Owen remembered from Reynald's time.

How long had it been since he'd sat in this room? Since before Elin killed Reynald. Since the Vikings captured him. Now, belatedly, it came to him that he'd won.

Won the struggle he'd begun so long ago with Hakon and his Vikings. Count Anton hadn't survived it; Reynald hadn't survived it. But he, who wouldn't have given copper for his own chances, had survived. Not only survived but won. Hakon was in his hand. Everything Hakon held was in his hand. The only question now was what to do with his victory.

He leaned over and spoke softly to Enar. "Hakon's gate guards?"

Enar grinned. He'd been having a wonderful time all day. This was victory in the high style to him. Riding beside a man so clever he'd outwitted his enemy completely. "In one of the storerooms fettered. Denis and two of the boys are looking after them."

"Those skinning the game?"

Enar chortled happily. "I sent them a hog's head of Elspeth's best dark brown brew. They aren't drunk, but unsteady and slightly glassy-eyed. They hadn't eaten in a long while. The beer went down on some empty stomachs."

"Then there is nothing else."

"No." Enar shook his head.

The small, dark man across from Owen spoke. "What will you do with us?"

"Nothing," Owen replied. "I will disturb none of Reynald's people, either their persons or land tenure. All rights and privileges will remain the same."

Just then, Owen felt a stirring around him.

At the high table, Elin led the procession to the hall. She was seated next to Hakon, and he stepped forward and pulled the heavy armchair for her.

Ranulf, Tosi, and Alfric were at her left. Owen approved. Hakon—or Elspeth—was showing a certain tact. She deserved the protection of his people. Elspeth was seated at Hakon's right; near her, those of Hakon's men who'd been at the butchering. They were all, as Enar had said, glassy-eyed. And also damp and clean. They'd been bathing in the horse trough.

As they seated themselves, Bettena entered carrying a tray of cups and a wine bottle. Hakon and Elspeth began speaking to each other in low voices.

Elin looked out over the hall. She saw Owen and smiled. Their eyes met, and he returned the smile. He was as a man wandering in the desert for many months at the mercy of brackish ponds and muddy holes who is suddenly offered a beaker of clear, sweet water. He could drink in the beauty of that smile, be lost forever in the clear, sea-blue eyes. For that moment they were oddly alone together. No one else realized the secret message passing between them. The moment of absolute love. There had been some lines of strain in her features when she'd entered, but they disappeared as her face was transfigured by happiness.

Food was being served at the tables now, first wine, then soup. Owen noticed Elin received only a bowl of clear broth, some bread and salt. He understood.

She sprinkled salt on the bread, dipped part of it into the broth, and ate. Then she looked at him.

He nodded almost imperceptibly. She agreed with his decision. He'd have gone ahead with it in any case, but he was pleased to see she'd reached the same conclusion he had.

He could see Elspeth was distracting Hakon, but that wouldn't last long. Owen studied the man. He had tremendous magnetism and presence. Today, Owen had caught him unaware. He knew he would not be caught so again.

Hakon's eyes wandered over the hall. Some of the serving girls were coming out, bringing wine to the low tables.

Owen watched as comprehension flooded Hakon's face. He knew.

"Ah," Enar whispered with delight, "he knows he is a hooked fish."

"Owen!" Hakon shouted. "Where are you?"

Owen rose and walked away from the tables into the light. He stood only about ten feet from the high table. He was wearing a leather cap of the type Elin's people wore. He pulled it off. At the same moment, the archers raised their bows. They were not pointed at anyone, but Hakon could see that if Owen gave the order, within a moment everyone Owen wanted dead would be dead.

Hakon glanced over at Elspeth. One of her hands rested on his wrist, the other was on her breast. Her eyes were closed.

Hakon and Owen confronted each other over the high table. Hakon tried to move his right hand toward his sword. Elspeth's fingers tightened. He realized she was right. The only thing drawing his sword right now would do would be to get him killed.

"What do you want, Owen?" he asked.

Owen answered calmly, dispassionately. "I want my wife and my friends."

Hakon nodded. "Certainly, since you put your request so forcefully. I must acquiesce. Anything else?"

"My, what nerve!" Enar whispered with delight.

"You have two choices, Hakon. The first is we come here as your guests." So saying, he bowed, pressing the leather cap to his heart. "The second is that we have come here as your enemies and your stronghold has fallen. With my host, I will negotiate a peace for the river and the valley. But my enemy I will kill. And I will take all he has. Choose!"

To almost everyone's surprise, Hakon began laughing.

"Wonderful," Enar whispered. "But then no one ever said he was a coward."

"How was it done?" he asked savagely. "Treachery?"

"No," Owen said. "Never think that about those around you. Your lake just isn't as deep as you think it is . . . in some places. All, all are loyal to you. None offered to compound with us even after they were captured. But the men were hostage for the women and the women for the men."

Hakon nodded. Then he lifted Elspeth's hand from his sword arm and kissed it. She saw the darkness in his face. She didn't speak. She knew he would want her to try to dissuade him, but two tears gathered at the corners of her eyes, flowed down, and tasted wet and salty at her lips.

Elin assessed Hakon, frowning. *He's going to go for that sword,* she thought. A pregnant woman doesn't have much to fight with, but she has weight, and Elin used hers, at the same time hoping she wouldn't have a labor pain and frighten Owen.

She rose and turned as Hakon reached for his sword. She drove the full weight of her elbow and hip into his stomach, then slammed the heel of her hand into his chest. The impact knocked the wind out of him for a few seconds.

She stood over him, palm outspread on his chest. "No," she told him in an outraged tone. "No, you will not fight my husband or die at the hands of his bowmen. I won't permit it. I won't permit it because already you have deeper roots here than you know. In the secret darkness of your wife's womb, your seed made life. In a few weeks, she'll feel it kick. It will be a girl, and a lucky one.

"No, Hakon, you will not leave your wife here, weeping while her belly swells with your seed. And, no, you will not destroy yourself and leave her to be handed like a sack of salt to the first Owen trusts enough to wed her and obey him. If you dare to do such a thing, I will put a curse on you, a woman's curse, and the queen of darkness will set her furies on you. For a thousand years your soul will not lie quiet in its grave. I promise you!"

A gasp of horror rose from the benches, and a babble of talk broke out in the room.

"Damnation!" Godwin roared above the din. He strode to the fore and stood next to Owen. Hakon was on his feet embracing a weeping Elspeth. Godwin pointed at Hakon. "You're not going to let that rogue and his wench escape so—"

At that moment there was a crash that reminded everyone of the smith's hammer striking the forge. Complete silence fell.

Ivor strode forward. He'd come with Godwin. Owen had noticed they got along well. The two were close friends. Christian or not, Ivor was a berserk. No one knew what he might do. He was wearing the black mantle over his head. Now he dropped it.

"Look at me, Jarl Godwin," he shouted. "Look! And you also, Hakon, arrogant killer of men."

Odd, Owen thought, *how everyone has forgotten that Ivor's face is a ruin.* He'd been struck by a mace that nearly killed him. One eye was sunken, milky. The cheekbone was shattered. Most of the teeth on that side were wicked-looking stubs or missing. The shattered eye and socket oozed mucous, flowing down the side of his face.

"Look well on me," Ivor bellowed again as he made a striding circuit of the hall's center. "I am the face of war! Is there not enough in this beautiful valley for us all? If we are generous to one another, may we not have peace?"

Owen watched with wry amusement as the starch went out of both Godwin and Hakon. Victory! Not the one he'd always sought, but victory nonetheless.

Ranulf helped Elin down from the low dais, and she walked toward Owen.

The men stepped aside for her, and silence fell again. Or did it? Owen never knew. All he ever did remember about the moment was Elin, beautiful in Elspeth's ample brown dress walking toward him, smiling.

There were those who did say, a long time after, that a strange darkness invaded the hall at that moment. Not an evil or unholy darkness, but the sweet beauty of a summer night limned with fireflies, when the warm air is heavy with the fragrance of honeysuckle, wild roses, and flowering trees. Others claimed to hear distant strains of music. They felt as though they stood at land's end, and looked far out to sea as the day turned into night, and heard, borne by the wind, the songs sung by those who dwell in the western paradise where only singers and heroes are welcomed.

But perhaps this was all the mist of illusion, the shadow of an empty dream. But then, aren't those who dream such dreams all the luckier for having been allowed to imagine something so beautiful?

Then she reached him, and the dream vanished.

He was only a small, dark man she'd met reconnoitering a Viking camp long ago, who'd slowed his horse and risked his life to rescue a very dirty-looking slave. And she was only a dark woman whose sole striking feature was her deep blue eyes, who was heavy with her first pregnancy.

He took her hand and kissed it. "I can't get any closer," he joked quietly as he rested his hand on her belly.

"Presently," she said. "I'm already in labor. Soon you'll be able to get as close as you want to. Closer, in fact. I'll need you to help me. The men among my people help their wives give birth."

He surprised her by knowing about the custom. "Alshan told me. I'm prepared."

Then they walked away together, hand in hand, toward the room Elspeth had set up as a birthing chamber. They had everything in the world to say to each other and nothing to say to one another. Now that they were together again, nothing much else mattered. They had all the time in creation for both the long silences, and the even longer conversations, of love.

Elin delivered the child near dawn. Her labor was a painful struggle, since first childbirths are apt to be difficult. But she came through it well. The baby was a girl. As much as can be told about an infant at birth suggested she would be dark like Elin, but with the equally dark eyes of her grandmother, Wilsa. Indeed, she seemed, to Elin's eyes, to favor her grandmother more than anyone else.

Elspeth's evening was a series of minor shocks. First, she was shocked by Owen, who refused to leave the chamber and insisted on helping even with the most intimate details of childbirth. Then, by Elin, who gave birth squatting, clinging to her husband. And third, by the appearance of Sybilla, who arrived unannounced. Elspeth simply turned and found the small forest woman sitting on the side of the bed. She screeched and frightened Sybilla as much as Sybilla had frightened her.

When the afterbirth was delivered, Owen shocked Elspeth by sponging Elin off, washing her clean of perspiration and blood, and even braiding her hair, which had come loose during labor. Then he helped her into a fresh linen gown and even assisted her to pad herself with clean clothes. He and Elspeth put her to bed.

"I have to look in on Godwin, Hakon, Enar, and Alfric," he said.

"How did it go?" Elspeth asked.

"Well," Owen said. "At first Hakon and Godwin snarled at each other like a pair of angry dogs. But then Alfric and Enar began telling funny stories. I know I've had them work their wiles on me. They are damn near irresistible when they get started. Soon they had Hakon and Godwin both in stitches. Enar poured beer. Alfric served roast beef. It turned into a carouse. Then Alfric pulled out his parchment and pens. I think Hakon should look at what he agreed to, sober and by day. The same is true of Godwin.

I gave Alfric strict orders not to let either man sign anything.

"Hakon and Godwin and most of the household went to bed in their boots hours ago, but I still have archers on guard in the hall and at the gate. Judith sent a message that her traveling carriage is on its way for Elin. Now I need to check with my men. I'll be back soon," he promised, and left, blowing a kiss to Elin.

Elspeth hugged Elin. "What you did was very generous."

"I did it for you," Elin answered. "Your people speak well of you. They would have been nothing but trouble to Owen."

Elspeth kissed Elin good night and then left. She was nearly dropping with exhaustion.

Sybilla sat on a chest in the corner. Elin beckoned to her and whispered in her ear. Sybilla left.

Elin put the child to her breast. She suckled for a few moments, but then, after the manner of healthy newborns, she drifted off to sleep, accepting her change in fortune from the warm, wet womb to the bright, confusing world of taste, touch, smell, filled with almost painful lights accompanied by loud noises and odd shapes that came and went. The womb had not been bad; perhaps this wouldn't be, either.

She snuggled warmly against her mother and slept. She still slept even when Sybilla returned. Elin crowned her downy head with apple blossoms as Sybilla eased silently out of the room, leaving Elin alone.

Owen returned. For a long moment he stood looking at Elin cradling her child, basking in the deep golden glow of the last candle of the night. And he knew life sometimes does bless us with perfect happiness. Then he approached the bed and stood over her.

"Remember," she said. "Remember when you told me you wished you could be sure of the springtime? Remember when you told me you felt locked in perpetual winter and would never see the earth turn green again? Well, God is He who turns the night of death into morning."

He sat on the bed and she placed the child, crowned

with apple blossoms, in his arms. The little one suckled a hand, then reached out to clutch his exploring finger in one tiny fist.

"Here," she whispered, "here is your springtime."